ARCHETYPAL THEMES IN
THE MODERN STORY

Edited by Jack Matthews

ARCHETYPAL THEMES IN THE MODERN STORY

St. Martin's Press
NEW YORK

ACKNOWLEDGMENTS

p. 34: "Love and Death" by Joyce Carol Oates. Reprinted by permission
of the author and Blanche C. Gregory, Inc. Copyright © 1970 by Joyce Carol
Oates.

p. 51: "Smith and Jones" by Conrad Aiken. Reprinted by permission of The
World Publishing Company from *The Collected Short Stories of Conrad
Aiken.* Copyright 1922, 1923, 1924, 1925, 1927, 1928, 1929, 1930, 1931, 1932, 1933,
1934, 1935, 1941, 1950, 1952, 1953, 1955, 1956, 1957, 1958, 1959, 1960 by Conrad
Aiken.

p. 59: "A Last Word" by William Sansom. Copyright © 1947, 1950, 1953,
1957, 1960, 1963 by William Sansom. From *The Stories of William Sansom* by
William Sansom, by permission of Atlantic-Little, Brown and Co.

p. 65: "Circe" by Eudora Welty. From *The Bride of the Innisfallen,*
copyright © 1955 by Eudora Welty. Reprinted by permission of Harcourt
Brace Jovanovich, Inc.

p. 71: "The Tailor's Daughter," Chapter II, in *The Confessions of Edward
Dahlberg* by Edward Dahlberg. Reprinted by permission of the author.

p. 95: "Master Richard" by John Wain. Reprinted by permission of Curtis
Brown, Ltd.

p. 114: "The Legacy of Leontis" by Harry Mark Petrakis. Published by
permission of the author from *Pericles on 31st Street,* published by Quadrangle
Books.

p. 121: "The Prison Window," pp. 125–143, in *The Second Choice,* by Louis
Auchincloss. Reprinted by permission of Houghton Mifflin Company.

iv

p. 132: "The Broken Lyre" by Bryan MacMahon. From *The Red Petticoat and Other Stories* by Bryan MacMahon. Reprinted by permission of Curtis Brown, Ltd. Copyright © 1972.

p. 137: "Sonny's Blues" by James Baldwin. Copyright 1948, 1951, © 1957, 1958, 1960, 1965 by James Baldwin. Reprinted by permission of Robert Lantz-Candida Donadio Literary Agency Inc.

p. 181: "Since When Do They Charge Admission?" by Wright Morris. Reprinted by permission of the author.

p. 191: "Nina" by Anaïs Nin. From *Collages* by Anaïs Nin. Copyright © 1964 by Anaïs Nin. Published by The Swallow Press. Reprinted by permission of the Author's representative, Gunther Stuhlmann.

p. 196: "The Sky Is Gray" by Ernest J. Gaines. From *Bloodline* by Ernest J. Gaines. Copyright © 1963, 1964, 1968 by Ernest J. Gaines. Reprinted by permission of the publisher, The Dial Press.

p. 217: "Walk in the Moon Shadows" by Jesse Stuart. Reprinted by permission of the author.

p. 224: "Thus the Early Gods" by George Garrett. Copyright © 1959, 1961 by George Garrett. Reprinted by permission of the author.

p. 235: "I'm a Fool" by Sherwood Anderson. Reprinted by permission of Harold Ober Associates Incorporated. Copyright 1922 by Dial Publishing Company. Renewed 1949 by Eleanor Copenhaver Anderson.

p. 244: "Traven" by David Madden. Reprinted by permission of the author.

p. 267: "Frail Vessel," pp. 280–302, in *Collected Stories,* by Mary Lavin. Reprinted by permission of Houghton Mifflin Company and the author.

p. 283: "Song of the First and Last Beatnik" by Herbert Gold from *The Magic Will.* Copyright © 1971 by Herbert Gold. Reprinted by permission of Random House, Inc.

p. 295: "The Agony of A. Boscas" by Patrick Boyle. Reprinted by permission of the author.

p. 300: "The Magic Telephone" by Garrison Keillor. Reprinted by permission from *The Carleton Miscellany,* copyrighted by Carleton College.

p. 309: "The Blind Man" by D. H. Lawrence. From *The Complete Short Stories of D. H. Lawrence,* Vol. II. Copyright 1922 by Thomas B. Seltzer Inc., 1950 by Frieda Lawrence. All rights reserved. Reprinted by permission of the Viking Press, Inc.

p. 323: "The Best of Everything" by Richard Yates. Reprinted by permission of Monica McCall, International Famous Agency. Copyright © 1954 Richard Yates.

p. 333: "Shadow Show" by Clifford Simak. Reprinted by permission of the author.

p. 361: "Incest" by John Updike. Copyright © 1957 by John Updike from *The Same Door.* Reprinted by permission of Alfred A. Knopf, Inc. First appeared in *The New Yorker.*

p. 371: "The Sword" by Doris Betts. Reprinted by permission of the author.

p. 379 : "The Girl at the Window" by Jack Matthews. Reprinted by permission of the author.

Contents

INTRODUCTION 1

THE CONTEST 5
    Bartleby the Scrivener / Herman Melville 7
    Love and Death / Joyce Carol Oates 34
    Smith and Jones / Conrad Aiken 51
    A Last Word / William Sansom 59
    Circe / Eudora Welty 65
    The Tailor's Daughter / Edward Dahlberg 71

THE SCAPEGOAT 79
    My Kinsman, Major Molineux / Nathaniel Hawthorne 81
    Master Richard / John Wain 95
    The Legacy of Leontis / Harry Mark Petrakis 114
    The Prison Window / Louis Auchincloss 121
    The Broken Lyre / Bryan MacMahon 132
    Sonny's Blues / James Baldwin 137

METAMORPHOSIS 161
    The Open Boat / Stephen Crane 163
    Since When Do They Charge Admission? / Wright Morris 181
    Nina / Anaïs Nin 191
    The Sky Is Gray / Ernest J. Gaines 196
    Walk in the Moon Shadows / Jesse Stuart 217
    Thus the Early Gods / George Garrett 224

THE TRICKSTER 233
    I'm a Fool / Sherwood Anderson 235
    Traven / David Madden 244
    Frail Vessel / Mary Lavin 267
    Song of the First and Last Beatnik / Herbert Gold 283
    The Agony of A. Boscas / Patrick Boyle 295
    The Magic Telephone / Garrison Keillor 300

TABOO   307
   The Blind Man / D. H. Lawrence   309
   The Best of Everything / Richard Yates   323
   Shadow Show / Clifford Simak   333
   Incest / John Updike   361
   The Sword / Doris Betts   371
   The Girl at the Window / Jack Matthews   379

ARCHETYPAL THEMES IN THE MODERN STORY

INTRODUCTION

THESE ARE EXCITING TIMES FOR BOTH WRITERS AND READERS. THE modern short story has not only opened up new vistas of experience (in step with the proliferation of theories and ideas in the sciences) but it has been emancipated from censorship and the tyranny of *genre*. Today it seems that as long as a story possesses some kind of tension or conflict almost anything goes; and this expansion of the form is virtually worldwide. In France, Robbe-Grillet writes stories in which nothing overt *happens,* and in Argentina Borges writes stories in the form of philosophical essays. Stories are written in present tense, in different voices signaled by changes in typography, even in the form of questionnaires. And not only are writers experimenting vigorously with new modes of telling stories but they are assured of readers, or at least of publication, if they do it well enough.

But in spite of the great emphasis on experimentation in contemporary literature, and the accompanying value placed on "originality," we must remember an important counter truth. The writer who strives for originality is likely to end up with nothing more than novelty, and a story that does not rise above mere novelty will be superseded immediately by the next novelty.

In the narrowest sense, Homer was not original, nor were Sophocles and Shakespeare, for they all took up old tales and motifs and revitalized them with their genius. They were, in an important sense, *retellers* rather than tellers of tales. If the poet is "the maker," as the word *poiētēs* meant in classical Greek, he is not himself the maker of stories but the conveyer of stories; what he makes are cunning and meaningful variations. Stories from myth and folklore, told long ago by Homer, Aesop, Plutarch, and a thousand anonymous storytellers, are still very much alive today, appearing in the pages of *The New Yorker* and *The Malahat Review,* in the books of John Updike, Saul Bellow, and Joyce Carol Oates.

To acknowledge that he is as much a "passer on" of stories as a creator of them should not cause the serious writer to despair. Nor should recognition of that fact disappoint the reader. It is gratifying to understand to what extent, and in what ways, the stories we experience are celebrations of old meanings, perpetuated and revitalized from generation to generation according to the unique customs, preoccupations, and materials of the day.

1

The "old meanings" I am speaking of are the archetypal themes of this book's title. The term *archetype* may evoke ideas of the racial unconscious and the theories of C. J. Jung, but I do not mean to tie this book to a particular doctrine or psychological school. The premise of this book is simply that certain story patterns clearly have within them the power to symbolize vital concerns from culture to culture and from era to era, and, further, that the contemplation of modern fiction in terms of these enduring themes yields special values and insights.

How many archetypes are there? How many should one settle on? This is a little bit like asking how many pieces there are in a pie, or how many colors in the spectrum: it depends on how you divide them. Professor George Polti classified all story patterns into "thirty-six dramatic situations" (these he viewed as archetypes). At the other end of the scale, someone else once said that all stories are variations on the Cinderella theme.

In this book I have sought to avoid the reductionist error of making all modern stories seem to fit the procrustean bed of a few selected archetypes. I settled on the five themes that organize this collection—The Contest, The Scapegoat, Metamorphosis, The Trickster, Taboo—because these are among the oldest of the themes that are still vital in today's literature. In addition, they contrast strongly with one another so that their basic configurations are vividly apparent. And by limiting them to five I could include a sufficient number of stories to show something of the variety and range possible within each theme. But I am aware that in selecting such archetypes an editor must be somewhat impressionistic, even intuitive, and must have the honesty and humility to admit it.

Not all ancient themes are archetypal in the sense that they are vitally present in the stories of today. The theme of the Hero Slaying the Dragon, for example, which Jung found so important in the literature of the past, has all but disappeared—even if one tries to see the Dragon metaphorically reborn as Guilt or The Establishment. One of the reasons we do not celebrate the Hero-Slaying-the-Dragon theme as we once did is that we no longer have a culturally vivid sense of the Hero. Figures comparable to Aeneas, Beowulf, and Roland are virtually nonexistent in modern stories. The old-fashioned Hero was the champion of his "Establishment"—his fatherland, his family, and the institutions that supported him and gave him meaning *as* a hero. By contrast, today's fictional protagonist is frequently pictured in revolt against the institutions around him; the practice of identifying with the sacred ideals of one's family and one's culture—what the Romans termed *pietas*—no longer qualifies as heroic and has accordingly lost the power to evoke celebration in stories. Of course, it may turn out that this ancient, seemingly defunct theme is not dead after all; given the right sort of social chemistry, it may once again prove vital.

On the other hand, there are many themes that are virtually unique to the modern writer. Among these are the Romantic or Glamorized Misfit (the nearest thing to a current version of the Hero); the Bifurcation of Self (in which a conflict is internalized and enacted within the psyche of a character); and its obverse theme, the Opposable Self (in which a character projects upon another his own obsessions and reacts against him accordingly). There is the theme of the Initiation into Irony, showing a character emerging from a state of innocence into an awareness of the multiple meanings of things he once thought simple. And there are stories without number that celebrate the One Against the Many or the Triumph of the Underdog—two themes that, though closely related, have subtly different emphases. All these themes have proved valuable to modern writers in structuring fictional experiences, and, in fact, the alert reader will find all of them represented to some degree in stories in this book.

But whether or not any of these themes could properly be termed archetypal (and in my judgment all are too modern), they are not the *dominant* themes in the stories present here. And this brings us to the question of how the stories in this book "ought" to be approached.

To arrange thirty stories under five thematic headings, as I have done, is to apply "labels"; and, as the English philosopher Dean William Inge said, "Every label is a libel." It is important to keep this bit of wisdom in mind, for glib labeling of any sort is the enemy of good reading. On the other hand, labels are essential to our ability to think abstractly—so obviously essential that Dean Inge was forced to use words, or verbal labels, to communicate the idea that every label conceals qualities that limit and oppose the particular truth it conveys. Here is a paradox like the one embedded in the familiar Chinese proverb, "One picture is worth a thousand words"—it takes words to say this.

Perhaps it is most useful to think of the five archetypal themes of this book as lenses, each of which is capable of revealing inner consistencies and focusing particular meanings within a story. One lens will prove irrelevant to a specific tale and focus nothing; another will reveal interestingly different meanings among the stories upon which it is turned. What is to be avoided at all costs is the reductionist error that is most obviously signaled by the words "nothing but"—as in the statement, "Hawthorne's story 'My Kinsman, Major Molineux' is nothing but the Scapegoat tale in early American dress." Such formulas lie. Nothing is "nothing but." In working with archetypal themes, the essential thing is to recognize not only how a story embodies a particular theme but how, and in what ways, the story *resists* the theme.

Moreover, archetypes—along with the human values they express—are so subtly entangled with one another that they can appear in all sorts of combinations: a contest might involve two trickster figures, one of whom might play the role of scapegoat. If there were such a story, it would incorporate three of the five archetypal themes I have decided upon. However, the themes in a story are seldom equally dominant, and it is precisely in seeking to discern and account for differences in emphasis among them that a reader may discover essential meanings that might otherwise remain obscure. The reader who begins by asking, "Whose story is this?" and follows out all of the implications of that question is well on the way to placing the themes in meaningful relationships to one another and arriving at the most powerful interpretation of the story.

As he proceeds, the reader will find that he is participating with the writer in forming an experience—collecting information about the characters and their plight, receiving cues concerning how the events of the story are to be viewed, how one is to feel about them. Are certain things hinted at as forthcoming in the narrative? Are there events, or characters, that are referred to more often than the practical demands of the narrative would seem to justify? If so, what is the significance of such references: do they point toward deeper meanings that are perhaps concealed from the reader or from the characters or from both? How are the events in a particular scene—and in the story as a whole—related to the title? The title itself is a kind of "label"; but, as we have said, a label is often most useful in calling attention to the ways in which the thing labeled resists the description applied to it.

To return, finally, to our five archetypal themes: they are among the most ancient, and yet at least five of the six authors represented in each of the following sections are actively writing, and experimenting, today. The originality we seek in these modern stories is no different from what readers (or listeners) in all ages have valued. It consists in what the storytellers have *made* of the themes that are available to them in their heritage, and it comes only with the writers' achievement of honesty and depth. As the word suggests, originality is the origin of something: it generates, it moves, it affects. The best way to approach a story, then, is with an open responsiveness, a sense of adventure in launching forth upon the particular journey the story represents. If the reader is responsive and the story a good one, there will be no question that the journey has been worthwhile.

THE CONTEST

IN SPITE OF RECENT EXPERIMENTATION, ALL STORIES MUST HAVE CON-flict of some kind, or we don't refer to them as stories at all—we call them tone poems, or essays, or mood pieces, or something else. In one important sense, conflict *is* the story; it forms the vortex of interest in the story, and it is often the force that propels the narrative movement.

Since it is an essential feature of stories, conflict cannot reasonably be considered a theme. In one of its forms, however—the Contest motif—it constitutes a primordial situation, a truly archetypal theme. While a single character may experience "inner conflict," it would be strange indeed to speak of his "inner contest." In the Contest, there are two characters of comparable power who more or less knowingly enter some sort of arena in a struggle with each other. Often this struggle is highly symbolic, insofar as the characters themselves seem vested with larger meaning.

David and Goliath, Hector and Achilles, Dimmesdale and Chillingworth, Eliza and W. O. Gant (in Thomas Wolfe's *Look Homeward, Angel*), Fast Eddie and Minnesota Fats (in Walter Tevis' *The Hustler*) are all participants in contests, are all Contest figures. Sometimes the contest is overt and physi-cal; at other times it is concealed and confused, as in the marriage of Eliza and W. O. Gant—a marriage that is itself an arena of strife between two life styles.

Much more than a conflict between life styles is at stake in Herman Melville's strange and fascinating story, "Bartleby the Scrivener." The law-yer and Bartleby come together in the arena of an office of law—a place that exists in service of dialectic, of rational debate for the sake of truth. But Bartleby's challenge is a deeper, more unsettling one: he does not seem to care for reason, or dialectic, or truth. He is a spirit of awesome negation, and the contest is entered upon the instant his employer (the narrator of the story) determines to force Bartleby not simply to go to work but to "see things his way." In the playing out of the long, strange drama of struggle, Bartleby's insistent preference "not to" makes us feel that he achieves a kind of humble nobility, even though our social and rational sentiments must belong to the kindly but exasperated lawyer who tells the story.

The variations on the Contest theme seem almost endless. Joyce Carol Oates claims that most of her stories have to do with the Contest motif. Her "Love and Death," like Eudora Welty's hauntingly subtle "Circe," involves

5

one of the oldest contests around (and still, at this writing, undecided)—that between man and woman. William Sansom's story, on the other hand, is a colorful and honest journey into the implications of two old men entering the whimsical arena of who-can-out-miser-the-other, and the whimsical triumph of a protagonist who is suddenly deprived of his antagonist.

A few of the many classic short stories that are concerned with the theme of the Contest are "The Pupil" by Henry James, "The Short Happy Life of Francis Macomber" by Ernest Hemingway, "The Bride Comes to Yellow Sky" by Stephen Crane, and "The Secret Sharer" by Joseph Conrad.

Herman Melville
Bartleby the Scrivener

I AM A RATHER ELDERLY MAN. THE NATURE OF MY AVOCATIONS, FOR THE last thirty years, has brought me into more than ordinary contact with what would seem an interesting and somewhat singular set of men, of whom, as yet, nothing, that I know of, has ever been written—I mean, the law-copyists, or scriveners. I have known very many of them, professionally and privately, and, if I pleased could relate divers histories, at which good-natured gentlemen might smile, and sentimental souls might weep. But I waive the biographies of all other scriveners, for a few passages in the life of Bartleby, who was a scrivener, the strangest I ever saw, or heard of. While, of other law-copyists, I might write the complete life, of Bartleby nothing of that sort can be done. I believe that no materials exist, for a full and satisfactory biography of this man. It is an irreparable loss to literature. Bartleby was one of those beings of whom nothing is ascertainable, except from the original sources, and, in his case, those are very small. What my own astonished eyes saw of Bartleby, *that* is all I know of him, except, indeed, one vague report, which will appear in the sequel.

Ere introducing the scrivener, as he first appeared to me, it is fit I make some mention of myself, my *employés,* my business, my chambers, and general surroundings; because some such description is indispensable to an adequate understanding of the chief character about to be presented. Imprimis: I am a man who, from his youth upwards, has been filled with a profound conviction that the easiest way of life is the best. Hence, though I belong to a profession proverbially energetic and nervous, even to turbulence, at times, yet nothing of that sort have I ever suffered to invade my peace. I am one of those unambitious lawyers who never address a jury, or in any way draw down public applause; but, in the cool tranquillity of a snug retreat, do a snug business among rich men's bonds, and mortgages, and title-deeds. All who know me, consider me an eminently *safe* man. The late John Jacob Astor, a personage little given to poetic enthusiasm, had no hesitation in pronouncing my first grand point to be prudence; my next, method. I do not speak it in vanity, but simply record the fact, that I was not unemployed in my profession by the late John Jacob Astor; a name which, I admit, I love to repeat; for it hath a rounded and orbicular sound to it, and rings like unto bullion. I will freely add, that I was not insensible to the late John Jacob Astor's good opinion.

Some time prior to the period at which this little history begins, my avocations had been largely increased. The good old office, now extinct in the State of New York, of a Master in Chancery, had been conferred upon me. It was not a very arduous office, but very pleasantly remunerative. I seldom lose my temper; much more seldom indulge in dangerous indignation at wrongs and outrages; but I must be permitted to be rash here and declare, that I consider the sudden and violent abrogation of the office of Master in Chancery, by the new Constitution, as a—premature act; inasmuch as I had counted upon a life-lease of the profits, whereas I only received those of a few short years. But this is by the way.

My chambers were up stairs, at No.—Wall Street. At one end, they looked upon the white wall of the interior of a spacious sky-light shaft, penetrating the building from top to bottom.

This view might have been considered rather tame than otherwise, deficient in what landscape painters call "life." But, if so, the view from the other end of my chambers offered, at least, a contrast, if nothing more. In that direction, my windows commanded an unobstructed view of a lofty brick wall, black by age and everlasting shade; which wall required no spy-glass to bring out its lurking beauties, but, for the benefit of all near-sighted spectators, was pushed up to within ten feet of my window-panes. Owing to the great height of the surrounding buildings, and my chambers being on the second floor, the interval between this wall and mine not a little resembled a huge square cistern.

At the period just preceding the advent of Bartleby, I had two persons as copyists in my employment, and a promising lad as an office-boy. First, Turkey; second, Nippers; third, Ginger Nut. These may seem names, the like of which are not usually found in the Directory. In truth, they were nicknames, mutually conferred upon each other by my three clerks, and were deemed expressive of their respective persons or characters. Turkey was a short, pursy Englishman, of about my own age—that is, somewhere not far from sixty. In the morning, one might say, his face was of a fine florid hue, but after twelve o'clock, meridian—his dinner hour—it blazed like a grate full of Christmas coals; and continued blazing—but, as it were, with a gradual wane—till six o'clock, P.M., or thereabouts; after which, I saw no more of the proprietor of the face, which, gaining its meridian with the sun, seemed to set with it, to rise, culminate, and decline the following day, with the like regularity and undiminished glory. There are many singular coincidences I have known in the course of my life, not the least among which was the fact, that, exactly when Turkey displayed his fullest beams from his red and radiant countenance, just then, too, at that critical moment, began the daily period when I considered his business capacities as seriously disturbed for the remainder of the twenty-four hours. Not that he was absolutely idle, or averse to business then; far from it. The difficulty was, he was apt to be altogether too energetic. There was a strange, inflamed, flurried, flighty recklessness of activity about him. He would be incautious in dipping his pen into his inkstand. All his blots upon my documents were dropped there after twelve o'clock, meridian. Indeed, not only would he be reckless, and sadly given to making blots in the afternoon, but, some days, he went further, and was rather noisy. At such times, too, his face flamed with augmented blazonry, as if cannel coal had been heaped on anthracite. He made an unpleasant racket with his chair; spilled his sand-box; in mending his pens, impatiently split them all to pieces, and threw them on the floor in a sudden passion; stood up, and leaned over his table, boxing his papers about in a most indecorous manner, very sad to behold in an elderly man like him. Nevertheless, as he was in many ways a most valuable person to me, and all the time before twelve o'clock, meridian, was the quickest, steadiest creature, too, accomplishing a great deal of work in a style not easily to be matched—for these reasons, I was willing to overlook his eccentricities, though, indeed, occasionally, I remonstrated with him. I did this very gently, however, because, though the civilest, nay, the blandest and most reverential of men in the morning, yet, in the afternoon, he was disposed, upon provocation, to be slightly rash with his tongue—in fact, insolent. Now, valuing his morning services as I did, and resolved not to lose them—yet, at the same time, made uncomfortable by his inflamed ways after twelve o'clock—and being a man of peace, unwilling by my admonitions to call forth unseemly retorts from him, I took upon me, one Saturday noon (he was always worse on Saturdays) to hint to him, very kindly, that, perhaps, now that he was growing old, it might be well to abridge his labors; in short, he need not come to my chambers after twelve o'clock, but, dinner over, had best go home to his lodgings, and rest himself till tea-time. But no; he insisted upon his afternoon devotions. His countenance became intolerably fervid, as he oratorically assured me—gesticulating with a long ruler at the other end of the room—that if his services in the morning were useful, how indispensable, then, in the afternoon?

"With submission, sir," said Turkey, on this occasion, "I consider myself your right-hand man. In the morning I but marshal and deploy my columns; but in the afternoon I put myself at their head, and gallantly charge the foe, thus"—and he made a violent thrust with the ruler.

"But the blots, Turkey," intimated I.

"True; but, with submission, sir, behold these hairs! I am getting old. Surely, sir, a blot or two of a warm afternoon is not to be severely urged against gray hairs. Old age—even if it blot the page—is honorable. With submission, sir, we *both* are getting old."

This appeal to my fellow-feeling was hardly to be resisted. At all events, I saw that go he would not. So, I made up my mind to let him stay, resolving, nevertheless, to see to it that, during the afternoon, he had to do with my less important papers.

Nippers, the second on my list, was a whiskered, sallow, and, upon the whole, rather piratical-looking young man, of about five-and-twenty. I always deemed him the victim of two evil powers—ambition and indigestion. The ambition was evinced by a certain impatience of the duties of a mere copyist, an unwarrantable usurpation of strictly professional affairs, such as the origi-nal drawing up of legal documents. The indigestion seemed betokened in an occasional nervous testiness and grinning irritability, causing the teeth to audibly grind together over mistakes committed in copying; unnecessary maledictions, hissed, rather than spoken, in the heat of business; and especially by a continual discontent with the height of the table where he worked. Though of a very ingenious mechanical turn, Nippers could never get this table to suit him. He put chips under it, blocks of various sorts, bits of paste-board, and at last went so far as to attempt an exquisite adjustment, by final pieces of folded blotting-paper. But no invention would answer. If, for the sake of easing his back, he brought the table-lid at a sharp angle well up towards his chin, and wrote there like a man using the steep roof of a Dutch house for his desk, then he declared that it stopped the circulation in his arms. If now he lowered the table to his waistbands, and stooped over it in writing, then there was a sore aching in his back. In short, the truth of the matter was, Nippers knew not what he wanted. Or, if he wanted anything, it was to be rid of a scrivener's table altogether. Among the manifestations of his diseased ambition was a fondness he had for receiving visits from certain ambiguous-looking fellows in seedy coats, whom he called his clients. Indeed, I was aware that not only was he, at times, considerable of a ward-politician, but he occasionally did a little business at the justices' courts, and was not unknown on the steps of the Tombs. I have good reason to believe, however, that one individual who called upon him at my chambers, and who, with a grand air, he insisted was his client, was no other than a dun, and the alleged title-deed, a bill. But, with all his failings, and the annoyances he caused me, Nippers, like his compatriot Turkey, was a very useful man to me; wrote a neat, swift hand; and, when he chose, was not deficient in a gentlemanly sort of deportment. Added to this, he always dressed in a gentlemanly sort of way; and so, incidentally, reflected credit upon my chambers. Whereas, with respect to Turkey, I had much ado to keep him from being a reproach to me. His clothes were apt to look oily, and smell of eating-houses. He wore his pantaloons very loose and baggy in summer. His coats were execrable; his hat not to be handled. But while the hat was a thing of indifference to me, inasmuch as his natural civility and deference, as a dependent Englishman, always led him to doff it the moment he entered the room, yet his coat was another matter. Concerning his coats, I reasoned with him; but with no effect. The truth was, I suppose, that a man with so small an income could not afford to sport such a lustrous face and a lustrous coat at one and the same time. As Nippers once observed, Turkey's money went chiefly for red ink. One winter day, I presented Turkey with a highly respectable-looking coat of my own—a padded gray coat, of a most comfortable warmth, and which buttoned straight up from the knee to the neck. I thought Turkey would appreciate the favor, and abate his rashness and obstreperousness of afternoons. But no; I verily believe that buttoning himself up in so downy and blanket-like a coat had a pernicious effect upon him—upon the same principle that too much oats are bad for horses. In fact, precisely as a rash, restive horse is said to feel his oats, so Turkey felt his coat. It made him insolent. He was a man whom prosperity harmed.

Though, concerning the self-indulgent habits of Turkey, I had my own private surmises, yet, touching Nippers, I was well persuaded that, whatever might be his faults in other respects, he was, at least, a temperate young man. But, indeed, nature herself seemed to have been his vintner, and, at his birth, charged him so thoroughly with an irritable, brandy-like disposition, that all subsequent potations were needless. When I consider how, amid the stillness of my chambers, Nippers would sometimes impatiently rise from his seat, and stooping over his table, spread his arms wide apart, seize the whole desk, and move it, and jerk it, with a grim, grinding motion on the floor, as if the table were a perverse voluntary agent, intent on thwarting and vexing him, I plainly perceive that, for Nippers, brandy-and-water were altogether superfluous.

It was fortunate for me that, owing to its peculiar cause—indigestion—the irritability and consequent nervousness of Nippers were mainly observable in the morning, while in the afternoon he was comparatively mild. So that, Turkey's paroxysms only coming on about twelve o'clock, I never had to do with their eccentricities at one time. Their fits relieved each other, like guards. When Nipper's was on, Turkey's was off; and *vice versa*. This was a good natural arrangement, under the curcumstances.

Ginger Nut, the third on my list, was a lad, some twelve years old. His father was a carman, ambitious of seeing his son on the bench instead of a cart, before he died. So he sent him to my office, as student at law, errand-boy, cleaner and sweeper, at the rate of one dollar a week. He had a little desk to himself, but he did not use it much. Upon inspection, the drawer exhibited a great array of the shells of various sorts of nuts. Indeed, to this quick-witted youth, the whole noble science of the law was contained in a nutshell. Not the least among the employments of Ginger Nut, as well as one which he discharged with the most alacrity, was his duty as cake and apple purveyor for Turkey and Nippers. Copying law-papers being proverbially a dry, husky sort of business, my two scriveners were fain to moisten their mouths very often with Spitzenbergs, to be had at the numerous stalls nigh the Custom House and Post Office. Also, they sent Ginger Nut very frequently for that peculiar cake—small, flat, round, and very spicy—after which he had been named by them. Of a cold morning, when business was but dull, Turkey would gobble up scores of these cakes, as if they were mere wafers—indeed, they sell them at the rate of six or eight for a penny—the scrape of his pen blending with the crunching of the crisp particles in his mouth. Rashest of all the fiery afternoon blunders and flurried rashnesses of Turkey, was his once moistening a ginger-cake between his lips, and clapping it on to a mortgage, for a seal. I came within an ace of dismissing him then. But he mollified me by making an oriental bow, and saying—

"With submission, sir, it was generous of me to find you in stationery on my own account."

Now my original business—that of a conveyancer and title hunter, and drawer-up of recondite documents of all sorts—was considerably increased by receiving the Master's office. There was now great work for scriveners. Not only must I push the clerks already with me, but I must have additional help.

In answer to my advertisement, a motionless young man one morning stood upon my office threshold, the door being open, for it was summer. I can see that figure now—pallidly neat, pitiably respectable, incurably forlorn! It was Bartleby.

After a few words touching his qualifications, I engaged him, glad to have among my corps of copyists a man of so singularly sedate an aspect, which I thought might operate beneficially upon the flighty temper of Turkey, and the fiery one of Nippers.

I should have stated before that ground-glass folding-doors divided my premises into two parts, one of which was occupied by my scriveners, the other by myself. According to my humor, I threw open these doors, or closed them. I resolved to assign Bartleby a corner by the folding-doors, but on my side of them, so as to have this quiet man within easy call, in case any trifling thing was to be done. I placed his desk close up to a small side-window in that part of the room, a window which originally had afforded a lateral view of certain grimy brickyards and bricks, but which, owing to subsequent erections, commanded at present no view at all, though it gave some light. Within three feet of the panes was a wall, and the light came down from far above, between two lofty buildings, as from a very small opening in a dome. Still further to a satisfactory arrangement, I procured a high green folding screen, which might entirely isolate Bartleby from my sight, though not remove him from my voice. And thus, in a manner, privacy and society were conjoined.

At first, Bartleby did an extraordinary quantity of writing. As if long famishing for something to copy, he seemed to gorge himself on my documents. There was no pause for digestion. He ran a day and night line, copying by sunlight and by candle-light. I should have been quite delighted with his application, had he been cheerfully industrious. But he wrote on silently, palely, mechanically.

It is, of course, an indispensable part of a scrivener's business to verify the accuracy of his copy, word by word. Where there are two or more scriveners in an office, they assist each other in this examination, one reading from the copy, the other holding the original. It is a very dull, wearisome, and lethargic affair. I can readily imagine that, to some sanguine temperaments, it would be altogether intolerable. For example, I cannot credit that the mettlesome poet, Byron, would have contentedly sat down with Bartleby to examine a law document of, say five hundred pages, closely written in a crimpy hand.

Now and then, in the haste of business, it had been my habit to assist in comparing some brief document myself, calling Turkey or Nippers for this purpose. One object I had, in placing Bartleby so handy to me behind the screen, was, to avail myself of his services on such trivial occasions. It was on the third day, I think, of his being with me, and before any necessity had arisen for having his own writing examined, that, being much hurried to complete a small affair I had in hand, I abruptly called to Bartleby. In my haste and natural expectancy of instant compliance, I sat with my head bent over the original on my desk, and my right hand sideways, and somewhat nervously extended with the copy, so that, immediately upon emerging from his retreat, Bartleby might snatch it and proceed to business without the least delay.

In this very attitude did I sit when I called to him, rapidly stating what it was I wanted him to do—namely, to examine a small paper with me. Imagine my surprise, nay, my consternation, when, without moving from his privacy, Bartleby, in a singularly mild, firm voice, replied, "I would prefer not to."

I sat awhile in perfect silence, rallying my stunned faculties. Immediately it occurred to me that my ears had deceived me, or Bartleby had entirely misunderstood my meaning. I repeated my request in the clearest tone I could assume; but in quite as clear a one came the previous reply, "I would prefer not to."

"Prefer not to," echoed I, rising in high excitement, and crossing the room with a stride. "What do you mean? Are you moon-struck? I want you to help me compare this sheet here—take it," and I thrust it towards him.

"I would prefer not to," said he.

I looked at him steadfastly. His face was leanly composed; his gray eye dimly calm. Not a wrinkle of agitation rippled him. Had there been the least uneasiness, anger, impatience or impertinence in his manner; in other words, had there been anything ordinarily human about him, doubtless I should have violently dismissed him from the premises. But as it was, I should have as soon thought of turning my pale plaster-of-paris bust of Cicero out of doors. I stood gazing at him awhile, as he went on with his own writing, and then reseated myself at my desk. This is very strange, thought I. What had one best do? But my business hurried me. I concluded to forget the matter for the present, reserving it for my future leisure. So, calling Nippers from the other room, the paper was speedily examined.

A few days after this, Bartleby concluded four lengthy documents, being quadruplicates of a week's testimony taken before me in my High Court of Chancery. It became necessary to examine them. It was an important suit, and great accuracy was imperative. Having all things arranged, I called Turkey, Nippers and Ginger Nut, from the next room, meaning to place the four copies in the hands of my four clerks, while I should read from the original. Accordingly, Turkey, Nippers, and Ginger Nut had taken their seats in a row, each with his document in his hand, when I called to Bartleby to join this interesting group.

"Bartleby! quick, I am waiting."

I heard a slow scrape of his chair legs on the uncarpeted floor, and soon he appeared standing at the entrance of his hermitage.

"What is wanted?" said he, mildly.

"The copies, the copies," said I, hurriedly. "We are going to examine them. There"—and I held towards him the fourth quadruplicate.

"I would prefer not to," he said, and gently disappeared behind the screen.

For a few moments I was turned into a pillar of salt, standing at the head of my seated column of clerks. Recovering myself, I advanced towards the screen, and demanded the reason for such extraordinary conduct.

"*Why* do you refuse?"

"I would prefer not to."

With any other man I should have flown outright into a dreadful passion, scorned all further words, and thrust him ignominiously from my presence. But there was something about Bartleby that not only strangely disarmed me, but, in a wonderful manner, touched and disconcerted me. I began to reason with him.

"These are your own copies we are about to examine. It is labor saving to you, because one examination will answer for your four papers. It is common usage. Every copyist is bound to help examine his copy. Is it not so? Will you not speak? Answer!"

"I prefer not to," he replied in a flute-like tone. It seemed to me that, while I had been addressing him, he carefully revolved every statement that I made; fully comprehended the meaning; could not gainsay the irresistible conclusion; but, at the same time, some paramount consideration prevailed with him to reply as he did.

"You are decided, then, not to comply with my request—a request made according to common usage and common sense?"

He briefly gave me to understand, that on that point my judgment was sound. Yes: his decision was irreversible.

It is not seldom the case that, when a man is browbeaten in some unprecedented and violently unreasonable way, he begins to stagger in his own plainest faith. He begins, as it were, vaguely to surmise that, wonderful as it may be, all the justice and all the reason is on the other side. Accordingly, if any disinterested persons are present, he turns to them for some reinforcement for his own faltering mind.

"Turkey," said I, "what do you think of this? Am I not right?"

"With submission, sir," said Turkey, in his blandest tone, "I think that you are."

"Nippers," said I, "what do *you* think of it?"

"I think I should kick him out of the office."

(The reader of nice perceptions will here perceive that, it being morning, Turkey's answer is couched in polite and tranquil terms, but Nippers replies in ill-tempered ones. Or, to repeat a previous sentence, Nipper's ugly mood was on duty, and Turkey's off.)

"Ginger Nut," said I, willing to enlist the smallest suffrage in my behalf, "what do *you* think of it?"

"I think, sir, he's a little *luny*," replied Ginger Nut, with a grin.

"You hear what they say," said I, turning towards the screen, "come forth and do your duty."

But he vouchsafed no reply. I pondered a moment in sore perplexity. But once more business hurried me. I determined again to postpone the consideration of this dilemma to my future leisure. With a little trouble we made out to examine the papers without Bartleby, though at every page or two Turkey deferentially dropped his opinion, that this proceeding was quite out of the common; while Nippers, twitching in his chair with a dyspeptic nervousness, ground out, between his set teeth, occasional hissing maledictions against the stubborn oaf behind the screen. And for his (Nippers's) part, this was the first and the last time he would do another man's business without pay.

Meanwhile Bartleby sat in his hermitage, oblivious to everything but his own peculiar business there.

Some days passed, the scrivener being employed upon another lengthy work. His late remarkable conduct led me to regard his ways narrowly. I observed that he never went to dinner; indeed, that he never went anywhere. As yet I had never, of my personal knowledge, known him to be outside of my office. He was a perpetual sentry in the corner. At about eleven o'clock though, in the morning, I noticed that Ginger Nut would advance toward the opening in Bartleby's screen, as if silently beckoned thither by a gesture invisible to me where I sat. The boy would then leave the office, jingling a few pence, and reappear with a handful of ginger-nuts, which he delivered in the hermitage, receiving two of the cakes for his trouble.

He lives, then, on ginger-nuts, thought I; never eats a dinner, properly speaking; he must be a vegetarian, then, but no; he never eats even vegetables, he eats nothing but ginger-nuts. My mind then ran on in reveries concerning the probable effects upon the human constitution of living entirely on ginger-nuts. Ginger-nuts are so called, because they contain ginger as one of their peculiar constituents, and the final flavoring one. Now, what was ginger? A hot, spicy thing. Was Bartleby hot and spicy? Not at all. Ginger, then, had no effect upon Bartleby. Probably he preferred it should have none.

Nothing so aggravates an earnest person as a passive resistance. If the individual so resisted be of a not inhumane temper, and the resisting one perfectly harmless in his passivity, then, in the better moods of the former, he will endeavor charitably to construe to his imagination what proves impossible to be solved by his judgment. Even so, for the most part, I regarded Bartleby and his ways. Poor fellow! thought I, he means no mischief; it is plain he intends no insolence; his aspect sufficiently evinces that his eccentricities are involuntary. He is useful to me. I can get along with him. If I turn him away, the chances are he will fall in with some less indulgent employer, and then he will be rudely treated, and perhaps driven forth miserably to starve. Yes. Here I can cheaply purchase a delicious self-approval. To befriend Bartleby; to humor him in his strange wilfulness, will cost me little or nothing, while I lay up in my soul what will eventually prove a sweet morsel for my conscience. But this mood was not invariable with me. The passiveness of Bartleby sometimes irritated me. I felt strangely goaded on to encounter him in new opposition—to elicit some angry spark from him answerable to my own. But, indeed, I might as well have essayed to strike fire with my knuckles against a bit of Windsor soap. But one afternoon the evil impulse in me mastered me, and the following little scene ensued:

"Bartleby," said I, "when those papers are all copied, I will compare them with you."

"I would prefer not to."

"How? Surely you do not mean to persist in that mulish vagary?"

No answer.

I threw open the folding-doors near by, and turning upon Turkey and Nippers, exclaimed:

"Bartleby a second time says, he won't examine his papers. What do you think of it, Turkey?"

It was afternoon, be it remembered. Turkey sat glowing like a brass boiler; his bald head steaming; his hands reeling among his blotted papers.

"Think of it?" roared Turkey. "I think I'll just step behind his screen, and black his eyes for him!"

So saying, Turkey rose to his feet and threw his arms into a pugilistic position. He was hurrying away to make good his promise, when I detained him, alarmed at the effect of incautiously rousing Turkey's combativeness after dinner.

"Sit down, Turkey," said I, "and hear what Nippers has to say. What do you think of it, Nippers? Would I not be justified in immediately dismissing Bartleby?"

"Excuse me, that is for you to decide, sir. I think his conduct quite unusual, and, indeed, unjust, as regards Turkey and myself. But it may only be a passing whim."

"Ah," exclaimed I, "you have strangely changed your mind, then—you speak very gently of him now."

"All beer," cried Turkey; "gentleness is effects of beer—Nippers and I dined together to-day. You see how gentle *I* am, sir. Shall I go and black his eyes?"

"You refer to Bartleby, I suppose. No, not to-day, Turkey," I replied; "pray, put up your fists."

I closed the doors, and again advanced towards Bartleby. I felt additional incentives tempting me to my fate. I burned to be rebelled against again. I remembered that Bartleby never left the office.

"Bartleby," said I, "Ginger Nut is away; just step around to the Post Office, won't you?" (it was but a three minutes' walk) "and see if there is anything for me."

"I would prefer not to."

"You *will* not?"

"I *prefer* not."

I staggered to my desk, and sat there in a deep study. My blind inveteracy returned. Was there any other thing in which I could procure myself to be ignominiously repulsed by this lean, penniless wight?—my hired clerk? What added thing is there, perfectly reasonable, that he will be sure to refuse to do?

"Bartleby!"

No answer.

"Bartleby," in a louder tone.

No answer.

"Bartleby," I roared.

Like a very ghost, agreeably to the laws of magical invocation, at the third summons, he appeared at the entrance of his hermitage.

"Go to the next room, and tell Nippers to come to me."

"I prefer not to," he respectfully and slowly said, and mildly disappeared.

"Very good, Bartleby," said I, in a quiet sort of serenely-severe self-possessed tone, intimating the unalterable purpose of some terrible retribution very close at hand. At the moment I half intended something of the kind. But upon the whole, as it was drawing towards my dinner-hour, I thought it best to put on my hat and walk home for the day, suffering much from perplexity and distress of mind.

Shall I acknowledge it? The conclusion of this whole business was, that it soon became a fixed fact of my chambers, that a pale young scrivener, by the name of Bartleby, had a desk there; that he copied for me at the usual rate of four cents a folio (one hundred words); but he was permanently exempt from examining the work done by him, that duty being transferred to Turkey and Nippers, out of compliment, doubtless, to their superior acuteness; moreover, said Bartleby was never, on any account, to be dispatched on the most trivial errand of any sort; and that even if entreated to take upon him such a matter, it was generally understood that he would "prefer not to"—in other words, that he would refuse point-blank.

As days passed on, I became considerably reconciled to Bartleby. His steadiness, his freedom from all dissipation, his incessant industry (except when he chose to throw himself into a standing revery behind his screen), his great stillness, his unalterableness of demeanor under all circumstances, made him a valuable acquisition. One prime thing was this—*he was always there* —first in the morning, continually through the day, and the last at night. I had a singular confidence in his honesty. I felt my most precious papers perfectly safe in his hands. Sometimes, to be sure, I could not, for the very soul of me, avoid falling into sudden spasmodic passions with him. For it was exceeding difficult to bear in mind all the time those strange peculiarities, privileges, and unheard-of exemptions, forming the tacit stipulations on Bartleby's part under which he remained in my office. Now and then, in the eagerness of dispatching pressing business, I would inadvertently summon Bartleby, in a short, rapid tone, to put his finger, say, on the incipient tie of a bit of red tape with which I was about compressing some papers. Of course, from behind the screen the usual answer, "I prefer not to," was sure to come; and then, how could a human creature, with the common infirmities of our nature, refrain from bitterly exclaiming upon such perverseness—such unreasonableness? However, every added repulse of this sort which I received only tended to lessen the probability of my repeating the inadvertence.

Here it must be said, that, according to the custom of most legal gentlemen occupying chambers in densely-populated law buildings, there were several keys to my door. One was kept by a woman residing in the attic, which person weekly scrubbed and daily swept and dusted my apartments. Another was kept by Turkey for convenience sake. The third I sometimes carried in my own pocket. The fourth I knew not who had.

Now, one Sunday morning I happened to go to Trinity Church, to hear a celebrated preacher, and finding myself rather early on the ground I thought

I would walk round to my chambers for a while. Luckily I had my key with me; but upon applying it to the lock, I found it resisted by something inserted from the inside. Quite surprised, I called out; when to my consternation a key was turned from within; and thrusting his lean visage at me, and holding the door ajar, the apparition of Bartleby appeared, in his shirtsleeves, and otherwise in a strangely tattered deshabille, saying quietly that he was sorry, but he was deeply engaged just then, and—preferred not admitting me at present. In a brief word or two, he moreover added, that perhaps I had better walk round the block two or three times, and by that time he would probably have concluded his affairs.

Now, the utterly unsurmised appearance of Bartleby, tenanting my law-chambers of a Sunday morning, with his cadaverously gentlemanly *nonchalance,* yet withal firm and self-possessed, had such a strange effect upon me, that incontinently I slunk away from my own door, and did as desired. But not without sundry twinges of impotent rebellion against the mild effrontery of this unaccountable scrivener. Indeed, it was his wonderful mildness chiefly, which not only disarmed me, but unmanned me, as it were. For I consider that one, for the time, is somehow unmanned when he tranquilly permits his hired clerk to dictate to him, and order him away from his own premises. Furthermore, I was full of uneasiness as to what Bartleby could possibly be doing in my office in his shirt-sleeves, and in an otherwise dismantled condition of a Sunday morning. Was anything amiss going on? Nay, that was out of the question. It was not to be thought of for a moment that Bartleby was an immoral person. But what could he be doing there?—copying? Nay again, whatever might be his eccentricities, Bartleby was an eminently decorous person. He would be the last man to sit down to his desk in any state approaching to nudity. Besides, it was Sunday; and there was something about Bartleby that forbade the supposition that he would by any secular occupation violate the proprieties of the day.

Nevertheless, my mind was not pacified; and full of a restless curiosity, at last I returned to the door. Without hindrance I inserted my key, opened it, and entered. Bartleby was not to be seen. I looked round anxiously, peeped behind his screen; but it was very plain that he was gone. Upon more closely examining the place, I surmised that for an indefinite period Bartleby must have ate, dressed, and slept in my office, and that too without plate, mirror, or bed. The cushioned seat of a rickety old sofa in one corner bore the faint impress of a lean, reclining form. Rolled away under his desk, I found a blanket; under the empty grate, a blacking box and brush; on a chair, a tin basin, with soap and a ragged towel; in a newspaper a few crumbs of ginger-nuts and a morsel of cheese. Yes, thought I, it is evident enough that Bartleby has been making his home here, keeping bachelor's hall all by himself. Immediately then the thought came sweeping across me, what miserable friendlessness and loneliness are here revealed! His poverty is great; but his solitude, how horrible! Think of it. Of a Sunday, Wall Street is deserted as Petra; and every night of every day it is an emptiness. This building, too, which of week-days hums with industry and life, at nightfall echoes with sheer vacancy, and all through Sunday is forlorn. And here Bartleby makes his home; sole spectator of a solitude which he has seen all populous—a sort of innocent and transformed Marius brooding among the ruins of Carthage!

For the first time in my life a feeling of overpowering stinging melancholy seized me. Before, I had never experienced aught but a not unpleasing sadness. The bond of a common humanity now drew me irresistibly to gloom. A fraternal melancholy! For both I and Bartleby were sons of Adam. I remembered the bright silks and sparkling faces I had seen that day, in gala trim, swan-like sailing down the Mississippi of Broadway; and I contrasted them with the pallid copyist, and thought to myself, Ah, happiness courts the light, so we deem the world is gay; but misery hides aloof, so we deem that misery there is none. These sad fancyings—chimeras, doubtless, of a sick and silly brain—led on to other and more special thoughts, concerning the eccentricities of Bartleby. Presentiments of strange discoveries hovered round me. The scrivener's pale form appeared to me laid out, among uncaring strangers, in its shivering winding-sheet.

Suddenly, I was attracted by Bartleby's closed desk, the key in open sight left in the lock.

I mean no mischief, seek the gratification of no heartless curiosity, thought I; besides, the desk is mine, and its contents, too, so I will make bold to look within. Everything was methodically arranged, the papers smoothly placed. The pigeon-holes were deep, and removing the files of documents, I groped into their recesses. Presently I felt something there, and dragged it out. It was an old bandanna handkerchief, heavy and knotted. I opened it, and saw it was a savings bank.

I now recalled all the quiet mysteries which I had noted in the man. I remembered that he never spoke but to answer; that, though at intervals he had considerable time to himself, yet I had never seen him reading—no, not even a newspaper; that for long periods he would stand looking out, at his pale window behind the screen, upon the dead brick wall; I was quite sure he never visited any refectory or eating-house; while his pale face clearly indicated that he never drank beer like Turkey, or tea and coffee even, like other men; that he never went anywhere in particular that I could learn; never went out for a walk, unless, indeed, that was the case at present; that he had declined telling who he was, or whence he came, or whether he had any relatives in the world; that though so thin and pale, he never complained of ill-health. And more than all, I remembered a certain unconscious air of pallid —how shall I call it?—of pallid haughtiness, say, or rather an austere reserve about him, which had positively awed me into my tame compliance with his eccentricities, when I had feared to ask him to do the slightest incidental thing for me, even though I might know, from his long-continued motionlessness, that behind his screen he must be standing in one of those dead-wall reveries of his.

Revolving all these things, and coupling them with the recently discovered fact, that he made my office his constant abiding place and home, and not forgetful of his morbid moodiness; revolving all these things, a prudential feeling began to steal over me. My first emotions had been those of pure melancholy and sincerest pity; but just in proportion as the forlornness of Bartleby grew and grew to my imagination, did that same melancholy merge into fear, that pity into repulsion. So true it is, and so terrible, too, that up to a certain point the thought or sight of misery enlists our best affections; but, in certain special cases, beyond that point it does not. They err who would assert that invariably this is owing to the inherent selfishness of the human heart. It rather proceeds from a certain hopelessness of remedying excessive and organic ill. To a sensitive being, pity is not seldom pain. And when at last it is perceived that such pity cannot lead to effectual succor, common sense bids the soul be rid of it. What I saw that morning persuaded me that the scrivener was the victim of innate and incurable disorder. I might give alms to his body; but his body did not pain him; it was his soul that suffered, and his soul I could not reach.

I did not accomplish the purpose of going to Trinity Church that morning. Somehow, the things I had seen disqualified me for the time from church-going. I walked homeward, thinking, what I would do with Bartleby. Finally, I resolved upon this—I would put certain calm questions to him the next morning, touching his history, etc., and if he declined to answer them openly and unreservedly (and I supposed he would prefer not), then to give him a twenty dollar bill over and above whatever I might owe him, and tell him his services were no longer required; but that if in any other way I could assist him, I would be happy to do so, especially if he desired to return to his native place, wherever that might be, I would willingly help to defray the expenses. Moreover, if, after reaching home, he found himself at any time in want of aid, a letter from him would be sure of a reply.

The next morning came.

"Bartleby," said I, gently calling to him behind his screen.

No reply.

"Bartleby," said I, in a still gentler tone, "come here; I am not going to ask you to do anything you would prefer not to do—I simply wish to speak to you."

Upon this he noiselessly slid into view.

"Will you tell me, Bartleby, where you were born?"

"I would prefer not to."

"Will you tell me *anything* about yourself?"

"I would prefer not to."

"But what reasonable objection can you have to speak to me? I feel friendly towards you."

He did not look at me while I spoke, but kept his glance fixed upon my bust of Cicero, which, as then sat, was directly behind me, some six inches above my head.

"What is your answer, Bartleby?" said I, after waiting a considerable time for a reply, during which his countenance remained immovable, only there was the faintest conceivable tremor of the white attenuated mouth.

"At present I prefer to give no answer," he said, and retired into his hermitage.

It was rather weak in me I confess, but his manner, on this occasion, nettled me. Not only did there seem to lurk in it a certain calm disdain, but his perverseness seemed ungrateful, considering the undeniable good usage and indulgence he had received from me.

Again I sat ruminating what I should do. Mortified as I was at his behavior, and resolved as I had been to dismiss him when I entered my office, nevertheless I strangely felt something superstitious knocking at my heart, and forbidding me to carry out my purpose, and denouncing me for a villain if I dared to breathe one bitter word against this forlornest of mankind. At last, familiarly drawing my chair behind his screen, I sat down and said: "Bartleby, never mind, then, about revealing your history; but let me entreat you, as a friend, to comply as far as may be with the usages of this office. Say now, you will help to examine papers to-morrow or next day: in short, say now, that in a day or two you will begin to be a little reasonable:—say so, Bartleby."

"At present I would prefer not to be a little reasonable," was his mildly cadaverous reply.

Just then the folding-doors opened, and Nippers approached. He seemed suffering from an unusually bad night's rest, induced by severer indigestion than common. He overheard those final words of Bartleby.

"*Prefer not,* eh?" gritted Nippers—"I'd *prefer* him, if I were you, sir," addressing me—"I'd *prefer* him; I'd give him preferences, the stubborn mule! What is it, sir, pray, that he *prefers* not to do now?"

Bartleby moved not a limb.

"Mr. Nippers," said I, "I'd prefer that you would withdraw for the present."

Somehow, of late, I had got into the way of involuntarily using this word "prefer" upon all sorts of not exactly suitable occasions. And I trembled to think that my contact with the scrivener had already and seriously affected me in a mental way. And what further and deeper aberration might it not yet produce? This apprehension had not been without efficacy in determining me to summary measures.

As Nippers, looking very sour and sulky, was departing, Turkey blandly and deferentially approached.

"With submission, sir," said he, "yesterday I was thinking about Bartleby here, and I think that if he would but prefer to take a quart of good ale every day, it would do much towards mending him, and enabling him to assist in examining his papers."

"So you have got the word, too," said I, slightly excited.

"With submission, what word, sir?" asked Turkey, respectfully crowding himself into the contracted space behind the screen, and by so doing, making me jostle the scrivener. "What word, sir?"

"I would prefer to be left alone here," said Bartleby, as if offended at being mobbed in his privacy.

"*That's* the word, Turkey," said I—"*that's* it."

"Oh, *prefer?* oh yes—queer word. I never use it myself. But, sir, as I was saying, if he would but prefer—"

"Turkey," interrupted I, "You will please withdraw."

"Oh certainly, sir, if you prefer that I should."

As he opened the folding-door to retire, Nippers at his desk caught a glimpse of me, and asked whether I would prefer to have a certain paper copied on blue paper or white. He did not in the least roguishly accent the word "prefer." It was plain that it involuntarily rolled from his tongue. I thought to myself, surely I must get rid of a demented man, who already has in some degree turned the tongues, if not the heads of myself and clerks. But I thought it prudent not to break the dismission at once.

The next day I noticed that Bartleby did nothing but stand at his window in his dead-wall revery. Upon asking him why he did not write, he said that he had decided upon doing no more writing.

"Why, how now? what next?" exclaimed I, "do no more writing?"

"No more."

"And what is the reason?"

"Do you not see the reason for yourself?" he indifferently replied.

I looked steadfastly at him, and perceived that his eyes looked dull and glazed. Instantly it occurred to me, that his unexampled diligence in copying by his dim window for the first few weeks of his stay with me might have temporarily impaired his vision.

I was touched. I said something in condolence with him. I hinted that of course he did wisely in abstaining from writing for a while; and urged him to embrace that opportunity of taking wholesome exercise in the open air. This, however, he did not do. A few days after this, my other clerks being absent, and being in a great hurry to dispatch certain letters by the mail, I thought that, having nothing else earthly to do, Bartleby would surely be less inflexible than usual, and carry these letters to the post office. But he blankly declined. So, much to my inconvenience, I went myself.

Still added days went by. Whether Bartleby's eyes improved or not, I could not say. To all appearance, I thought they did. But when I asked him if they did, he vouchsafed no answer. At all events, he would do no copying. At last, in reply to my urgings, he informed me that he had permanently given up copying.

"What!" exclaimed I; "suppose your eyes should get entirely well—better than ever before—would you not copy then?"

"I have given up copying," he answered, and slid aside.

He remained as ever, a fixture in my chamber. Nay—if that were possible —he became still more of a fixture than before. What was to be done? He would do nothing in the office; why should he stay there? In plain fact, he had now become a millstone to me, not only useless as a necklace, but afflictive to bear. Yet I was sorry for him. I speak less than the truth when I say that, on his own account, he occasioned me uneasiness. If he would but have named a single relative or friend, I would instantly have written, and urged their taking the poor fellow away to some convenient retreat. But he seemed alone, absolutely alone in the universe. A bit of wreck in the mid-Atlantic. At length, necessities connected with my business tyrannized over all other considerations. Decently as I could, I told Bartleby that in six days' time he must unconditionally leave the office. I warned him to take measures, in the interval, for procuring some other abode. I offered to assist him in this endeavor, if he himself would but take the first step towards a removal. "And when you finally quit me, Bartleby," added I, "I shall see that you go not away entirely unprovided. Six days from this hour, remember."

At the expiration of that period, I peeped behind the screen, and lo! Bartleby was there.

I buttoned up my coat, balanced myself; advanced slowly towards him, touched his shoulder, and said, "The time has come; you must quit this place; I am sorry for you; here is money; but you must go."

"I would prefer not," he replied, with his back still towards me.

"You *must*."

He remained silent.

Now I had an unbounded confidence in this man's common honesty. He had frequently restored to me sixpences and shillings carelessly dropped upon the floor, for I am apt to be very reckless in such shirt-button affairs. The proceeding, then, which followed will not be deemed extraordinary.

"Bartleby," said I, "I owe you twelve dollars on account; here are thirty-two; the odd twenty are yours—Will you take it?" and I handed the bills towards him.

But he made no motion.

"I will leave them here, then," putting them under a weight on the table. Then taking my hat and cane and going to the door, I tranquilly turned and added—"After you have removed your things from these offices, Bartleby, you will of course lock the door—since every one is now gone for the day but you—and if you please, slip your key underneath the mat, so that I may have it in the morning. I shall not see you again; so good-bye to you. If, hereafter, in your new place of abode, I can be of any service to you, do not fail to advise me by letter. Good-bye, Bartleby, and fare you well,"

But he answered not a word; like the last column of some ruined temple, he remained standing mute and solitary in the middle of the otherwise deserted room.

As I walked home in a pensive mood, my vanity got the better of my pity. I could not but highly plume myself on my masterly management in getting rid of Bartleby. Masterly I call it, and such it must appear to any dispassionate thinker. The beauty of my procedure seemed to consist in its perfect quietness. There was no vulgar bullying, no bravado of any sort, no choleric hectoring, and striding to and fro across the apartment, jerking out vehement commands for Bartleby to bundle himself off with his beggarly traps. Nothing of the kind. Without loudly bidding Bartleby depart—as an inferior genius might have done—I *assumed* the ground that depart he must; and upon that assumption built all I had to say. The more I thought over my procedure, the more I was charmed with it. Nevertheless, next morning, upon awakening, I had my doubts—I had somehow slept off the fumes of vanity. One of the coolest and wisest hours a man has is just after he awakes in the morning. My procedure seemed as sagacious as ever—but only in theory. How it would prove in practice—there was the rub. It was truly a beautiful thought to have assumed Bartleby's departure; but, after all, that assumption was simply my own, and none of Bartleby's. The great point was, not whether I had assumed that he would quit me, but whether he would prefer so to do. He was more a man of preferences than assumptions.

After breakfast, I walked down town, arguing the probabilities *pro* and *con*. One moment I thought it would prove a miserable failure, and Bartleby would be found all alive at my office as usual; the next moment it seemed certain that I should find his chair empty. And so I kept veering about. At the corner of Broadway and Canal Street, I saw quite an excited group of people standing in earnest conversation.

"I'll take odds he doesn't," said a voice as I passed.

"Doesn't go?—done!" said I, "put up your money."

I was instinctively putting my hand in my pocket to produce my own, when I remembered that this was an election day. The words I had overheard bore no reference to Bartleby, but to the success or non-success of some candidate for the mayoralty. In my intent frame of mind, I had, as it were, imagined that all Broadway shared in my excitement, and were debating the same question with me. I passed on, very thankful that the uproar of the street screened my momentary absent-mindedness.

As I had intended, I was earlier than usual at my office door. I stood listenting for a moment. All was still. He must be gone. I tried the knob. The door was locked. Yes, my procedure had worked to a charm; he indeed must be vanished. Yet a certain melancholy mixed with this: I was almost sorry for my brilliant success. I was fumbling under the door mat for the key, which Bartleby was to have left there for me, when accidentally my knee knocked against a panel, producing a summoning sound, and in response a voice came to me from within—"Not yet; I am occupied."

It was Bartleby.

I was thunderstruck. For an instant I stood like the man who, pipe in mouth, was killed one cloudless afternoon long ago in Virginia, by summer lightning; at his own warm open window he was killed, and remained leaning out there upon the dreamy afternoon, till some one touched him, when he fell.

"Not gone!" I murmured at last. But again obeying that wondrous ascendancy which the inscrutable scrivener had over me, and from which ascendancy, for all my chafing, I could not completely escape, I slowly went down stairs and out into the street, and while walking round the block, considered what I should next do in this unheard-of perplexity. Turn the man out by an actual thrusting I could not; to drive him away by calling him hard names would not do; calling in the police was an unpleasant idea; and yet, permit him to enjoy his cadaverous triumph over me—this, too, I could not think of. What was to be done? Or, if nothing could be done, was there anything further that I could *assume* in the matter? Yes, as before I had prospectively assumed that Bartleby would depart, so now I might retrospectively assume that departed he was. In the legitimate carrying out of this assumption, I might enter my office in a great hurry, and pretending not to see Bartleby at all, walk straight against him as if he were air. Such a proceeding would in a singular degree have the appearance of a home-thrust. It was hardly possible that Bartleby could withstand such an application of the doctrine of assumptions. But upon second thoughts the success of the plan seemed rather dubious. I resolved to argue the matter over with him again.

"Bartleby," said I, entering the office, with a quietly severe expression, "I am serious displeased. I am pained, Bartleby. I had thought better of you. I had imagined you of such a gentlemanly organization, that in any delicate dilemma a slight hint would suffice—in short, an assumption. But it appears I am deceived. Why," I added, unaffectedly starting, "you have not even touched that money yet," pointing to it, just where I had left it the evening previous.

He answered nothing.

"Will you, or will you not, quit me?" I now demanded in a sudden passion, advancing close to him.

"I would prefer *not* to quit you " he replied, gently emphasizing the *not.*

"What earthly right have you to stay here? Do you pay any rent? Do you pay my taxes? Or is this property yours?"

He answered nothing.

"Are you ready to go on and write now? Are your eyes recovered? Could you copy a small paper for me this morning? or help examine a few lines? or step round to the post-office? In a word, will you do anything at all, to give a coloring to your refusal to depart the premises?"

He silently retired to his hermitage.

I was now in such a state of nervous resentment that I thought it but prudent to check myself at present from further demonstrations. Bartleby and I were alone. I remembered the tragedy of the unfortunate Adams and the still more unfortunate Colt in the solitary office of the latter; and how poor Colt, being dreadfully incensed by Adams, and imprudently permitting himself to get wildly excited, was at unawares hurried into his fatal act—an act which certainly no man could possibly deplore more than the actor himself. Often it had occurred to me in my ponderings upon the subject that had that altercation taken place in the public street, or at a private residence, it would not have terminated as it did. It was the circumstance of being alone in a solitary office, up stairs, of a building entirely unhallowed by humanizing domestic associations—an uncarpeted office, doubtless, of a dusty, haggard sort of appearance—this it must have been, which greatly helped to enhance the irritable desperation of the hapless Colt.

But when this old Adam of resentment rose in me and tempted me concerning Bartleby, I grappled him and threw him. How? Why, simply by recalling the divine injunction: "A new commandment give I unto you, that ye love one another." Yes, this it was that saved me. Aside from higher considerations, charity often operates as a vastly wise and prudent principle—a great safeguard to its possessor. Men have committed murder for jealousy's sake, and anger's sake, and hatred's sake, and selfishness' sake, and spiritual pride's sake; but no man, that ever I heard of ever committed a diabolical murder for sweet charity's sake. Mere self-interest, then, if no better motive can be enlisted, should, especially with high-tempered men, prompt all beings to charity and philanthropy. At any rate, upon the occasion in question, I strove to drown my exasperated feelings towards the scrivener by benevolently construing his conduct. Poor fellow, poor fellow! thought I, he don't mean anything; and besides, he has seen hard times, and ought to be indulged.

I endeavored, also, immediately to occupy myself, and at the same time to comfort my despondency. I tried to fancy, that in the course of the morning, at such time as might prove agreeable to him, Bartleby, of his own free accord, would emerge from his hermitage and take up some decided line of march in the direction of the door. But no. Half-past twelve o'clock came; Turkey began to glow in the face, overturn his inkstand, and become generally obstreperous; Nippers abated down into quietude and courtesy; Ginger Nut munched his noon apple; and Bartleby remained standing at his window in one of his profoundest dead-wall reveries. Will it be credited? Ought I to acknowledge it? That afternoon I left the office without saying one further word to him.

Some days now passed, during which, at leisure intervals I looked a little into "Edwards on the Will," and "Priestley on Necessity." Under the circumstances, those books induced a salutary feeling. Gradually I slid into the persuasion that these troubles of mine, touching the scrivener, had been all predestinated from eternity, and Bartleby was billeted upon me for some mysterious purpose of an all-wise Providence, which it was not for a mere mortal like me to fathom. Yes, Bartleby, stay there behind your screen, thought I; I shall persecute you no more; you are harmless and noiseless as any of these old chairs; in short, I never feel so private as when I know you are here. At last I see it, I feel it; I penetrate to the predestinated purpose of my life. I am content. Others may have loftier parts to enact; but my mission in this world, Bartleby, is to furnish you with office-room for such period as you may see fit to remain.

I believe that this wise and blessed frame of mind would have continued with me, had it not been for the unsolicited and uncharitable remarks obtruded upon me by my professional friends who visited the rooms. But thus it often is, that the constant friction of illiberal minds wears out at last the best resolves of the more generous. Though to be sure, when I reflected upon it, it was not strange that people entering my office should be struck by the peculiar aspect of the unaccountable Bartleby, and so be tempted to throw out some sinister observations concerning him. Sometimes an attorney, having business with me, and calling at my office, and finding no one but the scrivener there, would undertake to obtain some sort of precise information from him touching my whereabouts; but without heeding his idle talk, Bartleby would remain standing immovable in the middle of the room. So after contemplating him in that position for a time, the attorney would depart, no wiser than he came.

Also, when a reference was going on, and the room full of lawyers and witnesses, and business driving fast, some deeply-occupied legal gentleman present, seeing Bartleby wholly unemployed, would request him to run round to his (the legal gentleman's) office and fetch some papers for him. Thereupon, Bartleby would tranquilly decline, and yet remain idle as before. Then the lawyer would give a great stare, and turn to me. And what could I say? At last I was made aware that all through the circle of my professional acquaintance, a whisper of wonder was running round, having reference to the strange creature I kept at my office. This worried me very much. And as the idea came upon me of his possibly turning out a long-lived man, and keep occupying my chambers, and denying my authority; and perplexing my visitors; and scandalizing my professional reputation; and casting a general gloom over the premises; keeping soul and body together to the last upon his savings (for doubtless he spent but half a dime a day), and in the end perhaps outlive me, and claim possession of my office by right of his perpetual occupancy: as all these dark anticipations crowded upon me more and more, and my friends continually intruded their relentless remarks upon the apparition in my room; a great change was wrought in me. I resolved to gather all my faculties together, and forever rid me of this intolerable incubus.

Ere revolving any complicated project, however, adapted to this end, I first simply suggested to Bartleby the propriety of his permanent departure. In a calm and serious tone, I commended the idea to his careful and mature consideration. But, having taken three days to meditate upon it, he apprised me, that his original determination remained the same; in short, that he still preferred to abide with me.

What shall I do? I now said to myself, buttoning up my coat to the last button. What shall I do? what ought I to do? what does conscience say I *should* do with this man, or, rather, ghost. Rid myself of him, I must; go, he shall. But how? You will not thrust him, the poor, pale, passive mortal—you will not thrust such a helpless creature out of your door? you will not dishonor yourself by such cruelty? No, I will not, I cannot do that. Rather would I let him live and die here, and then mason up his remains in the wall. What, then, will you do? For all your coaxing, he will not budge. Bribes he leaves under your own paper-weight on your table; in short, it is quite plain that he prefers to cling to you.

Then something severe, something unusual must be done. What! surely you will not have him collared by a constable, and commit his innocent pallor to the common jail? And upon what ground could you procure such a thing to be done?—a vagrant, is he? What! he a vagrant, a wanderer, who refuses to budge? It is because he will *not* be a vagrant, then, that you seek to count him *as* a vagrant. That is too absurd. No visible means of support: there I have him. Wrong again: for indubitably he does support himself, and that is the only unanswerable proof that any man can show of his possessing the means so to do. No more, then. Since he will not quit me, I must quit him. I will change my offices; I will move elsewhere, and give him fair notice, that if I find him on my new premises I will then proceed against him as a common trespasser.

Acting accordingly, next day I thus addressed him: "I find these chambers too far from the City Hall; the air is unwholesome. In a word, I propose to remove my offices next week, and shall no longer require your services. I tell you this now, in order that you may seek another place."

He made no reply, and nothing more was said.

On the appointed day I engaged carts and men, proceeded to my chambers, and, having but little furniture, everything was removed in a few hours. Throughout, the scrivener remained standing behind the screen, which I directed to be removed the last thing. It was withdrawn; and, being folded up like a huge folio, left him the motionless occupant of a naked room. I stood in the entry watching him a moment, while something from within me upbraided me.

I re-entered, with my hand in my pocket—and—and my heart in my mouth.

"Good-bye, Bartleby; I am going—good-bye, and God some way bless you; and take that," slipping something in his hand. But it dropped upon the floor, and then—strange to say—I tore myself from him whom I had so longed to be rid of.

Established in my new quarters, for a day or two I kept the door locked, and started at every footfall in the passages. When I returned to my rooms, after any little absence, I would pause at the threshold for an instant, and attentively listen, ere applying my key. But these fears were needless. Bartleby never came nigh me.

I thought all was going well, when a perturbed-looking stranger visited me, inquiring whether I was the person who had recently occupied rooms at No. —Wall Street.

Full of forebodings, I replied that I was.

"Then, sir," said the stranger, who proved a lawyer, "you are responsible for the man you left there. He refuses to do any copying; he refuses to do anything; he says he prefers not to; and he refuses to quit the premises."

"I am very sorry, sir," said I, with assumed tranquillity, but an inward tremor, "but, really, the man you allude to is nothing to me—he is no relation or apprentice of mine, that you should hold me responsible for him."

"In mercy's name, who is he?"

"I certainly cannot inform you. I know nothing about him. Formerly I employed him as a copyist; but he has done nothing for me now for some time past."

"I shall settle him, then—good morning, sir."

Several days passed, and I heard nothing more; and, though I often felt a charitable prompting to call at the place and see poor Bartleby, yet a certain squeamishness, of I know not what, withheld me.

All is over with him, by this time, thought I, at last, when, through another week, no further intelligence reached me. But, coming to my room the day after, I found several persons waiting at my door in a high state of nervous excitement.

"That's the man—here he comes," cried the foremost one, whom I recognized as the lawyer who had previously called upon me alone.

"You must take him away, sir, at once," cried a portly person among them, advancing upon me, and whom I knew to be the landlord of No.—Wall Street. "These gentlemen, my tenants, cannot stand it any longer; Mr. B——," pointing to the lawyer, "has turned him out of his room, and he now persists in haunting the building generally, sitting upon the banisters of the stairs by day, and sleeping in the entry by night. Everybody is concerned; clients are leaving the offices; some fears are entertained of a mob; something you must do, and that without delay."

Aghast at this torrent, I fell back before it, and would fain have locked myself in my new quarters. In vain I persisted that Bartleby was nothing to me—no more than to any one else. In vain—I was the last person known to have anything to do with him, and they held me to the terrible account. Fearful, then, of being exposed in the papers (as one person present obscurely threatened), I considered the matter, and, at length, said, that if the lawyer would give me a confidential interview with the scrivener, in his (the lawyer's) own room, I would, that afternoon, strive my best to rid them of the nuisance they complained of.

Going up stairs to my old haunt, there was Bartleby silently sitting upon the banister at the landing.

"What are you doing here, Bartleby?" said I.

"Sitting upon the banister," he mildly replied.

I motioned him into the lawyer's room, who then left us.

"Bartleby," said I, "are you aware that you are the cause of great tribulation to me, by persisting in occupying the entry after being dismissed from the office?"

No answer.

"Now one of two things must take place. Either you must do something, or something must be done to you. Now what sort of business would you like to engage in? Would you like to re-engage in copying for some one?"

"No; I would prefer not to make any change."

"Would you like a clerkship in a dry-goods store?"

"There is too much confinement about that. No, I would not like a clerkship; but I am not particular."

"Too much confinement," I cried, "why, you keep yourself confined all the time!"

"I would prefer not to take a clerkship," he rejoined, as if to settle that little item at once.

"How would a bar-tender's business suit you? There is no trying of the eye-sight in that."

"I would not like it at all; though, as I have said before, I am not particular."

His unwonted wordiness inspirited me. I returned to the charge.

"Well, then, would you like to travel through the country collecting bills for the merchants? That would improve your health."

"No, I would prefer to be doing something else."

"How, then, would going as a companion to Europe, to entertain some young gentleman with your conversation—how would that suit you?"

"Not at all. It does not strike me that there is anything definite about that. I like to be stationary. But I am not particular."

"Stationary you shall be, then," I cried, now losing all patience, and, for the first time in all my exasperating connection with him, fairly flying into a passion. "If you do not go away from these premises before night, I shall feel bound—indeed, I *am* bound—to—to quit the premises myself!" I rather absurdly concluded, knowing not with what possible threat to try to frighten his immobility into compliance. Despairing of all further efforts, I was precipitately leaving him, when a final thought occurred to me—one which had not been wholly unindulged before.

"Bartleby," said I, in the kindest tone I could assume under such exciting circumstances, "will you go home with me now—not to my office, but my dwelling—and remain there till we can conclude upon some convenient arrangement for you at our leisure? Come, let us start now, right away."

"No: at present I would prefer not to make any change at all."

I answered nothing; but, effectually dodging every one by the suddenness and rapidity of my flight, rushed from the building, ran up Wall Street towards Broadway, and, jumping into the first omnibus, was soon removed from pursuit. As soon as tranquillity returned, I distinctly perceived that I had now done all that I possibly could, both in respect to the demands of the landlord and his tenants, and with regard to my own desire and sense of duty, to benefit Bartleby, and shield him from rude persecution. I now strove to be entirely care-free and quiescent; and my conscience justified me in the attempt; though, indeed, it was not so successful as I could have wished. So fearful was I of being again hunted out by the incensed landlord and his exasperated tenants, that, surrendering my business to Nippers, for a few days, I drove about the upper part of the town and through the suburbs, in my rockaway; crossed over to Jersey City and Hoboken, and paid fugitive visits to Manhattanville and Astoria. In fact, I almost lived in my rockaway for the time.

When again I entered my office, lo, a note from the landlord lay upon the desk. I opened it with trembling hands. It informed me that the writer had sent to the police, and had Bartleby removed to the Tombs as a vagrant. Moreover, since I knew more about him than any one else, he wished me to appear at that place, and make a suitable statement of the facts. These tidings had a conflicting effect upon me. At first I was indignant; but, at last, almost approved. The landlord's energetic, summary disposition, had led him to adopt a procedure which I do not think I would have decided upon myself; and yet, as a last resort, under such peculiar circumstances, it seemed the only plan.

As I afterwards learned, the poor scrivener, when told that he must be conducted to the Tombs, offered not the slightest obstacle, but, in his pale, unmoving way, silently acquiesced.

Some of the compassionate and curious by-standers joined the party; and headed by one of the constables arm-in-arm with Bartleby, the silent procession filed its way through all the noise, and heat, and joy of the roaring thoroughfares at noon.

The same day I received the note, I went to the Tombs, or, to speak more properly, the Halls of Justice. Seeking the right officer, I stated the purpose of my call, and was informed that the individual I described was, indeed, within. I then assured the functionary that Bartleby was a perfectly honest man, and greatly to be compassionated, however unaccountably eccentric. I narrated all I knew, and closed by suggesting the idea of letting him remain in as indulgent confinement as possible, till something less harsh might be done—though, indeed, I hardly knew what. At all events, if nothing else could be decided upon, the alms-house must receive him. I then begged to have an interview.

Being under no disgraceful charge, and quite serene and harmless in all his ways, they had permitted him freely to wander about the prison, and, especially, in the inclosed grass-platted yards thereof. And so I found him there, standing all alone in the quietest of the yards, his face towards a high wall, while all around, from the narrow slits of the jail windows, I thought I saw peering out upon him the eyes of murderers and thieves.

"Bartleby!"

"I know you," he said, without looking round—"and I want nothing to say to you."

"It was not I that brought you here, Bartleby," said I, keenly pained at his implied suspicion. "And to you, this should not be so vile a place. Nothing reproachful attaches to you by being here. And see, it is not so sad a place as one might think. Look, there is the sky, and here is the grass."

"I know where I am," he replied, but would say nothing more, and so I left him.

As I entered the corridor again, a broad meat-like man, in an apron, accosted me, and, jerking his thumb over his shoulder, said—"Is that your friend?"

"Yes."

"Does he want to starve? If he does, let him live on the prison fare, that's all."

"Who are you?" asked I, not knowing what to make of such an unofficially speaking person in such a place.

"I am the grub-man. Such gentlemen as have friends here, hire me to provide them with something good to eat."

"Is this so?" said I, turning to the turnkey.

He said it was.

"Well, then," said I, slipping some silver into the grub-man's hands (for so they called him), "I want you to give particular attention to my friend there; let him have the best dinner you can get. And you must be as polite to him as possible."

"Introduce me, will you?" said the grub-man, looking at me with an expression which seemed to say he was all impatience for an opportunity to give a specimen of his breeding.

Thinking it would prove of benefit to the scrivener, I acquiesced; and, asking the grub-man his name, went up with him to Bartleby.

"Bartleby, this is a friend; you will find him very useful to you."

"Your sarvant, sir, your sarvant," said the grub-man, making a low salutation behind his apron. "Hope you find it pleasant here, sir; nice grounds—cool apartments—hope you'll stay with us some time—try to make it agreeable. What will you have for dinner to-day?"

"I prefer not to dine to-day," said Bartleby, turning away. "It would disagree with me; I am unused to dinners." So saying, he slowly moved to the other side of the inclosure, and took up a position fronting the dead-wall.

"How's this?" said the grub-man, addressing me with a stare of astonishment. "He's odd, ain't he?"

"I think he is a little deranged," said I, sadly.

"Deranged? deranged is it? Well, now, upon my word, I thought that friend of yourn was a gentleman forger; they are always pale and genteel-like, them forgers. I can't help pity 'em—can't help it, sir. Did you know Monroe Edwards?" he added, touchingly, and paused. Then, laying his hand piteously on my shoulder, sighed, "he died of consumption at Sing-Sing. So you weren't acquainted with Monroe?"

"No, I was never socially acquainted with any forgers. But I cannot stop longer. Look to my friend yonder. You will not lose by it. I will see you again."

Some few days after this, I again obtained admission to the Tombs, and went through the corridors in quest of Bartleby; but without finding him.

"I saw him coming from his cell not long ago," said a turnkey, "may be he's gone to loiter in the yards."

So I went in that direction.

"Are you looking for the silent man?" said another turnkey, passing me. "Yonder he lies—sleeping in the yard there. 'Tis not twenty minutes since I saw him lie down."

The yard was entirely quiet. It was not accessible to the common prisoners. The surrounding walls, of amazing thickness, kept off all sounds behind them. The Egyptian character of the masonry weighed upon me with its gloom. But a soft imprisoned turf grew under foot. The heart of the eternal pyramids, it seemed, wherein, by some strange magic, through the clefts, grass-seed, dropped by birds, had sprung.

Strangely huddled at the base of the wall, his knees drawn up, and lying on his side, his head touching the cold stones, I saw the wasted Bartleby. But nothing stirred. I paused; then went close up to him; stooped over, and saw that his dim eyes were open; otherwise he seemed profoundly sleeping. Something prompted me to touch him. I felt his hand, when a tingling shiver ran up my arm and down my spine to my feet.

The round face of the grub-man peered upon me now. "His dinner is ready. Won't he dine to-day, either? Or does he live without dining?"

"Lives without dining," said I, and closed the eyes.

"Eh!—He's asleep, ain't he?"

"With kings and counselors," murmured I.

There would seem little need for proceeding further in this history. Imagination will readily supply the meagre recital of poor Bartleby's interment. But, ere parting with the reader, let me say, that if this little narrative has sufficiently interested him, to awaken curiosity as to who Bartleby was, and what manner of life he led prior to the present narrator's making his acquaintance, I can only reply, that in such curiosity I fully share, but am wholly unable to gratify it. Yet here I hardly know whether I should divulge one little item of rumor, which came to my ear a few months after the scrivener's decease. Upon what basis it rested, I could never ascertain; and hence, how true it is I cannot now tell. But, inasmuch as this vague report has not been without a certain suggestive interest to me, however sad, it may prove the same with some others; and so I will briefly mention it. The report was this: that Bartleby had been a subordinate clerk in the Dead Letter Office at Washington, from which he had been suddenly removed by a change in the administration. When I think over this rumor, hardly can I express the emotions which seize me. Dead letters! does it not sound like dead men? Conceive a man by nature and misfortune prone to a pallid hopelessness, can any business seem more fitted to heighten it than that of continually handling these dead letters, and assorting them for the flames? For by the cart-load they are annually burned. Sometimes from out the folded paper the pale clerk takes a ring—the finger it was meant for, perhaps, moulders in the grave; a bank-note sent in swiftest charity—he whom it would relieve, nor eats nor hungers any more; pardon for those who died despairing; hope for those who died unhoping; good tidings for those who died stifled by unrelieved calamities. On errands of life, these letters speed to death.

Ah, Bartleby! Ah, humanity!

Joyce Carol Oates
Love and Death

IN FEBRUARY, 1963, A MAN NAMED MARSHALL HUGHES RETURNED TO HIS hometown to visit his father, a widower. This is not really the beginning of the story—that is, not the true beginning; but it would be his idea of the beginning.

His father lived alone with an older sister, who was his housekeeper and nurse. His name was also Marshall; he had been "big Marshall" at one time; now it was Marshall, Jr., who was big and his father who was small, though perhaps that was just a trick of the light. "No, keep that shut," his father kept saying, wagging his fingers toward the window, "it hurts my eyes." He sat up in bed, or in a big armchair near the bed, reading newspapers. He was a sharp, petulant old man who still had money, coming in from sources he was secretive about. Good for him, Marshall thought, as if his father's financial stability protected them both from something; good, let him stay that way, let him die happy.

The family house was large and drafty, Victorian in style. It struck Marshall as the prototype for houses in the cartoons of certain sophisticated magazines—cartoons meaningful only to a generation who have abandoned such houses, with nostalgia. His wife could look back at such a family home too. Marshall and his wife were well matched, both intelligent and pleasant and accustomed to certain delicacies that are the result of money—money kept invisible, of course. They had both belonged to the same kind of social group; they had gone to the same kind of schools, had the same kind of teachers. They were bound together before they had even met by the queer pleasing network of names that made up their world.

Marshall and Fran had been married for nine years in 1963, and they had three children. Marshall worked for a company that made electrical parts for other companies, an excellent business. And he needed to work, too, because the money that came to him and Fran from various sources was no more than seven or eight thousand a year, and he felt a strange satisfaction at the thought of "having to work," because there was a kind of settledness in that thought, a sense of safety. They went to a Presbyterian church mainly for their children's sakes. And they lived in an excellent suburb in the Midwest, several hundred miles from their families and, it would seem, centuries beyond the influence of the past.

So Marshall went back to visit. His conscience nudged him, his wife said,

34

"Why don't you. . . ?", and he made up his mind to return, since his father wasn't well and it would be only a matter of time until the old man died. Marshall was worried that his father knew this. That was perhaps why his father kept saying sourly, "I'm going back to the office when the weather clears. This winter lasts too long."

"How is Dr. Fitzgerald?" Marshall said.

"Competent."

"Is his son doing well?"

"I wouldn't know about his son."

In such ways was Marshall's generation shouldered aside, squeezed out, ignored. Marshall, sensitive to his father's pride in himself and his power, never pursued any subjects that led to the forbidden subterranean world of time and mortality and death.

On the first evening of his visit he called Fran and was relieved to hear her voice—that cool, sane, immensely charming voice, which summoned up for him the elegant world of his home, his friends, his children, his wife. Whatever his father's people had achieved, there was none of the comfort of the new generation in it: its victories were grim, like its antique furniture. There was little joy in that generation. "How are the children?" Marshall asked over the telephone. Tears often stung his eyes when he called home from his business trips, asking about the children. He thought of them mainly when he was away; when he was home they somehow eluded his concern.

"Oh, they all miss you. They love you," Fran said.

"Tell them to be good."

There were odd embarrassed moments when he and Fran could not think of the next thing to say. This was not in spite of their politeness with each other but because of it.

"Please take care of yourself," Marshall said.

"Take care of your*self,*" his wife answered.

The next morning he went out for a walk. He was prepared to see a decline in the neighborhood, but things weren't too bad. One or two of the old places were obviously vacant, another looked as if it must be a nursing home of some kind. It was a mild, sunny day, suggesting spring. Marshall went all the way down to the post office, which looked smaller than he remembered; there were four windows inside but only one was open, so he had to stand in line, and he noticed a woman near the front of the line who looked familiar. He stared at the back of her head. She wore a cloth coat of a cheap cut. A flimsy pink scarf was tied about her hair, which was in no particular style, though bleached blond. Marshall himself wore a topcoat of a good, dark material and gloves, and his expensive shoes were protected by rubbers. He was a tall, fairly handsome man of about forty. When the woman turned away from the window he caught his breath—yes, he did remember her.

She went over to one of the closed windows and set her purse down on the counter, so that she could put stamps on some envelopes. He watched her. She had a thin, frail, careless profile, not quite as he had remembered. He had remembered her as more solid. She licked the stamps and put them on the envelopes, oblivious of anyone around her. Marshall wondered whom she was writing to. He saw that her coat, which looked new, was too short for her skirt, which hung down an inch or so in an untidy way.

He kept watching her and thought surely she would notice him. He was almost at the window when she picked up her purse and turned to go, without seeing him. So there was nothing for him to do but follow her—he didn't want to call after her, and he didn't want her to get away. At the door he caught up with her and said, "Hello, it's Cynthia, isn't it? Cynthia?"

She turned and stared at him. He saw that she recognized him, and he saw also the sudden recoiling gesture, the half-demure protestation, as if he had caught her at a bad moment. "Oh, Marshall," she said flatly. Her eyes were a cold, critical gray. "Marshall Hughes."

He laughed in embarrassment, breathlessly. "I was sure it was you . . ."

"Are you back home again?"

"I'm visiting."

The corners of her mouth turned up, but not in a smile. Her lips were quite red. He was struck by the flat, blatant, tired look she was giving him, a look that must have been defensive. Her bleached hair, inside the scarf, had a festive and rather ludicrous appearance, framing so cold a face. Several strands of hair had been combed down onto her forehead in a style that was a little too girlish for her. Her nose was long, as he had remembered it, giving her a slightly hungry, impatient look, her nostrils were thin, nervous, her mouth sharply and ironically defined, with the shadows of lines at its corners. It was an intelligent look somehow imposed upon an ordinarily pretty woman's frail, conventional look; her plucked, arched eyebrows could have belonged to any unstylish woman, but that mouth looked as if it might have something to say.

"Well, it was a surprise, seeing you . . . I was sure it was you," Marshall said vaguely. The woman laughed in a short, humorless way, as if he had said something funny. "Do you still live around here? I mean—with your mother?"

"With my mother?" She laughed.

"Yes, I thought—I mean, weren't you living with her?" He was conscious of having said something stupid, having confused facts. She stared at him mockingly. "Well, where do you live? Nearby?"

"Yes, nearby," she said. Her irony was crude; he felt a pang of revulsion toward her.

"Well, how are you?" he said.

"All right."

"I live in Kansas City now myself. My wife and I have three children."

"That's nice."

"And you, are you married?"

"I was married."

He tried to smile, wanting her to smile. There was something cruel about her mouth. He resented her coldness and the proud, indifferent way in which she kept him there, asking her questions. The very look of his clothes embar-

rassed him; she looked so shabby, so sad, and there was no failure of his own
that he could offer her.

"Where are you going now?" he said suddenly.

"Back."

"Back. . . ?"

"A few blocks away."

She moved toward the door. He followed, awkwardly. "Did you walk all
the way down here, from your father's house?" she said.

"Yes. It's a fine day for a walk."

They descended the steps. He had the idea she wanted to get away, and he
was anxious to keep her with him. He had to think of something to say. Years
ago they had been involved with each other casually, and he had forgotten
her, and yet now he did not want her to get away; her indifference made him
uneasy.

"Could I buy you some coffee? Or lunch?"

"It's too early for lunch."

"It's after eleven."

"I didn't get up till ten."

Again he experienced a slight tug of revulsion. He himself always got up
at seven, never slept later. "Some coffee then, down the street?"

"All right."

They went to a small restaurant which Marshall believed he could
remember. The woman sat down and unbuttoned her coat and let it fall
over the back of her chair as if she were quite accustomed to the place. She
wore a deep pink sweater that was too tight for her, and with the coat off
she looked younger, more gentle. The sweater was cheap, its neck stretched
and a little soiled, but it cast up onto her face a soft pink tone that was
flattering.

"How have you been all these years?" Marshall said.

"I've gotten along."

"It was quite an accident, running into you . . ."

"Yes," she said sarcastically. She was not yet smiling. Marshall was relieved when the waitress came to take their order. They were sitting across
from each other at a small, wobbly table. The woman had not pulled her chair
in, conscious of the smallness of the table, and so she sat back awkwardly.
Marshall folded his coat neatly over a nearby chair, and with a deft movement
that looked unplanned he pushed the table in toward her and drew his own
chair up to it.

"Yes, it's quite a surprise," he said, rubbing his hands.

"Christ, do you have to keep saying that?"

"But I mean it." He flushed, as if embarrassed by her profanity. She had
so much strength, mysterious strength, and he had none. Her eyes regarded
him with an unsurprised, calculating look, a look he had never seen in any
other woman, and he noticed with satisfaction that there were slight hollows
beneath those eyes. She was about thirty-five now. In a few years she would
age suddenly, and there would be no strength then, none of this sullen

independence. He could not understand why he had followed her out of the post office.

"Did you say you were married now?" he said.

"Who wants to know?"

"I do. I want to know," he said weakly.

"Maybe I am, what difference does it make? Maybe I kicked him out. It's the same old story; anyway what difference does it make?"

"You certainly don't mean it makes no difference to you."

"No. I mean to you."

"But I care. I'm anxious to hear about you."

"Oh, Christ," she said. Her eyes moved about behind him with a remote, amused look, as if she were searching out someone to laugh with her over him. Marshall remembered that—he remembered this woman breaking off their conversation to gaze around in that stupid, indifferent, placid way, pretending she had better things to think about.

"How is your brother?" he said.

"Which one, Davey?" she said, more gently.

"Yes, what happened to him?"

"He's the same, he's married now. Working a night shift."

"And what about your mother?"

"Look, you know my mother died a long time ago. You know that."

Marshall frowned. He did not remember, and yet in a way he did remember. There was something sluggish about him. The woman leaned forward, crossing her arms at the wrists; her wrists were girlish and delicate. She said, "You certainly do remember. You're lying."

"What, lying?"

"You're lying." She smiled sourly. "Now tell me about your wife."

"But I want to talk about you."

She laughed. The waitress brought their coffee, and Marshall resented the distraction. The woman said, "You want to talk about me? Why the hell about me? Do you have a cigarette?"

He took out his package of cigarettes at once, anxious to please her. Unwrapping the package, jerking the red cellophane strip around, he was nervous, thinking that there was something vaguely obscene about what he was doing. He finally got a cigarette to stick out, and she took it. Lighting her cigarette was another awkward thing, but at last it was accomplished.

"So your brother is still in town?"

"Yes. You liked him, didn't you?" she said curiously.

"Why do you ask?"

"You liked him because he kept his nose out of our business. That was what you liked about him, and what you didn't like about my mother."

This stirred some memory in him; he nodded slowly. It would be better to agree.

"Your own mother, of course, was a bitch of another type. We won't mention her."

"You never saw my mother."

"I certainly did."

"When did you see her?"

"My God, you know very well—we saw her one day downtown, the two of us. We saw her with some other fat bitches, all dressed up, and you pointed her out to me. I remember that."

Marshall was a little shocked, but he made himself smile. "But if you only saw her . . . ?"

"I knew all about her. You told me. And is your father still alive?"

"Yes."

"You're here visiting him?"

"Yes."

"How long are you going to stay?" But then she tapped ashes from the cigarette onto the floor, nervously, as if conscious of having said something wrong but not wanting to correct it.

"A few more days." He pushed the coffee cup aside, he had no desire for coffee. He watched her impatiently. "Well, never mind about that," he said. "What about you, are you married?"

"In a way."

"What does that mean?"

She shrugged her shoulders. With her thumb and two fingers she picked up the coffee cup, a precise little gesture of affectation that struck him. She was a pretty woman in spite of everything. Her hair was disheveled but clean, gleaming in the light from the window. He liked her hair. It was vulgar, that color, and showed that she wasn't so clever after all—what a phony color— but still he liked it on her.

He said, "Your hair looks good."

She lifted one shoulder in a lazy gesture of indifference.

"You used to wear it long. . . ?"

They sat for a while in silence. Then she said, "I have to leave now." She spoke stubbornly, as if arguing. Marshall said, hardly knowing what he would hear, "But where are you going?" Home, she told him. He asked what that meant; whom did she live with? By herself, she said, she lived by herself; but she worked in the evening, and she had some things to do, she had to wash things, go shopping. He asked her if he could come along. She swore in a gentle, weary, unsurprised way, staring at him; she shook her head. Marshall fumbled for the pack of cigarettes and put them away, nervously. The woman kept looking at him. He felt guilty suddenly and had to fight down an impulse to look over his shoulder, to see if anyone had heard.

They had met many years ago in a bar. She had been with one crowd, he with another. He had been introduced to her, asked her her name and telephone number, and a few days later had called her up. She had lived then in a big ugly house, a very old house. He remembered that house, and his shyness, and the girl's carefully made-up, mocking face, and the very high heels of the shoes that she wore.

"No, I have to leave," she said.

He helped her with her coat and put on his own, not bothering to button it.

"Where are you going now?"

"I told you, home."

"Where is that?"

"Close by." She looked sideways at him and smiled. "Do you want to walk me there?"

Her apartment was in a six-story building, an old building. For some reason Marshall was in a hurry, his heartbeat was choked and rapid. On the stairs his feet ached to carry him up fast, faster than he was going. The woman kept glancing sideways at him, ironically. On the banister her bare hand moved in jerks, a few inches at a time, and he watched this movement out of the corner of his eye.

At her door he watched as she put the key into the lock. This startled him, the way it went into the lock, forcing itself in and then turning easily. She said, "You should go back down," indicating with a jerk of her head the stairs behind them.

"Couldn't I stay awhile? Talk to you?"

"Oh, talk, what do you want to talk about? Talk!" she said in disgust.

"Could I see you later, then? Tonight?"

She had opened the door. She seemed impatient to get away, yet something made her linger; like him, she felt a peculiar tugging between them, an undefined force that would not release her. Marshall waited. He remembered her making him wait, in the old days, this sluttish girl who had nothing, really nothing, except what men like himself wanted to give her. Her profile, nearly overwhelmed by the bunch of blond hair that looked resilient and unreal as a dummy's wig, put him in mind of his wife's profile for an instant. But the two women were quite different. His wife had a healthy, wholesome, friendly face, she played golf with women like herself, she dressed with simple, excellent taste. What reminded him of her, in this woman, was no more than the fact that he was standing close to the woman. He had been close to few people in his life.

"Could I come in now? For a few minutes?"

He was perspiring, he was not himself. Her fingers, tapping impatiently on the doorknob, seemed to be tapping against his body, teasing him. He said, begging, "I won't stay long."

He had no impression of the room except that it was small. Windows at one end with their shades drawn; mingled odors of food. He felt as if he had broken through to something, liberated and floating in a way he could not control. It was a strange feeling. All his life he had said silently to others, Let me alone, don't touch me, talk to me but don't touch me, because I'm afraid of—afraid of what? He was afraid, that was enough. He and his wife said this to each other, silently, Let me alone, don't touch me—Cynthia took off her coat angrily and looked around at him. "I don't know why the hell you're here. Do you think it's still fifteen years ago?"

This shocked him. "Fifteen years? Nothing ever happened—that long ago—" he said dizzily. He moved toward her. He put his arms around her, clumsy in his coat, and she stood there with a kind of contemptuous patience, a mockery of patience. "I don't think so much time went by—"

"All right."

"I've thought about you a great deal—"

"All right, sure."

"Could we go in there? Is that another room, could we go in there?"

"You'll have to give me some money."

"Yes."

"You used to give me money, right?"

"I don't know, yes, maybe—I don't remember. Did I give you money?" he asked, surprised.

"Certainly."

"I gave you money?"

"I was in love with you, sure, but I was never stupid," she said, in her flat amused voice. "What makes you think I'm stupid? Because I'm poor? Because I don't dress like your wife?"

"No, you're not stupid."

"Then give me some money, now."

He took out his wallet. He had the idea that she was degrading him in this manner, degrading herself, in order to block out the memory of their love together—that was all right, he understood her. She was protecting herself. He took out a number of bills, and smiling foolishly, handed them to her. She took them and began to smile too. "Yes, you gave me money," she said. "Otherwise why should I have bothered with you?"

They went into the other room. Marshall stopped thinking. When he began to think again, a while later, his mind was precise, and he looked around the room as if memorizing it. And when they went back out into the larger room, the woman yawning and indifferent at his side, he looked around that room too. He saw the cheap modern furniture, blond wood and green cushions, a table with a formica top, flowered drapes, a worn-out rug. He felt dislocated and quite empty. The room was so ugly that it saddened him.

"Let me see you again. I want to see you again," he said.

"You can take me to dinner tonight."

"Dinner? Really?"

"Yes, dinner. Good-bye."

He had to make excuses at home, saying he had met an old friend on his walk. When his aunt asked who this friend was, in her dry, suspicious spinster's voice, he really could not think of a name for several seconds. It was embarrassing. His father luckily paid no attention; he was reading newspapers. Marshall watched the old man, jealous of the attention he paid to all those papers when his son had traveled so far to see him. He noticed the way the old man pursed his lips, reading, working his lips as if mumbling secret words to himself, flexing his jaws. There was something outlandish and too intimate, almost indecent, in the way he worked his lips. Marshall looked away. Then he looked back, fascinated.

Marshall called his wife again that afternoon. He asked how the children were, how Fran was. Fine, fine. But one of the boys had cut his leg. Out playing. No, he hadn't been pushed, it was just an accident. Marshall tried to keep talking and listening. It was easier to talk than to listen. His wife's voice was very far away; the book-lined study in which he sat seemed somehow very far away too, its indistinct walls confining the air of another, older time, into which he had stepped accidentally. And he would step out of it again in a moment.

When he came to the woman's apartment that evening he was very nervous. She said, amused, "What's wrong with you? In the post office you were another person; now you're back to what you were fifteen years ago."

"But what was I, fifteen years ago?"

"What you are now."

"But what is that?"

"I can't tell you. How can I describe you to yourself?"

They had dinner in a dark, ordinary restaurant. A big air-conditioning unit was perched up above them on the wall, silent and ominous. As they ate their dinner, uninteresting food he barely tasted, he kept asking her about what she had meant, earlier. "Did I really give you money?"

"Yes, of course."

"And you took it?"

"Why wouldn't I take it?"

"Do you remember how we met? The first time?"

"You came in a certain bar to make a telephone call. Your friends were outside, waiting. You saw me and asked me something—asked me for change, for the telephone. You talked to me. Then you went out and told your friends to drive on without you, and you came back in, and the two of us went somewhere . . ." She paused, thinking. "Yes. We went to this place I sometimes stayed at, a flat a friend of mine rented."

"But it wasn't that way at all," Marshall said quickly.

"No? How was it, then?"

"Didn't I call you up, later? Didn't I get your telephone number?"

"Yes. You asked me for my number, after we went back to that flat."

"Only after that?"

"Yes, don't you remember?"

He stared at her. Slowly, reluctantly, he began to remember. She had been a thin girl in a black dress, trying to look older than she was. She had been sitting at a table near the telephone booth, in a corner. "So we went back to a flat? A friend of yours had a flat?"

"Yes. We only went there once."

"It wasn't someone else?"

"You mean, instead of you? There were other men, yes, but it was you as well."

"But you say we only went there once?"

"I lived at home then. I was with my family."

"Yes. I remember that, of course."

"You remember my mother."

"Yes."

Her mother had screamed at him one day, a fat drunken woman who accused him of taking advantage of her daughter. Marshall had had to push her away, she had tried to strike him and scratch his face . . . Yes, he remembered that fat bitch of a woman; he was glad she was dead.

"You were glad when she died," Cynthia said.

"I wouldn't say that . . ."

"Yes, I would say it," Cynthia said flatly.

After dinner he said, "Why haven't you done more with yourself? Why are you still living in the same neighborhood, after so long?"

"I don't have any ambitions."

"You never got married?"

"I didn't say that."

"Or have children?"

"My real life isn't of any interest to you, it's nothing. What do you care if I did get married? All right, I did. Then it was ended, like that. No children. I'm not like people you know, I don't have any ambition. I don't care."

"It seems impossible . . ."

"But I wouldn't want to be your wife. I wouldn't want that."

"You wouldn't want to marry me?"

She laughed. "No, I wouldn't. I mean that I wouldn't want to be the woman who is your wife, now—I wouldn't want to be that woman."

Marshall had to think for a moment, recalling his wife. His heart fluttered as if he were in danger.

"You are two very different people," he said slowly.

They went back to her apartment. Near as he could come to her she always held him off, in a sense, observing him coldly. He could never get past the icy circle of her mind; she was always thinking about him, holding him apart from her. "What was your husband like?" he said. "Like anyone. An ordinary man," she said. "He didn't have money, did he?" he said. "Of course not," she said, "nobody has money except you."

He was reluctant to leave her; he wanted to stay all night, but his father would wonder about him; a vision of that ugly old mansion rose in his mind and made him stir guiltily. In the dark, it was difficult for him to know who he was. And yet it was a darkness that was not unfamiliar.

She snapped on the light. "I hope that from now on we can be friends, and forget each other."

"Why should we forget each other?"

"But you forgot me before. You never sent me any money."

"I didn't know you wanted money."

"You must have known. Everyone wants money," she said, without bothering to emphasize any of her words, just pronouncing them. He felt that she did not believe this, that it was nothing more than a means of holding him off. She had a strange face, this woman, an unhappy, brooding, and yet careless look, which her makeup seemed to parody. He was uncomfortable beneath her gaze. She might have been assessing any man, himself or a stranger, making no distinction between them.

"I can send you some money, when I get home."

She said nothing. Marshall went on, anxiously, "I want to ask you something before I leave. Why do you think I came over to you?"

"When, today? Or the first time?"

"Either time."

"Because you liked me, I suppose."

"But why—why do you think I like you?"

She shut her eyes wearily. "You mean, it seems crazy to you that you should be here? All right, yes, it is crazy. But I do know why you're here, as a matter of fact."

"Why?"

"Don't you know? Can't you guess?"

He felt a slight pang of terror, at the very softness of her voice. "What? What is it?"

"Do you remember what you said to me, the first time we met? I mean after we went back to that flat."

"No. What did I say?"

"You asked me my age, how long I had been doing that sort of thing. You asked me about the men I knew. You were very curious, very excited. Of course, you were a young man then—"

"And you were young too," he said nervously.

"Not in the same way. You were always pestering me then, back then—don't you remember?"

"I think you're mixing me up with someone else."

"Oh, hell," she laughed. "Go on home, then."

"No, please. Couldn't you be mixing me up with someone else?"

"I don't forget things. There was a time when I loved you, and this time is closed off from what came before and what came after, and I can look back at it and remember it perfectly. What's strange is that you don't remember it."

"But I want to remember it."

"You asked me about the other men. You came to see me all the time, it was crazy. You wrote me letters though we lived in the same city, you gave me presents—jewelry and clothes—you were always bothering me. You liked to tease me about those other men, you'd sit on the edge of the bed and ask me questions. lots of questions. Don't you remember that?"

"No," Marshall said dully. But even as he spoke he knew it was true, and a sense of revulsion and anger stirred inside him.

"What do you remember, then?"

"I asked you your telephone number, and I called you up, a few days later," he said, as if reciting something. "I went to your house—your brother was working on his car, in the driveway. You introduced me to your mother. I think it was a Sunday, Sunday afternoon."

"But we met on Saturday night."

"This was the next day. You introduced me to your mother."

"Did you like that?"

"I thought that was nice."

"But you must have known I did it to make fun. My mother was always drunk, and I wanted to see how you'd act. Didn't you know that?"

Marshall was silent for a moment. Then he said, "But I don't remember any flat."

"Of course you remember."

"I think you're mixing me up with someone else."

"So, you called me up, you met my mother, what else?"

"And then . . . we started seeing each other."

"What did we do?"

"We went to movies, out to dinner. We went dancing." He thought about this, watching her uneasily. Then his mind cleared, and he remembered that it was Fran he had done those things with.

"We went to rooms, to hotels," she said. "We drove around in your car."

"But you didn't seem to mind—"

"Why should I mind? You paid me."

"I remember that vaguely—"

"Vaguely, hell!"

She wanted him to leave, but he was reluctant. He clutched at something: "But you lied to me too. You said you had to work tonight."

"Did I?"

"I think you said that."

"Yes, I work some evenings. I have a real job; I'm a hostess in a restaurant. But I took tonight off."

"For me?"

She shrugged her shoulders. Of course, he had given her money—but he did not think that was significant.

She saw him to the door. He turned to leave, his face burning. It seemed to him that something was wrong, something was threatening. When he was out in the hall she said, in her low teasing voice, "Here's something else you won't remember either—how when we went out you talked to me about my life, how I was trapped, I had nowhere to go, no future—I'd get diseased or some maniac would kill me. You said you loved me, because I was just a tramp and my mother was a drunk and so on—and you really did love me, but you don't remember any of it."

He made up his mind not to see her again, and the rest of his visit was spent in the old house. He sat with his father while the old man read his papers, the two of them quite oblivious of one another. Except from time to time Marshall glanced at his father and saw that queer silent smacking of his father's lips—again and again—and his very bowels seemed stirred by it, stirred to anger. He called Fran, as if in desperation. But her voice was distant, and what she spoke of seemed trivial. He wondered whether, if he put the receiver down gently, he might cut her out from his life altogether.

But of course this was nonsense. He was frightened at himself, at such thoughts. He had never in his life had such thoughts before. And he found himself recalling certain moments of his lovemaking with that woman when he had thought of the possibility of her being diseased and of the great risk he was taking. It excited him, to think of this risk. Yet that was all nonsense, all disgusting. He was anxious to return home again.

A strange thing: he began seeing things that weren't there. Or, rather, a foreign vision imposed itself upon them, distorting them violently. One day his aunt—a woman of over sixty, hefty, vague, sour, very religious—was cutting meat when he walked into the kitchen. He was eager to talk with someone. She was slicing pieces of raw meat off a large, fatty hunk, and something about her wet, blood-stained fingers and the tender pink meat and the flashing of the knife terrified him. He was almost sick. His aunt did not care to talk, and so he passed on through to the breakfast room and safely away . . . And another time at dinner he watched his father finish a glass of water, lifting it to his mouth and drinking in rather audible gasps until nothing was left, and Marshall thought: In just that way do people make love. It was not a thought that made sense. But it flashed clearly through his mind, as he watched his father empty the crystal goblet.

He was not going to call Cynthia, but on the last day he did. They talked vaguely as if they had nothing in common. "Now I'm leaving. I probably won't see you again," he said cautiously. She said, "Yes, good luck. I hope your father is well." The mention of his father startled him, for certainly she was thinking that he had to be back—didn't he?—when his father got worse, when his father died, he had to be back then, and he'd call her up, wouldn't he? He was trapped. So he said irritably, "Of course he's well. And now I'm going back. You'll see—a person can do one thing and then do the opposite thing, it doesn't matter. I won't be seeing you again."

He arrived back home in time for a dinner party. Everything was confused, gaily muddled. He had to tell his wife about the visit while they dressed, the two of them already late, a little giddy with the prospect of a familiar excellent evening before them. Marshall felt good; he felt quite safe. He kept chatting to his wife about all sorts of things, and she in her turn chatted about the latest news, which friends she had had lunch with, who was in town. He was amazed at how rich and complex and yet safe this life was, out here.

It was several hours before he even remembered that woman. At about ten o'clock they went in to dinner, into an elegant dining room, and their host opened a bottle of wine. He worked at the cork, making jokes, and seemed to be looking at Marshall as if Marshall were somehow the main point of the joke. Marshall felt sweat break out on his body. He couldn't quite make out the joke, but he did watch with a kind of terror the man's fingers working at the cork. Something was straining for release, something threatened to spurt out—Then the moment passed, it was over. Wine was poured into glasses in an ordinary way, and there was nothing behind it.

For more than a week he continued as his usual self, and then he had an overwhelming impulse to write to Cynthia. He was at his office, and he used business stationery, with the firm's Kansas City address on it. Let her see it. He wanted to give her proof of how successful he was. He wrote her a long, aimless, unplanned letter. It was chatty and superficial. Rereading it, however, he saw that the letter was quite obviously a disguise for something left unsaid—but he did not know what that was.

She did not reply to it.

Angered, he wrote again. This time he asked her specific questions, about her ex-husband, about her "present mode of living," about her plans for the future. This letter was five pages long, an inspired letter. Marshall had never been able to write to anyone and had always telephoned if he had anything to say, so he was both pleased and a little disturbed that he could write so much to that woman. She was so unimportant, after all.

He included in the letter a check for several hundred dollars, and this time she replied. She thanked him for the money and wrote a few more lines, just to be polite. He was enraged at this but did not know what he had expected. So he wrote again at once, ending his letter: "Write back. I want to hear anything you have to say. Tell me about your job, about your mother or anything."

As an afterthought he took some bills out of his wallet and slid them into the envelope. His fingers were shaking.

Her letter came a few weeks later. In ball-point ink she had written a few lines, mentioning the money. This was followed by a paragraph in pencil, evidently written at a later time, in which she did talk about her mother: "You both hated each other, and yet you were curious about each other. She knew you had money, and, who knows, she might end up with it herself—I'm sure that crossed her mind. And then, on the day she died, you had to hear everything about her and go right into her bedroom, though the poor woman had been in that bed a few hours before. And yet you two never really met except that one time and never talked to each other."

He read this and a fine dizzying film passed before his eyes. In such flat, blatant language, just as she spoke—what had she told him? Her mother's bedroom, what about that? Something seemed to be blocking his memory. So he wrote her again, careful to include a check this time (she had reproved him for sending money through the mail), and asked for more information. He waited eagerly for her to reply. But no reply came. He wondered if she had received the letter. When his wife mentioned that she had heard from a friend in Boston, Marshall turned to stare at her in amazement. Because it seemed to him that she was about to confront him with her knowledge of Cynthia, and he was excited not by the danger of his position but by the possibility of her having discovered a letter, having somehow intercepted it, and he would have allowed that if it meant he would at last hear from Cynthia . . . But no, the letter was truly from a friend, no irony was intended.

He wrote Cynthia again, begging and demanding that she answer. He sent her another check, this time for a thousand dollars. Angry, frustrated, he believed that she was blackmailing him and that she was a criminal; she ought

to be arrested and punished. He hated her for her power over him and thought
of revenge he might take upon her. He would do something, yes. He did hate
her. And yet when her letter arrived his heart thudded as if he were indeed
in love.

She wrote: "You asked me about her room, about that apartment. You
remember the living room—the ugly furniture, the religious junk on the walls.
All right. My mother died of some kind of seizure while she was in bed. I went
in and found her. Her face was awful, it was not her face at all or any human
face. Her eyes were bulging. I went up to her and saw how it was, and so I
went out to call the police. That night you came over. You wanted to take
care of me, you said I must be very upset. You looked around the living room
and asked me if you could see the bedroom. So I took you in. You were very
quiet, you seemed sad. In that room you asked me about her, whether she'd
known about me, how she had died, and you were very interested in hearing
about it—because you hated her, I think that was the reason. Then you
comforted me and put your arms around me, and you insisted that we make
love in that bed. You insisted upon that. You begged me. I didn't care because
a person can do one thing, and then do the opposite, as you know. I didn't
have a guilty conscience because I had been good to my mother, so I didn't
care. And while we were making love you asked me about her, about her eyes
in particular, which had especially frightened me. Like what? What did she
look like? you kept asking. Doesn't this all make you laugh, now?"

He was sickened by that letter. "She's lying," he muttered, but at once he
thought, "Yes, it was like that."

Feeling her power over him across the country he began to send her things,
to buy her off. He sent her some clothes, having them mailed from expensive
shops. That ought to please her. And notes with checks enclosed, now and
then, anything to buy her off, shut her up. What was terrifying was that he
had no way of knowing whether this would work, or whether his desperation
would make her more bold. Suppose she wrote directly to his wife? Or went
to see his father? He had given so much of himself to her, surrendered so
much of his power, that she could destroy him if she wanted. And she never
replied. What did her silence mean? He reread her letters again and again,
lingering over the last one, sometimes lured into an erotic daze and unable
to rouse himself—it was so vivid now, so real. Yes, he had certainly done that.
He wanted very much to do it again. With Fran he was always too busy to
talk, too tired to make love to her, and certainly this was a relief to her—she
was not that kind of woman at all—yet his thoughts were preoccupied with
his own body and its needs.

He thought, "When my father dies I'll have to go back." But his father did
not die. His father never wrote either. He had to depend for news upon his
own telephone calls, put through every Sunday evening. But he kept calling,
faithfully. He had become quite a dutiful son now. And finally, Fran said
again, "Would you like to visit your father?"

He had overheard her talking with a woman friend one evening, about how
hard it was for men to take their father's deaths. Fran had been assured that,

according to Freud, it was the single most traumatic event in a man's life; therefore, with Marshall, she had to be as sympathetic as possible. His father was not dying yet, Marshall thought, but that seemed almost irrelevant. The old man would die someday—perhaps. He pretended to think it over, knowing all along that he would give in and take the trip. It had been nearly a year since the last visit.

Planning for it, he was overcome with a strange lassitude. He would sit in his office, and daydreams forced themselves into his mind, as if he were being invaded by an alien, sordid force. He thought of that old flat—which he now remembered clearly—and its clutter, the dishes and underwear lying around, the stockings drying in the bathroom, he thought of Cynthia and what they had done together, which was not at all what he and Fran had ever done together, he thought of the money he had given that woman—it gave him pleasure to think of this—and, lingeringly, he thought of her mother's death, which seemed somehow to have taken place in the room with Cynthia and himself. He was tremendously excited by this. He did not understand it except to know that his body ached and seemed now to be the body of another man. It was hard to maneuver it, even to walk normally. He felt that at any moment he might take a false step, lunge off a sidewalk, bump someone. It was especially difficult to get through an evening with friends, because, where once he had been able to imagine himself as a certain person, a successful business executive named Marshall Hughes, now he felt that his internal self had become impatient, as if waking from a long sleep, and might demand recognition.

The more his wife chatted about her friends and the bridge circle, the more he felt that he loved her and could forget about her. When she talked about the children, she was his wife, she belonged to him. She could never disturb him. Their affection was the affection of friends or companions, there was nothing passionate or brutal about it. He loved her. He hated that woman who was blackmailing him, and his body stirred at the thought of her, excited and furious at the same time. Yes, he had to have his revenge on her! He could not spend the rest of his life being blackmailed by a prostitute. And yet, at this thought, he would fall off into another of his disturbing dreams, recalling her, shaking his head at the memory of her hair and her plucked eyebrows, she was so common, really, and he had to urge himself awake to get where he was going, to do his work, or to reply to his wife, who had begun to look at him a little strangely. So he decided to go back to visit his father.

He wanted to talk with her just once more, to say good-bye. He would ask for his letters. Why should she have anything against him? He was prepared to write out one more check, a sizable check, and all she would have to do would be to return his indiscreet letters and promise to forget him—it disturbed him to think that she might not forget him. On the plane he sat rigid, thinking. It was not quite thinking, perhaps, but planning, groping, inching along as if with his fingers. Of his father he hardly thought; the old man could take care of himself. What did that old man, or any other old man, know of the terrible dangers of life? Marshall nearly wept to think that he had so many years to go before he drifted into the sanctity of old age and death, the final safety, far safer than his suburban life and marriage. "Those old bastards don't let us through. They block things up. They don't move along," he thought in anguish.

At the airport he took a taxi at once to her neighborhood. But for some reason, he asked to be let out a few blocks away. Marshall's palms were damp with sweat, his entire body was damp, he seemed in a kind of vague, outraged daze. He was both lunging forward and holding himself back. He did not think at all, except to say to himself: "I'll talk her out of it." He walked the several blocks quickly and then stood for a while staring up at her lighted windows. Again he thought of nothing, not really. His body seemed to be thinking for him. It was protecting all the people who stood behind him, his father, his family, the people who worked for him, the people who were his friends. After a while he went inside and up the stairs to her door. He knocked on it. The knocking echoed jarringly in his brain, and he thought of all the letters he had written, so recklessly, and yet perhaps on purpose?—and he thought of the hours he had spent with that woman, losing himself in her, groveling in the darkness of her body and the mastery of her soiled, ugly life, and yet coming from her with no knowledge and no affection, nothing.

The door opened. A child of about twelve, a girl, leaned out and looked at him. "Whatdaya want?" she said.

"Who lives here?" Marshall said. "What—what happened to—Where is—?"

"You want my father?" the girl said.

"But—when did you move in here?"

"Last summer." The girl looked at him, chewing gum. She seemed to see something interesting in his face. "You looking for somebody else?"

He turned away. He began to weep. His breath came in great gulps, as if he had just saved himself from a terrible danger. Descending the stairs, he grasped the banister and remembered the way she had held onto it, indifferently, lightly, and how, even then, he had wanted to reach over and snap her wrist. But it was better not to think of that. He would never think of it again, nor would he think of his having come to this apartment straight from the airport, drenched in sweat, his body stiffened and monstrous with desire; he would not think of that. When he felt better he called another taxi and went to his father's house.

The old man was about the same, perhaps getting senile. Not much change. He did not die for six years, and then his death was sudden. Marshall was nearly forty-seven at this time, and his own health was unsteady, so he had an excuse not to go to his father's funeral. But no one in the family believed him, even Fran did not really believe him, and they held it against him all his life: he was a man who hadn't even bothered with his father's death.

Conrad Aiken

Smith and Jones

SMITH AND JONES, AS FAR AS ONE COULD TELL IN THE DARKNESS, LOOKED almost exactly alike. Their names might have been interchangeable. So might their clothes, which were apparently rather shabby, though, as they walked quickly and the night was cloudy, it was difficult to be sure. Both of them were extraordinarily articulate. They were walking along the muddy road that led away from a large city and they talked as they went.

"As far as I'm concerned," said Smith, "it's all over. No more women for me. There's nothing in it. It's a damned swindle. Walk right up, gentlemen, and make your bets! The hand is quicker than the eye. Where is the elusive little pea? Ha ha! Both ends against the middle."

He struck a match and lit his pipe; his large pale unshaven face started out of the night.

Jones grumbled to himself. Then turning his head slightly toward Smith, in a somewhat aggressive way, as if he were showing a fang, he began to laugh in a peculiar soft insolent manner.

"Jesus! One would think you were an adolescent. No more women! If there aren't it'll be because you're dead. You were born to be made a fool of by women. You'll buzz round the honey-pot all your days. You have no sense in these matters, you've never had the courage or the intelligence once and for all to *realize* a woman. Look! here's a parable for you. There are an infinite number of little white clouds stretching one after another across blue space, just like sweet little stepping stones. To each of them is tethered a different-colored child's balloon—I know that would rather badly fracture the spectrum, but never mind. And behold, our angel-child, beautiful and trustful, flies to the first little cloud-island, and seizes the first balloon, enraptured. It's pink. But then he sees the next island, and the next balloon, which is orange. So he lets the first one go, which sails away, and flies vigorously to the next little island. From there he catches sight of a different shade of pink—sublime! intoxicating! and again dashes across an abyss. . . . This lovely process goes on forever. It will never stop."

Smith splashed into a puddle and swore.

"Don't be so damned patronizing, with your little angel-child and toy balloons. I know what I'm talking about. Adolescent? Of course I am—who isn't? The point is, exactly, that I *have* at last realized a woman. That's more, I'll bet, than you've done—you, with your damned negativism!"

"Negativism!—how? But never mind that. Tell me about your woman."

"It must be experienced to be understood."

"Of course—so must death."

"What can I tell you then? You, who have always made it a principle to experience as little as possible! Your language doesn't, therefore, extend to the present subject. You are still crawling on your hands and knees, bumping into chairs, and mistaking your feet for a part of the floor, or your hands for a part of the ceiling. Stand up! Be a man! It's glorious."

"Was she blonde or brunette?"

"If you insist, she was a Negress tattooed with gold and silver. Instead of earrings, she wore brass alarm clocks in her ears, and for some unexplained reason she had an ivory thimble in her left nostril."

Jones laughed; there was a shade of annoyance in his laughter.

"I see. . . . I forgot to mention, by the way, that when the angel-child flew so vigorously from cloud to cloud his wings made a kind of whimpering sound. . . . But go on."

"No, she was neither blonde nor brunette, but, as you suggested, imaginary. She didn't really exist. I thought she did, of course—I had seen her several times quite clearly. She had a voice, hands, eyes, feet—in short, the usual equipment. In point of size she was colossal; in point of speed, totally incommensurable. She walked, like Fama, with her head knocking about among the stars. She stepped casually, with one step, from town to town, making with the swish of her skirts so violent a whirlwind that men everywhere were sucked out of houses."

"I recognize the lady. It was Helen of Troy."

"Not at all. Her name, as it happened, was Gleason."

Jones sighed. The two men walked rapidly for some time in silence. The moon, like a pale crab, pulled clouds over itself, buried itself in clouds with a sort of awkward precision, and a few drops of rain fell.

"Rain!" said Jones, putting up one hand.

"To put out the fires of conscience."

"Gleason? She must be—if your description is accurate—in the theatrical profession? A lady acrobat, a trapeze artist, or a Pullman portress?"

"Wrong again, Jones—if error were, as it ought to be, punishable by death, you'd be a corpse. . . . Suffice it to say that Gleason loved me. It was like being loved by a planet."

"Venus?"

"Mars. She crushed me, consumed me. Her love was a profounder and more fiery abyss than the inferno which Dante, in the same sense, explored. It took me days of circuitous descent to get even within sight of the bottom; and then, as there were no ladders provided, I plunged headlong. I was at once ignited and became a tiny luminous spark, which, on being cast forth to the upper world again on a fiery exhalation, became an undistinguished cinder."

"To think a person named Gleason could do all that!"

"Yes, it's a good deal, certainly. I feel disinclined for further explorations of the sort."

"Temporarily, you mean. . . . You disliked the adventure?"

"Oh, no—not altogether! Does one dislike life altogether? Do we hate this walk, this road, the rain, ourselves, the current of blood which, as we walk and talk, our hearts keep pumping and pumping? We like and dislike at the same time. It's like an organism with a malignant fetid cancer growing in it. Cut out the cancer, which has interlaced its treacherous fibers throughout every part, and you extinguish life. What's to be done? In birth, love, and death, in all acts of violence, all abrupt beginnings and abrupt cessations, one can detect the very essence of the business—there one sees, in all its ambiguous nakedness, the beautiful obscene."

Jones reflected; one could make out that his head was bowed. Smith walked beside him with happy alacrity. It began to rain harder, the trees dripped loudly, but the two men paid no attention.

"The beautiful obscene!" said Jones, suddenly lifting his head. "Certainly that's something to have learned *chez* Gleason! . . . It suggests a good deal. It's like this road—it's dark, but it certainly leads somewhere."

"Where?"

"That's what we'll discover. Is it centrifugal or centripetal? The road is the former, of course. It leads, as we know, away from civilization into the wilderness, the unknown. But that's no reason for supposing the same to be true of your diagnosis—is it? And yet I wonder."

He wondered visibly, holding his coat-collar about his throat with one hand, and showed a disposition to slacken his pace. But Smith goaded him.

"Look here, we've got to keep moving, you know."

"Yes, we've got to keep moving."

They walked for a mile in complete silence. The rain kept up a steady murmur among the leaves of trees, the vague heaving shoulders of which they could see at right and left, and they heard the tinkling of water in a ditch. Their shoes bubbled and squelched, but they seemed to be indifferent to matters so unimportant. However, from time to time they inclined their heads forward and allowed small reservoirs of rain to slide heavily off their felt hats. It was Jones, finally, who began talking again. After a preliminary mutter or two, and a hostile covert glance at his companion, he said:

"Like all very great discoveries, this discovery of yours affords opportunities for a new principle of behavior. You are not a particularly intelligent man, as I've often told you, and as you yourself admit; so you probably don't at all see the implications of your casual observation. As often occurs to you, in the course of your foolish, violent, undirected activity, you have accidentally bumped your head and seen a star. You would never think, however, of hitching your wagon to such a star—which is what I propose to do."

Smith glanced sharply at his companion, and then began laughing on a low meditative note which gradually became shrill and derisive; he even lifted one knee and slapped it. It was obviously a tremendous joke.

"Just like you, Jones! You're all brain to the soles of your feet. *What* do you propose to do?"

"Don't be a simpleton, or I'll begin by murdering you—instead of ending by doing so."

This peculiar remark was delivered, and received, with the utmost sobriety.

"Of course," said Smith. "You needn't dwell on that, as it's an unpleasant necessity which is fully recognized between us. It doesn't in the least matter whether the event is early or late, does it?"

"What I mean is, that if you are right, and the beautiful obscene is the essence of the business, then obviously one should pursue that course of life which would give one the maximum number of—what shall I say?—perfumed baths of that description. . . . You say that this essence is most clearly to be detected in the simpler violences. In love, birth, death, all abrupt cessations and beginnings. Very good. Then if one is to live completely, to realize life in the last shred of one's consciousness, to become properly incandescent, or *identical* with life, one must put oneself in contact with the strongest currents. One should love savagely, kill frequently, eat the raw, and even, I suppose, be born as often as possible."

"A good idea!"

"I propose to do all these things. It has long been tacitly understood that sooner or later I will murder you, so as you tactfully suggest, I won't dwell on that. But I shall be glad to have Gleason's address . . . beforehand."

"Certainly; whenever you like. Telephone Main 220-W (I always liked that W) and ask for Mary."

"The question is: what's to be done about thought? . . . You see, this road of reflection is, after all, centripetal. It involves, inevitably a return to the center, an identification of one's self with the All, with the unconscious *primum mobile*. But thought, in its very nature, involves a separation of one's self from the—from the—"

"Unconscious?"

"From the unconscious. . . . We must be careful not to go astray at this point. One shouldn't begin by trying to *be* unconscious—not at all! One might as well be dead. What one should try to get rid of is consciousness of *self*. Isn't that it?"

Smith gave a short laugh, at the same time tilting his head to let the rain run off onto his feet. "Anything you say, professor. I trust you blindly. Anyway, I know that my pleasantest moments with Gleason were those in which I most completely lost my awareness of personality, of personal identity. Yes, it's beautiful and horrible, the way one loses, at such moments, everything but a feeling of animal force. . . . Analogously, one should never permit conversation at meals. And it was decidedly decadent of Cyrano to carry on an elaborate monologue in couplets while committing a murder— oh, decidedly. Quite the wrong thing! One's awareness, on such occasions, should be of nothing, nothing but murder—there should be no overlapping fringe which could busy itself with such boyisms as poetry or epigram. One should, in short, *be* a murder. . . . Do I interpret you correctly?"

Jones, at this, looked at Smith with a quick uneasiness. Smith appeared to be unconscious of this regard, and was as usual walking with jaunty alacrity.

The way he threw out his feet was extremely provocative—the angle of his elbows was offensive. His whole bearing was a deliberate, a calculated insult.

"Quite correctly," said Jones sharply, keeping his eye on Smith.

"Here's a haystack," replied the latter, equably, but also a little sneeringly. "Shall we begin with arson? We can go on, by degrees, to murder."

"By all means."

The two men could be seen jumping the ditch, and laboriously climbing over a slippery stone wall. Several matches sputtered and went out, and then a little blaze lighted the outstretched hands and solemn intent faces of Jones and Smith. They drew out and spread the dry hay over the blaze, the flames fed eagerly, and the stone wall and the black trunk of an elm tree appeared to stagger toward them out of the darkness.

"I think that will do," observed Smith cheerfully.

They climbed back over the wall and resumed their walk. The rain had become a drizzle, and the moon, in a crack between the clouds, showed for a second the white of an eye. Behind them, the fire began to spout, and they observed that they were preceded, on the puddled road, by oblique drunken shadows. They walked rapidly.

"A mere bagatelle," Smith went on, after a time. "But there's a farm at the top of the hill, so we can, as it were, build more stately mansions. . . . Were you aware, at the moment of ignition, of a kind of co-awareness with the infinite?"

"Don't be frivolous."

"Personally, I found it a little disappointing. . . . I don't like these deliberate actions. Give me the spontaneous, every time. That's one thing I particularly like about Gleason. The dear thing hasn't the least idea what she's doing, or what she's going to do next. If she decided to kill you, you'd never know it, because you'd be dead. . . . Not at all like you, Jones. You've got a devil of a lot to unlearn!"

Jones reflected. He took off his hat and shook it. His air was profoundly philosophical.

"True. I have. I'll put off a decision about the farm till we get to it. I suppose, by the same token, you'd like me to give up my habit of strict meditation on the subject of *your* death?"

"Oh, just as you like about that!" . . . Smith laughed pleasantly. "I assure you it's not of the smallest consequence. . . . It occurs to me, by the way, somewhat irrelevantly, that in your philosophy of incandescent sensation one must allow a place for the merely horrible. I never, I swear, felt more brilliantly alive than when I saw, once, a Negro sitting in a cab with his throat cut. He unwound a bloody towel for the doctor, and I saw, in the chocolate color, three parallel red smiles—no, gills. It was amazing."

"A domestic scene? . . . *Crime passionnelle?*"

"No—a trifling misunderstanding in a barber shop. This chap started to take out a handkerchief; the other chap thought it was a revolver; and the razor was quicker than the handkerchief. . . . The safety razor ought to be abolished, don't you think?"

Jones, without answer, jumped the ditch and disappeared in the direction of the farm. Smith leaned against the wall, laughing softly to himself. After a while there were six little spurts of light one after another in the darkness, hinting each time at a nose and fingers, and then four more. Nothing further happened. The darkness remained self-possessed, and presently Jones reappeared, muttering.

"No use! It's too wet, and I couldn't find any kindling."

"Don't let that balk you, my dear Jones! Ring the doorbell and ask for a little kerosene. Why not kill the old man, ravish his daughter, and then burn up the lot? It would be a good night's work."

"Damn you! You've done enough harm already."

There was something a little menacing in this, but Smith was unperturbed.

"What the devil do you mean?" he answered. "Intellectually I'm a child by comparison with you. I'm an adolescent."

"You know perfectly well what I mean—all this," and Jones gave a short ugly sweep of his arm toward the blazing haystack and, beyond that, the city. The moon came out, resting her perfect chin on a tawny cloud. The two men regarded each other strangely.

"Nonsense!" Smith then exclaimed. "Besides you'll have the satisfaction of killing me. That ought to compensate. And Gleason! think of Gleason! She'll be glad to see you. She'll revel in the details of my death."

"Will she?"

"Of course, she will. . . . She's a kind of sadist, or something of the sort. . . . How, by the way, do you propose to do it? We've never—come to think of it—had an understanding on that point. Would you mind telling me, or do you regard it as a sort of trade secret? . . . Just as you like!"

Jones seemed to be breathing a little quickly.

"No trouble at all—but I don't know! I shall simply, as you suggest, wait for an inspiration."

"How damned disquieting! Also, Jones, it's wholly out of character, and you'll have to forgive me if, for once, I refuse to believe you. What the deuce is this walk for, if not for your opportunity? You're bound to admit that I was most compliant. I accepted your suggestion without so much as a twitter —didn't I? Very unselfish of me, I think! . . . But, of course, it had to come."

The two men were walking, by tacit agreement, at opposite sides of the road; they had to raise their voices. Still, one would not have said that it was a quarrel.

"Oh yes, it had to come. It was clearly impossible that both of us should live!"

"Quite. . . . At the same time this affair is so exquisitely complex, and so dislocated, if I may put it so, into the world of the fourth dimension, that I'm bound to admit that while I recognize the necessity I don't quite grasp the cause. . . ."

"You're vulgar, Smith."

"Am I? . . . Ah, so that's it—I'm vulgar, I seize life by the forelock! . . . I go about fornicating, thieving, card-cheating, and murdering, in my persistent, unreflective, low-grade sort of way, and it makes life insupportable for you. Here, now, is Gleason. How that must simply infuriate you! Three days in town, and I have a magnificent planetary love affair like that—burnt to a crisp! Ha ha! And you, all the while, drinking tea and reading Willard Gibbs. I must say it's damned funny."

Jones made no reply. His head was thrust forward—he seemed to be brooding. His heavy breathing was quite audible, and Smith, after an amused glance toward him, went on talking.

"Lots of lights suddenly occur to me—lights on this extraordinary, impenetrable subject—take down my words, Jones, this is my death-bed speech! . . . I spoke, didn't I, of the beautiful obscene, and of the inextricable manner in which the two qualities are everywhere bound up together? The beautiful and the obscene. The desirable and the disgusting. I also compared this state of things with an organism in which a cancer was growing—which one tries to excise. . . . Well, Jones, you're the beautiful and I'm the obscene; you're the desirable and I'm the disgusting; and in some rotten way we've got tangled up together. . . . You, being the healthy organism, insist on having the cancer removed. But remember: I warned you! If you do so, it's at your own peril. . . . However, it's silly to warn you, for of course you have no more control over the situation than I have, or Gleason has. The bloody conclusion lies there, and we walk soberly toward it. . . . Are you sorry?"

"No!"

"Well then, neither am I. Let's move a little faster! . . . Damn it all, I *would* like to see Gleason again! You were perfectly right about that. . . . Do you know what she said to me?"

Smith, at this point, suddenly stopped, as if to enjoy the recollection at leisure. He opened his mouth and stared before him, in the moonlight, with an odd bright fixity. Jones, with the scantiest turn of his head, plodded on, so that Smith had, perforce, to follow.

"She said she'd like to live with me—that she'd support me. By George! What do you think of that? . . . 'You're a dear boy,' she said, 'you fascinate me!' 'Fascinate!' That's the best thing I do. Don't I fascinate you, Jones? Look at my eyes! Don't I fascinate you? . . . Ha, ha! . . . Yes, I have the morals of a snake. I'm graceful, I'm all curves, there's nothing straight about me. Gleason got dizzy looking at me, her head swayed from side to side, her eyes were lost in a sort of mist, and then she fell clutching at me like a paralytic, and talking the wildest nonsense. Could you do that, Jones, do you think? . . . Never! It's all a joke to think of your going to see Gleason. And if you told her what had happened she'd kill you. Yes, you'd look like St. Sebastian when Gleason got through with you. . . . Say something! Don't be so damned glum. Anybody'd suppose it was *your* funeral."

"Oh, go on talking! I like the sound of your voice."

"And then to think of your pitiful attempt to set that barn on fire! Good Lord, with half a dozen matches. . . . That's what comes of studying symbolic logic and the rule of phase. . . . Really, I don't know what you'll do without me, Jones! You're like a child, and when I'm dead, who's going to show you, as the wit said, how to greet the obscene with a cheer? . . . However, I wouldn't bother about that rock if I were you—aren't you premature?"

This last observation sounded a little sharp.

Jones had certainly appeared to be stooping toward a small loose fragment of rock by the roadside, but he straightened up with smiling alacrity.

"My shoelace," he said, cynically, "It's loose. I think I'll retie it."

"Pray do! Why not?"

"Very well! If you don't mind waiting!"

Jones gave a little laugh. He stooped again, fumbled for a second at his shoe, then suddenly shot out a snakelike hand toward the rock. But Smith meanwhile had made a gleaming gesture which seemed to involve Jones's back.

"Ah!" said Jones, and slid softly forward into a puddle.

"Are you there?"

Smith's query was almost humorous. As it received no reply, and Jones lay motionless in his puddle, Smith took him by the coat-collar, dragged him to the edge of the ditch, and rolled him in. The moon poured a clear green light on this singular occurrence. It showed Smith examining his hands with care, and then wiping them repeatedly on the wet grass and rank jewelweed. It showed him relighting his pipe—which had gone out during the rain—with infinite leisure. One would have said, at the moment, that he looked like a tramp. And, finally, it showed him turning back in the direction he had come from, and setting off cheerfully toward the city; alone, but with an amazing air, somehow, of having always been alone.

William Sansom

A Last Word

THE HOUSE WAS OWNED BY HENRY CADWALLER. IT WAS TALL AND GREY and windowed black; it rose, and was now falling, in the Fulham area, and its presently visible name, DWALLER HO, suggested much of its function— a dwelling-house where people might dawdle to death, with a Ho to summon the aged and weary to its door.

Henry Cadwaller was a man of thrift, and the old gold letters lost from the fanlight of the original HOUSE had never been replaced, nor had half the black-and-white tiles on the steps, nor the stained-glass lights to his hallway. These red and yellow and purple panes, patched nowadays with wood and cardboard, shed a more Gothic gloom than ever: indeed, the whole house was patched, its large Victorian rooms were partitioned with papered three-ply— each lodger lay and stared at his own piece of ceiling frieze, coming from nowhere and disappearing with mad pupose—and the curtains of many of the windows had once patently been tablecloths—or why the ink-stain at the top, why the vertical fringe?—and the bedcovers were unmistakably made from old curtains—or should bedcovers have ring-slots, and widen towards one end? Plaster fell freely from the grey façade, and was helped on its way by abandoned wireless aerials that flapped wearily down the walls from window-sills lined with meat-safes and milk-bottles; the garden at the back was a rot of thistles, crates, cans and the shattered glass of the old conservatory, now a plywood bathroom; on the roof the chimneys chatted in all directions, and cowled ventilators sprouted anywhere on the walls like an iron mushroom growth; in the old hallway the little fireplace once used to warm the footman's rump now held empty bottles and a pair of goloshes, and on the front door there were pinned, like the notes of a white up-ended dulcimer, thin strips of card announcing the names, against bakelite bell-pushes, of fifteen lodgers.

These bells were a source of much irritation to Mr. Cadwaller: a long time ago he had had them fixed to save himself trouble at the front door—but had overlooked the fact that each time a bell rang the cost of a small electric impulse went down on his bill. There were some days—on Monday morning when various laundries called, or on Saturday when the coming and going was something appalling—when he sat in his front room holding his hands over his ears to deafen this costly tolling. And sometimes, driven to absurd measures, he would run to the door when he saw a van arrive simply to save that insistent ringing whose every vibration cost money—yet never without his

59

pan and brush, in case a horse had passed to drop manure for his window-box. He liked milk-carts, and only ordered coal from a company that still employed the old drays.

Of all these bells, one angered him more than any other: and that was Mr. Horton's. Mr. Horton, a retired merchant, seldom had visitors; but always —and Mr. Cadwaller knew well by now that it was out of malice—he rang his bell before entering the house. To test it, he explained.

Mr. Horton was the scourge of Mr. Cadwaller's life: and thus perhaps its main stimulus. A feud had begun months previously, shortly after Mr. Horton had arrived, in the bathroom. Throughout the house, Cadwaller had had the overflow-holes in each bath reset three inches lower: expensive, but a reasonable outlay thus to lower authoritatively the level of each lodger's bath and save on the cost of hot water. And then one morning he had entered a bathroom just quitted by Mr. Horton. And he had seen the dark ring left high up above the overflow line.

He studied it, had the overflow tested, and then lay in wait. Each time Mr. Horton had a bath he left the same high ring. At length Cadwaller could stand it no longer. "You put your foot over it!" he said, catching Mr. Horton in the passage.

"Beg pardon?"

"Your foot!" He pointed through the door to the bath. "You keep it there."

It was a second of enormous understanding. Each man sized the other, recognized his intention, grasped his game.

Mr. Horton made no attempt to prevaricate, he closed his eyelids and sighed, before passing along the passage.

"I cannot, Mr. Cadwaller, help my sponge floating to the further end of the bath. If," his voice rose, "you can call it a bath."

From then on it was war, cold and subtle war. Cadwaller considered, of course, serving Mr. Horton his notice. But the rooms were not all full, it would be his own loss; and did he really want Mr. Horton to go? For that flash of mutual understanding had been of deep significance—as though twins of some kind had found each other. Each recognized his brother in thrift— and both were as suddenly aware of a physical resemblance. Their thrift, their almost acrobatic thrift—what others might call "meanness," though where does meanness begin and and thrift end?—might have been apparent before: Mr. Cadwaller might have noticed the amount of free samples that made up most of Mr. Horton's mail, and Mr. Horton might have taken more notice of Mr. Cadwaller's brush and pan. Indeed, idly they must have remarked these and a number of other matters; for now, in a sudden retrogressive flash, each totted up the other's account—and such was the intensity of the moment that each realized for the first time something else, they recognized their more than strong physical resemblance. Standing in the dim, daylit, room-smelling passage—the one in an old brown dressing-gown, the other in his tweed jacket fortified everywhere with leather—they faced each other like mirrors, two tall stooping grey-haired gentlemen each mumbling on a long jutting, petulant, prognathous jaw. On a long pale turnip of a jaw, on small bottom teeth monkeying forwards and under a drooping grey moustache disguising the short hare-like upper lip. It was as if, in the pale light of some curious asylum out of time and place, Valentin-le-désossé had met the Habsburg Charles II.

The formation of Charles II's jaw compelled that poor man to eat no solid food, he was fed on liquid hominies. Not so Mr. Horton: he liked his liquids, and the stronger the better, but he liked to eat too. This proved a matter of further contention; for Mr. Cadwaller ran a profitable dining-room downstairs, and Mr. Horton liked his food, when he ate it there, very well done. But Mr. Cadwaller liked his guests to eat their food half-raw, it saved gas. And here was this Horton consistently sending his back to be burnt! That is, when he ate it there. For upstairs there was a no-cooking-in-the-rooms rule: and from beneath Mr. Horton's door there crept into the linoleumed lincrustaed passage the most eloquent odours. Yet how could this be done? No trivet for the gas-fire, no gas-ring. Cadwaller even looked outside the window, as if Horton might have been an alcoholic hanging out his bottle, his gas-ring on a nail. However carefully Mr. Cadwaller searched, he never found the answer. For Mr. Horton cooked, beneath a tent of sheets, on an electric blanket.

Thus these two long-jawed gentlemen went to war: finesse of economy became their touchstone, they tried to outdo each other at every move—and the sphere widened, they openly criticized each other's tactics in fields outside any personal engagement. Thus, when on one morning of strong sunshine Mr. Horton looked in on Cadwaller and found him sitting in a chair in front of which was spread newspaper to prevent the sunshine fading the carpet, and moreover moving round the room with the newspaper and his chair as the poisonous beautiful sunlight travelled round, and moreover trying to do his pools at the same time—Mr. Horton was able to scoff at him for dispersing his concentrative powers. "You'll never hit the jackpot that way," he said. "Why not spread the paper all over?"

"Because I like to look at my carpet," Cadwaller growled. "What's the use of buying a carpet and not looking at it? Besides, I need the paper for the boiler."

"You could burn the paper later."

"Eh?" Cadwaller hadn't thought of that. But quickly, "I suppose you want me to go out and *buy* papers to put on the carpet?"

"Chuck away seventy thousand quid if you like. I don't care."

And for a moment Mr. Cadwaller would think he was really losing seventy thousand; and they would pause facing each other wildly, big turnip chins raised and trembling like the masks of warrior-ants.

All such arguments, absurd as they always became, were distinguished by the cardinal difference between them: Cadwaller's thrift was immediate, the act of expenditure itself gave him unbearable pain; while Horton held the long view, he never minded shelling out if finally profits might be reaped. He liked to foresee things. Thus Horton would with much misgiving pay the registration fee on a parcel, realizing the payment that otherwise must be made in time, fares and shoe-leather: but Cadwaller could not put that shilling on the counter—and took instead tenpence worth of bus fares, and lost time and shoe-leather into a bad bargain. And while Cadwaller wore his old coat out and stitched leather into the elbow-holes, cuffs and neck—Horton foresaw the necessity of this and simply had the arms from his chairs removed. (Trouble there, they were Cadwaller's chairs; but Horton made him a footstool of the arms, to save the wear and tear of bedroom slippers.)

As is natural, this common ground brought them much together, not as friends, not exactly as enemies—perhaps more like passionate chess-players. They could never resist each other's company. Their blood rose to each meeting. They went to the Sales together, where there was much argument as to what was true "clearance" and what was cheap stock brought in for the sale: and whereas neither bought much, Cadwaller would fall eventually for something he did not want at all, simply because it was so very heavily reduced, while Horton bought necessities, seeing the heat of summer through a winter's fog, or even buying two things, like a piece of mirror and a picture-frame, which he could put together to make something of three times the original value.

On such expeditions they would sometimes lunch together, and both, as often happens with "mean" people, wanted a taste off each other's plates. And so after a few hair-raising encounters when one or the other was served a larger or more appetizing helping, they agreed to order two plates of different dishes and two empty plates as well and then divide exactly both taste and helping. It proved an efficient solution—and if a more plentiful helping of something else passed them on its way to another table, then it was bad luck, it was painful and as pain must be forgotten. What could not be forgotten was a difference between them on the matter of alcohol. Needless to say that they paid for their own: Cadwaller always ordered mild beer, slow long pints of mild beer, perhaps three, but each occasioning an equally mild outlay and each worth its weight in drinking-time: but Horton ordered a small whisky in a large glass, believing in the greater toxic value of spirits, and watched with joy the publican's knuckles whiten as he pressed home the free soda-water. His joy was thus only confined by Cadwaller's presence, for Cadwaller too enjoyed the publican's discomfort, but at his, Horton's, expense.

Thus life continued, in and out of Dwaller Ho. The two great chins, the downdrawn moustaches faced each other and fiddled, fought it out. Ring up TIM? Nonsense, ring up a friend, combine a chat with the time. Take out your sister? Take her in a *taxi* to a cheap restaurant—the taxi'll do all the plinthing she needs. Keep the veg. water for soup? But what of the reducing costs, the expanding gas-bill? Tip the waiter a bit more to get a bigger helping next time? But what if all that money goes in a common pool? Switch out the hall-lights when no one's there? But the poor filaments they make these days—and what of the switches anyway, what of *deterioration*, wear, my God, and tear? And keep the Ascot pilot flame going to warm the place.

As time went on, and in early summer, that fruitfuul time that follows the mortal months, Cadwaller killed himself.

They had argued about horse-shoes and motor-tyres: shoeing a horse cost

exactly twice the cost of motor-tyres over the same distance. Four treads each.
Deep in this and adjacent problems of shoe-leather, Cadwaller, during a
particularly wet April, refused to have his walking-shoes repaired until the
holes achieved a reasonable importance, like the size of the yolk of a flat-fried
egg: one could walk on inclined welts. But welts or no, those holes let in water,
he caught cold, it lingered, he refused fires and hot-water bottles during the
deepening bronchial troubles, there were developments, and in the latter
middle of a starless night he died all by himself in the dark, not wishing to
turn the light on or ring for his nurse.

Birds were singing in those days. The guests at Dwaller Ho were upset,
despite the discomfort to which, in their creaking partitions, amid their
personal sounds and their occasional smells, they had always been put. But
even so most of them felt more for poor Mr. Horton than for the dead
Cadwaller himself. For they knew that neither could live happily without the
other. They had all recognized how much each had meant to the other;
neither old man had ever tried to hide their curious rivalry, and it was a local
joke. Yet not only a joke, it was touching, too, in its way—and now there was
poor Mr. Horton alone, bereft of his adversary, his playmate. He sat at his
window, the early summer sunshine too fresh for his worn skin and his grey
hair, and more than ever that long jaw seemed to press his mouth closed,
always as if he were offended and refused to speak, as if he were the little boy
left out of the game, alone and with no one to play with.

But if the sight of him then was touching, his fellow-guests were really
moved on the day of the funeral. For early that morning Mr. Horton was seen
to pick his way through the broken glass and old crates and rubbish of the
garden to a single flowering bush at the end wall. He carried a knife. He stood
by the bush for some minutes, staring at it, then looking at the knife in his
hand, as if he were considering whether it was worthwhile to risk the blade.
Then his shoulders suddenly shook—the poor old fellow couldn't be weeping?
—and he bent down and cut off a branch of flowers. Another and another.
And finally turned, his head bowed, and carried back to the house an armful
of blossom.

Everyone knew his intention. And though they smiled to see this final
economy and murmured that Cadwaller would turn six feet beneath when
these, his own flowers cut free of charge, touched his grave—nevertheless they
were deeply moved by old Horton's thought.

The day of the funeral was one of sunshine and fresh warmth, a pale and
lovely day of early flowering summer. There were few mourners: but when
the hearse drew up at the cemetery gates, and the little file of people came
in ones and twos up the asphalt path, lost and at a loss among so vast a civic
sea of marble and granite—Mr. Horton was already there standing at a
respectful distance away from the yellow mound of new-turned clay. The
grave was like any hole in the ground—only the mourners, and they much
more than the coffin, gave it presence and meaning. And of the mourners, Mr.
Horton, a sad figure and the older for the fresh blossom held in his hand,
seemed, in his resemblance to the dead man and in the memory the others

had of the two together, to sanctify the moment more than the priest, the fair weather, the grave.

A short service was read, the coffin lowered, and then, when the carpet of green grass had been finally placed over the grave, Mr. Horton went forward alone to place his flowers on his old companion's last resting-place. He stood for a minute, head bowed, in silent prayer. Then turned and walked, a solitary figure, away into the years of loneliness.

They watched him go, they saw the last of him turn out through the cemetery gates. But nobody, naturally, saw the giant chuckle beneath Mr. Horton's bowed shoulders: nobody knew the true nature of his last tribute, his bloom, his last word, *Rubus Idacus,* the common raspberry.

Eudora Welty

Circe

NEEDLE IN AIR, I STOPPED WHAT I WAS MAKING. FROM THE UPPER CASE-
ment, my lookout on the sea, I saw them disembark and find the path; I heard
that whole drove of mine break loose on the beautiful strangers. I slipped
down the ladder. When I heard men breathing and sandals kicking the stones,
I threw open the door. A shaft of light from the zenith struck my brow, and
the wind let out my hair. Something else swayed my body outward.

"Welcome!" I said—the most dangerous word in the world.

Heads lifted to the smell of my bread, they trooped inside—and with such
a grunting and frisking at their heels to the very threshold. Star-gazers! They
stumbled on my polished floor, strewing sand, crowding on each other, sizing
up the household for gifts (thinking already of sailing away), and sighted
upwards where the ladder went, to the sighs of the island girls who peeped
from the kitchen door. In the hope of a bath, they looked in awe at their
hands.

I left them thus, and withdrew to make the broth.

With their tear-bright eyes they watched me come in with the great winking
tray, and circle the room in a winding wreath of steam. Each in turn with
a pair of black-nailed hands swept up his bowl. The first were trotting at my
heels while the last still reached with their hands. Then the last drank too,
and dredging their snouts from the bowls, let go and shuttled into the company.

That moment of transformation—only the gods really like it! Men and
beasts almost never take in enough of the wonder to justify the trouble. The
floor was swaying like a bridge in battle. "Outside!" I commanded. "No dirt
is allowed in this house!" In the end, it takes phenomenal neatness of
housekeeping to put it through the heads of men that they are swine. With
my wand seething in the air like a broom, I drove them all through the door
—twice as many hooves as there had been feet before—to join their brothers,
who rushed forward to meet them now, filthily rivaling, but welcoming. What
tusks I had given them!

As I shut the door on the sight, and drew back into my privacy—deathless
privacy that heals everything, even the effort of magic—I felt something from
behind press like the air of heaven before a storm, and reach like another
wand over my head.

I spun round, thinking, O gods, it has failed me, it's drying up. Before everything, I think of my power. One man was left.

"What makes you think you're different from anyone else?" I screamed; and he laughed.

Before I'd believe it, I ran back to my broth. I had thought it perfect—I'd allowed no other woman to come near it. I tasted, and it was perfect—swimming with oysters from my reef and flecks of golden pork, redolent with leaves of bay and basil and rosemary, with the glass of island wine tossed in at the last: it has been my infallible recipe. Circe's broth: all the gods have heard of it and envied it. No, the fault had to be in the drinker. If a man remained, unable to leave that magnificent body of his, then enchantment had met with a hero. Oh, I know those prophecies as well as the back of my hand —only nothing is here to warn me when it is *now.*

The island girls, those servants I support, stood there in the kitchen and smiled at me. I threw kettle and all at their withering heels. Let them learn that unmagical people are put into the world to justify and serve the magical —not to smile at them!

I whirled back again. The hero stood as before. But his laugh had gone too, after his friends. His gaze was empty, as though I were not in it—I was invisible. His hand groped across the rushes of a chair. I moved beyond him and bolted the door against the murmurous outside. Still invisibly, I took away his sword. I sent his tunic away to the spring for washing, and I, with my own hands, gave him his bath. Then he sat and dried himself before the fire—carefully, the only mortal man on an island in the sea. I rubbed oil on his shadowy shoulders, and on the rope of curls in which his jaw was set. His rapt ears still listened to the human silence there.

"I know your name," I said in the voice of a woman, "and you know mine by now."

I took the chain from my waist, it slipped shining to the floor between us, where it lay as if it slept, as I came forth. Under my palms he stood warm and dense as a myrtle grove at noon. His limbs were heavy, braced like a sleep-walker's who has wandered, alas, to cliffs above the sea. When I passed before him, his arm lifted and barred my way. When I held up the glass he opened his mouth. He fell among the pillows, his still-open eyes two clouds stopped over the sun, and I lifted and kissed his hand.

It was he who in a burst of speech announced the end of day. As though the hour brought a signal to the wanderer, he told me a story, while the owl made comment outside. He told me of the monster with one eye—he had put out the eye, he said. Yes, said the owl, the monster is growing another, and a new man will sail along to blind it again. I had heard it all before, from man and owl. I didn't want his story, I wanted his secret.

When Venus leaned at the window, I called him by name, but he had talked himself into a dream, and his dream had him fast. I now saw through the cautious herb that had protected him from my broth. From the first, he had found some way to resist my power. He must laugh, sleep, ravish, he must talk and sleep. Next it would be he must die. I looked an age into that face above the beard's black crescent, the eyes turned loose from mine like the statues' that sleep on the hill. I took him by the locks of his beard and hair, but he rolled away with his snore to the very floor of sleep—as far beneath my reach as the drowned sailor dropped out of his, in the tale he told of the sea.

I thought of my father the Sun, who went on his divine way untroubled, ambitionless—unconsumed; suffering no loss, no heroic fear of corruption through his constant shedding of light, needing no story, no retinue to vouch for where he has been—even heroes could learn of the gods!

Yet I know they keep something from me, asleep and awake. There exists a mortal mystery, that, if I knew where it was, I could crush like an island grape. Only frailty, it seems, can divine it—and I was not endowed with that property. They live by frailty! By the moment! I tell myself that it is only a mystery, and mystery is only uncertainty. (There is no mystery in magic! Men are swine: let it be said, and no sooner said than done.) Yet mortals alone can divine where it lies in each other, can find it and prick it in all its peril, with an instrument made of air. I swear that only to possess that one, trifing secret, I would willingly turn myself into a harmless dove for the rest of eternity!

When presently he leapt up, I had nearly forgotten he would move again —as a golden hibiscus startles you, all flowers, when you are walking in some weedy place apart.

Yes, but he would not dine. Dinner was carried in, but he would not dine with me until I would undo that day's havoc in the pigsty. I pointed out that his portion was served in a golden bowl—the very copy of that bowl my own father the Sun crosses back in each night after his journey of the day. But he cared nothing for beauty that was not of the world, he did not want the first taste of anything new. He wanted his men back. In the end, it was necessary for me to cloak myself and go down in the dark, under the willows where the bones are hung to the wind, into the sty; and to sort out and bring up his friends again from their muddy labyrinth. I had to pass them back through the doorway as themselves. I could not skip or brush lightly over one—he named and counted. Then he could look at them all he liked, staggering up on their hind legs before him. Their jaws sank asthmatically, and he cried, "Do you know me?"

"It's Odysseus!" I called, to spoil the moment. But with a shout he had already sprung to their damp embrace.

Reunions, it seems, are to be celebrated. (I have never had such a thing.) All of us feasted together on meat and bread, honey and wine, and the fire roared. We heard out the flute player, we heard out the story, and the fair-haired sailor, whose name is now forgotten, danced on the table and pleased them. When the fire was black, my servants came languishing from the kitchen, and all the way up the ladder to the beds above they had to pull the drowsy-kneed star-gazers, spilling laughter and songs all the way. I could hear them calling away to the girls as they would call them home. But the pigsty was where they belonged.

Hand in hand, we climbed to my tower room. His cheeks were grave and his eyes black, put out with puzzles and solutions. We conversed of signs, omens, premonitions, riddles and dreams, and ended in fierce, cold sleep. Strange man, as unflinching and as wound up as I am. His short life and my long one have their ground in common. Passion is our ground, our island—do others exist?

His sailors came jumping down in the morning, full of themselves and stories. Preparing the breakfast, I watched them tag one another, run rough-and-tumble around the table, regaling the house. "What did *I* do? How far did *I* go with it?" and in a reckless reassurance imitating the sounds of pigs at each other's backs. They were certainly more winsome now than they could ever have been before; I'd made them younger, too, while I was about it. But tell me of one that appreciated it! Tell me one now who looked my way until I had brought him his milk and figs.

When he made his appearance, we devoured a god's breakfast—all, the very sausages, taken for granted. The kitchen girls simpered and cried that if this went on, we'd be eaten out of house and home. But I didn't care if I put the house under greater stress for this one mortal than I ever dreamed of for myself—even on those lonely dull mornings when mist wraps the island and hides every path of the sea, and when my heart is black.

But a stir was upon them all from the moment they rose from the table. Treading on their napkins, tracking the clean floor with honey, they deserted me in the house and collected, arms wound on each other's shoulders, to talk beneath the sky. There they were in a knot, with him in the center of it. He folded his arms and sank his golden weight on one leg, while every ear on the island listened. I stood in the door and waited.

He walked up and said, "Thank you, Circe, for the hospitality we have enjoyed beneath your roof."

"What is the occasion for a speech?" I asked.

"We are setting sail," he said. "A year's visit is visit enough. It's time we were on our way."

Ever since the morning Time came and sat on the world, men have been on the run as fast as they can go, with beauty flung over their shoulders. I ground my teeth. I raised my wand in his face.

"You've put yourself to great trouble for us. You may have done too much," he said.

"I undid as much as I did!" I cried. "That was hard."

He gave me a pecking, recapitulating kiss, his black beard thrust at me like a shoe. I kissed it, his mouth, his wrist, his shoulder, I put my eyes to his eyes, through which I saw seas toss, and to the cabinet of his chest.

He turned and raised an arm to the others. "Tomorrow."

The knot broke and they wandered apart to the shore. They were not so forlorn when they could eat acorns and trot quickly where they would go.

It was as though I had no memory, to discover how early and late the cicadas drew long sighs like the playing out of all my silver shuttles. Wasn't it always the time of greatest heat, the Dog Star running with the Sun? The sea the color of honey looked sweet even to the tongue, the salt and vengeful sea. My grapes had ripened all over again while we stretched and drank our wine, and I ordered the harvest gathered and pressed—but this wine, I made clear to the servants, was to store. Hospitality is one thing, but I must consider how my time is endless, how I shall need wine endlessly. They smiled; but magic is the tree, and intoxication is just the little bird that flies in it to sing and flies out again. But the wanderers were watching the sun and waiting for the stars.

Now the night wind was rising. I went my way over the house as I do by night to see if all is well and holding together. From the rooftop I looked out. I saw the vineyards spread out like wings on the hill, the servants' huts and the swarthy groves, the sea awake, and the eye of the black ship. I saw in the moonlight the dance of the bones in the willows. "Old, displeasing ones!" I sang to them on the wind. "There's another now more displeasing than you! Your bite would be sweeter to my mouth than the soft kiss of a wanderer." I looked up at Cassiopeia, who sits there and needs nothing, pale in her chair in the stream of heaven. The old Moon was still at work. "Why keep it up, old woman?" I whispered to her, while the lions roared among the rocks; but I could hear plainly the crying of birds nearby and along the mournful shore.

I swayed, and was flung backward by my torment. I believed that I lay in disgrace and my blood ran green, like the wand that breaks in two. My sight returned to me when I awoke in the pigsty, in the red and black aurora of flesh, and it was day.

They sailed from me, all but one.

The youngest—Elpenor was his name—fell from my roof. He had forgotten where he had gone to sleep. Drunk on the last night, the drunkest of them all—so as not to be known any longer as only the youngest—he'd gone to sleep on the rooftop, and when they called him, his step went off into air. I saw him beating down through the light with rosy fists, as though he'd never left his mother's side till then.

They all ran from the table as though a star had fallen. They stood or they crouched above Elpenor fallen in my yard, low-voiced now like conspirators —as indeed they were. They wept for Elpenor lying on his face, and for themselves, as *he* wept for them the day they came, when I had made them swine.

He knelt and touched Elpenor, and like a lover lifted him; then each in turn held the transformed boy in his arms. They brushed the leaves from his face, and smoothed his red locks, which were still in their tangle from his brief attempts at love-making and from his too-sound sleep.

I spoke from the door. "When you dig the grave for that one, and bury him in the lonely sand by the shadow of your fleeing ship, write on the stone: 'I died of love.' "

I thought I spoke in epitaph—in the idiom of man. But when they heard me, they left Elpenor where he lay, and ran. Red-limbed, with linens sparkling, they sped over the windy path from house to ship like a rainbow in the sun, like new butterflies turned erratically to sea. While he stood in the prow and shouted to them, they loaded the greedy ship. They carried off their gifts from me—all unappreciated, unappraised.

I slid out of their path. I had no need to see them set sail, knowing as well as if I'd been ahead of them all the way, the far and wide, misty and islanded, bright and indelible and menacing world under which they all must go. But foreknowledge is not the same as the last word.

My cheek against the stony ground, I could hear the swine like summer thunder. These were with me still, pets now, once again—grumbling without meaning. I rose to my feet. I was sickened, with child. The ground fell away before me, blotted with sweet myrtle, with high oak that would have given me a ship too, if I were not tied to my island, as Cassiopeia must be to the sticks and stars of her chair. We were a rim of fire, a ring on the sea. His ship was a moment's gleam on a wave. The little son, I knew, was to follow—follow and slay him. That was the story. For whom is a story enough? For the wanderers who will tell it—it's where they must find their strange felicity.

I stood on my rock and wished for grief. It would not come. Though I could shriek at the rising Moon, and she, so near, would wax or wane, there was still grief, that couldn't hear me—grief that cannot be round or plain or solid-bright or running on its track, where a curse could get at it. It has no heavenly course; it is like mystery, and knows where to hide itself. At last it does not even breathe. I cannot find the dusty mouth of grief. I am sure now grief is a ghost—only a ghost in Hades, where ungrateful Odysseus is going —waiting on him.

Edward Dahlberg
The Tailor's Daughter

I joye in grief, and doo detest all joyes.
— Sir Philip Sidney

I HAD DISCLOSED TO MY HARD-WORKING MOTHER THAT I HOPED SHORTLY
to be a famous man of letters, and with charred distrust asked her if she could
send me fifteen dollars a week. When word came there was a money order
for me at Western Union at first I tarried. Should I refuse to accept it, for
was I not filching her poor savings? Such was my plight: I had to gull my
mother so that I would not be a gross person. I have always burned in the
furnace of shame when I recall how I diminished her addle purse.

At last I bent my way toward the telegraph office, asking my mother to
forgive her son. I wore my guilt on my face and on my back.

A young woman behind the counter asked me to identify myself. Absorbed
in her toothsome, plump hands and the cleft in her dainty chin, I began to
gently boil and my head turned to other impressions. As I gazed at her chin,
and the glen in it, I was sure this was proof of a blessed cranny. Yet esteeming
her chastity I misliked my riggish heat.

Awakened from this sleepy vagary I heard her say: "What is your name,
please? Sir, will you kindly show me your driver's license? Doubtless you are
a propertied man."

"Lovely Madonna," I said, "I am Anybody's Miserable Chagrin."

"How much life insurance do you carry? Perhaps the company will guarantee that you are Anybody's Miserable Chagrin."

My tone altered. "Lady, I belong to the wormwood fraternity of penniless
authors, a parasite according to our shop-keeping nation." Then with more
bile I said: "Do you expect me to own a twenty-story building in order to
collect fifteen dollars? How can I prove that I am I? So many parts of me are
dissimilar I believe they must belong to someone else. I beg you on bended
knees, don't ask me who I am; I really don't know. Let my countenance
deliver the angelic or brutish message."

I handed her a card on which a printer had engraved:

ANYBODY'S MISERABLE CHAGRIN
Castaway Author of America

What delicate pips she had, a pair of roses or two bunches of violets, I
guessed. And the little nose of a Sabine virgin. Already I chanted Chaucer's
"For pitie renneth sone in gentil hearte."

She turned from the counter to go to her desk, and I devoured her milked calves and was set afire by the rump Venus had given her to placate the hungry tribe of males. Filled with her untasted myrrh I yearned to gather her mouth unto me.

Giddily I told her my imperial companions George Gissing, Flaubert, Gautier, Andreyev, Gogol and Baudelaire would not be reluctant to be a surety of my character.

The manager, who had a bean-shaped nose and vulpine mouth, picked up the phone and asked for the number of the charity hospital for the insane, but she stopped him from proceeding further. After she had given me the fifteen dollars I called out to him: "Do you know *The Death of Ivan Ilyitch* by Count Leo Tolstoy?" Bewildered, he gave me several low bows, declaring he had not realized I was on intimate terms with the nobility.

As I stood by the counter, for I was loath to leave, I considered the difference between her seraphic hinder parts and the pin-buttocks of Aeschylus and Euripides, which a poet must have to compose *Prometheus* and *The Bacchae*. Immune to a female with stingy flat posteriors, I was now full of my knowledge of women, the cause of so many scabbed follies. My easily stung flesh was my sole hovel which was never sufficient to cover my feelings. Still what a delightful udder she was.

My hesitation to ask her name was so thinly wrapped up that she herself told me she was Mary C——, and that I might call on her at her home the following evening. When she opened her lips I inspected her teeth as edible as the inner white skin of an apple, and noticed with a quantum of despair that one of them was fungused. Then to reappraise her and sustain my amorous desires I observed her wrist, for women who are hairy are as unpleasant to kiss as Methuselah in his nine-hundredth year. My heart was mirthful; her skin had no bristles and she did not secretly shave herself.

I walked away in my sodden shoes with a spruce gait. What a windfall the hour had been. A superstitious animal, I was minded to believe that good luck is gregarious as evil occurrences. Why does one receive five letters from different people on a single day, and then none for a fortnight? Should one receive a civil salutation from a bare acquaintance that also was a good sign and likely to be followed by another agreeable incident. Then if a passer-by steps on your foot, and you apologize to him, and he scowls at you, be sure the entire day is a fit of gloom. Doubtless nature is as unreasonable as man. I had won this virgin, and so pampered up was I by my triumph I now felt I was to acquire some credit in this world.

The night I was to visit Mary I polished my secondhand shoes so that they would not appear to be a pair of misfortunes. Then I spat on my sleeves and endeavored to sharpen the crease in my trousers, for I did not want my pants and jacket to show their murrain traits at once. Yet my clothes did not despise me, for my crumpled sharkskin suit and I had grown so close to one another we could be said to be blood relations. My cravat gave me a musty look, but I let that pass. I hid the ragged end and was ready to be the fop and beau.

Deeply smitten, though somewhat unnerved by the memory of that fungused tooth, I had the most pious faith in my lady's body. As I gazed out the window of the streetcar I hoped she was an orphan. A family was sure to be a galloping consumption to a mendicant suitor. At last the tram was near the city's limits; I got off and strolled, having an unusual fondness for the trees because they were neighbors of humble cottages. No avarice could dwell here, and the air was not pestered with the rotten fever of wealth.

At the door I was introduced to a slight stump of a father who straightway took a rare interest in my suit. Neither he nor my suit seemed to be getting along together. Fingering my coat he asked: "Where did you get this drowned animal?" With a vein of hauteur I quoted a sixteenth-century author: "The richest garments are subject to time's moth-frets."

My cravat also was scornful of him; it was still damp with my saliva. "Has your necktie a bad cold or bronchitis?" he asked, and without warning he put his nose against my sleeve. Dolefully he shook his head. "Never have I seen a coat so filled with sorrow. Was it beaten up lately?" Then with some display of propriety he touched the spectral seams of my trousers.

Without further preamble he stated that he was a tailor and demanded that I be plain with him since I showed myself all too clearly.

"Sir," I replied, "I did not come here to decieve you. My sharkskin suit is just as sincere and outspoken as I am."

The tailor was himself a piece of tallow wrinkled dotage, with a hump on his back and a head scrawled with a few miserable hairs. But Mary was standing close to me and I was so delirious I begged the universe for help, little knowing that he who looks for alms is certain to receive carrion woes. I was resolved to marry her, though my purse suffered from catarrh. I felt sure we could maintain ourselves with the fifteen dollars I would receive each week from my mother added to Mary's wages.

Shortly I heard her father saying: "I didn't catch your name." Misliking this fetid obstacle to my ecstasy, I gave him his deserts: "I don't lend my name at once. Wait until I am assured we can rely upon one another." Then in another mood I answered him: "Suppose you borrow my name, and then discover you are holding Mr. Hypocrisy, or Mr. Deceit, or Sir Knavishness, what sort of a match would I be for your daughter?

"We've had a bad start," I began again. "Now let me be frank with you. My prospects are more than you could discover at first blush. I have a score of glorious disappointments. Don't be put off; you can't imagine what good can come of bad luck."

In return for my efforts to please him the tailor gave me a smile that had long since died. Then he proffered me a mawky grimace, but I was in a high gale of self-confidence. "To repeat," I said, "I'm not promiscuous, and just don't allow the first person I meet to handle my name. Such a name is a whore, a summer resort companion, a pimp. Look, I am ready to esteem you. After all, now that I think on it, you are Honorable Father-in-Law. Please bear in mind I offer your precious flower all that I possess, good clean poverty, a carcass of my simplicity and my clove-scented anticipations. Don't frown on such Arcadian gifts. Now that we know each other better, you may use my Christian name, *Anybody's*, and when the occasion is ripe you may disclose to a few intimate friends my surname, *Miserable Chagrin.*"

The fuddled tailor stared wildly at me, and then in a vein nearly humble, beseeched me: "Have you a family?"

"No, sir," I replied, "I live with me."

He nodded. "That must age a man. Your face seems to gray your hair."

Musing, I said: "Well, so much has happened to me though there are no events in my life. I'm not a mediocre tradesman. I account bakers, dairymen, cobblers, robbers, and though they grow fortunes Venus shall hate them and the caterpillars devour their houses, wives and mistresses. As for my own vocation, when the spell is on me I go out into the streets bawling: 'A harp for sorrow, a sackbutt to soothe those diseased with melancholia, and true fresh garden maidenheads for the impoverished.' "

"You call that work. A man must sweat for a living."

"Sir, I perspire for your daughter."

"Look to your manners, lunatic. This is not a sporting house. Simple-minded as you must be, you know where the door is."

Mary stepped between us, and the tailor lowered his tone: "Let us pass that over. But tell me, who takes care of you?"

Somewhat battered, I asserted: "On Sundays, when I have totally forsaken myself, I write a letter to my mother. I have learned it is human nature to abandon others. A few months ago, realizing this, I got a divorce from society."

"How is your health?"

"I'm in poor shape, but I despise a man who has a sound constitution; he is sure to take advantage of it and have a short life. Besides, he is so concerned with his diet, digestion and how many bowel movements he should have a week that he has no time for others."

At this point the benumbed tailor pinched himself. "What have you done with your youth," he moaned. "You look a good sixty to seventy to me."

"Tell me, what has my youth done for me? You're seasoned enough yourself to understand how experience ages a man."

"Yes, but who gave you the right to be that experienced? If I may say so in a word or two, you've been hard on life. I can't help pity you. Your sharkskin suit looks homeless, pain has peeled most of your socks, your shirt is a waif and should be sent to an orphanage. But don't come to any fond conclusions. Be truthful and soft-spoken: how long have you worn your clothes? They are ailing if not dying. When did your shoes have their last meal? Never has a customer handed me such a pair of pants. Does your jacket give up bile before breakfast? Could you see the back of yourself you would carry your suit to a charity ward. Why are you so unkind to your collar that it hangs so hopeless about your neck?"

Mary had disappeared, and I felt as though I had gone back to my own cell supperless. Had she that feminine comprehension of a long rapturous quarrel which cannot be interrupted without causing more quarrels? Whatever was occurring within her swollen breast I feared the planet, Cancer, had affected me and would presently eat up even foul denials. Oh, the influences of storms, winds and constellations opposed to my manly purposes. Then I caught sight of her primping in the bedroom, and I was stirred up as I saw her put on a violet-granite blouse.

Meanwhile our argument had so heated the tailor he had removed his shirt, and when Mary came out she scolded him. "Father," she cried, wringing her tender palatable hands, "are you out of your head? It is not eleven o'clock and you act as if you were in Mother's bedchamber. You show not a whit of respect for her household, and she cleaned and scoured the walls and floors all morning. Good heavens, you're as naked as Adam and in your wife's own home."

By now this unboweled cottage had chastised me. Certain venomous spirits haunted the furniture and the mourning December drapes, as the tailor continued his monotonous catechism: "Why is the seat of your pants so tired? You do nothing, and yet your suit is all in. Wake up, mister. I can hear the threads snore, and wheeze in vain for a needle. Everything you're wearing looks dead. God forbid, I should have a corpse in my house. You keep on rattling about books that probably died centuries ago. Are they buried or lepers, for I never met a single person who touched one. Does reading make a skeleton of a man?"

"What can I do?" I muttered. "I'm thin as dust. Like the Essenes I eat so little I have evacuations only once a week."

This seemed to infuriate him. "Idler! Don't tell me your bowels are too lazy to move."

Mary was once more in her boudoir powdering her face and completing her mouth. Slyly I peered at her, while I watched an apocryphal mouse playing in the muggy, sour channels of her father's right chap. I was stricken by the shameful works of my blood. No wonder it is fabled that Venus has her abode beneath the celestial roof of Scorpion, who stings men until they are covered with love scabs which they scrape with Job's potsherd only to burn the more. Give me danewort, I silently begged, or a purgation, or let me vomit forth all my salt deprivations. Where is there the physic for my corrupt sighs? What ravenous beasts are within proud upright citizens who go abroad like counterfeit principles?

The tailor had not lost sight of my furtive gaze and was determined to protect his fledgling, but I not noticing him tottered about in an amorous swoon—yea I was love drunk and there was no help for it. "Are you a street animal," he exploded, "that you dare enter my front room to suck up the breath of my daughter's skirts?"

"Forgive me," I begged, "but I could be the lamb of God did she not move about so much. It's the motion that makes me lewd. She takes one tiny step and I'm ignited. Oh, Father Tailor, give me leave to touch her finger, but that will fury me the more. Who can deliver me from this venereal affliction?"

"Mary, open the windows, I'm suffocating," he cried, and turned to me and demanded that I go outside and throw my mean and sotted desires into the street. Then abruptly he altered his tone. "Perhaps you're unemployed because you've just got out of college."

"Sir, I do not propose to be textual and have a student address me as Professor Footnote. All is over if you expect me to be a university buffoon with pocky wits."

"How did you get an educated language? Simply listening to you has made a lunatic of me. I'm so dizzy I forget what we were talking about. What did you tell me your occupation is?"

"I think."

"Is that work? Explain, what do you think about? And don't load me with any more of your piggish feelings."

"I think about thought. Believe me, there's no more cruel labor than that, for no matter how hard you think, you're likely to be thoughtless. Suppose one has an idea in January, by February it has chilblains, bunions or is gouty. Although I am by nature and creed pensive, what is the result? Nothing, which is as good as thinking about something. With all veneration for you, what do you do that's better? You toil to make a suit to order for a glutton, a miser, a usurious banker, a shark in a life insurance company. It's your turn, Reverend Tailor. Is it right that you should labor to cover the seven cardinal sins?"

He was pacing the floor to tether his irritation. Now he paused abruptly to turn to me. "Loafer," he screamed, "don't let me lose control of myself. I'm gentle, tender—ask any customer how soft and amiable I am—but am I to stand here while you expectorate on my sacred trade? Right from the start, I believed you were so bad you couldn't be worse, but who doesn't make mistakes? Come to the point. Don't you even like money? Be careful, you've already gone the limit."

"The real question is," I protested, "does money care for me? Besides, the sight of it makes me squeamish; everybody handles it. Wouldn't you admit it's like a secondhand womb? Would you marry one? Could you fall in love with what's false and sneaky? Look at it this way; whenever I happen to clap my eyes on money it slinks into somebody else's pocket. Without any cant I am able to admit I never wronged lucre. Answer me, why does that creeping mole despise me? I have more charity than you'll ever know, yet though I pity everything on this earth I abhor money. Anyway, since I'm more out of this world than in it, I decided to be a foundling singer of the purgatory of poverty."

Seeing no way out of this enigma, the tailor waxed insolent. "Do you know what you look like?" he said, to which I weakly replied: "Who is brave enough to see himself? Not even Helen of Troy had a mirror. Could a man know his own face it might ruin his whole life. Regardless of your uncivil manner, I am a religious of fanatical fancies that don't thrive in a merchant's lukewarm land. We're a carcass of a nation, a decayed lion where businessmen, electricians, plumbers and landlords get their money; American morals are Cash on the Spot, respectability. Whatever you call me, don't say I'm Mr. Shrewd Mammon."

"Never mind Grace, Sarah or Helen and their looking glass. Just reply in three words: you're self-employed."

"Who else would hire me? Despite all my crushing doubts, I trust myself more than society does, and so I work for me. You ask why? Once I took my head, by no means brand-new, to a junk dealer who obviously was on the lookout for exhausted goods of any sort. When I offered to sell him my head at a bargain price he called a policeman, and not finding one, bellowed: 'Madman, criminal, murderer, thief, spoiler of our country's virgins.' "

Panting, I continued: "Why should a peddler of junk, who buys up scrap iron and lead pipes, refuse to give a penny for a brain? Why, I could sell unkindness, knavery, dissembling, savagery and every quibble could they be marketed as wares. At times I have the most woeful shrieking dreams that gush up out of my sleep, and when I attempt to slubber over the miserable remnants of such a dark watery agony that has been pictured upon my closed eyelids I am certain this is the paint of death. The whole dismal globe is in a suffering and slumbering grave daubed in divers colors just to befool maundering dunces who have not even the skill to perceive that the sun merely rouges the sky, and that the morning's crimson-robed light and the white evening stars are funeral torches. We are and we are not, and this is the disease that killeth up resolution.

"What pains I have are in all greedy, shaking limbs. Remember, this is a tale of worshipful books and a maiden chaste as a ring dove. The game is at an end; shrive my authors and me, for Nature is our enemy. Not all is my fault; your bed and hinges have eclipsed my sober hours. Already past my prime, I bring you the ashes of my youth in an urn. Still, one writer, Porphyry of sacred memory, has said that a crab is lured out of a chink by sounds produced from reeds. Since I am your obedient servant, why can't I enter one?"

The tailor was in the throes of melancholia, and he muttered, with some hardship: "Do you live for flesh and bed, mister?"

"No, I die for it."

"Ancient boy, I doubt you know the time."

"A time-server either wants to get rid of you or himself. It's his manner of hurrying into a winding sheet. Besides, clocks are likely to render a man impotent."

He gasped at this. "In truth, you're God's riddle, you come out of nothing. Have you any character references?"

"Just write to Hunger, Desolation and Rueful Expectations, three doughty and steadfast citizens of our republic, and you'll see I'm no ordinary gutter bird. You should bless me, for as one poet of olden times says, 'Poverty is hateful good.'

"Nor am I so indigent as you deem me," I went on. "I have bountiful compassion. How I pity a weeping, vacant purse I see lying in the gutter. In a way, I could be the compendium of perfection did I not want to void my seed in one glorious vessel. Tell me, why did you beget her? Oh, proud cloth-mender, you've been lofty with me, but I could not even patronize a slug. I know I'm a bladder of arrogance. I only cleave to my raffish foibles because they are so devoted to me. But I apologize, and pledge that solely because you produced such a tasty morsel of a minion, I'll compose a dudgeon epitaph for you. I admit I am of contrary moods. Would that I were a jot whimsical, and gentle and lamed in the middle." And I recited this:

"Christ was a mayde, and shapen as a man."

Again I shouted forth: "Take a caveat from your son-in-law: avoid your closest friends, Greed and Optimism. Never set foot in a bank. As you can see, I have a pocket full of precepts, and you consider me a pauper."

The fuddled tailor was running around the room; my words were driving him senseless. But then it is said that commoners cannot understand Angels who only talk Latin.

"Daughter," he howled, "not even I can stitch this fool together. What man in my trade ever had material like this to mend?"

Mary hastened to us, and overwhelmed by the sight of a snippet of her russet petticoat, I vowed I would walk barefoot to the sepulchre of Christ and lay a gillyflower there as a jot of penance for my unruly corporal desires.

The tailor reeled. "Daughter, his eyes are sewers gluttonously lapping you up. Is it too much to expect that he show some skill in hiding his disrespect?"

"Gentle sir, pardon me," I begged. "I cannot stop up my pores. A blind man taps the pavement and knows where he is going, but to see hurts me. What can I do? My shoulders, my neck, my feet have ferret sight. Soon as one announces his morals his vices appear, and from nowhere. I would be virtuous did it not become a vicious habit. All precepts I have studied have racked my sore pulses. What lilied lepers of human goodness range the town. Oh, God shame good conduct, lest bare grinning principles show themselves."

The tailor's spleen rose and fell like the Ephesian sod. "What do you expect of a reverend father? Everyone wants my daughter's precious vessel. Either I guard her virginity or let her be a streetwalker."

"A pair of whoremasters, I swear," whimpered Mary. "If I repeated such unclean toilet language to Mother her blushing ears would flee."

THE SCAPEGOAT

WHEN IS A PERSON NOT HIMSELF? ANSWER: WHEN HE REMINDS YOU, consciously or unconsciously, of someone else, and you can't see the living presence because of the remembered image. Or when, through accident or muddled design, he begins to embody our own secret fears. In psychology, this is termed projection; in a story or folktale, it is a celebration of the Scapegoat theme.

Ancient kings were said to have ordered the execution of messengers who brought news of disaster, and some modern commentators feel that very much the same sort of motivation is operating underneath the sentencing, and especially the execution, of criminals. Possibly a similar form of projection takes place to the *benefit* of the recipient, but I can't at the moment think of any reference in literature to this happy situation.

References to the other sort of projection are, however, common: Jonah, victimized when he was thrown from the ship as a sacrificial offering to God or the sea; Cinderella, victimized by her hateful half sisters; Tom Jones, victimized by the envious Thwackum and Square; Huck Finn; "the great" Gatsby; Holden Caulfield. All are more or less innocent (at least in the particular context of their suffering); all are eminently, dramatically available as scapegoats.

No one can grow up into a full-fledged, card-carrying Human Being without having experienced the bitter taste of innocence-wrongly-abused; accordingly, we have a great capacity for understanding the Scapegoat in almost any situation. The dark counter truth is that we have all participated in the persecution of an Innocent, performing actions that seem almost beyond our control. And so we can readily understand the vicious mechanism at the heart (or heartlessness) of this kind of projection.

Hawthorne's use of the Scapegoat motif in "My Kinsman, Major Molineux" may at first strike a reader as strange and even unwarranted. But a closer reading will show how the boy, Robin, feels he has suffered anxiety and humiliation because of, almost *through*, the absence of his powerful uncle. We are of course often ready to make unreasonable demands upon others, at least in our secret thoughts; and so far as he can tell, Robin's suffering is related to the Major's simply "not being there" to protect him with his power. The fact that his kinsman was innocent of wronging or neglecting him does not make any difference to a childish mind—or to a mind that has, under stress, reverted to childlike responses.

The naiveté of Robin's comments and their quality of black humor are significant; his Uncle had obviously been a celebrated man not long before, and we must understand that the "celebrity" and "scapegoat" are two aspects of symbolic projection (and consequent dehumanizing of the one who fills the role). There is also in the story a growing ambivalence towards the Major, very much like that of many young boys towards their fathers, so that by the time the Major is shown tarred and feathered as he is being ridden out of town, the hero of the story is quite ready to join in mocking him, with his shout of laughter "the loudest there."

The characters in the other stories are innocent, as they must be in a scapegoat situation, and we see them from two different perspectives: from that of their persecutors and from the outside. We do not see them directly as they see themselves. A first-person story by one who has been wronged is a natural, in some ways; but its danger is that of special pleading—the character complaining too ardently of how he's been wronged and thereby depriving the audience of its right to sympathy.

"A rose is a rose is a rose," says Gertrude Stein in her most famous utterance. It is truly a pity that we cannot understand that a person is a person is a person. For few of us, outside of the myopic vision of those who label us according to their own fears and resentments, are lieutenants of threatening alien armies.

Some of the famous short stories written in English that have to do with the Scapegoat theme are "The Blue Hotel" by Stephen Crane, "Counterparts," by James Joyce, "The Lottery" by Shirley Jackson, "Red Leaves" by William Faulkner, and "Guests of the Nation" by Frank O'Connor.

Nathaniel Hawthorne
My Kinsman, Major Molineux

AFTER THE KINGS OF GREAT BRITAIN HAD ASSUMED THE RIGHT OF AP-
pointing the colonial governors, the measures of the latter seldom met with
the ready and generous approbation which had been paid to those of their
predecessors, under the original charters. The people looked with most jealous scrutiny to the exercise of power which did not emanate from themselves,
and they usually rewarded their rulers with slender gratitude for the compli-
ances by which, in softening their instructions from beyond the sea, they had
incurred the reprehension of those who gave them. The annals of Massachu-
setts Bay will inform us, that of six governors in the space of about forty years
from the surrender of the old charter, under James II, two were imprisoned
by a popular insurrection; a third, as Hutchinson inclines to believe, was
driven from the province by the whizzing of a musket-ball; a fourth, in the
opinion of the same historian, was hastened to his grave by continual bicker-
ings with the House of Representatives; and the remaining two, as well as
their successors, till the Revolution, were favored with few and brief intervals
of peaceful sway. The inferior members of the court party, in times of high
political excitement, led scarcely a more desirable life. These remarks may
serve as a preface to the following adventures, which chanced upon a summer
night, not far from a hundred years ago. The reader, in order to avoid a long
and dry detail of colonial affairs, is requested to dispense with an account of
the train of circumstances that had caused much temporary inflammation of
the popular mind.

It was near nine o'clock of a moonlight evening, when a boat crossed the
ferry with a single passenger, who had obtained his conveyance at that
unusual hour by the promise of an extra fare. While he stood on the landing
place, searching in either pocket for the means of fulfilling his agreement, the
ferryman lifted a lantern, by the aid of which, and the newly-risen moon, he
took a very accurate survey of the stranger's figure. He was a youth of barely
eighteen years, evidently country-bred, and now, as it should seem, upon his
first visit to town. He was clad in a coarse gray coat, well worn, but in
excellent repair; his under garments were durably constructed of leather, and
fitted tight to a pair of serviceable and well-shaped limbs; his stockings of blue
yarn were the incontrovertible work of a mother or a sister; and on his head
was a three-cornered hat, which in its better days had perhaps sheltered the
graver brow of the lad's father. Under his left arm was a heavy cudgel, formed

81

of an oak sapling, and retaining a part of the hardened root; and his equipment was completed by a wallet, not so abundantly stocked as to incommode
the vigorous shoulders on which it hung. Brown, curly hair, well-shaped
features, and bright, cheerful eyes, were nature's gifts, and worth all that art
could have done for his adornment.

The youth, one of whose names was Robin, finally drew from his pocket
the half of a little province bill of five shillings, which, in the depreciation of
that sort of currency, did but satisfy the ferryman's demand, with the surplus
of a sexangular piece of parchment, valued at three pence. He then walked
forward into the town, with as light a step as if his day's journey had not
already exceeded thirty miles, and with as eager an eye as if he were entering
London city, instead of the little metropolis of a New England colony. Before
Robin had proceeded far, however, it occurred to him that he knew not
whither to direct his steps; so he paused, and looked up and down the narrow
street, scrutinizing the small and mean wooden buildings that were scattered
on either side.

"This low hovel cannot be my kinsman's dwelling," thought he, "nor
yonder old house, where the moonlight enters at the broken casement; and
truly I see none hereabouts that might be worthy of him. It would have been
wise to inquire my way of the ferryman, and doubtless he would have gone
with me, and earned a shilling from the Major for his pains. But the next man
I meet will do as well."

He resumed his walk, and was glad to perceive that the street now became
wider, and the houses more respectable in their appearance. He soon discerned a figure moving on moderately in advance, and hastened his steps to
overtake it. As Robin drew nigh, he saw that the passenger was a man in
years, with a full periwig of gray hair, a wide-skirted coat of dark cloth, and
silk stockings rolled above his knees. He carried a long and polished cane,
which he struck down perpendicularly before him at every step; and at regular
intervals he uttered two successive hems, of a peculiarly solemn and sepulchral intonation. Having made these observations, Robin laid hold of the skirt
of the old man's coat, just when the light from the open door and windows
of a barber's shop fell upon both their figures.

"Good evening to you, honored sir," said he, making a low bow, and still
retaining his hold of the skirt. "I pray you tell me whereabouts is the dwelling
of my kinsman, Major Molineux."

The youth's question was uttered very loudly; and one of the barbers, whose
razor was descending on a well-soaped chin, and another who was dressing
a Ramillies wig, left their occupations, and came to the door. The citizen, in
the mean time, turned a long-favored countenance upon Robin, and answered
him in a tone of excessive anger and annoyance. His two sepulchral hems,
however, broke into the very centre of his rebuke, with most singular effect,
like a thought of the cold grave obtruding among wrathful passions.

"Let go my garment, fellow! I tell you, I know not the man you speak of.
What! I have authority, I have—hem, hem—authority; and if this be the
respect you show for your betters, your feet shall be brought acquainted with
the stocks by daylight, tomorrow morning!"

Robin released the old man's skirt, and hastened away, pursued by an ill-mannered roar of laughter from the barber's shop. He was at first considerably surprised by the result of his question, but, being a shrewd youth, soon thought himself able to account for the mystery.

"This is some country representative," was his conclusion, "who has never seen the inside of my kinsman's door, and lacks the breeding to answer a stranger civilly. The man is old, or verily—I might be tempted to turn back and smite him on the nose. Ah, Robin, Robin! even the barber's boys laugh at you for choosing such a guide! You will be wiser in time, friend Robin."

He now became entangled in a succession of crooked and narrow streets, which crossed each other, and meandered at no great distance from the water-side. The smell of tar was obvious to his nostrils, the masts of vessels pierced the moonlight above the tops of the buildings, and the numerous signs, which Robin paused to read, informed him that he was near the centre of business. But the streets were empty, the shops were closed, and lights were visible only in the second stories of a few dwelling-houses. At length, on the corner of a narrow lane, through which he was passing, he beheld the broad countenance of a British hero swinging before the door of an inn, whence proceeded the voices of many guests. The casement of one of the lower windows was thrown back, and a very thin curtain permitted Robin to distinguish a party at supper, round a well-furnished table. The fragrance of the good cheer steamed forth into the outer air, and the youth could not fail to recollect that the last remnant of his travelling stock of provision had yielded to his morning appetite, and that noon had found, and left him, dinnerless.

"Oh, that a parchment three-penny might give me a right to sit down at yonder table!" said Robin, with a sigh. "But the Major will make me welcome to the best of his victuals; so I will even step boldly in, and inquire my way to his dwelling."

He entered the tavern, and was guided by the murmur of voices, and the fumes of tobacco, to the public room. It was a long and low apartment, with oaken walls, grown dark in the continual smoke, and a floor, which was thickly sanded, but of no immaculate purity. A number of persons—the larger part of whom appeared to be mariners, or in some way connected with the sea—occupied the wooden benches, or leather-bottomed chairs, conversing on various matters, and occasionally lending their attention to some topic of general interest. Three or four little groups were draining as many bowls of punch, which the West India trade had long since made a familiar drink in the colony. Others, who had the appearance of men who lived by regular and laborious handicraft, preferred the insulated bliss of an unshared potation, and became more taciturn under its influence. Nearly all, in short, evinced a predilection for the Good Creature in some of its various shapes, for this is a vice to which, as Fast Day sermons of a hundred years ago will testify, we have a long hereditary claim. The only guests to whom Robin's sympathies inclined him were two or three sheepish countrymen, who were using the inn somewhat after the fashion of a Turkish caravansary; they had gotten themselves into the darkest corner of the room, and heedless of the Nicotian atmosphere, were supping on the bread of their own ovens, and the bacon cured in their own chimney-smoke. But though Robin felt a sort of brotherhood with these strangers, his eyes were attracted from them to a person who stood near the door, holding whispered conversation with a group of ill-dressed associates. His features were separately striking almost to grotesqueness, and the whole face left a deep impression on the memory. The forehead bulged out into a double prominence, with a vale between; the nose came boldly forth in an irregular curve, and its bridge was of more than a finger's breadth; the eyebrows were deep and shaggy, and the eyes glowed beneath them like fire in a cave.

While Robin deliberated of whom to inquire respecting his kinsman's dwelling, he was accosted by the innkeeper, a little man in a stained white apron, who had come to pay his professional welcome to the stranger. Being in the second generation from a French Protestant, he seemed to have inherited the courtesy of his parent nation; but no variety of circumstances was ever known to change his voice from the one shrill note in which he now addressed Robin.

"From the country, I presume, sir?" said he, with a profound bow. "Beg leave to congratulate you on your arrival, and trust you intend a long stay with us. Fine town here, sir, beautiful buildings, and much that may interest a stranger. May I hope for the honor of your commands in respect to supper?"

"The man sees a family likeness! the rogue has guessed that I am related to the Major!" thought Robin, who had hitherto experienced little superfluous civility.

All eyes were now turned on the country lad standing at the door, in his worn three-cornered hat, gray coat, leather breeches, and blue yarn stockings, leaning on an oaken cudgel, and bearing a wallet on his back.

Robin replied to the courteous innkeeper, with such an assumption of confidence as befitted the Major's relative. "My honest friend," he said, "I shall make it a point to patronize your house on some occasion, when"—here he could not help lowering his voice—"when I may have more than a parchment three-pence in my pocket. My present business," continued he, speaking with lofty confidence, "is merely to inquire my way to the dwelling of my kinsman, Major Molineux."

There was a sudden and general movement in the room, which Robin interpreted as expressing the eagerness of each individual to become his guide. But the innkeeper turned his eyes to a written paper on the wall, which he read, or seemed to read, with occasional recurrences to the young man's figure.

"What have we here?" said he, breaking his speech into little dry fragments. "Left the house of the subscriber, bounden servant, Hezekiah Mudge,—had on, when he went away, gray coat, leather breeches, master's third-best hat. One pound currency reward to whosoever shall lodge him in any jail of the province. Better trudge, boy; better trudge!"

Robin had begun to draw his hand towards the lighter end of the oak cudgel, but a strange hostility in every countenance induced him to relinquish his purpose of breaking the courteous innkeeper's head. As he turned to leave the room, he encountered a sneering glance from the bold-featured personage whom he had before noticed; and no sooner was he beyond the door, than he heard a general laugh, in which the innkeeper's voice might be distinguished, like the dropping of small stones into a kettle.

"Now, is it not strange," thought Robin, with his usual shrewdness,—"is it not strange that the confession of an empty pocket should outweigh the name of my kinsman, Major Molineux? Oh, if I had one of those grinning rascals in the woods, where I and my oak sapling grew up together, I would teach him that my arm is heavy though my purse be light!"

On turning the corner of the narrow lane, Robin found himself in a spacious street, with an unbroken line of lofty houses on each side, and a steepled building at the upper end, whence the ringing of a bell announced the hour of nine. The light of the moon, and the lamps from the numerous shop-windows, discovered people promenading on the pavement, and amongst them Robin had hoped to recognize his hitherto inscrutable relative. The result of his former inquiries made him unwilling to hazard another, in a scene of such publicity, and he determined to walk slowly and silently up the street, thrusting his face close to that of every elderly gentleman, in search of the Major's lineaments. In his progress, Robin encountered many gay and gallant figures. Embroidered garments of showy colors, enormous periwigs, gold-laced hats, and silver-hilted swords glided past him and dazzled his optics. Travelled youths, imitators of the European fine gentlemen of the period, trod jauntily along, half dancing to the fashionable tunes which they hummed, and making poor Robin ashamed of his quiet and natural gait. At length, after many pauses to examine the gorgeous display of goods in the shop-windows, and after suffering some rebukes for the impertinence of his scrutiny into people's faces, the Major's kinsman found himself near the steepled building, still unsuccessful in his search. As yet, however, he had seen only one side of the thronged street; so Robin crossed, and continued the same sort of inquisition down the opposite pavement, with stronger hopes than the philosopher seeking an honest man, but with no better fortune. He had arrived about midway towards the lower end, from which his course began, when he overheard the approach of some one, who struck down a cane on the flagstones at every step, uttering, at regular intervals, two sepulchral hems.

"Mercy on us!" quoth Robin, recognizing the sound.

Turning a corner, which chanced to be close at his right hand, he hastened to pursue his researches in some other part of the town. His patience now was wearing low, and he seemed to feel more fatigue from his rambles since he crossed the ferry, than from his journey of several days on the other side. Hunger also pleaded loudly within him, and Robin began to balance the propriety of demanding, violently, and with lifted cudgel, the necessary guidance from the first solitary passenger whom he should meet. While a resolution to this effect was gaining strength, he entered a street of mean appearance, on either side of which a row of ill-built houses was straggling towards the harbor. The moonlight fell upon no passenger along the whole extent, but in the third domicile which Robin passed there was a half-opened door, and his keen glance detected a woman's garment within.

"My luck may be better here," said he to himself.

Accordingly, he approached the door, and beheld it shut closer as he did so; yet an open space remained, sufficing for the fair occupant to observe the stranger, without a corresponding display on her part. All that Robin could discern was a strip of scarlet petticoat, and the occasional sparkle of an eye, as if the moonbeams were trembling on some bright thing.

"Pretty mistress," for I may call her so with a good conscience, thought the shrewd youth, since I know nothing to the contrary,—"my sweet pretty mistress, will you be kind enough to tell me whereabouts I must seek the dwelling of my kinsman, Major Molineux?"

Robin's face was plaintive and winning, and the female, seeing nothing to be shunned in the handsome country youth, thrust open the door, and came forth into the moonlight. She was a dainty little figure, with a white neck, round arms, and a slender waist, at the extremity of which her scarlet petticoat jutted out over a hoop, as if she were standing in a balloon. Moreover, her face was oval and pretty, her hair dark beneath the little cap, and her bright eyes possessed a sly freedom, which triumphed over those of Robin.

"Major Molineux dwells here," said this fair woman.

Now, her voice was the sweetest Robin had heard that night, yet he could not help doubting whether that sweet voice spoke Gospel truth. He looked up and down the mean street, and then surveyed the house before which they stood. It was a small, dark edifice of two stories, the second of which projected over the lower floor, and the front apartment had the aspect of a shop for petty commodities.

"Now, truly, I am in luck," replied Robin, cunningly, "and so indeed is my kinsman, the Major, in having so pretty a housekeeper. But I prithee trouble him to step to the door; I will deliver him a message from his friends in the country, and then go back to my lodgings at the inn."

"Nay, the Major has been abed this hour or more," said the lady of the scarlet petticoat; "and it would be to little purpose to disturb him to-night, seeing his evening drought was of the strongest. But he is a kind-hearted man, and it would be as much as my life's worth to let a kinsman of his turn away from the door. You are the good old gentleman's very picture, and I could swear that was his rainy-weather hat. Also he has garments very much resembling those leather small-clothes. But come in, I pray, for I bid you hearty welcome in his name."

So saying, the fair and hospitable dame took our hero by the hand; and the touch was light, and the force was gentleness, and though Robin read in her eyes what he did not hear in her words, yet the slender-waisted woman in the scarlet petticoat proved stronger than the athletic country youth. She had drawn his half-willing footsteps nearly to the threshold, when the opening of a door in the neighborhood startled the Major's housekeeper, and leaving the Major's kinsman, she vanished speedily into her own domicile. A heavy yawn preceded the appearance of a man, who, like the Moonshine of Pyramus and

Thisbe, carried a lantern, needlessly aiding his sister luminary in the heavens. As he walked sleepily up the street, he turned his broad, dull face on Robin, and diplayed a long staff, spiked at the end.

"Home, vagabond, home!" said the watchman, in accents that seemed to fall asleep as soon as they were uttered. "Home, or we'll set you in the stocks, by peep of day!"

"This is the second hint of the kind," thought Robin. "I wish they would end my difficulties, by setting me there to-night."

Nevertheless, the youth felt an instinctive antipathy towards the guardian of midnight order, which at first prevented him from asking his usual question. But just when the man was about to vanish behind the corner, Robin resolved not to lose the opportunity, and shouted lustily after him,—

"I say, friend! will you guide me to the house of my kinsman, Major Molineux?"

The watchman made no reply, but turned the corner and was gone; yet Robin seemed to hear the sound of drowsy laughter stealing along the solitary street. At that moment, also, a pleasant titter saluted him from the open window above his head; he looked up, and caught the sparkle of a saucy eye; a round arm beckoned to him, and next he heard light footsteps descending the staircase within. But Robin, being of the household of a New England clergyman, was a good youth, as well as a shrewd one; so he resisted temptation, and fled away.

He now roamed desperately, and at random, through the town, almost ready to believe that a spell was on him, like that by which a wizard of his country had once kept three pursuers wandering, a whole winter night, within twenty paces of the cottage which they sought. The streets lay before him, strange and desolate, and the lights were extinguished in almost every house. Twice, however, little parties of men, among whom Robin distinguished individuals in outlandish attire, came hurrying along; but, though on both occasions, they paused to address him, such intercourse did not at all enlighten his perplexity. They did but utter a few words in some language of which Robin knew nothing, and perceiving his inability to answer, bestowed a curse upon him in plain English and hastened away. Finally, the lad determined to knock at the door of every mansion that might appear worthy to be occupied by his kinsman, trusting that perseverance would overcome the fatality that had hitherto thwarted him. Firm in this resolve, he was passing beneath the walls of a church, which formed the corner of two streets, when, as he turned into the shade of its steeple, he encountered a bulky stranger, muffled in a cloak. The man was proceeding with the speed of earnest business, but Robin planted himself full before him, holding the oak cudgel with both hands across his body as a bar to further passage.

"Halt, honest man, and answer me a question," said he, very resolutely. "Tell me, this instant, whereabouts is the dwelling of my kinsman, Major Molineux!"

"Keep your tongue between your teeth, fool, and let me pass!" said a deep, gruff voice, which Robin partly remembered. "Let me pass, or I'll strike you to the earth!"

"No, no, neighbor!" cried Robin, flourishing his cudgel, and then thrusting its larger end close to the man's muffled face. "No, no, I'm not the fool you take me for, nor do you pass till I have an answer to my question. Whereabouts is the dwelling of my kinsman, Major Molineux?"

The stranger, instead of attempting to force his passage, stepped back into the moonlight, unmuffled his face, and stared full into that of Robin.

"Watch here an hour, and Major Molineux will pass by," said he.

Robin gazed with dismay and astonishment on the unprecedented physiognomy of the speaker. The forehead with its double prominence, the broad hooked nose, the shaggy eyebrows, and fiery eyes, were those which he had noticed at the inn, but the man's complexion had undergone a singular, or, more properly, a two-fold change. One side of the face blazed an intense red, while the other was black as midnight, the division line being in the broad bridge of the nose; and a mouth which seemed to extend from ear to ear was black or red, in contrast to the color of the cheek. The effect was as if two individual devils, a fiend of fire and a fiend of darkness, had united themselves to form this infernal visage. The stranger grinned in Robin's face, muffled his parti-colored features, and was out of sight in a moment.

"Strange things we travellers see!" ejaculated Robin.

He seated himself, however, upon the steps of the church-door, resolving to wait the appointed time for his kinsman. A few moments were consumed in philosophical speculations upon the species of man who had just left him; but having settled this point shrewdly, rationally, and satisfactorily, he was compelled to look elsewhere for his amusement. And first he threw his eyes along the street. It was of more respectable appearance than most of those into which he had wandered, and the moon, creating, like the imaginative power, a beautiful strangeness in familiar objects, gave something of romance to a scene that might not have possessed it in the light of day. The irregular and often quaint architecture of the houses, some of whose roofs were broken into numerous little peaks, while others ascended, steep and narrow, into a single point, and others again were square; the pure snow-white of some of their complexions, the aged darkness of others, and the thousand sparklings, reflected from bright substances on the walls of many; these matters engaged Robin's attention for a while, and then began to grow wearisome. Next he endeavored to define the forms of distant objects, starting away, with almost ghostly indistinctness, just as his eye appeared to grasp them; and finally he took a minute survey of an edifice which stood on the opposite side of the street, directly in front of the church-door, where he was stationed. It was a large, square mansion, distinguished from its neighbors by a balcony, which rested on tall pillars, and by an elaborate Gothic window, communicating therewith.

"Perhaps this is the very house I have been seeking," thought Robin.

Then he strove to speed away the time, by listening to a murmur which swept continually along the street, yet was scarcely audible, except to an unaccustomed ear like his; it was a low, dull, dreamy sound, compounded of many noises, each of which was at too a great a distance to be separately heard. Robin marvelled at this snore of a sleeping town, and marvelled more whenever its continuity was broken by now and then a distant shout, apparently loud where it originated. But altogether it was a sleep-inspiring sound, and, to shake off its drowsy influence, Robin arose, and climbed a window-frame, that he might view the interior of the church. There the moonbeams came trembling in, and fell down upon the deserted pews, and extended along the quiet aisles. A fainter yet more awful radiance was hovering around the pulpit, and one solitary ray had dared to rest upon the open page of the great Bible. Had nature, in that deep hour, become a worshipper in the house which man had builded? Or was that heavenly light the visible sanctity of the place, —visible because no earthly and impure feet were within the walls? The scene made Robin's heart shiver with a sensation of loneliness stronger than he had ever felt in the remotest depths of his native woods; so he turned away and sat down again before the door. There were graves around the church, and now an uneasy thought obtruded into Robin's breast. What if the object of his search, which had been so often and so strangely thwarted, were all the time mouldering in his shroud? What if his kinsman should glide through yonder gate, and nod and smile to him in dimly passing by?

"Oh that any breathing thing were here with me!" said Robin.

Recalling his thoughts from this uncomfortable track, he sent them over forest, hill, and stream, and attempted to imagine how that evening of ambiguity and weariness had been spent by his father's household. He pictured them assembled at the door, beneath the tree, the great old tree, which had been spared for its huge twisted trunk, and venerable shade, when a thousand leafy brethren fell. There, at the going down of the summer sun, it was his father's custom to perform domestic worship, that the neighbors might come and join with him like brothers of the family, and that the wayfaring man might pause to drink at that fountain, and keep his heart pure by freshening the memory of home. Robin distinguished the seat of every individual of the little audience; he saw the good man in the midst, holding the Scriptures in the golden light that fell from the western clouds; he beheld him close the book and all rise up to pray. He heard the old thanksgivings for daily mercies, the old supplications for their continuance, to which he had so often listened in weariness, but which were now among his dear remembrances. He perceived the slight inequality of his father's voice when he came to speak of the absent one; he noted how his mother turned her face to the broad and knotted trunk; how his elder brother scorned, because the beard was rough upon his upper lip, to permit his features to be moved; how the younger sister drew down a low hanging branch before her eyes; and how the little one of all, whose sports had hitherto broken the decorum of the scene, understood the prayer for her playmate, and burst into clamorous grief. Then he saw them go in at the door; and when Robin would have entered also, the latch tinkled into its place, and he was excluded from his home.

"Am I here, or there?" cried Robin, starting; for all at once, when his thoughts had become visible and audible in a dream, the long, wide, solitary street shone out before him.

He aroused himself, and endeavored to fix his attention steadily upon the large edifice which he had surveyed before. But still his mind kept vibrating between fancy and reality; by turns, the pillars of the balcony lengthened into the tall, bare stems of pines, dwindled down to human figures and settled again into their true shape and size, and then commenced a new succession of changes. For a single moment, when he deemed himself awake, he could have sworn that a visage—one which he seemed to remember, yet could not absolutely name as his kinsman's—was looking towards him from the Gothic window. A deeper sleep wrestled with and nearly overcame him, but fled at the sound of footsteps along the opposite pavement. Robin rubbed his eyes, discerned a man passing at the foot of the balcony, and addressed him in a loud, peevish, and lamentable cry.

"Hallo, friend! must I wait here all night for my kinsman, Major Molineux?"

The sleeping echoes awoke, and answered the voice; and the passenger, barely able to discern a figure sitting in the oblique shade of the steeple, traversed the street to obtain a nearer view. He was himself a gentleman in his prime, of open, intelligent, cheerful, and altogether prepossessing countenance. Perceiving a country youth, apparently homeless and without friends, he accosted him in a tone of real kindness, which had become strange to Robin's ears.

"Well, my good lad, why are you sitting here?" inquired he. "Can I be of service to you in any way?"

"I am afraid not, sir," replied Robin, despondingly; "yet I shall take it kindly, if you'll answer me a single question. I've been searching, half the night, for one Major Molineux; now, sir, is there really such a person in these parts, or am I dreaming?"

"Major Molineux! The name is not altogether strange to me," said the gentleman, smiling. "Have you any objection to telling me the nature of your business with him?"

Then Robin briefly related that his father was a clergyman, settled on a small salary, at a long distance back in the country, and that he and Major Molineux were brothers' children. The Major, having inherited riches, and acquired civil and military rank, had visited his cousin, in great pomp, a year or two before; had manifested much interest in Robin and an elder brother, and, being childless himself, had thrown out hints respecting the future establishment of one of them in life. The elder brother was destined to succeed to the farm which his father cultivated in the interval of sacred duties; it was therefore determined that Robin should profit by his kinsman's generous intentions, especially as he seemed to be rather the favorite, and was thought to possess other necessary endowments.

"For I have the name of being a shrewd youth," observed Robin, in this part of his story.

"I doubt not you deserve it," replied his new friend, good-naturedly; "but pray proceed."

"Well, sir, being nearly eighteen years old, and well-grown, as you see," continued Robin, drawing himself up to his full height, "I thought it high time to begin the world. So my mother and sister put me in handsome trim, and my father gave me half the remnant of his last year's salary, and five days ago I started for this place, to pay the Major a visit. But, would you believe it, sir! I crossed the ferry a little after dark, and have yet found nobody that would show me the way to his dwelling;—only, an hour or two since, I was told to wait here, and Major Molineux would pass by."

"Can you describe the man who told you this?" inquired the gentleman.

"Oh, he was a very ill-favored fellow, sir," replied Robin, "with two great bumps on his forehead, a hook nose, fiery eyes,—and, what struck me as the strangest, his face was of two different colors. Do you happen to know such a man, sir?"

"Not intimately," answered the stranger, "but I chanced to meet him a little time previous to your stopping me. I believe you may trust his word, and that the Major will very shortly pass through this street. In the mean time, as I have a singular curiosity to witness your meeting, I will sit down here upon the steps, and bear you company."

He seated himself accordingly, and soon engaged his companion in animated discourse. It was but of brief continuance, however, for a noise of shouting, which had long been remotely audible, drew so much nearer that Robin inquired its cause.

"What may be the meaning of this uproar?" asked he. "Truly, if your town be always as noisy, I shall find little sleep, while I am an inhabitant."

"Why, indeed, friend Robin, there do appear to be three or four riotous fellows abroad to-night," replied the gentleman. "You must not expect all the stillness of your native woods, here in our streets. But the watch will shortly be at the heels of these lads, and—"

"Ay, and set them in the stocks by peep of day," interrupted Robin, recollecting his own encounter with the drowsy lantern-bearer. "But, dear sir, if I may trust my ears, an army of watchmen would never make head against such a multitude of rioters. There were at least a thousand voices went up to make that one shout."

"May not a man have several voices, Robin, as well as two complexions?" said his friend.

"Perhaps a man may; but Heaven forbid that a woman should!" responded the shrewd youth, thinking of the seductive tones of the Major's housekeeper.

The sounds of a trumpet in some neighboring street now became so evident and continual, that Robin's curiosity was strongly excited. In addition to the shouts, he heard frequent bursts from many instruments of discord, and a wild and confused laughter filled up the intervals. Robin rose from the steps, and looked wistfully towards a point whither people seemed to be hastening.

"Surely some prodigious merry-making is going on," exclaimed he. "I have laughed very little since I left home, sir, and should be sorry to lose an opportunity. Shall we step round the corner by the darkish house, and take our share of the fun?"

"Sit down again, sit down, good Robin," replied the gentleman, laying his hand on the skirt of the gray coat. "You forget that we must wait here for your kinsman; and there is reason to believe that he will pass by, in the course of a very few moments."

The near approach of the uproar had now disturbed the neighborhoood; windows flew open on all sides; and many heads, in the attire of the pillow, and confused by sleep suddenly broken, were protruded to the gaze of whoever had leisure to observe them. Eager voices hailed each other from house to house, all demanding the explanation, which not a soul could give. Half-dressed men hurried towards the unknown commotion, stumbling as they went over the stone steps that thrust themselves into the narrow foot-walk. The shouts, the laughter, and the tuneless bray, the antipodes of music, came onwards with increasing din, till scattered individuals, and then denser bodies, began to appear round a corner at the distance of a hundred yards.

"Will you recognize your kinsman, if he passes in this crowd?" inquired the gentleman.

"Indeed, I can't warrant it, sir; but I'll take my stand here, and keep a bright look-out," answered Robin, descending to the outer edge of the pavement.

A mighty stream of people now emptied into the street, and came rolling slowly towards the church. A single horseman wheeled the corner in the midst of them, and close behind him came a band of fearful wind-instruments, sending forth a fresher discord, now that no intervening buildings kept it from the ear. Then a redder light disturbed the moonbeams, and a dense multitude of torches shone along the street, concealing, by their glare, whatever object they illuminated. The single horseman, clad in a military dress, and bearing a drawn sword, rode onward as the leader, and, by his fierce and variegated countenance, appeared like war personified: the red of one cheek was an emblem of fire and sword; the blackness of the other betokened the mourning that attends them. In his train were wild figures in the Indian dress, and many fantastic shapes without a model, giving the whole march a visionary air, as if a dream had broken forth from some feverish brain, and were sweeping visibly through the midnight streets. A mass of people, inactive, except as applauding spectators, hemmed the procession in; and several women ran along the side-walk, piercing the confusion of heavier sounds with their shrill voices of mirth or terror.

"The double-faced fellow has his eye upon me," muttered Robin, with an indefinite but an uncomfortable idea that he was himself to bear a part in the pageantry.

The leader turned himself in the saddle, and fixed his glance full upon the country youth, as the steed went slowly by. When Robin had freed his eyes from those fiery ones, the musicians were passing before him, and the torches were close at hand; but the unsteady brightness of the latter formed a veil which he could not penetrate. The rattling of wheels over the stones sometimes found its way to his ear, and confused traces of a human form appeared at intervals, and then melted into the vivid light. A moment more, and the leader thundered a command to halt: the trumpets vomited a horrid breath, and then held their peace; the shouts and laughter of the people died away, and there remained only a universal hum, allied to silence. Right before Robin's eyes was an uncovered cart. There the torches blazed the brightest, there the moon shone out like day, and there, in tar-and-feathery dignity, sat his kinsman, Major Molineux!

He was an elderly man, of large and majestic person, and strong, square features, betokening a steady soul; but steady as it was, his enemies had found means to shake it. His face was pale as death, and far more ghastly; the broad forehead was contracted in his agony, so that his eyebrows formed one grizzled line; his eyes were red and wild, and the foam hung white upon his quivering lip. His whole frame was agitated by a quick and continual tremor, which his pride strove to quell, even in those circumstances of overwhelming humiliation. But perhaps the bitterest pang of all was when his eyes met those of Robin; for he evidently knew him on the instant, as the youth stood witnessing the foul disgrace of a head grown gray in honor. They stared at each other in silence, and Robin's knees shook, and his hair bristled, with a mixture of pity and terror. Soon, however, a bewildering excitement began to seize upon his mind; the preceding adventures of the night, the unexpected appearance of the crowd, the torches, the confused din and the hush that followed, the spectre of his kinsman reviled by that great multitude,—all this, and, more than all, a perception of tremendous ridicule in the whole scene, affected him with a sort of mental inebriety. At that moment a voice of sluggish merriment saluted Robin's ears; he turned instinctively, and just behind the corner of the church stood the lantern-bearer, rubbing his eyes, and drowsily enjoying the lad's amazement. Then he heard a peal of laughter like the ringing of silvery bells; a woman twitched his arm, a saucy eye met his, and he saw the lady of the scarlet petticoat. A sharp, dry cachinnation appealed to his memory, and, standing on tiptoe in the crowd, with his white apron over his head, he beheld the courteous little innkeeper. And lastly, there sailed over the heads of the multitude a great, broad laugh, broken in the midst by two sepulchral hems; thus, "Haw, haw, haw,—hem, hem,—haw, haw, haw, haw!"

The sound proceeded from the balcony of the opposite edifice, and thither Robin turned his eyes. In front of the Gothic window stood the old citizen, wrapped in a wide gown, his gray periwig exchanged for a night-cap, which was thrust back from his forehead, and his silk stockings hanging about his legs. He supported himself on his polished cane in a fit of convulsive merriment, which manifested itself on his solemn old features like a funny inscription on a tomb-stone. Then Robin seemed to hear the voices of the barbers, of the guests of the inn, and of all who had made sport of him that night. The contagion was spreading among the multitude, when, all at once, it seized upon Robin, and he sent forth a shout of laughter that echoed through the street;—every man shook his sides, every man emptied his lungs, but Robin's shout was the loudest there. The cloud-spirits peeped from their silvery islands, as the congregated mirth went roaring up the sky! The Man in the

Moon heard the far bellow. "Oho," quoth he, "the old earth is frolicsome tonight!"

When there was a momentary calm in that tempestuous sea of sound, the leader gave the sign, the procession resumed its march. On they went, like fiends that throng in mockery around some dead potentate, mighty no more, but majestic still in his agony. On they went, in counterfeited pomp, in senseless uproar, in frenzied merriment, trampling all on an old man's heart. On swept the tumult, and left a silent street behind.

"Well, Robin, are you dreaming?" inquired the gentleman, laying his hand on the youth's shoulder.

Robin started, and withdrew his arm from the stone post to which he had instinctively clung, as the living stream rolled by him. His cheek was somewhat pale, and his eye not quite as lively as in the earlier part of the evening.

"Will you be kind enough to show me the way to the ferry?" said he, after a moment's pause.

"You have, then, adopted a new subject of inquiry?" observed his companion, with a smile.

"Why, yes, sir," replied Robin, rather dryly. "Thanks to you, and to my other friends, I have at last met my kinsman, and he will scarce desire to see my face again. I begin to grow weary of a town life, sir. Will you show me the way to the ferry?"

"No, my good friend Robin,—not to-night, at least," said the gentleman. "Some few days hence, if you wish it, I will speed you on your journey. Or, if you prefer to remain with us, perhaps, as you are a shrewd youth, you may rise in the world without the help of your kinsman, Major Molineux."

John Wain

Master Richard

ALL CLEAR? ARE MY DEFENCES IN ORDER, IS MY CAMOUFLAGE SKILFULLY applied? I think so: the kiddies' Encyclopaedia is my largest book, and if I keep it propped up in front of me I'm fairly secure against anyone coming in through the door, which faces me; and since I've taken care not to sit with my back to the window, there's no danger of any interfering fool looking over my shoulder. I can start writing.

Not that conditions are perfect, of course. It annoys me intensely, for instance, to reflect that there's a perfectly good portable typewriter standing in the corner, which it's out of the question for me to touch; I could get along much faster, once I got the hang of the thing, and in any case the precisian in me would greatly prefer the sight of a neat stack of typewritten sheets to this grubby notebook. But it won't do. The grubby notebook is my only chance of being able to write at all. If I so much as laid a finger on the typewriter, the first person who came in the door would swoop and drag me away from it. Of course there'd be the usual cluckings, and pseudo-reticent boastings, about my precocity. "Doesn't play with ordinary toys—not he! Why, the other day he made a bee-line for the *typewriter!*" "Mechanically minded, I suppose," I can just hear some fool of a visitor saying. "No, far from it," they'd answer. "It's the writing aspect that fascinates him. We just can't keep him away from books and papers. He's going to be a real professor, you wait!"

But what am I thinking of? Use a typewriter—me? To begin with, my arms haven't enough strength to drag the thing up on to the table, and if I did get it up, my fingers are probably too small to work the keys. I watched Him typing a letter on it the other day: He was only using two fingers, and probably slamming the thing much too hard—His great horny digits were coming down like sledge-hammers—but even if half the force would have been enough, I could tell I'd never be able to manage it. It's bad enough holding this damned pencil; my hand aches before I've written a page, and in any case the beastly thing loses its point so soon that I have to keep twisting it round to get the lead at a fresh angle. Just as I get really started, I expect, it'll give out altogether and I'll have to go and hunt about for a replacement. Because, of course, I'm not supposed to be able to *sharpen* one. There's no sharpener, anyway, and I can imagine the hullaballoo if I tried to get hold of a knife. I practically have to laugh at the very idea.

No, there's nothing for it but to scrawl away with this thing. Why do I bother? What is it that drives me to try to put my thoughts on paper at all? —But even as I ask that question I can see how obvious is the answer. *Of course* I must write my thoughts down, if only to get the illusion of communicating with someone, somewhere, somehow. It's what all prisoners do —and I, after all, am in a very real sense a prisoner. There's no possible chance of my getting away from these surroundings, from the maddening surveillance of Him, Her, and the rest of them, at any time in the next ten years at least. Ten years!—it fills me with despair to name the term of my sentence. And it's not only the length, but the appalling complication of the circumstances, that numbs me. If all I had to do was to stick it out for ten years, and then be released and free to behave normally, I think I could face it. But it's the problem of how to adapt, the eternal difficulty of gauging how much development I can permit myself each succeeding year, that makes me feel I'll never manage to keep my sanity.

Let me put it quite baldly. At the time of writing I've just had my fifth birthday. That is, the body into which my intelligence has somehow strayed has lived five years since emerging from the womb—Her womb. As far as I can judge, from comparison with the other children I meet, I seem to be a normal enough five-year-old, physically; I can run about quite nimbly, my organs of speech will pronounce a complete vocabulary (I have to keep a watch on myself there, of course, and it's an intolerable strain all the time), I can dress myself (though I make a show of not being able to manage buttons unless they're in front, and not always then), and my voice will sing an octave. But *my mind*—how old is that? At a guess, I should say I had the mind of a man of about thirty-five. It's hard to say, of course, because I've none of the ordinary means of guessing. An ordinary thirty-five-year-old would be able to estimate his own age, should it ever be in dispute, by the things he could remember: his clear memories would go back about thirty years, and in any case he would recall countless events to which a definite date could be attached. What makes my situation so eerie is the blankness—rather like amnesia, I suppose. I feel that my interests are those of a man of thirty-five, but I can only feel it in a generalized way. That's about how old He is, I suppose, and I do know that when He has friends in to dinner, and I manage to sneak within hearing range, the things they are saying are usually pretty well on my wave-length. They don't fit in exactly with my interests, but they do sound like a smaller, duller and more repetitive version of the conversations I'd like to be having. Like? I'd give my right arm to be able to talk normally with men of my own age—my mind's own age, that is. I already get plentiful doses of the company of my fellow five-year-olds: little pixies, the apples of their parents' eyes. In other words, a lot of snotty-nosed, egocentric brats, each one the centre of its own stuffy little universe.

Need I dwell on the agonies I go through? She, being a sensible modern mother (that is, just literate enough to spell out the child-welfare articles in the Sunday papers), takes me several afternoons a week to visit other s.m.m.'s —the drill being to put the kids down where they can play together without breaking anything valuable, while the women let their hair down and criticise their husbands. I must say I've had an amusing moment or two, even amid that welter of desperate boredom and loneliness, when I've crawled near enough to hear them go on. The inadequacies they find in the poor devils they're tied to!—it's enough to make me, at the age of five, resolve never to marry. But, of course, I don't get a chance to sit and hear a whole chapter of marital grievances; there's always the kid—or as I suppose I should say, the other kid—toddling about, alternately gooing and howling, and I'm expected to pull my weight and join in. It certainly is a peculiar kind of hell. You know the sort of hopeless bewilderment that comes naturally over an adult male when he's left in charge of a young child?—an aching, apprehensive helplessness, arising from the well-founded suspicion that, before many minutes are up, the little cherub will begin to scream uncontrollably, or swallow something and choke, or just go black in the face for no special reason. Well, I feel all that, but it's made a thousand times worse by physical helplessness; being no bigger, heavier, or stronger than the kids I play with, I can't even fall back on the adult's one last defence—his size. And the mental strain! It's unbelievable. I nearly wrote "it's worse than anything I've ever known," but I remembered in time that, on the contrary, it's just about the only thing I *have* known. In terms of recallable experience, that is. Every conversation I can actually bring to mind has either been with some ga-ga-ing infant or with some fool of an adult who tries to reproduce infantile talk so as to put us on the same footing. And I don't know which is worse.

Of course, I must admit that a kindly Providence has spared me the ultimate horror. At least I didn't have an adult intelligence during my years of actual helplessness—or, if I did, I don't remember it. All the time I was having to wear nappies, live on pap, and all the rest of that disgusting business, I knew nothing of the plight I was in. I can't say exactly at what moment I first realized the appalling practical joke that fate had played on me: it was somewhere in the latter part of my fourth year, I think. I was talking by then, and I think language was the key that unlocked the whole wretched situation to me. I simply realized, one day, that the speech of the grown-ups, when I happened to overhear it, fell more naturally on my ear than the kind of babble I was supposed to be capable of. But, even as I realized it, an instinct warned me not to let anyone else into the secret. I don't think I consciously reasoned about it; I just talked as little as possible, and when I had to say something I'd take time to vet it beforehand, to stop myself coming out with anything too precocious.

Because—and this, if anything can, will save some rags of sanity for me— I was, and am, utterly determined not to be a child prodigy, a freak, a side-show attraction. Of course, She and He are not the type of people who would actually put me in a side-show; they seem to be good solid *bourgeoisie* —He's in Insurance or something of the kind. It would more probably be a matter of being the wonder of the medical world. And what's that but a scientific version of the same thing? If I don't want yokels crowding into a tent to gasp at my feats of memory, still less do I want professors and Harley

Street types looking at me through their bifocals and making little notes. No, as God is my witness I'm going to grow up a normal boy, a little brighter than most at his school work perhaps, but no freak.

All the same, it's going to be a struggle. Impatience is my big pitfall. For instance, I found it quite intolerable to have to pretend that I couldn't read. There isn't much to read in the house, goodness knows, but I thought that if I could once get over the hump, and make it an officially accepted fact that I could read, I might get access to library books or something. I have such a damned hunger for *information*. I swear I could read anything, but anything at all, provided it was (a) in a language intelligible to me, and (b) contained some solid facts to sink my teeth in.

Anyway, as soon as I had fairly grasped the nature of my situation, I set about the job of getting it accepted that I could read. The pencil would crumble into acrid dust if I tried to describe the sickening subterfuges I had to resort to. I began, naturally, by pulling books out of the shelves and going through the motions of playing about with them, with signs of both incomprehension and delight. At first, it worked fairly well. "How fond he is of books!" they squawked. I don't know which of them was the more pleased. Nobody set foot inside the house who wasn't told about my fondness for books, and how I'd make a bee-line for them to the neglect of ordinary toys, and all the rest of it. I began to be afraid of getting known as a Child Genius, but it couldn't be helped. I had to carry on with the scheme. The next step, of course, was to climb up on to the lap of anyone I saw reading anything—like a kitten—and start pestering to be shown what the writing said. "I want to read!" I lisped, ready to puke at the sound of my own artless prattle. "I want to read!"

It never worked with Her. She never did sit down to read anything, in any case, when she was alone; sometimes she'd pick up an illustrated paper, but but if I clambered up and started the "I-want-to-read" routine she'd just get hold of me absent-mindedly, keeping her eyes on the page, and dump me on the floor again. It used to make me boil. More than once I've prayed for the strength to brain her. What I found particularly maddening was her way of never giving me more than half her attention. Of course, mothers do get like that, with young children, and I suppose the child doesn't notice. But I noticed, by God, and more than once I've gone off to the other end of the kitchen and deliberately smashed a cup. Not just any cup, either, but an expensive bone-china one. It got so that there wasn't an intact set in the house. That shifted her, naturally, and then she'd smack me till I yelled. The funny thing was, I would cry just like a real five-year-old. I mean the thing seemed to be geared physically rather than mentally. In moments of annoyance or fright, I can no more stop myself from wailing and blubbering than an adult can prevent himself from sneezing or coughing. I—the real "I"—stand apart from it, and listen to myself setting up a racket, but all the same I can't stop it. When She leathered me, I'd squall the place down, till the neighbours must have thought she was killing a pig.

After a time, I gave up on Her and concentrated my efforts on Him. He was a push-over. I'd crawl on to his lap, poke my finger at the book (which always seemed to be some shoddy detective-novel) and look up into his face with an appealing "Show me the writing, Daddy! I want to read!" I gave him the full works. Well, of course, he was delighted. "That's a," he would say, having hunted about and found an a. "It says *aa*. This one's b: it says *buh.*" And I would repeat the sounds, and pick out other occurrences of those letters, and we got along fine. After two or three sessions I found it possible to go and sit in a corner with a book; provided I didn't turn the pages too quickly, it passed as a harmless form of play; I was just fascinated by print, and was trying to remember the things He had told me.

I'm leaving out a lot of the details; the act I had to put on was too nauseating. But it was worth it. By the time my fifth birthday came along, I had gained the point; it didn't occasion any surprise if I sat with a book, not just looking at it but demonstrably reading it. Of course, that still left the problem of what books I could get access to. My birthday brought me a crop of nauseating children's picture-books. I had to pore over them, naturally, and show every sign of delight in owning some books all to myself. And God, what muck they were! The only way I could reconcile myself to staring at them for the required number of hours was to make up obscene versions of the rhymes under the pictures. But that wasn't much fun, when I thought how I might be spending the time reading something interesting.

My task was a delicate one: to drive into their heads the idea that I liked reading more than playing with bricks and plasticine, but to do it without getting the reputation of a prodigy. It was like the problem of talking. As a matter of fact, I never really mastered the talking business. It's such a strain that I sometimes wonder whether I shan't come out of the whole thing a raving lunatic. I keep my sentences short, and stick to very simple words, but I have to admit that the result doesn't sound much like the unending stream of drivel that pours from the lips of the other five-year-olds I meet.

But one thing is clear—I'm going through with it. There simply is no way out except forward. Sometimes, in the night, I used to lie and stare up at the ceiling and think how maddening and monstrous and absurd the whole thing was. Why should I be punished like this? I used to wonder. Is it a practical joke, or a heartless experiment, on the part of some hellish unmerciful God? Or is it simply an accident somewhere among the obscure machinery of the universe: did I wander innocently down a wrong turning in the time-corridor? And in any case, what has become of the body that used to house this mind? The thirty-five-year-old man who used to be me—where is he now? Dead? Or mumbling and playing with his fingers in some institution somewhere, having suddenly switched minds with a child of five? These questions used to hammer through my mind until I'd suddenly decide I couldn't stand it any more, and resolve to get out of bed that minute, put my clothes on, escape from the house and wander about the streets until I saw a doctor's brass plate, then go in and give myself up to his protection. "I appeal to you in the name of medical science," I pictured myself saying. "I don't know the reason, but I'm an adult who finds himself encased in the body of a child. *Do* something, for God's sweet sake!"

But always, at this stage, I would be pulled up by the thought: what *could* he do? What doctor, what specialist, what congress of specialists recruited from every corner of the earth, could possibly help me? And I would sink back, into despair. There was nothing that could help me except time—time and patience.

Here comes somebody I must stop

Well, here I am again. God knows why I go on taking the risk. If these sheets should ever be discovered, I daren't think of the mess I'd be in. Naturally, I hide them pretty carefully, among the litter of kiddies' books in my toy-box, but it's a constant worry—my heart thumps whenever I hear Her, or the daily help, clumping about in my room. It's enough to give me ulcers. Yes, perhaps I'll end up as the only five-year-old ever known to have had a duodenal ulcer. *That* ought to focus the attention of the medical profession, even if my precocity doesn't.

There isn't much to report, outwardly. I'm going to skip all the tedious little details (e.g. of the God-awful seaside holiday we had last month). Suffice it to say that three months have gone by since I last wrote, and only one new thing has emerged: namely, that it can now be taken as absolutely certain that I shall go mad. The strain of this dual perception of life is simply too much. My mind knows too many things that my body doesn't. The other day, for instance, I was horrified to find that I could experience lust. She had a rather good-looking young matron to tea; most of Her friends are dowdy and uninteresting, but this was a girl of about twenty-six, I'd say, who knew how to dress and had kept herself smart. I sat looking at her, while her own two kids squalled together in a corner, and I suddenly found myself imagining her sex-life. She looks as if she got plenty of the right stuff, I thought. And all of a sudden I began leering and drooling over the thought, exactly like a man of eighty. Which is, of course, a fairly exact parallel. And instead of trying to check myself, I went on, letting my thoughts rove, till I started imagining what I'd like to do to her myself. God, it was horrible—loathsome. There were no physical manifestations, naturally; no erection or anything like that. It was all so completely *cerebral.*

I went to bed that night in a state of complete despair. My life is ruined in advance, I thought. I calculated the years that must go by before I could have a hope of starting any normal sexual life; thirteen at least. If this were a Latin country, I could cut that down to six or seven; another example of my luck—if I had to be a five-year-old, why couldn't I be a little Sicilian or Argentinian?

So I lay there, Facing the prospect. If I could experience physical desire already, what was it going to be like when I got a bit older? Year after year of hell, till finally my mind gives way and I become a sexual maniac. Or a raving homosexual—that's another possibility, especially if they send me to a boarding-school.

Self-pity engulfed me, and I lay and snuffled. The tears brought me some kind of relief, so that I might have drifted off to sleep, but I was just getting drowsy when suddenly, it came.

Banging down on me like a rafter from the ceiling came a huge, cold, heavy weight of fear. Not just anxiety, but sheer panic, clutching at my heart. I sat up in bed: it was all I could do not to scream.

The reason for my fear? Simply that a thought had occurred to me, a terrible, obsessing thought that had, mercifully, not struck me before. But now that it *had* come, I knew I should never get out from under its chilling shadow. It was just this: how do I know what life-span my mind can expect? If it starts thirty years ahead of my body, why shouldn't it end thirty years sooner? When my body is forty, my mind will be seventy; why shouldn't it get tired and die? Think of it as I thought of it—a man of forty, crawling about with a dead mind. No memory, no speech, no *character*. Like someone who's had frontal lobotomy, only a hundred times worse.

Of course, it also occurred to me that my body might simply be unable to survive the death of my mind. Without a mind to co-ordinate and direct its impulses, a body can hardly go on functioning. Or should I, perhaps, be left with just enough mental co-ordination to keep me alive as a kind of idiot?

I had to scream, really *needed* to, this time. I put my hand over my mouth, but it was no good. The screams came, as loud and sudden as train whistles in a confined space between walls. Once I had started, I took my hand away and just let rip. Scream upon scream upon scream—it was all I had left, the only relief, the only way I could tell the horrible torturing universe what I thought of it.

And then, of course, we had all the usual commotion; it wasn't very late, and some people who had come to dinner were still there downstairs, and He rushed in, smelling of cigar-smoke, and She followed him up the stairs as fast as She could on Her high heels, and it was picking me up and "There, there!" and "He's had a nightmare!" and speculation about what I'd had to eat that could have disagreed with me.

I stopped screaming. But that was the first moment I realized that I hated them.

Well, here we go. She's pregnant. I knew it as soon as they did, but that wasn't difficult; the doctor only confirmed it three days ago, and already the whole town must know. Neither of them can talk of anything else, of course. You'd think He was the first man ever to get results out of a woman, the way he struts about. Bloated ass! Why, in addition to my other sorrows, did I have to get landed with an inane fool for a father? Not to speak of a mindless, blinkered, tiny-souled milch-cow for a mother, who's never had a thought in her life that didn't concern her own physical functions, directly or indirectly. I only have to look at her and I can see her whole mental history in that round, inexpressive face with its wide-spaced eyes and narrow forehead. From the age of six months till her wedding-day, how to get a man: from that day onwards, her own role as a viviparous mammal. It's all too brutally squalid.

I don't see what either of them is doing wearing clothes or walking upright. And how they misuse the divine gift of speech, real adult speech that I'd give anything to enjoy for ten minutes! As I loll about on the rug, pretending to play with toys, and listen to the grunting and lowing that passes for conversation between them, I feel really mad with anger that these two blockheads should have the use of this precious instrument when I don't.

And now, if you please, they're worried about me. Yes, worried. They've noticed me behaving strangely, as they call it. One or two of the other modern young mothers have said that I don't seem to act like a five-year-old. This, after all my efforts: there's ingratitude for you! If they only knew, the impersonation of a five-year-old that I put on every day, non-stop for hour after hour, is the greatest acting performance they'll ever witness. I've studied the other little horrors very closely (God, what a treatise I could write on infantile psychology!—not that I shall; my one ambition is to be able to forget about the whole subject), and in the interests of a realistic performance I've isolated the two characteristics that essentially indicate the five-year-old *homo sapiens*. The first, of course, is egotism. Morally, the little dears I have to play with are at the same stage as a new-born baby. They're aware of needs and instincts, but nothing beyond. They don't understand the concepts of gratitude, loyalty, affection, anything that cuts across the immediate appetite of the moment. The second feature is charm. No, let me give it a capital: Charm, bogus, phony, oozing Charm. That's one respect in which the child of five really has moved a long way from the new-born baby. When a baby wants anything, he stretches out his arms and yells. When a boy or girl of five (the sexes are alike in this) wants anything, the Charm comes into play. To see these little matinée-idols look up at their parents and flutter their eyelashes and smile, when they want to twist them round their little fingers!—it's incredible. And I don't blame them; the parents are such a push-over, the idiots. Any detached observer can see that the children are just making fools of them, but they never see it themselves. It's as if they were hypnotized.

The other day, I was "playing" with a blubber-lipped booby of my own age, the son of a woman whose house we were visiting for tea. The weather's good just now, and this kid and I had been pushed outside into the back yard, which the pretentious fool of a woman called "the patio." Everything went smoothly for a time—he was absorbed in some fantasy-world or other and I didn't take much notice of him. But presently, his private world built up to a point where, it seemed, he needed some cups and saucers. Don't ask me why; perhaps he was seeing himself as a butler or something. Anyway, he trots into the house, and I can hear the rattling of crockery and an argument going on. His mother, the poor fool, is trying to persuade him not to take cups and saucers outside, or, if he must, not to take the best ones but to wait while she hunts up some old cracked ones. Backwards and forwards they yap about it for a bit, then the woman's voice stops; evidently she's gone off to find some old cups for him. The next thing, of course, is that he appears in the doorway with a pile of cups and saucers balanced unsteadily in his hands. Behind him, clucking a bit but not daring to oppose his wishes, the pie-faced little lord and master,

I can see Her, my mum, watching uneasily as he blandly disregards his mother's orders. Coming out into the yard, he puts the cups and saucers down on the bricks and starts filling them with sand or something of that kind. The mother came back, and the two women came out and stared uneasily for a bit, but he just ignored them. They hovered, trying to pluck up courage to grab the cups and saucers and face the bawling that he'd inevitably set up, but finally they cheered each other up by saying that he seemed to be playing quite nicely with them, and didn't seem likely to break them, and decided to leave him to it. I even heard Her say, as they went back into the house, that it would be useful for him to get into the habit of handling thin china. "Richard's a terror for that," she said. "Always breaking my best things. It's the only really naughty thing he does."

Richard. That's what they call me. Just the sort of good, bourgeois, middle-of-the-road name they'd think suitable.

Well, peace descended. The nipper went on messing about with the crocks and mumbling some rigmarole to himself: he'd won his battle of wills, and he was quite satisfied. And suddenly—I can't quite describe how—a cold rage welled up inside me. Silly, flaccid cows! I thought. Why do they let him get away with it? What they need is a sharp lesson. And I walked straight over to the crocks and kicked a couple of them for six. Splinters of china flew everywhere; in fact, the things just disintegrated as my foot hit them. It was one of those rather satisfying sensations, like treading on acorns. The kid set up a yowl, of course, but before the avenging matrons appeared in the door-way I was over on the other side of the yard, playing with a ball. Of course, he sobbed out that narsy ole Richard had come and smashed his cups, but children of five aren't supposed to be truthful, and with a bit of wide-eyed innocence I was able to make him look like a bare-faced liar.

I felt better all evening. It made me feel that I'd struck a blow for more disciplined upbringing, and altogether that I wasn't as powerless in the grip of the adult world as I'd thought myself.

Well, the months have rolled by somehow; I shall soon be six, and at about the same time the population of the household will be increased by one. Arithmetically, that is; if you put it in terms of proportion, you'd have to say that the population was going up by about fifteen hundred per cent. The sheer amount of equipment!—the plastic buckets and the nappies and the Carricot and the pram (a gleaming new job big enough to hold a walrus), and the tiny garments and the tins of powder and the rolls of bandage and mysterious tonics lining the bathroom window-sill! The whole house is in a state of siege.

Meanwhile, I've started school. At any other time I suppose that might have been the occasion of a little mild rejoicing, but as things are it went pretty well unnoticed. The arrangements were duly made, I was taken out shopping and fitted up with clothes and a satchel, and that was that. When the day came, I was taken along by Him on his way to the office, dumped inside the school building, and left to sink or swim. At least, to be strictly accurate, He did come inside for a few minutes and make the teacher a little speech, all about what a genius I was. "You'll find he can read already, Miss Briggs," he said, cooing bashfully and trying not to look too much like a man who'd grown a prize-winning marrow. "Taught himself, with a little help from me now and again!" "Yes," says Miss Briggs (prolonging the conversation, I suppose, because she doesn't often get a chance to be within six feet of a man), "the headmistress was telling me about Richard. It's *very* rare for a child to be able to read before having any schooling at all! We're all very excited to have charge of such a prodigy!"

That's torn it, I thought. I nearly kicked her on the ankle to make her shut up. The word "prodigy" was exactly what I'd been trying to avoid. Being a word of more than one syllable neither He nor She would dredge it up of their own accord; but once they had it put into their mouths by someone else they'd be using it all day long. "Our elder child," they'd be saying airily to everyone they met, "is a Prodigy." And before long, I'd be irretrievably consigned to the glass case as a freak.

As it turned out, I needn't have worried. I went into school with my heart in my boots, but when I went home for lunch I could see at once that the whole subject had been well and truly buried. He didn't even remember talking to the woman, as far as I could see; the conversation was just baby, baby, baby, as usual. They did ask me, perfunctorily, how I'd got on at school, and I said all right, and they went back straightaway to baby, baby, baby again.

I was glad, of course, though naturally there's always a certain let-down when you've steeled yourself to fight something and then the fight is called off. I'd made up my mind, during the morning, that if there was any danger of this prodigy business I was going to redouble my efforts to look like a normal child of my age, including a good slab of downright bad behaviour, even if it meant a smack or two. I was five years old, by their calendar, and I wasn't going to get them forget it. I could see, now, that the act wasn't going to be necessary, but I had got steam up for it, so I decided to go ahead. No harm in being on the safe side. I knocked over a glass of milk, and when a new one was brought I promptly knocked that over too, taking care to let it run down on to His suit. Then, as soon as He got back from mopping himself up, I declared that I was hungry and wanted some more fish—that was what we were having that day. There wasn't any more fish, as I perfectly well knew, so I threw a good fit of the sulks and ended up by snatching some from Her plate. Even this didn't rouse them; they clucked a bit, and disapproved, but She didn't even bother to retrieve the fish. It was as if I'd suddenly become invisible, hidden behind the giant bulk of the baby, who hadn't even got himself born yet. Suddenly, I couldn't stand it any longer. I let out a succession of piercing yells, shied the stolen fish at Him (it caught him right across the face, I'm glad to say), and generally ran amok. At one point I even seized the table-cloth and began dragging at it, hoping to sweep the whole God-damned meal on to the floor, but He was too quick for me. So then, of course, I got a smack, and was put outside the door, and was generally in disgrace until it was time to go back to school. He chauffeured me, again. At first, when we climbed into the car, He was doing His more-in-sorrow I'm-surprised-at-you act, but during the ten minutes it took us to get there He must have decided that I was under strain, first day at school and all that, and He spoke to me gently and said I mustn't try too hard at school but just take things as they came. And when He opened the car door to let me out He gave my arm a squeeze with His big meaty hand. And I walked straight into school and grabbed a ruler and started beating hell out of the kid nearest me, and the teacher grabbed me, and I started yelling, and then suddenly I stopped yelling and threw up all over the floor, before they could get me out of the room, and I remember wishing all the time that I could just throw up my guts once and for all and lie down and die and be rid of the whole bloody business.

Tonight She is bearing the child. I know it although I am not supposed to understand what birth is. They've given me the usual routine: Mummy is going away for a few days. I shall wake up one morning and find Her gone. Soon She will be back and I shall have a nice little brother or sister to play with. *Which will it be?* I asked, lying my way through the part of a six-year-old, choking down the black fog of rage and sorrow that crawled up my gullet and tried to burst out of my mouth. *Nobody knows, till She gets there.*

And now, as I lie here, She is getting there. I know tonight is the birth because they took Her off at about nine o'clock. He went too, and left some fool of a woman here to look after me. One of the ones She takes me to tea with. Now it's about three in the morning. The woman is asleep downstairs. Several times she has been to the telephone and spoken to the hospital. The last time was about midnight, and I heard her say "So it's started? Good!"

I lie here twisting like a trapped snake. It's started. This is the birth that should have been me. This child will be normal, I know it. No kink in the time-corridor for him. He'll be nought years old to-night, one year old in a year's time, and six when his body grows to be like mine. He'll discover the world gradually, step by step; it will be terrifying, of course, it always is; but at least the world will keep pace with him as he grows up. There'll be no terrible loneliness such as I suffer and must always suffer, and no abyss of fear that what has happened once to me might happen again. The new one will be the right one. They always wanted to breed, to have children to save them from their own ordinariness, to have a miracle bursting in and happening right there in the centre of their lives. What, us? Ordinary? Pig-faced? Dreary? *But we live with a miracle!* And now they've got it. I might have been it, but I was a miracle that went wrong. The old conjurer up there was nodding off to sleep, or thinking of something else: he waved his wand, but he waved it a little too much to one side, or gave it one wiggle too many. Result—a monster. Like a photograph when you forget to turn the film before you take a fresh picture. Blurred, superimposed. A ghost walking on the same plate that records the clear, rehearsed smile of every day. How do I know that? I never handled a camera, I'm too young. I'd break it. How do I know? *How do I know anything?*

But I do. I know things, I know every crevice and corner of this life to which I am being introduced like a hesitant stranger. I am the ghost on the photographic plate. That's Mother at the fountain. And that's Uncle Phil standing by his new car. And who's looking over Uncle's shoulder, walking right through Mother, spoiling the picture? It's me, me, me, me, me. I didn't ask to be a ghost. They made me. Ghosts don't like being ghosts. They just find themselves forced into it when they get superseded. Up to now I've just been a monster, but now I'm a ghost. The baby will take over my life. He has my body, my soul. He is I and not-I. He has come to restore the balance, to provide a baby who shall be a baby all through, not a fake. He is the child they should have had when they had me. He is being born in my stead—but too late! I am here already! They should have labelled him "Useless if Delayed." He is coming, savagely fighting his way into the world of air and light, ready to kill or be killed rather than stop his blind, crazy struggle to get out into this world. Go back, you fool! What makes you think it's so good out here? Who told you you'd like it? But it's too late: he's coming—not too late for himself, not too late for Them, but too late for me.

The earth is spinning aimlessly round the sun, and I am lost. The universe contains no home for me. I cling to the gnarled surface of the earth, I lie here in this bed and think of the millions of miles of frozen darkness between the stars: I might as well be out there. The cold would kill my body, but my mind could not die with it. That neat, predictable timing, that cosy precision, has been denied me. My mind will die when its own independent life-span is over. Where is the body it used to inhabit? Dead and decomposed, or living on without a mind? I keep wondering, but no one can ever tell me. And now the personality that should have been mine is launching itself upon the world. The mother is thrashing and bulging with pain, her eyeballs bursting, her veins cut to ribbons from within. Or she is lying comatose, between spasms, her silent torturer, whom she loves so dearly, choosing his own moment to clutch and rack her anew. She loves him, her bully, perhaps her murderer: the more he savages her, the closer he comes to killing her, the more she loves and wants him. I know it because I am there. If he is I, I am also he. I kick on my bed as she kicks on hers: I am there as well as here: sleek and murderous as a fish, I am forcing my way down that red, blubbery chute: with the fangs of a shark I tear her flesh like wet paper, with the fingers of a baby I caress her skin. My head butts out of her belly, her walls collapse, her veins wilt, she has suffered too much, it is over, she cannot find strength to breathe, she lies back, happy that I have overpowered her. Already I am her son. If she dies now I shall still be her son: her lover, devourer, crucifier: her parasite and saviour.

I am born! He is born! Siamese twins of the spirit: he takes the place that was his from the beginning, and it is time for me to move over, but I cannot: there is nowhere for me to move, not even into death. There is no place for me, even in nothingness: I must stay here in darkness, in solitude, in hatred.

In darkness, because every particle of light that shines on the surface of my body casts its own particle of shadow into the silent centre where I lurk, shrinking from discovery, hunched over my decaying secret.

In solitude, because I am an outcast, totally and for ever outside the law, hurled into my own damnation beyond the reach even of the simplest and most primal fellowship, that of time.

In hatred, because I hate, I hate, I hate, I hate, I hate.

Now I am cold. Cold, hard and shiny: I am stainless steel, I am glass, I am metal and chemical. The hysteria has passed. It took time; I was ill for weeks, too ill to be moved, and then I was sent to some kind of children's convalescent hospital. It was a peaceful time; I lay in an iron cot, out of doors. There were other children there, but I could ignore them and just sleep. I needed rest, long weeks of it. I had been trying to contain the emotions of a mature man within the body of a six-year-old, which is impossible. My tender fibres were ripped and split by my hard, spiny feelings. I felt as guilty as a man who sees red and beats a child—only the child I was beating was myself. I savaged my own body till I broke it, reduced it to a pale, scarcely breathing little heap of limpness, pale as the shed skin of an eel, lying trembling and weeping on a cot.

Rest has restored me. Everyone was kind. He came out to see me at week-ends, often, and She came, too, when She could get away. But mostly She had to stay at home with the baby. And now the baby is about six months old. Soon he will be crawling about the floor; already they leave him unattended, in his play-pen, to kick his legs in the summer air and wallow about, glad to be alive and to have limbs that move.

I'm glad he exists. The official theory of my illness connects it with jealousy at the birth of the baby, and they still watch me, anxiously trying to ward off any renewed signs of jealous hatred. But I never give a sign of it. Why should I? I'm grateful to the baby for coming into the world. By doing so, he has solved a problem for me, a moral problem. I am no longer in doubt. I know what I have to do.

Briefly, there is no way for me to go except downwards. The coming of the baby, with his normality, has finally revealed me to myself as a monster. Originally, I hoped that by concealing my unsynchronized intelligence from those about me, by marking time, so to speak, until my body grew up and fell into step with my mind, I might one day cease to be an oddity. With every year that passed I could grow nearer and nearer to a blessed state in which I could lower my guard, say whatever came into my head and begin to take life on normal terms. But now I know that I was idly dreaming. Such bliss is not for me. I am a monster, hurled beyond the bounds of normal human life and condemned to live in a metaphysical wilderness, a dark, tangled place lit only by flashes of red fire. As far as I know, I am alone in this wilderness —but the time may come when I shall meet other denizens of it, and then God knows what unimaginably horrible and pitiable beings they will prove to be! Yes, God—that far-off engineer of cruelties, whose ear is stopped to the cries of those he has created only to whirl them beyond the reach of his own memory!

I'm getting carried away. I mustn't. Calm, calm, everything I do and think must proceed from calm and tend towards calm again. Only in that way can I accomplish anything. I know what excited me: the sensation of holding a pencil, writing on these lovely blank pages, after all those months away from it. This notebook is the only friend I have. But what a friend! Always receptive, always patient. I am so eager to talk to it that I scribble away, faster and faster, so impatiently fast that my little hands can hardly form the letters properly and the result looks like some sort of code—but never mind! I can read it, and that is all that matters. There is no one else in my world. Already I find that I'm less and less frightened about the risk of discovery. I used to sweat with fear if I heard anyone moving about in the room where I hide this book: but nowadays, I don't care. I hardly trouble to hide it. The possibility of its being read by other eyes simply isn't real to me. I write myself, for myself to read; the knowledge that these pages exist is the only thing that saves me from that aching corroding loneliness. No, there is one other thing: there is my Plan.

My notebook, and my Plan! My past, and my future! By writing this account of the phases of my suffering, I put my experience into some sort of order, leaving a snail's track behind me that, wavering and tormented as it is, I can still look back on. What lies ahead is chaotic, but what lies behind is at least caught and fixed in some sort of order, held and objectified in the words I have found for it. And my future? At least I can prophesy one thing, that whatever my future contains it will contain my Plan. Nothing short of total annihilation will make me let go of that. It gives purpose to my life, direction to my thoughts, even—at times—a kind of happiness to my misery.

For consider. The moral law, as every thoughtful person knows, is the same as the law of nature. To be true to one's own nature: there is the one basic duty. A man must not behave like a dog, nor a bird like an insect. I, being a monster, must fulfil my destiny, which is to act monstrously, to achieve monstrous things. Before my illness I fell apart under the pressure of trying to decide how to view the world, what objects to strive for, and what fulfilment to seek. Now, it is all settled. And here is the perfect instrument, put into my hands. This baby. He will grow up, six years my junior, looking to me as the chief intermediary between himself and the world. A little kindness on my part, and he will love and admire me without reserve. His parents, devotedly as they may watch over him, can never be as close to him as I shall be, for I share his child-nature at the same time as I participate in adult-nature. *He is mine.* And if he is mine, so are He and She. Their happiness is hinged on this one question of how their offspring grow up. Anything is possible: pride, contentment, a rapturous unfolding of new lives, in whose every phase they can share: or misery, humiliation, shame. They already have one monster among their brood, but they shall never know it; I will guard every look, every gesture; nothing shall give me away. No, it is he who will be the monster. I shall mould him into an instrument of their destruction. If ever a completely corrupt human being walked the earth, such—I guarantee it—this child will be. I shall write on the snowy surface of his mind as copiously and as gleefully as I write on these pages. I shall be circumspect;

he will shock, wound, offend, and finally betray. He will sell his parents into spiritual captivity to buy a handful of scented cachous. He will roll their eyeballs in the gutter for marbles. He will spit into the graves they are patiently digging for themselves. Nothing will be too terrible for him to inflict on them! And I, all the time that I am planning his crimes, suggesting them to him, pushing him gently down the slope whenever I see him falter—I shall be discreet, and smile, and look grave and worried when things go wrong.

This is my Plan. And thus I join battle not with three puny, inoffensive human beings, unworthy of a monster's strength, but with that God who has dared to challenge and affront me!

A fresh start. You'll notice that a great wodge of pages has been torn out. (I say "you," though even as I write I realize that it steadily becomes more unthinkable that any eye but my own should light on these pages. Still, it seems natural, if one's talking or writing, to *address* somebody. Perhaps the "you" in question is oneself at a later time; fair enough, if so.) Anyway, two years have gone by since the last entry I've left intact. Slightly more, in fact; the nipper is two-and-a-half, and it's summer time again.

I *had* to tear those pages out and burn them. They served their purpose, no doubt, at the time they were written; but to-day, re-reading them, I felt soiled, sticky, humiliated. All that thick, syrupy self-pity! I can see, looking calmly back on it, that the last two years have been very hard ones to get over. Sometimes I seem to have been out of my mind, quite literally, for weeks, even months at a time. Fortunately, children aren't expected to behave sanely! An adult, under the pressures I've been under, would have been certified and put away. And the verbal vomit, the emotional pus I've suppurated over the pages of this notebook! (In such quantities, by the way, that I shall soon be on Vol. II. What a thought! I can see an infinite shelf of painfully written notebooks stretching away to infinity, every page covered with my sufferings.)

It wasn't exactly disgust, however, that led me to scrap those pages. I realize, for that matter, that I'm no more "sane," as the word is commonly interpreted, at this moment than during the worst of my raving spells. No nearer, that is, to a normal mental organization, normal motives, normal "feelings." My Plan is still with me, cherished and worked out in detail more and more lovingly as time goes by. No, what sickened me about that part of the notebook was the impurity of my feelings. I don't mean lustfulness; I mean, in the chemical sense, that my feelings were impure, contaminated. I wasn't single-minded enough. Time and time again, for instance, I caught myself indulging in fits of sheer jealousy—the kind of black, mountainous jealousy that children suffer from. As if *I*, a grown man in everything but physique, could feel jealous of a squalling, nappy-wetting baby! And yet, many times over, I *was* jealous—that's the fact and I can't get away from it.

Perhaps I ought not to blame myself too much. It's as if there were bits of seven-year-old psychology lurking in odd corners of my being. The contrast between my mature mind and my infantile body isn't a clean-cut one; how could it be? I noticed, years ago, that when She smacked me I couldn't stop

myself from wailing just as passionately as a real child. The crying seemed
to be geared to my physical system rather than my mental one. And perhaps
the same thing applies to this business of jealousy. After all, I have all the
physical appetites of a child; I wolf things like cake and blanc-mange, that
no self-respecting adult would do more than toy with, and though I know,
as a matter of strict fact, that (say) dry sherry is better worth drinking than
lemonade, I also know that I shouldn't *like* it any better. Condemned as I
am to live the life of a small boy with a baby brother, I can't help feeling
twinges of the sort of jealousy that such a situation gives rise to.

Very well, I forgive myself; but the pages on which this jealousy had vented
itself, so passionately and so copiously, had, all the same, to go into the fire.
I must purge myself of those inferior emotions. My intention, which was
formed coldly, which grew up in coldness, and which by this time is as hard
and bright as a tool forged from stainless steel, is to use this child as the
instrument of my vengeance on the universe. That vengeance, which will be
a terrible one—as terrible, if I can make it so, as the initial crime of the
universe against me—will necessarily involve the child himself, in the first
instance, before it can spread to the parents and thence, through ever-widen-
ing circles of metaphysical implication, to God. So, without flinching, I must
first make a complete ruin of the child. But I must, at whatever cost in terms
of self-control, banish any kind of personal feeling. My hatred is not for the
child—not, even, for Him and Her. It is their misfortune that they have been
placed within the orbit of my rage. The same devilish spite that ruined me,
will ruin them. I can feel the sadness of their plight; in more exalted moments,
it strikes me almost as keenly as the sadness of my own. But there is no escape,
for them any more than for me.

So, of course, it follows that I must turn my back on all that pitiful record
of childish tears and tantrums. That I should ever have experienced them is
one of the plagues an implacable fate has laid on me. But to dwell on them,
to allow the record of them to stand even in a notebook which no one else
will ever read, is unthinkable.

A curse, an eternity of curses on this unstable spirit within me! Nobody will
ever know, nothing could ever describe, the intensity of my struggle to keep
the purity of my vision and the singleness of my motives from blurring and
melting into a formless mush. But it seems that, struggle as I may, weakness
and multiplicity will creep in; not unawares, but right out in the open, before
my very eyes as I struggle with every drop of my energy for strength and
singleness!

Let me put down the pitiful story. A week has passed since I wrote that
last entry, making all those high-minded resolutions about impersonality and
metaphysical vengeance. And now, so soon, to fall into pettiness and spite,
to behave as if it were not the universe, but my little brother, that I hated!
To crack, to crumble, just because of an expression in his eyes! But let me pull
myself together and calmly write out what happened. At least that will
objectify it.

I came back from school this afternoon, feeling, for once, more or less contented. The sun was shining, had been shining all day, and the part of town we live in is pleasant enough, with wide tree-lined streets. I swung in at the gate, eager to dump my school kit and go outside to play for half an hour, before being called in to the table. But as soon as I entered the garden, there he was, my brother, waiting for me. Not only waiting, but standing there as if he'd been rooted to the spot for hours, waiting for me to come home.

He can run about fairly well now, and talk, after a fashion. It's only in the last few months that he's shown much power of connected thought, but lately the development has been quite rapid. Anyway, I could see that he was waiting for me and that he had something to show me.

"Itchard!" And he bounded up to me, all shining. (He can't say "R," so he mostly just leaves it out.) "Come and see my house!"

I thought at first it was just some figment of imagination; like every child of that age, he seems able to wander across the border into make-believe and back again without knowing he's been away. So I said, to humour him, "Fine! A great house!" or words to that effect.

"No, no," he said, and began pulling at my wrist. Evidently he really had made something, in another part of the garden, and he wanted me to go and see it.

I made him wait while I took my school satchel inside and hung it up. But, though I didn't hurry, when I came outside he was waiting, dancing up and down with a kind of joyous impatience, and beaming.

"My house! I'll show you!" he piped; not getting the words quite right, but coming close enough for me to understand him.

As we went down the garden path, with my cold, half-disdainful hand in his little eager one, I suddenly felt my heart turn over in my chest, like a dying fish leaping up for the last time. A cold heaviness settled on my limbs, and I wanted to lie down, there in the middle of the gravel path, and howl like an animal. It was as if someone had crept up and injected a monstrous dose of some horrible poison into me. Which, of course, was just what had happened. He, my brother, was so full of love for me, so full of joy at seeing me and being able to share with me his triumph at having created something, that he was, quite literally, killing me. Because love, when you don't want it or can't use it, is lethal.

He felt me stiffen and looked up at me, with his eyes full of trust and joyfulness, and it was as if he had sandbagged me. His love for me was burning my skin, choking my veins, bringing my heart to a standstill; every breath I drew was more difficult than the last, because I was gulping down the thick, choking fumes of his love.

Oh, you who happen on this notebook, if anyone by chance should ever do so: you who wonder what kind of feelings pierced and throbbed in this tormented soul, learn from me one lesson, before I am swallowed up! Never, *never* arouse, or permit, love in any being, human or animal, if you cannot love that being in return. Remember this, or you will suffer as I do now—

and I say solemnly, against the backdrop of all eternity, that no matter what deeper and darker caverns of misery await me, this is the worst of my agonies!

I didn't collapse on the gravel; it would have been better if I had. But a long habit of self-control forced my limbs onward, and we reached the furthest corner of the garden, a favourite playground for both of us because of the bushes that screened it from view of the house.

We stopped; and there it was, his house. He had searched about until he had found half-a-dozen sticks of more or less equal length, and then leaned them together and put a bit of rag over the top. It looked more like a tent than a house, though you couldn't truthfully say that it *resembled* even that. The sticks were, obstinately, just sticks, and the rag was nothing but a piece of rag. Still, there it was, his house. The first thing he had ever made. And he had waited for me to come home, to show it to me, because he loved me as his brother.

"Look, Itchard!" he crooned, pointing, as if the house were two hundred yards off instead of there in front of us. "Look!"

I looked. I pictured his trotting about the garden, searching for sticks, then having to try about two hundred times before he could get them to stand up in that shape; then going and getting a piece of cloth from the house and draping it over the top. Love! That's what the house expressed: love of the world, of life, love of sticks and bits of rag, love of houses, love of making something, love of breathing and moving about. But, over and above everything, what he was expressing was love of me. He wanted to make something so that he could show it to me and I would be pleased, and I would love him, too.

My heart was dead. The sky was black, and rain was falling through the dry, hateful crevices of my heart. I shook his hand from mine, stood motionless for an instant staring at the house he had made, then moved forward slowly and purposefully and trod on it. Poor little house, it didn't take much treading down; the first touch of my foot sent it flying, and the thin sticks cracked under my feet as I stamped up and down on them. I ground the piece of rag into the mud with my heel, and the job was done. No more house. No more love. *How about that, God?*

Then I turned to face him. I knew I was being a fool, because my Plan required that I should gain his confidence, and I ought to have played along with him about the house and everything else, till I could start the job of corrupting his instincts. Cruel disappointments might have to be engineered, but it was quite out of order for me to be obviously the source of them. But I couldn't help myself. Love, as I say, is a deadly weapon when turned against someone who can't reciprocate it; and his love was burning, choking, poisoning me. I wanted him to fly into a rage, to shriek with anger and fly at me with his little fists waving; or, better still, to run sobbing to his mother and get me a good thrashing. At that moment I positively asked for physical punishment: what a liberation it would be, to feel the sharp rhythm of blows on my backside, stinging and scalding, driving out the love that was breaking my heart!

I can hardly write the rest of the story. When I think of it, I feel faint, I tremble and weep. Because,
>> he didn't
>>> get angry
>>>> at all:
>>>>> he just
>>>>>> stood and
looked at me with those big eyes that had just been so bright with happiness and now they were all sad and brimming with tears, but he didn't say anything and I waited for him to say something and he just stood there and looked at me and then he looked down at what was left of his house that he had been so proud to show me only nothing was left of it nothing I had trodden on it and he still loved me that was the terrible thing he still loved me listen are you there can you hear me God I am coming up there and I am going to spit right in your face because you beat me you threw the one thing at me that nobody can duck. You made me sorry I kicked his house down. I was sorry because he loved me. Nobody can fight against love and that's why I am coming up there God to spit at you because you never fight fair and you have fought me so dirty with the love that I had to see in his eyes.

And now it is after tea and he didn't say anything all through tea and he just looked at his plate and She took his temperature because they both thought he must be ill and now I am by myself and everyone is busy She is bathing the little sad one upstairs and He is messing about somewhere and it is over

it is over

when I have written this I am going to go to the kitchen because nobody can fight against love and I have got to fight against it or die so I am going to die and I am going to the kitchen to get the big long sharp carving knife and I am going to drive it into my throat and I hope I cut my head off

it is over

Harry Mark Petrakis
The Legacy of Leontis

LEONTIS MARNAS MARRIED ANGELIKI WHEN HE WAS FIFTY-EIGHT YEARS
old. She was twenty-four. She had been in the United States only a little over
two years. All that time she spent working from dawn to dark in the house
of an older brother who had paid her passage from Greece. Her days were
endured scrubbing floors and caring for his children. In addition, the unhappy
girl did not get along with her brother's wife, who was a sullen and unfriendly
woman.

Leontis was not aware at that time of how desperately Angeliki wished for
liberation from her bondage. When he visited the house in the evening to play
cards with her brother, she released upon him all the smoldering embers of
her despair. He would have been ashamed to admit that he mistook her
attention for affection and her desperation for passion. He was bewildered and
yet wished ardently to believe that a young and comely woman could find him
attractive. He could not help being flattered and soon imagined that he was
madly in love.

In the twenty-eight years since Leontis emigrated from Greece to the
United States, he had made a number of attempts to marry. Several times he
almost reached the altar, but in the end these efforts were always unsuccessful.
Even when he was a young man the bold girls had frightened him, and the
shy sweet girls to whom he was attracted lacked the aggressiveness to encour-
age him. He was without sufficient confidence to make the first move, and as
a result always lost his chance.

Sometimes despair and restlessness drove him to women that he paid for
affection. As he grew older, however, these visits became much more infre-
quent, and when he realized they burdened rather than satisfied him, he gave
them up.

A year came when he was forced to concede to himself that he would never
marry. This caused him a good deal of remorse and self-reproach, but secretly
he was also relieved to be spared additional disappointment. His mother, of
whom he often said, God rest her departed soul, had affirmed that keeping
busy prevented melancholia. He became active in a Hellenic lodge and spon-
sored the education of several war orphans overseas. He rearranged all the
stock in his grocery at least twice in each six months. On Sundays, the hardest
day of the week for him to sustain, he rode the trolley from one end of the
city to the other. He visited museums and spent many hours at the zoo. He

114

was strangely drawn to the monkey house and quietly marveled at his apparent resemblance to one somber old male in a corner of a cage who seemed untouched by the climate of social amiability that prevailed all around him.

During the week, after closing the store in the evening, he sometimes played cards with fellow members of his lodge. In the beginning, this was his reason for visiting the house of Angeliki's brother. Afterwards, although it took a while to admit it to himself, he went only to see her.

Later, in remembering that time, Leontis often considered how ridiculous his conviction that Angeliki loved him must have appeared to her brother. Perhaps he saw their union as an answer to his concern for the future of his sister. But whatever his reasons, her brother gave his approval and completed the alchemy created by the loneliness of Leontis and Angeliki's wish for freedom.

In the early spring of that year, with the first buds breaking in slim green shoots upon the trees, Angeliki and Leontis were married. But it did not take long for the poor girl to realize she had merely substituted one form of despair for another. He could offer her every advantage but the one of youth to match her own. Leontis knew she must have considered him ancient and unattractive, but his presence in the rooms in which she bathed and slept must have created in her an awareness of her body, and perhaps excited her as well. She could see that he admired and adored her, and at the same time he could not blame her impatience with his fumblings.

She could not comprehend how difficult it was for him to value himself as a participant in the act of love. He had too long lived vicariously on the perimeter of life. Yet he desired her fervently and made a valiant effort to play the role of lover. On a number of occasions he did manage to fulfill the functions expected of him. But Angeliki grew petulant and bitter at his inadequacies and began to ridicule his age and appearance. A day came when his own long-suffering patience wore thin, and they exchanged hot and furious words.

"You married me for my money!" he said, and he knew that was not true, but anger selects its own truth.

"No." She laughed bitterly. "I married you because you were young and handsome."

He felt the black bile of despair through his body, and he was tempted to strike her but understood helplessly that she could not deny herself the release of some of her frustration.

"I married you because you were handsome!" she shrieked. "A Greek god with a golden body!"

"Enough," he said, and suddenly his anger was gone and he was only weary. He saw in that moment the absurdity of his delusion and how much more he was to blame than she.

He fled down the stairs. In the store, Thomas Sarris, the young man who worked for him, was stacking cans of coffee. Leontis was ashamed and wondered if Thomas had heard them quarreling.

Upstairs, Angeliki slammed a door, a loud and angry slam. Thomas Sarris pretended he did not hear.

The following spring, a son was born to them. Through the months of Angeliki's pregnancy, observing her body curving incredibly into the shape of a pear, Leontis felt sure the doctor had made a mistake. For a long time he had accepted that he would never have a wife. The prospect of becoming a father had been additionally remote. Not until the moment in the hospital shortly after Angeliki returned from the delivery room was he able to accept the conception as real. He was shocked at the sight of her pale cheeks and her dark moist hair, combed stiffly, in the way of hair on a corpse. Fifty-nine years on earth without awareness of the struggle of birth had not prepared him for the emotion. He could not speak. A great tenderness for his young wife possessed him. He touched her cheeks softly and struggled vainly to find words to explain that he understood the ordeal she had endured alone.

When they brought the baby to Angeliki to be nursed, he was rooted with reverence and wonder. He had seen babies before, not quite as small and wrinkled, but that this baby should be a part of his flesh, a blossom of his passion, filled him with a wild strength. As if in some strange and secretive way he had cultivated a garden beyond the reaches of his own death.

Back at home, Angeliki was a devoted mother and cared diligently for the baby. She was dismayed and fretful at the disorderly abundance of affection Leontis showered upon the child. But he could not help himself. He worked in the store, and whether or not he was alone, a moment came when he was filled with an overwhelming longing to see his son. He would run up the stairs and burst through the kitchen into the room where the baby played. Angeliki would follow him, nagging fiercely, but he paid her no attention. He would bend over the baby and marvel at how beautiful he was. He would kiss the top of his soft head and kiss each of his tiny warm feet. The bell in the store rang endlessly.

Angeliki drove him finally from the room.

"You are mad! I will have you put away. You think of nothing but that baby. Your store, your wife—nothing matters. We will end up in the street!"

He kept a few feet ahead of her, and puffing heavily he hurried down the stairs.

A few weeks before the baby's first birthday they baptized him in the Greek Orthodox Church on Laramie Street. Leontis planned a gigantic party. He had several whole lambs roasted, and fifty gallons of wine, and forty trays of honey-nut sweets. He rented the large Masonic hall and invited almost all of the congregation of the church to attend. It was a wild and festive night, and everyone appeared to marvel at the way Leontis danced. Angeliki at last caught him in a corner.

"What an old fool! You will drop dead in the air. Everyone is laughing at you. They think you are crazy."

But full of wine and lamb and gratitude, Leontis just smiled. He danced and sang for love of his son, and he did not care what others thought.

Now, in that month of his son's baptism, sleeplessness, which had troubled Leontis for years, grew worse. He lay wakeful and still beside Angeliki and stared into the dark, and sweats came, and chills, and strange forebodings rode his restless dreams. He went secretly to his friend Doctor Spiliotis. The old physician examined him silently and spoke without sugar off his square tongue.

"Have you made out a will? If not, go home and attend to it."

"I have a will made," Leontis said. "Thank you, old friend, for the advice."

"No thanks to me," the doctor said brusquely. "Thank that heart of yours, which had endured all the abuse you could heap upon it. Many men have weak hearts. They live long lives by taking care. You seem determined to leave as quickly as possible."

"I have lived a long time," Leontis said. "Looking back, it seems to me there is nothing but time."

The doctor looked down and stabbed fiercely with his hand through the air.

"I only treat physical ailments," he said. "They have specialists now for sickness of the mind. For aberrations of old men who marry strong young girls."

"You should have been a diplomat, old friend," Leontis said.

"Understand me, Leontis," the doctor said. "The time is past for jokes. Unless you go to bed at once and move very little for six months or a year, I do not think you have long to live."

In that moment, Leontis understood the tangled emotion a man feels who hears sentence of his death. At the same time, it seemed his decision was clear.

"Who will attend the store?" Leontis asked. "Who will walk my son in the park in the afternoons? Who will sit with my family in church on Sunday mornings?" He paused for breath. "And if I go to bed, can this insure I will live a long time?"

"We can be sure of nothing on this earth," the doctor said.

"Then I will wait in the way I wish," Leontis said.

"Get out," the doctor said, but the affection of their long friendship softened his words. "I will send you a wreath, a big one, fit for a horse. It will be inscribed 'Athenian Fool.'"

"Save your wreath for someone less fortunate," Leontis said. "I have lived long enough, and I have a son who will carry on my name."

With the knowledge of his impending death, a strange calm descended upon Leontis. Recalling his sixty-odd years as dispassionately as he could did not permit him any reason for garish grief. He knew that except for his son there was nothing in his life worthy of exultation or outrage.

He was certain of Angeliki as a devoted mother who would love and attend the child. To provide them with economic security in addition to the store, he had been purchasing bonds in considerable quantity for years. Therefore, only the possibility of Angeliki's remarriage to a man who might mistreat the child caused him anxiety.

He began carefully studying the clerk in his store, Thomas Sarris. A young man of strong build and pleasant manner. On a number of occasions, Leontis had noticed him discreetly admiring Angeliki when she entered the store. For an instant, the thought of Thomas Sarris or any man replacing him as father to his son brought a terrible pang to his body, but reason calmed him. Thomas was not wild, as were many of the young men. He did not wish to be more than a good grocer, but he worked hard and would care for his own. He would know how to sweeten a girl like Angeliki and remove the memory of her bitterness in marriage to an old man.

He spoke cautiously to Thomas one afternoon.

"How old are you, Thomas?"

"Twenty-eight," Thomas said.

"Twenty-eight," Leontis repeated, and kept busy bagging loaves of fresh bread so that Thomas would not notice his agitation. "How is it you are not married yet? Many young men are in a great hurry to marry these days."

Thomas easily swung a heavy sack of potatoes from the floor to the counter.

"I have not found the right girl."

"Are you looking?" Leontis asked.

"I will be ready when I find her," Thomas said. "But I am intent on getting myself established first. Get a store of my own."

Leontis felt his pulse beat more quickly.

"Do you like this store?" he asked in what he felt was a casual voice.

Thomas shook his head enthusiastically.

"A wonderful store," he said. "A fine business. I would give anything to have one like it someday."

Leontis turned away so that Thomas would not see the sly and pleased smile that he was sure showed on his face.

From that day he brought the baby and Angeliki and Thomas together. He invited the young man to dinner and afterwards encouraged him to play with the baby. He was gratified when Thomas was gentle and tolerant with the child. And the presence of the young man seemed to act as a balm upon Angeliki. She spoke more softly and laughed easily, and there was a strange sparkle in her eyes. Sometimes, in the course of those evenings, it seemed to Leontis that Angeliki and Thomas and the baby were the family and he the intruder. Awareness of this jolted him, and forgetting for an instant that this was his design, he would flee with the child to another room. He would sit in the dark, holding the child tightly in his arms, and with the bitter knowledge of their separation roweling his flesh, he sometimes cried, softly, so that Angeliki and Thomas would not hear.

Summer passed and autumn swept brown crisp leaves along the streets beside the torn scraps of newspaper. In the morning, opening the store, Leontis felt the strange turning of the earth and endured the vision of the sun growing paler each day.

He knew that it was too late; but he suddenly took great care not to exert himself and called to Thomas to move even the smallest box. More and more often, he left the younger man alone in the store and spent most of the day upstairs with Angeliki and the baby. In the beginning she reproached him for neglecting the store, but after a while she seemed to sense his weariness and left him alone. He sat and watched her work about the rooms and listened to the baby make soft squealing sounds at play. Sometimes Angeliki brought him the baby to hold, and they would sit together by the window, looking out upon the winter street.

One afternoon when it rained and the dark heavy sky filled him with unrest, he spoke to her for the first time of what was in his mind.

"Angeliki," he said, "If I died, what would you do?"

She looked up and paused in sewing a button on the sweater of the baby.

"What is the matter with you?" she answered sharply. "What makes you talk of dying?"

"I am getting older," he said. "It should be considered."

"I will not listen to nonsense," she said.

"Would you marry again?" he asked. "I would want you to marry again."

She did not answer, but bent again over her sewing.

"Thomas is a fine young man," he said. "He works hard in the store. He is gentle with the baby. He would make a fine father and husband."

Angeliki snapped down her sewing.

"What nonsense is this?" she said impatiently. "I have better things to do than sit here and listen to you talk of nonsense." She rose to leave the room, but a slight flush had entered her cheeks at mention of the young man.

There was a night he woke with a strange pain in his chest. He looked fearfully at the clock on the stand beside the bed, as if in some senseless way he hoped to arrest time. He was about to cry out, but the pain eased almost as quickly as it had come.

Later the baby cried in his sleep, a thin wail that echoed in the silent room. Angeliki got up and brought the child to their bed and placed him between them. In another moment, her breathing eased evenly again into sleep.

Leontis turned on his side and comforted the child and fell asleep with the warmth of the child within his arms. A noise within his body woke him. His eyes opened as if his eyelids were curtains on all of life. He cried out in despair.

Angeliki sat up in bed beside the baby.

"Leontis, what is the matter?"

He was bathed in a terrible sweat, and his heart seemed to be fluttering wings like a trapped bird to escape from the cage of his body.

"Leontis!" she cried. "Leontis!"

He knew he was dying. Not fear or anxiety, as he had known many times in the past months, but knowledge, swift and real as if seared in flame across his flesh.

"Leontis!" she cried. "You must not die before you forgive me!"

He touched the baby's face. He felt his nose, small and warm, and his eyes, and the soft strands of his hair.

"Forgive me!" she shrieked. "Forgive me!"

Her hands were on his face and then they were lost within the crest of a mighty wave that tossed his body. He tried to hug the boy with all of his soul, and the last great swell exploded from his eyes.

The Prison Window

Louis Auchincloss

"YOU ALWAYS FORGET, AILEEN, THAT WE'RE NOT AN ART INSTITUTE. Perhaps it would be more fun if we were, but we're not. The Museum of Colonial America, as its name implies, exists for a very specific purpose. We're a history museum. That doesn't mean, of course, that there aren't a great many ways of accomplishing that purpose, such as awakening the young to a proper sense of their heritage and revitalizing the old forms of communication . . ."

"I know, I know," Aileen Post interrupted. It was not the thing to do for a curator to interrupt the director, but when the curator was middle-aged and female and the director male and very young, exceptions had to be admitted. "I know all the jargon. I realize that we have to be 'relevant' and 'swinging" and 'up to the minute.' I understand very clearly that we have to be everything on God's earth but simply beautiful!"

"History is not always beautiful, Aileen."

"Oh, Tony! Don't be sententious. Save it for the trustees. You know what I mean. The *illustrations* of history should be beautiful! We can read about the horrors. We don't have to look at them. Why should there be any but lovely things in my gallery? Why should I have to put *that* in the same room with the Bogardus tankard and the Copley portrait of Lillian van Rensselaer?"

Here she pointed a scornful finger at an ancient rusted piece of iron grillwork that might have fitted into a small window space, two feet by two, which lay on a pillow of yellow velvet on the table by Tony Side's desk.

"Because it's a sacred relic," Tony replied, with the half-mocking smile, that as a modern director, he was careful to assume in discussing serious topics. "Because tradition has it that it covered a window on the ground floor of the Ludlow House in Barclay Street. During the Revolution it was the sole outlet to a large, dark storage room in which Yankee prisoners were miserably and sometimes fatally confined."

If the distressed virgin curator of beautiful things suggested too much the past, her superior was almost too redolent of the present and future. He had long chestnut locks—as long as his trustees would tolerate, perhaps half an inch longer—that fell oddly about a pale, hawklike face and greenish eyes that fixed his interlocutor with the expression of being able to take in any enormity. Tony twisted his long arms in a curious ravel and nodded his head

121

repeatedly as if to say, "Ah, yes, keep on, keep going. I'm way ahead of you, *way* ahead!" It might have been the point of his act to be both emperor and clown.

"It's not that I haven't any feeling for those poor wretches," Aileen protested, her face clouding as it always did at the thought of pain. "God knows, it isn't that. But must their agony be commemorated in *my* gallery? It isn't as if there weren't memorials enough everywhere to dead patriots."

Aileen herself might have been an academic painting of a martyr. One could imagine viewing the long, gray, osseous face and those large, gray, desperately staring eyes raised heavenward, through the smoke of a heretic's pyre. It seemed a wasteful fate that had cast her, tall and bony, with neatly set hair and black dresses, in the role of priestess of antiques.

"Your concept of history is too limited, too snobbish," Tony warned her. "It's odd, for you're completely unsnobbish yourself. But be objective for once and take a new look at your eighteenth century. Aileen Post's eighteenth century. Isn't it all tankards and silverware and splendid portraits and mahogany furniture? Doesn't it boil down to the interior decoration of the rich? Where are your butchers and grocers? Where are your beggars? Where are your slaves?"

"But you shouldn't judge beautiful artifacts by their owners!" Aileen exclaimed with passion. "They represent the aspirations of the age! The way the spire of a Gothic cathedral represents the thrust of man's soul toward heaven! What is history but the story of his reaching? Do you want a museum to show the whips and manacles, the starvation, the failure? Leave that to Madame Tussaud and the printed record. I want the person who comes into my gallery to breathe in the inspiration of the past!"

"Tut, tut, Aileen," Tony warned her, wagging a finger. "You're playing with nemesis. In your books the rich and mighty enjoy not only the delights of this world but the respect of posterity. What is left for the wretched but that pie in the sky they no longer believe in? Watch out! Those wretched can be very determined. They want their bit of the here and now."

"Who? The dead? The dead poor?"

"Why not?" Tony smiled broadly. "Aren't I helping them right now? By setting up the prison window in the very center of your gallery?" He got up and made her a little bow. "Those are orders, my dear."

Aileen left the room without another word. She knew that, mock bow or no, his orders were to be obeyed. Tony Side, under his perpetual smile, was a very serious young man who had no idea of staying in the Colonial Museum for more than a few years. It was too obvious that he was headed for greater things. He would keep his name before the eyes of other institutes—and particularly before the eyes of their trustees—by arranging shows that need have only slender ties to the colonial era. Already he had achieved a considerable success with a gaudy display of eighteenth-century balloons and primitive flying machines against a background of blown-up photographs of Cape Canaveral. It had even been written up in *Life*.

Traversing the Ludlow Gallery of decorative arts on her way back to her office, Aileen noted bitterly that there were only two people in it. Two visitors on a Saturday morning in the middle of the biggest city of the nation! It spoke little for the much touted "cultural revival." Aileen scorned the huge, mute, unthinking crowds that pushed by the high-priced masterpieces of the Metropolitan and the shaggy youths and pert-eyed, trousered girls who gawked at abstracts in the Whitney and the Modern. She told her friends at the Cosmopolitan Club that beauty was obsolete and fashion despot. She nodded grimly when they laughed at her. They would live to see their idols perish as hers was perishing.

When she had first come to the Colonial Museum, twenty-five years before, it had seemed a symbol of permanence in an ever-changing city. The great memorial plaques in the front hall, the names of benefactors carved on stone, the portraits of former presidents and directors had heralded one into the glittering collection as a released soul might be heralded into perpetual bliss. The institution had seemed to rise above its paucity of visitors; its dignity had waxed with its noble and solemn emptiness. The solitary wanderer was rewarded by the rich sustaining silence in which he found himself embraced. It was as if the museum, with its high task of preserving beauty for eternity, could afford the luxury of being capriciously choosy as its votaries.

But now all that was over. Modern New York had repudiated the concept of permanence. No grave, no shrine, no cache of riches was any longer safe. No quantity of carved names on marble, no number of " irrevocable" trust instruments drawn up by long dead legal luminaries, no assemblage of conditions, prayers, engraved stipulations or printed supplications could arrest the erosion of endowments or the increase of costs. The "dead hand" of the past became as light as dust when the money it once represented had slipped away. Aileen found herself faced with the probability that she might survive her own selected tomb.

It was unthinkable. The treasures of the Ludlow Gallery were like so many members of her family. At least a third of them had come to the museum as a direct result of her own detective work and solicitations. The great Beekman breakfront she had discovered in a storage house; the tea service of Governor Winthrop had been redeemed at a sheriff's sale; the Benjamin Wests of the Jarvis family had come as one man's tribute to the "ardor and faith" of Aileen Post. She could smell out eighteenth-century artifacts through stone walls; she could track them down in the dreariest and most massive accumulations of Victorians. How she pitied people who spoke of her misguided adoration of the inanimate! As if a Copley portrait could be dead! As if a coffee urn from Westover could be without life! Only ugliness was dead, and it was Aileen's passionate faith that it should never be resurrected.

Certainly nothing seemed deader than the iron window. Tony, who for all his vulgarisms was a gentleman at heart, had allowed her to choose its site in the gallery, but she knew that he would correct her if she tried to hide it. She had placed it finally, framed in dark polished mahogany, upright, in a glass case, in front of the Wollaston portrait of Valerian Ludlow, the owner of the house from which it had come. Certainly it was conspicuous enough there, in the very center of the gallery. Peering through it, on his first inspection, Tony was pleased.

"It makes it look as if old Ludlow were behind bars," he pointed out with a chuckle. "Very likely he deserved to be."

Aileen at first tried not to see the window when she passed through the gallery. She would keep her eyes averted and quicken her pace as she approached the hated object. But she found that this made it worse. What good was it to banish it from her vision if she only succeeded in summoning it to fill her mind? Somehow she would have to make her peace with it, before it became an obsession.

She then adopted the practice, each time that she had to pass it, of making herself pause to look at it, or really to look through it, for there was nothing to see but its rusted blackness. She observed that one side was slightly more rugged than the other and had probably been the external side, facing on Barclay Street. Gazing through it, as if from inside the Ludlow house, she tried to imagine that thoroughfare as it must have appeared to an incarcerated patriot. Then she would walk around the grille and peer in, as if from the street, to visualize, with a shudder, the dark, fetid hole where the prisoners might have been penned. Sometimes visitors in the gallery would stop to watch her, and, when she had finished, take her place to stare through the window to see what she had been noting. Aileen, amused, became almost reconciled to her new "artifact."

One morning, however, when she was alone in the gallery and looking through the grille from the "prison cell" side she had a curious and rather frightening experience. Ordinarily, she had not looked through the bars *at* anything in particular, but rather at her imagined reconstruction of an eighteenth-century street. That day when she happened to glance at the portrait of Valerian Ludlow, it struck her that he would have often passed that barred cellar window, in his own house, on the way to his own front door, and she attempted to picture him as he might have appeared striding by, viewed at knee height. The portrait helped her by showing him full length, standing by an open window, looking out to a sea on which floated two little vessels, presumably his own, with wind-puffed sails. The expression on his round face (the cheeks seemed to repeat the puffed sails) was one of mercantile complacency. Mr. Ludlow had obviously been one of the blessed of earth.

But now Aileen seemed to see something in his countenance that she had not noticed before. The eyes, instead of being merely opaque, either because of the artist's inadequacy or the subject's lack of expression, had a hard, black glitter. They changed the whole aspect of the portrait from one of seemingly harmless self-satisfaction to one of almost sinister acquisitiveness. At the same time the quality of the paint seemed to have lost its richness and glow. Mr. Ludlow's red velvet coat now had a shabby look, and the sea on which his vessels bobbed was brown rather than a lustrous green. Yet these changes, instead of making the whole picture more trenchant, more interesting, as they might have, seemed instead to push it back into an earlier era of clumsy primitives. Ludlow was now not only disagreeable; he was badly painted. Was his new degradation of character simply the artist's error? Had he come out mean, in the way of a clown drawn by a child? Or was Aileen seeing the real Ludlow for the first time?

Walking now quickly around the grilled window, with a conscious effort of will—for she was distinctly frightened—she turned suddenly and looked through it from the other side. She gave a little cry and then stopped her own mouth, for the sensation that had abruptly appalled her had as abruptly ceased. She had, for two seconds, stared into an absolute blackness, and at the same time her nostrils had been filled with a suffocating stench. Now she smelled nothing, and she was looking once more through the window toward the great glass case that housed the tankard collection.

Badly shaken, she returned to her office to go back to work on her article for the museum magazine on Dutch silver. But she was clear now that she would have to deal strongly with this preoccupation. In future she would walk by the window, not with consciously averted eye, not with undue attention, but simply taking it in casually, as she might take in any other exhibit. She would not flatter it with her fear or with her disdain. She would treat it, if its emanations compelled her to pause, with an icy disapproval, as she might treat a snoopy guard, set there by a jealous director to catch her out in something wrong.

By staying away from the window, she avoided any repetition of the shock of the sinister Ludlow and the black pit (figments, she assured herself, of her overcharged imagination), but she was not sure that she had eliminated all of the window's influence. She still had a sense, whenever she passed it, of some small, crouching, indistinguishable creature, some huge insect or tiny rodent, humped there by its base. And whenever she had to work near it, in the center of the gallery, she was conscious of something in the air, an aroma or maybe just a thickening of the atmosphere, that at once depressed her. If she looked about at the treasures of the gallery from any spot in the immediate circumference of the window, they appeared unaccountably drab. The silver seemed to thicken and tarnish and to lose the special elegance of its century. Bowls, plates, urns suddenly resembled the kind of ugly testimonials given to railroad presidents in the era following the Civil War. The beautiful carved wooden lady of victory that had once adorned the prow of a clipper ship might have been a widening, middle-aging nursemaid in Central Park. And the portraits, *all* the portraits, not only Valerian Ludlow's, seemed to have hardened into so many dusty merchants and merchants' wives as might have choked the wall of the Chamber of Commerce.

Sometimes she would watch visitors furtively from the door of her office to see, when they were standing near the prison window, if they noticed what she had noticed, but if they did, they showed no sign of it. Yet how could she be sure, if the things actually had changed, that they would notice it? Perhaps what she saw, under the malign influence of whatever the squatting creature was, was simply *their* vision of beautiful things. Perhaps that was the mystic significance of the window: that, peering through it, one saw art as it appeared to the Philistine! Aileen's mind had become a sea of hateful speculations.

One afternoon, at her desk, she looked up and gave a start to see an old lady standing before her. She had not heard anyone come in. It took her two or three seconds before she realized that she knew who it was. It was Mrs. Ada Ludlow Sherry, one of those "old New Yorkers" who made life for the curators both difficult and possible. She gave money and she gave things, but her gifts were hardly a *quid pro quo* for her almost daily interference. She was small and bent but very strong, and her skin, enamellike, and her hair, falsely red, gave the impression of having been preserved by a dipping in some hardening unguent. Her agate eyes snapped at Aileen.

"Are you aware, Miss Post, that an atrocious act of vandalism has been committed in your gallery?"

"Oh, no!"

"Some villain has poked a hole in my great-great-grandfather! Don't you ever check up on your portraits? There's a ghastly, gaping rip where his left eye was!"

"In Valerian Ludlow!" Aileen jumped up and ran into the gallery to the Wollaston painting. Sure enough, old Ludlow blinked at her with one black eye and one blue, the latter being the color of the wall on which he was hung. Aileen gave a little scream of panic.

"This was done within the hour!" she cried. "He had both eyes when I last went by!"

Tony Side was summoned, the alarm was rung and all guards were questioned. Nothing was discovered, and after an hour of futile excitement Aileen was back again at her desk, depleted and scared, with the irate Mrs. Sherry, who refused now to depart. Aileen felt nothing but antipathy as she listened to the old lady's animadversions. Obviously, Mrs. Sherry cared far more for the grudge than for the grievance. She had none of Aileen's nausea at the damage to a beautiful object or her despair for the soul of the perpetrator.

"Some black boy, of course," Mrs. Sherry was grumbling. "Unless it was a Puerto Rican. They're always prating about the hard times they've had, always griping about how they've been deprived of education and opportunities. Is *this* what they want opportunities for? I'd like to see the cat-o'-nine-tails brought back. I'd like to see these boys lashed before the public in Times Square! What do they exist for but to tear our world apart? They don't care that they have nothing to put in its place! It's revenge, pure and simple."

"Revenge," Aileen murmured thoughtfully, glancing apprehensively through the doorway toward the iron grille. Could it be the revenge of a Yankee prisoner of war? But why? Revenge against whom?

"Everybody's too soft and sentimental with them," Mrs. Sherry continued. "If it *is* softness. If it isn't just cowardice, as I suspect it is. Where have our guts gone to, Miss Post? Where are our men, that we are exposed to all this? I tell you one thing, young lady. Nobody would have poked an eye out of Valerian Ludlow's portrait in his day!"

"What would he have done?"

"Don't you know what he would have done? Haven't you read his journal? *He* knew how to handle insubordinates!"

As Aileen watched the terrible old woman, she had just for a second the same eerie sense of blackness that she had experienced in peering through the iron grille. Then, as it passed, she felt a sudden, odd detachment from the immediate scene. She found herself observing Mrs. Sherry as if the latter had been a monologist performing at a private party. She noted the protuberance of the front molars and the drops of saliva at the corners of the thin lips. She marked how the almost transparent, onionskin eyelids snapped up and down and how hatefully dark were the merciless eyes. Except for the teeth Mrs. Sherry might have been a bird, a big, dark bird of rich, subdued colors whose feathers only made more horrible its dark face and beak, a condor tearing at a carcass. Both of Aileen's hands went to her lips in horror as she saw her world in a sudden new light. The feathers, the feathers alone, were art. The head, the beak, the glazed eyes, the talons were—man!

"Oh, be quiet! Be quiet, please!"

Mrs. Sherry stared down at Aileen incredulously. "I beg your pardon?"

When Aileen, stunned, gathered that she must have actually uttered her reproach aloud, she desperately summoned up the courage to go on. "You're saying the most dreadful things, and you have no business to. You don't know who damaged that portrait. You have no idea. It might have been a guard. It might have been me. It might have been you, yourself!" Aileen rose as if propelled by two strong hands clutching her elbows, and she spoke with a passionate urgency, a wondering, bemused prisoner of her own new flow of eloquence. "How do I know that you're not just trying to get someone in trouble? Or a whole race of people in trouble? How do I know what mad, twisted motives you may have? Look at your umbrella. You might have done it with *that!* But, my God, there's something sticking to it!" She seized the umbrella and rushed out into the gallery crying, "Guard! Guard!" When the bewildered man hurried up to her she shouted, "I've got her! The vandal! She did it with this! Look!"

Here she held the umbrella up to the portrait, the tip toward the hole. Then she lowered it slowly, dumbly, apologetically, looking shamefaced at the shamefaced guard. For the round tip of the umbrella had a thick rubber cover. Mrs. Sherry must have made it do double duty as a walking stick. Pushed into a canvas, it would have made a much bigger hole than the one in Valerian Ludlow's left eye.

"And now, Miss Post, will you be so good as to return my property? And let me ask this gentleman to conduct me to the director of this institution that I may complain of your insane behavior?"

Mrs. Sherry was so carried away that, turning from the stricken Aileen after she had snatched back her umbrella, she made the mistake of taking the guard's arm. Her exit was comic rather than magnificent. But nothing could console Aileen.

Tony, when he came, was very kind. He said that the vandalism had obviously unnerved her. He regretted that so important a member of the museum as Mrs. Sherry should have been insulted, but he hoped that she could be placated. He suggested that Aileen would do well to take a few days off and get a good rest.

"No, I'm all right, I really am," she insisted in a stony voice. "I promise, you won't have to worry about me."

When Tony had left, obviously much concerned about her, Aileen sat for ten minutes, absolutely still. Then she rose and strode with a new resolution to the middle of the gallery. As she leaned slowly down and stared into the hated window, she whispered hoarsely:

"Who are you, in there? Why have you come back to haunt us? Are you the spirit of some poor boy who died in that black chamber?" As she listened, she felt her first impulse of sympathy for whatever might be behind those bars. She had a vision of a thin, undernourished face, that of some nineteen-year-old Yankee boy, with long light hair and eyes liquid with homesickness, pressed up against the bars. "Were you left behind in General Washington's retreat? Was that how the British caught you? But why do you hate the Ludlows? Wasn't their house requisitioned by the governor? Was that their fault?" In the silence, as she listened intently, she had again that eerie sense of a close malevolence. "Or do you know something about them that we don't know? Was Valerian Ludlow a secret Tory? Was he a traitor?"

The blackness that she imagined behind the bars seemed now to lift, and her eyes fell upon the great portrait in the corner of the gallery of General Cornwallis, his hand on a globe on which the eastern shoreline of the thirteen colonies was clearly visible. Aileen straightened up and returned to her office. There would be no further revelations that day.

The following morning she was greeted by the doorman with the news: "There's been another of them vandals in your gallery, Miss Post." When she arrived at her floor, breathless, after running up two flights, she found Tony and three guards standing before the glass case of the silver tankards. He silently pointed to something as she hurried to his side. On the top tray one of the tankards lay toppled over. Its cover had been wrenched off the hinges and had fallen to the bottom of the case. The coat of arms had been gashed several times by a heavy instrument, possibly a stone. She did not have to look twice to recognize the Ludlow crest.

"Nobody's to touch it until the detective from the police department comes," Tony explained. "This is a weird one. The glass, you see, has not been removed." He put his arm around Aileen's shoulders and led her out of earshot of the guards. "It had to be an inside job," he told her. "Whoever did it must have got the key to the case from your office. But we've checked, and your key case is locked. He may have slipped into your office one day when it was open, taken the key, had it duplicated and put it back. It might have been the same guy who used your umbrella to poke the hole in the Ludlow portrait while you were out to lunch."

"*My* umbrella!"

"Well, I didn't want to upset you, but we found a smitch of canvas by the rack in your office where you keep your pink umbrella. It has to be some nut, of course, with some fantastic grudge against the Ludlow family."

"Oh, you've put that together, have you?" she murmured. "You've recognized the Ludlow tankard?"

"My dear Aileen. Even though I'm a museum director, I'm not a complete nincompoop."

Aileen was seized with a fit of violent trembling. She felt the same fierce prosecuting excitement that she had experienced when she had denounced Mrs. Sherry to the guard. Pulling Tony further away down the gallery, she whispered desperately, "Maybe *I* did it! Maybe I poked the hole in the portrait and then tried to throw the blame on Mrs. Sherry! Maybe I came here last night and let myself into the gallery and scraped the tankard!"

Tony's little smile never failed him, but she could tell by the way it seemed just to flicker that he did not wholly dismiss the theory. "But assuming all this, my dear, what on earth would be your motive?"

"I had no motive."

"Then why would you do it?"

"Because I'm the instrument of a fiend! The fiend that you brought in when you made me take *that!*"

Tony took in the little barred window, and at last even his smile ceased. "I said before that you needed a rest," he replied in his kindest tone. "This time I insist upon it. I want you to take three weeks off, and I want you to see a doctor."

Aileen was surprised and heartened by her own reaction to this disaster. Instead of crumpling before circumstance, she discovered that her spirit was strong and her emotional state serene. When Tony told her that the police detective had said that the force used in rubbing the stone or other substance against the crest of the Ludlow tankard had been greater than that of a woman, she had merely nodded and taken her dignified leave of him. She had recovered faith in her own sanity and did not need the confirmation of a cop. She had promised that she would consult a psychiatrist, but she was already resolved that she would not. There was no use in a confrontation between the world of medicine and the occult. It could result only in her commitment to a lunatic asylum.

She was grateful for the solitude of her enforced vacation and of the time that it afforded her to deal with her ghostly opponent. For she knew now that she had one. No human being could help her. It was her grim and lonely task to track down and outwit the sinister spirit that was seeking to destroy her gallery.

She spent her days in the library of the New-York Historical Society, reading everything that there was to be read on the history of the Ludlow family. The material was rich. She found considerable evidence of a curious effeminate streak in the Ludlow males of the eighteenth century. The first Ludlow in New York, a royal governor, had insisted on wearing woman's robes while presiding at the council, on the theory that he thus more appropriately represented his sovereign, Queen Anne. A generation later, his son had been criticized for making his more muscular African slaves wait on table half-naked, and this son's son, in turn, incurred the resentment of society by keeping exotic birds, expensively imported from Rio, loose in the house where they pecked his guests. The wives of all these gentlemen, on the other hand, had been big, blocky, plainly dressed women, such as one might expect in a community that was still, after all, almost the frontier.

Aileen, like many old-maid scholars, was as sophisticated about the past as she was timid about the present, and she perfectly understood that there might have been a streak of cruelty, or even sadism, in such eccentrics as the male Ludlows. But nowhere could she find the slightest evidence that any of them had been guilty of any public or private injustice, and the record of Valerian Ludlow in the Revolution seemed to repudiate the least imputation of Toryism. She had come almost to the end of her documents when a librarian asked her if she would like to see the microfilm of the manuscript of Valerian Ludlow's journal.

"I should like to look at it, of course," she replied. "I've read it so often in print, I know it almost by heart."

"You mean the DeLancey Tyler edition."

"Well, yes. Isn't that the only one? It's supposed to be complete."

"*Supposed* to be."

Aileen looked more closely at the young man. "You mean it isn't?"

He shrugged. "Tyler was a great-grandson of the journalist. He published his book in 1900. You know how prudish people were in those days."

Aileen knew by the bound of her heart that her search was over. She spent the next two days tensely reading the diary of Valerian Ludlow on the microfilm machine. The librarian had been quite right. There were substantial sections omitted in the Tyler edition. Ludlow had been a vain and easily offended gentleman of exquisite tastes and domineering manner. He had entered in the journal every slight that he had imagined himself to have received, and he had carefully recorded every punishment meted out to a servant. His descendant and editor had left in all his purchases of artifacts, all his recorded dealings with architects and decorators, all his conversations with the great, but he had carefully suppressed the invidious details of the correction of his staff and family. Aileen read breathlessly as she cranked the machine, turning the pages of the neat, flowing, somehow merciless handwriting. The realization that she was on the threshold of her revelation was actually painful.

She found at last this entry, dated July 30, 1747:

> I have neglected my journal for a week because of a disturbing episode which, through God's grace, has now ended happily for most but not all. A group of slaves last Tuesday seized a farm on Lydecker Street and held it against the bailiff and his men for twenty-four hours. What the purpose of these ignorant fellows was we do not know, and they all fled. One constable, however, was killed when his own rifle blew up in his face. Public feeling has been very passionate, and on Thursday morning a large mob called here to demand my Rolfe. I met the leaders at the doorstep, and, I must say, they were very civil. They explained their reasons for believing that Rolfe had

been the leading insurrectionist. I found these reasons convincing, the more so as I had had to confine Rolfe to the storeroom only that morning for insubordination. I delivered him up for what I understood was to be a trial, but I doubt that he had one. What is sure is that the mob burnt him alive in Bowling Green. It was a slow fire, and they say the poor fellow's bellows could be heard for six hours. I have discussed this unfortunate matter with Attorney Reynolds, and he advises me that if no trial occurred, I may be able to demand the price of Rolfe from the City Council, as he was taken under a show of authority.

Aileen turned from the machine with a gasp and rocked to and fro in her agony. For minutes she writhed as if she had been that wretched creature on the fire. How could flesh endure it? Six *hours?* The tears came at last to her eyes as she gave herself up to the relief of hating mankind. Mankind? Could she hate Rolfe, too, bellowing hour after hour, bound over a small flame like a sausage? Could she hate the man who must have listened, agonized, at that storeroom window while his master negotiated with the mob? Oh, God, God! But there was no God. There was only beauty, and whatever commiseration she felt for Rolfe she had to prevent him from destroying that. She jumped up as she came out of her daze. If she were only in time!

When her taxi arrived at the museum she fled up the steps and jammed her way through the revolving door.

"Is everything all right, Tom?" she asked the doorman.

"Never a dull moment these days, Miss Post. We had quite a scare an hour ago in your gallery. There was some defective wiring in the broom closet that started a small fire. We've had the chief and hook and ladder and all. Some excitement! But it's all out now."

She bounded up the two flights to her office and fumbled crazily among her keys until she found the one for the prison window's case. Then she sped down the gallery and opened it. She paused for just a moment as she faced the hated bars, and murmuring, "Forgive me, Rolfe," she picked them up and bore them to the window over the courtyard. Looking down to be sure there was no one beneath, she shoved them out, closing her eyes as she heard the clangor of the smashing to a hundred pieces.

For a moment she felt as if someone were pulling her over the sill, dragging her after it. With a violent effort she bounded back and stared about her. She was alone, perfectly alone, although below she could hear the shouts of the alarmed guards. In a moment they would come up, and all would be over. She would lose the job that was simply her whole life. As the inky depression began to surge and bubble about her, like rising water in a filthy tub, she saw at last what it was that the squatting spirit had been after.

"Why me?" she could only groan. "Why, in God's name, me? Was it such a crime to think that even their possessions were beautiful?"

Bryan MacMahon

The Broken Lyre

THE DARK-FACED MELODEON-PLAYER, HIS INSTRUMENT SLUNG FROM A strap over his left shoulder, hurried through the town where the cattle fair had long since ended. Stravaging behind him came his red-haired wife, recurrently freeing her forearms from the irk of her red-green tartan shawl and shrieking coarse insults at her husband in the savage hope that he would turn and strike her. Farmers standing at pub doors watched the pair with amusement.

The musician turned the corner leading into the Market Square. As, momentarily, he was out of his wife's sight, he moved swiftly in the direction of the caravans and carts that were halted beside a small church in mid-square, the walls of which were aflame with the red-gold of Virginia creeper. The woman turned the corner; then, her anger further whetted by the trick her husband had played on her, she gave a cry of animal anger and ran full pelt after him. Sensing her approach the melodeon-player veered away from the caravans and strode quickly toward the door of a public house. His manhood would not allow him to run; thus it was that the panting woman readily caught up with him. Grasping his jacket by the shoulder, she swung him around. The man raised his right arm to strike his wife, but, thinking better of it, allowed the arm to droop wearily by his side.

"Say it ag'in!" the woman screamed.

"Go 'way from me!" the husband said darkly.

Dancing with anger, the woman shrieked: "Call it to me now, where there's witnesses to hear it!"

The musician wearily raised his head. In each wicked eye a small ember blazed. "If you don't go 'way, I'll hang for you!" he said quietly, but with full venom.

As he turned away, the woman, still screaming incoherently, snatched at him. He dragged himself away, leaving in her grasp a rag of his jacket for hostage. Again she stumbled before him. Panting, the pair eyed one another. The twin crescents of white in the melodeon-player's eyes indicated that he was secretly watching the watching farmers.

As his wife readied her talons to claw his face, the musician said desperately: "If you don't let me be, I swear to you in God that I'll kick the gadget!"

"I dar' you!" the woman screamed. Then, her talons ready, her hair mad, and her shawl trailing unheeded in the dirt, she rushed at him. He dodged accurately as she sped by him on high-heeled shoes that were relics of cast-off finery.

When he had made an angle from which she could not readily renew her attack, he deftly grasped his swinging melodeon, flicked off the clasps, and, as its red bellows were discovered in the sunlight, he let the instrument fall from him to the ground. He then drove his heavy shoe fairly through the raucous chord of protest to which the instrument was giving vent. Again and again he lashed out savagely. Once the boot was trapped in the melodeon's middle. This added to the traveling man's anger; he wrenched it free and with a final kick reduced the instrument to two disparate black boards to each of which rags of corrugated cardboard were still attached.

The onlookers were silent. With everything of the earth in their stolidity they continued to watch.

The woman's new-toned scream came from one who sees her fire and food being destroyed. As the scream wheeled downwards to lamentation, the woman began ceremoniously to draw her talons through the tangles of her red hair. She tossed her head, extended her rigid hands and allowed her nostrils fully to flare. Stiff and erect she stood above the flung brilliance of her shawl. Stolid and black-dog-like, her husband, with lowered head, continued to watch her—objectively almost—as if comparing the quality of this rage with that of other rages he had known.

In the midst of her trance the woman shed her rigidity and became astonishingly lissom. When at last she came flying at her husband, he waited for her and struck her full in the face. As she returned to the attack he struck her again and again with that strange accuracy that lies beyond desperation. The woman sobbed, reeled and fell.

An ex-soldier had pushed his way out from the adjoining publichouse. He was wearing a soft hat pinched to a crude tricorn; on the back of each of his hands were the muted cobalt patterns of tatooing. With a curse, he buttoned his jacket and advanced on the melodeon-player.

"Hey, there!" he called out in a tone of tipsy outrage.

"Keep out!" the melodeon-player warned.

"You savage!" the ex-soldier said, staggering the musician with a direct blow.

Fierce, mauling fighting began. Fist met flesh and rang the bone behind it. The traveling man had youth on his side but the irregular food of the road had sapped his body's strength. That the ex-soldier had learned the elements of boxing was evident from his stance and guard; yet it seemed that advancing age detracted somewhat from the advantage of his experience. After a few moments of indecisive fighting it became clear that the ex-soldier still possessed sufficient skill to gain victory over a travelling man whose face was by this time utterly bloodied.

The woman had sunk to the kerb-stone. Her palms kept fondling her bewildered cheeks. For a time she seemed awed by the fire her anger had lighted. Realizing that her man tottered on the edge of defeat, dullness disappeared from her face. She glanced quickly about her. One of the farmers in the circle of bystanders was loosely holding a strong ash crop between his fingers. Rising and moving with agility the woman snapped the crop out of the farmer's hand. The farmer laughed and let her have the weapon.

Grasping the stick by its lighter end the woman moved catlike to where the ex-soldier had his back turned to her. Her reeling husband put all he had into an attack designed to fling the ex-soldier within the range of his wife's stick. The ruse was successful; viciously the woman brought the crop down on the ex-soldier's head. The crimped hat was sent flying to the cowdung of the street.

The ex-soldier did not fall. Bareheaded, hair cropped close to its black roots, his eyes still on his enemies, he crouched and drew apart. The crowd dully watched him shake his head free of vertigo. Then, as he feigned terror of a sudden drop into unconsciousness, he shambled for a few steps like a sick ape. When he had interposed the melodeon-player between him and the woman, he rushed with ferocity at the man and with two swift blows knocked him senseless on the roadway.

As the woman closed with him he grasped the stick she held and tried furiously to wrest it from her. The stick cracked in their grasp—the ex-soldier tossed it aside and hurtled the swaying woman from him—she keeled over and fell on her rump, to be up again quickly like a clever toy. This time, however, instead of coming at him she stood apart, her eyes fully ablaze. Then she began to cry out for help in the secret language of the Irish roads.

The doors of the caravans under the steeple were torn open and the square became suddenly peopled with red-headed men wearing bright plaid shirts. As they meshed out in a quick arc, the ex-soldier's mouth opened in terror of the semi-known. He dared not stoop to retrieve his hat lest this action should brand him as the musician's assailant.

He tried to back away in the direction of the black asphalt road that raced out of the square and downhill between high demesne walls into the open country of the south. In his agitation he turned; then the blood slow-running from his crown readily identified him as the culprit: if this were insufficient the woman cursing him loudly and pointing frenziedly in his direction was more than enough to make her friends come after him and kill him. The tinkers came running. The farmers continued to remain aloof.

Realizing that his danger was now extreme, the ex-soldier took to his heels and ran pell-mell out of the square. The tinkers came lumbering after, crying out with the cry of hounds close on their quarry. Two young tinkers, who were last out of the caravans, laughed suddenly and sprang lithely on to the body of a flat spring-cart. One stood up straight in the vehicle and, using the free loop of the rein as whip, lashed out at the piebald pony where it slumbered beneath the glitter of gee-gawed harness: the other, a thin smile on his lips and a heavy-ended ash crop in easy equipoise between the thumb and finger of his right hand, vaulted smilingly to the sideboard of the vehicle.

This then was the chase: the bloody-polled ex-soldier in front, the running tinkers lumbering after, and the harnessed spring-cart, all silver and bells, moving swiftly behind.

The ex-soldier gave promise of outdistancing his immediate pursuers: the farmers watching from the crest of the height observed his head move downwards through the evening sun that had brought the left-hand demesne wall to the full color of orange. As the spring-cart outdistanced them, the tinkers on foot slowed up.

The ex-soldier, whose recurrent backward glances of terror had been directed at those who pursued him on foot, suddenly realized the menace of the approaching vehicle. For a few dazed moments he hesitated—the piebald pony, the flashing harness and the chiaroscuro on the lighted wall seemed to add to his befuddlement. As, with a final fearful glance over his shoulder, he noticed the young standing tinker, his supple body swaying with every movement of the headlong vehicle, and also the seated tinker with the surety of the kill inherent in his indolent poise and the anticipation of the kill implicit in the smile on his cruel lips, the ex-soldier cried out in his agony. The unshod pony drew closer upon him: the ex-soldier glanced in anguish to left and right, seeking in vain to find a breach in the merciless walls.

The sitting tinker spat into the palm of the hand holding the weapon. His eyes never left his quarry. Skilfully the driver veered to the right, forcing the ex-soldier to keep close to the left wall or be run down. The ex-soldier then tried a trick of which the pair of young tinkers had foreknowledge: stopping suddenly by the wall he crouched and laced his fingers about his blood-pied poll. Immediately the driver drew on the reins and brought the vehicle as close to the wall as was necessary for his comrade's purpose.

The seated tinker made no error: he gathered his body to tautness, allowed the weapon to droop over his shoulder and, as the spring-cart hammered past, he drove the heavy knob of his weapon fair through the wickerwork of flesh to crunch audibly on the ex-soldier's skull. For a moment or two the crouching position of the ex-soldier seemed unaltered, then what was a taut ball of humanity disintegrated. The broken body keeled and fell ignominiously on its head.

The pair of tinkers rode on for a short distance, then, glancing behind them, the shouts of victory died on their lips as they saw the cap-badges of the advancing Guards. Furiously they lashed the pony and rode into the open southlands.

The melodeon-player had picked himself up and escaped in the mêlée. Glancing neither to right nor to left and with his cap drawn well down over his injured features, he moved swiftly through the streets. His wife, brazening out her innocence, moved at some little distance behind him. Carefully she followed her husband as he made out of the town by the north road that wound its way into the uplands. The golden evening light was everywhere and the rooks moved overhead in a regiment.

Soon they had reached the warm farmlands where long shadows in the stubble vouched for the cumulative majesty of the corn stooks. There was no one on the road but the man and the woman. After a while she ventured to call out his name. When he did not indicate that he had heard her, her voice grew more piteous in its appeal. She hastened her steps but her high-heeled shoes broke her gait. At length, drawing almost level with him, she walked with him for a while, keeping the half-pace of subjection behind his shoulder.

Walking thus, they reached the parapet of an old limestone bridge. The woman laid her hand on her husband's forearm.

"I'll wash your face, Mick!" she said, quietly. She gentled him down by the boreen that led from the bridge end to the stream below. He was listless and remote. At her bidding he knelt on the gravel at the stream's edge. She knelt beside him and, as her shawl slipped from her shoulder, she dipped her gown-end into the stream and began to pat his damaged face. He allowed her to do so, yet did not break his silence.

When his face was washed, she patted him dry. He remained in the same listless attitude. As he looked down at his empty hands his face showed a tendency to break. At this the woman stroked the track the melodeon-strap had burned on the shoulder of his jacket. Then slowly her lips came apart and her face moved toward his. She brought her teeth tenderly to caress his ear-rim.

"Me an' you, Mick," she whispered, "an' the world ag'in us!"

He nodded comprehendingly.

They remained there kneeling in that small vessel of the dusk. In the little stream beside them the pebbles rang faintly. Then, with that brisk exclamation of throwing trouble away that all women use on occasion, the musician's wife stood up.

"Come!" she said.

Slowly he rose. For a moment or two as they stood breast to breast the man and woman were burnished with evening gold.

James Baldwin

Sonny's Blues

I READ ABOUT IT IN THE PAPER, IN THE SUBWAY, ON MY WAY TO WORK. I read it, and I couldn't believe it, and I read it again. Then perhaps I just stared at it, at the newsprint spelling out his name, spelling out the story. I stared at it in the swinging lights of the subway car, and in the faces and bodies of the people, and in my own face, trapped in the darkness which roared outside.

It was not to be believed and I kept telling myself that as I walked from the subway station to the high school. And at the same time I couldn't doubt it. I was scared, scared for Sonny. He became real to me again. A great block of ice got settled in my belly and kept melting there slowly all day long, while I taught my classes algebra. It was a special kind of ice. It kept melting, sending trickles of ice water all up and down my veins, but it never got less. Sometimes it hardened and seemed to expand until I felt my guts were going to come spilling out or that I was going to choke or scream. This would always be at a moment when I was remembering some specific thing Sonny had once said or done.

When he was about as old as the boys in my classes his face had been bright and open, there was a lot of copper in it; and he'd had wonderfully direct brown eyes, and great gentleness and privacy. I wondered what he looked like now. He had been picked up, the evening before, in a raid on an apartment downtown, for peddling and using heroin.

I couldn't believe it: but what I mean by that is that I couldn't find any room for it anywhere inside me. I had kept it outside me for a long time. I hadn't wanted to know. I had had suspicions, but I didn't name them, I kept putting them away. I told myself that Sonny was wild, but he wasn't crazy. And he'd always been a good boy, he hadn't ever turned hard or evil or disrespectful, the way kids can, so quick, so quick, especially in Harlem. I didn't want to believe that I'd ever see my brother going down, coming to nothing, all that light in his face gone out, in the condition I'd already seen so many others. Yet it had happened and here I was, talking about algebra to a lot of boys who might, every one of them for all I knew, be popping off needles every time they went to the head. Maybe it did more for them than algebra could.

I was sure that the first time Sonny had ever had horse, he couldn't have been much older than these boys were now. These boys, now, were living as we'd been living then, they were growing up with a rush and their heads bumped abruptly against the low ceiling of their actual possibilities. They were filled with rage. All they really knew were two darknesses, the darkness of their lives, which was now closing in on them, and the darkness of the movies, which had blinded them to that other darkness, and in which they now, vindictively, dreamed, at once more together than they were at any other time, and more alone.

When the last bell rang, the last class ended, I let out my breath. It seemed I'd been holding it for all that time. My clothes were wet—I may have looked as though I'd been sitting in a steam bath, all dressed up, all afternoon. I sat alone in the classroom a long time. I listened to the boys outside, downstairs, shouting and cursing and laughing. Their laughter struck me for perhaps the first time. It was not the joyous laughter which—God knows why—one associates with children. It was mocking and insular, its intent was to denigrate. It was disenchanted, and in this, also, lay the authority of their curses. Perhaps I was listening to them because I was thinking about my brother and in them I heard my brother. And myself.

One boy was whistling a tune, at once very complicated and very simple, it seemed to be pouring out of him as though he were a bird, and it sounded very cool and moving through all that harsh, bright air, only just holding its own through all those other sounds.

I stood up and walked over to the window and looked down into the courtyard. It was the beginning of the spring and the sap was rising in the boys. A teacher passed through them every now and again, quickly, as though he or she couldn't wait to get out of that courtyard, to get those boys out of their sight and off their minds. I started collecting my stuff. I thought I'd better get home and talk to Isabel.

The courtyard was almost deserted by the time I got downstairs. I saw this boy standing in the shadow of a doorway, looking just like Sonny. I almost called his name. Then I saw that it wasn't Sonny, but somebody we used to know, a boy from around our block. He'd been Sonny's friend. He'd never been mine, having been too young for me, and, anyway, I'd never liked him. And now, even though he was a grown-up man, he still hung around that block, still spent hours on the street corner, was always high and raggy. I used to run into him from time to time and he'd often work around to asking me for a quarter or fifty cents. He always had some real good excuse, too, and I always gave it to him, I don't know why.

But now, abruptly, I hated him. I couldn't stand the way he looked at me, partly like a dog, partly like a cunning child. I wanted to ask him what the hell he was doing in the school courtyard.

He sort of shuffled over to me, and he said, "I see you got the papers. So you already know about it."

"You mean about Sonny? Yes, I already know about it. How come they didn't get you?"

He grinned. It made him repulsive and it also brought to mind what he'd looked like as a kid. "I wasn't there. I stay away from them people."

"Good for you." I offered him a cigarette and I watched him through the smoke. "You come all the way down here just to tell me about Sonny?"

"That's right." He was sort of shaking his head and his eyes looked strange, as though they were about to cross. The bright sun deadened his damp dark brown skin and it make his eyes look yellow and showed up the dirt in his conked hair. He smelled funky. I moved a little away from him and I said, "Well, thanks. But I already know about it and I got to get home."

"I'll walk you a little ways," he said. We started walking. There were a couple of kids still loitering in the courtyard and one of them said good night to me and looked strangely at the boy beside me.

"What're you going to do?" he asked me. "I mean, about Sonny?"

"Look. I haven't seen Sonny for over a year, I'm not sure I'm going to do anything. Anyway, what the hell *can* I do?"

"That's right," he said quickly, "ain't nothing you can do. Can't much help old Sonny no more, I guess."

It was what I was thinking and so it seemed to me he had no right to say it.

"I'm surprised at Sonny, though," he went on—he had a funny way of talking, he looked straight ahead as though he were talking to himself—"I thought Sonny was a smart boy, I thought he was too smart to get hung."

"I guess he thought so too," I said sharply, "and that's how he got hung. And how about you? You're pretty goddamn smart, I bet."

Then he looked directly at me, just for a minute. "I ain't smart," he said. "If I was smart, I'd have reached for a pistol a long time ago."

"Look. Don't tell *me* your sad story, if it was up to me, I'd give you one." Then I felt guilty—guilty, probably, for never having supposed that the poor bastard *had* a story of his own, much less a sad one, and I asked, quickly, "What's going to happen to him now?"

He didn't answer this. He was off by himself some place. "Funny thing," he said, and from his tone we might have been discussing the quickest way to get to Brooklyn, "when I saw the papers this morning, the first thing I asked myself was if I had anything to do with it. I felt sort of responsible."

I began to listen more carefully. The subway station was on the corner, just before us, and I stopped. He stopped, too. We were in front of a bar and he ducked slightly, peering in, but whoever he was looking for didn't seem to be there. The juke box was blasting away with something black and bouncy and I half watched the barmaid as she danced her way from the juke box to her place behind the bar. And I watched her face as she laughingly responded to something someone said to her, still keeping time to the music. When she smiled one saw the little girl, one sensed the doomed, still-struggling woman beneath the battered face of the semi-whore.

"I never *give* Sonny nothing," the boy said finally, "but a long time ago I come to school high and Sonny asked me how it felt." He paused, I couldn't bear to watch him, I watched the barmaid, and I listened to the music which seemed to be causing the pavement to shake. "I told him it felt great." The music stopped, the barmaid paused and watched the juke box until the music began again. "It did."

All this was carrying me some place I didn't want to go. I certainly didn't want to know how it felt. It filled everything, the people, the houses, the music, the dark, quicksilver barmaid, with menace; and this menace was their reality.

"What's going to happen to him now?" I asked again.

"They'll send him away some place and they'll try to cure him." He shook his head. "Maybe he'll even think he's kicked the habit. Then they'll let him loose"—He gestured, throwing his cigarette into the gutter. "That's all."

"What do you mean, that's *all?*"

But I knew what he meant.

"I *mean,* that's *all.*" He turned his head and looked at me, pulling down the corners of his mouth. "Don't you know what I mean?" he asked, softly.

"How the hell *would* I know what you mean?" I almost whispered it, I don't know why.

"That's right," he said to the air, "how would *he* know what I mean?" He turned toward me again, patient and calm, and yet I somehow felt him shaking, shaking as though he were going to fall apart. I felt that ice in my guts again, the dread I'd felt all afternoon; and again I watched the barmaid, moving about the bar, washing glasses, and singing. "Listen. They'll let him out and then it'll just start all over again. That's what I mean."

"You mean—they'll let him out. And then he'll just start working his way back in again. You mean he'll never kick the habit. Is that what you mean?"

"That's right," he said, cheerfully. "*You* see what I mean."

"Tell me," I said at last, "why does he want to die? He must want to die, he's killing himself, why does he want to die?"

He looked at me in surprise. He licked his lips. "He don't want to die. He wants to live. Don't nobody want to die, ever."

Then I wanted to ask him—too many things. He could not have answered, or if he had, I could not have borne the answers. I started walking. "Well, I guess it's none of my business."

"It's going to be rough on old Sonny," he said. We reached the subway station. "This is your station?" he asked. I nodded. I took one step down. "Damn!" he said, suddenly. I looked up at him. He grinned again. "Damn if I didn't leave all my money home. You ain't got a dollar on you, have you? Just for a couple of days, is all."

All at once something inside gave and threatened to come pouring out of me. I didn't hate him any more. I felt that in another moment I'd start crying like a child.

"Sure," I said. "Don't sweat." I looked in my wallet and didn't have a dollar, I only had a five. "Here," I said. "That hold you?"

He didn't look at it—he didn't want to look at it. A terrible, closed look came over his face, as though he were keeping the number on the bill a secret from him and me. "Thanks," he said, and now he was dying to see me go. "Don't worry about Sonny. Maybe I'll write him or something."

"Sure," I said. "You do that. So long."
"Be seeing you," he said. I went on down the steps.

And I didn't write Sonny or send him anything for a long time. When I
finally did, it was just after my little girl died, he wrote me back a letter which
made me feel like a bastard.

Here's what he said:

> Dear brother,
> You don't know how much I needed to hear from you. I wanted to write
> you many a time but I dug how much I must have hurt you and so I didn't
> write. But now I feel like a man who's been trying to climb up out of some
> deep, real deep and funky hole and just saw the sun up there, outside. I got
> to get outside.
> I can't tell you much about how I got here. I mean I don't know how to
> tell you. I guess I was afraid of something or I was trying to escape from
> something and you know I never never been very strong in the head (smile).
> I'm glad Mama and Daddy are dead and can't see what's happened to their
> son and I swear if I'd known what I was doing I would never have hurt you
> so, you and a lot of other fine people who were nice to me and who believed
> in me.
> I don't want you to think it had anything to do with me being a musician.
> It's more than that. Or maybe less than that. I can't get anything straight in
> my head down here and I try not to think about what's going to happen to
> me when I get outside again. Sometime I think I'm going to flip and never
> get outside and sometime I think I'll come straight back. I tell you one thing,
> though, I'd rather blow my brains out than go through this again. But that's
> what they all say, so they tell me. If I tell you when I'm coming to New York
> and if you could meet me, I sure would appreciate it. Give my love to Isabel
> and the kids and I was sure sorry to hear about little Gracie. I wish I could
> be like Mama and say the Lord's will be done, but I don't know it seems to
> me that trouble is the one thing that never does get stopped and I don't know
> what good it does to blame it on the Lord. But maybe it does some good if
> you believe it.
>
> Your brother,
>
> SONNY

Then I kept in constant touch with him and I sent him whatever I could
and I went to meet him when he came back to New York. When I saw him
many things I thought I had forgotten came flooding back to me. This was
because I had begun, finally, to wonder about Sonny, about the life that Sonny
lived inside. This life, whatever it was, had made him older and thinner and
it had deepened the distant stillness in which he had always moved. He looked
very unlike my baby brother. Yet, when he smiled, when we shook hands, the
baby brother I'd never known looked out from the depths of his private life,
like an animal waiting to be coaxed into the light.

"How you been keeping?" he asked me.

"All right. And you?"

"Just fine." He was smiling all over his face. "It's good to see you again."

"It's good to see you."

The seven years' difference in our ages lay between us like a chasm: I wondered if these years would ever operate between us as a bridge. I was remembering, and it made it hard to catch my breath, that I had been there when he was born; and I had heard the first words he had ever spoken. When he started to walk, he walked from our mother straight to me. I caught him just before he fell when he took the first steps he ever took in this world.

"How's Isabel?"

"Just fine. She's dying to see you."

"And the boys?"

"They're fine, too. They're anxious to see their uncle."

"Oh, come on. You know they don't remember me."

"Are you kidding? Of course they remember you."

He grinned again. We got into a taxi. We had a lot to say to each other, far too much to know how to begin.

As the taxi began to move, I asked, "You still want to go to India?"

He laughed. "You still remember that. Hell, no. This place is Indian enough for me."

"It used to belong to them," I said.

And he laughed again. "They damn sure knew what they were doing when they got rid of it."

Years ago, when he was around fourteen, he'd been all hipped on the idea of going to India. He read books about people sitting on rocks, naked, in all kinds of weather, but mostly bad, naturally, and walking barefoot through hot coals and arriving at wisdom. I used to say that it sounded to me as though they were getting away from wisdom as fast as they could. I think he sort of looked down on me for that.

"Do you mind," he asked, "if we have the driver drive alongside the park? On the west side—I haven't seen the city in so long."

"Of course not," I said. I was afraid that I might sound as though I were humoring him, but I hoped he wouldn't take it that way.

So we drove along, between the green of the park and the stony, lifeless elegance of hotels and apartment buildings, toward the vivid, killing streets of our childhood. These streets hadn't changed, though housing projects jutted up out of them now like rocks in the middle of a boiling sea. Most of the houses in which we had grown up had vanished, as had the stores from which we had stolen, the basements in which we had first tried sex, the rooftops from which we had hurled tin cans and bricks. But houses exactly like the houses of our past yet dominated the landscape, boys exactly like the boys we once had been found themselves smothering in these houses, came down into the streets for light and air and found themselves encircled by disaster. Some escaped the trap, most didn't. Those who got out always left something of themselves behind, as some animals amputate a leg and leave it in the trap. It might be said, perhaps, that I had escaped, after all, I was a schoolteacher; or that Sonny had, he hadn't lived in Harlem for years. Yet, as the cab moved uptown through streets which seemed, with a rush, to darken with dark people, and as I covertly studied Sonny's face, it came to me that what we both were seeking through our separate cab windows was that part of ourselves which had been left behind. It's always at the hour of trouble and confrontation that the missing member aches.

We hit 110th Street and started rolling up Lenox Avenue. And I'd known this avenue all my life, but it seemed to me again, as it had seemed on the day I'd first heard about Sonny's trouble, filled with a hidden menace which was its very breath of life.

"We almost there," said Sonny.

"Almost." We were both too nervous to say anthing more.

We live in a housing project. It hasn't been up long. A few days after it was up it seemed uninhabitably new, now, of course, it's already rundown. It looks like a parody of the good, clean, faceless life—God knows the people who live in it do their best to make it a parody. The beat-looking grass lying around isn't enough to make their lives green, the hedges will never hold out the streets, and they know it. The big windows fool no one, they aren't big enough to make space out of no space. They don't bother with the windows, they watch the TV screen instead. The playground is most popular with the children who don't play at jacks, or skip rope, or roller skate, or swing, and they can be found in it after dark. We moved in partly because it's not too far from where I teach, and partly for the kids; but it's really just like the houses in which Sonny and I grew up. The same things happen, they'll have the same things to remember. The moment Sonny and I started into the house I had the feeling that I was simply bringing him back into the danger he had almost died trying to escape.

Sonny has never been talkative. So I don't know why I was sure he'd be dying to talk to me when supper was over the first night. Everything went fine, the oldest boy remembered him, and the youngest boy liked him, and Sonny had remembered to bring something for each of them; and Isabel, who is really much nicer than I am, more open and giving, had gone to a lot of trouble about dinner and was genuinely glad to see him. And she's always been able to tease Sonny in a way that I haven't. It was nice to see her face so vivid again and to hear her laugh and watch her make Sonny laugh. She wasn't, or, anyway, she didn't seem to be, at all uneasy or embarrassed. She chatted as though there were no subject which had to be avoided and she got Sonny past his first, faint stiffness. And thank God she was there, for I was filled with that icy dread again. Everything I did seemed awkward to me, and everything I said sounded freighted with hidden meaning. I was trying to remember everything I'd heard about dope addiction and I couldn't help watching Sonny for signs. I wasn't doing it out of malice. I was trying to find out something about my brother. I was dying to hear him tell me he was safe.

"Safe!" my father grunted, whenever Mama suggested trying to move to a neighborhood which might be safer for children. "Safe, hell! Ain't no place safe for kids, nor nobody."

He always went on like this, but he wasn't, ever, really as bad as he sounded, not even on weekends, when he got drunk. As a matter of fact, he was always on the lookout for "something a little better," but he died before he found it. He died suddenly, during a drunken weekend in the middle of the war, when Sonny was fifteen. He and Sonny hadn't ever got on too well. And this was partly because Sonny was the apple of his father's eye. It was because he loved Sonny so much, and was frightened for him, and that he was always fighting with him. It doesn't do any good to fight with Sonny. Sonny just moves back, inside himself, where he can't be reached. But the principal reason that they never hit it off is that they were so much alike. Daddy was big and rough and loud-talking, just the opposite of Sonny, but they both had —that same privacy.

Mama tried to tell me something about this, just after Daddy died. I was home on leave from the army.

This was the last time I ever saw my mother alive. Just the same, this picture gets all mixed up in my mind with pictures I had of her when she was younger. The way I always see her is the way she used to be on a Sunday afternoon, say, when the old folks were talking after the big Sunday dinner. I always see her wearing pale blue. She'd be sitting on the sofa. And my father would be sitting in the easy chair, not far from her. And the living room would be full of church folks and relatives. There they sit, in chairs all around the living room, and the night is creeping up outside, but nobody knows it yet. You can see the darkness growing against the windowpanes and you hear the street noises every now and again, or maybe the jangling beat of a tambourine from one of the churches close by, but it's real quiet in the room. For a moment nobody's talking, but every face looks darkening, like the sky outside. And my mother rocks a little from the waist, and my father's eyes are closed. Everyone is looking at something a child can't see. For a minute they've forgotten the children. Maybe a kid is lying on the rug, half asleep. Maybe somebody's got a kid in his lap and is absent-mindedly stroking the kid's head. Maybe there's a kid, quiet and big-eyed, curled up in a big chair in the corner. The silence, the darkness coming, and the darkness in the faces frightens the child obscurely. He hopes that the hand which strokes his forehead will never stop—will never die. He hopes that there will never come a time when the old folks won't be sitting around the living room, talking about where they've come from, and what they've seen, and what's happened to them and their kinfolk.

But something deep and watchful in the child knows that this is bound to end, is already ending. In a moment someone will get up and turn on the light. Then the old folks will remember the children and they won't talk any more that day. And when light fills the room, the child is filled with darkness. He knows that every time this happens he's moved just a little closer to that darkness outside. The darkness outside is what the old folks have been talking

about. It's what they've come from. It's what they endure. The child knows
that they won't talk any more because if he knows too much about what's
happened to *them,* he'll know too much too soon, about what's going to
happen to *him.*

The last time I talked to my mother, I remember I was restless. I wanted
to get out and see Isabel. We weren't married then and we had a lot to
straighten out between us.

There Mama sat, in black, by the window. She was humming an old church
song, "Lord, you brought me from a long ways off." Sonny was out somewhere. Mama kept watching the streets.

"I don't know," she said, "if I'll ever see you again, after you go off from
here. But I hope you'll remember the things I tried to teach you."

"Don't talk like that," I said, and smiled. "You'll be here a long time yet."

She smiled, too, but she said nothing. She was quiet for a long time. And
I said, "Mama, don't you worry about nothing. I'll be writing all the time,
and you be getting the checks. . . ."

"I want to talk to you about your brother," she said, suddenly. "If anything
happens to me he ain't going to have nobody to look out for him."

"Mama," I said, "ain't nothing going to happen to you *or* Sonny. Sonny's
all right. He's a good boy and he's got good sense."

"It ain't a question of his being a good boy," Mama said, "nor of his having
good sense. It ain't only the bad ones, nor yet the dumb ones that gets sucked
under." She stopped, looking at me. "Your daddy once had a brother," she
said, and she smiled in a way that made me feel she was in pain. "You didn't
never know that, did you?"

"No," I said, "I never knew that," and I watched her face.

"Oh, yes," she said, "your daddy had a brother." She looked out of the
window again. "I know you never saw your daddy cry. But *I* did—many a
time, through all these years."

I asked her, "What happened to his brother? How come nobody's ever
talked about him?"

This was the first time I ever saw my mother look old.

"His brother got killed," she said, "when he was just a little younger than
you are now. I knew him. He was a fine boy. He was maybe a little full of
the devil, but he didn't mean nobody no harm."

Then she stopped and the room was silent, exactly as it had sometimes been
on those Sunday afternoons. Mama kept looking out into the streets.

"He used to have a job in the mill," she said, "and, like all young folks,
he just liked to perform on Saturday nights. Saturday nights, him and your
father would drift around to different places, go to dances and things like that,
or just sit around with people they knew, and your father's brother would
sing, he had a fine voice, and play along with himself on his guitar. Well, this
particular Saturday night, him and your father was coming home from some
place, and they were both a little drunk and there was a moon that night, it
was bright like day. Your father's brother was feeling kind of good, and he
was whistling to himself, and he had his guitar slung over his shoulder. They

was coming down a hill and beneath them was a road that turned off from the highway. Well, your father's brother, being always kind of frisky, decided to run down this hill, and he did, with that guitar banging and clanging behind him, and he ran across the road, and he was making water behind a tree. And your father was sort of amused at him and he was still coming down the hill, kind of slow. Then he heard a car motor and that same minute his brother stepped from behind the tree, into the road, in the moonlight. And he started to cross the road. And your father started to run down the hill, he says he don't know why. This car was full of white men. They was all drunk, and when they seen your father's brother they let out a great whoop and holler and they aimed the car straight at him. They was having fun, they just wanted to scare him, the way they do sometimes, you know. But they was drunk. And I guess the boy, being drunk, too, and scared, kind of lost his head. By the time he jumped it was too late. Your father says he heard his brother scream when the car rolled over him, and he heard the wood of that guitar when it give, and he heard them strings go flying, and he heard them white men shouting, and the car kept on a-going and it ain't stopped till this day. And, time your father got down the hill, his brother weren't nothing but blood and pulp."

Tears were gleaming on my mother's face. There wasn't anything I could say.

"He never mentioned it," she said, "because I never let him mention it before you children. Your daddy was like a crazy man that night and for many a night thereafter. He says he never in his life seen anything as dark as that road after the lights of that car had gone away. Weren't nothing, weren't nobody on that road, just your daddy and his brother and that busted guitar. Oh, yes. Your daddy never did really get right again. Till the day he died he weren't sure but that every white man he saw was the man that killed his brother."

She stopped and took out her handkerchief and dried her eyes and looked at me.

"I ain't telling you all this," she said, "to make you scared or bitter or to make you hate nobody. I'm telling you this because you got a brother. And the world ain't changed."

I guess I didn't want to believe this. I guess she saw this in my face. She turned away from me, toward the window again, searching those streets.

"But I praise my Redeemer," she said at last, "that He called your daddy home before me. I ain't saying it to throw no flowers at myself, but, I declare, it keeps me from feeling too cast down to know I helped your father get safely through this world. Your father always acted like he was the roughest, strongest man on earth. And everybody took him to be like that. But if he hadn't had *me* there—to see his tears!"

She was crying again. Still, I couldn't move. I said, "Lord, Lord, Mama, I didn't know it was like that."

"Oh, honey," she said, "there's a lot that you don't know. But you are going to find it out." She stood up from the window and came over to me. "You got to hold on to your brother," she said, "and don't let him fall, no matter what it looks like is happening to him and no matter how evil you gets with him. You going to be evil with him many a time. But don't you forget what I told you, you hear?"

"I won't forget," I said. "Don't you worry, I won't forget. I won't let nothing happen to Sonny."

My mother smiled as though she were amused at something she saw in my face. Then, "You may not be able to stop nothing from happening. But you got to let him know you's *there.*"

Two days later I was married, and then I was gone. And I had a lot of things on my mind and I pretty well forgot my promise to Mama until I got shipped home on a special furlough for her funeral.

And after the funeral, with just Sonny and me alone in the empty kitchen, I tried to find out something about him.

"What do you want to do?" I asked him.

"I'm going to be a musician," he said.

For he had graduated, in the time I had been away, from dancing to the juke box to finding out who was playing what, and what they were doing with it, and he had bought himself a set of drums.

"You mean, you want to be a drummer?" I somehow had the feeling that being a drummer might be all right for other people but not for my brother Sonny.

"I don't think," he said, looking at me very gravely, "that I'll ever be a good drummer. But I think I can play a piano."

I frowned. I'd never played the role of the older brother quite so seriously before, had scarcely ever, in fact, *asked* Sonny a damn thing. I sensed myself in the presence of something I didn't really know how to handle, didn't understand. So I made my frown a little deeper as I asked: "What kind of musician do you want to be?"

He grinned. "How many kinds do you think there are?"

"Be *serious,*" I said.

He laughed, throwing his head back, and then looked at me. "I *am* serious."

"Well, then, for Christ's sake, stop kidding around and answer a serious question. I mean, do you want to be a concert pianist, you want to play classical music and all that, or—or what?" Long before I finished he was laughing again. "For Christ's *sake,* Sonny!"

He sobered, but with difficulty. "I'm sorry. But you sound so—*scared!*" and he was off again.

"Well, you may think it's funny now, baby, but it's not going to be so funny when you have to make your living at it, let me tell you *that.*" I was furious because I knew he was laughing at me and I didn't know why.

"No," he said, very sober now, and afraid, perhaps, that he'd hurt me, "I don't want to be a classical pianist. That isn't what interests me. I mean"— he paused, looking hard at me, as though his eyes would help me to under-

stand, and then gestured helplessly, as though perhaps his hand would help
—"I mean, I'll have a lot of studying to do, and I'll have to study *everything*,
but, I mean, I want to play *with*—jazz musicians." He stopped. "I want to
play jazz," he said.

Well, the word had never before sounded as heavy, as real, as it sounded
that afternoon in Sonny's mouth. I just looked at him and I was probably
frowning a real frown by this time. I simply couldn't see why on earth he'd
want to spend his time hanging around night clubs, clowning around on
bandstands, while people pushed each other around a dance floor. It seemed
—beneath him, somehow. I had never thought about it before, had never been
forced to, but I suppose I had always put jazz musicians in a class with what
Daddy called "good-time people."

"Are you *serious?*"

"Hell, *yes,* I'm serious."

He looked more helpless than ever, and annoyed, and deeply hurt.

I suggested, helpfully: "You mean—like Louis Armstrong?"

His face closed as though I'd struck him. "No. I'm not talking about none
of that old-time, down-home crap."

"Well, look, Sonny, I'm sorry, don't get mad. I just don't altogether get
it, that's all. Name somebody—you know, a jazz musician you admire."

"Bird."

"Who?"

"Bird! Charlie Parker! Don't they teach you nothing in the goddamn
army?"

I lit a cigarette. I was surprised and then a little amused to discover I was
trembling. "I've been out of touch," I said. "You'll have to be patient with
me. Now. Who's this Parker character?"

"He's just one of the greatest jazz musicians alive," said Sonny, sullenly,
his hands in his pockets, his back to me. "Maybe *the* greatest," he added,
bitterly, "that's probably why *you* never heard of him."

"All right," I said, "I'm ignorant. I'm sorry. I'll go out and buy all the cat's
records right away, all right?"

"It don't," said Sonny, with dignity, "make any difference to me. I don't
care what you listen to. Don't do me no favors."

I was beginning to realize that I'd never seen him so upset before. With
another part of my mind I was thinking that this would probably turn out
to be one of those things kids go through and that I shouldn't make it seem
important by pushing it too hard. Still, I didn't think it would do any harm
to ask: "Doesn't all this take a lot of time? Can you make a living at it?"

He turned back to me and half leaned, half sat, on the kitchen table.
"Everything takes time," he said, "and—well, yes, sure, I can make a living
at it. But what I don't seem to be able to make you understand is that it's
the only thing I want to do."

"Well, Sonny," I said, gently, "you know people can't always do exactly
what they *want* to do—"

"*No,* I don't know that," said Sonny, surprising me. "I think people *ought*
to do what they want to do, what else are they alive for?"

"You getting to be a big boy," I said desperately, "it's time you started thinking about your future."

"I'm thinking about my future," said Sonny grimly. "I think about it all the time."

I gave up. I decided, if he didn't change his mind, that we could always talk about it later. "In the meantime," I said, "you got to finish school." We had already decided that he'd have to move in with Isabel and her folks. I knew this wasn't the ideal arrangement because Isabel's folks are inclined to be dicty and they hadn't especially wanted Isabel to marry me. But I didn't know what else to do. "And we have to get you fixed up at Isabel's."

There was a long silence. He moved from the kitchen table to the window. "That's a terrible idea. You know it yourself."

"Do you have a *better* idea?"

He just walked up and down the kitchen for a minute. He was as tall as I was. He had started to shave. I suddenly had the feeling that I didn't know him at all.

He stopped at the kitchen table and picked up my cigarettes. Looking at me with a kind of mocking, amused defiance, he put one between his lips. "You mind?"

"You smoking already?"

He lit the cigarette and nodded, watching me through the smoke. "I just wanted to see if I'd have the courage to smoke in front of you." He grinned and blew a great cloud of smoke to the ceiling. "It was easy." He looked at my face. "Come on, now. I bet you was smoking at my age, tell the truth."

I didn't say anything but the truth was on my face, and he laughed. But now there was something very strained in his laugh. "Sure. And I bet that ain't all you was doing."

He was frightening me a little. "Cut the crap," I said. "We already decided that you was going to go and live at Isabel's. Now what's got into you all of a sudden?"

"*You* decided it," he pointed out. "*I* didn't decide nothing." He stopped in front of me, leaning against the stove, arms loosely folded. "Look, brother. I don't want to stay in Harlem no more, I really don't." He was very earnest. He looked at me, then over toward the kitchen window. There was something in his eyes I'd never seen before, some thoughtfulness, some worry all his own. He rubbed the muscle of one arm. "It's time I was getting out of here."

"Where do you want to *go*, Sonny?"

"I want to join the army. Or the navy, I don't care. If I say I'm old enough, they'll believe me."

Then I got mad. It was because I was so scared. "You must be crazy. You goddamn fool, what the hell do you want to go and join the *army* for?"

"I just told you. To get out of Harlem."

"Sonny, you haven't even finished *school*. And if you really want to be a musician, how do you expect to study if you're in the *army*?"

He looked at me, trapped, and in anguish. "There's ways. I might be able to work out some kind of deal. Anyway, I'll have the G.I. Bill when I come out."

"*If* you come out." We stared at each other. "Sonny, please. Be reasonable. I know the setup is far from perfect. But we got to do the best we can."

"I ain't learning nothing in school," he said. "Even when I go." He turned away from me and opened the window and threw his cigarette out into the narrow alley. I watched his back. "At least, I ain't learning nothing you'd want me to learn." He slammed the window so hard I thought the glass would fly out, and turned back to me. "And I'm sick of the stink of these garbage cans!"

"Sonny," I said, "I know how you feel. But if you don't finish school now, you're going to be sorry later that you didn't." I grabbed him by the shoulders. "And you only got another year. It ain't so bad. And I'll come back and I swear I'll help you do *whatever* you want to do. Just try to put up with it till I come back. Will you please do that? For me?"

He didn't answer and he wouldn't look at me.

"Sonny. You hear me?"

He pulled away. "I hear you. But you never hear anything *I* say."

I didn't know what to say to that. He looked out of the window and then back at me. "OK," he said, and sighed. "I'll try."

Then I said, trying to cheer him up a little, "They got a piano at Isabel's. You can practice on it."

And as a matter of fact, it did cheer him up for a minute. "That's right," he said to himself. "I forgot that." His face relaxed a little. But the worry, the thoughtfulness, played on it still, the way shadows play on a face which is staring into the fire.

But I thought I'd never hear the end of that piano. At first, Isabel would write me, saying how nice it was that Sonny was so serious about his music and how, as soon as he came in from school, or wherever he had been when he was supposed to be at school, he went straight to that piano and stayed there until suppertime. And, after supper, he went back to that piano and stayed there until everybody went to bed. He was at that piano all day Saturday and all day Sunday. Then he bought a record player and started playing records. He'd play one record over and over again, all day long sometimes, and he'd improvise along with it on the piano. Or he'd play one section of the record, one chord, one change, one progression, then he'd do it on the piano. Then back to the record. Then back to the piano.

Well, I really don't know how they stood it. Isabel finally confessed that it wasn't like living with a person at all, it was like living with sound. And the sound didn't make any sense to her, didn't make any sense to any of them —naturally. They began, in a way, to be afflicted by this presence that was living in their home. It was as though Sonny were some sort of god, or monster. He moved in an atmosphere which wasn't like theirs at all. They fed him and he ate, he washed himself, he walked in and out of their door; he certainly wasn't nasty or unpleasant or rude, Sonny isn't any of those things; but it was as though he were all wrapped up in some cloud, some fire, some vision all his own; and there wasn't any way to reach him.

At the same time, he wasn't really a man yet, he was still a child, and they had to watch out for him in all kinds of ways. They certainly couldn't throw him out. Neither did they dare to make a great scene about that piano because even they dimly sensed, as I sensed, from so many thousands of miles away, that Sonny was at that piano playing for his life.

But he hadn't been going to school. One day a letter came from the school board and Isabel's mother got it—there had, apparently, been other letters but Sonny had torn them up. This day, when Sonny came in, Isabel's mother showed him the letter and asked where he'd been spending his time. And she finally got it out of him that he'd been down in Greenwich Village, with musicians and other characters, in a white girl's apartment. And this scared her and she started to scream at him and what came up, once she began— though she denies it to this day—was what sacrifices they were making to give Sonny a decent home and how little he appreciated it.

Sonny didn't play the piano that day. By evening, Isabel's mother had calmed down but then there was the old man to deal with, and Isabel herself. Isabel says she did her best to be calm but she broke down and started crying. She says she just watched Sonny's face. She could tell, by watching him, what was happening with him. And what was happening was that they penetrated his cloud, they had reached him. Even if their fingers had been a thousand times more gentle than human fingers ever are, he could hardly help feeling that they had stripped him naked and were spitting on that nakedness. For he also had to see that his presence, that music, which was life or death to him, had been torture for them and that they had endured it, not at all for his sake, but only for mine. And Sonny couldn't take that. He can take it a little better today than he could then but he's still not very good at it and, frankly, I don't know anybody who is.

The silence of the next few days must have been louder than the sound of all the music ever played since time began. One morning, before she went to work, Isabel was in his room for something and she suddenly realized that all of his records were gone. And she knew for certain that he was gone. And he was. He went as far as the navy would carry him. He finally sent me a postcard from some place in Greece and that was the first I knew that Sonny was still alive. I didn't see him any more until we were both back in New York and the war had long been over.

He was a man by then, of course, but I wasn't willing to see it. He came by the house from time to time, but we fought almost every time we met. I didn't like the way he carried himself, loose and dreamlike all the time, and I didn't like his friends, and his music seemed to be merely an excuse for the life he led. It sounded just that weird and disordered.

Then we had a fight, a pretty awful fight, and I didn't see him for months. By and by I looked him up where he was living, in a furnished room in the Village, and I tried to make it up. But there were lots of other people in the room and Sonny just lay on his bed, and he wouldn't come downstairs with me, and he treated these other people as though they were his family and I weren't. So I got mad and then he got mad, and then I told him that he might just as well be dead as live the way he was living. Then he stood up and he told me not to worry about him any more in life, that he *was* dead as far as I was concerned. Then he pushed me to the door and the other people looked on as though nothing were happening, and he slammed the door behind me. I stood in the hallway, staring at the door. I heard somebody laugh in the room and then the tears came to my eyes. I started down the steps, whistling to keep from crying, I kept whistling to myself, "You going to need me, baby, one of these cold, rainy days."

I read about Sonny's trouble in the spring. Little Grace died in the fall. She was a beautiful little girl. But she only lived a little over two years. She died of polio and she suffered. She had a slight fever for a couple of days, but it didn't seem like anything and we just kept her in bed. And we would certainly have called the doctor, but the fever dropped, she seemed to be all right. So we thought it had just been a cold. Then, one day, she was up, playing; Isabel was in the kitchen fixing lunch for the two boys when they'd come in from school, and she heard Grace fall down in the living room. When you have a lot of children you don't always start running when one of them falls, unless they start screaming or something. And, this time, Grace was quiet. Yet, Isabel says that when she heard that *thump* and then that silence, something happened in her to make her afraid. And she ran to the living room and there was little Grace on the floor, all twisted up, and the reason she hadn't screamed was that she couldn't get her breath. And when she did scream, it was the worst sound, Isabel says, that she'd ever heard in all her life, and she still hears it sometimes in her dreams. Isabel will sometimes wake me up with a low, moaning, strangled sound and I have to be quick to awaken her and hold her to me and where Isabel is weeping against me seems a mortal wound.

I think I may have written Sonny the very day that little Grace was buried. I was sitting in the living room in the dark, by myself, and I suddenly thought of Sonny. My trouble made his real.

One Saturday afternoon, when Sonny had been living with us, or, anyway, been in our house, for nearly two weeks, I found myself wandering aimlessly about the living room, drinking from a can of beer, and trying to work up the courage to search Sonny's room. He was out, he was usually out whenever I was home, and Isabel had taken the children to see their grandparents. Suddenly I was standing still in front of the living room window, watching Seventh Avenue. The idea of searching Sonny's room made me still. I scarcely dared to admit to myself what I'd be searching for. I didn't know what I'd do if I found it. Or if I didn't.

On the sidewalk across from me, near the entrance to a barbecue joint, some people were holding an old-fashioned revival meeting. The barbecue cook, wearing a dirty white apron, his conked hair reddish and metallic in the pale sun and a cigarette between his lips, stood in the doorway, watching them. Kids and older people paused in their errands and stood there, along with some older men and a couple of very tough-looking women who watched everything that happened on the avenue, as though they owned it, or were maybe owned by it. Well, they were watching this, too. The revival was being carried on by three sisters in black, and a brother. All they had were their voices and their Bibles and a tambourine. The brother was testifying and while he testified two of the sisters stood together, seeming to say Amen, and the third sister walked around with the tambourine outstretched and a couple of people dropped coins into it. Then the brother's testimony ended and the sister who had been taking up the collection dumped the coins into her palm and transferred them to the pocket of her long black robe. Then she raised both hands, striking the tambourine against the air, and then against one hand, and she started to sing. And the two other sisters and the brother joined in.

It was strange, suddenly, to watch, though I had been seeing these street meetings all my life. So, of course, had everybody else down there. Yet, they paused and watched and listened and I stood still at the window. "Tis the old ship of Zion," they sang, and the sister with the tambourine kept a steady, jangling beat, "it has rescued many a thousand!" Not a soul under the sound of their voices was hearing this song for the first time, not one of them had been rescued. Nor had they seen much in the way of rescue work being done around them. Neither did they especially believe in the holiness of the three sisters and the brother, they knew too much about them, knew where they lived, and how. The woman with the tambourine, whose voice dominated the air, whose face was bright with joy, was divided by very little from the woman who stood watching her, a cigarette between her heavy, chapped lips, her hair a cuckoo's nest, her face scarred and swollen from many beatings, and her black eyes glittering like coal. Perhaps they both knew this, which was why, when, as rarely, they addressed each other, they addressed each other as Sister. As the singing filled the air the watching, listening faces underwent a change, the eyes focusing on something within; the music seemed to soothe a poison out of them; and time seemed, nearly, to fall away from the sullen, belligerent, battered faces, as though they were fleeing back to their first condition, while dreaming of their last. The barbecue cook half shook his head and smiled, and dropped his cigarette and disappeared into his joint. A man fumbled in his pockets for change and stood holding it in his hand impatiently, as though he had just remembered a pressing appointment further up the avenue. He looked furious. Then I saw Sonny, standing on the edge of the crowd. He was carrying a wide, flat notebook with a green cover, and it made him look, from where I was standing, almost like a schoolboy. The coppery sun brought out the copper in his skin, he was very faintly smiling, standing very still. Then the singing stopped, the tambourine turned into a collection plate again. The furious man dropped in his coins and vanished, so did a couple of the women, and Sonny dropped some change in the plate, looking directly at the woman with a little smile. He started across the avenue, toward the house. He has a slow, loping walk, something like the way Harlem hipsters walk, only he's imposed on this his own half-beat. I had never really noticed it before.

I stayed at the window, both relieved and apprehensive. As Sonny disappeared from my sight, they began singing again. And they were still singing when his key turned in the lock.

"Hey," he said.

"Hey, yourself. You want some beer?"

"No. Well, maybe." But he came up to the window and stood beside me, looking out. "What a warm voice," he said.

They were singing "If I could only hear my mother pray again!"

"Yes," I said, "and she can sure beat that tambourine."

"But what a terrible song," he said, and laughed. He dropped his notebook on the sofa and disappeared into the kitchen. "Where's Isabel and the kids?"

"I think they went to see their grandparents. You hungry?"

"No." He came back into the living room with his can of beer. "You want to come someplace with me tonight?"

I sensed, I don't know how, that I couldn't possibly say No. "Sure. Where?"

He sat down on the sofa and picked up his notebook and started leafing through it. "I'm going to sit in with some fellows in a joint in the Village."

"You mean, you're going to play, tonight?"

"That's right." He took a swallow of his beer and moved back to the window. He gave me a sidelong look. "If you can stand it."

"I'll try," I said.

He smiled to himself and we both watched as the meeting across the way broke up. The three sisters and the brother, heads bowed, were singing "God be with you till we meet again." The faces around them were very quiet. Then the song ended. The small crowd dispersed. We watched the three women and the lone man walk slowly up the avenue.

"When she was singing before," said Sonny, abruptly, "her voice reminded me for a minute of what heroin feels like sometimes—when it's in your veins. It makes you feel sort of warm and cool at the same time. And distant. And —and sure." He sipped his beer, very deliberately not looking at me. I watched his face. "It makes you feel—in control. Sometimes you've got to have that feeling."

"Do you?" I sat down slowly in the easy chair.

"Sometimes." He went to the sofa and picked up his notebook again. "Some people do."

"In order," I asked, "to play?" And my voice was very ugly, full of contempt and anger.

"Well"—he looked at me with great, troubled eyes, as though, in fact, he hoped his eyes would tell me things he could never otherwise say—"they *think* so. And *if* they think so—!"

"And what do *you* think?" I asked.

He sat on the sofa and put his can of beer on the floor. "I don't know," he said, and I couldn't be sure if he were answering my question or pursuing his thoughts. His face didn't tell me. "It's not so much to *play*. It's to *stand* it, to be able to make it at all. On any level." He frowned and smiled. "In order to keep from shaking to pieces."

"But these friends of yours," I said, "they seem to shake themselves to pieces pretty goddamn fast."

"Maybe." He played with the notebook. And something told me that I should curb my tongue, that Sonny was doing his best to talk, that I should listen. "But of course you only know the ones that've gone to pieces. Some don't—or at least they haven't *yet* and that's just about all *any* of us can say." He paused. "And then there are some who just live, really, in hell, and they know it and they see what's happening and they go right on. I don't know." He sighed, dropped the notebook, folded his arms. "Some guys, you can tell from the way they play, they on something *all* the time. And you can see that, well, it makes something real for them. But of course," he picked up his beer from the floor and sipped it and put the can down again, "they *want* to, too, you've got to see that. Even some of them that say they don't—*some,* not all."

"And what about you?" I asked—I couldn't help it. "What about you? Do *you* want to?"

He stood up and walked to the window and remained silent for a long time. Then he sighed. "Me," he said. Then: "While I was downstairs before, on my way here, listening to that woman sing, it struck me all of a sudden how much suffering she must have had to go through—to sing like that. It's *repulsive* to think you have to suffer that much."

I said: "But there's no way not to suffer—is there, Sonny?"

"I believe not," he said, and smiled, "but that's never stopped anyone from trying." He looked at me. "Has it?" I realized, with this mocking look, that there stood between us, forever, beyond the power of time or forgiveness, the fact that I had held silence—so long!—when he had needed human speech to help him. He turned back to the window. "No, there's no way not to suffer. But you try all kinds of ways to keep from drowning in it, to keep on top of it, and to make it seem—well, like *you.* Like you did something, all right, and now you're suffering for it. You know?" I said nothing. "Well, you know," he said, impatiently, "why *do* people suffer? Maybe it's better to do something to give it a reason, *any* reason."

"But we just agreed," I said, "that there's no way not to suffer. Isn't it better, then, just to—take it?"

"But nobody just takes it," Sonny cried, "that's what I'm telling you! *Everybody* tries not to. You're just hung up on the *way* some people try—it's not *your* way!"

The hair on my face began to itch, my face felt wet. "That's not true," I said, "that's not true. I don't give a damn what other people do, I don't even care how they suffer. I just care how *you* suffer." And he looked at me. "Please believe me," I said, "I don't want to see you—die—trying not to suffer."

"I won't," he said, flatly, "die trying not to suffer. At least, not any faster than anybody else."

"But there's no need," I said, trying to laugh, "is there? in killing yourself."

I wanted to say more, but I couldn't. I wanted to talk about will power and how life could be—well, beautiful. I wanted to say that it was all within; but was it? Or, rather, wasn't that exactly the trouble? And I wanted to promise that I would never fail him again. But it would all have sounded—empty words and lies.

So I made the promise to myself and prayed that I would keep it.

"It's terrible sometimes, inside," he said, "that's what's the trouble. You walk these streets, black and funky and cold, and there's not really a living ass to talk to, and there's nothing shaking, and there's no way of getting it out—that storm inside. You can't talk it and you can't make love with it, and when you finally try to get with it and play it, you realize *nobody's* listening. So *you've* got to listen. You got to find a way to listen."

And then he walked away from the window and sat on the sofa again, as though all the wind had suddenly been knocked out of him. "Sometimes you'll do *anything* to play, even cut your mother's throat." He laughed and looked at me. "Or your brother's." Then he sobered. "Or your own." Then: "Don't worry. I'm all right now and I think I'll *be* all right. But I can't forget—where I've been. I don't mean just the physical place I've been, I mean where I've *been*. An *what* I've been."

"What have you been, Sonny?" I asked.

He smiled—but sat sideways on the sofa, his elbow resting on the back, his fingers playing with his mouth and chin, not looking at me. "I've been something I didn't recognize, didn't know I could be. Didn't know anybody could be." He stopped, looking inward, looking helplessly young, looking old. "I'm not talking about it now because I feel *guilty* or anything like that—maybe it would be better if I did, I don't know. Anyway, I can't really talk about it. Not to you, not to anybody," and now he turned and faced me. "Sometimes, you know, and it was actually when I was most *out* of the world, I felt that I was in it, that I was *with* it, really, and I could play or I didn't really have to *play*, it just came out of me, it was there. And I don't know how I played, thinking about it now, but I know I did awful things, those times, sometimes, to people. Or it wasn't that I *did* anything to them—it was that they weren't real." He picked up the beer can; it was empty; he rolled it between his palms: "And other times—well, I needed a fix, I needed to find a place to lean, I needed to clear a space to *listen*—and I couldn't find it, and I—went crazy, I did terrible things to *me*, I was terrible *for* me." He began pressing the beer can between his hands, I watched the metal begin to give. It glittered, as he played with it, like a knife, and I was afraid he would cut himself, but I said nothing. "Oh well. I can never tell you. I was all by myself at the bottom of something, stinking and sweating and crying and shaking, and I smelled it, you know? *my* stink, and I thought I'd die if I couldn't get away from it and yet, all the same, I knew that everything I was doing was just locking me in with it. And I didn't know," he paused, still flattening the beer can, "I didn't know, I still *don't* know, something kept telling me that maybe it was good to smell your own stink, but I didn't think that *that* was what I'd been trying to do—and—who can stand it?" and he abruptly dropped the ruined beer can, looking at me with a small, still smile, and then rose, walking to the window as though it were the lodestone rock. I watched his face, he watched the avenue. "I couldn't tell you when Mama died—but the reason I wanted to leave Harlem so bad was to get away from drugs. And then, when I ran away, that's what I was running from—really. When I came back, nothing had changed, *I* hadn't changed, I was just—older." And he stopped, drumming with his fingers on the windowpane. The sun had vanished, soon darkness would fall. I watched his face. "It can come again," he said, almost as though speaking to himself. Then he turned to me. "It can come again," he repeated. "I just want you to know that."

"All right," I said, at last. "So it can come again. All right."

He smiled, but the smile was sorrowful. "I had to try to tell you," he said.

"Yes," I said. "I understand that."

"You're my brother," he said, looking straight at me, and not smiling at all.

"Yes," I repeated, "yes. I understand that."

He turned back to the window, looking out. "All that hatred down there," he said, "all that hatred and misery and love. It's a wonder it doesn't blow the avenue apart."

We went to the only night club on a short, dark street, downtown. We squeezed through the narrow, chattering, jam-packed bar to the entrance of the big room, where the bandstand was. And we stood there for a moment, for the lights were very dim in this room and we couldn't see. Then, "Hello, boy," said a voice and an enormous black man, much older than Sonny or myself, erupted out of all that atmospheric lighting and put an arm around Sonny's shoulder. "I been sitting right here," he said, "waiting for you."

He had a big voice, too, and heads in the darkness turned toward us.

Sonny grinned and pulled a little away, and said, "Creole, this is my brother. I told you about him."

Creole shook my hand. "I'm glad to meet you, son," he said, and it was clear that he was glad to meet me *there,* for Sonny's sake. And he smiled, "You got a real musician in *your* family," and he took his arm from Sonny's shoulder and slapped him, lightly, affectionately, with the back of his hand.

"Well. Now I've heard it all," said a voice behind us. This was another musician, and a friend of Sonny's, a coal-black, cheerful-looking man, built close to the ground. He immediately began confiding to me, at the top of his lungs, the most terrible things about Sonny, his teeth gleaming like a lighthouse and his laugh coming up out of him like the beginning of an earthquake. And it turned out that everyone at the bar knew Sonny, or almost everyone; some were musicians, working there, or nearby, or not working, some were simply hangers-on, and some were there to hear Sonny play. I was introduced to all of them and they were all very polite to me. Yet, it was clear that, for them, I was only Sonny's brother. Here, I was in Sonny's world. Or, rather: his kingdom. Here, it was not even a question that his veins bore royal blood.

They were going to play soon and Creole installed me, by myself, at a table in a dark corner. Then I watched them, Creole, and the little black man, and Sonny, and the others, while they horsed around, standing just below the bandstand. The light from the bandstand spilled just a little short of them and,

watching them laughing and gesturing and moving about, I had the feeling
that they, nevertheless, were being most careful not to step into that circle of
light too suddenly: that if they moved into the light too suddenly, without
thinking, they would perish in flame. Then, while I watched, one of them, the
small, black man, moved into the light and crossed the bandstand and started
fooling around with his drums. Then—being funny and being, also, extremely
ceremonious—Creole took Sonny by the arm and led him to the piano. A
woman's voice called Sonny's name and a few hands started clapping. And
Sonny, also being funny and being ceremonious, and so touched, I think, that
he could have cried, but neither hiding it nor showing it, riding it like a man,
grinned, and put both hands to his heart and bowed from the waist.

Creole then went to the bass fiddle and a lean, very bright-skinned brown
man jumped up on the bandstand and picked up his horn. So there they were,
and the atmosphere on the bandstand and in the room began to change and
tighten. Someone stepped up to the microphone and announced them. Then
there were all kinds of murmurs. Some people at the bar shushed others. The
waitress ran around, frantically getting in the last orders, guys and chicks got
closer to each other, and the lights on the bandstand, on the quartet, turned
to a kind of indigo. Then they all looked different there. Creole looked about
him for the last time, as though he were making certain that all his chickens
were in the coop, and then he jumped and struck the fiddle. And there they
were.

All I know about music is that not many people ever really hear it. And
even then, on the rare occasions when something opens within, and the music
enters, what we mainly hear, or hear corroborated, are personal, private,
vanishing evocations. But the man who creates the music is hearing something else, is dealing with the roar rising from the void and imposing order
on it as it hits the air. What is evoked in him, then, is of another order, more
terrible because it has no words, and triumphant, too, for that same reason.
And his triumph, when he triumphs, is ours. I just watched Sonny's face. His
face was troubled, he was working hard, but he wasn't with it. And I had the
feeling that, in a way, everyone on the bandstand was waiting for him, both
waiting for him and pushing him along. But as I began to watch Creole, I
realized that it was Creole who held them all back. He had them on a short
rein. Up there, keeping the beat with his whole body, wailing on the fiddle,
with his eyes half closed, he was listening to everything, but he was listening
to Sonny. He was having a dialogue with Sonny. He wanted Sonny to leave
the shore line and strike out for the deep water. He was Sonny's witness that
deep water and drowning were not the same thing—he had been there, and
he knew. And he wanted Sonny to know. He was waiting for Sonny to do the
things on the keys which would let Creole know that Sonny was in the water.

And, while Creole listened, Sonny moved, deep within, exactly like someone in torment. I had never before thought of how awful the relationship must
be between the musician and his instrument. He has to fill it, this instrument,
with the breath of life, his own. He has to make it do what he wants it to do.
And a piano is just a piano. It's made out of so much wood and wires and

little hammers and big ones, and ivory. While there's only so much you can do with it, the only way to find out is to try to try and make it do everything.

And Sonny hadn't been near a piano for over a year. And he wasn't on much better terms with his life, not the life that stretched before him now. He and the piano stammered, started one way, got scared, stopped; started another way, panicked, marked time, started again; then seemed to have found a direction, panicked again, got stuck. And the face I saw on Sonny I'd never seen before. Everything had been burned out of it, and, at the same time, things usually hidden were being burned in, by the fire and fury of the battle which was occurring in him up there.

Yet, watching Creole's face as they neared the end of the first set, I had the feeling that something had happened, something I hadn't heard. Then they finished, there was scattered applause, and then, without an instant's warning, Creole started into something else, it was almost sardonic, it was "Am I Blue." And, as though he had been commanded, Sonny began to play. Something began to happen. And Creole let out the reins. The dry, low, black man said something awful on the drums, Creole answered, and the drums talked back. Then the horn insisted, sweet and high, slightly detached perhaps, and Creole listened, commenting now and then, dry, and driving, beautiful and calm and old. Then they all came together again, and Sonny was part of the family again. I could tell this from his face. He seemed to have found, right there beneath his fingers, a damn brand-new piano. It seemed that he couldn't get over it. Then, for a while, just being happy with Sonny, they seemed to be agreeing with him that brand-new pianos certainly were a gas.

Then Creole stepped forward to remind them that what they were playing was the blues. He hit something in all of them, he hit something in me, myself and the music tightened and deepened, apprehension began to beat the air. Creole began to tell us what the blues were all about. They were not about anything very new. He and his boys up there were keeping it new, at the risk of ruin, destruction, madness, and death, in order to find new ways to make us listen. For, while the tale of how we suffer, and how we are delighted, and how we may triumph is never new, it always must be heard. There isn't any other tale to tell, it's the only light we've got in all this darkness.

And this tale, according to that face, that body, those strong hands on those strings, has another aspect in every country, and a new depth in every generation. Listen, Creole seemed to be saying, listen. Now these are Sonny's blues. He made the little black man on the drums know it, and the bright, brown man on the horn. Creole wasn't trying any longer to get Sonny in the water. He was wishing him Godspeed. Then he stepped back, very slowly, filling the air with the immense suggestion that Sonny speak for himself.

Then they all gathered around Sonny and Sonny played. Every now and again one of them seemed to say, Amen. Sonny's fingers filled the air with life, his life. But that life contained so many others. And Sonny went all the way back, he really began with the spare, flat statement of the opening phrase of the song. Then he began to make it his. It was very beautiful because it wasn't hurried and it was no longer a lament. I seemed to hear with what burning he had made it his, with what burning we had yet to make it ours, how we could cease lamenting. Freedom lurked around us and I understood, at last, that he could help us to be free if we would listen, that he would never be free until we did. Yet, there was no battle in his face now. I heard what he had gone through, and would continue to go through until he came to rest in earth. He had made it his: that long line, of which we knew only Mama and Daddy. And he was giving it back, as everything must be given back, so that, passing through death, it can live forever. I saw my mother's face again, and felt, for the first time, how the stones of the road she had walked on must have bruised her feet. I saw the moonlit road where my father's brother died. And it brought something else back to me, and carried me past it, I saw my little girl again and felt Isabel's tears again, and I felt my own tears begin to rise. And I was yet aware that this was only a moment, that the world waited outside, as hungry as a tiger, and that trouble stretched above us, longer than the sky.

Then it was over. Creole and Sonny let out their breath, both soaking wet, and grinning. There was a lot of applause and some of it was real. In the dark, the girl came by and I asked her to take drinks to the bandstand. There was a long pause, while they talked up there in the indigo light and after a while I saw the girl put a Scotch and milk on top of the piano for Sonny. He didn't seem to notice it, but just before they started playing again, he sipped from it and looked toward me, and nodded. Then he put it back on top of the piano. For me, then, as they began to play again, it glowed and shook above my brother's head like the very cup of trembling.

METAMORPHOSIS

THE THEME OF METAMORPHOSIS IS BOTH THE MOST PERVASIVE AND ELU-sive of those represented in the present book. Change is everywhere a fact of life; and whether reality is "process" or not, actuality certainly is.

Traditionally, the short story is not concerned with process and change, but rather with a "moment in time"—a moment whose history is implicit in the particular characters and stage setting of the event and whose implications transcend the literal scope of the action. Characters in novels often change under the long term of our scrutiny. (Indeed, some critics feel that they *must* change to be real; but this is debatable, and the critical turns of the debate concern the meaning of "change.") There are characters in the short story and folktale, however, who are suddenly *confronted* with the reality of change, either in themselves or in their condition, and when this confrontation is part of what the story is essentially about, then we can say that the story celebrates the theme of Metamorphosis. Often the story is about this change as it is reflected inside a character, in which case we have Initiation, an important variation on the Metamorphosis theme.

Metamorphosis is change, and at the heart of change is time. That is to say, we cannot conceive of time without change, or change without time—each requires the other. And if a story is about an experience so powerful that whoever undergoes it does not come out of it quite the same person and if the story is *about* this quality of the experience, then we are talking about the theme of Metamorphosis.

Such an experience is concentrated time, as it were. For example, in the simple words of Stephen Crane (who actually underwent an ordeal like the one recounted in his story), "A night on the sea in an open boat is a long night." "The Open Boat" is a story about such a deep and elemental change, focused basically through the sensibility of the "Correspondent" (suggestive of Crane himself, of course). Such a deep change as this, however, is not simple and isolated; rather, it is a changing relationship between oneself and the world, or even the universe: "When it occurs to man that Nature does not regard him as important, and that she feels she would not maim the universe by disposing of him, he at first wishes to throw bricks at the temple, and he hates deeply the fact that there are no bricks and no temples." The complex truth of this utterance (note that it says something not only about Nature but also about what are deemed man's irrelevant institutions and structures—

such as religion—and about himself as an irrelevancy) is what is learned during a "night on the sea in an open boat." It is an initiation into a darker truth than was known before, and the psychological distance between the beginning and the end of the story is somewhat measurable as the difference between *knowing* that every man is expendable (for surely there was nothing so abstract as this learned in the open boat about the human condition) and understanding the full terrible, existential reality which knowing only vaguely conveys. Men are vulnerable, exposed, helpless, like survivors in an *open* (great emphasis, here) boat, and they do not understand how profoundly true this is until they have gone through an ordeal similar to that in Crane's story.

Odysseus' homeward journey and homecoming, the "Metamorphoses" of Ovid, Prince Hal's perceptible transformation into Henry V, the adventures of Gulliver, and the initiation of Frederic Henry into the reality of death (the death of a beloved woman) are all stories of that dramatic, focused, and elemental change, either in oneself or one's world, that constitutes metamorphosis.

Sometimes, even within the confines of the short story, we understand that this metamorphosis is itself habitual in one's character, and therefore (paradoxically) a sort of constant, as in Anaïs Nin's story "Nina." Again, it can be an initiation into the evanescence of life and the abiding nearness of its opposite, death, as in Jesse Stuart's story, or into the evanescence of seemingly durable social habits and mores, as in the stories by Wright Morris and Ernest J. Gaines.

Famous stories that have to do with the theme of Metamorphosis are "Araby" and "The Dead" by James Joyce; "The Jolly Corner" by Henry James, "Sophistication" by Sherwood Anderson, "Youth" by Joseph Conrad, "Big Two-Hearted River" and "The Killers" by Ernest Hemingway, and "Ligeia" by Edgar Allan Poe.

Stephen Crane

The Open Boat

I

NONE OF THEM KNEW THE COLOR OF THE SKY. THEIR EYES GLANCED level, and were fastened upon the waves that swept toward them. These waves were of the hue of slate, save for the tops, which were of foaming white, and all of the men knew the colors of the sea. The horizon narrowed and widened, and dipped and rose, and at all times its edge was jagged with waves that seemed thrust up in points like rocks. Many a man ought to have a bath-tub larger than the boat which here rode upon the sea. These waves were most wrongfully and barbarously abrupt and tall, and each froth-top was a problem in small-boat navigation.

The cook squatted in the bottom and looked with both eyes at the six inches of gunwale which separated him from the ocean. His sleeves were rolled over his fat forearms, and the two flaps of his unbuttoned vest dangled as he bent to bail out the boat. Often he said: "Gawd! That was a narrow clip." As he remarked it he invariably gazed eastward over the broken sea.

The oiler, steering with one of the two oars in the boat, sometimes raised himself suddenly to keep clear of water that swirled in over the stern. It was a thin little oar and it seemed often ready to snap.

The correspondent, pulling at the other oar, watched the waves and wondered why he was there.

The injured captain, lying in the bow, was at this time buried in that profound dejection and indifference which comes, temporarily at least, to even the bravest and most enduring when, willy nilly, the firm fails, the army loses, the ship goes down. The mind of the master of a vessel is rooted deep in the timbers of her, though he commanded for a day or a decade, and this captain had on him the stern impression of a scene in the grays of dawn of seven turned faces, and later a stump of a top-mast with a white ball on it that slashed to and fro at the waves, went low and lower, and down. Thereafter there was something strange in his voice. Although steady, it was deep with mourning, and of a quality beyond oration or tears.

"Keep 'er a little more south, Billie," said he.

" 'A little more south,' sir," said the oiler in the stern.

A seat in this boat was not unlike a seat upon a bucking broncho, and by the same token, a broncho is not much smaller. The craft pranced and reared, and plunged like an animal. As each wave came, and she rose for it, she seemed like a horse making at a fence outrageously high. The manner of her scramble over these walls of water is a mystic thing, and, moreover, at the top of them were ordinarily these problems in white water, the foam racing down from the summit of each wave, requiring a new leap, and a leap from the air. Then, after scornfully bumping a crest, she would slide, and race, and splash down a long incline, and arrive bobbing and nodding in front of the next menace.

A singular disadvantage of the sea lies in the fact that after successfully surmounting one wave you discover that there is another behind it just as important and just as nervously anxious to do something effective in the way of swamping boats. In a ten-foot dingey one can get an idea of the resources of the sea in the line of waves that is not probable to the average experience which is never at sea in a dingey. As each slaty wall of water approached, it shut all else from the view of the men in the boat, and it was not difficult to imagine that this particular wave was the final outburst of the ocean, the last effort of the grim water. There was a terrible grace in the move of the waves, and they came in silence, save for the snarling of the crests.

In the wan light, the faces of the men must have been gray. Their eyes must have glinted in strange ways as they gazed steadily astern. Viewed from a balcony, the whole thing would doubtless have been weirdly picturesque. But the men in the boat had not time to see it, and if they had had leisure there were other things to occupy their minds. The sun swung steadily up the sky, and they knew it was broad day because the color of the sea changed from slate to emerald-green, streaked with amber lights, and the foam was like tumbling snow. The process of the breaking day was unknown to them. They were aware only of this effect upon the color of the waves that rolled toward them.

In disjointed sentences the cook and the correspondent argued as to the difference between a life-saving station and a house of refuge. The cook had said: "There's a house of refuge just north of the Mosquito Inlet Light, and as soon as they see us, they'll come off in their boat and pick us up."

"As soon as who see us?" said the correspondent.

"The crew," said the cook.

"Houses of refuge don't have crews," said the correspondent. "As I understand them, they are only places where clothes and grub are stored for the benefit of shipwrecked people. They don't carry crews."

"Oh, yes, they do," said the cook.

"No, they don't," said the correspondent.

"Well, we're not there yet, anyhow," said the oiler, in the stern.

"Well," said the cook, "perhaps it's not a house of refuge that I'm thinking of as being near Mosquito Inlet Light. Perhaps it's a life-saving station."

"We're not there yet," said the oiler, in the stern.

II

As the boat bounced from the top of each wave, the wind tore through the hair of the hatless men, and as the craft plopped her stern down again the spray splashed past them. The crest of each of these waves was a hill, from the top of which the men surveyed, for a moment, a broad tumultuous expanse, shining and wind-riven. It was probably splendid. It was probably glorious, this play of the free sea, wild with lights of emerald and white and amber.

"Bully good thing it's an on-shore wind," said the cook. "If not, where would we be? Wouldn't have a show."

"That's right," said the correspondent.

The busy oiler nodded his assent.

Then the captain, in the bow, chuckled in a way that expressed humor, contempt, tragedy, all in one.

"Do you think we've got much of a show now, boys?" said he.

Whereupon the three were silent, save for a trifle of hemming and hawing. To express any particular optimism at this time they felt to be childish and stupid, but they all doubtless possessed this sense of the situation in their minds. A young man thinks doggedly at such times. On the other hand, the ethics of their condition was decidedly against any open suggestion of hopelessness. So they were silent.

"Oh, well," said the captain, soothing his children, "we'll get ashore all right."

But there was that in his tone which made them think, so the oiler quoth: "Yes! If this wind holds!"

The cook was bailing: "Yes! If we don't catch hell in the surf."

Canton-flannel gulls flew near and far. Sometimes they sat down on the sea, near patches of brown seaweed that rolled on the waves with a movement like carpets on a line in a gale. The birds sat comfortably in groups, and they were envied by some in the dingey, for the wrath of the sea was no more to them than it was to a covey of prairie chickens a thousand miles inland. Often they came very close and stared at the men with black bead-like eyes. At these times they were uncanny and sinister in their unblinking scrutiny, and the men hooted angrily at them, telling them to be gone.

One came, and evidently decided to alight on the top of the captain's head. The bird flew parallel to the boat and did not circle, but made short sidelong jumps in the air in chicken-fashion. His black eyes were wistfully fixed upon the captain's head. "Ugly brute," said the oiler to the bird. "You look as if you were made with a jack-knife." The cook and the correspondent swore darkly at the creature. The captain naturally wished to knock it away with the end of the heavy painter; but he did not dare do it, because anything resembling an emphatic gesture would have capsized this freighted boat, and so with his open hand, the captain gently and carefully waved the gull away. After it had been discouraged from the pursuit the captain breathed easier on account of his hair, and others breathed easier because the bird struck their minds at this time as being somehow gruesome and ominous.

In the meantime the oiler and the correspondent rowed. And also they rowed.

They sat together in the same seat, and each rowed an oar. Then the oiler took both oars; then the correspondent took both oars; then the oiler; then the correspondent. They rowed and they rowed. The very ticklish part of the business was when the time came for the reclining one in the stern to take his turn at the oars. By the very last star of truth, it is easier to steal eggs from under a hen than it was to change seats in the dingey. First the man in the stern slid his hand slong the thwart and moved with care, as if he were of Sèvres. Then the man in the rowing seat slid his hand along the other thwart. It was all done with the most extraordinary care. As the two sidled past each other, the whole party kept watchful eyes on the coming wave, and the captain cried: "Look out now! Steady there!"

The brown mats of seaweed that appeared from time to time were like islands, bits of earth. They were traveling, apparently, neither one way nor the other. They were, to all intents, stationary. They informed the men in the boat that it was making progress slowly toward the land.

The captain, rearing cautiously in the bow, after the dingey soared on a great swell, said that he had seen the lighthouse at Mosquito Inlet. Presently the cook remarked that he had seen it. The correspondent was at the oars then, and for some reason he too wished to look at the lighthouse, but his back was toward the far shore and the waves were important, and for some time he could not seize an opportunity to turn his head. But at last there came a wave more gentle than the others, and when at the crest of it he swiftly scoured the western horizon.

"See it?" said the captain.

"No," said the correspondent slowly, "I didn't see anything."

"Look again," said the captain. He pointed. "It's exactly in that direction."

At the top of another wave, the correspondent did as he was bid, and this time his eyes chanced on a small still thing on the edge of the swaying horizon. It was precisely like the point of a pin. It took an anxious eye to find a lighthouse so tiny.

"Think we'll make it, captain?"

"If this wind holds and the boat don't swamp, we can't do much else," said the captain.

The little boat, lifted by each towering sea, and splashed viciously by the crests, made progress that in the absence of seaweed was not apparent to those in her. She seemed just a wee thing wallowing, miraculously top-up, at the mercy of five oceans. Occasionally, a great spread of water, like white flames, swarmed into her.

"Bail her, cook," said the captain serenely.

"All right, captain," said the cheerful cook.

III

It would be difficult to describe the subtle brotherhood of men that was here established on the seas. No one said that it was so. No one mentioned it. But it dwelt in the boat, and each man felt it warm him. They were a captain, an oiler, a cook, and a correspondent, and they were friends, friends in a more curiously iron-bound degree than may be common. The hurt captain, lying against the water-jar in the bow, spoke always in a low voice and calmly, but he could never command a more ready and swiftly obedient crew than the motley three of the dingey. It was more than a mere recognition of what was best for the common safety. There was surely in it a quality that was personal and heartfelt. And after this devotion to the commander of the boat there was this comradeship that the correspondent, for instance, who had been taught to be cynical of men, knew even at the time was the best experience of his life. But no one said that it was so. No one mentioned it.

"I wish we had a sail," remarked the captain. "We might try my overcoat on the end of an oar and give you two boys a chance to rest."

So the cook and the correspondent held the mast and spread wide the overcoat. The oiler steered, and the little boat made good way with her new rig. Sometimes the oiler had to scull sharply to keep a sea from breaking into the boat, but otherwise sailing was a success.

Meanwhile the lighthouse had been growing slowly larger. It had now almost assumed color, and appeared like a little gray shadow on the sky. The man at the oars could not be prevented from turning his head rather often to try for a glimpse of this little gray shadow.

At last, from the top of each wave the men in the tossing boat could see land. Even as the lighthouse was an upright shadow on the sky, this land seemed but a long black shadow on the sea. It certainly was thinner than paper. "We must be about opposite New Smyrna," said the cook, who had coasted this shore often in schooners. "Captain, by the way, I believe they abandoned that life-saving station there about a year ago."

"Did they?" said the captain.

The wind slowly died away. The cook and the correspondent were not now obliged to slave in order to hold high the oar. But the waves continued their old impetuous swooping at the dingey, and the little craft, no longer under way, struggled woundily over them. The oiler or the correspondent took the oars again.

Shipwrecks are *à propos* of nothing. If men could only train for them and have them occur when the men had reached pink condition, there would be less drowning at sea.

Of the four in the dingey none had slept any time worth mentioning for two days and two nights previous to embarking in the dingey, and in the excitement of clambering about the deck of a foundering ship they had also forgotten to eat heartily.

For these reasons, and for others, neither the oiler nor the correspondent was fond of rowing at this time. The correspondent wondered ingenuously how in the name of all that was sane could there be people who thought it amusing to row a boat. It was not an amusement; it was a diabolical punishment, and even a genius of mental aberrations could never conclude that it was anything but a horror to the muscles and a crime against the back. He mentioned to the boat in general how the amusement of rowing struck him, and the weary-faced oiler smiled in full sympathy. Previously to the foundering, by the way, the oiler had worked double-watch in the engine-room of the ship.

"Take her easy, now, boys," said the captain. "Don't spend yourselves. If we have to run a surf you'll need all your strength, because we'll sure have to swim for it. Take your time."

Slowly the land arose from the sea. From a black line it became a line of black and a line of white, trees and sand. Finally, the captain said that he could make out a house on the shore.

"That's the house of refuge, sure," said the cook. "They'll see us before long, and come out after us."

The distant lighthouse reared high. "The keeper ought to be able to make us out now, if he's looking through a glass," said the captain. "He'll notify the life-saving people."

"None of those other boats could have got ashore to give word of the wreck," said the oiler, in a low voice. "Else the life-boat would be out hunting us."

Slowly and beautifully the land loomed out of the sea. The wind came again. It had veered from the north-east to the south-east.

Finally, a new sound struck the ears of the men in the boat. It was the low thunder of the surf on the shore. "We'll never be able to make the lighthouse now," said the captain. "Swing her head a little more north, Billie," said he.

" 'A little more north,' sir," said the oiler.

Whereupon the little boat turned her nose once more down the wind, and all but the oarsman watched the shore grow. Under the influence of this expansion doubt and direful apprehension was leaving the minds of the men. The management of the boat was still most absorbing, but it could not prevent a quiet cheerfulness. In an hour, perhaps, they would be ashore.

Their backbones had become thoroughly used to balancing in the boat, and they now rode this wild colt of a dingey like circus men. The correspondent thought that he had been drenched to the skin, but happening to feel in the top pocket of his coat, he found therein eight cigars. Four of them were soaked with sea-water; four were perfectly scatheless. After a search, somebody produced three dry matches, and thereupon the four waifs rode impudently in their little boat, and with an assurance of an impending rescue shining in their eyes, puffed at the big cigars and judged well and ill of all men. Everybody took a drink of water.

IV

"Cook," remarked the captain, "there don't seem to be any signs of life about your house of refuge."

"No," replied the cook. "Funny they don't see us!"

A broad stretch of lowly coast lay before the eyes of the men. It was of dunes topped with dark vegetation. The roar of the surf was plain, and sometimes they could see the white lip of a wave as it spun up the beach. A tiny house was blocked out black upon the sky. Southward, the slim lighthouse lifted its little gray length.

Tide, wind, and waves were swinging the dingey northward. "Funny they don't see us," said the men.

The surf's roar was dulled, but its tone was, nevertheless, thunderous and mighty. As the boat swam over the great rollers, the men sat listening to this roar. "We'll swamp sure," said everybody.

It is fair to say here that there was not a life-saving station within twenty miles in either direction, but the men did not know this fact, and in consequence they made dark and opprobrious remarks concerning the eyesight of the nation's life-savers. Four scowling men sat in the dingey and surpassed records in the invention of epithets.

"Funny they don't see us."

The lightheartedness of a former time had completely faded. To their sharpened minds it was easy to conjure pictures of all kinds of incompetency and blindness and, indeed, cowardice. There was the shore of the populous land, and it was bitter and bitter to them that from it came no sign.

"Well," said the captain, ultimately, "I suppose we'll have to make a try for ourselves. If we stay out here too long, we'll none of us have strength left to swim after the boat swamps."

And so the oiler, who was at the oars, turned the boat straight for the shore. There was a sudden tightening of muscle. There was some thinking.

"If we don't all get ashore——" said the captain. "If we don't all get ashore, I suppose you fellows know where to send news of my finish?"

They then briefly exchanged some addresses and admonitions. As for the reflections of the men, there was a great deal of rage in them. Perchance they might be formulated thus: "If I am going to be drowned—if I am going to be drowned—if I am going to be drowned, why, in the name of the seven mad gods who rule the sea, was I allowed to come thus far and contemplate sand and trees? Was I brought here merely to have my nose dragged away as I was about to nibble the sacred cheese of life? It is preposterous. If this old ninny-woman, Fate, cannot do better than this, she should be deprived of the management of men's fortunes. She is an old hen who knows not her intention. If she has decided to drown me, why did she not do it in the beginning and save me all this trouble? The whole affair is absurd. . . . But no, she cannot mean to drown me. She dare not drown me. She cannot drown me. Not after all this work." Afterward the man might have had an impulse to shake his fist at the clouds: "Just you drown me, now, and then hear what I call you!"

The billows that came at this time were more formidable. They seemed always just about to break and roll over the little boat in a turmoil of foam. There was a preparatory and long growl in the speech of them. No mind unused to the sea would have concluded that the dingey could ascend these sheer heights in time. The shore was still afar.

The oiler was a wily surfman. "Boys," he said swiftly, "she won't live three minutes more, and we're too far out to swim. Shall I take her to sea again, captain?"

"Yes! Go ahead!" said the captain.

This oiler, by a series of quick miracles, and fast and steady oarsmanship, turned the boat in the middle of the surf and took her safely to sea again.

There was a considerable silence as the boat bumped over the furrowed sea to deeper water. Then somebody in gloom spoke. "Well, anyhow, they must have seen us from the shore by now."

The gulls went in slanting flight up the wind toward the gray desolate east. A squall, marked by dingy clouds, and clouds brick-red, like smoke from a burning building, appeared from the south-east.

"What do you think of those life-saving people? Ain't they peaches?"

"Funny they haven't seen us."

"Maybe they think we're out here for sport! Maybe they think we're fishin'. Maybe they think we're damned fools."

It was a long afternoon. A changed tide tried to force them southward, but the wind and wave said northward. Far ahead, where coast-line, sea, and sky formed their mighty angle, there were little dots which seemed to indicate a city on the shore.

"St. Augustine?"

The Captain shook his head. "Too near Mosquito Inlet."

And the oiler rowed, and then the correspondent rowed. Then the oiler rowed. It was a weary business. The human back can become the seat of more aches and pains than are registered in books for the composite anatomy of a regiment. It is a limited area, but it can become the theater of innumerable muscular conflicts, tangles, wrenches, knots, and other comforts.

"Did you ever like to row, Billie?" asked the correspondent.

"No," said the oiler. "Hang it!"

When one exchanged the rowing-seat for a place in the bottom of the boat, he suffered a bodily depression that caused him to be careless of everything save an obligation to wiggle one finger. There was cold sea-water swashing to and fro in the boat, and he lay in it. His head, pillowed on a thwart, was within an inch of the swirl of a wave crest, and sometimes a particularly obstreperous sea came in-board and drenched him once more. But these matters did not annoy him. It is almost certain that if the boat had capsized he would have tumbled comfortably out upon the ocean as if he felt sure that it was a great soft mattress.

"Look! There's a man on the shore!"

"Where?"

"There! See 'im? See 'im?"

"Yes, sure! He's walking along."

"Now he's stopped. Look! He's facing us!"

"He's waving at us!"

"So he is! By thunder!"

"Ah, now we're all right! Now we're all right! There'll be a boat out here for us in half-an-hour."

"He's going on. He's running. He's going up to that house there."

The remote beach seemed lower than the sea, and it required a searching glance to discern the little black figure. The captain saw a floating stick and they rowed to it. A bath-towel was by some weird chance in the boat, and, tying this on the stock, the captain waved it. The oarsman did not dare turn his head, so he was obliged to ask questions.

"What's he doing now?"

"He's standing still again. He's looking, I think . . . There he goes again. Toward the house . . . Now he's stopped again."

"Is he waving at us?"

"No, not now! he was, though."

"Look! There comes another man!"

"He's running."

"Look at him go, would you."

"Why, he's on a bicycle. Now he's met the other man. They're both waving at us. Look!"

"There comes something up the beach."

"What the devil is that thing?"

"Why, it looks like a boat."

"Why, certainly it's a boat."

"No, it's on wheels."

"Yes, so it is. Well, that must be the life-boat. They drag them along shore on a wagon."

"That's the life-boat, sure."

"No, by——, it's—it's an omnibus."

"I tell you it's a life-boat."

"It is not! It's an omnibus. I can see it plain. See? One of these big hotel omnibuses."

"By thunder, you're right. It's an omnibus, sure as fate. What do you suppose they are doing with an omnibus? Maybe they are going around collecting the life-crew, hey?"

"That's it, likely. Look! There's a fellow waving a little black flag. He's standing on the steps of the omnibus. There comes those other two fellows. Now they're all talking together. Look at the fellow with the flag. Maybe he ain't waving it."

"That ain't a flag, is it? That's his coat. Why, certainly, that's his coat."

"So it is. It's his coat. He's taken it off and is waving it around his head. But would you look at him swing it."

"Oh, say, there isn't any life-saving station there. That's just a winter resort hotel omnibus that has brought over some of the boarders to see us drown."

"What's that idiot with the coat mean? What's he signaling, anyhow?"

"It looks as if he were trying to tell us to go north. There must be a life-saving station up there."

"No! He thinks we're fishing. Just giving us a merry hand. See? Ah, there, Willie!"

"Well, I wish I could make something out of those signals. What do you suppose he means?"

"He don't mean anything. He's just playing."

"Well, if he'd just signal us to try the surf again, or to go to sea and wait, or go north, or go south, or go to hell—there would be some reason in it. But look at him. He just stands there and keeps his coat revolving like a wheel. The ass!"

"There come more people."

"Now there's quite a mob. Look! Isn't that a boat?"

"Where? Oh, I see where you mean. No, that's no boat."

"That fellow is still waving his coat."

"He must think we like to see him do that. Why don't he quit it? It don't mean anything."

"I don't know. I think he is trying to make us go north. It must be that there's a life-saving station there somewhere."

"Say, he ain't tired yet. Look at 'im wave."

"Wonder how long he can keep that up. He's been revolving his coat ever since he caught sight of us. He's an idiot. Why aren't they getting men to bring a boat out? A fishing boat—one of those big yawls—could come out here all right. Why don't he do something?"

"Oh, it's all right, now."

"They'll have a boat out here for us in less than no time, now that they've seen us."

A faint yellow tone came into the sky over the low land. The shadows on the sea slowly deepened. The wind bore coldness with it, and the men began to shiver.

"Holy smoke!" said one, allowing his voice to express his impious mood, "If we keep on monkeying out here! If we've got to flounder out here all night!"

"Oh, we'll never have to stay here all night! Don't you worry. They've seen us now, and it won't be long before they'll come chasing out after us."

The shore grew dusky. The man waving a coat blended gradually into this gloom, and it swallowed in the same manner the omnibus and the group of people. The spray, when it dashed uproariously over the side, made the voyagers shrink and swear like men who were being branded.

"I'd like to catch the chump who waved the coat. I feel like soaking him one, just for luck."

"Why? What did he do?"

"Oh, nothing, but then he seemed so damned cheerful."

In the meantime the oiler rowed, and then the correspondent rowed, and then the oiler rowed. Gray-faced and bowed forward, they mechanically, turn by turn, plied the leaden oars. The form of the lighthouse had vanished from the southern horizon, but finally a pale star appeared, just lifting from the sea. The streaked saffron in the west passed before the all-merging darkness, and the sea to the east was black. The land had vanished, and was expressed only by the low and drear thunder of the surf.

"If I am going to be drowned—if I am going to be drowned—if I am going to be drowned, why, in the name of the seven mad gods who rule the sea, was I allowed to come this far and contemplate sand and trees? Was I brought here merely to have my nose dragged away as I was about to nibble the sacred cheese of life?"

The patient captain, drooped over the water-jar, was sometimes obliged to speak to the oarsman.

"Keep her head up! Keep her head up!"

" 'Keep her head up,' sir." The voices were weary and low.

This was surely a quiet evening. All save the oarsman lay heavily and listlessly in the boat's bottom. As for him, his eyes were just capable of noting the tall black waves that swept forward in a most sinister silence, save for an occasional subdued growl of a crest.

The cook's head was on a thwart, and he looked without interest at the water under his nose. He was deep in other scenes. Finally he spoke. "Billie," he murmured, dreamfully, "What kind of pie do you like best?"

V

"Pie," said the oiler and the correspondent, agitatedly. "Don't talk about those things, blast you!"

"Well," said the cook, "I was just thinking about ham sandwiches, and——"

A night on the sea in an open boat is a long night. As darkness settled finally, the shine of the light, lifting from the sea in the south, changed to full gold. On the northern horizon a new light appeared, a small bluish gleam on the edge of the waters. These two lights were the furniture of the world. Otherwise there was nothing but waves.

Two men huddled in the stern, and distances were so magnificent in the dingey that the rower was enabled to keep his feet partly warmed by thrusting them under his companions. Their legs indeed extended far under the rowing-seat until they touched the feet of the captain forward. Sometimes, despite the efforts of the tired oarsmen, a wave came piling into the boat, an icy wave of the night, and the chilling water soaked them anew. They would twist their bodies for a moment and groan, and sleep the deep sleep once more, while the water in the boat gurgled about them as the craft rocked.

The plan of the oiler and the correspondent was for one to row until he lost the ability, and then arouse the other from his sea-water couch in the bottom of the boat.

The oiler plied the oars until his head dropped forward, and the overpowering sleep blinded him. And he rowed yet afterward. Then he touched a man in the bottom of the boat, and called his name. "Will you spell me for a little while?" he said, meekly.

"Sure, Billie," said the correspondent, awakening and dragging himself to a sitting position. They exchanged places carefully, and the oiler, cuddling down in the sea-water at the cook's side, seemed to go to sleep instantly.

The particular violence of the sea had ceased. The waves came without snarling. The obligation of the man at the oars was to keep the boat headed so that the tilt of the rollers would not capsize her, and to preserve her from filling when the crests rushed past. The black waves were silent and hard to be seen in the darkness. Often one was almost upon the boat before the oarsman was aware.

In a low voice the correspondent addressed the captain. He was not sure that the captain was awake, although this iron man seemed to be always awake. "Captain, shall I keep her making for that light north, sir?"

The same steady voice answered him. "Yes. Keep it about two points off the port bow."

The cook had tied a life-belt around himself in order to get even the warmth which this clumsy cork contrivance could donate, and he seemed almost stove-like when a rower, whose teeth invariably chattered wildly as soon as he ceased his labor, dropped down to sleep.

The correspondent, as he rowed, looked down at the two men sleeping under-foot. The cook's arm was around the oiler's shoulders, and, with their fragmentary clothing and haggard faces, they were the babes of the sea, a grotesque rendering of the old babes in the wood.

Later he must have grown stupid at his work, for suddenly there was a growling of water, and a crest came with a roar and a swash into the boat, and it was a wonder that it did not set the cook afloat in his lifebelt. The cook continued to sleep, but the oiler sat up, blinking his eyes and shaking with the new cold.

"Oh, I'm awful sorry, Billie," said the correspondent contritely.

"That's all right, old boy," said the oiler, and lay down again and was asleep.

Presently it seemed that even the captain dozed, and the correspondent thought that he was the one man afloat on all the oceans. The wind had a voice as it came over the waves, and it was sadder than the end.

There was a long, loud swishing astern of the boat, and a gleaming trail of phosphorescence, like blue flame, was furrowed on the black waters. It might have been made by a monstrous knife.

Then there came a stillness, while the correspondent breathed with the open mouth and looked at the sea.

Suddenly there was another swish and another long flash of bluish light, and this time it was alongside the boat, and might almost have been reached with an oar. The correspondent saw an enormous fin speed like a shadow through the water, hurling the crystalline spray and leaving the long glowing trail.

The correspondent looked over his shoulder at the captain. His face was hidden, and he seemed to be asleep. He looked at the babes of the sea. They certainly were asleep. So being bereft of sympathy, he leaned a little way to one side and swore softly into the sea.

But the thing did not then leave the vicinity of the boat. Ahead or astern, on one side or the other, at intervals long or short, fled the long sparkling streak, and there was to be heard the whirroo of the dark fin. The speed and power of the thing was greatly to be admired. It cut the water like a gigantic and keen projectile.

The presence of this biding thing did not affect the man with the same horror that it would if he had been a picnicker. He simply looked at the sea dully and swore in an undertone.

Nevertheless, it is true that he did not wish to be alone. He wished one of his companions to awaken by chance and keep him company with it. But the captain hung motionless over the water-jar and the oiler and the cook in the bottom of the boat were plunged in slumber.

VI

"If I am going to be drowned—if I am going to be drowned—if I am going to be drowned, why, in the name of the seven mad gods who rule the sea, was I allowed to come thus far and contemplate sand and trees?"

During this dismal night, it may be remarked that a man would conclude that it was really the intention of the seven mad gods to drown him, despite the abominable injustice of it. For it was certainly an abominable injustice to drown a man who had worked so hard, so hard. The man felt it would be a crime most unnatural. Other people had drowned at sea since galleys swarmed with painted sails, but still—

When it occurs to a man that Nature does not regard him as important, and that she feels she would not maim the universe by disposing of him, he at first wishes to throw bricks at the temple, and he hates deeply the fact that there are no bricks and no temples. Any visible expression of Nature would surely be pelleted with jeers.

Then, if there be no tangible thing to hoot, he feels, perhaps, the desire to confront a personification and indulge in pleas, bowed to one knee, and with hands supplicant, saying: "Yes, but I love myself."

A high cold star on a winter's night is the word he feels that she says to him. Thereafter he knows the pathos of his situation.

The men in the dingey had not discussed these matters, but each had, no doubt, reflected upon them in silence and according to his mind. There was seldom any expression upon their faces save the general one of complete weariness. Speech was devoted to the business of the boat.

To chime the notes of his emotion, a verse mysteriously entered the correspondent's head. He had even forgotten that he had forgotten this verse, but it suddenly was in his mind.

"A soldier of the Legion lay dying in Algiers,
There was lack of woman's nursing, there was dearth of woman's tears;
But a comrade stood beside him, and he took that comrade's hand,
And he said: 'I never more shall see my own, my native land.'"

In his childhood, the correspondent had been made acquainted with the fact that a soldier of the Legion lay dying in Algiers, but he had never regarded the fact as important. Myriads of his school-fellows had informed him of the soldier's plight, but the dinning had naturally ended by making him perfectly indifferent. He had never considered it his affair that a soldier of the Legion lay dying in Algiers, nor had it appeared to him as a matter for sorrow. It was less to him than the breaking of a pencil's point.

Now, however, it quaintly came to him as a human, living thing. It was no longer merely a picture of a few throes in the breast of a poet, meanwhile drinking tea and warming his feet at the grate; it was an actuality—stern, mournful, and fine.

The correspondent plainly saw the soldier. He lay on the sand with his feet out straight and still. While his pale left hand was upon his chest in an attempt to thwart the going of his life, the blood came between his fingers. In the far Algerian distance, a city of low square forms was set against a sky that was faint with the last sunset hues. The correspondent, plying the oars and dreaming of the slow and slower movements of the lips of the soldier, was moved by a profound and perfectly impersonal comprehension. He was sorry for the soldier of the Legion who lay dying in Algiers.

The thing which had followed the boat and waited, had evidently grown bored at the delay. There was no longer to be heard the slash of the cut-water, and there was no longer the flame of the long trail. The light in the north still glimmered, but it was apparently no nearer to the boat. Sometimes the boom of the surf rang in the correspondent's ears, and he turned the craft seaward then and rowed harder. Southward, some one had evidently built a watch-fire on the beach. It was too low and too far to be seen, but it made a shimmering roseate reflection upon the bluff back of it, and this could be discerned from the boat. The wind came stronger, and sometimes a wave suddenly raged out like a mountain-cat, and there was to be seen the sheen and sparkle of a broken crest.

The captain, in the bow, moved on his water-jar and sat erect. "Pretty long night," he observed to the correspondent. He looked at the shore. "Those life-saving people take their time."

"Did you see that shark playing around?"

"Yes, I saw him. He was a big fellow, all right."

"Wish I had known you were awake."

Later the correspondent spoke into the bottom of the boat.

"Billie!" There was a slow and gradual disentanglement. "Billie, will you spell me?"

"Sure," said the oiler.

As soon as the correspondent touched the cold comfortable sea-water in the bottom of the boat, and had huddled close to the cook's lifebelt he was deep in sleep, despite the fact that his teeth played all the popular airs. This sleep was so good to him that it was but a moment before he heard a voice call his name in a tone that demonstrated the last stages of exhaustion. "Will you spell me?"

"Sure, Billie."

The light in the north had mysteriously vanished, but the correspondent took his course from the wide-awake captain.

Later in the night they took the boat farther out to sea, and the captain directed the cook to take one oar at the stern and keep the boat facing the seas. He was to call out if he should hear the thunder of the surf. This plan enabled the oiler and the correspondent to get respite together. "We'll give those boys a chance to get into shape again," said the captain. They curled down and, after a few preliminary chatterings and trembles, slept once more the dead sleep. Neither knew they had bequeathed to the cook the company of another shark, or perhaps the same shark.

As the boat caroused on the waves, spray occasionally bumped over the side and gave them a fresh soaking, but this had no power to break their repose. The ominous slash of the wind and the water affected them as it would have affected mummies.

"Boys," said the cook, with the notes of every reluctance in his voice, "she's drifted in pretty close. I guess one of you had better take her to sea again." The correspondent, aroused, heard the crash of the toppled crests.

As he was rowing, the captain gave him some whisky-and-water, and this steadied the chills out of him. "If I ever get ashore and anybody shows me even a photograph of an oar—"

At least there was a short conversation.

"Billie . . . Billie, will you spell me?"

"Sure," said the oiler.

VII

When the correspondent again opened his eyes, the sea and the sky were each of the gray hue of the dawning. Later, carmine and gold was painted upon the waters. The morning appeared finally, in its splendor, with a sky of pure blue, and the sunlight flamed on the tips of the waves.

On the distant dunes were set many little black cottages, and a tall white windmill reared above them. No man, nor dog, nor bicycle appeared on the beach. The cottages might have formed a deserted village.

The voyagers scanned the shore. A conference was held in the boat. "Well," said the captain, "if no help is coming we might better try a run through the surf right away. If we stay out here much longer we will be too weak to do anything for ourselves at all." The others silently acquiesced in this reasoning. The boat was headed for the beach. The correspondent wondered if none ever ascended the tall windtower, and if then they never looked seaward. This tower was a giant, standing with its back to the plight of the ants. It represented in a degree, to the correspondent, the serenity of Nature amid the struggles of the individual—Nature in the wind, and Nature in the vision of men. She did not seem cruel to him then, nor beneficent, nor treacherous, nor wise. But she was indifferent, flatly indifferent. It is, perhaps, plausible that a man in this situation, impressed with the unconcern of the universe, should see the innumerable flaws of his life, and have them taste wickedly in his mind and wish for another chance. A distinction between right and wrong seems absurdly clear to him, then, in this new ignorance of the grave-edge, and he understands that if he were given another opportunity he would mend his conduct and his words, and be better and brighter during an introduction or at a tea.

"Now, boys," said the captain, "she is going to swamp, sure. All we can do is to work her in as far as possible, and then, when she swamps, pile out and scramble for the beach. Keep cool now, and don't jump until she swamps sure."

The oiler took the oars. Over his shoulder he scanned the surf. "Captain," he said, "I think I'd better bring her about, and keep her head-on to the seas and back her in."

"All right, Billie," said the captain. "Back her in." The oiler swung the boat then and, seated in the stern, the cook and the correspondent were obliged to look over their shoulders to contemplate the lonely and indifferent shore.

The monstrous in-shore rollers heaved the boat high until the men were again enabled to see the white sheets of water scudding up the slanted beach. "We won't get in very close," said the captain. Each time a man could wrest his attention from the rollers, he turned his glance toward the shore, and in the expression of the eyes during this contemplation there was a singular quality. The correspondent, observing the others, knew that they were not afraid, but the full meaning of their glances was shrouded.

As for himself, he was too tired to grapple fundamentally with the fact. He tried to coerce his mind into thinking of it, but the mind was dominated at this time by the muscles, and the muscles said they did not care. It merely occurred to him that if he should drown it would be a shame.

There were no hurried words, no pallor, no plain agitation. The men simply looked at the shore. "Now, remember to get well clear of the boat when you jump," said the captain.

Seaward the crest of a roller suddenly fell with a thunderous crash, and the long white comber came roaring down upon the boat.

"Steady now," said the captain. The men were silent. They turned their eyes from the shore to the comber and waited. The boat slid up the incline, leaped at the furious top, bounced over it, and swung down the long back of the wave. Some water had been shipped and the cook bailed it out.

But the next crest crashed also. The tumbling, boiling flood of white water caught the boat and whirled it almost perpendicular. Water swarmed in from all sides. The correspondent had his hands on the gunwale at this time, and when the water entered at that place he swiftly withdrew his fingers, as if he objected to wetting them.

The little boat, drunken with this weight of water, reeled and snuggled deeper into the sea.

"Bail her out, cook! Bail her out!" said the captain.

"All right, captain," said the cook.

"Now, boys, the next one will do for us, sure," said the oiler. "Mind to jump clear of the boat."

The third wave moved forward, huge, furious, implacable. It fairly swallowed the dingey, and almost simultaneously the men tumbled into the sea. A piece of life-belt had lain in the bottom of the boat, and as the correspondent went overboard he held this to his chest with his left hand.

The January water was icy, and he reflected immediately that it was colder than he had expected to find it on the coast of Florida. This appeared to his dazed mind as a fact important enough to be noted at the time. The coldness of the water was sad; it was tragic. This fact was somehow so mixed and confused with his opinion of his own situation that it seemed almost a proper reason for tears. The water was cold.

THE OPEN BOAT (STEPHEN CRANE)

When he came to the surface he was conscious of little but the noisy water. Afterward he saw his companions in the sea. The oiler was ahead in the race. He was swimming strongly and rapidly. Off to the correspondent's left, the cook's great white and corked back bulged out of the water, and in the rear the captain was hanging with his one good hand to the keel of the overturned dingey.

There is a certain immovable quality to a shore, and the correspondent wondered at it amid the confusion of the sea.

It seemed also very attractive, but the correspondent knew that it was a long journey, and he paddled leisurely. The piece of life preserver lay under him, and sometimes he whirled down the incline of a wave as if he were on a hand-sled.

But finally he arrived at a place in the sea where travel was beset with difficulty. He did not pause swimming to inquire what manner of current had caught him, but there his progress ceased. The shore was set before him like a bit of scenery on a stage, and he looked at it and understood with his eyes each detail of it.

As the cook passed, much farther to the left, the captain was calling to him, "Turn over on your back, cook! Turn over on your back and use the oar."

"All right, sir." The cook turned on his back, and, paddling with an oar, went ahead as if he were a canoe.

Presently the boat also passed to the left of the correspondent with the captain clinging with one hand to the keel. He would have appeared like a man raising himself to look over a board fence, if it were not for the extraordinary gymnastics of the boat. The correspondent marvelled that the captain could still hold to it.

They passed on, nearer to shore—the oiler, the cook, the captain—and following them went the water-jar bouncing gaily over the seas.

The correspondent remained in the grip of this strange new enemy—a current. The shore, with its white slope of sand and its green bluff, topped with little silent cottages, was spread like a picture before him. It was very near to him then, but he was impressed as one who in a gallery looks at a scene from Brittany or Holland.

He thought: "I am going to drown? Can it be possible? Can it be possible? Can it be possible?" Perhaps an individual must consider his own death to be the final phenomenon of nature.

But later a wave perhaps whirled him out of this small, deadly current, for he found suddenly that he could again make progress toward the shore. Later still, he was aware that the captain, clinging with one hand to the keel of the dingey, had his face turned away from the shore and toward him, and was calling his name. "Come to the boat! Come to the boat!"

In his struggle to reach the captain and the boat, he reflected that when one gets properly wearied, drowning must really be a comfortable arrangement, a cessation of hostilities accompanied by a large degree of relief, and he was glad of it, for the main thing in his mind for some months had been horror of the temporary agony. He did not wish to be hurt.

Presently he saw a man running along the shore. He was undressing with most remarkable speed. Coat, trousers, shirt, everything flew magically off him.

"Come to the boat," called the captain.

"All right, captain." As the correspondent paddled, he saw the captain let himself down to bottom and leave the boat. Then the correspondent performed his one little marvel of the voyage. A large wave caught him and flung him with ease and supreme speed completely over the boat and far beyond it. It struck him even then as an event in gymnastics, and a true miracle of the sea. An overturned boat in the surf is not a plaything to a swimming man.

The correspondent arrived in water that reached only to his waist, but his condition did not enable him to stand for more than a moment. Each wave knocked him into a heap, and the undertow pulled at him.

Then he saw the man who had been running and undressing, and undressing and running, coming bounding into the water. He dragged ashore the cook, and then waded towards the captain, but the captain waved him away, and sent him to the correspondent. He was naked, naked as a tree in winter, but a halo was about his head, and he shone like a saint. He gave a strong pull, and a long drag, and a bully heave at the correspondent's hand. The correspondent, schooled in the minor formulae, said: "Thanks, old man." But suddenly the man cried: "What's that?" He pointed a swift finger. The correspondent said: "Go."

In the shallows, face downward, lay the oiler. His forehead touched sand that was periodically, between each wave, clear of the sea.

The correspondent did not know all that transpired afterward. When he achieved safe ground he fell, striking the sand with each particular part of his body. It was as if he dropped from a roof, but the thud was grateful to him.

It seems that instantly the beach was populated with men with blankets, clothes, and flasks, and women with coffee-pots and all the remedies sacred to their minds. The welcome of the land to the men from the sea was warm and generous, but a still and dripping shape was carried slowly up the beach, and the land's welcome for it could only be the different and sinister hospitality of the grave.

When it came night, the white waves paced to and fro in the moonlight, and the wind brought the sound of the great sea's voice to the men on shore, and they felt that they could then be interpreters.

Wright Morris
Since When Do They Charge Admission?

ON THE MORNING THEY LEFT KANSAS, MAY HAD TUNED IN FOR THE weather and heard of the earthquake in San Francisco, where her daughter, Janice, was seven months pregnant. So she had called her. Her husband, Vernon Dickey, answered the phone. He was a native Californian so accustomed to earthquakes he thought nothing of them. It was the wind he feared.

"When I read about those twisters," he said to May, "I don't know how you people stand it." He wouldn't believe that May had never seen a twister till she saw one on TV, and that one in Missouri.

"Ask him about the riots," Cliff had asked her.

"What riots, Mrs. Chalmers?"

It was no trouble for May to see that Janice could use someone around the house to talk to. She was like her father, Cliff, in that it took children to draw her out. Her sister, Charlene would talk the leg off a stranger but the girls 'had never talked much to each other. But now they would, once the men got out of the house. It had been Cliff's idea to bring Charlene along since she had never been out of Kansas. She had never seen an ocean. She had never been higher than Estes Park.

On their way to the beach, Charlene cried, "Look! Look!" She pointed into the sunlight; May could see the light shimmering on the water.

"That's the beach," said Janice.

"Just *look,*" Charlene replied.

"You folks come over here often?" asked Cliff.

"On Vernon's days off," replied Janice.

"If it's a weekday," said May, "you wouldn't find ten people on a beach in Merrick County."

"You wouldn't because there's no beach for them to go to," said Janice.

Cliff liked the way Janice spoke up for California, since that was what she was stuck with. He didn't like it, himself. Nothing had its own place. Hardly any of the corners were square. All through the Sunday morning service he could hear the plastic propellers spinning at the corner gas station, and the loud bang when they checked the oil and slammed down the hood. Vernon Dickey took it all in his stride, the way he did the riots.

Janice said, "Vernon's mother can't understand anybody who lives where they have dust storms."

"I'd rather see it blow than feel it shake," said Cliff.

181

"Ho—ho!" said Vernon.

"I suppose it's one thing or another," said May. "When I read about India I'm always thankful."

Cliff honked his horn at the sharp turns in the road. The fog stood offshore just far enough to let the sun shine yellow on the beach sand. At the foot of the slope the beach road turned left through a grove of trees. Up ahead of them a chain, stretched between two posts, blocked the road. On the left side a portable contractor's toilet was brightly painted with green and yellow flowers. A cardboard sign attached to the chain read, *Admission 50¢.*

"Since when do they charge admission?" Janice asked. She looked at her husband, a policeman on his day off. As Cliff stopped the car a young man in the booth put out his head.

"In heaven's name," May said. She had never seen a man with such a head of hair outside of *The National Geographic.* He had a beard that seemed to grow from the hair on his chest. A brass padlock joined the ends of a chain around his neck.

"How come the fifty-cent fee?" said Vernon. "It's a public beach."

"It's a racket," said the youth. "You can pay it or not pay it." He didn't seem to care. At his back stood a girl with brown hair to her waist, framing a smiling, vacant, pimpled face. She was eating popcorn; the butter and salt greased her lips.

"I don't know why anyone should pay it," said May. "Cliff, drive ahead."

Cliff said, "You like to lower the chain?"

When the boy stepped from the booth he had nothing on but a jockstrap. The way his plump buttocks were tanned it was plain that was all he was accustomed to wear. He stooped with his backside toward the car, but the hood was between him and the ladies. As the chain slacked Cliff drove over it, slowly, into the parking lot.

"What in the world do you make of *that?*" asked May.

"He's a hippie," said Janice. "They're hippies."

"Now I've finally seen one," said May. She twisted in the seat to take a look back.

"Maybe they're having a love-in down here," said Vernon, and guffawed. Cliff had never met a man with a sense of humor that stayed within bounds.

"Park anywhere," said Janice.

"You come down here alone?" asked May.

Vernon said, "Mrs. Chalmers, you don't need to worry. They're crazy but they're not violent."

Cliff maneuvered between the trucks and cars to where the front wheels thumped against a driftwood log. The sand began there, some of it blowing in the offshore breeze. The tide had washed up a sandbar, just ahead, that concealed the beach and most of the people on it. Way over, maybe five or ten miles, was the coastline just west of the Golden Gate, with the tier on tier of houses that Cliff knew to be Daly City. From the bridge, on the way over, Vernon had pointed it out. Vernon and Janice had a home there, but they wanted something more out in the open, nearer the beach. As a matter of fact, Cliff had come up with the idea of building them something. He was a builder. He and May lived in a house that he had built. If Vernon would come up with the piece of land, Cliff would more or less promise to put a house on it. Vernon would help him on the weekends, and his days off.

"What about a little place over there," said Cliff, and wagged his finger at the slope near the beach. Right below it were the huge rocks black as the water, but light on their tops. That was gull dung. One day some fellow smarter than the rest would make roof tiles or fertilizer out of it.

"Most of the year it's cold and foggy," said Vernon, "too cold for the kids."

"What good is a cold, windy beach?" said May. She had turned to take the whip of the wind on her back. No one answered her question. It didn't seem the right time to give it much thought. Cliff got the picnic basket out of the rear and tossed the beach blanket to Vernon. There was enough sand in it, when they shook it, to blow back in his face.

"Just like at home," Cliff said to Vernon, who guffawed.

Vernon had been born and raised in California, but he had got his Army training near Lubbock, Texas, where the dust still blew. Now he led off toward the beach, walking along the basin left where the tide had receded. Charlene trailed along behind him wearing the flowered pajama suit she had worn since they left Colby, on the fourth of June. They had covered twenty-one hundred and forty-eight miles in five days and half of one night, Cliff at the wheel. Charlene could drive, but May didn't feel she could be trusted on the interstate freeways, where they drove so fast. There was a time, every day, about an hour after lunch, when nothing Cliff could think or do would keep him from dozing off. He'd jerk up when he'd hear the sound of gravel or feel the pull of the wheel on the road's shoulder. Then he'd be good for a few more miles till it happened again. The score of times that happened Cliff might have killed them all but he couldn't bring himself to pull over and stop. It scared him to think of the long drive back.

"Except where it was green, in Utah," said May, "it's looked the same to me since we left home."

"Mrs. Chalmers," said Vernon, "you should've sat on the other side of the car."

It was enlightening to Cliff, after all he'd heard about the population explosion, to see how wide open and empty most of the country was. In the morning he might feel he was all alone in it. The best time of day was the forty miles or so he got in before breakfast. They slipped by so easy he sometimes felt he would just like to drive forever, the women in the car quiet until he stopped for food. Anything May saw before she had her coffee was lost on her. After breakfast Cliff didn't know what seemed longer: the day he put in waiting for the dark, or the long night he put in waiting for the light. He had forgotten about trains until they had to stop for the night.

Vernon said, "I understand that when they take the salt out of the water there'll be no more water problems. Is that right, Mr. Chalmers?"

Like her mother, Charlene said, "There'll just be others." Was there anything Cliff had given these girls besides a poor start? He turned to see how Janice, who was seven months pregnant, was making out. The way her feet had sunk into the sand she was no taller than her mother. With their backsides to the wind both women looked broad as a barn. One day Janice was a girl—the next day you couldn't tell her from her mother. That part of her life that she looked old would prove to be the longest, but seem the shortest. Her mother hardly knew a thing, or cared, about what had happened since the war. The sight of anything aging, or anything just beginning, like that unborn child she was lugging, affected Cliff so strongly he could wet his lips and taste it. Where did people get the strength to do it all over again? He turned back to face the beach and the clumps of people who were sitting around, or lying. One played a guitar. A wood fire smoked in the shelter of a few smooth rocks. Vernon said, "It's like the coast of Spain. Cliff could believe it might well be true: it looked old and bleak enough. Where the sand was wet about half a dozen dogs ran up and down, yapping like kids.

"Dogs are fun! They just seem to know almost everything." This side of Charlene made her good with her kids, but Cliff sometimes wondered about her husband.

"How's this?" said Vernon, taking Cliff by the arm, and indicated where he thought they should spread the blanket. On one side were two boys, stretched out on their bellies, and nearer at hand was this blanket-covered figure, his back humped up. His problem seemed to be that he couldn't find a spot in the sand to his liking. He squirmed a good deal. Now and then his backside rose and fell. Cliff took one end of the blanket and Vernon the other, and they managed to hold it against the wind, flatten it to the sand. Charlene plopped down on it to keep it from blowing. It seemed only yesterday that Cliff and his father would put her in a blanket and toss her like a pillow, scaring her mother to death. Charlene was one of those girls who was more like a boy in the way nothing fazed her. Out of the water, toward Vernon, a girl came running so wet and glistening she looked naked.

"Look at that!" said Cliff, and then stood there, his mouth open, looking. She was actually naked. She ran right up and passed him, her feet kicking wet sand on him, then she dropped to lie for a moment on her face, then roll on her back. Only the gold-flecked sand clung to her white belly and breasts. Grains of the sand, cinnamon colored, clung to her prominent, erectile nipples. Her eyes were closed, her head tipped to the left to avoid the wind. For a long moment Cliff gazed at her body as if in thought. When he blinked his eyes the peculiar thing was that he was the one who felt in the fishbowl. Surrounded by them. What did they think of a man down at the beach with all his clothes on? He was distracted by a tug on the blanket and turned to see Vernon pointing at the women. They waddled along like turtles. All he could wonder was what had ever led them to come to a beach. Buttoned at the collar, Janice's coat draped about her like a tent she was dragging. Cliff just stood there till they came along beside him, and May put out a hand to lean on him. Sand powdered her face.

"It's always so windy?" she asked Vernon.

"You folks call this windy?" May looked closely at him to see if he meant to be taken seriously. He surely knew, if he knew anything, that she knew more about wind than he did.

"Get Cliff to tell you how it blows around Chadron," she said. "It blows the words right out of your mouth if you'd let it." Cliff was silent, so she added, "Don't it Cliff?"

"Don't it what?" he answered. He allowed himself to turn so that his eyes went to the humped squirming figure, under the blanket. The humping had pulled it up so the feet were uncovered. Four of them. Two of them were toes down, with tar spots on the bottoms; two of them were toes up, the heels dipped into the sand. In a story Cliff had heard but never fully understood the point had hinged on the four-footed monster. Now he got the point.

"Blow the words right out of your mouth if you'd let it," said May. At a loss for words, Cliff moved to stand so he blocked her view. He took a grip on her hands and let her sag, puffing sour air at him, down to the blanket. "It's hard enough work just to get here," she said, and raised her eyes to squint at the water. "Charlene, you wanted to see the ocean: well, there it is."

Cliff was thinking that Charlene looked no older than the summer she was married. It was hard to understand her. She had had three children without ever growing up.

"If I'd know the sand was going to blow," said May, "we'd have stayed home to eat, then come over later. I hate sand in my food. Charlene, you going to sit down?"

Charlene stood there staring at a girl up to her ankles in the shallow water. She stooped to hold a child pressed to her front, the knees buckled up as if she squeezed it. A stream of water arched from the slit between the child's legs. The way she held it, pressed to her front, it was like squeezing juice from a bladder. There was nothing Cliff could do but wait for it to stop. Charlene's handbag dangled to where it almost dragged in the sand.

"That's Farrallon Island," said Vernon, pointing. Without his glasses Cliff couldn't see it. Janice tipped forward, as far as she could, to cup handfuls of sand over her ankles: she couldn't reach her feet. "We hear and read so much about the California beaches, but nothing about their being so dirty," said May.

"It's the hippies," said Vernon. "They've taken it over."

Why was he such a fool as to say so? Even Cliff, who knew what he would see, twisted his head on his neck and looked all around him. The stark naked girl had dried a lighter color: she didn't look so good. The sand sprinkled her like brown sugar, but the mole-colored nipples were flat on her breasts, like they'd been snipped off. At her feet, using her legs as a backrest, a lank-haired boy, chewing blowgum, sunned his pimpled face. On his hairless chest someone had painted his nipples to look like staring eyes. Now that Cliff was seated it was plainer than ever what was going on under the blanket: the heels of the two of the feet thrust deep into the sand, piling it up. Cliff felt the eyes of Janice on the back of his head, but he missed those of her mother. Where were they?

"Cliff," she said.

He did not turn to look.

"Cliff," she repeated.

At the edge of the water a dappled horse galloped with two long-haired naked riders. If one was a boy, Cliff couldn't tell which was which.

"Who's ready for a beer?" asked Vernon, and peeled the towel off the basket. When no one replied he said, "Mr. Dickey, have yourself a beer," and took one. He moved the basket of food to where both Cliff and the women could reach it. Along with the bowl of potato salad there were two broiled chickens from the supermarket. The chickens were still warm.

"All I've done since we left home is eat," Cliff said.

"We just ate," said Janice.

"We didn't drag all this stuff here," said Cliff, "just to turn around and drag it back." He took out the bowl of salad. He fished around in the basket for the paper cups and plates. He didn't look up at May until he knew for certain she had got her head and eyes around to the front. The sun glinted on her glasses. Absent-mindedly she raked her fingers across her forehead for loose strands of hair. "We eat the salad first or along with the chicken?"

None of the women made any comment. One of the maverick beach dogs, his coat heavy with sand, stood off a few yards and sniffed at the chicken. "They shouldn't allow dogs on a beach," said Cliff. "They run around and get hot and can't drink the water. In the heat they go mad."

"There's salt in there somewhere," said Janice. "I don't put all the salt I could on the salad."

Cliff took out one of the chickens, and using his fingers pried the legs off the body. He then broke the drumsticks off the thighs, and placed the pieces on one of the plates.

"You still like the dark meat?" he said to Charlene. She nodded her head. He peeled the plastic cover off the potato salad and forked it out on the paper plates. "Eat it before the sand gets at it," he said, and passed a plate to May. Janice reached to take one, and placed it on the slope of her lap. Vernon took the body of one of the birds, tore off the wings, and tossed one to the dog.

"I can't stand to see a dog watch me eat," he said.

"Vernon was in Korea for a year," said Janice.

Cliff began to eat. After the first few swallows it tasted all right. He hadn't been hungry at all when he started, but now he ate like he was famished. When he traveled all he seemed to do was sit and eat. He glanced up to see that they were all eating except for May, who just sat there. She had her head cocked sidewise as if straining to hear something. Not twenty yards away a boy plucked a guitar but Cliff didn't hear a sound with the wind against him. Two other boys, with shorts on, one with a top on, lay out on their bellies with their chins on their hands. One used a small rock to drive a short piece of wood into the sand. It was the idle sort of play Cliff would expect from a kid about six, not one about twenty. On the sand before them a shadow flashed and eight or ten feet away a bird landed, flapping its wings. Cliff had never set eyes on a bigger crow. He was shorter in the leg but as big as the gulls that strutted on the firm sand near the water. A little shabby at the tail, big glassy hatpin eyes. Cliff watched him dip his beak into the sand like one of these glass birds that go on drinking water, rocking on the perch. One of the boys said, "Hey, you, bird, come here!" and wiggled a finger at him. When the bird did just that Cliff couldn't believe his eyes. He had a stiff sort of strut, pumping his head, and favored one leg more than the other. No more than two feet away from the heads of those boys he stopped and gave them a look. Either one of them might have reached out and touched him. Cliff had never seen a big, live bird as tame as that. The crows around Chadron were smarter than most people and had their own meetings and cawed crow language. They had discussions. You could hear them decide what to do next. The boy with the rock held it out toward him and damn if the crow didn't peck at it. Cliff could hear the click of his beak tapping the rock. He turned to see if May had caught that, but her eyes were on the plate in her lap.

"May, look—" he said.

Her eyes down she said, "I've seen all I want to see the rest of my life."

"The crow—" said Cliff, and took another look at him. He had his head cocked to one side, like a parrot, and his beak clamped down on one of the sticks driven into the sand. He tried to wiggle it loose as he tugged at it. He braced his legs and strained back like a robin pulling a worm from a hole. So Vernon wouldn't miss it, Cliff put out his hand to nudge him. "Well, I'll be damned," Vernon said.

Two little kids, one with a plastic pail, ran up to within about a yard of the bird, stopped and stared. He stared right back at them. Who was to say which of the two looked the strangest. The kids were naked as the day they were born. One was a boy. Whatever they had seen before they had never seen a crow that close up.

"Come on, bird," said the boy with the rock, and waved it. Nobody would ever believe it, but that bird took a tug at the stick, then rocked back and cawed. He made such a honk the kids were frightened. The little girl backed off and giggled. The crow clamped his beak on the stick again and had another try. A lanky-haired hippie girl, just out of the water, ran up and said, "Sam —are they teasing you Sam?" She had on no top at all but a pair of blue-jean shorts on her bottom. "Come on bird!" yelled the boy with the rock, and pounded his fists on the sand. That crow had figured out a way to loosen up the stick by clamping down on it, hard, then moving in a circle, like he was drilling a well. He did that twice, then he pulled it free, clamped one claw on it, and cawed. "Good bird!" said the boy, and tried to take it from him, but that crow wouldn't let him. He backed off, flapped his wings, and soared off with his legs dangling. Cliff could see what it took a big bird like that to fly.

"What does he do with it?" said the girl. She looked off toward the cliffs where the bird had flown. Somewhere up there he had a lot of sticks: no doubt about that.

"Buries it," said the boy, "He thinks it's a bone."

The little girl with the plastic pail said, "Why don't you give him a real bone, then?" The boy and girl laughed. The hippie girl said, "Can I borrow a comb?" and the boy replied, "If you don't get sand in it." He moved so he could reach the comb in his pocket, and stroked it on his sleeve as he passed it to her. Combing her hair, her head tipped back, Cliff might have mistaken her for a boy. The little girl asked, "When will he do it again?"

"Soon as he's buried it," said the boy.

Cliff didn't believe that. He had watched crows all his life, but he had never seen a crow behave like that. He wanted to bring the point up, but how could he discuss it with a girl without her clothes on?

"Here he comes," said the boy, and there he was, his shadow flashing on the sand before them. He made a circle and came in for a landing on the firm sand. What if he did bury those sticks? His beak was shiny yellow as a banana. "Come here, bird!" said the boy, and held out the rock, but the girl leaned forward and grabbed it from him.

"You want to hurt him?" she cried. "Why don't you give him a real bone?" She looked around as if she might see one, raking the sand with her hands.

"Here's one, Miss!" said Cliff, and held the chicken leg out toward her. He could no more help himself than duck when someone took a swing at him. On her hands and knees the girl crawled toward him to where she could reach it. Her lank hair framed her face.

"There's meat on it," she said.

"Don't you worry," said Cliff, "crows like meat. They're really good meat eaters."

She looked at him closely to see how he meant that. About her neck a fine gold-colored chain dangled an ornament. Cliff saw it plainly. Two brass nails were twisted to make some sort of puzzle. She looked at the bone Cliff had given her, the strip of meat on it, and turned to hold it out to the bird. He limped forward like he was trained and took it in his beak. Cliff caught his eye, and what worried him was that he might want to crow over it and drop it. He didn't want him to drop it and have to gulp down sandy meat. But that bird actually knew he had something unusual since he didn't put it down to clamp his claws on it. Instead he strutted. Up and down he went, like a sailor with a limp. Vernon laughed so hard he gave Cliff a slap on the knee. "Don't laugh *at* him," said the girl, and when she put out her hand he limped toward her to where she could touch him, stroking with her fingers the flat top of his head. The little boy suddenly yelled and ran around them in a circle, kicking up sand, and hooting. The crow took off. The heavy flap of his wings actually stirred the hair of the boy who was lying there, nearest to him; he raised one of his hands to wave as the bird soared away.

"I never seen anything like it!" said Vernon.

"Maybe you'd like to come oftener." Janice picked at the bread crumbs in her lap.

"Did you see him?" asked Cliff. "You get to see him?"

"We can go now if you men have eaten." May made a wad of the napkin and scraps in her lap, put them under the towel and plates in the basket.

Vernon said, "Honey, you see that crazy bird?"

Janice shaded her eyes with one hand, peered at the sky. Up there, high, a bird was wheeling. Cliff took it for a gull. The wind had caked the color she put on her lips, and sand powdered the wrinkles around her eyes. Cliff remembered they were called crow's feet, which was how they looked. Now she lowered her hand and held it out to Vernon to pull her up. The sand caught up in the folds of her dress blew over May and the girl lying behind her, one arm across her face.

"People must be crazy to come and eat on a beach," said May.

Cliff pushed himself to his feet, sand clinging to his chicken-sticky fingers. He helped Vernon with the blanket, walking toward the water where they could shake it and not disturb people. A bearded youth without pants, but with a striped T-shirt, sat with crossed legs on the edge of the water. The horse that had galloped off to the south came galloping back with just one rider on it. Cliff could see it was a girl. Janice and her mother had begun the long walk back toward the car. Along the way they passed the naked girl, still sprawled on her back.

"She's going to get herself a sunburn," said Vernon.

To Charlene Cliff said, "You see that bird?" Charlene nodded. "Just remember you did, when I ask you. Nobody back in Chadron is going to believe me if you don't."

"What bird was it?" asked May.

"A crow," said Cliff.

"I would think you'd seen enough of crows," said May.

At the car Cliff turned for a last look at the beach. The tide had washed up a sort of reef so that he could no longer see the water. The girl and the dogs that ran along it were like black paper cutouts. Nobody would know if she had her clothes on or off. He had forgotten to check on the two of them who had been squirming under the blanket. One still lay there. The other one crouched with lowered head, as if reading something. From the back Cliff wouldn't know which one was the girl.

May said, "I've never before really believed it when I said that I can't believe my eyes, but now I believe it."

"You wouldn't believe them if you'd seen that crow," said Cliff.

"I didn't come all this way to look at a crow," she replied.

They all got into the car, and Cliff put the picnic basket into the rear. He took a moment, squinting, to see if the crazy bird had come back for more bones. If he had just thought, he would have given the girl the other two legs to feed him.

"I'd like a cup of coffee," said May, "but I'm willing to wait till we get home for it."

Vernon said, "Mr. Chalmers, you like me to drive?" Cliff agreed that he would. They went out through the gate where they had entered but the boy and the girl had left the booth. The chain was already half-covered with drifting sand.

"It's typical of your father," said May, "to drive all the way out here and look at a crow."

Charlene said, "Wait until I tell Leonard!" They looked to see what she would tell him. On the dry slope below them a small herd of cattle were being fed from a hovering helicopter. Bundles of straw were dropped to spread on the slope.

"If I were you," said May, "I'd tell him about *that* and nothing else."

Cliff felt his head wagging. He stopped it and said, "Charlene, now you tell him about that crow. What's a few crazy people to one crow in a million?"

There was no comment.

"We're going up now," said Vernon. "You feel that poppin' in your ears?"

Anaïs Nin

Nina

BRUCE AND RENATE ENTERED A DIMLY-LIT CAFE WHERE ANYONE COULD sit on the small stage and sing folk songs, and if he sang well would be kept there by applause and, if not, quickly encouraged to leave. The tables were beer-stained and sticky with Coca-Cola. The waitresses were heavily made up with Cleopatra eyes, and they wore sack dresses and black stockings. The spotlight on the singers was red and made them appear pale and condemned to sing. The shadows were so strong that when they bent over their guitar it seemed intimate and not like a song one must listen to. A few figures stood in the shadows on the side, and from this vague group a woman sprang towards them and, touching Renate's arm, said in a chanting voice: "You are Renate," giving to the name all the musical resonances it contained and adding, with a perfect lyrical illogic: "I am Nina," as if a woman called Nina must of course address a woman called Renate. Renate hesitated because she was trying to remember where she had seen Nina and yet she could not remember, and this was so manifest on her face that Nina said: "Of course you could not remember, there are fourteen women in me, you may have met only one of them, perhaps on the stage, when I acted at the Playwright's Theatre, do you remember that? I was the blind girl."

"Yes, of course I remember her, but you do not seem like the same woman, and even now you do not seem like the same woman who first came out to speak to me."

It was true that she changed so quickly that already Renate had seen in her a beautiful Medea because of the flowing hair, but a Medea without jealousy, and the next moment she seemed like a wandering Ophelia who had never known repose. It was impossible to imagine her asleep or drowned. She held her head proudly on a very slender neck; she used her hands like puppets, each finger with an important role to play. She was without sadness and so light she seemed almost weightless, as if performing on a stage alone, while her eyes scanned the entire room, her quick-winged words a monologue about to be interrupted. She thrust out her shoulders as if she had to push her way through a crowd and leave.

Bruce's speech and thoughts were agile, like those of a rootless person accustomed to pack and move swiftly from city to city, from home to home, and yet he could not follow her flights and vertiginous transitions. A touching, apologetic smile accompanied her incoherence. She herself did not get

191

lost in sudden turns and free associations, but she seemed wistful that others could not follow her.

"My name is Nina Gitana de la Primavera." She said "Gitana" as if she had been born in Spain, and "Primavera" as if she had been born in Italy, and one could see the Persian flowers on her cotton dress flowering.

"But these are my winter names. I change with the seasons. When the spring comes I no longer need to be Primavera. I leave that to the season. It is so far away." She threw her head back like a young horse trying to sniff the far off spring, so far back Renate thought her neck would snap.

"I am waiting for Manfred, but he is not coming. May I sit with you?"

"Who is Manfred?" asked Bruce.

She repeated the name but separated its syllables: "Manfred." As if she were examining its philological roots.

"Man-fred is the man I am going to love. He may not yet be born. I have often loved men who are not yet born."

Bruce, who never swerved in the path of a drunkard, who had once invited a potential burglar to come in for a coffee, was afraid of this beautiful undrowned Ophelia who borrowed her language from mythology. He feared she had the power to snap the cord which bound him securely to ordinary life.

He wanted to leave. But just then a new singer climbed the wooden stage, and began to talk before he sang as if to sell his own songs.

Nina never ceased talking except to stare at Renate and Bruce and touch their faces delicately with her fingertips as if she were still playing the blind girl on the stage. Then she spread open her hands and to each separate finger she said severely: "You talk too much."

Renate wondered how anyone had been able to put the words of playwrights in her mouth when her own overflowed so profusely. But she was able to quote Gertrude Stein accurately and sing a Mozart theme when she mentioned the composer. So her memory was not lost in this multitude of disconnected selves.

Bruce asked her questions as if he were a reporter interviewing her, but a reporter accustomed to deal with the poetics of space, air and water.

"Say something I will always remember," he asked, thinking that in this way he might solve the elusive nature of her talk.

She meditated silently and then gracefully made five gestures. She touched her forehead, her lips, her breasts, the center of her throat, then placed her hand under her elbow and held it there and said: "Remember this."

"As-tar-te," she murmured. "Every word has several personalities enclosed in it, and if you separate the syllables you can catch all its aspects. Bruce is too short for you. It does not describe you. Have you ever noticed how short American names are? They are like lizards who have lost their tails. This happened when America was first settled. It was a rebellion against the long European names. You should have had a name like a merry-go-round. It should have a joyous sound, and it should *turn.*"

Her body was thin and supple. Her eyes large and green. She had a pure straight nose, finely designed lean cheeks, a tender but not too full mouth and beautiful teeth. Her long curled hair covered her shoulders. On stage she looked like Vivien Leigh. In life she looked as if she had dressed in old stage clothes, an Indian print cotton not made for her, which was off the shoulders and which she was too thin to hold up securely, covered by a dusty violet cape.

Every now and then she exposed her teeth, placed a finger on the middle tooth and hissed as if she wanted to let the breath out of her body, like a balloon about to fly. With a long thin finger she designed a large S on the bar table, explaining that this was the sign of the Infinite. The hiss had been a prologue to S S S S S.

"Julien and his wife do not want me to go out alone because they think I am mad and that the madhouse people will pick me up and that they will give a shock treatment to wake me up."

"You are dreaming awake," said Renate. "Many people dream awake. And some are jealous of having no dreams and they either drink or take pills to make them dream."

"I am not going home to Julien and Juliana tonight. I love them but that is not my home tonight. I must find my real home tonight. The police will not let me sit on trees. I did once at Pershing Square. I loved climbing the tree there, and listening to the preachers, and watching the hoboes who listen to the songs and the prayers. They were all lost people like me, and even their clothes did not belong to them. You could see they were dressed with what people gave to charity collections and from Thrift Shops. Each piece of clothing had belonged to a different human being. I sat up there for a whole evening but then I could not get down again. And when the police found me they took me to a big building and they gave me a shock to wake me up. Silver Fox said to me once, 'Nina, you have something to give to the world and the world has nothing to give you.' "

"Who is Silver Fox?" asked Bruce who was determined to find a key and had hopes that this story would make sense and that he might identify the characters.

Each word came out of her mouth caressed as if it were a beautiful word, a sensuous word. When Bruce asked his questions she looked as if her magic trick had failed. But she was indulgent towards his blindness.

She drank wine, and when the glass was empty she held it against her cheek as if to warm it and no one could have sworn they had seen her drink. Towards midnight she refused another glass but said she was hungry. She paused to try and remember when she had last eaten. "Oh, yes, last night."

So Bruce ordered a sandwich. It was a big Italian sandwich, clumsy and as large as her face. Before starting she pulled up her dress once more because her breasts were too small to hold its strapless top. Then she handled the sandwich as if it were a wafer. She looked mischievously at Bruce as if she knew he did not believe she would eat it, and he was amazed to see it vanish while her eyes remaining fixed on him seemed to say: "I will swallow it but you won't see me eat it."

"You have magical powers," said Renate, "and yet Bruce and I feel we must protect you. Bruce and I will take you wherever you want to go to-night."

Nina asked for the time, although Renate was sure she did not care. It was part of her exquisite politeness towards conventions. Nina braided her long hair and took her bracelet off in preparation for the journey.

"People are afraid of dreamers," she said. "They want to put me away."

On the pavement they found giant pipelines resting beside an excavated street. Nina bent over one of the openings and laughed into the drainpipe and then ran towards the other end to see if her laughter was coming out of it.

The friend she wanted to stay with was not in. So Renate and Bruce drove her to Malibu. She thought the room was small; then she opened the window and said: "Oh, but there is so much more to this room than I thought. It's enormous. There is a roar in my ears."

"It's the ocean," said Renate.

Then Nina asked for silver foil paper. "I always glue silver foil paper on the walls to make them beautiful."

She wanted to mop the tile floor with beer. "The foam will make it shine."

"Do you want to sleep?" asked Renate.

"I never sleep," said Nina. "Just give me a sheet."

She took the sheet and covered herself with it, and then slid to the floor saying: "Now I am invisible."

The next day she wanted to go to the theatre. There was a play she had already seen but wanted to see again.

She carried a brown paper bag with her which she would not allow Bruce to leave in the car when they entered the theatre.

During the play there was a scene at a dining-table. The actors sat around talking and eating. At this point Nina opened her brown paper bag, took out a sandwich and a pickle and began to eat in unison with the actors. She whispered to Renate: "The audience should not just watch actors eat. They should eat with them. They will feel less lonely."

Then she laughed softly: "I have a friend who says the best way to remember a beautiful city or a beautiful painting is to eat something while you are looking at it. The flavor really helps the image to penetrate the body. It fixes it as lacquer does a drawing."

After the performance she insisted on visiting the actors. "I don't know any of them but they like to see friendly faces."

A friend hailed her. He was a television actor. He took her arm and guided her out of the theatre.

Bruce and Renate did not see her for several days. Then she reappeared one day and she was wearing a new dress and new sandals.

"I got a job," she said. "Do you remember the young actor we met at the theatre? They had just finished a reading of a children's play for a radio show but the star could not laugh like a witch. He remembered that I had done this once to frighten people at a party I did not like. So they put me in this sound-proof room. I could see the men behind the glass windows running their machines. They wore earphones and never raised their eyes to see what

I was doing. They blinked some red lights and I heard a voice say: 'Now start laughing like a witch until I tell you to stop.' I felt that I must laugh, must keep on laughing and attract their attention, or else they would leave me in that room and forget all about me. I was all alone in a room without echoes. You don't know the loneliness of being in a room without echo. I had to laugh like a witch with nobody to laugh for, or to laugh at. To wind myself up I went to each corner of the room pretending each corner was a different person, and I laughed, laughed, and finally I was laughing so hard I was afraid I could not stop. I thought if no one comes into the room, if no human being comes in and says: 'It is enough,' I will not be able to stop. I watched the wheels turning and hoped the tape would give out. And finally it did give out and its tail rose up like the tail of a snake and it slapped the young man in the face, the young man who would not look at me. Then the young man opened the door and said to me: 'We got a lot of footage out of that,' and handed me a check. I bought this dress, do you like it? See, it is wide and loose like a tent. All I need to do is pull it up a little above my head, and then sink down, and I am completely covered and can go to sleep. And do you like my sandals? I brought you a present. I found her waiting for an audition."

It was Nobuko who came walking over the small stones of the patio with short, tiny steps. Though she had walked up the hill from the bus stop, no dust showed on her white socks and wooden sandals. She was carrying flowers she had picked up on the way, which she offered to Renate.

The Sky Is Gray

Ernest J. Gaines

I

GO'N BE COMING IN A FEW MINUTES. COMING 'ROUND THAT BEND DOWN there full speed. And I'm go'n get out my hankercher and I'm go'n wave it down, and us go'n get on it and go.

I keep on looking for it, but Mama don't look that way no more. She looking down the road where us jest come from. It's a long old road, and far's you can see you don't see nothing but gravel. You got dry weeds on both sides and you got trees on both sides, and fences on both sides, too. And you got cows in the pastures and they standing close together. And when us was coming out yer to catch the bus I seen the smoke coming out o' the cow's nose.

I look at my mama and I know what she thinking. I been with Mama so much, jest me and her, I know what she thinking all the time. Right now it's home—Auntie and them. She thinking if they got 'nough wood—if she left 'nough there to keep 'em warm till us get back. She thinking if it go'n rain and if any of 'em go'n have to go out in the rain. She thinking 'bout the hog —if he go'n get out, and if Ty and Val be able to get him back in. She always worry like that when she leave the house. She don't worry too much if she leave me there with the smaller ones 'cause she know I'm go'n look after 'em and look after Auntie and everything else. I'm the oldest and she say I'm the man.

I look at my mama and I love my mama. She wearing that black coat and that black hat and she looking sad. I love my mama and I want put my arm 'round her and tell her. But I'm not s'pose to do that. She say that's weakness and that's cry-baby stuff, and she don't want no cry-baby 'round her. She don't want you to be scared neither. 'Cause Ty scared of ghosts and she always whipping him. I'm scared of the dark, too. But I make 'tend I ain't. I make 'tend I ain't 'cause I'm the oldest, and I got to set a good sample for the rest. I can't ever be scared and I can't ever cry. And that's the reason I didn't ever say nothing 'bout my teef. It been hurting me and hurting me close to a month now. But I didn't say it. I didn't say it 'cause I didn't want act like no cry-baby, and 'cause I know us didn't have 'nough money to have it pulled. But, Lord, it been hurting me. And look like it won't start till at night when you trying to get little sleep. Then soon's you shet your eyes—umm-umm, Lord, Look like it go right down to your heart string.

196

"Hurting, hanh?" Ty'd say.

I'd shake my head, but I wouldn't open my mouth for nothing. You open your mouth and let that wind in, and it almost kill you.

I'd just lay there and listen to 'em snore. Ty, there, right 'side me, and Auntie and Val over by the fireplace. Val younger 'an me and Ty, and he sleep with Auntie. Mama sleep 'round the other side with Louis and Walker.

I'd just lay there and listen to 'em, and listen to that wind out there, and listen to that fire in the fireplace. Sometime it'd stop long enough to let me get little rest. Sometime it just hurt, hurt, hurt. Lord, have mercy.

II

Auntie knowed it was hurting me. I didn't tell nobody but Ty, 'cause us buddies and he ain't go'n tell nobody. But some kind o' way Auntie found out. When she asked me, I told her no, nothing was wrong. But she knowed it all the time. She told me to mash up a piece o' aspirin and wrap it in some cotton and jugg it down in that hole. I did it, but it didn't do no good. It stopped for a little while, and started right back again. She wanted to tell Mama, but I told her Uh-uh. 'Cause I knowed it didn't have no money, and it jest was go'n make her mad again. So she told Monsieur Bayonne, and Monsieur Bayonne came to the house and told me to kneel down 'side him on the fireplace. He put his finger in his mouth and made the sign of the Cross on my jaw. The tip of Monsieur Bayonne finger is some hard, 'cause he always playing on that guitar. If us sit outside at night us can always hear Monsieur Bayonne playing on his guitar. Sometime us leave him out there playing on the guitar.

He made the Sign of the Cross over and over on my jaw, but that didn't do no good. Even when he prayed and told me to pray some, too, that teef still hurt.

"How you feeling?" he say.

"Same," I say.

He kept on praying and making the Sign of the Cross and I kept on praying, too.

"Still hurting?" he say.

"Yes, sir."

Monsieur Bayonne mashed harder and harder on my jaw. He mashed so hard he almost pushed me on Ty. But then he stopped.

"What kind o' prayers you praying, boy?" he say.

"Baptist," I say.

"Well, I'll be—no wonder that teef still killing him. I'm going one way and he going the other. Boy, don't you know any Catholic prayers?"

"Hail Mary," I say.

"Then you better start saying it."

"Yes, sir."

He started mashing again, and I could hear him praying at the same time. And, sure 'nough, afterwhile it stopped.

Me and Ty went outside where Monsieur Bayonne two hounds was, and us started playing with 'em. "Let's go hunting," Ty say. "All right," I say; and us went on back in the pasture. Soon the hounds got on a trail, and me and Ty followed 'em all cross the pasture and then back in the woods, too. And then they cornered this little old rabbit and killed him, and me and Ty made 'em get back, and us picked up the rabbit and started on back home. But it had started hurting me again. It was hurting me plenty now, but I wouldn't tell Monsieur Bayonne. That night I didn't sleep a bit, and first thing in the morning Auntie told me go back and let Monsieur Bayonne pray over me some more. Monsieur Bayonne was in his kitchen making coffee when I got there. Soon's he seen me, he knowed what was wrong.

"All right, kneel down there 'side that stove," he say. "And this time pray Catholic. I don't know nothing 'bout Baptist, and don't want know nothing 'bout him."

III

Last night Mama say: "Tomorrow us going to town."

"It ain't hurting me no more," I say. "I can eat anything on it."

"Tomorrow us going to town," she say.

And after she finished eating, she got up and went to bed. She always go to bed early now. 'Fore Daddy went in the Army, she used to stay up late. All o' us sitting out on the gallery or 'round the fire. But now, look like soon's she finish eating she go to bed.

This morning when I woke up, her and Auntie was standing 'fore the fireplace. She say: " 'Nough to get there and back. Dollar and a half to have it pulled. Twenty-five for me to go, twenty-five for him. Twenty-five for me to come back, twenty-five for him. Fifty cents left. Guess I get a little piece o' salt meat with that."

"Sure can use a piece," Auntie say. "White beans and no salt meat ain't white beans."

"I do the best I can," Mama say.

They was quiet after that, and I made 'tend I was still sleep.

"James, hit the floor," Auntie say.

I still made 'tend I was sleep. I didn't want 'em to know I was listening.

"All right," Auntie say, shaking me by the shoulder. "Come on. Today's the day."

I pushed the cover down to get out, and Ty grabbed it and pulled it back.

"You, too, Ty," Auntie say.

"I ain't getting no teef pulled," Ty say.

"Don't mean it ain't time to get up," Auntie say. "Hit it, Ty."

Ty got up grumbling.

"James, you hurry up and get in your clothes and eat your food," Auntie say. "What time y'all coming back?" she say to Mama.

"That 'leven o'clock bus," Mama say. "Got to get back in that field this evening."

"Get a move on you, James," Auntie say.

I went in the kitchen and washed my face, then I ate my breakfast. I was having bread and syrup. The bread was warm and hard and tasted good. And I tried to make it last a long time.

Ty came back there, grumbling and mad at me.

"Got to get up," he say. "I ain't having no teef pulled. What I got to be getting up for."

Ty poured some syrup in his pan and got a piece of bread. He didn't wash his hands, neither his face, and I could see that white stuff in his eyes.

"You the one getting a teef pulled," he say. "What I got to get up for. I bet you if I was getting a teef pulled, you wouldn't be getting up. Shucks; syrup again. I'm getting tired of this old syrup. Syrup, syrup, syrup. I want me some bacon sometime."

"Go out in the field and work and you can have bacon," Auntie say. She stood in the middle door looking at Ty. "You better be glad you got syrup. Some people ain't got that—hard's time is."

"Shucks," Ty say. "How can I be strong."

"I don't know too much 'bout your strength," Auntie say; "but I know where you go'n be hot, you keep that grumbling up. James, get a move on you; your mama waiting."

I ate my last piece of bread and went in the front room. Mama was standing 'fore the fireplace warming her hands. I put on my coat and my cap, and us left the house.

IV

I look down there again, but it still ain't coming. I almost say, "It ain't coming, yet," but I keep my mouth shet. 'Cause that's something else she don't like. She don't like for you to say something just for nothing. She can see it ain't coming, I can see it ain't coming, so why say it ain't coming. I don't say it, and I turn and look at the river that's back o' us. It so cold the smoke just raising up from the water. I see a bunch of pull-doos not too far out—jest on the other side the lilies. I'm wondering if you can eat pull-doos. I ain't too sure, 'cause I ain't never ate none. But I done ate owls and black birds, and I done ate red birds, too. I didn't want kill the red birds, but she made me kill 'em. They had two of 'em back there. One in my trap, one in Ty trap. me and Ty was go'n play with 'em and let 'em go. But she made me kill 'em 'cause us needed the food.

"I can't," I say. "I can't."

"Here," she say. "Take it."

"I can't," I say. "I can't. I can't kill him, Mama. Please."

"Here," she say. "Take this fork, James."

"Please, Mama, I can't kill him," I say.

I could tell she was go'n hit me. And I jecked back, but I didn't jeck back soon enough.

"Take it," she say.

I took it and reached in for him, but he kept hopping to the back.

"I can't, Mama," I say. The water just kept running down my face. "I can't."

"Get him out o' there," she say.

I reached in for him and he kept hopping to the back. Then I reached in farther, and he pecked me on the hand.

"I can't Mama," I say.

She slapped me again.

I reached in again, but he kept hopping out my way. Then he hopped to one side, and I reached there. The fork got him on the leg and I heard his leg pop. I pulled my hand out 'cause I had hurt him.

"Give it here," she say, and jecked the fork out of my hand.

She reached and got the little bird right in the neck. I heard the fork go in his neck, and I heard it go in the ground. She brought him out and helt him right in front o' me.

"That's one," she say. She shook him off and gived me the fork. "Get the other one."

"I can't, Mama. I do anything. But I can't do that."

She went to the corner o' the fence and broke the biggest switch over there. I knelt 'side the trap crying.

"Get him out o'there," she say.

"I can't, Mama."

She started hitting me across the back. I went down on the ground crying.

"Get him," she say.

"Octavia," Auntie say.

'Cause she had come out o' the house and she was standing by the tree looking at us.

"Get him out o'there," Mama say.

"Octavia," Auntie say; "explain to him. Explain to him. Jest don't beat him. Explain to him."

But she hit me and hit me and hit me.

I'm still young. I ain't no more'an eight. But I know now. I know why I had to. (They was so little, though. They was so little. I 'member how I picked the feathers off 'em. and cleaned 'em and helt 'em over the fire. Then us all ate 'em. Ain't had but little bitty piece, but us all had little bitty piece, and ever'body jest looked at me 'cause they was so proud.) S'pose she had to go away? That's why I had to do it. S'pose she had to go away like Daddy went away? Then who was go'n look after us? They had to be somebody left to carry on. I didn't know it then, but I know it now. Auntie and Monsieur Bayonne talked to me and made me see.

V

Time I see it, I get out my handkercher and start waving. It still way down there, but I keep waving anyhow. Then it come closer and stop and me and Mama get on. Mama tell me go sit in the back while she pay. I do like she say, and the people look at me. When I pass the little sign that say White and Colored, I start looking for a seat. I just see one of 'em back there, but I don't take it, 'cause I want my mama to sit down herself. She come in the back and sit down, and I lean on the seat. They got seats in the front, but I know I can't sit there, 'cause I have to sit back o' the sign. Anyhow, I don't want sit there if my mama go'n sit back here.

They got a lady sitting 'side my mama and she look at me and grin little bit. I grin back, but I don't open my mouth, 'cause the wind'll get in and make that teef hurt. The lady take out a pack o' gum and reach me a slice, but I shake my head. She reach Mama a slice, and Mama shake her head. The lady jest can't understand why a little boy'll turn down gum and she reached me a slice again. This time I point to my jaw. The lady understand and grin little bit, and I grin little bit, but I don't open my mouth, though.

They got a girl sitting 'cross from me. She got on a red overcoat, and her hair plaited on one big plait. First, I make 'tend I don't even see her. But then I start looking at her little bit. She make 'tend she don't see me neither, but I catch her looking that way. She got a cold, and ever' now and then she hist that little handkercher to her nose. She ought to blow it, but she don't. Must think she too much a lady or something.

Ever' time she hist that little handkercher, the lady 'side her say something in her yer. She shake her head and lay her hands in her lap again. Then I catch her kind o' looking where I'm at. I grin at her. But think she'll grin back? No. She turn up her little old nose like I got some snot on my face or something. Well, I show her both o' us can turn us head. I turn mine, too, and look out at the river.

The river is gray. The sky is gray. They have pull-doos on the water. The water is wavey, and the pull-doos go up and down. The bus go 'round a turn, and you got plenty trees hiding the river. Then the bus go 'round another turn, and I can see the river again.

I look to the front where all the white people sitting. Then I look at that old gal again. I don't look right at her, 'cause I don't want all them people to know I love her. I jest look at her little bit, like I'm looking out that window over there. But she know I'm looking that way, and she kind o' look at me, too. The lady sitting 'side her catch her this time, and she lean over and say something in her yer.

"I don't love him nothing," that little old gal say out loud.

Ever'body back there yer her mouth, and all of 'em look at us and laugh.

"I don't love you, neither," I say. "So you don't have to turn up your nose, Miss."

"You the one looking," she say.

"I wasn't looking at you," I say. "I was looking out that window, there."

"Out that window, my foot," she say. "I seen you. Ever' time I turn 'round you look at me."

"You must o' been looking yourself if you seen me all them times," I say.

"Shucks," she say. "I got me all kind o' boyfriends."

"I got girlfriends, too," I say.

"Well, I just don't want you to get your hopes up," she say.

I don't say no more to that little old gal, 'cause I don't want have to bust her in the mouth. I lean on the seat where Mama sitting, and I don't even look that way no more. When us get to Bayonne, she jugg her little old tongue out at me. I make 'tend I'm go'n hit her, and she duck down side her mama. And all the people laugh at us again.

VI

Me and Mama get off and start walking in town. Bayonne is a little bitty town. Baton Rouge is a hundred times bigger 'an Bayonne. I went to Baton Rouge once—me, Ty, Mama, and Daddy. But that was 'way back yonder—'fore he went in the Army. I wonder when us go'n see him again. I wonder when. Look like he ain't ever coming home. . . . Even the pavement all cracked in Bayonne. Got grass shooting right out the sidewalk. Got weeds in the ditch, too; just like they got home.

It some cold in Bayonne. Look like it colder 'an it is home. The wind blow in my face, and I feel that stuff running down my nose, I sniff. Mama say use that hankercher. I blow my nose and put it back.

Us pass a school and I see them white children playing in the yard. Big old red school, and them children jest running and playing. Then us pass a café, and I see a bunch of 'em in there eating. I wish I was in there 'cause I'm cold. Mama tell me keep my eyes in front where they blonks.

Us pass stores that got dummies, and us pass another café, and then us pass a shoe shop, and that baldhead man in there fixing on a shoe. I look at him and I butt into that white lady, and Mama jeck me in front and tell me stay there.

Us come to the courthouse, and I see the flag waving there. This one yer ain't like the one us got at school. This one yer ain't got but a handful of stars. One at school got a big pile of stars—one for ever' state. Us pass it and us turn and there it is—the dentist office. Me and Mama go in, and they got people sitting ever' where you look. They even got a little boy in there younger 'an me.

Me and Mama sit on that bench, and a white lady come in there and ask me what my name. Mama tell her, and the white lady go back. Then I yer somebody hollering in there. And soon's that little boy hear him hollering, he start hollering, too. His mama pat him and pat him, trying to make him hush up, but he ain't thinking 'bout her.

The man that was hollering in there come out holding his jaw.

"Got it, hanh?" another man say.

The man shake his head.

"Man, I thought they was killing you in there," the other man say. "Hollering like a pig under a gate."

The man don't say nothing. He just head for the door, and the other man follow him.

"John Lee," the white lady say. "John Lee Williams."

The little boy jugg his head down in his mama lap and holler more now. His mama tell him go with the nurse, but he ain't thinking 'bout her. His mama tell him again, but he don't even yer. His mama pick him up and take him in there, and even when the white lady shet the door I can still hear him hollering.

"I often wonder why the Lord let a child like that suffer," a lady say to my mama. The lady's sitting right in front o' us on another bench. She got on a white dress and a black sweater. She must be a nurse or something herself, I reckoned.

"Not us to question," a man say.

"Sometimes I don't know if we shouldn't," the lady say.

"I know definitely we shouldn't," the man say. The man look like a preacher. He big and fat and he got on a black suit. He got a gold chain, too.

"Why?" the lady say.

"Why anything?" the preacher say.

"Yes," the lady say. "Why anything?"

"Not us to question," the preacher say.

The lady look at the preacher a little while and look at Mama again.

"And look like it's the poor who do most the suffering," she say. "I don't understand it."

"Best not to even try," the preacher say. "He works in mysterious ways. Wonders to perform."

Right then Little John Lee bust out hollering, and ever'body turn they head.

"He's not a good dentist," the lady say. "Dr. Robillard is much better. But more expensive. That's why most of the colored people come here. The white people go to Dr. Robillard. Y'all from Bayonne?"

"Down the river," my mama say. And that's all she go'n say, 'cause she don't talk much. But the lady keep on looking at her, and so she say: "Near Morgan."

"I see," the lady say.

VII

"That's the trouble with the black people in this country today," somebody else say. This one yer sitting on the same side me and Mama sitting, and he kind o'sitting in front of that preacher. He look like a teacher or somebody that go to college. He got on a suit, and he got a book that he been reading. "We don't question is exactly the trouble," he say. "We should question and question and question. Question everything."

The preacher jest look at him a long time. He done put a toothpick or something in his mouth, and he jest keep turning it and turning it. You can see he don't like that boy with that book.

"Maybe you can explain what you mean," he say.

"I said what I meant," the boy say. "Question everything. Every stripe, every star, every word spoken. Everything."

"It 'pears to me this young lady and I was talking 'bout God, young man," the preacher say.

"Question Him, too," the boy say.

"Wait," the preacher say. "Wait now."

"You heard me right," the boy say. "His existence as well as everything else. Everything."

The preacher jest look cross the room at the boy. You can see he getting madder and madder. But mad or no mad, the boy ain't thinking 'bout him. He look at the preacher jest's hard's the preacher look at him.

"Is this what they coming to?" the preacher say. "Is this what we educating them for?"

"You're not educating me," the boy say. "I wash dishes at night to go to school in the day. So even the words you spoke need questioning."

The preacher jest look at him and shake his head.

"When I come in this room and seen you there with your book, I said to myself, There's an intelligent man. How wrong a person can be."

"Show me one reason to believe in the existence of a God," the boy say.

"My heart tell me," the preacher say.

"My heart tell me," the boy say. "My heart tells me. Sure, my heart tells me. And as long as you listen to what your heart tells you, you will have only what the white man gives you and nothing more. Me, I don't listen to my heart. The purpose of the heart is to pump blood throughout the body, and nothing else."

"Who's your paw, boy?" the preacher say.

"Why?"

"Who is he?"

"He's dead."

"And your mom?"

"She's in Charity Hospital with pneumonia. Half killed herself working for nothing."

"And 'cause he's dead and she sick, you mad at the world?"

"I'm not mad at the world. I'm questioning the world. I'm questioning it with cold logic, sir. What do words like Freedom, Liberty, God, White, Colored mean? I want to know. That's why *you* are sending us to school, to read and to ask questions. And because we ask these questions, you call us mad. No, sir, it is not us who are mad."

"You keep saying 'us'?"

" 'Us' . . . why not? I'm not alone."

The preacher jest shake his head. Then he look at ever'body in the room —ever'body. Some of the people look down at the floor, keep from looking at him. I kind o' look 'way myself, but soon's I know he done turn his head, I look that way again.

"I'm sorry for you," he say.

"Why?" the boy say. "Why not be sorry for yourself? Why are you so much better off than I am? Why aren't you sorry for these other people in here? Why not be sorry for the lady who had to drag her child into the dentist office? Why not be sorry for the lady sitting on that bench over there? Be sorry for them. Not for me. Some way or other I'm going to make it."

"No, I'm sorry for you," the preacher say.

"Of course. Of course," the boy say, shaking his head. "You're sorry for me because I rock that pillar you're leaning on."

"You can't ever rock the pillar I'm leaning on, young man. It's stronger than anything man can ever do."

"You believe in God because a man told you to believe in God. A white man told you to believe in God. And why? To keep you ignorant, so he can keep you under his feet."

"So now, we the ignorant?"

"Yes," the boy say. "Yes." And he open his book again.

The preacher jest look at him there. The boy done forgot all about him. Ever'body else make 'tend they done forgot 'bout the squabble, too.

Then I see that preacher getting up real slow. Preacher a great big old man, and he got to brace hisself to get up. He come 'cross the room where the boy is. He jest stand there looking at him, but the boy don't raise his head.

"Stand up, boy," preacher say.

The boy look up at him, then he shet his book real slow and stand up. Preacher jest draw back and hit him in the face. The boy fall 'gainst the wall, but he straighten hisself up and look right back at that preacher.

"You forgot the other cheek," he say.

The preacher hit him again on the other side. But this time the boy don't fall.

"That hasn't changed a thing," he say.

The preacher jest look at the boy. The preacher breathing real hard like he jest run up a hill. The boy sit down and open his book again.

"I feel sorry for you," the preacher say. "I never felt so sorry for a man before."

The boy make 'tend he don't even hear that preacher. He keep on reading his book. The preacher go back and get his hat off the chair.

"Excuse me," he say to us. "I'll come back some other time. Y'all, please excuse me."

And he look at the boy and go out the room. The boy hist his hand up to his mouth one time, to wipe 'way some blood. All the rest o' the time he keep on reading.

VIII

The lady and her little boy came out the dentist, and the nurse call somebody else in. Then little bit later they come out, and the nurse call another name. But fast's she call somebody in there, somebody else come in the place where we at, and the room stay full.

The people coming in now, all of 'em wearing big coats. One of 'em say something 'bout sleeting, and another one say he hope not. Another one say he think it ain't nothing but rain. 'Cause, he say, rain can get awful cold this time o' year.

All 'cross the room they talking. Some of 'em talking to people right by 'em, some of 'em talking to people clare 'cross the room, some of 'em talking to anybody'll listen. It's a little bitty room, no bigger 'an us kitchen, and I can see ever'body in there. The little old room 's full of smoke, 'cause you got two old men smoking pipes. I think I feel my teef thumping me some, and I hold my breath and wait. I wait and wait, but it don't thump me no more. Thank God for that.

I feel like going to sleep, and I lean back 'gainst the wall. But I'm scared to go to sleep: Scared 'cause the nurse might call my name and I won't hear her. And Mama might go to sleep, too, and she be mad if neither us heard the nurse.

I look up at Mama. I love my mama. I love my mama. And when cotton come I'm go'n get her a newer coat. And I ain't go'n get a black one neither. I think I'm go'n get her a red one.

"They got some books over there," I say. "Want read one of 'em?"

Mama look at the books, but she don't answer me.

"You got yourself a little man there," the lady say.

Mama don't say nothing to the lady, but she must 'a' grin a little bit, 'cause I seen the lady grinning back. The lady look at me a little while, like she feeling sorry for me.

"You sure got that preacher out here in a hurry," she say to that other boy.

The boy look up at her and look in his book again. When I grow up I want be jest like him. I want clothes like that and I want keep a book with me, too.

"You really don't believe in God?" the lady say.

"No," he say.

"But why?" the lady say.

"Because the wind is pink," he say.

"What?" the lady say.

The boy don't answer her no more. He jest read in his book.

"Talking 'bout the wind is pink," that old lady say. She sitting on the same bench with the boy, and she trying to look in his face. The boy make 'tend the old lady ain't even there. He jest keep reading. "Wind is pink," she say again. "Eh, Lord, what children go'n be saying next?"

The lady 'cross from us bust out laughing.

"That's a good one," she say. "The wind is pink. Yes, sir, that's a good one."

"Don't you believe the wind is pink?" the boy say. He keep his head down in the book.

"Course I believe it, Honey," the lady say. "Course I do." She look at us and wink her eye. "And what color is grass, Honey?"

"Grass? Grass is black."

She bust out laughing again. The boy look at her.

"Don't you believe grass is black?" he say.

The lady quit laughing and look at him. Ever'body else look at him now. The place quiet, quiet.

"Grass is green, Honey," the lady say. "It was green yesterday, it's green today, and it's go'n be green tomorrow."

"How do you know it's green?"

"I know because I know."

"You don't know it's green. You believe it's green because someone told you it was green. If someone had told you it was black you'd believe it was black."

"It's green," the lady say. "I know green when I see green."

"Prove it's green."

"Surely, now," the lady say. "Don't tell me it's coming to that?"

"It's coming to just that," the boy say. "Words mean nothing. One means no more than the other."

"That's what it all coming to?" that old lady say. That old lady got on a turban and she got on two sweaters. She got a green sweater under a black sweater. I can see the green sweater 'cause some of the buttons on the other sweater missing.

"Yes, ma'am," the boy say. "Words mean nothing. Action is the only thing. Doing. That's the only thing."

"Other words, you want the Lord to come down here and show Hisself to you?" she say.

"Exactly, ma'am."

"You don't mean that, I'm sure?"

"I do, ma'am."

"Done, Jesus," the old lady say, shaking her head.

"I didn't go 'long with that preacher at first," the other lady say; "but now —I don't know. When a person say the grass is black, he's either a lunatic or something wrong."

"Prove to me that it's green."

"It's green because the people say it's green."

"Those same people say we're citizens of the United States."

"I think I'm a citizen."

"Citizens have certain rights. Name me one right that you have. One right, granted by the Constitution, that you can exercise in Bayonne."

The lady don't answer him. She jest look at him like she don't know what he talking 'bout. I know I don't.

"Things changing," she say.

"Things are changing because some black men have begun to follow their brains instead of their hearts."

"You trying to say these people don't believe in God?"

"I'm sure some of them do. Maybe most of them do. But they don't believe that God is going to touch these white people's hearts and change them tomorrow. Things change through action. By no other way."

Ever'body sit quiet and look at the boy. Nobody say a thing. Then the lady 'cross from me and Mama jest shake her head.

"Let's hope that not all your generation feel the same way you do," she say.

"Think what you please, it doesn't matter," the boy say. "But it will be men who listen to their heads and not their hearts who will see that your children have a better chance than you had."

"Let's hope they ain't all like you, though," the old lady say. "Done forgot the heart absolutely."

"Yes, ma'am, I hope they aren't all like me," the boy say. "Unfortunately I was born too late to believe in your God. Let's hope that the ones who come after will have your faith—if not in your God, then in something else, something definitely that they can lean on. I haven't anything. For me, the wind is pink; the grass is black."

IX

The nurse come in the room where us all sitting and waiting and say the doctor won't take no more patients till one o'clock this evening. My mama jump up off the bench and go up to the white lady.

"Nurse, I have to go back in the field this evening," she say.

"The doctor is treating his last patient now," the nurse say. "One o'clock this evening."

"Can I at least speak to the doctor?" my mama say.

"I'm his nurse," the lady say.

"My little boy sick," my mama say. "Right now his teef almost killing him."

The nurse look at me. She trying to make up her mind if to let me come in. I look at her real pitiful. The teef ain't hurting me a tall, but Mama say it is, so I make 'tend for her sake.

"This evening," the nurse say, and go back in the office.

"Don't feel 'jected, Honey," the lady say to Mama. "I been 'round 'em a long time—they take you when they want to. If you was white, that's something else; but you the wrong shade."

Mama don't say nothing to the lady, and me and her go outside and stand 'gainst the wall. It's cold out there. I can feel that wind going through my coat. Some of the other people come out of the room and go up the street. Me and Mama stand there a little while and start to walking. I don't know where us going. When us come to the other street us jest stand there.

"You don't have to make water, do you?" Mama say.

"No, ma'am," I say.

Us go up the street. Walking real slow. I can tell Mama don't know where she going. When us come to a store us stand there and look at the dummies. I look at a little boy with a brown overcoat. He got on brown shoes, too. I look at my old shoes and look at his'n again. You wait till summer, I say.

Me and Mama walk away. Us come up to another store and us stop and look at them dummies, too. Then us go again. Us pass a café where the white people in there eating. Mama tell me keep my eyes in front where they blonks, but I can't help from seeing them people eat. My stomach start to growling 'cause I'm hungry. When I see people eating, I get hungry; when I see a coat, I get cold.

A man whistle at my mama when us go by a filling station. She make 'tend she don't even see him. I look back and I feel like hitting him in the mouth. If I was bigger, I say. If I was bigger, you see.

Us keep on going. I'm getting colder and colder, but I don't say nothing. I feel that stuff running down my nose and I sniff.

"That rag," she say.

I git it out and wipe my nose. I'm getting cold all over now—my face, my hands, my feet, ever'thing. Us pass another little café, but this'n for white people, too, and us can't go in there neither. So us jest walk. I'm so cold now, I'm 'bout ready to say it. If I knowed where us was going, I wouldn't be so cold, but I don't know where us going. Us go, us go, us go. Us walk clean out o'Bayonne. Then us cross the street and us come back. Same thing I seen when I got off the bus. Same old trees, same old walk, same old weeds, same old cracked pave—same old ever'thing.

I sniff again.

"That rag," she say.

I wipe my nose real fast and jugg that hankercher back in my pocket 'fore my hand get too cold. I raise my head and I can see David hardware store. When us come up to it, us go in. I don't know why, but I'm glad.

It warm in there. It so warm in there you don't want ever leave. I look for the heater, and I see it over by them ba'ls. Three white men standing 'round the heater talking in Creole. One of 'em come to see what Mama want.

"Got any ax handle?" she say.

Me, Mama, and the white man start to the back, but Mama stop me when us come to the heater. Her and the white man go on. I hold my hand over the heater and look at 'em. They go all the way in the back, and I see the white man point to the ax handle 'gainst the wall. Mama take one of 'em and shake it like she trying to figure how much it weigh. Then she rub her hand over it from one end to the other. She turn it over and look at the other side, then she shake it again, and shake her head and put it back. She get another one and she do it jest like she did the first one, then she shake her head. Then she get a brown one and do it that, too. But she don't like this one neither. Then she get another one, but 'fore she shake it or anything, she look at me. Look like she trying to say something to me, but I don't know what it is. All I know is I done got warm now and I'm feeling right smart better. Mama shake this ax handle jest like she done the others, and shake her head and say something to the white man. The white man jest look at his pile of ax handle, and when Mama pass by him to come to the front, the white man jest scratch his head and follow her. She tell me come on, and us go on out and start walking again.

Us walk and walk, and no time at all I'm cold again. Look like I'm colder now 'cause I can still remember how good it was back there. My stomach growl and I suck it in to keep Mama from yering it. She walking right 'side me, and it growl so loud you can yer it a mile. But Mama don't say a word.

X

When us come up to the courthouse, I look at the clock. It got quarter to twelve. Mean us got another hour and a quarter to be out yer in the cold. Us go and stand side a building. Something hit my cap and I look up at the sky. Sleet falling.

I look at Mama standing there. I want stand close 'side her, but she don't like that. She say that's cry-baby stuff. She say you got to stand for yourself, by yourself.

"Let's go back to that office," she say.

Us cross the street. When us get to the dentist I try to open the door, but I can't. Mama push me on the side and she twist the knob. But she can't open it neither. She twist some more, harder, but she can't open it. She turn 'way from the door. I look at her, but I don't move and I don't say nothing. I done seen her like this before and I'm scared.

"You hungry?" she say. She say it like she mad at me, like I'm the one cause of ever'thing.

"No, ma'am," I say.

"You want eat and walk back, or you rather don't eat and ride?"

"I ain't hungry," I say.

I ain't jest hungry, but I'm cold, too. I'm so hungry and I'm so cold I want to cry. And look like I'm getting colder and colder. My feet done got numb. I try to work my toes, but I can't. Look like I'm go'n die. Look like I'm go'n stand right here and freeze to death. I think about home. I think about Val and Auntie and Ty and Louis and Walker. It 'bout twelve o'clock and I know they eating dinner. I can hear Ty making jokes. That's Ty. Always trying to make some kind o' joke. I wish I was right there listening to him. Give anything in the world if I was home 'round the fire.

"Come on," Mama say.

Us start walking again. My feet so numb I can't hardly feel 'em. Us turn the corner and go back up the street. The clock start hitting for twelve.

The sleet's coming down plenty now. They hit the pave and bounce like rice. Oh, Lord; oh, Lord, I pray. Don't let me die. Don't let me die. Don't let me die, Lord.

XI

Now I know where us going. Us going back o' town where the colored people eat. I don't care if I don't eat. I been hungry before. I can stand it. But I can't stand the cold.

I can see us go'n have a long walk. It 'bout a mile down there. But I don't mind. I know when I get there I'm go'n warm myself. I think I can hold out. My hands numb in my pockets and my feet numb, too, but if I keep moving I can hold out. Jest don't stop no more, that's all.

The sky's gray. The sleet keep falling. Falling like rain now—plenty, plenty. You can hear it hitting the pave. You can see it bouncing. Sometimes it bounce two times 'fore it settle.

Us keep going. Us don't say nothing. Us jest keep going, keep going.

I wonder what Mama thinking. I hope she ain't mad with me. When summer come I'm go'n pick plenty cotton and get her a coat. I'm go'n get her a red one.

I hope they make it summer all the time. I be glad if it was summer all the time—but it ain't. Us got to have winter, too. Lord, I hate the winter. I guess ever'body hate the winter.

I don't sniff this time. I get out my hankercher and wipe my nose. My hand so cold I can hardly hold the hankercher.

I think us getting close, but us ain't there yet. I wonder where ever'body is. Can't see nobody but us. Look like us the only two people moving 'round today. Must be too cold for the rest of the people to move 'round.

I can hear my teefes. I hope they don't knock together too hard and make that bad one hurt. Lord, that's all I need, for that bad one to start off.

I hear a church bell somewhere. But today ain't Sunday. They must be ringing for a funeral or something.

I wonder what they doing at home. They must be eating. Monsieur Bayonne might be there with his guitar. One day Ty played with Monsieur Bayonne guitar and broke one o' the string. Monsieur Bayonne got some mad with Ty. He say Ty ain't go'n never 'mount to nothing. Ty can go jest like him when he ain't there. Ty can make ever'body laugh mocking Monsieur Bayonne.

I used to like to be with Mama and Daddy. Us used to be happy. But they took him in the Army. Now, nobody happy no more. . . . I be glad when he come back.

Monsieur Bayonne say it wasn't fair for 'em to take Daddy and give Mama nothing and give us nothing. Auntie says, Shhh, Etienne. Don't let 'em yer you talk like that. Monsieur Bayonne say, It's God truth. What they giving his children? They have to walk three and a half mile to school hot or cold. That's anything to give for a paw? She's got to work in the field rain or shine jest to make ends meet. That's anything to give for a husband? Auntie say, Shh, Etienne, shh. Yes, you right, Monsieur Bayonne say. Best don't say it in front of 'em now. But one day they go'n find out. One day. Yes, s'pose so, Auntie say. Then what, Rose Mary? Monsieur Bayonne say. I don't know, Etienne, Auntie say. All us can do is us job, and leave ever'thing else in His hand. . . .

Us getting closer, now. Us getting closer. I can see the railroad tracks.

Us cross the tracks, and now I see the café. Jest to get in there, I say. Jest to get in there. Already I'm starting to feel little better.

XII

Us go in. Ahh, it good. I look for the heater; there 'gainst the wall. One of them little brown ones. I jest stand there and hold my hand over it. I can't open my hands too wide 'cause they almost froze.

Mama standing right 'side me. She done unbuttoned her coat. Smoke rise out of the coat, and the coat smell like a wet dog.

I move to the side so Mama can have more room. She open out her hands and rub 'em together. I rub mine together, too, 'cause this keeps 'em from hurting. If you let 'em warm too fast, they hurt you sure. But if you let 'em warm jest little bit at a time, and you keep rubbing 'em, they be all right ever' time.

They got jest two more people in the café. A lady back o' the counter, and a man on this side the counter. They been watching us ever since us come in.

Mama get out the hankercher and count the money. Both o' us know how much money she got there. Three dollars. No, she ain't got three dollars. 'Cause she had to pay us way up here. She ain't got but two dollars and a half left. Dollar and a half to get my teef pulled and fifty cents for us to go back on, and fifty cents worse o' salt meat.

She stir the money 'round with her finger. Most o' the money is change 'cause I can hear it rubbing together. She stir it and stir it. Then she look at the door. It still sleeting. I can yer it hitting 'gainst the wall like rice.

"I ain't hungry, Mama," I say.

"Got to pay 'em something for they heat," she say.

She take a quarter out the hankercher and tie the hankercher up again. She look over her shoulder at the people, but she still don't move. I hope she don't spend the money. I don't want her spend it on me. I'm hungry, I'm almost starving I'm so hungry, but I don't want her spending the money on me.

She flip the quarter over like she thinking. She must be thinking 'bout us walkin back home. Lord, I sure don't want walk home. If I thought it done any good to say something, I say it. But my mama make up her own mind.

She turn way from the heater right fast, like she better hurry up and do it 'fore she change her mind. I turn to look at her go to the counter. The man and the lady look at her, too. She tell the lady something and the lady walk away. The man keep on looking at her. Her back turn to the man, and Mama don't even know he standing there.

The lady put some cakes and a glass o' milk on the counter. Then she pour up a cup o' coffee and set it side the other stuff. Mama pay her for the things and come back where I'm at. She tell me sit down at that table 'gainst the wall.

The milk and the cakes for me. The coffee for my mama. I eat slow, and I look at her. She looking outside at the sleet. She looking real sad. I say to myself, I'm go'n make all this up one day. You see, one day, I'm go'n make all this up. I want to say it now. I want to tell how I feel right now. But Mama don't like for us to talk like that.

"I can't eat all this," I say.

They got just three little cakes there. And I'm so hungry right now, the Lord know I can eat a hundred times three. But I want her to have one.

She don't even look my way. She know I'm hungry. She know I want it. I let it stay there a while, then I get it and eat it. I eat jest on my front teefes, 'cause if it tech that back teef I know what'll happen. Thank God it ain't hurt me a tall today.

After I finish eating I see the man go to the juke box. He drop a nickel in it, then he jest stand there looking at the record. Mama tell me keep my eyes in front where they blonks. I turn my head like she say, but then I yer the man coming towards us.

"Dance, Pretty?" he say.

Mama get up to dance with him. But 'fore you know it, she done grabbed the little man and done throwed him 'side the wall. He hit the wall so hard he stop the juke box from playing.

"Some pimp," the lady back o' the counter say. "Some pimp."

The little man jump off the floor and start towards my mama 'Fore you know it, Mama done sprung open her knife and she waiting for him.

"Come on," she say. "Come on. I'll cut you from your neighbo to yor throat. Come on."

I go up to the little man to hit him, but Mama make me come and stand 'side her. The little man look at me and Mama and go back to the counter.

"Some pimp," the lady back o' the counter say. "Some pimp." She start laughing and pointing at the little man. "Yes, sir, you a pimp, all right. Yes, sir."

XII

"Fasten that coat. Let's go," Mama say.

"You don't have to leave," the lady say.

Mama don't answer the lady, and us right out in the cold again. I'm warm right now—my hands, my yers, my feet—but I know this ain't go'n last too long. It done sleet so much now you got ice ever'where.

Us cross the railroad tracks, and soon's us do, I get cold. That wind go through this little old coat like it ain't nothing. I got a shirt and a sweater under it, but that wind don't pay 'em no mind. I look up and I can see us got a long way to go. I wonder if us go'n make it 'fore I get too cold.

Us cross over to walk on the sidewalk. They got jest one sidewalk back here. It's over there.

After us go jest a little piece, I smell cooking. I look, then I see a baker shop. When us get closer, I can smell it more better. I shet my eyes and make 'tend I'm eating. But I keep 'em shet too long and butt up 'gainst a telephone post. Mama grab me and see if I'm hurt. I ain't bleeding or nothing and she turn me loose.

I can feel I'm getting colder and colder, and I look up to see how far us still got to go. Uptown is 'way up yonder. A half mile, I reckoned. I try to think of something. They say think and you won't get cold. I think of that poem, *Annabel Lee.* I ain't been to school in so long—this bad weather—I reckoned they done passed *Annabel Lee.* But passed it or not, I'm sure Miss Walker go'n make me recite it when I get there. That woman don't never forget nothing. I ain't never seen anybody like that.

I'm still getting cold. *Annabel Lee* or no *Annabel Lee,* I'm still getting cold. But I can see us getting closer. Us getting there gradually.

Soon's us turn the corner, I see a little old white lady up in front o' us. She the only lady on the street. She all in black and she got a long black rag over her head.

"Stop," she say.

Me and Mama stop and look at her. She must be crazy to be out in all this sleet. Ain't got but a few other people out there, and all of 'em men.

"Yall done ate?" she say.

"Jest finished," Mama say.

"Yall must be cold then?" she say.

"Us headed for the dentist," Mama say. "Us'll warm up when us get there."

"What dentist?" the old lady say. "Mr. Bassett?"

"Yes, ma'am," Mama say.

"Come on in," the old lady say. "I'll telephone him and tell him yall coming."

Me and Mama follow the old lady in the store. It's a little bitty store, and it don't have much in there. The old lady take off her head piece and fold it up.

"Helena?" somebody call from the back.

"Yes, Alnest?" the old lady say.

"Did you see them?"

"They're here. Standing beside me."

"Good. Now you can stay inside."

The old lady look at Mama. Mama waiting to hear what she brought us in here for. I'm waiting for that, too.

"I saw yall each time you went by," she say. "I came out to catch you, but you were gone."

"Us went back o' town," Mama say.

"Did you eat?"

"Yes, ma'am."

The old lady look at Mama a long time, like she thinking Mama might be jest saying that. Mama look right back at her. The old lady look at me to see what I got to say. I don't say nothing. I sure ain't going 'gainst my mama.

"There's food in the kitchen," she say to Mama. "I've been keeping it warm."

Mama turn right around and start for the door.

"Just a minute," the old lady say. Mama stop. "The boy'll have to work for it. It isn't free."

"Us don't take no handout," Mama say.

"I'm not handing out anything," the old lady say. "I need my garbage moved to the front. Ernest has a bad cold and can't go out there."

"James'll move it for you." Mama say.

"Not unless you eat," the old lady say. "I'm old, but I have my pride, too, you know."

Mama can see she ain't go'n beat this old lady down, so she jest shake her head.

"All right," the old lady say. "Come into the kitchen."

She lead the way with that rag in her hand. The kitchen is a little bitty thing, too. The table and the stove jest about fill it up. They got a little room to the side. Somebody in there laying cross the bed. Must be the person she was talking with: Alnest or Ernest—I forget what she call him.

"Sit down," the old lady say to Mama. "Not you," she say to me. "You have to move the cans."

"Helena?" somebody say in the other room.

"Yes, Alnest?" the old lady say.

"Are you going out there again?"

"I must show the boy where the garbage is," the old lady say.

"Keep that shawl over your head," the old man say.

"You don't have to remind me. Come boy," the old lady say.

Us go out in the yard. Little old back yard ain't no bigger 'an the store or the kitchen. But it can sleet here jest like it can sleet in any big back yard. And 'fore you know it I'm trembling.

"There," the old lady say, pointing to the cans. I pick up one of the cans. The can so light I put it back down to look inside o' it.

"Here," the old lady say. "Leave that cap alone."

I look at her in the door. She got that black rag wrapped 'round her shoulders, and she pointing one of her fingers at me.

"Pick it up and carry it to the front," she say. I go by her with the can. I'm sure the thing's empty. She could 'a carried the thing by herself, I'm sure.

"Set it on the sidewalk by the door and come back for the other one," she say.

I go and come back, Mama look at me when I pass her. I get the other can and take it to the front. I don't feel no heavier 'an the other one. I tell myself to look inside and see just what I been hauling. First, I look up and down the street. Nobody coming. Then I look over my shoulder. Little old lady done slipped there jest's quiet's mouse, watching me. Look like she knowed I was go'n try that.

"Ehh, Lord," she say. "Children, children. Come in here, boy, and go wash your hands."

I follow her into the kitchen, and she point, and I go to the bathroom. When I come out, the old lady done dished up the food. Rice, gravy, meat, and she even got some lettuce and tomato in a saucer. She even got a glass o' milk and a piece o' cake there, too. It look so good. I almost start eating 'fore I say my blessing.

"Helena?" the old man say.

"Yes, Alnest?" she say.

"Are they eating?"

"Yes," she say.

"Good," he say. "Now you'll stay inside."

The old lady go in there where he is and I can hear 'em talking. I look at Mama. She eating slow like she thinking. I wonder what's the matter now. I reckoned she think 'bout home.

The old lady come back in the kitchen.

"I talked to Dr. Bassett's nurse," she say. "Dr. Bassett will take you as soon as you get there."

"Thank you, ma'am," Mama say.

"Perfectly all right," the old lady say. "Which one is it?"

Mama nod towards me. The old lady look at me real sad. I look sad, too.

"You're not afraid, are you?" she say.

"No'm," I say.

"That's a good boy," the old lady say. "Nothing to be afraid of."

When me and Mama get through eating, us thank the old lady again.

"Helena, are they leaving?" the old man say.

"Yes, Alnest."

"Tell them I say good-by."

"They can hear you, Alnest."

"Good-by both mother and son," the old man say. "And may God be with you."

Me and Mama tell the old man good-by, and us follow the old lady in the front. Mama open the door to go out, but she stop and come back in the store.

"You sell salt meat?" she say.

"Yes."

"Give me two bits worse."

"That isn't very much salt meat," the old lady say.

"That'll be all I have," Mama say.

The old lady go back o' the counter and cut a big piece off the chunk. Then she wrap it and put it in a paper bag.

"Two bits," she say.

"That look like awful lot of meat for a quarter," Mama say.

"Two bits," the old lady say. "I've been selling salt meat behind this counter twenty-five years. I think I know what I'm doing."

"You got a scale there." Mama say.

"What?" the old lady say.

"Weigh it," Mama say.

"What?" the old lady say. "Are you telling me how to run my business?"

"Thanks very much for the food," Mama say.

"Just a minute," the old lady say.

"James," Mama say to me. I move towards the door.

"Just one minute, I said," the old lady say.

Me and Mama stop again and look at her. The old lady take the meat out of the bag and unwrap it and cut 'bout half o' it off. Then she wrap it up again and jugg it back in the bag and give it to Mama. Mama lay the quarter on the counter.

"Your kindness will never be forgotten," she say. "James," she say to me.

Us go out, and the old lady come to the door to look at us. After us go a little piece I look back, and she still there watching us.

The sleet's coming down heavy, heavy now, and I turn up my collar to keep my neck warm. My mama tell me turn it right back down.

"You not a bum," she say. "You a man."

Jesse Stuart
Walk in the Moon Shadows

"WHERE ARE WE GOIN', MOM?" I SAID, LOOKING UP AT MY TALL MOTHER. "Where can we go when the moon is up and the lightning bugs are above the meadows?"

Mom didn't answer me. She was braiding Sophia's hair. Sophia was my oldest sister, twelve years old with blue eyes, blonde hair, and tight lips. Sophia didn't ask Mom any questions. She stood still, never moving her head while Mom finished braiding her hair. Mom had dressed Sophia in a white dress and she wore a sash of red ribbon instead of a belt to her dress. The sash was tied in a big bowknot. Sophia was dressed like Mom dressed her when we went to Plum Grove's Children's Day once a year.

Mom had scrubbed me from head to foot. She had used more soap and water than she had ever used before. There couldn't have been a speck of dirt on me anyplace. Mom gave me the same kind of scrubbing she gave Sophia. That was the reason I asked her where we were going. Mom had combed my hair, parting it in a straight line, using the long comb for a straightedge to get the part straight.

Mom had dressed me the way she always had before Children's Day. She put on me a little pair of pants that came to my knees and buttoned to my shirt. Mom made all of the clothes that we wore.

"There's no use to go, Sal," my father said. He was sitting in a rocking chair in the room where Mom was getting us ready. Now and then he would turn his head slowly and watch Mom for a minute. Then he would turn his head back and face the empty fireplace. "You're dressin' the children for nothin'. They won't be there when you go. They never have been at home."

"Just because we've gone before, Mick, and they weren't at home, is not any sign they won't be there on an evening as pretty as this one," Mom said. "I'll keep on tryin' until I catch them at home!"

"Where are we goin', Mom?" I asked again.

"I'll tell you later, Shan," she said.

"Sal, we've been there several times since we've been married and we've never found them at home," my father said.

"Where are we goin', Mom?" I asked. Sophia remained silent, pressing her lips tighter than a turtle's. "Who are these people we are goin' to see?"

"Never mind, Shan," Mom said. "I must go in the other room and dress."

"Who are they, Pa?" I asked, turning to him when Mom left the room.

217

"Just people you don't know," he replied. "But your mother and I know them. And when we go to visit them, they're never there."

"Where do they live?" I asked as Sophia made a face at me.

"Up on a high hill," he told me.

Then I thought we might be going to see Sinnetts. They had two boys, Morris and Everett. If we went there, I'd have somebody to play with. Then, I thought we might be going to Welches. They had three boys, Jimmie, Walter, and Ernest. If we went there I'd have somebody to play with. But Sinnetts lived upon a little bank above Academy Branch and Welches lived in the saddle between the Buzzard-Roost Hills and the John-Collins Knolls. I thought we might be going to see Alf and Annie Dysard. They lived on a low Plum Grove hill and had a son, Jack, and I could play with him. I didn't have a brother to play with.

When Mom came from the backroom, she was dressed as fine as I had ever seen her dress. Mom's black hair was combed and laid in a big knot on the back of her head. Her hair was held there with combs that sparkled in the half darkness when she walked to the far corner of the big room away from the kerosene lamp. She was wearing a blue dress trimmed in white frilly laces. She had worn this dress before to our Fourth of July Celebration at Blakesburg. My mother was beautiful. Pa looked at her and he didn't turn away and look at the empty fireplace this time. He kept on looking at Mom.

"I'll take the children with me, Mick," she said. "You'd better go with us, Mick!"

"I've gone there too many times already," he said. "I've been disappointed too many times. Sal, they're never at home. Not when we go. So I say: What is the use to go? If they can't be at home, if we can never see them, why go and try to look them up? I don't see any use of pestering friends who try to dodge us."

"I want our children to see them," Mom said. "Come, Sophia! Come, Shan!"

"We're going to Sinnetts, Welches, or Dysards," I said happily. "I'll have somebody to play with."

Sophia made another face at me. She was trying to get me to keep still.

"Do you know where we're goin', Sophia?" I asked.

She didn't answer me.

"You'd better go too, Mick," Mom said as she walked toward the front door of the big room with Sophia and me following her. "Mick, I think you want to go but you're afraid."

"I'm not afraid to go either," Pa said. "We've never had better neighbors. As friendly a people as we ever lived by. What would they have against me now? That's where you're wrong, Sal. I'm not afraid. I just don't see any use of trying to catch them at home. I'll stay here this time and let you go."

We walked down the fieldstone rock walk in front of our big loghouse. Mom in front and Sophia and I behind. When we came to the winding joltwagon road that went up the hollow, I watched to see which way Mom would go. If she went up the hollow, we would be going to Sinnetts. If she went down the hollow we would be going in the direction of Dysards and Welches. Mom turned down the hollow on the joltwagon road.

"Not to Sinnetts but to Welches or Dysards," I said. "I'll get to play with Jimmie, Walter, and Ernest. Maybe I'll get to play with Jack."

Mom didn't say a word and Sophia didn't make a face to keep me from talking. Mom took big steps down the road and Sophia hurried to keep up with her and I had to run. Sophia was three years older than I was and she was taller. She could take longer steps. And I looked up at the moon in the high blue sky. It was a big moon the color of a ripe pumpkin I had helped my father gather from the newground cornfield and lay on a sled and haul home with our mule. There were a few dim stars in the sky but over the meadows, down where there were long moon shadows from the tall trees, thousands of lightning bugs lighted their ways, going here, there, and nowhere. Upon Press Moore's high hill where Pa had found a wild bee tree, and cut his initial on the bark, a whippoorwill began singing a lonesome song. Somewhere behind us, I heard another whippoorwill start singing too.

Less than a quarter-mile down the hollow, an old road turned right. This road was not used except by hunters. And when we came to this road, Mom turned right.

"Mom, where are we goin'?" I said. "We don't go to Welches or Dysards that way. We can't go anywhere on that road. Not anybody lives on it."

"That's what a lot of people think," Mom said. "But I know people do live on it."

"Do they have any boys?" I asked as I followed Mom over the old road, marked by gullies where the joltwagons once loaded with coal had rolled along, pulled by oxen and mules in years gone by. I'd never seen the oxen and mules pulling the big coal wagons but Pa had told me about it when he had gone this way in the autumn to shoot rabbits and he had taken me along to carry them.

"No, they don't have any boys," Mom said.

"Then why did you want me to go, Mom?" I asked.

"Shan, I want you to meet them and to remember," Mom replied. "You might see something you will never see again."

"What's that, Mom?" I asked as Sophia walked very close to Mom and she was as silent as one of the tall trees with the moon shadows.

"Some old friends," Mom said.

Mom wouldn't tell us where we were going. If Sophia knew where we were going she wouldn't tell me. Sophia pretended that she knew. But I never believed that she did because she was afraid of the dark woods on each side of the dim moonlighted wagonroad. I watched Sophia step from lighted spot to lighted spot along the road, dodging the deep ruts and the dark long shadows. But the shadows and the ruts didn't bother Mom. She walked proudly and she was as straight as an upright tree. She wasn't afraid of dark shadows and deep ruts. Mom could step over the deep ruts easily. My mother wasn't afraid of anything at night. She loved the night because I had heard her say she did so many times. I'd heard her talk about old roads beneath the moon and stars, roads where people had walked, ridden horseback, and driven horses hitched to express wagons, surreys, hug-me-tights, and rubber-tired buggies. I'd heard her say she loved the lonesome songs of the whippoor-wills and she loved the summer season when the lightning bugs made millions of lights on our meadows up and down the hollow. Mom often sat alone in our frontyard and watched them at night. But Pa wouldn't do it. He'd sit whittling, making ax handles of hickory, butter paddles of buckeye, hoe handles of sassafras, and window boxes of yellow locust for her wild flowers. Pa always wanted to make his time count. I knew he would make a window box for Mom while she had taken us on this visit.

"Mom, where in the world are we goin'?" I asked.

I had to run to keep up with her as we climbed gradually up the hill on this deserted road that wound among the tall trees.

"Keep quiet, Shan," Mom said. "We'll soon be there."

Then, Sophia turned around and put her fingers over her lips. She told me to keep quiet without using words.

In many places we ran into pockets of darkness under the trees. The moonlight couldn't filter through the dense green leaves rustled by the late April winds. I wondered where Mom was taking us. Soon, after we had staggered and stumbled along, I looked ahead and saw a vast opening beyond the trees. It was like leaving the night and walking into the day to leave the woods and walk into a vast space where only waist-high bushes grew.

"We'll soon be there," Mom said, breathing a little harder.

We followed Mom along the ridgeroad until she came to a stop. In front of us was an old house and around it were a few blooming apple trees. The apple blossoms were very white in the moonlight and more lightning bugs than we had seen above our meadows played over these old fields.

"This is the place," Mom said.

"People don't live there, do they, Mom?" I said. "Half the windowpanes are out, planks are gone from the gable-end and the doors are wide open!"

I could see the windowpanes still in the windows because they shone brightly in the moonlight. And there were deep dark holes where the panes were out.

"Yes, people live there," Mom whispered. "Be quiet, Shan."

"Mom," I whispered, "are we goin' in?"

"No, we'll just wait out here," she said softly.

"Are there any boys here for me to play with?" I said.

"No," she replied very softly as she took a few steps forward. She reached one of the big apple trees that looked like a low white cloud. Mom sat down on a gnarled root beneath the tree. Sophia sat down beside her. And I sat down on the grass.

"I don't guess anyone's at home," Mom said. "We'll wait for them."

"Who are they, Mom?" I asked in a whisper, for I was beginning to get afraid.

"Our neighbors and friends," she said.

"Looks like they'd hang some curtains to their windows, plow the garden, and cut the grass in the yard," I said. "Looks like they'd nail the planks back on the house and put panes back in the windows. Pa wouldn't let us live in a house like that."

Mom didn't say anything. She looked toward the front door as if she expected to see somebody walk in or come out.

"Who are they, Mom?" I asked again. I wanted to know.

"Dot and Ted Byrnes," she said. "That is the old Garthee house. Dot used to be Dot Garthee . . . the prettiest girl among these hills. She and Ted and Mick and I used to be young together. None of us were married then. Many a time we rode down the road we have just walked up in a two-horse surrey together. Many people have seen them at night on this ridge in a two-horse surrey. Old Alec told me he did. Jim Pennix saw them one Sunday morning in the hug-me-tight driving early toward Blakesburg. That's the way they used to go to church every Sunday morning."

"But why don't they ever visit us, Mom?" I asked.

"Because they're not here any longer," she said.

"You mean they're dead?"

"Yes, in 1917, the flu epidemic," Mom said. "They left this world only hours apart."

"I'm afraid of this place, Mom," I said.

"Shhh, be quiet!" she said. "They won't hurt you. If they come in or go out of that house, I'll call to them. I want you children to see them. And I want them to see my children."

"Is that the reason we are all dressed up like we were goin' to Children's Day?" I asked.

Mom didn't answer me. She never took her eyes off the front door. Sophia sat closer to Mom and I got up closer to Sophia. We sat there silently and no one spoke. The April wind shook down a few apple blossoms from the branches above us. And when I saw a white blossom zig-zag down toward us, I shivered.

"Mom, I don't believe we're goin' to see them," I said. "I don't believe they're comin' home."

"But they might be in the house," she said. "Dot's great-grandfather, Jim Garthee, built that house. Her grandfather, John, and her father, Jake, lived in that house and raised their families. The well in that yard is ninety feet deep and cut through solid rock. I remember this house when there was a lot of life here. I've had many good times here visiting Dot. Dot was the last Garthee ever to live here. Now, she's gone."

"Mom, they're not comin' out," I said. "They don't want to see us. Let's go back home."

Mom wouldn't answer. She sat silently and waited for Ted and Dot Byrnes. I stopped looking at the old house there under the blooming trees. I looked away over the fields where the night wind rustled the leafy tops of the bushes and there were little dots of light everywhere. These fields were covered with lightning bugs. I didn't want to think about Dot and Ted Byrnes. I didn't want to see them and I didn't want to think about them. I wanted to go home and get away from this place. The whippoorwills were singing lonesome songs on the ridges and their singing and the falling apple blossoms made me have strange feelings. I knew Sophia was scared too. I sat close enough to her to feel her shaking. Sophia would do what Mom told her and she would never ask Mom a question.

"When I come back here another life comes back." Mom's words were softer than the April winds. "I can see the buggies filled with young people and the surreys with families going for visits or Sunday drives. I can see young men and women on horseback riding along this ridge. People used to stop here and drink cold water from that well and sit under the shade of the apple trees."

"Did you used to ride horseback here, Mom?" I asked.

"Yes, Dot and I used to ride her father's horses from one end of this ridge to the other," Mom said, looking away from me toward the house. "I'd love to see Dot and Ted. I know they'll never leave here no matter what happened to 'em. If Dot knew I was here with my family waiting, I think she'd come up and speak to us."

"Look, the moon is going over the ridge and it will soon be dark in the woods," I said. "How'll we get home?"

"Don't worry about that," Mom said. "We'll get back all right. Let's wait a while longer. Ted and Dot might be out somewhere on the ridge. And we'll get to see them when they come back."

"Do you want to see them, Sophia?" I said.

Sophia didn't answer me. She shook more than the leaves and blossoms in the wind above us.

"I wonder if Dot will be wearing one of the pretty dresses she used to wear," Mom said. "I think I can remember every dress she wore. Dot was always so pretty in her nice clothes. She knew the colors to wear and she was beautiful."

"Mom, I'm getting cold sitting here in this April wind," I said. "I want to go home."

"Just a few more minutes," Mom said, in a louder voice. "Maybe they'll hear us and come out."

"Could we go in the house and find them?" I asked.

"No, we'd better not try that," Mom said. "Your father and I did that once just before you were born. We didn't find them. I think it's better to let them come to us. But let's watch and see if anyone goes in or out."

While Mom watched the house the moon went down behind the ridge. I knew it must be midnight, for roosters crowed at faraway farmhouses.

"I wish we could have seen 'em," Mom sighed as she got up to leave.

Sophia jumped up and hugged close to Mom.

Mom walked slowly along the ridge and we followed her. We couldn't see the moon now and it was very dark. But we could see better than we thought after we followed the winding road into the deep woods again. We saw Pa coming toward us.

"Sophia, why did we ever come out here to the old Garthee house?" I said.

Then, Sophia walked close to me. She whispered in my ear as Mom walked on with Pa. "Shan, Mom is going to have a baby. She did this before you were born. Pa said she did before I was born."

I couldn't answer Sophia as we ran in the darkness to catch up. A baby brother, I thought as I ran. I will have somebody to play with me now.

George Garrett
Thus the Early Gods

"DECENT PEOPLE JUST DON'T ACT LIKE THAT, HER MOTHER-IN-LAW SAID.

Jane's mother-in-law was Mrs. Grim. How aptly named! Jane was amused by the thought until she reminded herself that it was her name too.

Jane's husband mumbled assent and held up his highball glass and looked through it to change the sky from blue to amber. Lately everything was being so changed.

Jane herself wasn't paying much attention to Mrs. Grim's desultory monologue. She sat with the other two on the front porch and looked on beyond the path that crawled like a lazy snake from the cottage through the dunes to the beach, beyond the glare and dance of light on the white sand of the beach and beyond the flourish of the breaking waves, perfectly ironed creases that became immaculate explosions into the dizzying blue of the sky, cloudless and pure today. There was a line of pelicans, a slightly lopsided V with one arm stretched out longer than the other, and they flew by with a brown sturdy grace like a crew of oarsmen in a racing shell. They followed the leader at the point. He (she guessed it would *have* to be a male) would spread his wings to soar, and all soared likewise, rising and hovering with delicate balance on invisible currents of air, maintaining always the shape and direction of the formation though, like a single, trained, instantaneous muscular action, like part of a dance. When he pumped his wide wings with a smooth strong motion, the others followed in quick succession. She liked to see them fishing and alone: the twisty, angled high dive followed by a small flash of white, and then up bobbed the pelican to float contented a while before flying again. She had seen them up close too, perched like silly newel posts on the pilings near the Fish Market, long-beaked, drab-feathered, clowns. And she had been disappointed. They seemed grotesquely comic. But now as formations of them passed by the front porch, at home in their native element of air, they seemed to be made of it, to partake of all the wild, wide-flung, dazzling substance and mystery and marvel of the sky. They were creatures of skill and grace and beauty, and she wished she could paint them.

But, of course, her paints were still packed tight in the wooden box underneath the double bed. She wouldn't dream of bringing them out.

"But they're so beautiful!" she exclaimed.

"*Who?*" the gray-haired woman, firmly in the rocking chair beside her, asked. "Who? Those Quiglys?"

"No, no," Jane said, laughing. "I was thinking about the pelicans."

Her mother-in-law snorted.

"I was speaking of the Quiglys."

Harper, Jane's husband, merely chuckled and sipped his drink.

Mrs. Grim had been talking about the Quigly family steadily ever since they had arrived and opened the beach cottage a few days (how many has it been already?) before. She noticed right away that they had been using her outside shower. ("Lord knows what kind of a staggering water bill I'll have!") She observed that they let their children run wild and free and naked as four little jaybirds all over the dunes and on the beach. And she complained that all of them, the gaunt, grinning scarecrow of a father included, used her path to the beach as if they had a perfect right to, instead of going the longer way around to the public approach. It was clear, too, at the outset that they had no pride.

The Grims hadn't been in the cottage five minutes before the man was standing at the back door, beating on it with bony knuckles, grinning and asking if he could borrow a quarter pound of butter and an electric iron, not explaining why, or, indeed, even making some kind of mannerable small talk about the casual incongruity of the two requests. He didn't introduce himself. He didn't bother to ask who they might be. He just asked for butter and the iron and then stood there waiting until he was given what he wanted.

Mrs. Grim had been fuming about the Quiglys ever since.

"Oh, Mother," Jane had said, mildly amused at first. "What's wrong with them? I mean really. They seem pleasant enough."

Her mother-in-law had stiffened.

"You're not from these parts," she had answered flatly. "So you wouldn't be expected to know or make *distinctions*. They're trash, honey, that's all. Trash, pure and simple."

The element that added insult to injury for Mrs. Grim was the occupation of Joe Quigly, whom she insisted on calling The Man, never by name. It turned out that he was a bulldozer operator. Farther south, more than a mile down the beach, he was daily engaged in levelling the pristine dunes for something or other. A new subdivision of crackerbox houses maybe. Perhaps even a motel. She wouldn't condescend to inquire.

"It really shouldn't bother you," Jane had said. "There's so much space down there, and there's a whole mile between here and there."

"When we first built this place, my late husband and I," Mrs. Grim had told her, "there wasn't another cottage for miles. It was so peaceful. Now houses are popping up everywhere like the heat rash. Like pimples. They're tearing the dunes down, and new people—not the kind of people you'd care to have around if you had any say so about the matter—are coming here by the hordes to live. They're ruining the place. They're like a lot of weeds choking us out."

"You'd have to know how everything was in the beginning to appreciate what I mean," she added.

Of course, she never failed to remind Jane that she was an outsider, from the north, and wouldn't be expected to offer her opinions on subjects she couldn't possibly know anything about, among them the Quiglys. Jane never failed to resent this either.

At first, their very first night in the cottage, Harper, too, had been amused.

"Oh, you'll come to love her when you know her and understand her better," he said. "Everyone does. It's just that she was born out of her time or, anyway, that she had to live on beyond it. She's a lady living in a time when that word doesn't mean anything. And all she sees around her is change, change, change. Change and decay. The good, happy, comfortable world she grew up in turned inside out, turned into something else after the Depression and the War. She's just a minor, eccentric victim of the great social revolution. A bewildered mastodon wandering around in the postglacial age."

But by the next night he was past that kind of fancy speech-making.

"Quit getting in a stew about nothing," he said. "Don't pay it no never mind."

Which was both strange grammar and an unfamiliar accent coming from him. Jane's husband was a lawyer now in Philadelphia. It had taken him a day and a night to pick up the accent and the idiom of a speech he couldn't have used at all since he was a child, *if* he had used it then. It had taken another full day for him to lose the half irony that made his new guise acceptable. It had taken another day and a very bad night (But she was so *nervous* visiting here for the first time. Didn't he even understand *that?*) for him to start in drinking. And now he wasn't shaving any more or brushing his teeth or changing his clothes or bothering to go down to the beach. And now he was always taking his mother's side.

They *did* look something alike. (Strangely. For wasn't it always the daughter who was supposed to end up looking more and more like the mother?) Sitting together side by side on the front porch, she with her empty hands folded, he with his clasping the almost empty glass, short, square-bodied, long-torsoed, they were clearly cut from the same pattern. Sometimes Harper's lips turned tight and down in precisely the same expression of unspoken disapproval. Sometimes, now, his small, quick, pale blue eyes reminded her of Mrs. Grim's. And Jane, slender ("Honey, you'll have to eat plenty while you're down here and put some meat on those bones. Harp, boy, you ought to be ashamed to let your wife get so frail and wispy."), milk-skinned and long-limbed, was beginning to feel made out of another substance, a member of another race.

At this moment, inspired by the sight of the flying pelicans, images to her at once of rigor and beauty and harmony and freedom, she felt like arguing.

"Now that you mention it, the Quigly children *are* beautiful."

Mrs. Grim grunted at that.

"Well, if you think naked savages are beautiful, you might say so. Each one to her own taste, as the old lady said."

"As a matter of fact, I *have* seen photographs of naked savages which I thought were beautiful, the savages that is," Jane persisted.

Harper stood up, sighed, and stretched.

"Tell you what," he said. "You want to see some savages around here? You just drop over to Black Bottom about ten o'clock on a Saturday night."

"That would cure her of notions," Mrs. Grim said, chuckling. She said the word *notions* as if it signified some kind of physical disease, barely mentionable in polite company. "That surely would cure her."

"You'd get yourself a bellyful of beautiful savages," Harper said.

"Where are you going?" Jane said.

"To pour myself another little drink. *If* you don't mind."

"Suit yourself," she said. "It's your vacation."

"Did you say *vocation?*"

"I did not."

"Much obliged."

Harper's mother rocked busily and steadily, looking straight ahead. Jane turned again to watch the fine line of the waves rising, hovering, exploding on the sand in snowy profusion. She heard Harper stumble over something in the kitchen and curse. Well, there was nothing to be done about it.

A whoop and a holler! A shrill pandemonium of treble cries and then a burst of sun-bronzed flesh as four blonde naked Quigly children shot around the corner of the porch, scattered like a flushed covey of quail down the path, and vanished in the dunes. Mrs. Grim was half out of her rocking chair, rigid, her face etched in lines of anger. Harper leaned on the door frame shaking his head.

"They won't never learn," he said.

"I tried to speak to the mother (*if* she is the mother) yesterday. And do you know she was *drunk?* Stone drunk in the middle of the day. I mean staggering around inside of that trailer blind drunk. No wonder those poor little children have to run around wild without a soul to look after them."

"They seem to be getting along all right, considering," Jane said.

"It's a wonder to me they don't all drown in the ocean," Mrs. Grim said. "I'd feel kind of sorry for The Man, if he wasn't so common and worthless himself. They tell me when he gets home from work the two of them start drinking together and just keep on until they pass out cold. The children just have to fend for themselves."

"Who told you that?"

"A perfectly legitimate source. Someone who ought to know," Mrs. Grim said indignantly.

"She didn't mean it to sound that way, Mother," Harper said. "She was just wondering."

Not even Jane now. Just *she.*

"I *did* mean it to sound that way," Jane said. "Gossip makes me sick."

"Well!" Mrs. Grim said.

"What in hell got into *you?*" Harper said.

"I don't know. I'm sorry. I just don't know."

Jane brushed past him running back toward the bedroom, fighting the impulse to tears. She flung herself on the bed and pulled a pillow over her head. It was a silly, childish gesture. He wasn't going to come running behind her and try to comfort her. He and his mother would talk about it in low voices, and after a while he'd come back to the bedroom and talk to her. He wouldn't offer any sympathy. And she was furious with herself that what she wanted was his sympathy.

She was confused about all of it, she realized. It wasn't just the usual battle, the immemorial tug of war between mother-in-law and daughter-in-law. It was that all right, intensified by the inescapable fact that Harper was an only child. But it was other things as well. She was seeing her husband for the first time in his native environment, without the well-mannered, gentle, acquired protective coloration he wore in her world, a world of strangers to him. (What comouflage was there for her here?) He was different. He seemed to sense it too, to succumb in helpless fury to old pressures and forces. She felt that as long as they stayed here they were lost to each other. The man she had married and lived with was a ghost. The one in her bed at night now was not a very attractive stranger. In that sense Mrs. Grim had become in her eyes the evil enchantress of a child's fairy tale. But then, after all, the whole business was so childish!

Then there were the Quiglys, the Battleground. They lived, the whole tribe of them, in a small trailer behind the cottage and across a dirt road, just at the edge of a palmetto jungle. It was a sagging, worn-out trailer, set up on cinder blocks. And the yard, if you could call the littered and trampled space between the trailer and the road a yard, was a perfect mess. In the center of that space there was the cross-eyed wreck of an old Buick convertible. It never moved. Sun baked it and the sudden summer showers soaked it. Every day Joe Quigly came home from work and washed and sponged it down, apparently to protect the paint and chrome from the salt air that corroded everything under the sun before long. After he'd finished, he'd climb in the driver's seat and just sit there. It looked (from the distance of the bedroom window where she always watched him) as if he pretended to be driving it. Maybe he had wrecked it and it wouldn't run any more. Maybe he had bought it as is from a junk yard and it didn't even have an engine. Maybe he simply didn't have the money for gas. (Which would be an odd thing for a bulldozer operator. She had heard they made lots of money. Unless . . . unless, maybe, alas, Mrs. Grim was quite right, and both Joe Quigly and his poor, frazzle-haired slattern of a wife, who usually appeared once a day anyway wrapped in an oversize pink dressing gown and wearing sneakers, blinking in the hard sunlight and stumbling over to the topless garbage can by the road to dispose of a bundle of—empty bottles?—*were alcoholics.*) In any case, Joe Quigly seemed to love that automobile and to be very possessive about it. If he found his children playing in it when he came trudging up the dirt road home, he ran and chased them out and away with kicks and blows and curses. They didn't seem to mind. They laughed and ran away and left him his car.

The strange thing to Jane was that neither did she. She should have cared. A man who mistreats his children! Of course he didn't really mistreat them. He had a tantrum and they had to flee, but it didn't seem to mean anything to them or, seriously, to him. It seemed to be a kind of game. It made her uneasy to think that she might have tolerated such a blow or kick or curse coming from him in just that spirit, though she was sure that if Harper ever struck her she would be badly hurt. Quigly was a curious one. Long, lean, shaggy-haired, his face high-boned, deeply tanned and lined, he moved around with a clumsy grace like an animal trying to walk on its hind legs. He grinned a snaggle- and yellow-tooth grin at her if they happened to pass, and he ran a hand through his thick, unruly blonde hair. He was a kind of caricature of the country bumpkin. But—and this was what touched and troubled her—there was something else, indefinable, about him that was utterly alien, yet intriguing. It was as if the clothes, the flesh and bones, the face he wore were all composite parts of a disguise, donned by choice and for some reason. Somehow he communicated a sense of elemental shiftlessness, of sly, supple and insinuative and irresponsible endurance. Thus the early gods, she thought, must have taken on their guise of mortal flesh and moved among us.

She had tried unsuccessfully to express this complex thing that she sensed to Harper after she'd seen Joe Quigly standing at the back door waiting for his quarter pound of butter and the electric iron. Harper had laughed at her.

"You artists! Him? He's a typical cracker boy. That's the way they all are. Godlike, my ass! Not worth a damn. Crooked as a bunch of snakes."

Since the bad night and the others following it when Harper tumbled into his side of the bed, dead drunk, and snored as soon as his face touched the pillow, she had discovered that she was increasingly fascinated by the myth she had made up for Joe Quigly. Oh, not in the ordinary way, to be sure. Not *that* way. But as one might be attracted by some wonderful new beast on display at the zoo. There was nothing to it, she assured herself, beyond that simple feeling of curiosity and delight.

Then yesterday something had happened. With Harper drinking and Mrs. Grim deep in a historical novel and Jane restless and bored, she had gone for a long, lonely walk down the beach. She passed the last of the houses and the few bathers splashing in the surf, and she walked on, following the straight and narrow ribbon of soft sand that seemed to stretch, like some ultimate desert, to infinity. The sun felt warm and good. After a while, alone and happy, she sat down at the foot of a high dune to enjoy it, soon lay back and closed her eyes, dozing in the light. It seemed to penetrate her and fill her veins, and she imagined all her blood, streams, rivers, networks, and canals, as becoming a choir of pure molten gold. As she lay there in a complete blank pleasure, she heard at first dimly, then near and loud, a roaring sound, and she sat up just in time to avoid being buried alive by a falling mountain of sand. Choking and spluttering, she struggled to her feet with vague gestures like a drowning person and tried to brush away the sand which covered her. She looked around and then up above her. On top of the dune, poised perilously at the very edge of it, was the flat blade of the bull-dozer, and standing above and behind the blade, tall against the whirling sky, straddle-legged, with the afternoon sun glaring behind him, was Joe Quigly, his wild hair tousled by the sea breeze, his head tossed back laughing. Jane was furious. Though she was fully and modestly dressed in shorts and a T-shirt, she felt as if he'd been spying on her naked. And then to be covered up, nearly killed in fact, was no joke. Joe Quigly obviously felt differently about it, and, even if he guessed how she must feel, he didn't care. He was content to laugh at her, and she had to laugh too. She stood there looking up at him and laughing, and she shyly raised her hand to wave at him. He waved back, vanished, backed the bulldozer away from the edge and went to work again.

Neither of them had said a word. Yet she was as pleased as if he'd tossed her a bouquet of flowers.

She kept that story to herself, not daring to mention it to Harper now. He was sure to take a different view of it.

Jane heard the bedroom door close behind her. She turned her head and saw Harper standing over her.

"I don't know what gets into you sometimes."

"I don't either," she said. "I'm sorry."

"You ought to be. That was pretty rude."

"I know it and I really am sorry."

He dropped down on his hands and knees on the floor and crawled under the bed. She heard him fumbling among the luggage they had stored there.

"What are you doing?"

"Looking for your box of paints," he said.

"What on earth for?"

"I got to paint me a sign."

"With those? That's too expensive."

"I'd be glad to use some other paint," he said. "But it happens we ain't got none. We've told these folks for the last time. Now I'm putting up a 'Keep Off' sign."

"That's silly, Harper. You've been drinking and that's a silly idea."

He backed out and raised his head to the level of the bed.

"You don't understand. Not at all," he said. "There happens to be a *legal* problem involved. If they keep on using the path and we don't put up a sign, then it becomes a common pathway. We don't want that, do we?"

"I guess not."

"Want to help me?" he said. "You can letter a whole lot better than I can."

"No," she said. "Just help yourself. The paints are right there somewhere."

"Where are you going?"

"Just for a walk," she said, shutting the door behind her.

She took the public approach to the beach and avoided the path to save herself from having to pass under the gray scrutiny of Mrs. Grim. She set off south at a good pace, feeling the warm sand between her toes. The tide was coming in now. Jane liked high tide best, though it was hard to explain why, even to herself. Somehow when the tide was high you felt you knew, were familiar with the things the water covered and concealed. At low tide shallow sloughs were mysteries. If you waded you were apt to step on something hidden there, some submarine creature, a quick, brittle, scuttling crab, a jellyfish. (She remembered with a shiver a story of someone stepping on a corpse in the surf.) High tide, though, seemed to be a blessing, the blue waves breaking over and finally covering the beach. The natural impulse of water. It seemed like a fine idea for water to want to cover the land. Perhaps that's how old Noah looked at it, she thought.

She almost tripped over a dead pelican and started back a step in surprise. It lay on the sand, a crumpled mass of wet feathers, a beak slack as a drunk's jaw, as an idiot's, bloody peepholes for eyes (the little birds had already plucked them like grapes), and crawling with black flies and small bugs. She was stabbed with a chill omen. She had to hold her nose as she stepped by.

After the last houses and the last bather—a great fat bald-headed man in a two-piece bathing suit bobbing and splashing like a happy hippo—she felt liberated at last. The sun glared on the empty sand ahead of her. She imagined herself as a pilgrim lost in a far land. It was almost blinding it was so bright, and the breeze had died down so that she could feel the heat of the sun. She started to run. She ran along the beach at the foot of the dunes, ran breathless until she heard the bulldozer working nearby above her.

She was panting and dripping with sweat, for it had been a long run. With nervous, clumsy fingers she took off her clothes. She looked back once to where the last houses were like small toys and saw not a soul now on the beach. She threw her clothes aside and didn't care, was suddenly drunk with the sea and the sun and the sky and her lonely freedom. She lay back and closed her eyes and let the sun bathe her. Her brain was blank and heat-struck, and her flesh crawled with rivulets of sweat. Would he come to the edge of the dune and stand tall and see her now? Would he laugh then, or be struck blind? Would he bury her alive under mountains of sand? It was a strange sweet dream.

She must have been dozing literally, for when she came to herself, the sun had gone behind the dunes and she was in shadow. The breeze had sprung up cool. She was goose-pimpled. The sand was uncomfortable and she felt cold and ashamed. She covered herself quickly with her hands and arms and looked around. Still no one on the beach. No one, thank God, had seen her there. No one, she was sure. What in the world had possessed her to do something like that? Crouching over, she slipped into her clothing and noticed, dismayed, that in her distraction, in her fierce haste, she had ripped off half the buttons of her shorts. She must have been insane.

When she was dressed again and had brushed the sand off her arms and legs, she was ready to start the long walk back. It was then that she heard the laughter, soft and mocking, heard as if at a great distance of time and space, like the light laughter of a ghost, like the memory of laughter. She looked up just in time to see four small blond faces, haloed by light, the Quigly children peering over the edge of the dune, disappear into the camouflage of even blonder, blown sea wheat. Stiff and ashamed, she walked briskly away, following now in reverse the path her bare feet had made in the sand.

When she had to pass the dead pelican again, lapped at, tumbled and turned by the incoming tide, she was afraid she was going to be sick.

It was nearly dark when she came up the back way to the cottage. He was in the red shell of a car, hands gripping the steering wheel, mouth wide open, driving in some furious daydream, and he didn't see her pass by. Her feet were hurting and she limped a little, but he had nothing, not even pity, to offer her. Just at the edge of the path, facing the trailer was a sign, crudely lettered with great smears of her good paint (a half-empty tube lay by the path), multicolored, the squandered paint dripping away from the letters as if they had been written in blood:

KEEP OFF THIS HERE PATH!
This means you

And beneath this was drawn a skull and crossbones.

Jane opened the back door and went into the kitchen. She poured herself a drink of Harper's whiskey and tossed it off.

"Is that you?" he called.

"Yes" she said. "It's me. I mean it is I."

She walked through the house to the front porch. Harper was sitting in his mother's rocker with a double-barrel shotgun in his lap. He was vigorously cleaning it with an oily rag. Jane leaned against the door frame behind him in weariness and slack despair and watched him work. He jerked his head around and grinned at her.

"Did you see my sign? Did you see the sign I put up?"

"Yes," she said. "I saw it."

"I found Daddy's old shotgun in the closet," he went on. "Next time I'm going to shoot. They've been warned aplenty. The next time one of them sets a foot on this land, I'm going to get me some tailfeathers."

Just then Mrs. Grim came bustling through the living room. She brushed past Jane as if she didn't see her, and her eyes, her small, pale blue eyes, were bright with triumph and pleasure. She put a box at the feet of her son.

"Honey boy," she cried. "I found the shells for the gun. I knew they were here somewhere and I found them."

THE TRICKSTER

IT IS APPROPRIATE THAT THE TRICKSTER, WHO REPRESENTS ONE OF THE
oldest and strongest motifs in both literature and folktale, should appear so
nearly universally and in so many forms. It is part of his essential vitality
that he crops up in the most divergent cultures, as if even the theme embodies
the human spirit of energetic play, of cleverness, of the impulse to manipulate
others.

In folklore, the Trickster is often an animal, appearing as Br'er Rabbit
(and his descendant, Bugs Bunny), a Trickster-Monkey figure in both Chinese and West African folklore, the Coyote of the American Indian (along
with many other Indian Tricksters), Reynard the Fox, and a whole zoo of
others.

He is equally prominent in literature, appearing as Odysseus, Til Eulen-
spiegel, Falstaff, Iago, Colonel Sellers, and Gully Jimson, to name only a few.
What is his essential character? To what extent can he himself be a hero, or
be considered "innocent" or "good," and still retain the essential lineaments
of Trickery?

To begin to answer these questions, we should remind ourselves that at the
heart of the term is the idea of manipulating others, of using them, of deceiv-
ing them for one's own material purposes or for the simple thrills of pride and
wrongheadedness. (Of course, the tricked need not be a person: in my view,
the narrator of "The Magic Telephone" is a Trickster not because he deceives
another and not because he *institutes* a deception but because he boldly and
somewhat cleverly utilizes a neurotic error in the telephone system for his
own purposes.)

The Trickster is a marvelously vital figure, often, though not always, a
comic one; the comedy is, in fact, an expression of his exuberance, his
particular power. We find it easy to identify with him, because something very
near trickery is built into our forms, our ceremonies, and all those graceful
little hypocrisies that make civilized life possible. It is this that helps us
accept him and believe in his possible innocence: if we haven't actually
committed his precise deceptions, we have at least dreamed of doing so. And
even though the Trickster is knowing, almost by definition, we sometimes
perceive something like innocence in the very *naturalness* of his life style.
When the Trickster engages our sympathy or affection, it is often because he
seems unaffected by the inhibitions and moral probings that trouble most of

233

us. Sometimes we perceive in his antics things we would secretly like to do ourselves.

A common and important variation on the Trickster theme is that of the Trickster Tricked. Whether or not it is true in real life, in fiction the manipulations of the Trickster often call forth treatment in kind—usually to the dismay of the Trickster himself and the delight of the reader. This sort of comeuppance is often termed "poetic justice," indicating how right and felicitous such an outcome seems to be. The Trickster Tricked theme merges somewhat with that of the Contest, the distinction lying in the fact that the tricking of the Trickster is usually revealed at the end of a story, whereas the Contest motif is by definition a sustained and overt trial.

Sometimes the ironic reversal, the boomerang effect of the Trickster Tricked theme, is merely the consequence of a character's action. Thus it is in Sherwood Anderson's story, "I'm a Fool." The still ingenuous but more mature narrator who tells the story is fully aware not only that in his self-aggrandizement he had been creating an edifice of lies meant to impress (trick) the girl with his importance but that this very edifice was the barrier that kept him from ever getting to know her better. It would be easy to be moralistic about the story, to insist upon the truism that you can't build a sound relationship between people upon falsehood; but the moral quality of the story is much greater than such a simplistic, if generally true, observation. The fact is that we have all been caught up in the fury of lying to others, trying to make ourselves appear better, grander, more important than we are. Seldom, however, has the insidiousness of such trickery been more vividly exposed than in Anderson's tale of the adolescent boy whose admiration for the girl becomes a factor in his ironic self-betrayal.

To some extent Anderson's story resists the Trickster theme. The protagonist is an old-fashioned, small-town innocent. He is serious, idealistic, and unsophisticated. He is not "naturally" a Trickster and would seem to be the least likely person to manipulate others for his own satisfaction. But this is the point, for under the pressure of desire and pride, he is capable of telling the unequivocal lie that exiles him from the girl precisely as it succeeds. The equation might almost be: If *this* boy can be guilty of such deceit, how much likelier are the rest of us to trick and deceive others for our own purposes. The theme of Metamorphosis is also important in the story, for the narrator has undergone change, has been initiated; but the central action and ironic focus revolve around the lie. This is what the narrator himself keeps returning to in his account.

Other classic short stories that celebrate the theme of the Trickster are "The Man That Corrupted Hadleyburg" by Mark Twain, "Spotted Horses" by William Faulkner, "The Limping Lady" by A. E. Coppard, "Haircut" by Ring Lardner, and "The Catbird Seat" by James Thurber.

Sherwood Anderson
I'm a Fool

IT WAS A HARD JOLT FOR ME, ONE OF THE MOST BITTEREST I EVER HAD to face. And it all came about through my own foolishness, too. Even yet sometimes, when I think of it, I want to cry or swear or kick myself. Perhaps, even now, after all this time, there will be a kind of satisfaction in making myself look cheap by telling of it.

It began at three o'clock one October afternoon as I sat in the grandstand at the fall trotting and pacing meet at Sandusky, Ohio.

To tell the truth, I felt a little foolish that I should be sitting in the grandstand at all. During the summer before I had left my home town with Harry Whitehead and, with a nigger named Burt, had taken a job as swipe with one of the two horses Harry was campaigning through the fall race meets that year. Mother cried, and my sister Mildred, who wanted to get a job as a school-teacher in our town that fall, stormed and scolded about the house all during the week before I left. They both thought it something disgraceful that one of our family should take a place as a swipe with race-horses. I've an idea Mildred thought my taking the place would stand in the way of her getting the job she'd been working so long for.

But after all, I had to work, and there was no other work to be got. A big lumbering fellow of nineteen couldn't just hang around the house, and I had got too big to mow people's lawns and sell newspapers. Little chaps who could get next to people's sympathies by their sizes were always getting jobs away from me. There was one fellow who kept saying to everyone who wanted a lawn mowed or a cistern cleaned, that he was saving money to work his way through college, and I used to lay awake nights thinking up ways to injure him without being found out. I kept thinking of wagons running over him and bricks falling on his head as he walked along the street. But never mind him.

I got the place with Harry and I liked Burt fine. We got along splendid together. He was a big nigger with a lazy, sprawling body and soft, kind eyes, and when it came to a fight, he could hit like Jack Johnson. He had Bucephalus, a big black pacing stallion that could do 2.09 or 2.10 if he had to, and I had a little gelding named Doctor Fritz that never lost a race all fall when Harry wanted him to win.

We set out from home late in July in a boxcar with the two horses, and after that, until late November, we kept moving along to the race meets and the fairs. It was a peachy time for me, I'll say that. Sometimes now I think

235

that boys who are raised regular in houses, and never have a fine nigger like
Burt for best friend, and go to high schools and college, and never steal
anything, or get drunk a little, or learn to swear from fellows who know how,
or come walking up in front of a grandstand in their shirt-sleeves and with
dirty horsey pants on when the races are going on and the grandstand is full
of people all dressed up—What's the use of talking about it? Such fellows
don't know nothing at all. They've never had no opportunity.

But I did. Burt taught me how to rub down a horse and put the bandages
on after a race and steam a horse out and a lot of valuable things for any man
to know. He could wrap a bandage on a horse's leg so smooth that if it had
been the same color you would think it was his skin, and I guess he'd have
been a big driver, too, and got to the top like Murphy and Walter Cox and
the others if he hadn't been black.

Gee whizz, it was fun. You got to a county-seat town, maybe say on a
Saturday or Sunday, and the fair began the next Tuesday and lasted until
Friday afternoon. Doctor Fritz would be, say in the 2.25 trot on Tuesday
afternoon, and on Thursday afternoon Bucephalus would knock 'em cold in
the "free-for-all" pace. It left you a lot of time to hang around and listen to
horse talk, and see Burt knock some yap cold that got too gay, and you'd find
out about horses and men and pick up a lot of stuff you could use all the rest
of your life, if you had some sense and salted down what you heard and felt
and saw.

And then at the end of the week when the race meet was over, and Harry
had run home to tend up to his livery-stable business, you and Burt hitched
the two horses to carts and drove slow and steady across country, to the place
for the next meeting, so as to not overheat the horses, etc., etc., you know.

Gee whizz, Gosh amighty, the nice hickory-nut and beech-nut and oaks
and other kinds of trees along the roads, all brown and red, and the good
smells, and Burt singing a song that was called Deep River, and the country
girls at the windows of houses and everything. You can stick your colleges
up your nose for all me. I guess I know where I got my education.

Why, one of those little burgs of towns you come to on the way, say now
on a Saturday afternoon, and Burt says, "Let's lay up here." And you did.

And you took the horses to a livery stable and fed them, and you got your
good clothes out of a box and put them on.

And the town was full of farmers gaping because they could see you were
race-horse people, and the kids maybe never see a nigger before and was afraid
and run away when the two of us walked down their main street.

And that was before prohibition and all that foolishness, and so you went
into a saloon, the two of you, and all the yaps come and stood around, and
there was always someone pretended he was horsey and knew things and
spoke up and began asking questions, and all you did was to lie and lie all
you could about what horses you had, and I said I owned them, and then some
fellow said, "Will you have a drink of whiskey?" and Burt knocked his eye
out the way he could say, offhand like, "Oh, well, all right, I'm agreeable to
a little nip. I'll split a quart with you." Gee whizz.

But that isn't what I want to tell my story about. We got home late in November and I promised mother I'd quit the race-horses for good. There's a lot of things you've got to promise a mother because she don't know any better.

And so, there not being any work in our town any more than when I left there to go to the races, I went off to Sandusky and got a pretty good place taking care of horses for a man who owned a teaming and delivery and storage and coal and real estate business there. It was a pretty good place with good eats, and a day off each week, and sleeping on a cot in a big barn, and mostly just shoveling in hay and oats to a lot of big good-enough skates of horses, that couldn't have trotted a race with a toad. I wasn't dissatisfied and I could send money home.

And then, as I started to tell you, the fall races come to Sandusky and I got the day off and I went. I left the job at noon and had on my good clothes and my new brown derby hat, I'd just bought the Saturday before, and a stand-up collar.

First of all I went downtown and walked about with the dudes. I've always thought to myself, "Put up a good front," and so I did it. I had forty dollars in my pocket and so I went into the West House, a big hotel, and walked up to the cigar stand. "Give me three twenty-five-cent cigars," I said. There was a lot of horsemen and strangers and dressed-up people from other towns standing around in the lobby and in the bar, and I mingled amongst them. In the bar there was a fellow with a cane and a Windsor tie on, that it made me sick to look at him. I like a man to be a man and dress up, but not to go put on that kind of airs. So I pushed him aside, kind of rough, and had me a drink of whiskey. And then he looked at me, as though he thought maybe he'd get gay, but he changed his mind and didn't say anything. And then I had another drink of whiskey, just to show him something, and went out and had a hack out to the races, all to myself, and when I got there I bought myself the best seat I could get up in the grandstand, but didn't go in for any of these boxes. That's putting on too many airs.

And so there I was, sitting up in the grandstand as gay as you please and looking down on the swipes coming out with their horses, and with their dirty horsey pants on and the horse blankets swung over their shoulders, same as I had been doing all the year before. I liked one thing about the same as the other, sitting up there and feeling grand and being down there and looking up at the yaps and feeling grander and more important, too. One thing's about as good as another, if you take it just right. I've often said that.

Well, right in front of me, in the grandstand that day, there was a fellow with a couple of girls and they was about my age. The young fellow was a nice guy all right. He was the kind maybe that goes to college and then comes to be a lawyer or maybe a newspaper editor or something like that, but he wasn't stuck on himself. There are some of that kind are all right and he was one of the ones.

He had his sister with him and another girl and the sister looked around over his shoulder, accidental at first, not intending to start anything—she wasn't that kind—and her eyes and mine happened to meet.

You know how it is. Gee, she was a peach! She had on a soft dress, kind of a blue stuff and it looked carelessly made, but was well sewed and made and everything. I knew that much. I blushed when she looked right at me and so did she. She was the nicest girl I've ever seen in my life. She wasn't stuck on herself and she could talk proper grammar without being like a schoolteacher or something like that. What I mean is, she was O.K. I think maybe her father was well-to-do, but not rich to make her chesty because she was his daughter, as some are. Maybe he owned a drugstore or a drygoods store in their home town, or something like that. She never told me and I never asked.

My own people are all O.K. too, when you come to that. My grandfather was Welsh and over in the old country, in Wales he was—But never mind that.

The first heat of the first race come off and the young fellow setting there with the two girls left them and went down to make a bet. I knew what he was up to, but he didn't talk big and noisy and let everyone around know he was a sport, as some do. He wasn't that kind. Well, he come back and I heard him tell the two girls what horse he'd bet on, and when the heat was trotted they all half got to their feet and acted in the excited, sweaty way people do when they've got money down on a race, and the horse they bet on is up there pretty close at the end, and they think maybe he'll come on with a rush, but he never does because he hasn't got the old juice in him, come right down to it.

And then, pretty soon, the horses came out for the 2.18 pace and there was a horse in it I knew. He was a horse Bob French had in his string, but Bob didn't own him. He was a horse owned by a Mr. Mathers down at Marietta, Ohio.

This Mr. Mathers had a lot of money and owned some coal mines or something, and he had a swell place out in the country, and he was stuck on race-horses, but was a Presbyterian or something, and I think more than likely his wife was one, too, maybe a stiffer one than himself. So he never raced his horses hisself, and the story round the Ohio race-tracks was that when one of his horses got ready to go to the races, he turned him over to Bob French and pretended to his wife he was sold.

So Bob had the horses and he did pretty much as he pleased and you can't blame Bob, at least, I never did. Sometimes he was out to win and sometimes he wasn't. I never cared much about that when I was swiping a horse. What I did want to know was that my horse had the speed and could go out in front, if you wanted him to.

And, as I'm telling you, there was Bob in this race with one of Mr. Mathers' horses, was named "About Ben Ahem" or something like that, and was fast as a streak. He was a gelding and had a mark of 2.21, but could step in .08 or .09.

Because when Burt and I were out, as I've told you, the year before, there was a nigger Burt knew, worked for Mr. Mathers and we went out there one day when we didn't have no race on at the Marietta Fair and our boss Harry was gone home.

And so everyone was gone to the fair but just this one nigger and he took us all through Mr. Mathers' swell house and he and Burt tapped a bottle of wine Mr. Mathers had hid in his bedroom, back in a closet, without his wife knowing, and he showed us this Ahem horse. Burt was always stuck on being a driver, but didn't have much chance to get to the top, being a nigger, and he and the other nigger gulped that whole bottle of wine and Burt got a little lit up.

So the nigger let Burt take this About Ben Ahem and step him a mile in a track Mr. Mathers had all to himself, right there on the farm. And Mr. Mathers had one child, a daughter, kinda sick and not very good-looking, and she came home and we had to hustle and get About Ben Ahem stuck back in the barn.

I'm only telling you to get everything straight. At Sandusky, that afternoon I was at the fair, this young fellow with the two girls was fussed, being with the girls and losing his bet. You know how a fellow is that way. One of them was his girl and the other his sister. I had figured that out.

"Gee whizz," I says to myself, "I'm going to give him the dope."

He was mighty nice when I touched him on the shoulder. He and the girls were nice to me right from the start and clear to the end. I'm not blaming them.

And so he leaned back and I give him the dope on About Ben Ahem. "Don't bet a cent on this first heat because he'll go like an oxen hitched to a plow, but when the first heat is over go right down and lay on your pile." That's what I told him.

Well, I never saw a fellow treat any one sweller. There was a fat man sitting beside the little girl, that had looked at me twice by this time, and I at her, and both blushing, and what did he do but have the nerve to turn and ask the fat man to get up and change places with me so I could set with his crowd.

Gee whizz, craps amighty. There I was. What a chump I was to go and get gay up there in the West House bar, and just because that dude was standing there with a cane and that kind of a necktie on, to go and get all balled up and drink that whiskey, just to show off.

Of course she would know, me setting right beside her and letting her smell of my breath. I could have kicked myself right down out of that grandstand and all around that race track and made a faster record than most of the skates of horses they had there that year.

Because that girl wasn't any mutt of a girl. What wouldn't I have give right then for a stick of chewing gum to chew, or a lozenger, or some liquorice, or most anything. I was glad I had those twenty-five-cent cigars in my pocket and right away I give that fellow one and lit one myself. Then that fat man got up and we changed places and there I was, plunked right down beside her.

They introduced themselves and the fellow's best girl, he had with him, was named Miss Elinor Woodbury, and her father was a manufacturer of barrels from a place called Tiffin, Ohio. And the fellow himself was named Wilbur Wessen and his sister was Miss Lucy Wessen.

I suppose it was their having such swell names got me off my trolley. A fellow, just because he has been a swipe with a race-horse, and works taking care of horses for a man in the teaming, delivery, and storage business, isn't any better or worse than anyone else. I've often thought that, and said it too.

But you know how a fellow is. There's something in that kind of nice clothes, and the kind of nice eyes she had, and the way she had looked at me, awhile before, over her brother's shoulder, and me looking back at her, and both of us blushing.

I couldn't show her up for a boob, could I?

I made a fool of myself, that's what I did. I said my name was Walter Mathers from Marietta, Ohio, and then I told all three of them the smashingest lie you ever heard. What I said was that my father owned the horse About Ben Ahem and that he had let him out to this Bob French for racing purposes, because our family was proud and had never gone into racing that way, in our own name, I mean. Then I had got started and they were all leaning over and listening, and Miss Lucy Wessen's eyes were shining, and I went the whole hog.

I told about our place down at Marietta, and about the big stables and the grand brick house we had on a hill, up above the Ohio River, but I knew enough not to do it in no bragging way. What I did was to start things and then let them drag the rest out of me. I acted just as reluctant to tell as I could. Our family hasn't got any barrel factory, and, since I've known us, we've always been pretty poor, but not asking anything of any one at that, and my grandfather, over in Wales—but never mind that.

We set there talking like we had known each other for years and years, and I went and told them that my father had been expecting maybe this Bob French wasn't on the square, and had sent me up to Sandusky on the sly to find out what I could.

And I bluffed it through I had found out all about the 2.18 pace, in which About Ben Ahem was to start.

I said he would lose the first heat by pacing like a lame cow and then he would come back and skin 'em alive after that. And to back up what I said I took thirty dollars out of my pocket and handed it to Mr. Wilbur Wessen and asked him, would he mind, after the first heat, to go down and place it on About Ben Ahem for whatever odds he could get. What I said was that I didn't want Bob French to see me and none of the swipes.

Sure enough the first heat come off and About Ben Ahem went off his stride, up the back stretch, and looked like a wooden horse or a sick one, and come in to be last. Then this Wilbur Wessen went down to the betting place under the grandstand and there I was with the two girls, and when that Miss Woodbury was looking the other way once, Lucy Wessen kinda, with her shoulder you know, kinda touched me. Not just tucking down, I don't mean.

You know how a woman can do. They get close, but not getting gay either. You know what they do. Gee whizz.

And then they give me a jolt. What they had done, when I didn't know, was to get together, and they had decided Wilbur Wessen would bet fifty dollars, and the two girls had gone and put in ten dollars each, of their own money, too. I was sick then, but I was sicker later.

About the gelding, About Ben Ahem, and their winning their money, I wasn't worried a lot about that. It come out O.K. Ahem stepped the next three heats like a bushel of spoiled eggs going to market before they could be found out, and Wilbur Wessen had got nine to two for the money. There was something else eating at me.

Because Wilbur come back, after he had bet the money, and after that he spent most of his time talking to that Miss Woodbury, and Lucy Wessen and I was left alone together like on a desert island. Gee, if I'd only been on the square or if there had been any way of getting myself on the square. There ain't any Walter Mathers, like I said to her and them, and there hasn't ever been one, but if there was, I bet I'd go to Marietta, Ohio, and shoot him tomorrow.

There I was, big boob that I am. Pretty soon the race was over, and Wilbur had gone down and collected our money, and we had a hack downtown, and he stood us a swell supper at the West House, and a bottle of champagne beside.

And I was with that girl and she wasn't saying much, and I wasn't saying much either. One thing I know. She wasn't stuck on me because of the lie about my father being rich and all that. There's a way you know. . . . Craps amighty. There's a kind of girl, you see just once in your life, and if you don't get busy and make hay, then you're gone for good and all, and might as well go jump off a bridge. They give you a look from inside of them somewhere, and it ain't no vamping, and what it means is—you want that girl to be your wife, and you want nice things around her like flowers and swell clothes, and you want her to have the kids you're going to have, and you want good music played and no ragtime. Gee whizz.

There's a place over near Sandusky, across a kind of bay, and it's called Cedar Point. And after we had supper we went over to it in a launch, all by ourselves. Wilbur and Miss Lucy and that Miss Woodbury had to catch a ten-o'clock train back to Tiffin, Ohio, because, when you're out with girls like that, you can't get careless and miss any trains and stay out all night, like you can with some kinds of Janes.

And Wilbur blowed himself to the launch and it cost him fifteen cold plunks, but I wouldn't never have knew if I hadn't listened. He wasn't no tin-horn kind of a sport.

Over at the Cedar Point place, we didn't stay around where there was a gang of common kind of cattle at all.

There was big dance halls and dining places for yaps, and there was a beach you could walk along and get where it was dark, and we went there.

She didn't talk hardly at all and neither did I, and I was thinking how glad

I was my mother was all right, and always made us kids learn to eat with a fork at table, and not swill soup, and not be noisy and rough like a gang you see around a race track that way.

Then Wilbur and his girl went away up the beach and Lucy and I sat down in a dark place, where there was some roots of old trees the water had washed up, and after that the time, till we had to go back in the launch and they had to catch their trains, wasn't nothing at all. It went like winking your eye.

Here's how it was. The place we were setting in was dark, like I said, and there was the roots from that old stump sticking up like arms, and there was a watery smell, and the night was like—as if you could put your hand out and feel it—so warm and soft and dark and sweet like an orange.

I most cried and I most swore and I most jumped up and danced, I was so mad and happy and sad.

When Wilbur come back from being alone with his girl, and she saw him coming, Lucy she says, "we got to go to the train now," and she was most crying too, but she never knew nothing I knew, and she couldn't be so all busted up. And then, before Wilbur and Miss Woodbury got up to where we was, she put her face up and kissed me quick and put her head up against me and she was all quivering and—Gee whizz.

Sometimes I hope I have cancer and die. I guess you know what I mean. We went in the launch across the bay to the train like that, and it was dark, too. She whispered and said it was like she and I could get out of the boat and walk on the water, and it sounded foolish, but I knew what she meant.

And then quick we were right at the depot, and there was a big gang of yaps, the kind that goes to the fairs, and crowded and milling around like cattle, and how could I tell her? "It won't be long because you'll write and I'll write to you." That's all she said.

I got a chance like a hay barn afire. A swell chance I got.

And maybe she would write me, down at Marietta that way, and the letter would come back, and stamped on the front of it by the U.S.A. "There ain't any such guy," or something like that, whatever they stamp on a letter that way.

And me trying to pass myself off for a bigbug and a swell—to her, as decent a little body as God ever made. Craps amighty—a swell chance I got!

And then the train come in, and she got on it, and Wilbur Wessen he come and shook hands with me, and that Miss Woodbury was nice too and bowed to me, and I at her, and the train went and I busted out and cried like a kid.

Gee, I could have run after that train and made Dan Patch look like a freight train after a wreck, but, socks amighty, what was the use? Did you ever see such a fool?

I'll bet you what—if I had an arm broke right now or a train had run over my foot—I wouldn't go to no doctor at all. I'd go set down and let her hurt and hurt—that's what I'd do.

I'll bet you what—if I hadn't a drunk that booze I'd a never been such a boob as to go tell such a lie—that couldn't never be made straight to a lady like her.

I wish I had that fellow right here that had on a Windsor tie and carried a cane. I'd smash him for fair. Gosh darn his eyes. He's a big fool—that's what he is.

And if I'm not another you just go find me one and I'll quit working and be a bum and give him my job. I don't care nothing for working, and earning money, and saving it for no such boob as myself.

David Madden

Traven

DID I EVER TELL YOU ABOUT THE TIME I TRIED TO GET MY LITTLE brother off the Tennessee chain gang? Oh. I did. . . . Okay, I *will* tell it again.

I had a wonderful summer all set up. I'd persuaded the parents of this old girl friend of mine from our acting days at the University of Kentucky that while they were "doing" Spain, they'd be smart to let me stay in the house to keep the windows open and exercise the horses. So I had a mansion on River Road all to myself, and I was happy to be back home in Louisville. I was late finishing my master's thesis on Henry James because I had gotten side-tracked by a novel set in Louisville, but Translyvania College hired me with the understanding that I would finish the thesis before September.

The first thing that hit me was my mother. Coming down the gangplank of the Belle of Louisville after a Saturday night excursion, she tripped and broke a leg. So I had to taxi her all over Louisville in the sleek blue, broken-down Buick Streamliner I had bought in San Diego to cross country, because it suddenly hit me that I was getting too old looking to hitch-hike.

We were over at Mam'maw's for Sunday dinner, along with a slew of relatives, when we got this call from Stillwater, in the mountains of Tennessee. It was me that answered.

"Hollis, they gonna throw me on the chain gang," Cody said, in a whine vibrant with outrage.

Hell, it made *me* mad, too. After three years in the federal penitentiary, looks like Tennessee could forgive and forget. But, no, they were out to clear the books of those old charges.

"Prosecuting attorney said he might can drop the charges," said Cody, "if the people I passed them checks on will settle for restitution."

"Hello, Hollis?" somebody said, in a deep, lush drawl, "your brother could use a little he'p." Turned out to be the prosecuting attorney, Jack Babcock. I asked him how much it all came to, and he said, about one thousand dollars. Knowing I couldn't get a spark with two nickles, I said I'd see what I could do.

He said, "One problem."

I said, "What?"

"They all want Cody's ass," he said. "They wanna be able to take a Sunday drive down the highway and see where Cody's cut the grass."

"Didn't I read about some boys on that chain gang that busted each other's

244

feet with sledge hammers because they'd had more than they could take of that kind of life?"

"They run that story all the way up yonder?"

So I asked him what I *could* do, and he said, "Those people he passed the checks on, they're human. Cody says you gonna be a teacher and all—respectable citizen. Maybe if they got a look at his brother and talked to him . . . ."

I said, okay, and told him I'd see him, and got Cody back on to tell him to take it easy, I was on my way. After I hung up, I wondered what the public prosecutor was doing trying to keep Cody off the chain gang. Then I remembered that it was Cody's talent for worming his way into people's confidence that got him in this fix in the first place. A talent trained to performance by our older brother, Traven.

As for the thousand dollars, all I could scrape up was a hundred to show good faith. My folks are all as poor as the corn patches they left behind in the mountain hollers of Eastern Kentucky, so all they could fork over was the gas money. And I was broke, with no money coming in until October when I'd get my first check from Transylvania, and by that time Cody'd have shackle sores on his ankles. Daddy got Momma to turn loose of a dollar, and he threw that in as *his* share.

For the hundred, I crossed over to some kin we have on the other side of the tracks in Louisville. Whiskey kin. Millionaires, with a horse in every derby at Churchill Downs. Kin who left the hills before we did, rich already off moonshine, who bought into whiskey, then bought out the big shareholders. I never cared much for money myself, but I always wanted to meet those Weavers on an equal social basis—they standing on their bank books, me standing on a Pulitzer prize. But now I had to jump the gun, go to them begging, like I was fresh out of the holler. I used my daddy's name to get in the office—it worked like a password on the secretary, who remembered him well—because when *his* daddy was killed in the mines and his momma died of cancer of the breast a year later, daddy lit out for Louisville, and his rich uncle and all the wealthy Weavers took pity, and every time Daddy came around the factory, they'd slip him a fiver, but never a job. Daddy has the same arrangement now with the government: it slips him a twenty each week out of sympathy for his chronic failure to find work.

Great uncle Hollis Weaver didn't bat an eye when I told him my daddy named me after him. But when I told him the story of Cody's life, and showed him a picture, which favored daddy—the big Clark Gable ears, the grin that said, 'aw, hell, all I need's a few bucks'—it wasn't long before he was taking me on a tour of the distillery, watching me toss down samplers. And when I walked out the gates, I had a check for a hundred.

So four flats and a new carburetor later, I had passed through one of the worst rain storms ever to hit the Cumberland Mountains and was in Sharpsburg, the first town Cody hit, with a list of victims in my pocket.

I parked in front of the Sharpsburg Family Department store, erected 1813, the same feeling in my stomach I had when I played Biff in a college production of *Death of a Salesman.* It didn't take long to see what they'd do to get a little business. They'd even take a check from a stranger passing through. I was tempted to test this impression, but remembered that Cody already had.

Mr. Overby, the proprietor, leaned against the counter under a big, spread-eagle fan that hung from the high, pressed-tin ceiling. Mrs. Overby camped by the cash register. As I imagined Cody viewing this little tableaux, *his* thoughts ran through *my* head. Or were they Traven's? Because according to Cody's version, his big damn brother, Traven, was the one got him into this.

Mr. Overby wants to know if he can help me.

"Sir, my name is Hollis Weaver. I'm Cody Weaver's brother."

By the cash register, Mrs. Overby stirs. "And here I was trying to match you up with some folks from around *here,* cause soon's you come in the door, I knew I'd seen a likeness of that face before."

Then Mr. Overby squints against the glare of noon sunlight in the door and walks around me so he can get me in focus, and when he does, he says, "Cody waltzed in here dressed fit to kill and tried on four suits and took one, and cashed a payroll check."

"But I bet you favor your mother," says Mrs. Overby, her black and white polka-dot rayon dress shimmering in the light.

"Folks *say* I do."

"Because I think it was your walk more than your face. Something about the way Cody walked in here made you drop your guard and like him right away."

"I'm after his ass, myself," says Mr. Overby.

"Fred, daddy's old sign's going back on the wall if you don't curb your tongue."

"Well, it was the biggest I was ever took, and it just scalds my cheeks to think about it."

"I was in the army at the time, sir," I said, "and then I had to go on with my education, and now I'm about to start teaching, or I would have been here sooner to let you know that I'll do everything in my power to pay you back."

"You gonna make a teacher?"

"Yes, ma'am."

"Mr. Overby squinted his eyes, suspicious. "That state investigator told me *you* was a con man, too."

"That's Traven, my older brother."

"How come *you* ain't a crook, too?"

I tried hard to fascinate *him* with an answer to a question most people seem to find fascinating.

Then they ask me if I'm a Christian, and when I tell them how I was saved in a tent on sawdust, they invite me to supper.

For such a tacky store, they had a fine modern ranch style house, but what Mrs. Overby puts on the table is good ol' country food.

We're sitting around talking, and glancing at *Gunsmoke,* and I begin to tell about Cody. "He's several years younger than I am. Traven's two years older.

So while I was looking up to Traven, I was looking down at Cody. Used to have to take care of him while Momma was working in the cigarette factory and Daddy was in the Sahara in the signal corps. We passed most of our lives in movie theatres, soaking up dreams and nightmares.

"What I wanted to tell you is about stopping off in Springfield, Missouri to visit Cody on my way out to get my master's at the University of San Diego. They wouldn't let me through the gate because it wasn't visiting hours, but when I talked with Cody's psychiatric counselor on the phone and persuaded him it would do Cody good to see his brother, he put in a call to the gate. It's one of the biggest federal penitentiaries, where a lot of the mob leaders end up, but it looks like a state university, and Cody was an impressionable pupil.

"Watching the door for Cody to show, I kept seeing him come through all the different doors in all the different places from the time he was nine: the juvenile detention home, the institutions for wayward children, La Grange reformatory, and now here he was in the big time, like the prison where I visited Traven outside Chicago when I was in the army, enroute to Alaska. Well, here come Cody through the door, grinning and waving, and he gives me a shake and a hug, and we talk about old times on the streets of Louisville —the smell of the tobacco factories (which was right there in the Luckies I brought him) and the beer plants, the distilleries, and the big bakeries. Ah, well, let's not go into that. It was just so sad, it hurt all the way to San Diego."

"Let's do with*out* Gunsmoke one night," says Mrs. Overby, twisting the knob. Mr. Overby sunk in his chair like he'd been wounded.

"Anyway, a few months ago, I stopped off in El Reno, Oklahoma where they'd transferred him because they said he was cured of his 'nerves,' as he called it, and ought to learn a trade: how to make brooms. But before he got to fastening on the sweeping part, he flew off the handle and broke some guy's jaw." But I didn't tell the Overbys *why:* the joker wanted to be Cody's buddy after lights out. Cody's got a hair-trigger temper. Good thing the only tools of his trade were a fountain pen and a book of blank checks.

"In El Reno, they had Cody on tranquillizers and it broke me up, because he moved and talked like a zombie. What was worrying him was that Tennessee had a retainer on him for a whole string of checks he passed on his way into Georgia. Straddling the two states was what brought in the F.B.I. Georgia was satisfied with the three years, to cover the one check in Athens. But Tennessee wants to bring him to trial."

What Cody had hoped was that Tennessee wouldn't want to go to the expense of being there at the gate when he stepped out of the federal pen. But on that bright morning, there they stood.

For one thing, Cody wanted to track down Traven and get even with him somehow. Traven had just come out of a Texas prison, full of religion, and somehow he had got hold of a Mack truck and a tent and had gone on a faith-healing tour. I hope he's serious.

"You see, it was my older brother Traven that led Cody astray. How it happened was this: Cody had been out of the reform school for a year and doing all right, playing ball, in fact, and getting scouts interested in his pitching. He had one problem: an eye that was blinking out on him. How did he get *that?* The scar still shows where Traven hit him with a baseball bat when we were little. It was raining outside, so we were doing a dry run in the living room, with me pitching the imaginary ball, Traven at bat, with a real bat, and Cody, age three, catching. Traven swung back and Cody began to scream and hold his head and roll in a spreading puddle of blood. A week later, he slipped while walking a railroad track and broke the stitches. A month later, he fell off his tricycle and busted open the nearly healed wound. So he had a good pitching arm, but one strike against him: a bad eye. And the last I heard he was going deaf in one ear. The prison psychiatrist promised me the chain gang would drive him totally insane."

Mrs. Overby cried and I got to crying, too, and Mr. Overby kept saying, in a friendly way, "I'm gonna have his ass in a sling."

After Mr. Overby had gone to bed, Mrs. Overby told me the story of her life, harping on the theme of childlessness. She made me promise not to write her up in a story.

The next morning, Mr. Overby took me down to his favorite filling station and had them fill me up on his credit card, and as I idled the motor, about to set out for Stillwater, he leaned on the window and said, "You tell that prosecutor, okay, I'll settle for the money, and you tell Cody, it was just that it hurt mine and Mrs. Overby's feelings so much that he'd do us that way, after we took to him the way we did."

In Carsonville, a truck full of fresh peaches was backed up to the curb in front of the courthouse. As soon as I talked with Mr. Crigger, proprietor of the Red Dot Cafe, I was going to get me one of those sweet Georgia peaches from just over the line, maybe two. The waitress behind the counter had a bottom like two clinging halves of a plump peach, and when I see home-made peach cobbler on the menu, I order it first. But what I bit into was Melba peaches from a can. I resisted pointing out the irony of it to the waitress because Mr. Crigger, thin as a hopeless T.B. case, is sitting on a high stool behind the cash register looking right at me. Then he's staring. Then he gets down off the stool and lopes on his long legs out to the sidewalk and crosses the street. I got the funny notion he was going for fresh peaches to make me a decent pie. But a few minutes later, Mr. Crigger comes back and sits down again and does a bad job of acting nonchalant, and a deputy walks in and sits right beside me, no better an actor than Mr. Crigger. The deputy seems aware his performance is weak, but he goes at it with a kind of aw-hell attitude. After I pass him the sugar he asks for and he's got it thoroughly stirred up, he says, "You just passing through?"

I give it to him straight, and he gives Crigger a false-toothed grin. "Hey, Ef, this here's that Cody's brother!"

"Well, 'y God, I tell you it was that walk that throwed me."

"Ef thought we'd caught you. Hey, Ef, didn't I tell you they had Cody in the Stillwater jail?"

While Crigger leaned against the counter with a gleaming coffee urn behind him, I started in on them. But they were awful cynical and tough. After a while, I wasn't following the waitress' peachy bottom, I was sweating. I felt ashamed, guilty, and cheap, like the time I was twelve, ushering at the Rodeo Theatre and I walked off the job in the middle of the tenth showing of *The Razor's Edge* and struck out for India and ended up in Atlanta, bumming for eating money. It picked up a little when I got to the part Mrs. Overby's tears had cut short: how Traven got Cody *into* this fix.

". . . so just when Cody got the word that his physical defects ruled him out of a career in baseball, along comes Traven, just finished with a stretch in Montana. Momma's sick and has to have a breast tumor removed. She's in the hospital and it's Mother's Day, which Cody never fails to observe, and she's lying up there worrying how she's gonna pay the bills, and Traven puts his arm around Cody, and starts in on what a hard life he and Cody have given Momma. They owe it to her to take care of those bastards that're worrying her to death with bills." They salute the Mother-flag as I run it up the pole, and I realize I'm consciously trying to manipulate their responses, so when I got the waitress crying and Mr.Crigger said, "Jo Ann, you get back in the kitchen with that bellering! Can't hear what the man's saying," I knew I had them. "So," I says, "he tells Cody about this perfect method of passing checks without getting caught, which he learned from some guy on his cellblock in Montana. He steals a check-making gismo from RCA, and they hit the highway. Traven's method worked fine for Traven. You didn't see *him,* did you, Mr. Crigger? No, he let Cody pass the checks. So Cody spent three years in the pen, hating Traven's guts. Before that, all Cody had done was refuse to go to school (because, as it turned out, he could hardly see or hear) and swipe a few things."

They all shook their heads, and there was good ol' Jo Ann, leaning in the service window, shaking hers.

"Jo Ann was here," said Mr. Crigger, "weren't you, Jo Ann?"

"Yeah, I was here. I been telling you for three years he wasn't a bad kid."

"Cody caught me on a Saturday night just before closing and I just did have the two hundred fifty dollars to break his check," Mr. Crigger reminisced. "Said he had to get on home, 'cause his momma was in the hospital and he'd already missed Mother's Day, and a more pitiful sight, I never—"

"And you fell for it," says the deputy.

"You needn't rub it in."

"What would it have to be 'fore you could smell what it was?"

"Listen," Crigger leaned toward me. "I almost died of the T.B. last winter, and I know what being shut up in a room is, so I say, turn him loose. But not before I see that money. Who needs revenge? I got hospital bills to pay."

The deputy went out with me and leaned on the parking meter while I got started, and as I pulled away, going toward Mt. Galilee, I blinked at the red violation flag under the deputy's elbow.

In Mt. Galilee, twenty miles down the line, I pulled into Pap's Service Station, where Pap's eating his lunch out of a turn-of-the-century lunch pail. I told him I hated to interrupt his lunch but that I was Cody Weaver's brother and wanted to assure him that I'd make good the check Cody passed on him three years ago. He didn't even let me get started on my little softener.

"A body gets what he deserves," says Pap. "Any son-of-a-bitch greedy enough to take in a big check like that from a stranger just for an oil change *ought* to suffer. Well, I did. I suffered two hundred dollars worth, plus the oil, plus the skin off my knuckles where the wrench slipped on that damned oil pan plug. I learned *my* lesson, so I figure he ought to learn *his*."

"He has been, sir, for three years. And the psychiatrist at El Reno told me that if Cody went on that chain gang, it would kill him, he'd lose his mind." Then I got it in about the threat of mental illness and how Cody was right on the edge now.

"Hell, let him *talk* his way off the chain gang. I never heard such a line as that boy lassoed *me* with, and I ain't about to hear another one such as that, because I ain't sitting still long enough for somebody's brother to get started." I'm leaning against the soft drink box, absorbing the delicate chill through my fanny. I'm about to break the silence by going, when he says, "Come in here grinning like he was my long lost nephew. Why, if he'd wanted to be saddled with it, I bet he could have conned me out of the whole damned filling station, and my uniform throwed in." Then he laughs and slaps his crossed arms, hard, like he's giving himself a friendly whipping. That's where I slipped in with the story of Cody's life, stressing the bad influences, but also the loneliness.

"And talk about filling stations, sir, something about them always drew him to them, I don't know what. Maybe *you* do. Loved to watch the racks go up and shosh down when he's little, and press the button on the air hose. He'd sneak into car junk yards and play all day, trying out the driver's seats and turning the moldy keys and looking through shattered windshields at imaginary six-lane highways. He wandered around a lot, up and down streets and cobblestone alleys of Louisville, alone, looking for buried treasure in the trash cans. And one time I was on a streetcar and I looked out as it turned around at this little park and there he sat on Daniel Boone's head, like a little pigeon."

For some reason, that part of the story got to Pap more than the rest, and he says, "Son, I'll have me a talk with that prosecutor, and if he convinces me that Cody's got it in him to reform himself, I'll drop the charges and settle for restitution . . . . Now sit down and have a big orange with me." He splits his peanut butter and apple jelly sandwich with me, too. Then he points the nozzle of his orange drink at me and asks, "They's just one thing I want to get straight. How come your brothers end up convicts and you turn out a teacher and a story writer?"

I tell him all about it, and he loves it, and skips back in out of the sun from filling up cars to turn me on again. When I told him that a blank page can be just as exciting and alluring as an open road, and, provided that page doesn't bear the name of a bank, you won't end up in a cell, he said, "Son, you a card."

I'm in my car, the motor running, ready to head for Stillwater and I tell him to keep an eye out for my name as scriptwriter on some TV show, and when I say it might well be a western, he slaps the hood like he's putting the seal of certainty on it. As I'm driving away, he yells, "You get that boy out of there and you bring him by here to see me, you hear?"

Taking the manager of the Western Auto store in Stillwater, where Cody had cashed a check by putting ten dollars down on a plastic rowboat and requested delivery to 2395 Sweetcreek Road, was difficult at first, but once I convinced him that he wasn't the damn fool he apparently thought himself to be for having swallowed Cody's story, it was smooth sailing. Louis Carpetti was a bachelor who had volunteered to take the store in Stillwater and put it back on its feet, but he was homesick for the Bronx, and when I started going over the high moments in several of the Broadway shows of the late forties, he was fighting tears. When I showed up, he was closing the doors, so when we parted, it was in front of the drugstore, where I had a pineapple shake and he had a cherry smash.

By then it was twilight, so I drove around the square and saw the light in the barred windows upstairs over the jailhouse, catty-corner behind the courthouse.

Cody must have been looking and listening for me all day, because just as I shut off the motor, he shows at the window, grinning, bare-chested, his pants hanging loosely on his hips, his navel black. "Hey, Hollis, where'd you get that carrrrr, good buddy!"

In the soft Tennessee summer twilight, I guess that long baby blue body with the silver trimming looked like what he'd dreamed about in his cell, but in San Diego broad daylight, I got *took* for 500 bucks.

Cody yells, "Come on up, Hollis," like all I had to do was simply walk in, climb up.

On the screened-in porch, a woman in a starched cotton lavender dress sat on a rusty glider, snapping and stringing pole beans, dropping them into a black iron pot clamped between her ankles.

"Looking for the sheriff, ma'am."

"He's wandering over the country som'mers."

"When's visiting hours?"

"Who you looking for?"

"My brother, Cody Weaver."

"You come all the way from Louisville, Kentucky?"

"Yes, ma'am."

"Well, you get yourself in here and go see your brother. That poor thing's been hanging on that window for days."

In the dim hallway, she stands up on tip-toe to reach something on the top ledge of the door.

What she came down from the ledge with was a long key that she shoved into the lock, and she gives it a twist and yanks the door open.

She says, "Same key fits the one at the head of the stairs," and before I realize what she's doing, I've got the key in my hand and she's stepping aside for me.

I went on up, and there at the barred door stands Cody, posing for the millionth cliché photograph of the prisoner, hands clutching the bars. I unlock the door, step inside, lock it again, and drop the key in my pocket. Cody gives me a big hug and then we shake hands. "Well, Hollis," he says, looking me in the eye, "they really out to get me this time," with that tone of infinite injury. "They jumped me soon's I stepped through the gate at El Reno. Damned man from the T.B.I. and Sheriff Thompson."

"Brought you some stuff," I said, and gave him a bag full of Luckies samplers Momma sent, a pack of Wrigley's Spearmint gum, a Milky Way and a *True.*

"Thanks. But I can't hardly read, I'm so nervous." In Springfield and El Reno, he read all the Thomas Wolfe he could round up, because he knew Wolfe was my hero when I was about thirteen, and though I'd switched to Joyce long ago, he always liked to make sentimental allusions to Wolfe. He tried writing, too. War stories, at first, because he'd been in the Marines when he was fifteen and got kicked out, and he thought war stories would sell easy. Later, he wrote some things about kids in trouble and asked me to send them off for him and we'd split the profit, because he knew it would make the best seller list since it was all true.

Psychiatrists would say we had a traumatic childhood, and I guess the broken home, the bad environment, and all that, had the predictable effect on Traven and Cody, but *I* remember none of it with anything but affection. We were depression babies, and Traven and I had to carry our lunches in a lard pail, with our milk in a Mason jar, and I guess it was supposed to be humiliating. Traven, anyway, realizing that a boy deserved something better, would steal cans of pineapple from the A & P and at the lunch table he would pull them out and, with a big taunting smile on his face like the Joker in Batman comics, he'd open a can with a little stolen can opener and eat the pineapple and smack his lips while the well-to-do kids watched in envy.

Well, the kind of childhood we had, you'd think you'd want to forget, but even when I was six years old, I used to go to sleep after a ritual in two parts: first, I'd review my life until I sensed I was about to go to sleep, then I'd stop, and pick it up the next night like a serial, and then I'd talk to God in a chummy way, and that's how I'd drift off. So Cody in his cell stirred all that up in me.

"And remember that time we went to the show and the ticket man grabbed me as I ran in and ripped my shirt off and you picked up a cigarette butt urn and threatened to frail him? He thought I was going in without a ticket but I was so eager to see the next chapter of Spy Smasher that I just raced on in, and you screamed at him for tearing my only good shirt, and then when I wouldn't leave after the show was over, you started pulling at me and slapping me and I was screaming in the lobby and some man came up and said he was going to beat hell out of you if you didn't quit slapping that sweet little boy—*me.* Ha! Remember?"

I'd never forgotten. I says, "Yeah, and remember," trying to steer him my way, "that creek we always crossed on the way to the show?"

"Yeah. Fartso, the whale that lived in the creek and we'd throw popcorn down to him, and I kept trying to see him. That went on for five years, me believing there really was a whale that would give you presents if you were good." The Sheriff came in, and Cody asked him if it was okay if I spent my nights in the jail and he said why sure, ain't no reason why not.

Next morning, a backfiring truck woke me, and when I looked out the window, it was a peach truck, so I sneaked down to the square, using the key in my pocket, and got a sack full, and left all but one in the cell, and quietly locked Cody in the cell and put the key above the silver-painted door.

I started out walking to look for the county prosecutor's office. Somebody directed me down a steep hill from the square to an old white, wooden house. Grass stood high in the front yard and grasshoppers flew up as I went along the walk. Two black and white spotted dogs on the porch lifted their heads and started raising hell. A window shoots up to my right and a man sticks out his head, says, "Ace, I reckon you and Hoppy want me to dump another spittoon on your heads! Now hush!" in a voice louder than the dogs. His black-streaked gray hair stirred up on his head, his face red as a beet, his eyes swollen, his lips whitish—the look of him makes me turn away, sure I've got somebody's house, not a lawyer's office, but he says, "What *you* want so early?" and I say, "This where Jack Babcock's office is?"

"It's his bedroom till the office opens. You didn't fiddle around getting here, did you? Cody goes before Judge Stumbo Monday at two."

"Oh, you know who I—"

"With that face and that walk? Swing around the porch to the side door."

He comes to the door in wrinkled trousers and a white shirt open to his navel, showing a hairy pot, and the smell of him hits me below the belt.

"They all described him by his walk, and when I saw him amble into the courtroom with Sheriff Thompson for the indictment, I knew why. Half-cocky, half-friendly, half-better-look-out."

What I walked into was the image of an old-time law office, full of old-fashioned furniture, and what he pointed to when he said, "Sit down, Hollis," was an old cracked-leather couch. I felt Babcock's warm sleep in the seat of my pants. He went into the bathroom.

And when he comes out again, he has on a tie and his hair's combed perfectly, parted almost in the middle, with a wave on one side, and two cups of coffee steam, as if by magic, in his hands. I take one as he blows at his coffee and lets his broad butt and pot belly sink into the leather cushion.

"How's Cody?"

"Well, just waiting, sir."

"Aren't we all!"

I didn't look at him.

"Cody tells me you're a writer."

"I do write, yes, sir."

"Jack. I'm Jack, and you're Hollis, okay?"

"Okay, Jack."

"See all them books that's got you surrounded?"

"Law books?"

"Full, chock full of stories."

So he took me on a two hour tour of legal documents containing vivid testimony concerning various sexual exploits from mere exposure to rape, from 1821 to 1956, and then he shows me a revolver he used on a German prisoner near Buchenwald, and says, "Write a story about *that.*" And running all through it like a thread is Cody, and I imagined not only that Jack had done a production for *him,* but that I was merely an affable stand-in for a re-run.

Then we steered straight onto Cody, with Jack interrogating me about Cody's background, till his eyes were misty. "Steam from the cup," he said, blowing on the cold coffee. "But don't depend on Cody's sad story with Judge Stumbo. The first fact you got to face is that Stumbo's been to the end of the line and come back. The gooks chopped off his son's head in Korea, and if you see a sporty little red Ford convertible, that's all the old man's got left. And second fact is that he's *always* been mean, and he hates my guts almost as much as I hate his."

"Then I'm afraid even to ask you—"

"Asking's free."

"Whether you think he'll let me pay off these people a little at a time through the next year or so out of my teacher's pay."

"Hollis, we may as well kiss Cody goodbye."

When Saturday morning country people started coming in to see him, I told Jack I'd see him later.

Through the leaves of a low-hanging, spread-fingered limb of the oak, I saw Sheriff Thompson leaning on the sill of a wide window, smoking, waving. I waved, and he glanced around to someone deep in the cavey-cool and dark of the office and dusted his cigarette on the ground, where no grass grew. His clothes were a little wrinkled and slouchy but he had the ghost of Gary Cooper going for him. Then to his side, suddenly, steps a man in severely ironed and creased khaki uniform, and a glistening leather belt and holster and slick yellow hair give him a corseted look, and he waves me in.

"Come to get your brother off the chain gang. Right?" says the well-groomed cop, as I come in the door.

"To put it subtly, yes."

Says the Sheriff, "Weaver, this is Mr. McCoy of the Tennessee Bureau of Investigation. Me and him was the ones went to Oklahoma to bring back your brother."

"And me and Cody," says McCoy, "were the ones nursed this old coot back to life. Broke down on us in Kansas City and we had to sit around a hospital room three days before we could come on in."

"Sit around ever' Kansas City bar and strip joint ever was, you mean, while *I* was *dy*ing."

"I never heard *this* story," I says, so they tell it, together, with the precision, pace, and thrust of a duet.

"But my advice to *you*, son," says McCoy, "is to turn around and go right back to Louisville. Number One, that brother of yours is a habitual criminal. Guys can murder once, and stop. They can rob and stop, soooner or later. But you take your check passer or a con man, they don't *never* give it up. So you may as well give up on your brother, now as later."

"Well, I think there's hope for Cody. I know what you mean, Mr. McCoy. Traven's like that, but Cody can be saved. Traven can't. Cody's in it out of bewilderment—always getting the world's signals crossed. But Traven's in it for love. And it's the *only* love he knows."

"Aint' no love 'tween Cody and *him*. That long ride back, all I heard was how Cody was gonna make Traven sorry."

"We all got tickled, thinking up ways he could do it," says the Sheriff, "and it two a.m. on the highway and me sick as a hog in the back seat."

"You know, I once asked Traven, since he never seems to get away with it, why he does it—passes checks and stuff."

"It's the thrill of it," says McCoy.

"That's what *he* said."

"Hell, I didn't have to *ask* him."

"Way *he* put it was, 'You walk into a store and you fox a man into your confidence and you charm the money out of his pocket, and when I walk out,' he says, 'I feel great. It's not the money. Look,' he says, 'I take a chance. When I lose, that's *my* tough luck. Next time, I'll know how to get away with it.' He's never bitter toward—toward you guys, or the people who bring charges, or the prison officials. It's just tough, and that's his attitude."

"I like a guy with a good attitude, don't you, Frank?"

"I pre*fer* 'em."

I didn't go into Cody's attitude, how he's always, since he was little, felt the injustice of it all. Somehow or other, somebody has sold him out, led him astray; it's not his fault; he can't help it; it all started when he was too young to control it. The evidence in his favor is overwhelming. Besides, that's what he's been told all his life. And he believes everything he's told, by this authority and that—by me, and by Traven, and by books, and by ads, slogans, salutes, pledges, promises, all the home truths. But when he rams his hand into one of those Christmas stockings up to the elbow and the smell of what's in it hits him, he gets that look on his face of awed surprise and hurt.

I say, "Another thing about Traven. One time when he was just out, and I was going to the University of Kentucky, we took a ride through the old neighborhood and parked in front of the house, the one out of about twenty-five that we grew up in, where we lived the longest and had the most fun, set between the railroad underpass and the cigarette factory where Momma still works—the house where he broke open Cody's head with a baseball bat (but that's another story)—and I says, 'Well, Traven, I hope you've given it up for good.' 'Hollis,' he says, solemnly, 'I've learned my lesson. I'm through. I'd rather die than go back.' I says, 'You know, Traven, the thing that's always scared me is that when the F.B.I. is tracking you, you might take to a gun, and—' By the red light of the semaphore above us, I saw the hurt look on his face. 'Hollis! You think your own brother'd do a thing like that?' He likes to keep his image in as sharp a focus as the next man.

"At the time, he had a job driving a truck on a run to Texas. It paid well. He even urged me to accept a little loan of twenty bucks. A week later, they caught him smuggling marijuana back over the border."

McCoy says, "What your big brother's got is contagious and your little brother is infected with a full dose of it."

"Cody, hell," says the Sheriff. "What about *this* one? Here I should be out scrounging around a cornfield for that gun Pete used on his wife, and 'stead of that, I'm listening to bedtime stories at high noon."

"What *I'm* trying to figure out is what you doing here in the first place," said McCoy, "less you expect to work on the judge . . . . Hit it, didn't I? Well, forget it, son. You'd have better luck with that statue of Stumbo's greatgrandfather about to fall off his horse in front of the courthouse. Am I right, Frank?"

"I'd *swear* to it. *You* all make yourselves at home. I'm riding," says the Sheriff, like it was an all-occasion exit line.

"And not only that, what you got a lawyer for, if you gonna do the tear-jerking on your own?"

"What lawyer?"

"The one up from Florida."

"That's one more than *I* know anything about."

"Maybe your mamma hired him since you left Louisville?"

"Not likely, though to get Cody off that chain gang, she *could* have done *any*thing."

"Well, this lawyer came to see me this morning down in Knoxville where I'm based, and he was wearing a white Panama suit with a wide-brimmed Panama hat, driving a white 1942 Lincoln Mercury Zephyr in mint condition. Fellow with black hair and a mustache and a cigarette holder. And carrying a shiny, shiny briefcase."

"That's pretty good, Mr. McCoy, pretty funny. You're not a bad con man yourself, but you don't expect me to believe anybody'd be seen in public looking like *that,* do you?"

McCoy laughs and slaps me on the shoulder. "You really are a card, ain't you?"

When I told Cody what Jack and the Sheriff and McCoy said about the judge, and when I reviewed the possibilities, he started to cry. Because he had lain on the cot for a week, imagining me driving up to the rescue, getting him out of there.

I lingered with him until almost dark, then I went out and got Cody some hot dogs and a big orange, and then to pacify him, I put in a call to Louisville to see how Momma was.

Momma said she was doing okay, except that the cast was heavy and her crutches hurt her, and she wished she could go dancing. Then she asked if I thought she ought to come down to Stillwater. I told her I didn't see that it would do any good. She said, "But don't you think if I come down there on crutches, they'd see how much Cody's mother believed in him, and maybe they'd . . . . Well, you know. . . ." I told her I knew exactly what she meant, but that I had that angle pretty well under control.

I felt guilty locking Cody in and going to the movies, but I was bone weary, worrying about Judge Stumbo's personality.

I was about to open the door of the screened porch when Mrs. Thompson called to me from inside the house. She held the telephone out to me when I came into the room.

"It's your daddy—long distance from Louisville. Barely make out your name, he's so sloppy drunk."

He was drunker than that. "Hollis" was about all *I* could make out, and I've had years of practice, trying to net the little silver fish that leap out of the muddy stream of his drunken gibberish. The penalty for falling for the lovable drunk notion is that you've got to hold still for a lot of unlovely flotsam. As he let it flow, I remembered the bright Sunday morning a cop car pulled up in front of the house next to the cigarette factory and Momma had to take her bathrobe out to it so Daddy could get from the curb to the living room without the neighbors seeing he had on only his shorts and a hangover. The cops had found him under a viaduct, stripped of all but his shorts, into which he had probably peed in fright as they were stripping him. As his voice rose and fell on the phone, crooned and crowed, I remembered the year after he came back from the war and Momma had divorced him as hopeless—the nights when he would stand out in the streets or up on the railroad tracks that rose on a clay bank above our house and call for me. "Hollis! Hey, Hollis! Ho, Hollis! It's you daddy, son!" And Mamma'd finally say, "Go out to him, and pacify him, Hollis," and I'd go out at two a.m. to pacify him, and end up gathering material for stories, because as the track chilled my tail, he would tell about the way it was when he served under Patton. He had a theory that Patton was really murdered, because so many people thought he was a sonofabitch, and he'd kill anybody that said he was. Then he'd tell the story about sitting under a tree cutting his toenails with a bayonet and limping quickly over to the aid-tent when he stuck himself, and starting back for his boots just as a mortar shell shivered it to bits, and somehow I always connected that with Patton not being a sonofabitch. He mourned his failure to live up to such luck. "Son," he'd say, "if I could write stories, we'd *all* be rich." Finally he passed out on the phone, and I hung up, and I drove down to the next town and saw Robert Mitchum in "Thunder Road," about mountain moonshine runners, and it took a while to realize I was seeing a movie instead of more of the real thing, because it seemed such a short leap from Stillwater to moonshine.

The next day was Sunday, and all I did was sit around the jail with Cody, eating peaches. I got Henry James out of the car and tried to read in him a little just to keep in shape. I couldn't relax, I got worried about the way the judge would react when I offered to pay for crime on the installment plan.

So I went out and put through some phone calls to Cody's victims, hoping I could persuade them to agree to that arrangement. I had given them all the impression they would get the full amount tomorrow.

Mr. Overby said he was going to have Cody's ass in a sling, and Mr. Crigger said he had hospital bills to pay, and Pap declared that suffering was good for the soul—look at Job and what it did for him—and he wished it on all his friends, including me. And the Western Auto man said the company expected him to make an example of Cody. Since I'm no good on the telephone, I didn't try any kind of plea.

When I got back at about twilight, Cody was lying on his cot, gazing glassy-eyed at the ceiling.

"I just been laying here worrying about Momma," said Cody.

"Well, that's fine. She's probably awake worrying about you. And Traven's probably lying awake trying to figure a way to con somebody out of some change, and that'll be something else to keep Momma awake. String all the nights like this together and what do you get, Cody?"

"What the hell you mean by *that?*"

"Nothing. And don't give me that hurt look. Goodnight."

"Well, by god, you can go off and let them throw me on the chain gang, if *that's* the way you feel about it! Hell, I ain't begging *no* damn body!"

"Shut up and go to sleep," I said.

That night after it got dead quiet, I said, "Cody . . . Cody . . . Cody . . ."

"Yeah, what?"

"I called up all those people a while ago and tried to get them to agree to let me pay them a little each month, but they said they had to have the cold cash tomorrow." He didn't say anything. "Cody . . . Cody . . . Cody . . ."

I wanted to lull him to sleep with a solution, as, in our childhood, I often lulled him to sleep with a story. But I had no solution and he was beyond the consolation of a story. Then I got an idea, a verge-of-sleep idea that blended into a dream. To get the cash to pay off his victims, I could pass some bad checks in Chattanooga. With the completion of my dissertation, I would move progressively into a state of academic rigidity: tenure, marriage, kids, house, new car, the whole show—a bomb. But by passing the checks, I could save my brother, who, it was dead certain, would go berserk, plunge into a deep depression that could get him killed on the chain gang, where there were so many hair-trigger possibilities. And besides, I always wondered what it would be like to have unlimited time to write (and I wondered, too, whether I had my brothers' talent for controlling life, at least for the duration of a con), and as I fell asleep the names of Cervantes, Milton, Dostoyevski, Genet, and other great prison writers chimed in my mind.

But when I woke the next morning, my mind was on the judge. I let myself out before the others were awake, and I went up to the courthouse to work on Judge Stumbo.

The judge's secretary's long black pompadour took me back to the forties. In her blue skirt, white sleeveless blouse, spike heels, and stockings with a lustrous sheen in the dewy morning light, she had a hard-life, country-come-to-town prettiness, and misty eyes. That always does it for *me*—misty eyes.

"I'm Hollis Weaver," I said, as though using a password. It didn't pass with *her*. "Cody's brother."

"Who's Cody?" She lay outside the charmed circle.

"He's to face the judge this morning, and I'd appreciate a chance to talk to him."

"The mood *he's* in, you'll wish you hadn't." Putting it as a challenge that way makes me eager to get to him. But her brassy manner and loud voice, contradicting her misty eyes, make me nervous.

"Is he in there now?" I ask her, looking at the closed door.

"Yes. And be glad *you're* out *here*. Now get out, and I mean that in a nice way, because I'm doing you a favor, Mr.—"

"Weaver. Listen—"

That's just what the judge was doing—listening to her loud mouth. Because the door cracks a foot and he's standing in it, five feet high, with a face that defies description, an expression long ago set in concrete that was beginning now to crack.

"Did you say he was Cody Weaver's brother?" he asks, without, looked like to me, opening his mouth.

"Yes, sir."

"Get out of here," he says to me.

"That's what *I* told him, sir," she says, ripping a sheet from her type-writer.

"But, sir, I must talk to you before two o'clock." Desperate, I blurted out the theme: "The chain gang will kill my brother!"

Judge Stumbo nods from the waist up, his eyelids slam shut three times with gavel-like finality.

"But the prison psychiatrist said—"

"Never *believed* in psychiatrists."

"Please, sir, I'm just trying to be my brother's keeper—"

"You're a fool."

"Well, sir, the nation needs teachers, doesn't it? And I'm trying to become a teacher, but I left off work on my dissertation to come down here to—"

"This nation don't need another educated fool."

"Sir, please, sir, just let me tell you the story of Cody's childhood, and I think you can see—"

"I've heard too *many* stories. Besides, I lack imagination."

"Sir, at least think of my mother—"

"I have no desire to think of your mother."

"Sir, what can I say, what can I do, what can Cody do, to convince you—?"

"He has only to be born again and live his life over in a different way. As it *is*, he goes on the chain gang." The crack closed before I could open my mouth. But then I got to laughing. It was a great line.

"Hey, he's really a very funny judge, isn't he?"

"I thought it was funny, too," she says, throwing her carriage, "first time I heard it."

But when the morning sun hit me in the face on the courthouse steps, I wasn't laughing. I had only five hours to work a miracle. Then, although I had just experienced a failure to the contrary, I realized that my last thin chance was to approach the victims *personally* again, and beg them to accept monthly payments. An even thinner chance on the other side of that was that the judge would accept their decisions.

So I hopped into my Buick, started off and swerved, wobbling, into a service station—with a flat tire. They patched it up, and I set out for Sharpsburg with only five dollars left of the hundred I had when I left Louisville. I headed for the other end of the line so I could gage my time as I worked back toward the deadline at the courthouse.

As I drove along, I half-decided that if I had no luck by the time I got to the third victim, I'd start cashing checks in the next town. Time passed quickly as I imagined the effect of such a move on my life. At least, I could finish the novel I was working on.

Mr. Overby squints against the sunburst where I'm standing in the doorway of his store. He seems puzzled. "He just left," he says.

"*Who* just left?"

"Your lawyer—Cody's lawyer. Mr. French."

"Huh? Listen, I just came by to talk to you about the money Cody owes you and try—"

"He just paid it off. You s'pose to meet each other here?"

"Hold it, Mr. Overby. What's going on?"

"Mr. French just paid me, see," he says, pulling a check out of his big wallet, thonged to his hip pocket. "And I signed his paper."

"What paper?"

"The affidavit saying I don't want to see Cody prosecuted, I'm satisfied with restitution, plus the interest for three years, like it was a loan. And a big plus feature of the agreement was that I get to keep the money even if Judge Stumbo sentences Cody anyway—which he will."

"So you get your money on the hip and Cody's ass in a sling any way the cookie crumbles, huh?"

"Yeah." He grins, as if delighted with the justice of it all. "Plus, *plus*—I sold him three brand new suits, one his size, and two Cody's size, and about a hundred dollars of this and that."

"What did he look like?"

Then Mr. Overby gives me the exact same description McCoy of the T.B.I. gave me, each item in the same order, right down to the shiny briefcase. "I'm gonna get *me* a briefcase like his," says Mr. Overby.

Then Mrs. Overby comes in and carried on about what a handsome, dashing, though oddly dressed, fellow Mr. French was, and she made me promise to bring Cody by to see her, and I had to promise again not to put her life story in a book.

When I walked into Mr. Crigger's Red Dot Cafe, he's up on that stool smoking a big cigar with a two inch ash.

"You just missed him," he says, and I ask who, and we go through the whole routine, the description of French and all, the gist of which is that Mr. French came in and treated them both to Crigger's best porterhouse steak (since Crigger didn't know what French meant by Chateaubriand), and over their steaks they came to an agreement, and Crigger settled for Mr. French's terms, which were the same as Overby's.

I drove up to the pumps where Pap was white-washing the island. He looks up, double surprised to see me. "I know," I says, "I just missed him."

"By less than five minutes."

"Driving a 1942 white Lincoln Mercury Zephyr in mint condition, right?"

"With brand new rubber all around," he says. "I unloaded four new double-ply nylon tires on him." He gave the island a sloppy slap of white wash.

"Did you get a cigar out of him?"

"Smoke it after lunch. Ought to last the weekend."

I scratched gravel to catch up with Mr. French, but jerked to a stop at the edge of the lot—out of gas. I didn't have any money left. Out of the goodness of his heart, Pap exchanged a tank of gas for my spare tire, my hubcaps, and, since I wouldn't need it without the spare, my jack. He said I looked faint and shouldn't go without my lunch, so he threw in a pack of stale peanut butter crackers that I almost choked to death on before I got to Stillwater.

I had the feeling there wasn't much point in going back, certainly no need to check the Western Auto man. If it was humanly possible, this Mr. French would get Cody off.

In a "no parking" zone in front of the courthouse, aligned with the walkway, was parked the white Lincoln Zephyr. I parked behind it, confident Mr. French would take care of any fines. In front of the drugstore, a Greyhound bus was discharging passengers.

The Zephyr, though white, reminded me of the Green Hornet's car in the chapter play Traven took me to see the day Cody was born. Momma wanted us out of the house to spare us the shock of birth. Traven held my hand, and as we went over a bridge, he told me about Fartso the whale, who lived in the creek below. If I threw him a nickle, Traven said, Fartso would tell his gremlins to bring me a Buck Rogers gun. "Give it to me," he said, "and I'll throw it in." Later, watching the Green Hornet's car force the bad guy's car to swerve and smash into a gas pump, I wondered for a minute how it was that Traven hugged two bags of popcorn when he had thrown both our nickles into the water. Twenty years later, it suddenly dawned on me.

I stepped into Judge Stumbo's outer office and saw Traven hefting a dangling lock of the secretary's long black hair that took me back to the forties. As if verifying the testimony of witnesses, Traven's wearing a white panama suit and hat that bring the sunlight indoors, and green-tinted glasses, a mustache, a pink shirt with a white tie, and two-tone, brown and white shoes, and in a chair lies a shiny brief case with H. F. on the gold clasp. He doesn't see me, and he's saying, "Not many girls can wear such long hair and get away with it, but if you lived in New York, you'd be setting a style, brown eyes." Her misty blue eyes look up at Traven, and she's forgotten, like many other girls, what the hell color her eyes really are, and a feeble smirk is her only attempt to control the situation. I stayed quiet, dangling in the doorway.

I'd come in at the climax, because she gets up and goes into Judge Stumbo's office, and Traven turns and glances right *at* me, as though we had been together all morning and I had just stepped in after a brief trip to the john. So I try to match his cool.

The door opens, and the secretary steps aside to let Traven pass. She leaves the door ajar, so from where I stand, I watch Traven walk up to the desk and put out his hand at such a distance that the Judge has to get up and reach across his desk to shake it. I can't catch all the conversation, but I see the affidavits come out of the shiny briefcase and the Judge take them and peruse them, shaking his head negative.

". . . willing to pay the court costs," I hear Traven say, his voice becoming louder, stageworthy, as he builds the scene. "I realize that in a case like this the court costs are what some people might regard as exorbitant; nevertheless, we're willing to lay it on the line today, sir. Settle it out of court, if possible."

"Sir, everybody has been at me to handle this case out of court, but I don't handle, sir, and you may as well save your techniques of persuasion until court convenes—in exactly ten minutes. Now, if you'll excuse me. . . ."

I stare at the back of Traven's head as he remains seated, very still, and the judge stares at Traven's face.

"Pardon me for staring, sir," says Traven, "but isn't that—?" Then I see the color photograph of a young man in a Marine uniform. "I *thought* the name was familiar. Judge Stumbo. That name kept nagging at me all the way down the highway. That's Joe, isn't it?"

"Why—yes, but—what's that got to do with Cody Weaver?"

"Nothing, sir," says Traven, rising, still looking at the picture. "Nothing." Then, he jerks himself into a posture of efficiency, puts out his hand so the Judge has to get up again and reach out to it, and as they shake, the Judge says, "Mr. French, what were you about to say?"

"That I knew him. The machine gun—"

"Who told you about Joe?"

"Told *me!* Let me tell *you,* sir. I was there." The Judge's other hand reaches out and the four hands clasp in one fingery knot. "All I got to show is one bullet wound, but poor Joe. . . ."

Then I remember the scar under Traven's shoulder blade. In Texas, a prison guard bent over a water fountain and his pistol fell out of its holster and fired.

"What are you people doing out there?" says the judge. "Mr. Weaver, your lawyer will be with you in a moment." He pushed the door shut. "Now, sir. . . . What did you say your first name was?"

Muffled by the door come a few phrases: ". . . died in my arms. . . . I was delirious at the time . . . didn't know him well, but . . . last words were, 'Candyman, Candyman'. . . . That mean anything to you, sir?"

At the word 'Candyman,' the secretary frowns slightly, then, slowly, smiles cunningly, then shrugs, stops pretending to work, and sits with her arms folded, listening with me.

"Candyman Joe's nickname for his father?" I ask.

She smirks and nods her head. "How did *you* know?"

"Imagination," I say, and nod *my* head.

Twenty minutes later, the Judge comes out and says, "Mrs. Harmon, would you please write out a check for a hundred dollars? Mr. French needs some expense money to get back to Florida, and I'm afraid he can't cash a check locally without identification, but they'll cash one with *my* signature on it. And here's his check to cover court costs. We've settled it out of court, so strike Cody Weaver from the docket."

We all shook hands and the Judge hurried out to court, thirty minutes late, content with Traven's promise to return and spend a weekend with him some time.

"Show Mr. French the jail," says Mrs. Harmon to me, smirking.

"If there's a florist in this town," says Traven, posing in the doorway, "expect a dozen roses within an hour."

"I won't hold my breath."

As we're going down the steps toward his car, Traven says, "See you in jail," and I see there's a ticket on my windshield, none on his. I follow in my car, which I want *near* me up to the last minute. In the short drive around the square to the jail, I notice the new tires on Traven's car, the suits hanging neatly in the back, the boxes of other stuff stacked in the seat, and I think of all the checks he passed this morning, and hope each of the receivers got a cigar at least. And then I think, yeah, everybody but me.

By the time I climb out of my wreck of a car and reach the screen porch, Cody is already out there, a grin stretching from one of those big ears to the other, and Sheriff Thompson is folding a piece of paper, probably a note from the judge.

I stayed outside in the broiling sun, while Cody hugs the Sheriff's wife and shakes hands with Thompson. Traven gives the Sheriff a big cigar, then loads his own pearl-handled cigarette holder and feels for matches until the Sheriff lights it for him, then lights his own cigar. They all step out into the sunlight, shaking hands.

I follow the parade toward the cars, and Cody runs ahead and jumps behind the wheel of that white Lincoln Mercury Zephyr like it was Santa's sleigh.

"Follow *me,*" Traven says to me, as he gets in beside Cody. They take off as though they have a motorcycle escort. As, in every sense that matters, they have.

Just before I pull away from the curb, I look up at the window where I first saw Cody two days ago.

At the intersection where the caution light blinked in the sun's glare, I took the highway less traveled by, the one that offered a short cut over a curving route to the state line. Traven and his chauffeur, Cody, were borne along in their dreamboat down the superhighway toward the horizon.

This was eight years ago, and the last time I saw Cody was when I was in Idaho a few months ago for the world premiere—as the producer called it— of my play *Berserk*. A little theatre group was trying it out for us, and I had gotten leave from the University of Montana (I *didn't* stick at Transylvania after all) to be in on rehearsals. Opening night, a terrific snowstorm hit, and television cameras were set up to shoot first nighters—Boise high society—as they came in out of the blizzard. Three came in and one stepped back to hold the door open for a fourth, and in walked a tuxedo with you-know-who inside, and that grin, transported from the Sheriff's porch.

On camera, Cody was asked why he had made the trip up from Dallas in this terrible blizzard, and he replied, with a jut of his chin and a look of amazement, "Well, you don't think I'd miss my brother's play, do you?" What he missed, of course, was the character *in* the play, who resembled himself—at least in *my* imagination.

He was driving a 1941 green Hudson wasp, one of only 395 that were made that year. Living in the car, he travels all over the United States, constantly on the move, from one brief job to another, living by his wits, but apparently keeping out of trouble. He's been living that way for eight years, and I've taught in almost that many colleges, and he always shows up at least once or twice a year from a thousand miles away, and a few days later, he leaves, usually in a rain or snow storm, and I get a card several days after, saying, "Dear Hollis: Well, I made it to Laredo, okay. On my way to San Diego. All my love, your brother, Cody Weaver." On the back is a color photograph of an Indian in full costume or a buffalo, for my son's sake. And if you'll just be patient, I'm sure Cody will come knocking at that front door before too long.

Since Stillwater, Traven's served three stretches, in California, New Jersey, and Mississippi. But now *he's* going straight, too, living and working in Toronto, where he's married and has a family, and runs a tabernacle of the Holiness church. His wife sings, his little girl shakes the tambourine, and he scorches sinners alive with his visions of hell, and then leaves them in Jordan. Well, who can tell? Maybe, even if it's a con, he does some good.

Because Traven's the oldest rat in the barn. Traven sold us *all* a bill of goods. Not just the judge, the victims, the sheriff, but in the beginning, back home in Louisville—me and Cody. With that merchant marine outfit, standing like that at the front door with the September sun around his head, a nimbus of light, evoking far off places, far *out* episodes. I never told you about that? Then listen.

A smoky-red October afternoon. Me and little Cody and Traven playing marbles under the Indian cigar tree with a bunch of tough kids, and somebody says to Traven, "Okay, Big Chief Chew-tabacca, shoot!" and Traven stands up, hitches up his knickers like Humphrey Bogart and spits tobacco juice bull's-eye into the ring and says, "You all take it easy, you hear? I'm going swimming." And we all laugh like hell as he walks down the street past the flood gates, his pockets bulging with marbles, into the autumn sunset, by God.

Thirteen years old at the time, and went off with only a dime to his name. Didn't see him again until a year later, in September, when I looked up from reading Smiling Jack, and there he stood at the screen door with the sunlight behind him and a merchant seaman's cap cocked back to show his pompadour. Says, "Shhhh. Wanna surprise Momma," as if he didn't have twenty more years to do *that* in.

This one ends twenty years later—the summer before my first novel came out—and it'd been eight years since I had seen him last, in Stillwater. He'd just come from working in a Mississippi cotton patch, under the gun. And here *I* was, the first in the family on both sides to graduate from high school and even on through college, and making ten thousand a year teaching at a big university, and a novel coming out, and a clean record in the home-town and the F.B.I. files, and—You know I didn't want to show off and make him feel bad, I wanted to make him feel part *of* it, so here we were: two brothers having a reunion at Mam'maw's house—sort of the home place, you know, because Momma moved all over the city of Louisville when we were little— and Traven was out in the back yard, full of flowers, and he was lolling in the hammock under the mimosa trees, and smoking this fat-assed cigar and wearing the baggy clothes they let him out in. Swinging in that hammock, raising a cloud of Dutch Master, grinning at me.

So I sat in this white kitchen chair Mam'maw'd propped up the curtain stretchers with, and tried to make him feel a part of it all. When I told him about the teaching job, he says, "Listen, kid," in this Yankee accent he picked up and stuck to since his first trip to New York, "what you waste your time teaching English for? Why don't you become a doctor or a lawyer where the *big* money is?" It tipped me off balance, and I made some lame excuses, and he says, "What's this they tell me about you gotta novel going to be published?" "Yeah," I said, and broke out in a face-aching grin. And he says, "Listen, kid, you better watch out for these editors. They'll try to cheat you out of what you got coming to you. *I* know. What you need is an agent."

Well, I was still feeling the reunion scene, so none of this soaked in. I was thinking, here's where I'll make him feel he's a part of it all, and not just a three or four time loser con man fresh out of the pen. He was still kinda thin and hollow-eyed, you know. But 'bout that time, he says, "What's it about?" and I say, "'Bout when I was in the merchant marines." That made him give the hammock a good swing with his dangling foot and look at me squint-eyed through the cigar smoke. "Kid, when were *you* ever in the merchant marines?" Just before they drafted me into the army, I told him, but didn't remind him that I used to send him money orders for stamps and Bull Durham from Savannah and Mobile and Rio, then later from Fort Jackson, nor how he used to sign his letters, "Jesus is the only hope for today's youth," knowing the censors would get it back to the parole officer. I won't stress the fact that *I* believed him. "Whatever made you go in the merchant marines, kid?"

I got choked up a little because I was about to grab him with it. "Well, Traven, remember the time . . . ?" Then I filled him in on our childhood and the time he came back in the merchant seaman's outfit. "And you told me and Cody all about New York and shipping out to Panama and the West Indies. Remember, Traven? It got Cody to running off from school and taking little trips that finally landed him in a detention home. It stirred up the wanderlust in me, too, but good little ol' Hollis, you know, stayed home, and dreamed about it, and saw movies about it, and wrote novel scenarios projecting himself into it, and read Conrad, and finished high school first. Then I went to New York, worked at the White Tower hamburger joint by night, sat in the union hall in Brooklyn by day, till I finally got out on a ship to India day before Christmas. There was this man on the ship who kind of reminded me of you. In my novel that's coming out, he turns out to be a strange kind of hero, in a bass-ackward way, and I'm his witness."

Traven braked the hammock with his foot, and kept it still, one eye squeezed shut against the smoke from the Dutch Master hanging in the corner of his mouth. Then he gives the hammock a little push, takes a long draw, spews out the smoke, dusts the cigar, and smirks: "Why, kid, I ain't never been in no merchant marines."

I heard a mimosa blossom drop. "But—"

"But, hell," Traven said, "I just wore that outfit so I could hitch-hike across country easier."

Mary Lavin

Frail Vessel

WHO WOULD HAVE THOUGHT, AS THEY STOOD BY THEIR MOTHER'S OPEN grave, that they would both be married within the year? Why Liddy was only sixteen then! Wasn't it for Liddy's sake that she and Daniel had gone on with the arrangements for their own marriage? Wasn't it partly to give her little sister a home; a real family life again that they were getting married so soon? Everyone in town appreciated the fact that she wasn't in a position to postpone her marriage. And anyway, taking into consideration the precarious state of the business and the fact that it would have collapsed years ago only for Daniel's good management, everyone sympathized with the necessity for an immediate formal settlement. In their case, there was certainly no disrespect intended toward the dead.

But Liddy! Bedelia was shocked to find that Liddy had no regard at all: for the living or the dead.

Naturally she was opposed to the marriage. She made every effort to persuade Liddy to wait a while. But she soon saw her efforts were useless. Whatever came over Liddy, she could get no good of her at all. She was like a person that was light in the head.

As for Alphonsus Carmody, Bedelia could make nothing out of him from the start. To begin with she never could stand solicitors. You could never feel at ease with them. They were always too clever for you, no matter what you did. And then she never could think of Alphonsus Carmody as anything but a stranger. And what else was he?

He had been only a few months in the town; a total stranger, with no connections—and no office you might say, except the use of a room at the Central Hotel. He was a kind of laughingstock right from the start, sitting inside the hotel window and not a soul ever darkening the door. He made no effort to get to know people either. Their Liddy was the only one he ever saluted!

Daniel used to laugh at the child.

"He must expect to get a lot of business out of you, Liddy," he said.

That was the whole trouble: they treated the thing as a joke, both she and Daniel. And indeed, Liddy herself took it as a joke, in the start.

No one in his senses could have believed that it could turn into anything serious. No one could have foreseen that a young girl would lose her head to an old fellow like Carmody.

267

Not that Alphonsus was so old; it was more that he was odd than anything else. But he was certainly a bit old for a man said to have just qualified.

"Just qualified!" Bedelia cried. "But he's gray!"

Daniel, however, was able to explain. He said probably Carmody had been a law clerk.

"They have a hard time. So he mightn't be as old as he looked."

As a matter of fact Daniel was right. Alphonsus was a lot younger than he looked, but all the same it never occurred to Bedelia that there could be anything romantic about him. And the day that Liddy's face got so red when they were passing the Central Hotel, she simply could not account for it.

They had been out for a walk together, she and Liddy, and they were coming home. They were talking about her own wedding, as a matter of fact, when she noticed that Liddy wasn't paying attention. And when she looked at her she saw that she was blushing.

Whatever for? That was her first thought, and she looked around the street. It could only be some boy, she supposed, and she couldn't help feeling annoyed because Liddy seemed too much of a child for that kind of thing. But although she scanned the street up and down there wasn't a soul in sight except Alphonsus Carmody standing at the hotel door. It simply did not occur to her to attribute those blushes to him; she contented herself by thinking that they were due to embarrassment at the way the child was teased about him.

How differently she would have acted if there had been a boy in the street that day, a young man, that is to say. If there had been anyone presentable at all in sight it would have been a warning to her. And although she was nearly distracted, with plans for her own wedding, she would have kept a better eye on Liddy.

As things were, however, she did not give the incident another thought.

She did notice, however, that Mr. Carmody had taken to standing a lot at the door of the hotel, because whenever she paused to look out the window she saw him there.

One day when Daniel was dressing the window in the gable end, and she was looking out over his shoulder into the street, she commented on it.

"He's coming out of his shell," she said to Daniel.

"You'd feel sorry for him," Daniel said. "He can't be doing much of a practice."

Bedelia herself felt a bit sorry for him, but as Liddy came into the shop just then she thought she'd make her laugh.

"We're looking out at your friend Mr. Carmody," she said. "He's always standing in the doorway of the hotel. Maybe he's got a job as hotel porter."

"That must be it," said Liddy. And she laughed.

Yes, Liddy laughed at him too that day. That deceived them.

If she had shown the slightest annoyance or taken Carmody's part in any way they might have been suspicious. But she deceived them completely. Either that, or she really and truly did regard the whole thing as a joke at that time. She certainly didn't take his first proposal seriously. And no wonder!

As it happened, Bedelia herself was at the window, that day, and she saw him lean out as Liddy was passing and catch her by the plait.

She little knew what he had said to her!

"Well, Liddy?" she said, when the girl came running into the shop. "I saw you!" She was partly disapproving; partly amused.

"But you didn't hear what he said to me!" cried Liddy. "He told me to go home and ask you when you'd let me marry him!"

"Well, the cheek of him!" Bedelia cried. "I didn't think he had it in him to make a joke." Because, of course, she took it as a joke.

But when it became a regular thing for the fellow to pull Liddy's plait every time she went up or down the street, Bedelia felt obliged to speak to her.

Liddy didn't take it well though. Bedelia noticed that at once, and for the first time she felt uneasy.

"After all, Liddy, you must remember that I stand in your mother's place and I am responsible for you. I think this thing is going beyond a joke."

But her words were truer than she knew: it was already beyond a joke.

So when Liddy paid no heed to her at all, but continued to hang about the hotel door laughing and talking to the fellow, Bedelia decided to have it out with her. The next time they were together upstairs, in the big parlor over the shop, Bedelia jerked her head in the direction of the Central Hotel.

"If this nonsense doesn't stop, Liddy, I'll have to speak to Mr. Carmody."

That was all she said, and indeed she hadn't any intention of carrying out such a threat. But to her surprise Liddy said nothing. Something odd about the girl's silence made her look sharply at her.

Liddy's face was covered with blushes.

"I think he wants to speak to you too, Bedelia," she said. Bedelia saw that her hands were trembling.

"To speak to me?" She was astonished.

Liddy's head was bent, but with a great effort she forced herself to look her in the face.

"I think he's coming to see you—" she said "—today!"

Today?

But Liddy could control herself no longer.

"Oh, Bedelia!" she cried. And Bedelia honestly could not tell whether she was crying or laughing. "Oh, Bedelia—you know the way he was always going on—about asking you if you'd let him marry me—you remember we thought he was joking—didn't we? Well—he wasn't't!"

Bedelia could only gasp. And then, before she had time to get over the shock there was a loud rap on the hall door.

Never in her life was she thrown into such flurry. She stared at Liddy. Liddy's blushes had died away.

"I expect that's him now," she said, coolly, calmly, as if it were the most natural thing in the world.

In the few minutes before Bedelia went down to the little front parlor to see her prospective brother-in-law, she tried to gather her thoughts together.

She was bewildered. What was she to say to this—stranger?

Her first impulse was to run down the backstairs and call Daniel in from the shop. But it didn't seem fair to drag Daniel into it. Anyway, she doubted if he would be much use in this kind of situation. Daniel's talent was for figures; for keeping books and attending to the financial side of things. Of course, there was a financial side to this situation too. How was this fellow going to support a wife? Where was he going to bring his wife to live? These and several other questions ran through her head as she stood where Liddy had left her, but it was only her mind that was working; her practical common-sense mind. What she felt about the matter she did not know; as to feeling, she was absolutely numb.

Then her eyes fell on the plain serge suit which was intended for her own wedding. It had just that day come from the dressmaker, and she was suddenly shot through and through with irritation. Why did this business about Liddy have to blow up almost on the eve of her own wedding?

Goodness knows, she hadn't expected much fuss to be made about her own marriage, what with not being out of mourning, and Daniel having always lived in the house anyway; but it did seem a bit unfair to have this excitement blow up around Liddy.

Two rare, very rare, and angry tears squeezed out of Bedelia's pale eyes, and fell down her plain round cheeks. Because, of course, mourning or no mourning, a young girl like Liddy wasn't likely to get married in serge!

Bedelia felt that a mean trick had been played on her. After all I've done for that girl! she thought. After being a mother to her! But this last thought made her feel more bitter than ever because it seemed to her that this was the measure of the difference between them as brides. Already she could imagine the fuss there would be over Liddy—the exclamations and the sighs of pity and admiration. Such a lovely bride!

Whereas when she—oh, but it was so unfair because never at any time did she regard her own marriage as anything but a practical expedient. It was only that she hadn't counted on being up against a comparison. It was the comparison she minded.

But here Bedelia called herself to order. Of course a lot depended upon when the other two intended to bring their affairs to a head. After all Alphonsus Carmody couldn't have much money. Perhaps he only wanted her sanction to his suit? It might be years before he could get married.

Yes, of course. Of course. That was it. She was letting her imagination run away with her. It would probably be years before poor Carmody would take the final step. Running across the landing to her bedroom, and dipping the corner of her towel into the ewer of water on her washstand, Bedelia rubbed her face and darted a look into the mirror. Smart and all as Liddy was, she might be old enough by the time her beau was in a position to lead her up to the altar! Bedelia ran down the stairs.

But at the bottom of the stairs another aspect of the situation struck her. It was all very well for Daniel and herself to be making a home for Liddy when they regarded her as a child—but how would things be after this? Indeed if this had never occurred it might have been more awkward than they

realized to have another person in the house with them right from the start
—and another woman at that.

For the first time in her life, Bedelia felt bashful at the thought of the night
when Daniel would move out of the little return-room on the back landing,
where he had slept since he was a young apprentice, and, with his old alarm
clock under his arm, take up his position in her room. It was only then—only
at the last minute, with her hand on the knob of the parlor door, that it came
over her that things might not be so bad after all. In any case what could she
do about it? If they were bent on getting married, who could stop them?

It was all settled. It had taken less than five minutes, and yet everything
was arranged. Daniel had been sent for and although he was as much taken
by surprise as anyone, he was soon brought around more or less to Alphonsus
Carmody's viewpoint. That was what came of being a solicitor, Bedelia
supposed. They were so able. But I'll never like him, she thought. He could
build a nest in my ear.

And that was tantamount to what her new brother-in-law proposed to do.

It seemed that Liddy had told him about the little house at the end of the
street that the sisters owned; it was unoccupied, tumbling down in fact, but
it had never seemed worthwhile repairing, for the small rent they would get
for it.

It would be just the thing for himself and Liddy, Alphonsus said. With a
bit of paint, and something done about the bad spot on the roof, it would serve
until they had time to find something better, something more suitable.

"And it's so pretty," Liddy cried. "I always thought it was a dear little
house! I used to peep in through the shutters and wish I could go and live
in it"—she turned and smiled at Alphonsus—"all by myself."

But Bedelia had had enough without that. Such soppiness—and in front
of Daniel. Well, Liddy might play the lovebird, but there was no getting away
from the fact that the romantic Mr. Carmody was almost gray—whereas
Daniel had a head of hair like an infant. She turned around to Alphonsus on
an impulse.

"It's a wonder you never married before now, Mr. Carmody," she said, and
she looked archly at him to conceal the malice in her voice.

But perhaps he saw through her, because he put out his hand and drew
Liddy nearer.

"I suppose I was waiting for Liddy, here," he said, and it was impossible
to know whether he was serious or whether he was joking.

And it crossed Bedelia's mind that that was the way in which he had
wormed himself into Liddy's affections: by mixing up sentiment and mockery.
It was a kind of cheating, she thought. Nowadays people didn't go on with
nonsense like that about waiting for the right person to come along. There
was nothing like that between herself and Daniel! Daniel certainly didn't go
down on his knees to her! She would have thought he was daft if he did. But
all the same, as she looked at Alphonsus, she felt that he was the kind of a
man who might easily fall down on his knees in front of a girl as a kind of

joke—and she'd know he was joking or partly joking—but all the same it would bring a kind of sweetness into her life.

But Bedelia had to call herself to order again, because Alphonsus was reaching for his hat and they had to see him to the door.

Bedelia was the first to speak, after the door was closed and they were back in the downstairs parlor. "Well, everyone to his own taste," she said, "but I must say I don't know how on earth you can bear that sloppy manner. You know what I mean," Bedelia added impatiently. She tried to think of something sloppy he had said, but it was like trying to remember a smell—she could only remember that it was sloppy. But at last she laid hold on one phrase he had used. "You know—all that rubbish he went on with—about you being the only one in the world for him—and that he was waiting all those years for you. How can you stand that kind of talk? It's so meaningless."

Liddy had caught up the tablecloth and was just about to spread it on the table, but instead she lifted it up to her face, as if it were a veil behind which she smiled, a dreamy, secretive little smile.

"Oh, Bedelia, *I* knew what he meant," she said, and then, over the edge of the cloth, her eyes seemed to implore something from Bedelia—but Bedelia turned aside. Really this sentimentality was more than she could bear. Her eyes narrowed.

"Liddy," she said sharply, "I hope"—she paused—"you know how I have always felt toward you, like a mother—well anyway, like a guardian," she corrected, "but perhaps lately with my own plans taking up so much of my time I may not have given you as much supervision as I used—as much as you should perhaps have had—I can only hope that you haven't abused your freedom in any way?"

But Liddy had spread the cloth on the table and was bending across it smoothing out the folds. Had she been listening at all? Bedelia gave a clap with her hands.

"What I mean is that I hope you haven't made yourself cheap in any way? Men don't usually speak so sentimentally, unless—well, unless a girl has let them become—well—familiar!"

After she'd said the word she was a little daunted herself by its force, but to her surprise at first, and then to her unspeakable irritation, Liddy didn't realize its implications at all.

"Oh, but that's just it, Bedelia! I wanted to tell you! We've become *so* familiar really. Isn't it odd and to think that we've only known each other for a few weeks, and that this is the first time we've ever been together inside a house." She gave a little high-pitched laugh. And—yes—Bedelia could hardly bear it, she hugged herself. "But I feel as if we've known each other for years and years." A rapt look came into the girl's face. "Bedelia! you don't mind my saying it, do you, because you want me to be happy, don't you? But I feel more familiar with him than with you! I do, really! I know it sounds queer, but it's true—" She paused as if she was trying to think of some way to make herself clearer. Then her face lit up. She didn't see the danger signals in Bedelia's face. "Do you know what I was thinking last night?" She paused —to take courage?—and then she rushed on. "In bed," she said softly. "I was thinking about when I was small and used to sleep with you in your big brass bed. Oh, I used to love it, you know that! I used to be lonely when I got a room of my own: I was never able to go to sleep for ages, and I couldn't warm up for hours! But all the same, even when I loved sleeping with you—you don't mind my telling you this, do you? I used to hate if your—I used to hate if my—I mean I couldn't bear it if our feet touched!"

But here, her faint heart failed her again, and she had to rush over to Bedelia.

"You don't mind my telling you, do you?"

Bedelia drew back. She did mind. She didn't want to hear it. It sounded a lot of rubbish to her. Still, in spite of everything, she was curious.

"I must say I don't see the point!" she said coldly.

Liddy brightened.

"Oh, I'm coming to the point. It's that although I never saw Alphonsus without his shoes and stockings on, of course, it came into my mind—last night in bed—that I wouldn't mind a bit if our feet touched—his and mine, you know—after we were married I mean!" It was said. She had said it. For a moment her face was radiant. Then she looked at Bedelia. "Oh, Bedelia! What's the matter?" She ran over to her. She couldn't understand the look on her sister's face. "You're not hurt, are you?"

"Hurt?" Bedelia put out her two hands. "Keep back from me," she shouted. "Hurt indeed. Revolted would be more like it! Such talk from a young girl. Do you want to know what I think? Well, I think you're disgusting!"

The sisters had both been married six months when Liddy came back to the old house one afternoon and, passing through the shop with only a word for Daniel, went straight upstairs to Bedelia's room over the shop.

"I want to ask you something, Bedelia," she said, straight-away, without preamble. "Will you let us off our share of the rent of the little house—it's such a small sum to you and—well, it's not so small to us—and I know you were only charging us something as a formality—to make us feel independent and all that—but the fact of the matter is—" Nervously she had run on without stopping ever since she came into the room, but as Bedelia, who was sitting at the window, stood up, she broke off—Bedelia was looking so queerly at her.

"Why, Liddy," she said, "I must say this is very surprising. Not that the rent means anything to Daniel and me—you're quite right about that —as a matter of fact Daniel was saying only the other day that no rent could compensate us for the loss of store-space—though mind you, Liddy, I would never have mentioned that if you hadn't brought up the matter yourself—but as I was saying, it isn't a question of money—you know that—you know the standard of living in this house, and you know your little contribution wouldn't go far to maintain it! And it hasn't changed, I can tell you that, although I must say Daniel is very particular about my keeping accounts—"

But marriage had quickened Liddy's perceptions.

"You're not going to let us off?" she whispered, not caring that she was interrupting.

Was she going to run from the room? Bedelia put out her hand. "Wait a minute, Liddy," she cried. "Don't be so hasty. I didn't refuse you, did I?" she asked when she saw with relief that Liddy had come back into the room. "I was taken by surprise, that's all. It's such a wretched little house—I thought perhaps that you were going to tell me that you'd found something better—you know it was never supposed to be anything but a stopgap. I thought you'd be out of it long ago, but of course, if Alphonsus hasn't been able to better his position—if indeed, as it seems, he's come down a peg instead—well then I think the least he could do would be to come and see me himself and not leave you to do his begging for him."

"Begging! Oh!"

For a minute Liddy's stricken face swam in front of Bedelia, but the next minute she could hardly believe that it was her own little sister who suddenly drew herself up, her eyes blazing.

"I'm glad he didn't come to you, Bedelia," she said. "I wouldn't like anyone, much less Alphonsus, to be hurt like you've hurt me. But before I go, I want you to know one thing—Alphonsus didn't send me. He didn't even know I was coming. And he had no idea I was going to ask you for anything." She softened for a minute. "I was going to pretend you suggested it yourself," she said, almost in a whisper. Then she drew herself up again. "I'm sorry I bothered you, Bedelia. Goodbye." At the door she paused. "Please don't say anything about this to anyone, Bedelia. After all, we *are* sisters." She half turned away again and then she turned back. "And just in case you might change your mind, I want you to know I couldn't accept now."

It was the last cut that hit Bedelia hardest, because she had changed her mind and she was already planning how she'd scribble a note when Liddy was gone and send it up the street after her; to overtake her before she got inside the door of the wretched little house.

As if she read her mind, Liddy looked at her sadly.

"You see, Bedelia, I couldn't ever pretend now that you had done it of your own accord. It would be telling him a real lie now, not just managing things a little bit, making things easy—like I meant it to be!"

She was gone.

"Liddy!"

Bedelia made her way clumsily to the door to call after her, but she could hear the light feet on the stairs. The next minute she heard the front door clapped shut. There was no question of going after her now. Bedelia was heavy with child.

It was two months later. Bedelia was once again sitting in the big parlor upstairs, and she was thinking of Liddy. Except when she caught glimpses of her in the street, she had not seen her since she ran down the stairs and out of the house, her pathetic request ungranted.

Oh, how could she have refused that miserably small favor? How could she have refused her anything: Liddy, her little sister? Only, of course, it wasn't really Liddy she wanted to refuse that day, it was Carmody. It was him she had wanted to humiliate, it was Carmody. Oh, how she had grown to hate that fellow. How had she ever consented to his taking Liddy away from her, because, after the tepid experience of marriage with Daniel, Bedelia had begun to feel that no matter what, no one can ever be as near to you as your own flesh and blood. And although poor Liddy didn't seem to have discovered that fact yet, it only made Bedelia feel more drawn to her, and recalled all her old feelings of motherliness for the child! For to Bedelia as she herself grew heavier in pregnancy, Liddy, when she glimpsed her in the streets, seemed as childish as ever—thinner, if possible, than before she was married. Oh, what had possessed her that she didn't make more effort to keep her at home?

This was the question that Bedelia asked herself over and over again, and not only did she completely forget the last minute impulse of selfishness that had activated her decision, but she was beginning to think she had erred by being too selfless. And they were both the losers. Liddy's loss was only too obvious, but it was very hard for Bedelia to sit and think of all the help the girl could have been to her in these last few months. To think of the way she could have run up and down stairs, and stretched for things, and stooped for things. It would have been so different from asking the maids. The maids were so curious. It nearly drove her into a rage when she caught them covertly glancing at her swollen abdomen.

Vain regrets weren't much use, however, and the most she could hope for was that something or other would break Liddy's resolve, and that she would sometime start running in and out again like she did when she was first married, although it used to irritate her the way Liddy kept looking at a clock. Still, she'd love the briefest visit now. But the last words Liddy had flung at her as she ran out of the door were to the effect that she'd never set foot in the place again.

It was just as she was thinking of Liddy's last words that Bedelia heard the footsteps on the stairs, the unmistakable light little steps of her sister.

There was something wrong though. Bedelia's hand went to her heart. Always, she was susceptible to wild premonitions of trouble when she heard those flying feet, coming along a passage or as now, upon the stairs. But as she strained to get to her feet, she suddenly sank back again into the chair. For just as the protective waters within her lapped around her embryonic son, securing him from hurt, so too a protective instinct warned her against giving way to shock or distress.

Whatever was wrong, it was not her concern; unless indirectly. She must not let herself become upset. She sat still.

"Oh, Bedelia!"

It was an exclamation, not a greeting; it was a sigh, a gasp. And when Liddy came into the room, closing the door, she sank back against it exhausted. But the next minute she drew herself together, and even gave a little self-critical smile.

"I never thought I'd set foot in your house again, Bedelia," she said, and to Bedelia there was something preposterously confident and independent in the words, but the next minute Liddy's voice broke, and a more familiar dependent note came into it.

"But I had to come, Bedelia," she cried. "I had no one else to turn to— no one."

Oh, what satisfaction those words gave Bedelia.

"Well, what's the matter?" she said briskly. "Don't stand there—come over here and sit down."

Obediently Liddy moved forward into the room and sat down on the edge of a chair, but almost at once she stood up again.

"It's Alphonsus," she said. "We're in such trouble, Bedelia."

Bedelia tried to look more surprised than she felt.

"It was all my fault, really," Liddy cried. "Only for the way he's always trying to make things easier for me it would never have happened."

Bedelia always hated vagueness.

"What wouldn't have happened?" she asked, sharply.

But it was clear Liddy didn't know how to begin her story.

"Well, you see," she said falteringly, "when we got married Alphonsus wanted to do everything he could to increase his income and so he took on an insurance agency—temporarily, of course, although lots of solicitors do it. He thought he might work it up a bit and that it would bring in a little regular money until his practice grew—you needn't look so contemptuous, Bedelia," she interrupted suddenly, "the commission wasn't very much, but Alphonsus's idea was to get as many policies as we could and last month"—here a weak note of pride came into her voice—"last month he collected eleven premiums totaling forty-seven pounds."

Weak and watery as was that little note of pride, it angered Bedelia.

"I presume the forty-seven pounds was the amount of the premiums, not the commission," she said.

"Oh, the premiums of course," said Liddy, somewhat flatter, "the commission was only—" But here she paused, and almost as if some inspired voice had given her the cue she needed, just at the moment when it had seemed utterly impossible to go on with the story, she threw out her hands and rushed on eagerly. "That was the beginning of it all. The insurance company gives a percentage on each premium but the agent is supposed to make out the amounts himself, subtract his commission, and forward the balance to the head office. It's not fair you know, really—they have such a staff up there and everything, while poor Alphonsus has no one to do anything for him—not yet, I mean." At this point she hesitated. "And so he got things a bit mixed up—only in arrears really, but—" Here, however, her voice failed utterly. But Bedelia had heard enough.

"Do you mean to tell me he laid hands on it all—the policy money as well as the commission?" she cried, and in spite of nature's elaborate provisions against such contingency, Bedelia's heart began to palpitate, and a pulse began to beat in her temple. She wasn't so indirectly affected at all. She had thought it might be some trouble that would affect Carmody only—or at worst the pair of them. But if the fellow had converted this money to his own use—newspaper phrases flashed to her mind—well then he might easily bring disgrace on them all.

"Well, answer me! Did he?" she cried.

Although she herself was in a fury, she didn't like the way Liddy's face was quivering. "I'll have to know sooner or later," she said, more kindly, "you may as well tell me."

But Liddy was crying.

"It's the way you put it," she stammered. "As if he was a thief—"

Bedelia bit back the retort she would have liked to make, and instead she shrugged her shoulders.

"Well," she said then, "what do you want me to do?"

As if she had been running blindly down a wrong pathway and suddenly through the blinding branches had seen another way, the right way, Liddy ran back to Bedelia.

"Oh, Bedelia, all we need is to get an advance of the money—it isn't as if we had to ask you for it outright—it's not even a loan really, because the minute the premiums become due again we'll hand the commission straight over to you—of course it will take a little while, I expect, for it to accrue into the full amount, but you can see, can't you, that it's hardly a loan at all—just an advance."

"Advance—accrue! You've got very glib with financial phrases, I see."

Liddy smiled, or tried to smile. She had foreknown that it would be part of her purgatory to humor Bedelia.

"I've become quite a bookkeeper," she said, but as Bedelia said nothing, she looked at her sharply, and then drew back. "I should have known! You're not going to give it to us!" she said. "I can see by your eyes you're not," and she began to back away from those cold eyes, as from something destructive.

But she didn't go farther than the door, against which she shrank back exhausted. For where could she go?

Bedelia, however, had risen to her feet. Although she didn't believe Liddy had strength or spirit left to do what she did last time, flounce away in a temper, she just wasn't going to take any chances this time, and going over to a chest of drawers she took out a black tin box. Liddy knew that box. There was no need to say anything. Bedelia put it down on the table and let back the lid.

"How much did you say?" she said.

But Liddy was crying; silly hysterical tears.

"Forty-seven—oh, but that includes the commission and we don't have to make that up—Oh, Bedelia, I knew you wouldn't fail me—I was only afraid on account of that other time I came about the rent—and that's another thing —I wanted to tell you—you were right about that too—I told Alphonsus and he said you were right, that I shouldn't have asked you, not without telling him, anyway. Oh, you're so good—so kind—"

But Bedelia plunged her hand into the box.

"I'd like to get this settled," she said. "I want to lock away the box again. How much did you say?"

"Oh, dear—how much?"

Liddy tried to wipe away the silly tears, tried to think, to calculate. On her fingers she counted up a few figures and then she threw up her hands.

"I'll have to ask Alphonsus," she said. "You see, there's no immediate hurry: the inspector won't be here until the afternoon, I'll have plenty of time to get Alphonsus to tot up the exact amount." She paused. "I'll get him to write it down so I won't forget it," she said. She wanted Bedelia to see that she was going to be efficient about the whole thing right from the start.

"Liddy, I want to talk to you. Sit down."

Bedelia's voice was so odd that Liddy's eyes flew to the table, as if in doubt of all that had gone before, but no: the box was still there, with the bundle of notes in it held with tape. And to corroborate her previous words, Bedelia was stripping off note after note and counting them, forty, forty-five, fifty. But still, there was that strange, cold note in her voice. "Sit down," she said again.

Liddy sat down.

"I want to ask you something, Liddy. If I didn't give you this money, what were you going to do?"

For a minute there was silence, then Liddy spoke so low Bedelia had to bend her head to hear.

"Alphonsus would have to go away." Liddy said in a little dead voice, "until he gathered up the money somewhere," she added with a little more, but not much more, life. Then she looked up straight into Bedelia's eyes. "He would have to go on the four o'clock train this afternoon."

"And leave you to face the music?"

Liddy's face flushed all over. But it was the flush of courage, not shame.

"They couldn't do anything to me," she said, and then she sprang to her feet. "Why are you torturing me like this? Are you going to give it to me or not? Because I don't care! Do you hear that! I don't mind the disgrace. It couldn't be much worse than this. And in any case you'll come in for your share too. Do you think people won't know you refused us!"

"Hush, hush. Stop shouting! Who said I refused you? I didn't refuse you anything. I'm giving it to you." Feverishly and without finishing the counting, anything at all to stop her—Bedelia began to stuff the notes into her hands. "It's only that I want to do my best for you, Liddy. Surely you must know that," she cried, and as she felt the other soften again she led her over to the chair once more. "Liddy," she said softly, tenderly. "Liddy, I want you to ask yourself something. Do you believe in your heart of hearts that Alphonsus will never do this again?"

What is weakness? What is strength? Liddy had stood up to every taunt and vilification, but she wasn't proof against this tenderness.

"Oh, Bedelia," she whispered, and she began to cry again.

So many tears; she had shed so many and so many kinds, silly tears, tears of temper and tears of bewilderment, but these were tears of defeat. "I don't know," she said.

"Well, look here!" Bedelia took her hands. "This is the way I see it—I'm going to give you this money, but it's not enough to do just that, I want to do more for you. I want to help your poor husband if I can—help him to help himself, I mean."

Liddy didn't follow.

"Now, listen carefully to me," Bedelia ordered. "When I first agreed to help you, you spoke of conferring with Alphonsus. Well, that, I am afraid, I can't allow. This is going to be a matter between you and me"—she paused—"between you and me and the insurance company. I mean Alphonsus is not to know anything at all about it. In fact—he won't know because he will be gone on the four o'clock train. Do you follow?"

No, no! Liddy didn't follow, it would seem from the way she pressed her hands over her face. But when she took them down again it was clear she partly understood.

"But why?" she cried.

"It will test him out, Liddy. Can't you see that?" Bedelia said. "The other way would be making things too easy for him: it would be doing him harm; moral harm. But this way you save his name—you hand the money over to the company, with some excuse—you might even consider having the agency transferred to your name—but that's another matter—the important thing is you must let Alphonsus think that it has to be paid back—let him think that he has to send back the money, bit by bit, if necessary, until the whole debt is cleared. And in that way—"

But as at that moment the clock struck three, the sisters both started.

"Is this the only condition on which you'll give the money, Bedelia?" Liddy said quietly.

Bedelia's eyes ran over every cranny of her sister's face. For a minute she was afraid of what she was doing: afraid of the strain she was putting on the woman in front of her, so thin, so white; so beaten-looking.

But when she had got rid of Carmody, for a while anyway—and had taken the girl back into her own care again, she could make amends to her—make more than amends—for what she was doing now. Why, if there were nothing more gained than the opportunity—even for a few months—of feeding her properly and seeing that she had warmer clothes—there would be something to be said for her action. The girl could come home again, for the present. And with that thought Bedelia was so pleased that all vestige of doubt vanished from her mind, and she sank back into her chair.

And when, at that minute a button popped off her dress and rolled under the table, she caught herself up in the act of stooping for it. Liddy could do that.

It was two hours later when Liddy came back. The train had gone. Bedelia heard it give a short whistle as it went under the railway bridge at the end of the town, and then a long clear blast as it cut its way into the wide open country beyond the town. And then, only a few minutes afterward, there was a noise outside the parlor door, a sound of something heavy bumping, now against the stair treads, now against the banister.

"In the name of God, what is that noise?" Bedelia cried. She thought it was one of the servants.

It was Liddy, and dragging after her, as she came in the door, was their father's big portmanteau that she had taken to carry her things when she went away to be married.

"What on earth have you got in the portmanteau?" Bedelia cried. She hadn't thought Liddy would have taken her up so quickly about coming back. "You're welcome, of course," she said quickly, when Liddy, taken aback, began to explain. "I hope there's a bed ready for you, that's all," she said. "You know I can't do much these days. I'm doing more than I ought already." But as she saw Liddy's face fall, she tried to be warmer. "It's all right, you know," she said, "it's all right. I meant you to come, only I thought you'd have arrangements to make. I thought it would take you a few days to settle your things, although I dare say you wouldn't have much to attend to in that little poke-hole of a place—"

"Oh, I have lots to do," Liddy said proudly. "I've nothing done at all yet. I'll have to go back during the daytime, but—" she paused, and involuntarily her glance traveled toward the high window in the gable where the clouds could be seen foregathering in heavy masses on the western horizon.

Bedelia understood the glance all right, but some unanalyzed association of ideas irritated her.

"I thought it was only spinsters that were afraid at night!" she said, but immediately, prompted by a movement in her body, she knew she must not make remarks like that. They could upset herself as much as Liddy. If she was to get anything out of the situation; if she was to get any return for taking Liddy back into the house, she'd have to learn not to not give way to petty vexations. "Put down that heavy suitcase," she said abruptly.

Was the girl a fool that she was still holding it, her shoulder dragging down to one side. "Come over to the fire, can't you?" she said, "and sit down. You're tired, I expect. You're very white-looking. When did you eat any-thing? Are you hungry?"

She was trying to be considerate, but all her questions were irrelevant compared with the one question that she could not bring herself to ask. Ask it she must, however. "Well—how did he go off?"

For answer tears welled into Liddy's eyes.

"Oh, come now—it's not as bad as all that. You took the only course open to you, you must know that!" But as Liddy's tears still fell silently, Bedelia stood up and looked down at her. "Oh come, now," she said more kindly. "You'll be hearing from him in a few days; you may have a letter tomorrow if he gets to his destination in time to catch the post. By the way, I didn't ask where he went? Has he any people—any friends or relatives? We never heard of any, I know that," she added quickly, "but I suppose everyone in the world has somewhere to creep when they get into trouble." She stopped. "What's that?" she said.

For Liddy had spoken at last, but so softly, only a whisper, that again the other had to bend down close to hear.

"Like I crept back here," that was what Liddy had said.

Bedelia looked at her. Was she being clever; trying to get out of telling his whereabouts?

"You didn't say where he was going," she persisted doggedly. "Are you afraid to divulge his whereabouts in case something else comes to light about him? I'd hardly give him away—now!" It was cruel, but it wasn't cruel enough to make Liddy open her mouth. Bedelia stood over her. "Perhaps you don't know yourself," she said, moving still nearer. But she had to stand back suddenly as Liddy got to her feet unsteadily and swayed forward with her hand on her stomach.

"I think I'm going to be sick, Bedelia," she said, with a mawkish irrelevance.

It was such a shock. Bedelia gave a shout.

"Not on the carpet," she screamed, and frantically she pulled out a handkerchief from her sleeve. "Here, take this—try to swallow. Breathe—take a deep breath—it will pass off in a minute."

So it did; it was only a gust of nausea.

Liddy handed back the handkerchief and tried to smile bleakly through her tears.

"I'm all right now."

It was Bedelia who looked bad now. She sank down on a chair.

"I must say it's a queer way it took you!" she said crossly, and she placed her hand on her own stomach. "You gave me such a start."

Liddy saw the enormity of her offense.

"It must have been the portmanteau," she said apologetically, "the weight of it, I mean." Then gulping, she came to a quick decision. "I didn't tell you, Bedelia," she said, "but I'm not supposed to lift anything heavy just now—"

"Good God!"

Heavy and all as she was, awkward and clumsy, Bedelia was on her feet again in an instant.

"You don't mean—" Oh, but it was absolutely—oh, but absolutely unbelievable. It was the last straw. Why, she felt as if she had been tricked— as if between them they had made a fool of her, Liddy and Carmody, both of them. "Why didn't you tell me this before now?" she screamed, and as she screamed one question, others swarmed in her mind. What use would the creature be to her in this condition? This condition: it revolted her to think of them both—two of them!—in the same condition, in the one house—one as useless as the other as the days went on. And this brat? When he was born —what was going to become of him? Would she and Daniel have to rear him too, as well as their own child? And for how long?

Before her mind's eye, she saw the face of Alphonsus Carmody but it was as inscrutable as ever.

She swung around. "Might I ask one thing," she cried. "Did he know about this when he embezzled the funds, or did it come as a glorious surprise to him afterward?"

Liddy hesitated before she answered, but her tears had dried, and she looked steadily into Bedelia's eyes.

"He didn't know," she said calmly. "And he doesn't know even now! I didn't tell him at all!"

"You didn't what?" Bedelia's voice had gone; she could say nothing now except in a shrill scream.

"I didn't tell him," Liddy repeated quietly. Her voice was growing in confidence. "I was going to tell him the very night—the night he had to tell me about the money and so I didn't tell him after all!"

"Why?"

"I wanted to keep it till—"

Anyone—anyone could see why she waited: in the hope that the clouds would be dispelled and that the sun would shine again, and her secret be given its golden due.

Yes, Bedelia too could see that was why she waited: could see but could not bear what she saw.

"You fool," she cried. "There may be a time for sentimentality of that kind, but this wasn't the time! You let him get away without knowing the full extent of his responsibilities. What in the name of God were you thinking about?"

Liddy's mind, however, was in no confusion.

"I knew what I was doing, Bedelia," she said. "I wouldn't have told him for anything. I wouldn't have made things harder for him. He mightn't have been able to make up his mind if he knew—or not so quickly, anyway."

Just as on the day she announced that Carmody wanted to marry her, there was a radiance and glory about her that Bedelia could not but perceive. Yet she could not see whence came this ambience, nor why it should be Liddy's due.

"I must say it's easy to be noble at the expense of others," she said. "Have you thought about us—about me and my husband? It was one thing to have you here—for a while—by yourself—till he sent for you—you might even have been some help in the house—Daniel would have been only too pleased. But how will he take it now—when I have to tell him we're saddled with rearing another man's brat! And for how long? That's the question."

It was the all important question.

Yet Liddy never seemed to have pondered it at all. Her body, beautiful, frail for all its fertility, was still a vessel for some secret happiness Bedelia had never known. Bedelia thrust her face, that was swollen with the strain she had undergone, into the face, now so serene, in front of her.

"Do you know what I think?" she cried. "I think you've seen the last of him—do you hear me—the last of him!"

But she couldn't make out whether Liddy had heard or not. Certainly her reply, when it came in a whisper, was absolutely inexplicable.

"Even so!" Liddy whispered. "Even so!"

Herbert Gold
Song of the First and Last Beatnik

BACK IN 1957, IN SAN FRANCISCO, MY FRIEND THE FAMOUS BEAT POET wanted me to meet the champion beatnik of them all. This was during the finest rage of the holy barbarians, when North Beach, Chinatown and Telegraph Hill lay aswarm and abuzz with bongos, guitars, sandals, chicks, poets —and journalists watching everything—and San Francisco's Finest watching everyone. It was the golden age of the mimeographed manifesto and one girl for every ten geniuses, except when the tourists came out on weekends. Remember the beards? Remember red wine? Remember the revolutions? Remember poetry read to jazz?

Howard, one of the great men of the time, stood guard at his station on the sidewalk in front of the Co-Existence Bagel Shop on upper Grant, aslant on Telegraph Hill, revolving like a beacon in the fog. He was a tall, gangling, grinning, shambling young Negro possessed of that curious compulsion called logorrhea. He couldn't stop talking. He mumbled, he chanted, he discoursed; he was surely very strange with his baroque-sculptured, empty ears and hard-working mouth. But what he said had an odd off-wit; and unlike most madmen, Howard seemed to know what would please his hearers. He repeated a good story and discarded a bad one. He picked up the clues. He kept the faith that there are others out here.

When my friend the Famous Beat Poet introduced us, Howard said, "Howdya do. I got the water if you got the bucket."

To communicate was the beginning of misunderstanding. We stood in front of the Bagel Shop and talked. I listened. Someone mentioned the law. "Oh yes, oh yes, oh yes," he said. (I had heard that he was a disbarred lawyer.) "Tell you something right now. The man in the courtroom with the long hair is always the defendant. You better cut your hair, boy."

"I'm not on trial."

"Not so's you'd know it," he said, "but we are all on trial. Oh yes, oh *yes.* And for to be a prosecutor a man has to eat those *mean* pills all the day long. You get them in the little capsules. And that's another thing about the practice of the law. I was a dee-ay once, just starting out, an assistant dee-ay. But I'll tell you, friend, I was guilty of moral turpentine, I wiped out stains."

For just a moment he stopped speaking, leaving his mouth at the ready, and I saw the foam of saliva which all this talk stimulated. With an elaborate lean and smile he peered up the street toward a pretty, very young blond girl

283

in tooled cowboy boots and jeans who was strolling toward us. At the same time a finny police car swung around the corner, and the cops pulled over to study the action. Fins had just come in. The girl moved to lay her head against Howard's shoulder. He dodged away. "Lisa Subterranean," he said, introducing us. "That's a funny name, ain't it? And this is my friend's friend, his name is . . ." Oddly enough, he had remembered my name. He listened even while he talked and kept his eye on the policemen. Lisa again tried to snuggle and he danced away as if she were stepping on his shoeshine. "Listen, honey, you see those fuzz over there? Let me explain it to you, as if you didn't know. Contempt breeds familiarity. All right, so be nice. I do not want any trouble. In my *mind* there is no trouble. So you run along home now and put on the coffee and I'll be there as soon as I finish cutting up a jackpot with this here friend of my friend—okay now, baby?"

The girl ambled off. The cops looked sad. One blew his nose noisily, wadded up the Kleenex, and dropped it in our direction. The other one took down his clipboard and sat writing nothing. Howard smiled at me and said, "Sometimes I think I got the bucket *and* the water, but the most of the time I just got the water, and it run through my hands."

Howard had several wives and many children; he had many girl friends; he was chosen more than he chose. He was a renowned expert. Self-selected disciples fell by the Bagel Shop and chose him to eat with them; he ate. Girls came by and chose him to befriend them; he gave them a meaning in life and a revenge against parents. He was a maestro without a baton, a guru before krispie gurus came in packages from India. But what he really liked was to converse, just the simple flow, as birds sang in those distant mornings before DDT. It was his art form—like sneezing for a frustrated cop. Later there were those who claimed that Lenny Bruce was a better talker than Howard, but in 1957 Howard took the single's championship at monologue, standing and indoor, strolling and outdoor. He also carried sugar cubes in his pocket, stolen from the terrace of Enrico's Coffeehouse, to feed to beatnik, Italian, and Chinese kids on the street. And it was said that he had written a children's book, *The Cultivated Young Person's Garden of Hemp,* but this was probably an example of the heavy exaggeration of the Grant Avenue scene in those days. *On the Road* had replaced Senator McCarthy as a source of awe.

In 1960 the Bagel Shop was closed down (hassles, energy loss); the fickle beatniks were exchanging their guitars and bongos for washer-driers; an interval of complaint was passing, and the period of protest, peace march, Peace Corps, and civil rights was on its way. The few beatniks still shambling in the streets were morose, lonely and astigmatic; they did not see that they were the sediment left by history. The San Francisco police, the end of the Eisenhower epoch, and the dynamics of their style had done in the holy barbarians. But there remained, of course, the nuts, the nostalgia-ridden, the rearguard tourists, and the traditional bohemians who assimilated some of the beat ways. So there was a certain continuity, anyway—bookshops, coffeehouses, jazz, chess, and Howard. And other elements—sketch artists, sandal makers, jewelry makers, future in-writers and out-patients, perpetual students, would-be sex fiends, drinkers and smokers and health-food addicts, livers on the cheap. And Howard carried on.

But Howard also moved forward with the times.

Howard had taken to painting and religion. Since the sidewalk outside the Bagel Shop was now much changed (a dress shop had replaced the main office of the Beat Generation), he began to paint as he had once loitered, forgathered, and talked—with an intense passion which was both random and focused. Knowing nothing about painting, his style owed much to "Prince Valiant" and other comic strips; but his subject was pious. He planned a mural, depicting the Stations of the Cross, which he hoped to wrap around the nave of Grace Cathedral. Bishop Pike must have turned him down; he persisted, and found a storefront church in the Fillmore district—"The Moh," as it is sometimes called—which is San Francisco's Harlem. The bishop of the St. Booth Church of God in Every Soul, Inc., gave Howard the space on his walls. Howard had to supply the paint, but in return would be allowed to use the washroom for cleaning up afterward.

He painted the Stations of the Cross with Prince Valiant Romans and peasants out of "Peanuts" and a Christ who looked a little like Eddie Fisher. But of course this summary description cannot do justice to the passionate glow of his intentions. He worked all day, every day, and for nearly a year. Judas was white, Pilate was white, Christ was dark, and Mary was black. Howard gave up his girl friends. "The flesh is willing," he said, "but the spirit is weak." He still took sugar from Enrico's for the babies. He talked softly to himself, giving instructions, sketched cartoons and then projected them onto the walls, and painted as if paint could save his life. Lord knows how he ate. I think he borrowed some of the babies' sugar.

Sometimes I went to visit him as he worked. He wore blue jeans sawed off at the bottom, and padded about in bare feet. He was speckled with paint in his hair, on his arms, and on his grayish, horny toes. "Don't you get tired, standing up and reaching at the wall all day?" I asked him.

"It's easier'n sitting down if you have hemorrhoids or piles, and I have hemorrhoids and piles," he said. "I wish you wouldn't bother me with jivey questions like this was a courtroom. You see that Judas?"

"Yes."

"Negative. You don't see that Judas."

But I did. Judas was white. "What about that Judas?" I asked.

"You don't see him because I have trouble getting the expression. I ain't very good on the expressions. They come out stiff and cold. I ain't got the water."

He may not have had the water, but he almost finished the mural. Somehow, in the story of the Cross, he included lilacs, ailanthus trees, dusty roads, breezes blowing, the country of the South. There were meadows and distant hills. You could almost hear music—harmonicas, guitars. In the foreground was enacted the tragic tale, overwhelming the dreamy past in his soul with a set of fierce panels which covered three walls of the church. Within the intense circuit of his painting, Holy Rollers rolled and barkers barked and a falsetto bass-baritone bishop shrieked curses and warnings at his parishioners, promising doom three times a week, once each on Saturday and Sunday evenings, with a matinee Sunday afternoons. Soon the minister, Bishop Willy Bedford, brought darkness into Howard's life, and rage and misery, and trouble without end.

Someone told Bishop Willy that Howard was a lawyer and a mess-up, some kind of beatnik legal nut, and that he would surely demand payment for his year's work on the Stations of the Cross. Bishop Willy roared with indignation. An artist? For God? Money? "Mammon, oh Mammon!" he howled. He howled this word so often that the deacon answered to the name and began sweeping, but this time Bishop Willy's decision against sin had immediate practical consequences. By executive order Howard was barred from the St. Booth Church of God in Every Soul, Inc.

Howard came to work the next morning to find the door locked and three strong men waiting. They explained. He asked to use the telephone to call Bishop Willy. They explained again, and added that he could not use the pay telephone in the lobby. Mammon, the deacon, stood there with his broom to give the devil a jab if necessary.

Howard went to the record shop two doors down and called Bishop Willy. The bishop screamed "Mammon" at him. Howard, worried about the last problems of his mural, went home to brood. There were two important issues in his mind at this moment. He wanted to finish the Stations. And he began to fear that the bishop would have the mural painted out—ruining his life's labor, the vision and hope which had finally brought him regular hours and a sense of meaning. Even his speech had slowed down in recent months. He knew he was growing well, less sick; he was a mere sinner; the bishop had no right to deny God's will, working through him to create a masterpiece of art and a control on the flow of words. He could smell green and dusty roads when he painted; he was finding his way to putting human expression on the faces of Jews, Romans, Pharisees, women, judges. Bishop Willy had no such right.

He returned to the church the next morning, having spent a sleepless night conversing with himself, and again demanded admittance. "No," said the guards. Their arms in short-sleeved shirts were folded over their chests. No unnecessary violence was their collective plan. "Go 'way, man," said Mammon, choosing up sides with himself on the broom. Right hand won.

Howard heard noises within. Was some nonunion painter smearing pink wall paint over his Saviour? He thought he could hear drop cloths being dragged. He thought he heard laughter. Howard flung himself upon the guards, and without much trouble—his strength was as the strength of ten—broke through the line of mercenaries and past the deacon's broom. Inside, he bolted the door while they consulted without, on the sidewalk.

There was no one in the church. He had imagined the sounds of destruction and profanation. So much the better.

He ran cold water on his bruised hands, stirred up the thickened paints, and went back to work. Pilate's eyes gave him trouble. They stared but were not tormented, or they were tormented but did not stare. He needed both the staring and the torment in order to say what he wanted to say.

When the police came to expel him, there was a fight. "You gonna wuk me ovah?" he shouted at them from the window of the church. "Come on in heah, you mothahs, an' wuk me ovah." The parody of Southern speech must have been some little joke working in him almost without his knowledge. He fought them; they beat him, and used sharp jabs of their sticks in his groin when they had him pinned, in order to take the last fight out of him. The jab in the groin is good for subtraction in this problem of police arithmetic. Three of the arresting officers were Irish; one was a black man—new policy. The deacon, who had always hated the mess Howard made with his paints and brushes and drop cloths, tried to hit him with his broom. The police halted this infringement on their right.

Howard had made friends among the newspaper reporters covering North Beach. He was a charmer. Perhaps for this reason, he was released on his own recognizance a few days later. There was no precedent for the crime of painting the Stations of the Cross and resisting expulsion from a church. BEATNIK COMMITS HOLY TRESPASS ON WALL, said the early edition of the *Chronicle*.

The night after he was released, Howard returned to the church. He broke in—the lock had been changed—and lit up the whole building and stood surrounded at midnight by Jesus, Pilate, Mary, the Romans, the Jews, his Prince Valiant horses and chariots. Outside, the chicken and pork smells of Fillmore, and the angry traffic, and the shambling, ambling, lazy, desperate life of the Moh. Here—the permanence of a quest for meaning. He found his paints and brushes in the men's room and went back to his wall.

This time when they came for him he had barricaded the door. Also he had an automatic pistol, which he pointed menacingly from the high windows. Consultation outside. It seemed ridiculous to use tear gas on a mural painter. At the same time, it was an insult to the social order to let a crazyman turn an automatic pistol on anyone he chose. It could be loaded. The gathering of experts bore its complex fruit—sirens, loudspeakers, firemen, and trucks. Also Dr. Martin Bubkin from the Mount Zion psychiatric clinic nearby. At that time Dr. Bubkin was occupied in the divorce courts by a wife who spent her happiest hours contemplating the California community-property laws and thanking God that he had decided to do his residence in San Francisco. (He liked sailing and the hay-fever-free climate.) For his own reasons, Dr. Bubkin decided to try to settle matters with Howard without human or property damage. Howard was persuaded to admit the doctor alone through a side window. He crawled through, puffing, out of condition.

"I might run amuck, Doctor," Howard warned him.

"You couldn't make things any worse for me," Dr. Bubkin morosely replied.

For the first twenty minutes, Howard and Dr. Bubkin gossiped warily, complaining, keeping their deeper secrets, with no real meeting of spirit. The automatic pistol followed the psychiatrist's every movement. Then they got onto artistic matters, and the trouble with women, and the relation of the Jews to the crucifixion, and almost every topic that might occur to two intelligent, cultured young San Franciscans, except that they never bothered to discuss homosexuality, drugs, alcoholism, or Oakland.

"You know, Howard," said Dr. Bubkin, "you're the first person I've been able to talk to in months. I've been nervous."

"You jes' sayin' that so's I put down this here gun."

"That's true," admitted the doctor, "but I mean it, anyway. However, I'd be much obliged if you would stop waving it at me. Also—how come you slip in and out of dialect like that?"

Howard, nervous himself, didn't want the doctor to be nervous. It still hurt where he had been jabbed by a club between the legs, where he had been insulted by the Philistine bishop, where he had been disbarred and discommoded and bored and made anxious by his life on earth. He thought he might explain about his many dialects and talking so much. They sat in a pew and chatted while the firemen and policemen peeked in the windows. Many man-hours of public-servant time were expended; no one interfered, though a captain of detectives offered his commentary: "Serve that goddamn shrink right he get plugged by a mad rampaging colored gentleman."

His style was altered in midsentence, due to the neutral presence of a bunch of old envelopes in the hand of the jazz critic of the San Francisco *Bay Guardian*. The other hand was writing with a soft lead pencil.

The police captain watched the hands and tried to talk at a convenient speed. He liked giving interviews. It was one of the rewards of public service, in addition to the tax-free bags of cash from bookies.

In the meantime, inside, Howard and Dr. Bubkin, good friends by this time, were speaking of the doctor's unhappy marriage and Howard's troubles with the shouting preacher. Both of them had found their art forms. Howard's was painting and conversation; the doctor's had been sailing and interpersonal communication. Neither had known the greatest success. The doctor had been forced to sell his Spinniker. Now they sat in silence, grieving; at last Dr. Bubkin sighed and inquired if Howard would mind giving up the automatic pistol and going out and gettin committed to a nice clean insane asylum.

It didn't seem like much of an idea. Dr. Bubkin had little faith in it himself. He wasn't going to try to sell it hard to Howard, an artist and a good talker. Dr. Bubkin shrugged and let the matter drop.

"I guess so," said Howard, fatigued after the long day. Everyone has to make sacrifices in this vale of tears. Sailboats, machine pistols. It's lonely to be in conflict with society without institutional or ideological support. Even the college beatniks banded together. But no union for painters of the Stations of the Cross.

The crowd was hushed as, first, the doctor emerged, and then Howard. Dr. Bubkin squeezed Howard's hand, man to man, promised to see him soon, and handed him over to the police. They waited until the doctor drove off in his blue Chevelle convertible. Then they jabbed Howard between the legs with their clubs as preventative action against resisting arrest. He groaned and cried out, but bore them no animus. That, he knew, was the way of the world, and the cops could no more keep themselves from using their clubs after a period of strain than he could help his being a light mahogany in color. Negritude and coppiness are all part of man's fate—stations on the way to eternity.

From being treated as crazy so much, Howard began to act insane. His friend Dr. Bubkin did come to visit him several times, sitting on the edge of his bed and discussing life and assuring him that the occasional beatings to his groin would possibly cause no permanent harm and that he might even recover his virility. Then they discussed Dr. Bubkin's virility vis-à-vis his wife, or former wife. Howard urged Dr. Bubkin to stop thinking so much about sex and take up a hobby, such as painting or girls. After giving the doctor advice, Howard felt much better. He remarked to the psychiatrist, "Nice profession you got here."

"Yes, Howard. We strive to cure ourselves, and thus we get it both ways. Paid, too."

Perhaps Howard's situation tended to close his normally open nature. "You're getting paid for talking to me?"

"No, never mind, don't worry," said Dr. Bubkin. "You're my hobby, like you said. Painting, girls, or good conversation. I'd like to learn to be more spontaneous. Call me Albert."

"Well, that makes me feel better, Albert," said Howard.

"In you," declared Dr. Bubkin, "I am searching the I-thou relationship well described by the distinguished German philosopher of Mosaic extraction, Martin Buber."

"Hi there, Albert."

"A communication without reason, Howard, but telling of man's love for all nature, not excluding you. I don't think it's a joking matter, Howard."

Howard wished that he could blush. A little more Caucasian on his mother's side and he might have been able to manage it. Several of his children, especially the ones by Helga Swenson, knew how to blush.

"Spontaneous, you're so spontaneous, Howard," said Dr. Bubkin. "Even your kidding is like that. I truly admire your ability to kid spontaneously, Howard."

"There are many things I can't do," said Howard. "I'm limited by pigmentation, for example. Limited by all those limits."

Dr. Bubkin waited.

"Albert," he added.

Dr. Bubkin beamed. "Thank you, Howard, thank you," he said. "Now let's talk about you."

But it turned out that Albert's visits didn't do Howard enough good. From brooding about his inability to blush or paint, from the contrast between their easy conversations and the rest of Howard's life—shock treatment, camisoles, soilers, guards, therapists, pills, failure all about him—he began to grow weary and depressed. It took the form of objecting to being kept in a ward with Negroes. Howard insisted on a ward for the mulattoes. He explained that he had nothing against Negroes personally, as such, so long as they kept their place, but he wanted to associate with his own kind. "We mulattoes don't want our sisters to marry Negroes," he explained.

A kindly guard interrupted his breaking up the furniture with the promise of a dime and phone call to Dr. Bubkin.

"I'm desperate," said Howard, "Albert."

"Look, Howard," said Dr. Bubkin, "you haven't got a sister in there with you. Ergo, this is not a reality problem, don't you see?"

"I'm going to rip out this telephone. But first, Albert, did your wife get custody of the sailboat and the library?"

"She returned my textbooks, kept the *Horizons* and *American Heritages*. I have to pay her for the sailboat. Look, Howard, don't do anything till I get there. I'm coming down to interpersonally relate to you right now, okay? Now, you wait right there."

But by the time Dr. Bubkin arrived, his friend had gone into a rage, a brainstorm, a fury, a paranoid decline. Shock treatment. He turned against life, friendship, and painting. This was because painting, friendship, and life itself had let him down. But insulin and/or electricity remained faithful. More treatment. He received a series of twenty-four, plus a strained back from a leather thong left unsecured by an attendant who had been distracted by Howard's pleas for mercy. The presiding doctor interpreted the attendant's error as a covert act of hostility produced by a passive—dependent, but aggressive—character disorder. He recommended group therapy for the attendant. But Howard now had a slipped disc, which made him seem a little less loose and easy when he hobbled through the ward.

After a while the state and Howard grew weary of each other. He became tranquil; the state was appeased. The art critic of the San Francisco *Purveyor* wrote an article about the mural, and so many white visitors came to the St. Booth Church of God, etc., that Bishop Willy, sensitized as he was to the demands of Mammon, decided not to paint it out. When this good news was brought to Howard, he reacted with neither delight nor curiosity. He had lost interest in painting—another sign of cure. "We sometimes use the word 'cure,' " the head of the Service declared at the Monday morning conference, "when what we mean is 'remission.' That right, Howard? How do you feel, Howard?" Howard stood waiting before the amphitheater filled with doctors, residents, psychologists, technicians, and their friends. He didn't answer back. "I would call this a good remission," the doctor said.

He was let out on weekend passes. Friends in North Beach housed him. One friend was the mother of several of his children; others were colleagues from the Bagel Shop days. They had traded in their unemployment; they had jobs and shaving cream; some had good jobs, after-shave lotion, talcum powder. But they were nostalgic and happy to see Howard again. Parties,

quiet strolls down Grant Avenue, wry reminiscences about the good old days
when lentil soup at the Enigma was occasionally supplemented by steak tartar
at Enrico's, courtesy of a television producer or a visiting reporter. Bishop
Willy reported no sign of Howard in the vicinity of the Stations of the Cross.

After a few months of trial visits to the outside world, Howard was
released. He found a job as receptionist in a car wash. What the job consisted
of was this: standing in the street with a large white rag, grinning and waving
and flagging down motorists with the promise of clean windows and trim. But
Howard, gradually regaining his wits after the cleansing action of shock
treatment, liked to describe himself as a receptionist, like the girls out of Mills
College who couldn't type but wanted to work in fascinating jobs in advertis-
ing or finance.

The years sped by. A bit of gray appeared at Howard's temples. He seemed
well-adjusted to being part white; he bore no ill will against Negroes, Cauca-
sians, or mulattoes; he accepted himself. He sent Dr. Bubkin a wedding
present when he married his new wife in Tucson—an anthology of *The Best
from Show*. They corresponded. Howard opened his own car wash on money
saved and money borrowed. Dr. Bubkin took a small share as an investment.
The business prospered. Howard gave special rates on sports cars because of
their size. This was his contribution to the smog and traffic problems. He
encouraged the purchase of smaller cars. It was evident that a soupçon of his
previous reformism survived, but not enough to cause serious trouble or
indicate unbusinesslike attitudes. He was accepted. Only occasionally did
people remind themselves that he was a disbarred lawyer, a retired chief of
the beatniks, an expert on the Stations of the Cross. Now he was a Black
Capitalist.

He gave money to the mothers of his children when he could. The children
were mostly doing well in school. Several of the mothers had married—one
to a bearded photographer who told everyone how proud it made him that
Howard was the father of his children. "Howard comes from better stock
than me," said the photographer. "He's creative, intelligent. Eugenically I'm
inferior, and I consider it my ecological duty to have no children. But I'm
a good stepfather."

"Aw," said his wife. "Howard has flaws, too."

"No, dear," said the blond, silky-bearded photographer. "Flaws is one
thing, but talents is another. You read the article on the murals, didn't you,
dear? Actually, the camera is a secondary art form. Howard has gifted our
kids with primary talents and inner strength. You can't beat that for getting
ahead in life, dear."

Howard, who occasionally took tea with this happy couple, listened to the
discussion with embarrassment. Since he couldn't blush, he took the children
out for ice cream cones. He brought back a quart of lemon ice from the
Safeway to cool off the parents. Then he continued on his route up Telegraph
Hill to Union, where he had a child by a young lady formerly active in SNCC,
now getting involved in Women's Lib. She usually wanted to talk to him
about the Problem; she wondered if passive resistance is more truly vital than

rock throwing; he sighed and put up with it for the sake of the child. It was his youngest, a boy aged four, and the apple of his eye. He held the boy on his knees and told him stories. He liked to baby-sit while the mother went out passive-resisting. Lately she went out Gestetnering—a revolutionary duplicating process.

These strolls among his old friends in North Beach turned out to make more trouble. Perhaps life itself, plus the risks of having a personality and a soul, were the undoing of Howard. After the end of the beat movement, the new San Francisco Bohemia and the old Bohemia and the debris of the beatniks conspired to keep North Beach green. Hip was beginning to happen. Two bookstores, the Discovery and City Lights, still operated on Columbus Avenue near Broadway, separated by the Vesuvio Bar, which advertised its slogan, "We Are Itching to Get Away from Portland, Oregon," and kept booths for psychiatrists who wanted to study the clientele. The drug of choice became methedrine sulfate, a stimulant which constricts the blood vessels, causing rich fantasies and impotence, a confusing congeries of sensation. The methedrine addicts would steal books from the Discovery, sell them at City Lights for a few cents; then the owners of City Lights would return the books, or vice versa. This was a service the rival bookstores provided for each other. Otherwise they competed ferociously.

Howard, who had a keen eye for illegality, asked the owner of the Discovery, "Why don't yöu turn in those speed freaks?"

"Well, you know," he replied.

Watching a thief at City Lights, he remarked to Kellogg Kim, the bearded Korean poet and critic, who guarded the cash register, "Look, Kellogg, another booster."

"Yep," said Kellogg.

"So call the cops!"

"Aw, he's part of the family," said Kellogg, plucking at his package of Rice Krispies as the meth head strolled out toward the Discovery, his belt lined with paperbacks of James Baldwin, John Updike, Wolfgang Kohler, and a Sierra Club book about *Some Nice Walks under the Condemned Redwood Trees.*

Philosophy was not dead in Howard even though he was part owner of a car wash. He began to argue the relevance of this tolerance of criminality. He admitted that to steal for food and drink might be justified under certain circumstances, especially in an economy of abundance, but to steal for drugs . . . Kellogg answered that it was not his task to judge the needs of another . . . Howard said the moral man must make decisions . . . Kellogg said he had another code . . . Howard derogated this code . . . Kellogg gently insisted . . . Howard gently insisted . . . Kellogg reinsisted.

At this point in the discussion they both paused to watch another book thief leave the store in the direction of the Discovery. For Howard this was the last straw. He asked Kellogg for permission to stop him. Kellogg said no. Howard gave Kellogg one more chance. Kellogg turned away and opened a copy of Lawrence Ferlinghetti's *The Alligation,* a book about alligators. Howard hit Kellogg on the nose.

Bleeding, Kellogg said to Howard, "Look, I'm a Buddhist. I can't hit you back." A spot of blood dripped from his nose. It lengthened and hopped nimbly to his beard.

Howard danced about, saying, "You got to hit me back, Kellogg. I hit you. I ain't no Buddhist, I ain't no gentleman neither."

"I'm very strong," said Kellogg. "If I hit you, I'll kill you. That's why I'm a Buddhist."

"Hit me! Hit me!"—dancing about and jabbing the air, knocking over the racks of paperbacks, backing into a pile of *Ramparts* and *Partisan Reviews.*

"I can't," said Kellogg.

"Hit me, you yellow-skinned Jap!"

"I'm a Korean. Call me a gook. I'm a Buddhist." Somehow the discussants had been showered with Kellogg's Rice Krispies. They crunched underfoot; they were stuck in the Korean's beard. It looked like a Zen wedding in Battle Creek.

"You mutherfur!" screamed Howard.

Kellogg wiped some of the blood from his nose and beard. He looked at the blood on his shirt. "This stuff stains," he said softly. "But you're a part of the family."

Howard began to cry. He was not touched; he was frustrated. The long period of abstinence from sex, violence, drink, painting, and garrulity had left him fatigued in his soul. If only he and Kellogg could have enjoyed a good old family quarrel, exchanging a few family blows, Howard might have been spared another painful encounter with the police. If nonviolence doesn't work, give a man some violence. When Kellogg refused to strike back, Howard went out and stood on the corner of Columbus and Broadway to weep. He attracted a crowd tired of watching the topless dancers at the Condor. *Look, black tears, black man weeps!* was the general view of matters. He sobbed, he mewled, he showed all the signs of despair. When the police tried to lead him away—the crowd was blocking traffic—he refused to go. They shoved and pushed; he resisted. He held on to the door of the chili-teria.

Oh-oh, there it goes again, a small voice within warned him. Voice unheeded.

He refused to enter the paddy wagon. Voices unheeded.

More sticks to the groin.

A few days in jail, and then removal to Napa for therapy. Friends operated the car wash, but it went to pieces fast. Plumbing and finances all came apart. Howard's charm had kept people churning through for clean cars. The car wash passed into other hands. Howard seemed to be a permanent resident of Napa.

Nevertheless, he has attained a certain status as a patient. He enjoys weekend privileges. The last time I saw Howard, he was limping along Broadway with his friend Dr. Bubkin, who visits him whenever he comes to San Francisco. Howard is now a tall, gaunt, gray-haired man who looks like a mild bourgeois with his briefcase, his meticulous but shabby clothes, his tranquil smile and nod—*rational.* He doesn't have the rheumatiz, but he has a slipped disc. He talks a great deal again; it sounds as if he is doing it on purpose.

"I'd like you to meet my friend Dr. Bubkin," he said, introducing me.

"We know each other, Howard."

"I forgot. It's not fair."

"Anybody can forget things, Howard."

"I forget too much."

"Well, it'll happen that way, Howard."

He paused and looked toward the fog-shrouded Broadway tunnel. "I had girls, children, business. I had a painting—no, it was murals I did. I had lots of things. I used to be a lawyer. It's not fair."

"Well, what can you do?"

"I used to have the water, all I needed was the bucket. Now—"

The crowd near The Committee swept about us, students, tourists, lovers, hippie strollers filled with the joy of evening. A lovely blond dropout, maybe sixteen years old, was selling the *Barb*. There was the smell of woodsmoke and the sound of an amplified guitar. The Peppermint Tree invited dancers; the Balkan restaurant offered shish kabob, and baklava dripping with honeyed chopped nuts. Howard wore a tuft of cotton in each ear. He was protecting himself against the ocean damp.

"Now," said Howard, "I'm a mentally disturbed senior citizen. I'm a socially deprived. I ain't got the water."

Patrick Boyle

The Agony of A. Boscas

IT IS RELATED THAT AT THE FIRST OECUMENICAL COUNCIL OF THE BIRDS, held on the fifth day of Creation, each winged creature sought to justify his membership of the separate and unique sect to which he belonged. The peacock explained the significance of his ridiculous plumage, the owl his lunatic glare, the vulture his bald and corkscrew neck. Only the duck failed to vindicate his orthodoxy. After all, how account for an arse that is trailing the ground?

This prolapse of the croup—better known as Duck's Disease—is endemic amongst writers. But like *Anas boscas,* a writer can hardly explain that he is built nearer the ground than his neighbour, the better to savour the hum and reek of creation. Nor is he likely to admit to the morals of a tom-cat, the tenderness of Jack the Ripper, the respect for private property of a racecourse pickpocket—all virtues peculiar to the duck-arsed.

For the true *Anas boscas* will sell—dead meat or on the hoof—his family, his friends, his household gods. He will root up, assemble and set in motion the delicate bones of his grandmother (God rest her soul) with as little compunction as he would flay and dismember his doting wife. He will pillage, crib, despoil and plagiarise the work of the living and the dead, gobbling up words, phrases, ideas, to scutter them out later as genuine, home-produced, finest quality duck droppings.

He is a collector of trivia. His notebook contains classified sections headed: DEFINITIONS, DESCRIPTIONS, EXPRESSIONS. Each section is many pages long. There is a section labelled: OATHS, containing the basic swear words and their local refinements. It runs to a bare half page. There is a page of nicknames ranging from Scroggy, Gug, Parafoother to Choke the Rats. The longest section—CLICHÉS—the collected small talk of his friends provides the sawdust stuffing that will keep his characters from collapsing in a heap of empty rags. On the back page, under the heading: IDEAS FOR PLOTS, are six lines of small, deliberate writing:

The skivvy visiting the lodger. On business?
Uncle Willie Kiss-the-corpse.
The dying mouse lurching with stiff-legged dignity towards the waiting paw.
The Maggot and the uneconomic cow.
Who squirted the chewing tobacca juice over the corpse's face?
At the bottom of the page is a poem:

If you're starting off rich
And you want to be poor,
Keep a thorough-bred hunter
A hound and a hoor.

These occult messages have long since ceased to convey any meaning to him.

On the first page of his credo:

Pity the poor bastard on the horns of a dilemma. But for God's sake don't release him till he has himself roared out.

The notebook cost half a crown and had stiff covers until the contents of a bottle of stout softened the cardboard and loosened the binding.

Now for a glimpse of Anas at work. Crouched over the battered portable (he always types a first draft—the printed word carrying more hope of completion than the written scrawl) balding head sunk between dandruffed shoulders, he sits staring at the blank sheet of cheap 10″ x 8″, rolled into position for titling.

He has a beginning and an end, with only two thousand words of interior springing to pack in. It should not be beyond the wit of man to label it. The dandruff thickens on his shoulders as he scratches his head impatiently.

At last he decides to leave the titling until the work is under way. Briskly he shifts the paper up four double spaces, sets his margins and sits back, sighing contentedly—a man with a mission nearing completion.

But now what is happening? Once more he has slumped forward, elbows sprawling the typewriter, fisted knuckles rasping unshaven cheeks.

Where the hell is he to begin? In the past? The present? The future? Will he lead in with a proverb, pithy and apposite? Or a quotation from some minor poet? Will he himself act as narrator? Wheel around arsey-versey and address the back of his head as *You?* Stick to the God's-eye view of the third person singular? Should he treat the reader as an ignorant bloody yob who must have everything spelt out for him in words of one syllable? Or would it be safe to lay a trail of hints, suggestions and parables to keep the intelligent reader sniffing hungrily at his heels? Like this:

"You would have liked my Uncle Silas. A big paunchey Cork man with a bap-face and innocent butcher's-blue eyes. One look at him and you knew you had a buyer at last for that piner of a bullock that had been eating its head off this twelve months. How wrong you would be? A fly or any other creature of the insect world would never get toe-hold on Uncle Silas . . ."

Who would suspect that this was the opening paragraph to an article on entomology?

He sinks lower over his typewriter, brooding on the importance to the finished product of the opening paragraph. If it is not compelling enough, the reader will not stay button-holed. If too insistent, he becomes bored. If too long, he will skip.

At this hideous prospect Anas winces. He decides to leave the lead-in until the form is better. Those hot rums last night on top of a gutful of flat porter. Ugh! His stomach jerks uneasily like a dreaming dog.

Better map out the main body of the work. Always the easiest part of the job. Admitted there are certain small rules to be followed. But nothing to daunt a man in the whole of his health.

Take this little matter of the THEORY OF INDIRECT APPROACH. There should not be much trouble with that one.

Never try the front door. The back door might be on the latch or a window unsnibbed. If the back door is bolted, put your shoulder to it or kick it in. You'll more than likely discover the boss of the house on board the hired help or disturb him in the act of dismembering her pregnant corpse on the kitchen table. Don't back out, apologizing. Isn't this the kind of situation you've been trying to ferret out?

Never go direct from here to there. A fruitful deviation might be possible. Instead of skulking off when the tea-table is cleared, grabbing a hat from the hall-stand and closing the front door quietly, before setting off for the boozer, a detour to the scullery should be made, a dish cloth picked up and the little woman consulted:

"Can I help with the dishes, darling?"

Ignore the astonished silence. Make with the cloth. It's damp, it's dirty and it stinks—but no remarks, please. Keep talking. Introduce a little gentle badinage:

"Chatty this evening, aren't we, love?"

Never mind the deafening hush. Could be the old trouble again. Ear drums. Dewax them with elaborate sweeping gestures. Listen again with hand to ear. Still the same old silence. Pack it in, chum, and bugger off.

"I think I'll go as far as the Corner House and have a couple of jars."

Be sure and kiss wifey before leaving. Stoop down, lips puckered, eyes ajar. Oh-hoh! Something gone wrong here. Target for tonight seems to be the side of the jaw. Better get cracking before the storm breaks.

"Shan't be long dear."

Now step out briskly, shoulders back, slight swagger. Don't look round. Collect hat. Eyes front and stop whistling. The front door at last. And . . . SLAM IT SHUT.

From the foregoing, it would be reasonable to assume that our hero is not heading for the boozer. He has a date at the flat of a lady with the sinister name of Polk—Fay Rhyming-with-bloke-Polk—with whom he proposes to spend the next couple of hours in healthy, but not too arduous, activity of a sexual nature. He is married long enough to be bored with his wife, has neither chick nor child to bother him, and is a believer in the mental and physical stimulation of extra-marital nookey. From the behaviour of his wife it can be divined that she is not unaware of his infidelities.

Slumped in dejection, Anas stares at the blank paper, his mind a ferment of warnings and injunctions.

Avoid long paragraphs. You know better than to swig down a basin of porter without coming up once in a while for air.

Vary the sentence length so that it is impossible to read at cruising speed.

Work at the structure of each sentence until, besides making sense, it can be heard to walk, to trot, to gallop. If it fails to gather speed or develops a string-halt, there is nothing for it but to consult Roget.

Never use a highfaluting word where a commonplace one will serve. Occasionally an outrageously recondite word for something well known and trivial may prod awake a drowsy reader.

Monosyllables are the mostest.

This last assertion infuriates the duck-bottomed one. He jerks upright. Two-fingered he batters out:

"Balls.! BALLS.!.! B A L L S.!.!.!"

Scowling he stares at his handiwork. Slams back the carriage and starts again: "*Memo to Compositor.* Stop griping, bud. This rattley-box aint got no!. I get sick to my stomach hopping like a hunted flea from. to ! to hatch out!. So lay offa me.!.!.!

As he ponders the frustration of the artist, forever doomed to work with inferior tools, pity wells up in him. Tenderly he moistens parched and yearning lips. This, he decides, is an occasion for spiritual solace.

The Jameson bottle in the wall cupboard has a good gill of whiskey left, half of which he pours into the tumbler, topping it up from the cold tap in the bathroom.

The first three slugs he takes standing, bottle and glass in either hand. Heeling in the rest of the whiskey, he puts back the bottle and resumes his rigidly crouched position, poised over the typewriter. Waiting.

Empty metal brewery casks boom and clunk as they are rolled out and stacked along the pavement awaiting transport. A tuneless whistle passes keeping pace with shuffling feet. Children shout. Dogs bark. Singly and in chorus, sea-birds wail, screech, cackle.

He drinks again. Deep contented draughts savouring the stronger bite of the liquor. By the time the glass is empty, the old familiar glow has spread from the pit of his stomach to his tingling scalp. Soon the hum of the generator will fill his ear-drums.

Already he sees the finished work, quaking with fat, as it dangles from the slaughterhouse beams. Stepping back, he surveys its bulk. A flensing job is badly needed here. He spits on his hands, rubbing them together gleefully. A few final flicks of sharpening steel on skinning knife and Bob's your uncle.

First strip away the hide and get at the carcase. That's better! Now for the fat. Layer after layer of it. The gully, please. Thumb the knife edge. Sharp enough? Let's go! Collops of suet mound the floor. Kick them aside. Plenty more where they came from.

Still too much flesh on the brute. Time for the cleaver. Eh? And the meat saw.

Hacking, slashing, sawing, rending. Hewing through tendon and muscle, twisting at stubborn arteries, tearing away tissue.

At last he stands, tired, sweating, bloodied, gazing contentedly at the grinning, mangled skeleton.

Anas rolls on a fresh sheet of 10" x 8". In a welter of mixed metaphors, he fingers the keys of the typewriter, the pared-down work rising clearly before his mind's eye, spare and austere, like a giant gantry, able to support many times its own weight.

Eagerly he starts to type:

"It is related that at the oecumenical council of the birds . . ."

The Magic Telephone

Garrison Keillor

I SUBSCRIBE TO 18 MAGAZINES, AND MY NAME IS ON EVERY MAILING LIST in America. An armload of free offers, pornographic brochures, magazines, and other stuff is laid at my door every day but Sunday. I don't buy much. I just like to be asked. Also I edit a magazine and I like to keep up. Mainly, though, it gives me good impressions of my being around. Permanently. Here to stay. Believe me, I dread the day no mail comes. Either I'll be dead, or lost, or locked up. So it's a pleasure. My other pleasure is the telephone, which, when it rings, is for me (unless it's a wrong number) because I live by myself. I have a deep, cushy armchair by the telephone. It's "Hello, Janet, hello, Frank, hello, Jack," and I sink back into a warm bath of pleasantries and gags. I'm not conceited, but it's good to hear yourself when you talk so you can check on how you're doing. I never know just how I am unless I'm on the phone, then I can tell if I'm tired or angry, I can hear a snap in my voice, and many times I hear a pure light joy coming out of me. When you have somebody else right there in your house, you can't hear yourself. Even somebody else breathing in the room throws me off. A cough or sneeze is a kick in the head. But with a telephone, you jump into somebody's life, and jump back out. You talk, not to his eyes or her breasts but straight into the brain. I can call a girl in San Francisco (I'm in Minnesota), turn off the light, and zap! we're in bed and rapping over old times.

Nearly a year ago, I was stuck in Chicago where I was editor of a farm co-op journal. A mammoth 56-page weekly production that I had to sweat over like I was editing the Ten Commandments. I practically lived at the printer's, choking down Pepsis and nut bars over the galley proofs. Towards the end, I was planting hot ones on the jokes page, then I was asked to leave. I was ready to leave town, really I was all set to depart this life, the noise was getting me down. Every sort of noise, from the noise of machines to the noise when another body bangs into yours. But I needed another job, which I found with a hamburger chain that publishes a monthly magazine. That was almost as bad, until I found that all the stuff came in by mail and all of it went out by mail. So they let me go up to Minnesota, where it comes in and goes out just the same as in Chicago.

I chose this town for its name, Anoka, which is Indian for something, and rented a two-story grey frame house with an acre of yard, where I live now. When I have to see live people, I go to the college and paint scenery for the Playhouse. Most times, I keep to my property.

First thing, I ordered three telephones: black, white, green; office, kitchen, bedroom. When I got back from my last weekend fling in Chicago, the movers had set up the furniture, telephones installed, mail starting to arrive, every- thing perfect. Went to work on the hamburger editing, ordered a pizza, felt happy.

That evening, I remember, I called Janet in Los Angeles. She had just separated from her husband the reporter, David of UPI. Next night, a quick one to my father in Miami, and a long soul call to Joanne, my older sister, in California. I keep a running telephone bill in my head, and I know several other calls were made, some short, some long. I am an impulse caller. Leap to the phone, dial the number, and I'm resting comfortably in Boston or New Mexico, ear to ear with those I love. She isn't home, I'll talk to anybody wants to talk. Her mother, her kid, the plumber, it's all right, just me the anonymous caller wanting a friendly word.

My father's letter comes on the first of the month, his monthly statement: account payable. Then I looked through a circular for a book of sex secrets. Next on the pile was the telephone bill. I flipped it onto the bill pile and went through the details of how to build up your pectorals. After that was a fat envelope stuffed with contributions from the counter girls at our Dallas outlet, telling how much their jobs mean to them in terms of gaining experi- ence, which I'm always happy to hear about.

It was not until check writing day later that week that I actually opened the phone bill and held the computer card in my two hands. I was asked to pay $3.50, not including installation charges. My mind has a way of emitting a powerful laser beam when it is activated by any sort of typographical error, and this beam fastened on the figure of $3.50. My first feeling was purely professional, that I ought to cross it out and write $35.00 (or $350.00) above it, and send it back to the phone company. Then I realized what a personal honor had fallen to me, one among millions, to catch the Universal Telephone System with its decimal point off. Even so, I'm used to paying my own way, and I was prepared to call up the company manager and find out the right amount. I didn't, for two reasons: it would make trouble for the company, fishing around in its computer tapes to find the spot where the copper oxide was holding onto the right amount, and re-billing me; and I was innocent, since I have my own personal computer that makes out all my personal checks, and it makes them out to the amount requested by other computers, whether wrong or not. So I paid them $3.10, after deducting the tax that is burning women and children in Vietnam. All in a day for the phone company.

I should have laid off the long distance calls that month. Instead, I dialed as before—freely, to check on the Calfornia break-up, my father's kidney trouble and general regrets, and also to extend advice to an old girlfriend in Chicago who was shopping around for an abortionist. Not on my account, believe me. And I sang Happy Birthday to my nephew Jeffrey in California, who in person I scare out of his wits. So then it's August, which brings new letters from hamburger personnel all over the country describing their vaca- tions, and the telephone bill which I opened on receipt to find the computer still had me programmed for $3.50 which I paid (minus tax) with no complaint. Leaving out the details of my August days, I was billed the same amount in September. Same in October. In October, I threw caution to the wind and called long distance like mad. That month, all my friends of earlier college days were just assuming their places in the graduate schools of America from coast to coast. Sometimes it required an hour of telephone time to straighten out somebody's problem, which using other means would have required 10 letters and many months. I sat in my chair and took in the hot details of jerky love affairs, fights on the home front, spiritual hangovers, the pros and cons of earning a Ph.D., and I prescribed patience, love, sweetness, and, when it seemed appropriate, tested and guaranteed courses of action. Working in my own home, I was reaching out to the far corners of the land with a generosity that people never become accustomed to in life, with the subsidy from the telephone company which sent me a bill for $3.50 in November. I'd always been able and willing to pay for talking to faraway persons; now, with the help of AT&T, I could afford to sit and listen to them. I don't mind admitting that I thought of myself sometimes as a friendly God sitting in Minnesota, who could hear every prayer whether uttered in New York or San Diego and who would listen to it all the way through. Dear God, somebody was saying, please end this war, it is killing me. Dear God, I just want to talk to you. I'm sick. God, just lead me out of the Psychology Department into a cleaner, better life and I'll praise you all my days.

My friend Bobo, whom a fellowship dropped into Lawrence, Kansas, was one of many subscribers to me. I guessed Lawrence must be a bad town to be unhappy in, for when I talked to Bobo her voice was completely hollow, like "everything's O.K. but I'm sure glad you called anyway." I talked into her voice and back would come depth soundings that indicated all the good loving had dropped out the bottom of her. We had an arrangement; she called me and hung up after two rings. I called her right back. There followed her interminable description of some terribly interesting, tedious case study that had been laid on her that day. I followed her along, just watching the needle flying up into the red zone as her calm voice continued. She might have had a needle in one hand and a razor in the other, holding the phone under her chin, just waiting for the word from me to decide which to use. Believe me, I chose words with care. I spoke very carefully into that receiver. Long pauses while I parsed out my next thought. The calls ended with Bobo breaking up in hysterical laughter, like an alarm clock going off. Then it was day again. Bobo is alive in Lawrence.

Not that I was running a Suicide Center. It was my habit on the magic telephone to ring up Washington D.C. every two weeks or so and have an hour with T. R. Rudwick, Army Reserve psychological warrior, whom our government was keeping in check until a real national emergency when he would be sprung loose into the Asian hinterlands and persuade the natives to surrender peacefully. Maybe he could write them a poem, I don't know how the Army figured he would do it, since he couldn't read nor speak Asian. T. R. could hardly wait to get out into the villages and pacify all of peasantry. Handing out complimentary tubes of toothpaste, all smiles, and saying very

clearly so no peasant could fail to understand him: *you brush, we no bomb.*
At the time, T.R. was psychologizing his superiors at Army Reserve meetings. I could see him with his beads jingling on his brass buttons, standing
up in the middle of the armory, as he repeated for me over the telephone, "Sir,
I understand that our use of defoliants has actually increased the rice yield
in many areas." "I wonder, Sir, if you would go over once more slowly that
part about freedom." "Sir, is napalm odorless?" I ask T. R. when he is going
to desert, and he says, "Just as soon as they make us into a fighting unit."
His unit hadn't been issued ammunition since a rifle accidentally fired during
target practice, wounding an officer in the left buttock. T. R. gave me all his
nationwide telephone numbers from civilian anti-war days; with my telephone set-up, I could check in weekly with various outposts of the resistance
around the country and pass helpful information but mostly encouragement
between them. While Johnson was on the White House radio set bringing in
the bombers over Hanoi, I was on the telephone arranging places to sleep in
Montreal, telling Martha in Iowa City that so-and-so was available to speak
on the 18th, and meanwhile sending all my fraternal goodwill and best wishes
to Dave in St. Louis ("I read about the demonstration in Time"), to Jack the
A. J. Muste of Boston ("glad you were let go and don't get huffy about it"),
to Guffy the Madison mimeograph queen ("grass is $15 the lid from Box 343
Brooklyn"). No end of rainy day fun for me. With the aid of many information operators, I rang up Alfred Kazin, the White House ("Who shall I say
is calling?" "Bertrand Russell"), S. J. Perelman who wasn't home then,
Robert Lowell (Norman Mailer has an unlisted number), and the Oakland
Police ("I wish to report a demonstration"). I even had the urge to call up
some of the better contributors to my hamburger magazine: a carhop in
Shreveport who wrote a fine essay on the death of her father, Carole Hofstram
the Pittsburgh secretary and author of "soliloquy on Autumn," and Miss
Derby Crane who wrote "I feel about all the customers that they are *my*
customers." She was stationed in Wyoming.

This takes me up to Christmas Day when I spoke briefly to 221 individuals
in 24 states. It took all I had, and I believe I established an all-time long-
distance record, for which the telephone company would surely have sent me
a big plaque had it known.

My Christmas calls put me on a new line of thought. As I lay in bed upstairs
massaging my left ear, I understood that the telephone had become the center
of my existence and that without my license to dial free I wouldn't have the
chance of a bat in hell. How did I know of such a thing as the United States
without my talking to people around the land? I would only see faces on the
street, pictures in magazines, lines on TV, but on the telephone I seemed to
have a direct line to the part of me that hurt most and meant most to me.
Other people in the land could speak without charge to that part of me, like
I was taking free sun treatments. I put the phone to my head where it really
was hurting then, and good words entered in and shored me up awhile.
Without the telephone service gratis, I would be cut loose—for good, since
I was tapping small sources of goodness and mercy in all their towns, the

connection was a delicate one and broken once would be broken for all time. I would just come apart, I knew I would. Wander away and get lost in that territory of wild night that is 9/10 of the land mass of North America. You see, I've always been afraid of being a bum because I've moved frequently from city to city with little reason for it. I don't ever want to get to the place where the mail can't reach me and I can't be called to the telephone. That place, friends, is at the end of every road. And I knew I would never leave my home in Anoka so long as I had the magical telephone. I couldn't. I would never give it up.

My thoughts the next day were both generous and mean. I felt like I should share the telephone with others in my area, let them call their loved ones wherever they be for no money. I would put a classified ad in the paper: "Feeling lonely? Call—" Then explain my free offer over the phone. At least, I could offer the phone to the theatre students who were letting me paint their scenery. It might change their lives. Perhaps they would be so affected they would never pay for such things again but consider them rightfully theirs.

I was frying eggs and hash browns as this philanthropy occurred to me and right away, thoughts of danger and despair took me by force. Strangers would come into my house to use the telephone. They would bubble with thanks for my generosity, but underneath envy would be cooking. Perhaps they would be offended by this anomaly in the international telephone system and determine to set the world right. They could report me to the company, an anonymous call, "He's got a free phone." Or worse, somebody could make the mistake of calling person-to-person, thus giving my phone number to a live operator instead of a computer. The operator would jiggle the computer to bill me for the call, whereupon lights flash, computer cards fly out like snow, tapes spin, and blowing off a head of steam, the computer empties its bowels of all my misplaced long distance charges, and I get a bill the next day for $3½ million payable on the 10th.

I imagined being awakened by the fabled knock on the door, there to find a telephone company repairman. "I understand your phone is out of order," he says. "No, it works like a dream," says I. "We hear it's not working good at all," he says, one overshoe slipping over the doorsill. I try to block the way, but he breaks through and makes a dash for the phone. "Get off my property, you freak!" I scream, running behind. He holds up the telephone. "This is our property." "No, it's mine," I say, almost in tears, "It's mine." I snatch the phone away and dial the weather number. "See? Hear? Works like a charm." He gives me a crooked leer. I haven't heard ten other telephone repairmen, dressed in identical brown shirts and black leather riding boots, sneaking through the open door. My arms are pinned behind my back. I feel a screwdriver in my side. The repairmen take up my telephones, ripping them from their sockets. The wires have spread their roots into the walls and floor. The house seems to crumble like dirt. Without a word, the repairmen take away my loose leaf folder of a thousand telephone numbers. They bolt a huge black pay telephone high on the wall. There they leave me. I can't reach the coin slot and I don't have change.

This scene shot through me so, I locked the doors and promised myself I'd never tell a soul. This is the present condition of life in the U.S. that a good thing has to be kept under cover. An assassinating country, and me become a national underground telephone figure. The men who shot Kennedy are tracking down my telephone, the instrument of free press, by which a measure of good sense, love, and mercy are being spread to some parts of the nation. I don't mean to say I was watching the street, but I was high strung. I believe I don't live in the same country as the President and Congress, so much has been taken away—sane politics, courage, freedom, and something like the common assumption of good will—that I am reduced by the circumstances to whispering kind thoughts over the line instead of standing up as a public man as I might. I appreciate the mails, I certainly do. But I call it my right to keep this one line open, this freedom of speech, without which I am no more than an animal trapped in a bush. I wish others had the same, but whether or not, I believe it is essential to hold on to mine. This is something of what I was thinking that day, and also wondering if repairmen ever make service calls without your asking them. Maybe the company would fall into a fit of reorganizing and perfecting, and change everyone's number. What if? I'd be a dead man.

I couldn't stand the suspense, so I dialed DEWBLOSSOM, a word I had dialed weeks before and many times in the meantime, where there lived a sharp old woman on the top floor of a rotten apartment building a thousand miles away. She was never surprised to hear from me; she believed me to be her son. Over the weeks, I was keeping track of her doings, the cats Ralph and Phyllis who crapped in her flowerpots, the little boys who played under her window far below who she had named too, the names of cities Jasper Crystal Golden City Precious City Emerald Rosetown Highplace, the action on her street named House Street, and over again and over again, repeated as a rosary, the names of my beloved brothers and sisters Daley Sunny Bill Esther Mack Looby Pretty and the baby Lulu, and all we were doing and how proud and about our babies, all their names, new babies born every day. I never called her but what I was afraid somebody official had come around in the meantime and put her away in a little gray room. But there she was once more, going on about Esther's new job of rounding up lost cats and my new baby named Nevada. Daley was building a ship for us all to go around the world on, but she didn't want to go. I got in a word here and there about my worries with the telephone company and the war, meanwhile listening to her carrying on, carrying forward, bearing it all upward, and naming every part as she went along. She straightened me out in a minute. Oh yes, I mean she gave me a very good impression of my being around.

TABOO

TABOO AFFORDS ONE OF THE MOST INTENSE OCCASIONS FOR AMBIVA-
lence in our lives, for in its field of meaning we feel the presence of both
incomprehensible—even "supernatural"—power and an awful uncleanness.
Like the word "sterile," which suggests both a praiseworthy antisepsis and
a corresponding barrenness of life, "taboo" carries two meanings. As a word
of Polynesian origin, it signifies very much what the American Indian meant
by "medicine"; it also refers to a complementary excess of vital power so
great that it is awesomely dangerous for humans to contemplate, let alone
approach or participate in.

"The Blind Man," by D. H. Lawrence, can be read profitably as an interesting variation on the Contest motif, for Maurice (the "blind man" of the
title) and Bertie (a "normal," civilized man) are engaged in an elemental
conflict of world views as surely as Bartleby and the lawyer-narrator of
Melville's story are. But the contest between the two men is not all that the
story is about: the beginning and the end are both focused through the mind
of the blind man's wife, Isabel, and such emphases cannot be ignored. Although Isabel is to some extent a witness of the struggle between the dark
powers of the blood (as represented by her husband) and the conventional,
civilized power of the mind (as represented by Bertie), she is by habit and
training aligned with Bertie rather than her husband, and she shares his
uneasiness when faced with the blind man's testimony.

What is his testimony? The answer to this question rather than the question
of who will prevail in the contest between the two men (obviously, Maurice
"wins") lies at the very heart of the story. It is the testimony of the blood
against that institutionalized rationalism that underlies the conventional values of Western civilization. In both Isabel's and Bertie's witnessing of this
deep dark truth (notice that the story begins and ends in darkness, suggesting
that this, rather than light, is the abiding element) there is all of the fascination and wariness that characterizes one's experience of Taboo. The ugliness
of the blind man's scars make them "untouchable," just as his awful, blind
self-containment in his body make him something uncanny and fearful to the
two sighted people closest to him. Bertie undergoes something like initiation,
it is true (thus revealing one important variation upon the theme of Metamorphosis), but by the story's end he really hasn't changed very much. Isabel has
learned something more, one feels, but even this is hard to be sure of. The

fact is, both have been subjected to a power that is older than civilization—older than vision and light, even; and this power is ineffable, disturbing, and fascinating to them. It is capable of destroying or undermining almost all they understand of sanity, and yet it is inescapably "there"—as tangible as the blind man himself and as intimate as their own blood.

The theme of Taboo has apparently been with us from the beginning, whenever that was. The sad histories of Icarus, Pandora, Oedipus, Macbeth, Raskolnikov, and Joseph K. (of Kafka's *The Trial*) are only a few that are concerned totally or in part with Taboo. The object or act of taboo is insidious and powerful precisely because it is "unthinkable." Murder, incest, a violation of the privacy and/or integrity of another, the experiencing or manipulating of forces beyond our understanding and control are all subjects of taboo—not as literary subjects, of course, but as real or contemplated actions within the "real world" of the story. Of course, there is another taboo subject, which still stubbornly retains some of its old ambivalent power in spite of *Playboy* magazine and X-rated movies—sex. Richard Yates' story proves to be a fresh adaptation of this theme, for in the naive, roughhouse male world of the narrator, the prospect of his permanent coming together with a woman is almost paralyzing, a fact that the clumsy humor and inept clowning of the characters can scarcely conceal. And indeed sex has been the most widely exploited of subjects in modern fiction's celebration of Taboo, for its power is revealed, if not enhanced, by the sacredness of the generation of life implicit in even the, yes, "dirtiest" of stories.

Since the celebration of the Taboo motif in both literature and folklore constitutes such an old and enduring theme, it is interesting to observe that many of the science fiction stories written today make use of it, thereby presenting us with the phenomenon of one of the most modern *genres* utilizing a magic/mystic theme of impressive antiquity. Many of these stories are variations of what might be termed the "Frankenstein myth," in which a human meddles with the life force, manipulating that which is essentially beyond human understanding, and ultimately being destroyed, or at least chastened, as a result of his proud and foolish tinkering, his *hubris.* Because science fiction is an important part of our popular literature today, and that it is noteworthy for its exploitation of the theme of Taboo, I have included Clifford Simak's "Shadow Show," one of the better science fiction variations on the theme of Taboo.

Well-known English and American short stories that celebrate the Taboo theme are "Heart of Darkness" and "The Lagoon" by Joseph Conrad; "The Black Cat" by Edgar Allan Poe, "Rappaccini's Daughter" by Nathaniel Hawthorne, "The Beast in the Jungle" by Henry James, "The Monkey's Paw" by W.W. Jacobs, and "The Fly" by Katherine Mansfield.

D. H. Lawrence

The Blind Man

ISABEL PERVIN WAS LISTENING FOR TWO SOUNDS—FOR THE SOUND OF wheels on the drive outside and for the noise of her husband's footsteps in the hall. Her dearest and oldest friend, a man who seemed almost indispensable to her living, would drive up in the rainy dusk of the closing November day. The trap had gone to fetch him from the station. And her husband, who had been blinded in Flanders, and who had a disfiguring mark on his brow, would be coming in from the outhouses.

He had been home for a year now. He was totally blind. Yet they had been very happy. The Grange was Maurice's own place. The back was a farmstead, and the Wernhams, who occupied the rear premises, acted as farmers. Isabel lived with her husband in the handsome rooms in front. She and he had been almost entirely alone together since he was wounded. They talked and sang and read together in a wonderful and unspeakable intimacy. Then she reviewed books for a Scottish newspaper, carrying on her old interest, and he occupied himself a good deal with the farm. Sightless, he could still discuss everything with Wernham, and he could also do a good deal of work about the place—menial work, it is true, but it gave him satisfaction. He milked the cows, carried in the pails, turned the separator, attended to the pigs and horses. Life was still very full and strangely serene for the blind man, peaceful with the almost incomprehensible peace of immediate contact in darkness. With his wife he had a whole world, rich and real and invisible.

They were newly and remotely happy. He did not even regret the loss of his sight in these times of dark, palpable joy. A certain exultance swelled his soul.

But as time wore on, sometimes the rich glamour would leave them. Sometimes, after months of this intensity, a sense of burden overcame Isabel, a weariness, a terrible *ennui,* in that silent house approached between a colonnade of tall-shafted pines. Then she felt she would go mad, for she could not bear it. And sometimes he had devastating fits of depression, which seemed to lay waste his whole being. It was worse than depression—a black misery, when his own life was a torture to him, and when his presence was unbearable to his wife. The dread went down to the roots of her soul as these black days recurred. In a kind of panic she tried to wrap herself up still further in her husband. She forced the old spontaneous cheerfulness and joy to continue. But the effort it cost her was almost too much. She knew she could

309

not keep it up. She felt she would scream with the strain, and would give anything, anything, to escape. She longed to possess her husband utterly; it gave her inordinate joy to have him entirely to herself. And yet, when again he was gone in a black and massive misery, she could not bear him, she could not bear herself; she wished she could be snatched away off the earth altogether, anything rather than live at this cost.

Dazed, she schemed for a way out. She invited friends, she tried to give him some further connection with the outer world. But it was no good. After all their joy and suffering, after their dark, great year of blindness and solitude and unspeakable nearness, other people seemed to them both shallow, rattling, rather impertinent. Shallow prattle seemed presumptuous. He became impatient and irritated, she was wearied. And so they lapsed into their solitude again. For they preferred it.

But now, in a few weeks' time, her second baby would be born. The first had died, an infant, when her husband first went out to France. She looked with joy and relief to the coming of the second. It would be her salvation. But also she felt some anxiety. She was thirty years old, her husband was a year younger. They both wanted the child very much. Yet she could not help feeling afraid. She had her husband on her hands, a terrible joy to her, and a terrifying burden. The child would occupy her love and attention. And then, what of Maurice? What would he do? If only she could feel that he, too, would be at peace and happy when the child came! She did so want to luxuriate in a rich, physical satisfaction of maternity. But the man, what would he do? How could she provide for him, how avert those shattering black moods of his, which destroyed them both?

She sighed with fear. But at this time Bertie Reid wrote to Isabel. He was her old friend, a second or third cousin, a Scotchman, as she was a Scotchwoman. They had been brought up near to one another, and all her life he had been her friend, like a brother, but better than her own brothers. She loved him—though not in the marrying sense. There was a sort of kinship between them, an affinity. They understood one another instinctively. But Isabel would never have thought of marrying Bertie. It would have seemed like marrying in her own family.

Bernie was a barrister and a man of letters, a Scotchman of the intellectual type, quick, ironical, sentimental, and on his knees before the woman he adored but did not want to marry. Maurice Pervin was different. He came of a good old country family—the Grange was not a very great distance from Oxford. He was passionate, sensitive, perhaps over-sensitive, wincing—a big fellow with heavy limbs and a forehead that flushed painfully. For his mind was slow, as if drugged by the strong provincial blood that beat in his veins. He was very sensitive to his own mental slowness, his feelings being quick and acute. So that he was just the opposite to Bertie, whose mind was much quicker than his emotions, which were not so very fine.

From the first, the two men did not like each other. Isabel felt they had *ought* to get on together. But they did not. She felt that if only each could have the clue to the other there would be such a rare understanding between them. It did not come off, however. Bertie adopted a slightly ironical attitude, very offensive to Maurice, who returned the Scotch irony with English resentment, a resentment which deepened sometimes into stupid hatred.

This was a little puzzling to Isabel. However, she accepted it in the course of things. Men were made freakish and unreasonable. Therefore, when Maurice was going out to France for the second time, she felt that, for her husband's sake, she must discontinue her friendship with Bertie. She wrote to the barrister to this effect. Bertram Reid simply replied that in this, as in all other matters, he must obey her wishes, if these were indeed her wishes.

For nearly two years nothing had passed between the two friends. Isabel rather gloried in the fact; she had no compunction. She had one great article of faith, which was, that husband and wife should be so important to one another, that the rest of the world simply did not count. She and Maurice were husband and wife. They loved one another. They would have children. Then let everybody and everything else fade into insignificance outside this connubial felicity. She professed herself quite happy and ready to receive Maurice's friends. She was happy and ready: the happy wife, the ready woman in possession. Without knowing why, the friends retired abashed, and came no more. Maurice, of course, took as much satisfaction in this connubial absorption as Isabel did.

He shared in Isabel's literary activities, she cultivated a real interest in agriculture and cattle-raising. For she, being at heart perhaps an emotional enthusiast, always cultivated the practical side of life and prided herself on her mastery of practical affairs. Thus the husband and wife had spent the five years of their married life. The last had been one of blindness and unspeakable intimacy. And now Isabel felt a great indifference coming over her, a sort of lethargy. She wanted to be allowed to bear her child in peace, to nod by the fire and drift vaguely, physically, from day to day. Maurice was like an ominous thunder-cloud. She had to keep waking up to remember him.

When a little note came from Bertie, asking if he were to put up a tombstone to their dead friendship, and speaking of the real pain he felt on account of her husband's loss of sight, she felt a pang, a fluttering agitation of re-awakening. And she read the letter to Maurice.

"Ask him to come down," he said.

"Ask Bertie to come here!" she re-echoed.

"Yes—if he wants to."

Isabel paused for a few moments.

"I know he wants to—he'd only be too glad," she replied. "But what about you, Maurice? How would you like it?"

"I should like it."

"Well—in that case—But I thought you didn't care for him—"

"Oh, I don't know. I might think differently of him now," the blind man replied. It was rather abstruse to Isabel.

"Well, dear," she said, "if you're quite sure—"

"I'm sure enough. Let him come," said Maurice.

So Bertie was coming, coming this evening, in the November rain and darkness. Isabel was agitated, racked with her old restlessness and indecision. She had always suffered from this pain of doubt, just an agonizing sense of uncertainty. It had begun to pass off, in the lethargy of maternity. Now it returned, and she resented it. She struggled as usual to maintain her calm, composed, friendly bearing, a sort of mask she wore over all her body.

A woman had lighted a tall lamp beside the table and spread the cloth. The long dining-room was dim, with its elegant but rather severe pieces of old furniture. Only the round table glowed softly under the light. It had a rich, beautiful effect. The white cloth glistened and dropped its heavy, pointed lace corners almost to the carpet, the china was old and handsome, creamy-yellow, with a blotched pattern of harsh red and deep blue, the cups large and bell-shaped, the teapot gallant. Isabel looked at it with superficial appreciation.

Her nerves were hurting her. She looked automatically again at the high, uncurtained windows. In the last dusk she could just perceive outside a huge fir-tree swaying its boughs: it was as if she thought it rather than saw it. The rain came flying on the window panes. Ah, why had she no peace? These two men, why did they tear at her? Why did they not come—why was there this suspense?

She sat in a lassitude that was really suspense and irritation. Maurice, at least, might come in—there was nothing to keep him out. She rose to her feet. Catching sight of her reflection in a mirror, she glanced at herself with a slight smile of recognition, as if she were an old friend to herself. Her face was oval and calm, her nose a little arched. Her neck made a beautiful line down to her shoulder. With hair knotted loosely behind, she had something of a warm, maternal look. Thinking this of herself, she arched her eyebrows and her rather heavy eyelids, with a little flicker of a smile, and for a moment her grey eyes looked amused and wicked, a little sardonic, out of her transfigured Madonna face.

Then, resuming her air of womanly patience—she was really fatally self-determined—she went with a little jerk towards the door. Her eyes were slightly reddened.

She passed down the wide hall and through a door at the end. Then she was in the farm premises. The scent of dairy, and of farm-kitchen, and of farm-yard and of leather almost overcame her: but particularly the scent of dairy. They had been scalding out the pans. The flagged passage in front of her was dark, puddled, and wet. Light came out from the open kitchen door. She went forward and stood in the doorway. The farm-people were at tea, seated at a little distance from her, round a long, narrow table, in the centre of which stood a white lamp. Ruddy faces, ruddy hands holding food, red mouths working, heads bent over the tea-cups: men, land-girls, boys: it was tea-time, feeding-time. Some faces caught sight of her. Mrs. Wernham, going round behind the chairs with a large black teapot, halting slightly in her walk, was not aware of her for a moment. Then she turned suddenly.

"Oh, is it Madam!" she exclaimed. "Come in, then, come in! We're at tea." And she dragged forward a chair.

"No, I won't come in," said Isabel. "I'm afraid I interrupt your meal."

"No—no—not likely, Madam, not likely."

"Hasn't Mr. Pervin come in, do you know?"

"I'm sure I couldn't say! Missed him, have you, Madam?"

"No, I only wanted him to come in," laughed Isabel, as if shyly.

"Wanted him, did ye? Get up, boy—get up, now—"

Mrs. Wernham knocked one of the boys on the shoulder. He began to scrape to his feet, chewing largely.

"I believe he's in top stable," said another face from the table.

"Ah! No, don't get up. I'm going myself," said Isabel.

"Don't you go out of a dirty night like this. Let the lad go. Get along wi' ye, boy," said Mrs. Wernham.

"No, no," said Isabel, with a decision that was always obeyed. "Go on with your tea, Tom. I'd like to go across to the stable, Mrs. Wernham."

"Did ever you hear tell!" exclaimed the woman.

"Isn't the trap late?" asked Isabel.

"Why, no," said Mrs. Wernham, peering into the distance at the tall, dim clock. "No, Madam—we can give it another quarter or twenty minutes yet, good—yes, every bit of a quarter."

"Ah! It seems late when darkness falls so early," said Isabel.

"It do, that it do. Bother the days, that they draw in so," answered Mrs. Wernham. "Proper miserable!"

"They are," said Isabel, withdrawing.

She pulled on her overshoes, wrapped a large tartan shawl around her, put on a man's felt hat, and ventured out along the causeways of the first yard. It was very dark. The wind was roaring in the great elms behind the outhouses. When she came to the second yard the darkness seemed deeper. She was unsure of her footing. She wished she had brought a lantern. Rain blew against her. Half she liked it, half she felt unwilling to battle.

She reached at last the just visible door of the stable. There was no sign of a light anywhere. Opening the upper half, she looked in: into a simple well of darkness. The smell of horses, and ammonia, and of warmth was startling to her, in that full night. She listened with all her ears but could hear nothing save the night, and the stirring of a horse.

"Maurice!" she called, softly and musically, though she was afraid. "Maurice—are you there?"

Nothing came from the darkness. She knew the rain and wind blew in upon the horses, the hot animal life. Feeling it wrong, she entered the stable and drew the lower half of the door shut, holding the upper part close. She did not stir, because she was aware of the presence of the dark hindquarters of the horses, though she could not see them, and she was afraid. Something wild stirred in her heart.

She listened intensely. Then she heard a small noise in the distance—far away, it seemed—the chink of a pan, and a man's voice speaking a brief word. It would be Maurice, in the other part of the stable. She stood motionless, waiting for him to come through the partition door. The horses were so terryifyingly near to her, in the invisible.

The loud jarring of the inner door-latch made her start; the door was opened. She could hear and feel her husband entering and invisibly passing among the horses near to her, darkness as they were, actively intermingled. The rather low sound of his voice as he spoke to the horses came velvety to her nerves. How near he was, and how invisible! The darkness seemed to be in a strange swirl of violent life, just upon her. She turned giddy.

Her presence of mind made her call, quietly and musically:

"Maurice! Maurice—dea-ar!"

"Yes," he answered. "Isabel?"

She saw nothing, and the sound of his voice seemed to touch her.

"Hello!" she answered cheerfully, straining her eyes to see him. He was still busy, attending to the horses near her, but she saw only darkness. It made her almost desperate.

"Won't you come in, dear?" she said.

"Yes, I'm coming. Just half a minute. *Stand over—now!* Trap's not come, has it?"

"Not yet," said Isabel.

His voice was pleasant and ordinary, but it had a slight suggestion of the stable to her. She wished he would come away. Whilst he was so utterly invisible, she was afraid of him.

"How's the time?" he asked.

"Not yet six," she replied. She disliked to answer into the dark. Presently he came very near to her, and she retreated out of doors.

"The weather blows in here," he said, coming steadily forward, feeling for the doors. She shrank away. At last she could dimly see him.

"Bertie won't have much of a drive," he said, as he closed the doors.

"He won't indeed!" said Isabel calmly, watching the dark shape at the door.

"Give me your arm, dear," she said.

She pressed his arm close to her, as she went. But she longed to see him, to look at him. She was nervous. He walked erect, with face rather lifted, but with a curious tentative movement of his powerful, muscular legs. She could feel the clever, careful, strong contact of his feet with the earth, as she balanced against him. For the moment he was a tower of darkness to her, as if he rose out of the earth.

In the house-passage he wavered and went cautiously, with a curious look of silence about him as he felt for the bench. Then he sat down heavily. He was a man with rather sloping shoulders, but with heavy limbs, powerful legs that seemed to know the earth. His head was small, usually carried high and light. As he bent down to unfasten his gaiters and boots he did not look blind. His hair was brown and crisp, his hands were large, reddish, intelligent, the veins stood out in the wrists; and his thighs and knees seemed massive. When he stood up his face and neck were surcharged with blood, the veins stood out on his temples. She did not look at his blindness.

Isabel was always glad when they had passed through the dividing door into their own regions of repose and beauty. She was a little afraid of him, out there in the animal grossness of the back. His bearing also changed, as he smelt the familiar indefinable odour that pervaded his wife's surroundings, a delicate, refined scent, very faintly spicy. Perhaps it came from the potpourri bowls.

He stood at the foot of the stairs, arrested, listening. She watched him, and her heart sickened. He seemed to be listening to fate.

"He's not here yet," he said. "I'll go up and change."

"Maurice," she said, "you're not wishing he wouldn't come, are you?"

"I couldn't quite say," he answered. "I feel myself rather on the qui vive."

"I can see you are," she answered. And she reached up and kissed his cheek. She saw his mouth relax into a slow smile.

"What are you laughing at?" she said roguishly.

"You consoling me," he answered.

"Nay," she answered. "Why should I console you? You know we love each other—you know *how* married we are! What does anything else matter?"

"Nothing at all, my dear."

He felt for her face and touched it, smiling.

"*You're* all right, aren't you?" he asked anxiously.

"I'm wonderfully all right, love," she answered. "It's you I am a little troubled about, at times."

"Why me?" he said, touching her cheeks delicately with the tips of his fingers. The touch had an almost hypnotizing effect on her.

He went away upstairs. She saw him mount into the darkness, unseeing and unchanging. He did not know that the lamps on the upper corridor were unlighted. He went on into the darkness with unchanging step. She heard him in the bath-room.

Pervin moved about almost unconsciously in his familiar surroundings, dark though everything was. He seemed to know the presence of objects before he touched them. It was a pleasure to him to rock thus through a world of things, carried on the flood in a sort of blood-prescience. He did not think much or trouble much. So long as he kept this sheer immediacy of blood-contact with the substantial world he was happy, he wanted no intervention of visual consciousness. In this state there was a certain rich positivity, bordering sometimes on rapture. Life seemed to move in him like a tide lapping, lapping, and advancing, enveloping all things darkly. It was a pleasure to stretch forth the hand and meet the unseen object, clasp it, and possess it in pure contact. He did not try to remember, to visualize. He did not want to. The new way of consciousness substituted itself in him.

The rich suffusion of this state generally kept him happy, reaching its culmination in the consuming passion for his wife. But at times the flow would seem to be checked and thrown back. Then it would beat inside him like a tangled sea, and he was tortured in the shattered chaos of his own blood. He grew to dread this arrest, this throw-back, this chaos inside himself, when he seemed merely at the mercy of his own powerful and conflicting elements. How to get some measure of control or surety, this was the question. And when the question rose maddening in him, he would clench his fists as if he would *compel* the whole universe to submit to him. But it was in vain. He could not even compel himself.

Tonight, however, he was still serene, though little tremors of unreasonable exasperation ran through him. He had to handle the razor very carefully, as he shaved, for it was not at one with him, he was afraid of it. His hearing also was too much sharpened. He heard the woman lighting the lamps on the corridor, and attending to the fire in the visitors' room. And then, as he went to his room, he heard the trap arrive. Then came Isabel's voice, lifted and calling, like a bell ringing:

"Is it you, Bertie? Have you come?"

And a man's voice answered out of the wind:

"Hello, Isabel! There you are."

"Have you had a miserable drive? I'm so sorry we couldn't send a closed carriage. I can't see you at all, you know."

"I'm coming. No, I liked the drive—it was like Perthshire. Well, how are you? You're looking fit as ever, as far as I can see."

"Oh, yes," said Isabel. "I'm wonderfully well. How are you? Rather thin, I think—"

"Worked to death—everybody's old cry. But I'm all right, Ciss. How's Pervin?—isn't he here?"

"Oh, yes, he's upstairs changing. Yes, he's awfully well. Take off your wet things; I'll send them to be dried."

"And how are you both, in spirits? He doesn't fret?"

"No—no, not at all. No, on the contrary, really. We've been wonderfully happy, incredibly. It's more than I can understand—so wonderful: the nearness, and the peace—"

"Ah! Well, that's awfully good news—"

They moved away. Pervin heard no more. But a childish sense of desolation had come over him, and he heard their brisk voices. He seemed shut out—like a child that is left out. He was aimless and excluded, he did not know what to do with himself. The helpless desolation came over him. He fumbled nervously as he dressed himself, in a state almost of childishness. He disliked the Scotch accent in Bertie's speech, and the slight response it found on Isabel's tongue. He disliked the slight purr of complacency in the Scottish speech. He disliked intensely the glib way in which Isabel spoke of their happiness and nearness. It made him recoil. He was fretful and beside himself like a child, he had almost a childish nostalgia to be included in the life circle. And at the same time he was a man, dark and powerful and infuriated by his own weakness. By some fatal flaw, he could not be by himself, he had to depend on the support of another. And this very dependence enraged him. He hated Bertie Reid, and at the same time he knew the hatred was nonsense, he knew it was the outcome of his own weakness.

He went downstairs. Isabel was alone in the dining-room. She watched him enter, head erect, his feet tentative. He looked so strong-blooded and healthy and, at the same time, cancelled. Cancelled—that was the word that flew across her mind. Perhaps it was his scar suggested it.

"You heard Bertie come, Maurice?" she said.

"Yes—isn't he here?"

"He's in his room. He looks very thin and worn."

"I suppose he works himself to death."

A woman came in with a tray—and after a few minutes Bertie came down. He was a little dark man, with a very big forehead, thin, wispy hair, and sad, large eyes. His expression was inordinately sad—almost funny. He had odd, short legs.

Isabel watched him hesitate under the door, and glance nervously at her husband. Pervin heard him and turned.

"Here you are, now," said Isabel. "Come, let us eat."

Bertie went across to Maurice.

"How are you, Pervin?" he said, as he advanced.

The blind man stuck his hand out into space, and Bertie took it.

"Very fit. Glad you've come," said Maurice.

Isabel glanced at them, and glanced away, as if she could not bear to see them.

"Come," she said. "Come to table. Aren't you both awfully hungry? I am, tremendously."

"I'm afraid you waited for me," said Bertie, as they sat down.

Maurice had a curious monolithic way of sitting in a chair, erect and distant. Isabel's heart always beat when she caught sight of him thus.

"No," she replied to Bertie. "We're very little later than usual. We're having a sort of high tea, not dinner. Do you mind? It gives us such a nice long evening, uninterrupted."

"I like it," said Bertie.

Maurice was feeling, with curious little movements, almost like a cat kneading her bed, for his plate, his knife and fork, his napkin. He was getting the whole geography of his cover into his consciousness. He sat erect and inscrutable, remote-seeming. Bertie watched the static figure of the blind man, the delicate tactile discernment of the large, ruddy hands, and the curious mindless silence of the brow, above the scar. With difficulty he looked away, and without knowing what he did, picked up a little crystal bowl of violets from the table, and held them to his nose.

"They are sweet-scented," he said. "Where do they come from?"

"From the garden—under the windows," said Isabel.

"So late in the year—and so fragrant! Do you remember the violets under Aunt Bell's south wall?"

The two friends looked at each other and exchanged a smile, Isabel's eyes lighting up.

"Don't I?" she replied. *"Wasn't* she queer!"

"A curious old girl," laughed Bertie. "There's a streak of freakishness in the family, Isabel."

"Ah—but not in you and me, Bertie," said Isabel. "Give them to Maurice, will you?" she added, as Bertie was putting down the flowers. "Have you smelled the violets, dear? Do!—they are so scented."

Maurice held out his hand, and Bertie placed the tiny bowl against his large, warm-looking fingers. Maurice's hand closed over the thin white fingers of the barrister. Bertie carefully extricated himself. Then the two watched the blind man smelling the violets. He bent his head and seemed to be thinking. Isabel waited.

"Aren't they sweet, Maurice?" she said at last, anxiously.

"Very," he said. And he held out the bowl. Bertie took it. Both he and Isabel were a little afraid, and deeply disturbed.

The meal continued. Isabel and Bertie chatted spasmodically. The blind man was silent. He touched his food repeatedly, with quick, delicate touches of his knife-point, then cut irregular bits. He could not bear to be helped. Both Isabel and Bertie suffered: Isabel wondered why. She did not suffer when she was alone with Maurice. Bertie made her conscious of a strangeness.

After the meal the three drew their chairs to the fire, and sat down to talk. The decanters were put on a table near at hand. Isabel knocked the logs on the fire, and clouds of brilliant sparks went up the chimney. Bertie noticed a slight weariness in her bearing.

"You will be glad when your child comes now, Isabel?" he said.

She looked up to him with a quick wan smile.

"Yes, I shall be glad," she answered. "It begins to seem long. Yes, I shall be very glad. So will you, Maurice, won't you?" she added.

"Yes, I shall," replied her husband.

"We are both looking forward so much to having it," she said.

"Yes, of course," said Bertie.

He was a bachelor, three or four years older than Isabel. He lived in beautiful rooms overlooking the river, guarded by a faithful Scottish manservant. And he had his friends among the fair sex—not lovers, friends. So long as he could avoid any danger of courtship or marriage, he adored a few good women with constant and unfailing homage, and he was chivalrously fond of quite a number. But if they seemed to encroach on him, he withdrew and detested them.

Isabel knew him very well, knew his beautiful constancy, and kindness, and his incurable weakness, which made him unable ever to enter into close contact of any sort. He was ashamed of himself because he could not marry, could not approach women physically. He wanted to do so. But he could not. At the centre of him he was afraid, helplessly and even brutally afraid. He had given up hope, and ceased to expect any more that he could escape his own weakness. Hence he was a brilliant and successful barrister, also a *littérateur* of high repute, a rich man, and a great social success. At the centre he felt himself neuter, nothing.

Isabel knew him well. She despised him even while she admired him. She looked at his sad face, his little short legs, and felt contempt of him. She looked at his dark grey eyes, with their uncanny, almost childlike, intuition, and she loved him. He understood amazingly—but she had no fear of his understanding. As a man she patronized him.

And she turned to the impassive, silent figure of her husband. He sat leaning back, with folded arms, and face a little uptilted. His knees were straight and massive. She sighed, picked up the poker, and again began to prod the fire, to rouse the clouds of soft brilliant sparks.

"Isabel tells me," Bertie began suddenly, "that you have not suffered unbearably from the loss of sight."

Maurice straightened himself to attend but kept his arms folded.

"No," he said, "not unbearably. Now and again one struggles against it, you know. But there are compensations."

"They say it is much worse to be stone deaf," said Isabel.

"I believe it is," said Bertie. "Are there compensations?" he added, to Maurice.

"Yes. You cease to bother about a great many things." Again Maurice stretched his figure, stretched the strong muscles of his back, and leaned backwards, with uplifted face.

"And that is a relief," said Bertie. "But what is there in place of the bothering? What replaces the activity?"

There was a pause. At length the blind man replied, as out of a negligent, unattentive thinking:

"Oh, I don't know. There's a good deal when you're not active."

"Is there?" said Bertie. "What, exactly? It always seems to me that when there is no thought and no action, there is nothing."

Again Maurice was slow in replying.

"There is something," he replied. "I couldn't tell you what it is."

And the talk lapsed once more, Isabel and Bertie chatting gossip and reminiscence, the blind man silent.

At length Maurice rose restlessly, a big obtrusive figure. He felt tight and hampered. He wanted to go away.

"Do you mind," he said, "if I go and speak to Wernham?"

"No—go along, dear," said Isabel.

And he went out. A silence came over the two friends. At length Bertie said:

"Nevertheless, it is a great deprivation, Cissie."

"It is, Bertie. I know it is."

"Something lacking all the time," said Bertie.

"Yes, I know. And yet—and yet—Maurice is right. There is something else, something *there*, which you never knew was there, and which you can't express."

"What is there?" asked Bertie.

"I don't know—it's awfully hard to define it—but something strong and immediate. There's something strange in Maurice's presence—indefinable—but I couldn't do without it. I agree that it seems to put one's mind to sleep. But when we're alone I miss nothing; it seems awfully rich, almost splendid, you know."

"I'm afraid I don't follow," said Bertie.

They talked desultorily. The wind blew loudly outside, rain chattered on the window-panes, making a sharp drum-sound because of the closed, mellow-golden shutters inside. The logs burned slowly, with hot, almost invisible small flames. Bertie seemed uneasy, there were dark circles round his eyes.

Isabel, rich with her approaching maternity, leaned looking into the fire. Her hair curled in odd, loose strands, very pleasing to the man. But she had a curious feeling of old woe in her heart, old, timeless night-woe.

"I suppose we're all deficient somewhere," said Bertie.

"I suppose so," said Isabel wearily.

"Damned, sooner or later."

"I don't know," she said, rousing herself. "I feel quite all right, you know. The child coming seems to make me indifferent to everything, just placid. I can't feel that there's anything to trouble about, you know."

"A good thing, I should say," he replied slowly.

"Well, there it is. I suppose it's just Nature. If only I felt I needn't trouble about Maurice, I should be perfectly content—"

"But you feel you must trouble about him?"

"Well—I don't know—" She even resented this much effort.

The night passed slowly. Isabel looked at the clock. "I say," she said. "It's nearly ten o'clock. Where can Maurice be? I'm sure they're all in bed at the back. Excuse me a moment."

She went out, returning almost immediately.

"It's all shut up and in darkness," she said. "I wonder where he is. He must have gone out to the farm—"

Bertie looked at her.

"I suppose he'll come in," he said.

"I suppose so," she said. "But it's unusual for him to be out now."

"Would you like me to go out and see?"

"Well—if you wouldn't mind. I'd go, but—" She did not want to make the physical effort.

Bertie put on an old overcoat and took a lantern. He went out from the side door. He shrank from the wet and roaring night. Such weather had a nervous effect on him: too much moisture everywhere made him feel almost imbecile. Unwilling, he went through it all. A dog barked violently at him. He peered in all the buildings. At last, as he opened the upper door of a sort of intermediate barn, he heard a grinding noise, and looking in, holding up his lantern, saw Maurice, in his shirtsleeves, standing listening, holding the handle of a turnip-pulper. He had been pulping sweet roots, a pile of which lay dimly heaped in a corner behind him.

"That you, Wernham?" said Maurice, listening.

"No, it's me," said Bertie.

A large, half-wild grey cat was rubbing at Maurice's leg. The blind man stooped to rub its sides. Bertie watched the scene, then unconsciously entered and shut the door behind him. He was in a high sort of barn-place, from which, right and left, ran off the corridors in front of the stalled cattle. He watched the slow, stooping motion of the other man, as he caressed the great cat.

Maurice straightened himself.

"You came to look for me?" he said.

"Isabel was a little uneasy," said Bertie.

"I'll come in. I like messing about doing these jobs."

The cat had reared her sinister, feline length against his leg, clawing at his thigh affectionately. He lifted her claws out of his flesh.

"I hope I'm not in your way at all at the Grange here," said Bertie, rather shy and stiff.

"My way? No, not a bit. I'm glad Isabel has somebody to talk to. I'm afraid it's I who am in the way. I know I'm not very lively company. Isabel's all right, don't you think? She's not unhappy, is she?"

"I don't think so."

"What does she say?"

"She says she's very content—only a little troubled about you."

"Why me?"

"Perhaps afraid that you might brood," said Bertie, cautiously.

"She needn't be afraid of that." He continued to caress the flattened grey head of the cat wth his fingers. "What I am a bit afraid of," he resumed, "is that she'll find me a dead weight, always alone with me down here."

"I don't think you need think that," said Bertie, though this was what he feared himself.

"I don't know," said Maurice. "Sometimes I feel it isn't fair that she's saddled with me." Then he dropped his voice curiously. "I say," he asked, secretly struggling, "is my face much disfigured? Do you mind telling me?"

"There is the scar," said Bertie, wondering. "Yes, it is a disfigurement. But more pitiable than shocking."

"A pretty bad scar, though," said Maurice.

"Oh, yes."

There was a pause.

"Sometimes I feel I am horrible," said Maurice, in a low voice, talking as if to himself. And Bertie actually felt a quiver of horror.

"That's nonsense," he said.

Maurice again straightened himself, leaving the cat.

"There's no telling," he said. Then again, in an odd tone, he added: "I don't really know you, do I?"

"Probably not," said Bertie.

"Do you mind if I touch you?"

The lawyer shrank away instinctively. And yet, out of very philanthropy, he said, in a small voice: "Not at all."

But he suffered as the blind man stretched out a strong, naked hand to him. Maurice accidentally knocked off Bertie's hat.

"I thought you were taller," he said, starting. Then he laid his hand on Bertie Reid's head, closing the dome of the skull in a soft, firm grasp, gathering it, as it were; then, shifting his grasp and softly closing again, with a fine, close pressure, till he had covered the skull and the face of the smaller man, tracing the brows, and touching the full, closed eyes, touching the small nose and the nostrils, the rough, short moustache, the mouth, the rather strong chin. The hand of the blind man grasped the shoulder, the arm, the hand of the other man. He seemed to take him, in the soft, travelling grasp.

"You seem young," he said quietly, at last.

The lawyer stood almost annihilated, unable to answer.

"Your head seems tender, as if you were young," Maurice repeated. "So do your hands. Touch my eyes, will you?—touch my scar."

Now Bertie quivered with revulsion. Yet he was under the power of the blind man, as if hypnotized. He lifted his hand, and laid the fingers on the scar, on the scarred eyes. Maurice suddenly covered them with his own hand, pressed the fingers of the other man upon his disfigured eye-sockets, trembling in every fibre, and rocking slightly, slowly, from side to side. He remained thus for a minute or more, whilst Bertie stood as if in a swoon, unconscious, imprisoned.

Then suddenly Maurice removed the hand of the other man from his brow, and stood holding it in his own.

"Oh, my God," he said, "we shall know each other now, shan't we? We shall know each other now."

Bertie could not answer. He gazed mute and terror-struck, overcome by his own weakness. He knew he could not answer. He had an unreasonable fear, lest the other man should suddenly destroy him. Whereas Maurice was actually filled with hot, poignant love, the passion of friendship. Perhaps it was this very passion of friendship which Bertie shrank from most.

"We're all right together now, aren't we?" said Maurice. "It's all right now, as long as we live, so far as we're concerned?"

"Yes," said Bertie, trying by any means to escape.

Maurice stood with head lifted, as if listening. The new delicate fulfilment of mortal friendship had come as a revelation and suprise to him, something exquisite and unhoped-for. He seemed to be listening to hear if it were real.

Then he turned for his coat.

"Come," he said, "we'll go to Isabel."

Bertie took the lantern and opened the door. The cat disappeared. The two men went in silence along the causeways. Isabel, as they came, thought their footsteps sounded strange. She looked up pathetically and anxiously for their entrance. There seemed a curious elation about Maurice. Bertie was haggard, with sunken eyes.

"What is it?" she asked.

"We've become friends," said Maurice, standing with his feet apart, like a strange colossus.

"Friends!" re-echoed Isabel. And she looked again at Bertie. He met her eyes with a furtive, haggard look; his eyes were as if glazed with misery.

"I'm so glad," she said, in sheer perplexity.

"Yes," said Maurice.

He was indeed so glad. Isabel took his hand with both hers, and held it fast.

"You'll be happier now, dear," she said.

But she was watching Bertie. She knew that he had one desire—to escape from this intimacy, this friendship, which had been thrust upon him. He could not bear it that he had been touched by the blind man, his insane reserve broken in. He was like a mollusc whose shell is broken.

The Best of Everything

Richard Yates

NOBODY EXPECTED GRACE TO DO ANY WORK THE FRIDAY BEFORE HER wedding. In fact, nobody would let her, whether she wanted to or not.

A gardenia corsage lay in a cellophane box beside her typewriter—from Mr. Atwood, her boss—and tucked inside the envelope that came with it was a ten-dollar gift certificate from Bloomingdale's. Mr. Atwood had treated her with a special shy courtliness ever since the time she necked with him at the office Christmas party, and now when she went in to thank him he was all hunched over, rattling desk drawers, blushing and grinning and barely meeting her eyes.

"Aw, now, don't mention it, Grace," he said. "Pleasure's all mine. Here, you need a pin to put that gadget on with?"

"There's a pin that came with it," she said, holding up the corsage. "See? A nice white one."

Beaming, he watched her pin the flowers high on the lapel of her suit. Then he cleared his throat importantly and pulled out the writing panel of his desk, ready to give the morning's dictation. But it turned out there were only two short letters, and it wasn't until an hour later, when she caught him handing over a pile of Dictaphone cylinders to Central Typing, that she realized he had done her a favor.

"That's very sweet of you, Mr. Atwood," she said, "but I do think you ought to give me all your work today, just like any other."

"Aw, now, Grace," he said. "You only get married once."

The girls all made a fuss over her too, crowding around her desk and giggling, asking again and again to see Ralph's photograph ("Oh, he's *cute!*"), while the office manager looked on nervously, reluctant to be a spoilsport but anxious to point out that it was, after all, a working day.

Then at lunch there was the traditional little party at Schrafft's—nine women and girls, giddy on their unfamiliar cocktails, letting their chicken à la king grow cold while they pummeled her with old times and good wishes. There were more flowers and another gift—a silver candy dish for which all the girls had whisperingly chipped in.

Grace said "Thank you" and "I certainly do appreciate it" and "I don't know what to say" until her head rang with the words and the corners of her mouth ached from smiling, and she thought the afternoon would never end.

Ralph called up about four o'clock, exuberant. "How ya doin', honey?" he asked, and before she could answer he said, "Listen. Guess what I got?"

"I don't know. A present or something? What?" She tried to sound excited, but it wasn't easy.

"A bonus. Fifty dollars." She could almost see the flattening of his lips as he said "fifty dollars" with the particlar ernestness he reserved for pronouncing sums of money.

"Why, that's lovely, Ralph," she said, and if there was any tiredness in her voice he didn't notice it.

"Lovely, huh?" he said with a laugh, mocking the girlishness of the word. "Ya *like* that, huh Gracie? No, but I mean I was really surprised, ya know it? The boss siz, 'Here, Ralph,' and he hands me this envelope. He don't even crack a smile or nothin', and I'm wonderin', what's the deal here? I'm getting fired here, or what? He siz, 'G'ahead, Ralph, open it.' So I open it, and then I look at the boss and he's grinning a mile wide." He chuckled and sighed. "Well, so listen, honey. What time ya want me to come over tonight?"

"Oh, I don't know. Soon as you can, I guess."

"Well listen, I gotta go over to Eddie's house and pick up that bag he's gonna loan me, so I might as well do that, go on home and eat, and then come over to your place around eight-thirty, nine o'clock. Okay?"

"All right," she said. "I'll see you then, darling." She had been calling him "darling" for only a short time—since it had become irrevocably clear that she was, after all, going to marry him—and the word still had an alien sound. As she straightened the stacks of stationery in her desk (because there was nothing else to do), a familiar little panic gripped her: she couldn't marry him —she hardly even *knew* him. Sometimes it occurred to her differently, that she couldn't marry him because she knew him too well, and either way it left her badly shaken, vulnerable to all the things that Martha, her roommate, had said from the very beginning.

"Isn't he funny?" Martha had said after their first date. "He says 'terlet.' I didn't know people really said 'terlet.' " And Grace had giggled, ready enough to agree that it *was* funny. That was a time when she had been ready to agree with Martha on practically anything—when it often seemed, in fact, that finding a girl like Martha from an ad in the *Times* was just about the luckiest thing that had ever happened to her.

But Ralph had persisted all through the summer, and by fall she had begun standing up for him. "What don't you *like* about him, Martha? He's perfectly nice."

"Oh, everybody's perfectly nice, Grace," Martha would say in her college voice, making perfectly nice a faintly absurd thing to be, and then she'd look up crossly from the careful painting of her fingernails. "It's just that he's such a little—a little *white worm*. Can't you see that?"

"Well, I certainly don't see what his *complexion* has to do with—"

"Oh God, *you* know what I mean. Can't you see what I *mean*? Oh, and all those friends of his, his Eddie and his Marty and his George with their mean, ratty little clerks' lives and their mean, ratty little. . . . It's just that they're all *alike*, those people. All they ever say is 'Hey, wha' happen t'ya Giants?" and 'Hey, wha' happen t'ya Yankees?' and they all live way out in Sunnyside or Woodhaven or some awful place, and their mothers have those damn little china elephants on the mantelpiece." And Martha would frown over her nail polish again, making it clear that the subject was closed.

All that fall and winter she was confused. For a while she tried going out only with Martha's kind of men—the kind that used words like "amusing" all the time and wore small-shouldered flannel suits like a uniform; and for a while she tried going out with no men at all. She even tried that crazy business with Mr. Atwood at the office Christmas party. And all the time Ralph kept calling up, hanging around, waiting for her to make up her mind. Once she took him home to meet her parents in Pennsylvania (where she never would have dreamed of taking Martha), but it wasn't until Easter time that she finally gave in.

They had gone to a dance somewhere in Queens, one of the big American Legion dances that Ralph's crowd was always going to, and when the band played "Easter Parade" he held her very close, hardly moving, and sang to her in a faint, whispering tenor. It was the kind of thing she'd never have expected Ralph to do—a sweet, gentle thing—and it probably wasn't just then that she decided to marry him, but it always seemed so afterwards. It always seemed she had decided that minute, swaying to the music with his husky voice in her hair:

> "*I'll be all in clover
> And when they look you over
> I'll be the proudest fella
> In the Easter Parade. . . .*"

That night she had told Martha, and she could still see the look on Martha's face. "Oh, Grace, you're not—surely you're not *serious*. I mean, I thought he was more or less of a *joke*—you can't really mean you want to—"

"Shut up! You just shut up, Martha!" And she'd cried all night. Even now she hated Martha for it; even as she stared blindly at a row of filing cabinets along the office wall, half sick with fear that Martha was right.

The noise of giggles swept over her, and she saw with a start that two of the girls—Irene and Rose—were grinning over their typewriters and pointing at her. "*We* saw ya!" Irene sang. "*We* saw ya! Mooning again, huh Grace?" Then Rose did a burlesque of mooning, heaving her meager breasts and batting her eyes, and they both collapsed in laughter.

With an effort of will Grace resumed the guileless, open smile of a bride. The thing to do was concentrate on plans.

Tomorrow morning, "bright and early," as her mother would say, she would meet Ralph at Penn Station for the trip home. They'd arrive about one, and her parents would meet the train. "Good t'see ya, Ralph!" her father would say, and her mother would probably kiss him. A warm, homely love filled her: *they* wouldn't call him a white worm; *they* didn't have any ideas about Princeton men and "interesting" men and all the other kinds of men

Martha was so stuck-up about. Then her father would probably take Ralph out for a beer and show him the paper mill where he worked (and at least Ralph wouldn't be snobby about a person working in a paper mill, either), and then Ralph's family and friends would come down from New York in the evening.

She'd have time for a long talk with her mother that night, and the next morning, "bright and early" (her eyes stung at the thought of her mother's plain, happy face), they would start getting dressed for the wedding. Then the church and the ceremony, and then the reception (Would her father get drunk? Would Muriel Ketchel sulk about not being a bridesmaid?), and finally the train to Atlantic City, and the hotel. But from the hotel on she couldn't plan any more. A door would lock behind her and there would be a wild, fantastic silence, and nobody in all the world but Ralph to lead the way.

"Well, Grace," Mr. Atwood was saying, "I want to wish you every happiness." He was standing at her desk with his hat and coat on, and all around her were the chattering and scraping-back of chairs that meant it was five o'clock.

"Thank you, Mr. Atwood." She got to her feet, suddenly surrounded by all the girls in a bedlam of farewell.

"All the luck in the world, Grace."

"Drop us a card, huh Grace? From Atlantic City?"

"So long, Grace."

"G'night, Grace, and listen: the best of everything."

Finally she was free of them all, out of the elevator, out of the building, hurrying through the crowds to the subway.

When she got home Martha was standing in the door of the kitchenette, looking very svelte in a crisp new dress.

"Hi, Grace. I bet they ate you alive today, didn't they?"

"Oh no," Grace said. "Everybody was—real nice." She sat down, exhausted, and dropped the flowers and the wrapped candy dish on a table. Then she noticed that the whole apartment was swept and dusted, and the dinner was cooking in the kitchenette. "Gee, everything looks wonderful," she said. "What'd you do all this for?"

"Oh, well, I got home early anyway," Martha said. Then she smiled, and it was one of the few times Grace had ever seen her look shy. "I just thought it might be nice to have the place looking decent for a change, when Ralph comes over."

"Well," Grace said, "it certainly was nice of you."

The way Martha looked now was even more surprising: she looked awkward. She was turning a greasy spatula in her fingers, holding it delicately away from her dress and examining it, as if she had something difficult to say. "Look, Grace," she began. "You do understand why I can't come to the wedding, don't you?"

"Oh, sure," Grace said, although in fact she didn't, exactly. It was something about having to go up to Harvard to see her brother before he went into the Army, but it had sounded like a lie from the beginning.

"It's just that I'd hate you to think I—well, anyway, I'm glad if you do understand. And the other thing I wanted to say is more important."

"What?"

"Well, just that I'm sorry for all the awful things I used to say about Ralph. I never had a right to talk to you that way. He's a very sweet boy and I—well, I'm sorry, that's all."

It wasn't easy for Grace to hide a rush of gratitude and relief when she said, "Why, that's all right, Martha, I—"

"The chops are on fire!" Martha bolted for the kitchenette. "It's all right," she called back. "They're edible." And when she came out to serve dinner all her old composure was restored. "I'll have to eat and run," she said as they sat down. "My train leaves in forty minutes."

"I thought it was *tomorrow* you were going."

"Well, it was, actually," Martha said, "but I decided to go tonight. Because you see, Grace, another thing—if you can stand one more apology—another thing I'm sorry for is that I've hardly ever given you and Ralph a chance to be alone here. So tonight I'm going to clear out." She hesitated. "It'll be a sort of wedding gift from me, okay?" And then she smiled, not shyly this time but in a way that was more in character—the eyes subtly averted after a flicker of special meaning. It was a smile that Grace—through stages of suspicion, bewilderment, awe, and practiced imitation—had long ago come to associate with the word "sophisticated."

"Well, that's very sweet of you," Grace said, but she didn't really get the point just then. It wasn't until long after the meal was over and the dishes washed, until Martha had left for her train in a whirl of cosmetics and luggage and quick goodbyes, that she began to understand.

She took a deep, voluptuous bath and spent a long time drying herself, posing in the mirror, filled with a strange, slow excitement. In her bedroom, from the rustling tissues of an expensive white box, she drew the prizes of her trousseau—a sheer nightgown of white nylon and a matching negligee—put them on, and went to the mirror again. She had never worn anything like this before, or felt like this, and the thought of letting Ralph see her like this sent her into the kitchenette for a glass of the special dry sherry Martha kept for cocktail parties. Then she turned out all the lights but one and, carrying her glass, went to the sofa and arranged herself there to wait for him. After a while she got up and brought the sherry bottle over to the coffee table, where she set it on a tray with another glass.

When Ralph left the office he felt vaguely let down. Somehow, he'd expected more of the Friday before his wedding. The bonus check had been all right (though secretly he'd been counting on twice that amount), and the boys had bought him a drink at lunch and kidded around in the appropriate way ("Ah, don't feel too bad, Ralph—worse things could happen"), but still, there ought to have been a real party. Not just the boys in the office, but Eddie, and *all* his friends. Instead there would only be meeting Eddie at the White Rose like every other night of the year, and riding home to borrow Eddie's suitcase and to eat, and then having to ride all the way back to Manhattan just to see Gracie for an hour or two. Eddie wasn't in the bar when he arrived, which sharpened the edge of his loneliness. Morosely he drank a beer, waiting.

Eddie was his best friend, and an ideal best man because he'd been in on the courtship of Gracie from the start. It was in this very bar, in fact, that Ralph had told him about their first date last summer: "Ooh, Eddie—what a paira *knockers*!"

And Eddie had grinned. "Yeah? So what's the roommate like?"

"Ah, you don't want the roommate, Eddie. The roommate's a dog. A snob, too, I think. No, but this *other* one, this little *Gracie*—boy, I mean, she is *stacked.*"

Half the fun of every date—even more than half—had been telling Eddie about it afterwards, exaggerating a little here and there, asking Eddie's advice on tactics. But after today, like so many other pleasures, it would all be left behind. Gracie had promised him at least one night off a week to spend with the boys, after they were married, but even so it would never be the same. Girls never understood a thing like friendship.

There was a ball game on the bar's television screen and he watched it idly, his throat swelling in a sentimental pain of loss. Nearly all his life had been devoted to the friendship of boys and men, to trying to be a good guy, and now the best of it was over.

Finally Eddie's stiff finger jabbed the seat of his pants in greeting. "Whaddya say, sport?"

Ralph narrowed his eyes to indolent contempt and slowly turned around. "Wha' happen ta you, wise guy? Get lost?"

"Whaddya—in a hurry a somethin'?" Eddie barely moved his lips when he spoke. "Can't wait two minutes?" He slouched on a stool and slid a quarter at the bartender. "Draw one, there, Jack."

They drank in silence for a while, staring at the television. "Got a little bonus today," Ralph said. "Fifty dollars."

"Yeah?" Eddie said. "Good."

A batter struck out; the inning was over and the commercial came on. "So?" Eddie said, rocking the beer around in his glass. "Still gonna get married?"

"Why not?" Ralph said with a shrug. "Listen, finish that, willya? I wanna get a move on."

"Wait awhile, wait awhile. What's ya hurry?"

"C'mon, willya?" Ralph stepped impatiently away from the bar. "I wanna go pick up ya bag."

"Ah, bag schmagg."

Ralph moved up close again and glowered at him. "Look, wise guy. Nobody's gonna *make* ya loan me the goddamn bag, ya know. I don't wanna break ya *heart* or nothin'—"

"Arright, arright, arright. You'll getcha bag. Don't worry so much." He finished the beer and wiped his mouth. "Let's go."

Having to borrow a bag for his wedding trip was a sore point with Ralph; he'd much rather have bought one of his own. There was a fine one displayed in the window of a luggage shop they passed every night on their way to the subway—a big, tawny Gladstone with a zippered compartment on the side, at thirty-nine ninety-five—and Ralph had had his eye on it ever since Easter time. "Think I'll buy that," he'd told Eddie, in the same offhand way that a day or so before he had announced his engagement ("Think I'll marry the girl"). Eddie's response to both remarks had been the same: "Whaddya—crazy?" Both times Ralph had said, "Why not?" and in defense of the bag he had added, "Gonna get married, I'll *need* somethin' like that." From then on it was as if the bag, almost as much as Gracie herself, had become a symbol of the new and richer life he sought. But after the ring and the new clothes and all the other expenses, he'd found at last that he couldn't afford it; he had settled for the loan of Eddie's, which was similar but cheaper and worn, and without the zippered compartment.

Now as they passed the luggage shop he stopped, caught in the grip of a reckless idea. "Hey wait awhile, Eddie. Know what I think I'll do with that fifty-dollar bonus? I think I'll buy that bag right now." He felt breathless.

"Whaddya—crazy? Forty bucks for a bag you'll use maybe one time a year? Ya crazy, Ralph. C'mon."

"Ah—I dunno. Ya think so?"

"Listen, you better *keep* ya money, boy. You're gonna *need* it."

"Ah—yeah," Ralph said at last. "I guess ya right." And he fell in step with Eddie again, heading for the subway. This was the way things usually turned out in his life; he could never own a bag like that until he made a better salary, and he accepted it—just as he'd accepted without question, after the first thin sign, the knowledge that he'd never possess his bride until after the wedding.

The subway swallowed them, rattled and banged them along in a rocking, mindless trance for half an hour, and disgorged them at last into the cool early evening of Queens.

Removing their coats and loosening their ties, they let the breeze dry their sweated shirts as they walked. "So what's the deal?" Eddie asked. "What time we supposed to show up in this Pennsylvania burg tomorra?"

"Ah, suit yourself," Ralph said. "Any time in the evening's okay."

"So whadda we do then? What the hell can ya *do* in a hillbilly town like that, anyway?"

"Ah, I dunno." Ralph said defensively. "Sit around and talk, I guess; drink beer with Gracie's old man or somethin'; I dunno."

"Jesus," Eddie said. "Some weekend. Big, big deal."

Ralph stopped on the sidewalk, suddenly enraged, his damp coat wadded in his fist. "Look, you bastid. Nobody's gonna *make* ya come, ya know—you or Marty or George or any a the rest of 'em. Get that straight. You're not doin' *me* no favors, unnastand?"

"Whatsa matta?" Eddie inquired. "Whatsa matta? Can'tcha take a joke?"

"Joke," Ralph said. "You're fulla jokes." And plodding sullenly in Eddie's wake, he felt close to tears.

They turned off into the block where they both lived, a double row of neat, identical houses bordering the street where they'd fought and loafed and played stickball all their lives. Eddie pushed open the front door of his house and ushered Ralph into the vestibule, with its homely smell of cauliflower and overshoes. "G'wan in," he said, jerking a thumb at the closed living-room door, and he hung back to let Ralph go first.

Ralph opened the door and took three steps inside before it hit him like a sock on the jaw. The room, dead silent, was packed deep with grinning, red-faced men—Marty, George, the boys from the block, the boys from the office—everybody, all his friends, all on their feet and poised motionless in a solid mass. Skinny Maguire was crouched at the upright piano, his spread fingers high over the keys, and when he struck the first rollicking chords they all roared into song, beating time with their fists, their enormous grins distorting the words:

> "*Fa he's a jally guh fella*
> *Fa he's a jally guh fella*
> *Fa he's a jally guh fell-ah*
> *That nobody can deny!*"

Weakly Ralph retreated a step on the carpet and stood there wide-eyed, swallowing, holding his coat. "*That nobody can deny!*" they sang, "*That nobody can deny!*" And as they swung into the second chorus Eddie's father appeared through the dining-room curtains, bald and beaming, in full song, with a great glass pitcher of beer in either hand. At last Skinny hammered out the final line:

> "*That—no—bod—dee—can—dee—nye!*"

And they all surged forward cheering, grabbing Ralph's hand, pounding his arms and his back while he stood trembling, his own voice lost under the noise. "Gee, fellas—thanks. I—don't know what to—thanks, fellas. . . ."

Then the crowd cleaved in half, and Eddie made his way slowly down the middle. His eyes gleamed in a smile of love, and from his bashful hand hung the suitcase—not his own, but a new one: the big, tawny Gladstone with the zippered compartment on the side.

"*Speech!*" they were yelling. "*Speech! Speech!*"

But Ralph couldn't speak and couldn't smile. He could hardly even see.

At ten o'clock Grace began walking around the apartment and biting her lip. What if he wasn't coming? But of course he was coming. She sat down again and carefully smoothed the billows of nylon around her thighs, forcing herself to be calm. The whole thing would be ruined if she was nervous.

The noise of the doorbell was like an electric shock. She was halfway to the door before she stopped, breathing hard, and composed herself again. Then she pressed the buzzer and opened the door a crack to watch for him on the stairs.

When she saw he was carrying a suitcase, and saw the pale seriousness of his face as he mounted the stairs, she thought at first that he knew; he had come prepared to lock the door and take her in his arms. "Hello, darling," she said softly, and opened the door wider.

"Hi, baby." He brushed past her and walked inside. "Guess I'm late, huh? You in bed?"

"No." She closed the door and leaned against it with both hands holding the doorknob at the small of her back, the way heroines close doors in the movies. "I was just—waiting for you."

He wasn't looking at her. He went to the sofa and sat down, holding the suitcase on his lap and running his fingers over its surface. "Gracie," he said, barely above a whisper. "Look at this."

She looked at it, and then into his tragic eyes.

"Remember," he said, "I told you about that bag I wanted to buy? Forty dollars?" He stopped and looked around. "Hey, where's Martha? She in bed?"

"She's gone, darling," Grace said, moving slowly toward the sofa. "She's gone for the whole weekend." She sat down beside him, leaned close, and gave him Martha's special smile.

"Oh yeah?" he said. "Well anyway, listen. I said I was gonna borrow Eddie's bag instead, remember?"

"Yes."

"Well, so tonight at the White Rose I siz, 'C'mon, Eddie, let's go home pick up ya bag.' He siz, 'Ah, bag schmagg.' I siz, 'Whatsa matta?' but he don't say nothin', see? So we go home to his place and the living-room door's shut, see?"

She squirmed closer and put her head on his chest. Automatically he raised an arm and dropped it around her shoulders, still talking. "He siz, 'G'ahead, Ralph, open the door.' I siz, 'Whatsa deal?' He siz 'Never mind, Ralph, open the door.' So I open the door, and oh Jesus." His fingers gripped her shoulder with such intensity that she looked up at him in alarm.

"They was all there, Gracie," he said. "All the fellas. Playin' the piana, singin', cheerin'—" His voice wavered and his eyelids fluttered shut, their lashes wet. "A big surprise party," he said, trying to smile. "Fa me. Can ya beat that, Gracie? And then—then Eddie comes out and—Eddie comes out and hands me this. The very same bag I been lookin' at all this time. He bought it with his own money and he didn't say nothin', just to give me a surprise. 'Here, Ralph,' he siz. 'Just to let ya know you're the greatest guy in the world.' " His fingers tightened again, trembling. "I cried, Gracie," he whispered, "I couldn't help it. I don't think the fellas saw it or anything, but I was cryin'." He turned his face away and worked his lips in a tremendous effort to hold back the tears.

"Would you like a drink, darling?" she asked tenderly.

"Nah, that's all right, Gracie. I'm all right." Gently he set the suitcase on the carpet. "Only, gimme a cigarette, huh?"

She got one from the coffee table, put it in his lips and lit it. "Let me get you a drink," she said.

He frowned through the smoke. "Whaddya got, that sherry wine? Nah, I don't like that stuff. Anyway, I'm fulla beer." He leaned back and closed his eyes. "And then Eddie's mother feeds us this terrific meal," he went on, and his voice was almost normal now. "We had *steaks;* we had French-fried *potatas*"—his head rolled on the sofa-back with each item of the menu—

"lettuce-and-tomata *salad, pickles, bread, butter*—everything. The works."

"Well," she said. "Wasn't that nice."

"And afterwards we had ice cream and coffee," he said, "and all the beer we could drink. I mean, it was a real spread."

Grace ran her hands over her lap, partly to smooth the nylon and partly to dry the moisture on her palms. "Well, that certainly was nice of them," she said. They sat there silent for what seemed a long time.

"I can only stay a minute, Gracie," Ralph said at last. "I promised 'em I'd be back."

Her heart thumped under the nylon. "Ralph, do you—do you like this?"

"What, honey?"

"My negligee. You weren't supposed to see it until—after the wedding, but I thought I'd—"

"Nice," he said, feeling the flimsy material between thumb and index finger, like a merchant. "Very nice. Wudga pay fa this, honey?"

"Oh—I don't know. But do you like it?"

He kissed her and began, at last, to stroke her with his hands. "Nice," he kept saying. "Nice. Hey, I like this." His hand hesitated at the low neckline, slipped inside and held her breast.

"I do love you, Ralph," she whispered. "You know that, don't you?"

His fingers pinched her nipple, once, and slid quickly out again. The policy of restraint, the habit of months was too strong to break. "Sure," he said. "And I love you, baby. Now you be a good girl and get ya beauty sleep, and I'll see ya in the morning. Okay?"

"Oh, Ralph. Don't go. Stay."

"Ah, I promised the fellas, Gracie." He stood up and straightened his clothes. "They're waitin' fa me, out home."

She blazed to her feet, but the cry that was meant for a woman's appeal came out, through her tightening lips, as the whine of a wife: "Can't they wait?"

"Whaddya—*crazy?* " He backed away, eyes round with righteousness. She would *have* to understand. If this was the way she acted before the wedding, how the hell was it going to be afterwards? "Have a *heart,* willya? Keep the fellas waitin' *tonight?* After all they done fa *me?* "

After a second or two, during which her face became less pretty than he had ever seen it before, she was able to smile. "Of course not, darling. You're right."

He came forward again and gently brushed the tip of her chin with his fist, smiling, a husband reassured. " 'At's more like it," he said. "So I'll see ya, Penn Station, nine o'clock tomorra. Right, Gracie? Only, before I go—" he winked and slapped his belly. "I'm fulla beer. Mind if I use ya terlet?"

When he came out of the bathroom she was waiting to say goodnight, standing with her arms folded across her chest, as if for warmth. Lovingly he hefted the new suitcase and joined her at the door. "Okay, then, baby," he said, and kissed her. "Nine o'clock. Don't forget, now."

She smiled tiredly and opened the door for him. "Don't worry, Ralph," she said. "I'll be there."

Clifford Simak

Shadow Show

I

BAYARD LODGE, CHIEF OF LIFE TEAM NO. 3, SAT AT HIS DESK AND STARED across it angrily at Kent Forester, the team's psychologist.

"The Play must go on," said Forester. "I can't be responsible for what might happen if we dropped it even for a night or two. It's the one thing that holds us all together. It is the unifying glue that keeps us sane and preserves our sense of humor. And it gives us something to think about."

"I know," said Lodge, "but with Henry dead . . ."

"They'll understand," Forester promised. "I'll talk to them. I know they'll understand."

"They'll understand all right," Lodge agreed. "All of us recognize the necessity of the Play. But there is something else. One of those characters was Henry's."

Forester nodded. "I've been thinking of that, too."

"Do you know which one?"

Forester shook his head.

"I thought you might," said Lodge. "You've been beating out your brains to get them figured out, to pair up the characters with us."

Forester grinned sheepishly.

"I don't blame you," said Lodge. "I know why you're doing it."

"It would be a help," admitted Forester. "It would give me a key to every person here. Just consider—when a character went illogical . . ."

"They're all illogical," said Lodge. "That's the beauty of them."

"But the illogic runs true to a certain zany pattern," Forester pointed out. "You can use that very zaniness and set up a norm."

"You've done that?"

"Not as a graph," said Forester, "but I have it well in mind. When the illogic deviates it's not too hard to spot it."

"It's been deviating?"

Forester nodded. "Sharply at times. The problem that we have—the way that they are thinking . . ."

"Call it attitude," said Lodge.

For a moment the two of them were silent. Then Forester asked, "Do you mind if I ask why you insist on attitude?"

"Because it is an attitude," Lodge told him. "It's an attitude conditioned

333

by the life we lead. An attitude traceable to too much thinking, too much searching of the soul. It's an emotional thing, almost a religious thing. There's little of the intellectual in it. We're shut up too tightly. Guarded too closely. The importance of our work is stressed too much. We aren't normal humans. We're off balance all the time. How in the world can we be normal humans when we lead no normal life?"

"It's a terrible responsibility," said Forester. "They face it each day of their lives."

"The responsibility is not theirs."

"Only if you agree that the individual counts for less than the race. Perhaps not even then, for there are definite racial implications in this project, implications that can become terribly personal. Imagine making—"

"I know," said Lodge impatiently. "I've heard it from every one of them. Imagine making a human being not in the image of humanity."

"And yet it would be human," Forester said. "That is the point, Bayard. Not that we would be manufacturing life, but that it would be human life in the shape of monsters. You wake up screaming, dreaming of those monsters. A monster itself would not be bad at all, if it were no more than a monster. After centuries of traveling to the stars, we are used to monsters."

Lodge cut him off. "Let's get back to the Play."

"We'll have to go ahead," insisted Forester.

"There'll be one character missing," Lodge warned him. "You know what that might do. It might throw the entire thing off balance, reduce it to confusion. That would be worse than no Play at all. Why can't we wait a few days and start over, new again? With a new Play, a new set of characters."

"We can't do that," said Forester, "because each of us has identified himself or herself with a certain character. That character has become a part, an individual part, of each of us. We're living split lives, Bayard. We're split personalities. We have to be to live. We have to be because not a single one of us could bear to be himself alone."

"You're trying to say that we must continue the Play as an insurance of our sanity."

"Something like that. Not so grim as you make it sound. In ordinary circumstances there'd be no question we could dispense with it. But this is no ordinary circumstance. Every one of us is nursing a guilt complex of horrendous magnitude. The Play is an emotional outlet, a letdown from the tension. It gives us something to talk about. It keeps us from sitting around at night washing out the stains of guilt. It supplies the ridiculous in our lives —it is our daily comic strip, our chuckle or our belly laugh."

Lodge got up and paced up and down the room.

"I said attitude," he declared, "and it is an attitude—a silly, crazy attitude. There is no reason for the guilt complex. But they coddle it as if it were a thing that kept them human, as if it might be the one last identity they retain with the outside world and the rest of mankind. They come to me and they talk about it—as if I could do something about it. As if I could throw up my hands and say, well, all right, then, let's quit. As if I didn't have a job to do.

"They say we're taking a divine power into our hands, that life came to be by some sort of godly intervention, that it's blasphemous and sacrilegious for mere man to try to duplicate that feat.

"And there's an answer to that one—a logical answer, but they can't see the logic, or won't listen to it. Can Man do anything divine? If life is divine, then Man cannot create it in his laboratories no matter what he does, cannot put it on a mass production basis. If Man can create life out of his chemicals, out of his knowledge, if he can make one living cell by the virtue of his technique and his knowledge, then that will prove divine intervention was unnecessary to the genesis of life. And if we have that proof—if we know that a divine instrumentality is unnecessary for the creation of life, doesn't that very proof and fact rob it of divinity?"

"They are seeking an escape," said Forester, trying to calm him. "Some of them may believe what they say, but there are others who are merely afraid of the responsibility—the moral responsibility. They start thinking how it would be to live with something like that the rest of their lives. You had the same situation a thousand years ago when men discovered and developed atomic fission. They did it and they shuddered. They couldn't sleep at night. They woke up screaming. They knew what they were doing—that they were unloosing terrible powers. And we know what we are doing."

Lodge went back to his desk and sat down.

"Let me think about it, Kent," he said. "You may be right. I don't know. There are so many things that I don't know."

"I'll be back," said Forester.

He closed the door quietly when he left.

II

The Play was a never-ending soap opera, the *Old Red Barn* extended to unheard reaches of the ridiculous. It had a touch of Oz and a dash of alienness and it went on and on and on.

When you put a group of people on an asteroid, when you throw a space patrol around them, when you lead them to their laboratories and point out the problem to be solved, when you keep them at that problem day after endless day, you must likewise do something to preserve their sanity.

To do this there may be books and music, films, games, dancing of an evening—all the old standby entertainment values the race has used for millennia to forget its troubles.

But there comes a time when these amusements fail to serve their purpose, when they are not enough.

Then you hunt for something new and novel—and basic—for something in which each of the isolated group may participate, something with which they can establish close personal identity and lose themselves, forgetting for a time who they are and what may be their purpose.

That's where the Play came in.

In olden days, many years before, in the cottages of Europe and the pioneer farmsteads of North America, a father would provide an evening's entertainment for his children by means of shadow pictures. He would place a lamp or candle on a table opposite a blank wall, and sitting between the lamp and wall, he would use his hands to form the shadows of rabbit and of elephant, of horse and man and bear and many other things. For an hour or more the shadow show would parade across the wall, first one and then another—the rabbit nibbling clover, the elephant waving trunk and ears, the wolf howling on a hilltop. The children would sit quiet and spellbound, for these were wondrous things.

Later, with the advent of movies and of television, of the comic book and the cheap plastic dime-store toy, the shadows were no longer wondrous and were shown no longer, but that is not the point.

Take the principle of the shadow pictures, add a thousand years of know-how, and you have the Play.

Whether the long-forgotten genius who first conceived the Play had ever known of the shadow pictures is something that's not known. But the principle was there, although the approach was different in that one used his mind and thought instead of just his hands.

And instead of rabbits and elephants appearing in one-dimensional black-and-white, in the Play the characters were as varied as the human mind might make them (since the brain is more facile than the hand) and three-dimensional in full color.

The screen was a triumph in electronic engineering, with its memory banks, its rows of sonic tubes, its color selectors, ESP antennae and other gadgets, but it was the minds of the audience that did the work, supplying the raw material for the Play upon the screen. It was the audience that conceived the characters, that led them through their actions, that supplied the lines they spoke. It was the combined will of the audience that supplied the backdrops and dreamed up the properties.

At first the Play had been a haphazard thing, with the characters only half developed, playing at cross purposes, without personalities, and little more than cartoons paraded on the stage. At first the backdrops and the properties were the crazy products of many minds flying off at tangents. At times no fewer than three moons would be in the sky simultaneously, all in different phases. At times snow would be falling at one end of the stage and bright sunlight would pour down on palm trees at the other end.

But in time the Play developed. The characters grew to full stature, without missing arms and legs, acquired personalities, rounded out into full-blown living beings. The background became the result of a combined effort to achieve effective setting rather than nine different people trying desperately to fill in the blank spots.

In time direction and purpose had been achieved so that the action flowed smoothly, although there never came a time when any of the nine were sure of what would happen next.

That was the fascination of it. New situations were continually being introduced by one character or another, with the result that the human creators of the other characters were faced with the need of new lines and action to meet the changing situations.

It became in a sense a contest of wills, with each participant seeking advantages for his character, or, on the other hand, forced to backtrack to escape disaster. It became, after a time, a never-ending chess game in which each player pitted himself or herself against the other eight.

And no one knew, of course, to whom any of the characters belonged. Out of this grew up a lively guessing game and many jokes and sallies, and this was to the good, for that was what the Play was for: to lift the minds of the participants out of their daily work and worries.

Each evening after dinner the nine gathered in the theater, and the screen sprang into life and the nine characters performed their parts and spoke their lines: the Defenseless Orphan, the Mustached Villain, the Proper Young Man, the Beautiful Bitch, the Alien Monster and all the others.

Nine of them—nine men and women, and nine characters.

But now there would be only eight, for Henry Griffith had died, slumped against his bench with the notebook at his elbow.

And the Play would have to go on with one missing character—the character that had been controlled and motivated by the man who now was dead.

Lodge wondered which character would be the missing one. Not the Defenseless Orphan, certainly, for that would not have been down Henry's alley. But it might be the Proper Young Man or the Out-At-Elbows Philosopher or the Rustic Slicker.

Wait a minute there, said Lodge. Not the Rustic Slicker. The Rustic Slicker's me.

He sat idly speculating on which belonged to whom. It would be exactly like Sue Lawrence to dream up the Beautiful Bitch—a character as little like her prim, practical self as one could well imagine. He remembered that he had taunted her once concerning his suspicion and that she had been very cold to him for several days thereafter.

Forester said the Play must go on, and maybe he was right. They might adjust. God knows, they should be able to adjust to anything after participating in the Play each evening for months on end.

It was a zany thing, all right. Never getting anywhere. Not even episodic, for it never had a chance to become episodic. Let one trend develop and some joker was sure to throw in a stumbling block that upset the trend and sent the action angling off in some new direction.

With that kind of goings-on, he thought, the disappearance of a single character shouldn't throw them off their stride.

He got up from his desk and walked to the great picture window. He stood there looking out at the bleak loneliness of the asteroid. The curved roofs of the research center fell away beneath him, shining in the starlight, to the blackness of the cragged surface. Above the jagged northern horizon lay a flush of light and in a little while it would be dawn, with the weak, watch-sized sun sailing upward to shed its feeble light upon this tiny speck of rock. He watched the flushed horizon, remembering Earth, where dawn was morning and sunset marked the beginning of the night. Here no such scheme was possible, for the days and nights were so erratic and so short that they could not be used to divide one's time. Here morning came at a certain hour, evening came at another hour, regardless of the sun, and one might sleep out a night with the sun high in the sky.

It would have been different, he thought, if we could have stayed on Earth, for there we would have had normal human contacts. We would not have thought so much or brooded; we could have rubbed away the guilt on the hides of other people.

But normal human contacts would have meant the start of rumors, would have encouraged leaks, and in a thing of this sort there could be no leaks.

For the people of the Earth knew what they were doing, or, more correctly, what they were trying to do, they would raise a hubbub that might result in calling off the project.

Even here, he thought—even here, there are those who have their doubts and fears.

A human being must walk upon two legs and have two arms and a pair of eyes, a brace of ears, one nose, one mouth, be not unduly hairy. He must walk; he must not hop or crawl or slither.

A perversion of the human form, they said; a scrapping of human dignity; a going-too-far, farther than Man in all his arrogance was ever meant to go.

There was a rap upon the door. Lodge turned and called, "Come in."

It was Dr. Susan Lawrence. She stood in the open doorway, a stolid, dumpy, dowdy woman with an angular face that had a set of stubborness and of purpose in it. She did not see him for a moment and stood there, turning her head, trying to find him in the dusky room.

"Over here, Sue," he called.

She closed the door and crossed the room, and stood by his side looking out the window.

Finally she said, "There was nothing wrong with him, Bayard, Nothing organically wrong. I wonder . . ."

She stood there, silent, and Lodge could feel the practical bleakness of her thoughts.

"It's bad enough," she said, "when they die and you know what killed them. It's not so bad to lose them if you've had a fighting chance to save them. But this is different. He just toppled over. He was dead before he hit the bench."

"You've examined him?"

She nodded. "I put him in the analyzers. I've got three reels of stuff. I'll check it all—later. But I'll swear there was nothing wrong."

She reached out a hand and put it on his arm, her pudgy fingers tightening.

"He didn't want to live," she said. "He was afraid to live. He thought he was close to finding something and he was afraid to find it."

"We have to find it, Sue."

"For what?" she asked. "So we can fashion humans to live on planets where humans in their present form wouldn't have a chance. So we can take a human mind and spirit and enclose it in a monster's body, hating itself. . . ."

"It wouldn't hate itself," Lodge told her. "You're thinking in anthropomorphic terms. A thing is never ugly to itself because it knows itself. Have we any proof that bipedal man is any happier than an insect or a toad?"

"But why?" she persisted. "We do not need those planets. We have more now then we can colonize. Enough Earth-type planets to last for centuries. We'll be lucky if we even colonize them all, let alone develop them, in the next five hundred years."

"We can't take the chance," he said. "We must take control while we have the chance. It was all right when we were safe and snug on Earth, but that is true no longer. We've gone out to the stars. Somewhere in the universe there are other intelligences. There have to be. Eventually we'll meet. We must be in a strong position."

"And to get into that strong position we plant colonies of human monsters. I know, Bayard—it's clever. We can design the bodies, the flesh and nerves and muscles, the organs of communication—all designed to exist upon a planet where a normal human could not live a minute. We are clever, all right, and very good technicians, but we can't breathe the life into them. There's more to life than just the colloidal combination of certain elements. There's something else, and we'll never get it."

"We will try," said Lodge.

"You'll drive good technicians out of their sanity," she said. "You'll kill some of them—not with your hands, but with your insistence. You'll keep them cooped up for years and you'll give them a Play so they'll last the longer —but you won't find life, for life is not Man's secret."

"Want to bet? he asked, laughing at her fury.

She swung around and faced him.

"There are times," she said, "when I regret my oath. A little cyanide. . . ."

He caught her by the arm and walked her to the desk.

"Let's have a drink," he said. "You can kill me later."

III

They dressed for dinner.

That was a rule. They always dressed for dinner.

It was, like the Play, one of the many little habits that they cultivated to retain their sanity, not to forget that they were a cultured people as well as ruthless seekers after knowledge—a knowledge that any one of them would have happily forsworn.

They laid aside their scalpels and their other tools, they boxed their microscopes, they ranged the culture bottles neatly in place, they put the pans of saline solutions and their varying contents carefully away. They took their aprons off and went out and shut the door. And for a few hours they forgot, or tried to forget, who they were and what their labors were.

They dressed for dinner and assembled in the so-called drawing room for cocktails and then went in to dinner, pretending that they were no more than normal human beings—and no less.

The table was set with exquisite china and fragile glass, and there were flowers and flaming tapers. They began with an entree and their meal was served in courses by accomplished robots, and they ended with cheese and fruit and brandy and there were cigars for those who wanted them.

Lodge sat at the table's head and looked down the table at them and for a moment saw Sue Lawrence looking back at him and wondered if she were scowling or if the seeming scowl was no more than the play of candlelight upon her face.

They talked as they always talked at dinner—the inconsequential social chatter of people without worry and with little purpose. For this was the moment of forgetting and escape. This was the hour to wash away the guilt and to ignore the stain.

But tonight, he noticed, they could not pull themselves away entirely from the happenings of the day—for there was talk of Henry Griffith and of his sudden dying and they spoke of him in soft tones and with strained and sober faces. Henry had been too intense and too strange a man for anyone to know him well, but they held him in high regard, and although the robots had been careful to arrange the seating so his absence left no gap, there was a real and present sense that one of them was missing.

Chester Sifford said to Lodge, "We'll be sending Henry back?"

Lodge nodded. "We'll call in one of the patrol and it'll take him back to Earth. We'll have a short service for him here."

"But who?"

"Craven, more than likely. He was closer to Henry than any of the rest. I spoke to him about it. He agreed to say a word or two."

"Is there anyone on Earth? Henry never talked a lot."

"Some nephews and nieces. Maybe a brother or a sister. That would be all, I think."

Hugh Maitland said, "I understand we'll continue with the Play."

"That's right," Lodge told him. "Kent recommended it and I agreed. Kent knows what's best for us."

Sifford agreed. "That's his job. He's a good man at it."

"I think so, too," said Maitland. "Most psych-men stand outside the group. Posing as your conscience. But Kent doesn't work that way."

"He's a chaplain," Sifford said. "Just a goddamn chaplain."

Helen Gray sat to the left, and Lodge saw that she was not talking with anyone but only staring at the bowl of roses which this night served as a centerpiece.

Tough on her, he thought. For she had been the one who had found Henry dead and, thinking that he was merely sleeping, had taken him by the shoulder and shaken him to wake him.

Down at the other end of the table, sitting next to Forester, Alice Page was talking far too much, much more than she had ever talked before, for she was a strangely reserved woman, with a quiet beauty that had a touch of darkness in it. Now she leaned toward Forester, talking tensely, as if she might be arguing in a low tone so the others would not hear her, with Forester listening, his face masked with patience against a feeling of alarm.

They are upset, thought Lodge—far more than I had suspected. Upset and edgy, ready to explode.

Henry's death had hit them harder than he knew.

Not a lovable man, Henry still had been one of them. One of them, he thought. Why not one of us? But that was the way it always was—unlike Forester, who did his best work by being one of them, he must stand to one side, must keep intact that slight, cold margin of reserve which was all that preserved against an incident of crisis the authority which was essential to his job.

Sifford said, "Henry was close to something."

"So Sue told me."

"He was writing up his notes when he died," said Sifford. "It may be. . . ."

"We'll have a look at them," Lodge promised. "All of us together. In a day or two."

Maitland shook his head. "We'll never find it, Bayard. Not the way we're working. Not in the direction we are working. We have to take a new approach."

Sifford bristled. "What kind of approach?"

"I don't know," said Maitland. "If I knew. . . ."

"Gentlemen," said Lodge.

"Sorry," Sifford said. "I'm a little jumpy."

Lodge remembered Dr. Susan Lawrence, standing with him, looking out the window at the bleakness of the tumbling hunk of rock on which they lived and saying, "He didn't want to live. He was afraid to live."

What had she been trying to tell him? That Henry Griffith had died of intellectual fear? That he had died because he was afraid to live?

Would it actually be possible for a psychosomatic syndrome to kill a man?

IV

You could feel the tension in the room when they went to the theater, although they did their best to mask the tension. They chatted and pretended to be lighthearted, and Maitland tried a joke which fell flat upon its face and died, squirming beneath the insincerity of the laughter that its telling had called forth.

Kent was wrong, Lodge told himself, feeling a wave of terror washing over him. This business was loaded with deadly psychological dynamite. It would not take much to trigger it and it could set off a chain reaction that could wash up the team.

And if the team were wrecked the work of years was gone—the long years of education, the necessary months to get them working together, the constant, never-ending battle to keep them happy and from one another's throats. Gone would be the team confidence which over many months had replaced individual confidence and doubt, gone would be the smooth co-operation and co-ordination which worked like meshing gears, gone would be a vast percentage of the actual work they'd done, for no other team, no matter how capable it might be, could take up where another team left off, even with the notes of the first team to guide them on their way.

The curving screen covered one end of the room, sunken into the wall, with the flare of the narrow stage in front of it.

Back of that, thought Lodge, the tubes and generators, the sonics and computers—mechanical magic which turned human thought and will into the moving images that would parade across the screen. Puppets, he thought— puppets of the human mind, but with a strange and startling humanity about them that could not be achieved by carven hunks of wood.

And the difference, of course, was the difference between the mind and hand, for no knife, no matter how sharp, guided by no matter how talented and artistic a hand, could carve a dummy with half the precision or fidelity with which the mind could shape a human creature.

First, Man had created with hands alone, chipping the flint, carving out the bow and dish; then he achieved machines which were extensions of his hands and they turned out artifacts which the hands alone were incapable of making; and now, Man created not with his hands nor with extensions of his hands, but with his mind and extensions of his mind, although he still must use machinery to translate and project the labor of his brain.

Someday, he thought, it will be mind alone, without the aid of machines, without the help of hands.

The screen flickered and there was a tree upon it, then another tree, a bench, a duck pond, grass, a distant statue, and behind it all the dim, tree-broken outlines of city towers.

That was where they had left it the night before, with the cast of characters embarked upon a picnic in a city park—a picnic that was almost certain to remain a picnic for mere moments only before someone should turn it into something else.

Tonight, he hoped, they'd let it stay a picnic, let it run its course, take it easy for a change, not try any fancy stuff—for tonight, of all nights, there must be no sudden jolts, no terrifying turns. A mind forced to guide its character through the intricacies of a suddenly changed plot or some outlandish situation might crack beneath the effort.

As it was, there'd be one missing character and much would depend upon which one it was.

The scene stood empty, like a delicate painting of a park in springtime with each thing fixed in place.

Why were they waiting? What were they waiting for?

They had set the stage. What were they waiting for?

Someone thought of a breeze and you could hear the whisper of it, moving in the trees, ruffling the pond.

Lodge brought his character into mind and walked him on the stage, imagining his gangling walk, the grass stem stuck in his mouth, the curl of unbarbered hair above his collar.

Someone had to start it off. Someone—

The Rustic Slicker turned and hustled back off stage. He hustled back again, carrying a great hamper. "Forgot m' basket," he said, with rural sheepishness.

Someone tittered in the darkened room.

Thank God for that titter! It is going all right. *Come on, the rest of you!*

The Out-At-Elbows Philosopher strode on stage. He was a charming fellow, with no good intent at all—a cadger, a bum, a full-fledged fourflusher behind the façade of his flowered waistcoat, the senatorial bearing, the long, white, curling locks.

"My friend," he said. "My friend."

"Y' ain't m' friend," the Rustic Slicker told him, "till y' pay me back m' three hundred bucks."

Come on, the rest of you!

The Beautiful Bitch showed up with the Proper Young Man, who any moment now was about to get dreadfully disillusioned.

The Rustic Slicker had squatted on the grass and opened his hamper. He began to take out stuff—a ham, a turkey, a cheese, a vacuum jug, a bowl of Jello, a tin of kippered herring.

The Beautiful Bitch made exaggerated eyes at him and wiggled her hips. The Rustic Slicker blushed, ducking his head.

Kent yelled from the audience: "Go ahead and ruin him!"

Everyone laughed.

It was going to be all right. It would be all right.

Get the audience and the players kidding back and forth and it was bound to be all right.

"Ah think that's a good idee, honey," said the Beautiful Bitch. "Ah do believe Ah will."

She advanced upon the Slicker.

The Slicker, with his head still ducked, kept on taking things out of the hamper—more by far than could have been held in any ten such hampers.

He took out rings of bologna, stacks of wieners, mounds of marshmallows, a roast goose—and a diamond necklace.

The Beautiful Bitch pounced on the necklace, shrieking with delight.

The Out-At-Elbows Philosopher had jerked a leg off the turkey and was eating it, waving it between bites to emphasize the flowery oration he had launched upon.

"My friends—" he orated between bites—"my friends, in this vernal season it is right and proper, I said right and proper, sir, that a group of friends should forgather to commune with nature in her gayest aspects, finding retreat such as this even in the heart of a heartless city . . ."

He would go on like that for hours unless something intervened to stop him. The situation being as it was, something was almost bound to stop him.

Someone had put a sportive, if miniature, whale into the pond, and the whale, acting much more like a porpoise than a whale, was leaping about in graceful curves and scaring the hell out of the flock of ducks which resided on the pond.

The Alien Monster sneaked in and hid behind a tree. You could see with half an eye that he was bent upon no good.

"Watch out!" yelled someone in the audience, but the actors paid no attention to the warning. There were times when they could be incredibly stupid.

The Defenseless Orphan came on stage on the arm of the Mustached Villain (and there was no good intent in that situation, either) with the Extra-Terrestrial Ally trailing along behind them.

"Where is the Sweet Young Thing?" asked the Mustached Villain. "She's the only one who's missing."

"She'll be along," said the Rustic Slicker. "I saw her at the corner saloon building up a load—"

The Philosopher stopped his oration in midsentence, halted the turkey drumstick in midair. His silver mane did its best to bristle, and he whirled upon the Rustic Slicker.

"You are a cad, sir," he said, "to say a thing like that, a most contemptible cad!"

"I don't care," said the Slicker. "No matter what y' say, that's what she was doing."

"You lay off him," shrilled the Beautiful Bitch, fondling the diamond necklace. "He's mah frien' and you can't call him a cad."

"Now, B.B.," protested the Proper Young Man, "you keep out of this."

She spun on him. "You shut yoah mouth," she said. "You mealy hypocrite. Don't you tell me what to do. Too nice to call me by mah rightful name, but using just initials. You prissy-panted high-binder, don't you speak to me."

The Philosopher stepped ponderously forward, stooped down and swung his arm. The half-eaten drumstick took the Slicker squarely across the chops.

The Slicker rose slowly to his feet, one hand grasping the roast goose.

"So y' want to play," he said.

He hurled the goose at the Philosopher. It struck squarely on the flowered waistcoat. It was greasy and it splashed.

Oh, Lord, thought Lodge. Now the fat's in the fire for sure! Why did the Philosopher act the way he did? Why couldn't they have left it a simple, friendly picnic, just this once? Why did the person whose character the Philosopher was make him swing that drumstick?

And why had he, Bayard Lodge, made the Slicker throw the goose?

He went cold all over at the question, and when the answer came he felt a hand reach into his belly and start twisting at his guts.

For the answer was: He hadn't!

He hadn't made the Slicker throw the goose. He'd felt a flare of anger and a hard, cold hatred, but he had not willed his character to retaliatory action.

He kept watching the screen, seeing what was going on, but with only half his mind, while the other half quarreled with itself and sought an explanation.

It was the machine that was to blame—it was the machine that had made the Slicker throw the goose, for the machine would know, almost as well as a human knew, the reaction that would follow a blow upon the face. The machine had acted automatically, without waiting for the human thought. Sure, perhaps, of what the human thought would be.

It's logical, said the arguing part of his mind—it's logical that the machine would know, and logical once again that being sure of knowing, it would react automatically.

The Philosopher had stepped ceremoniously backward after he had struck the blow, standing at attention, presenting arms, after a manner of speaking, with the mangy drumstick.

The Beautiful Bitch clapped her hands and cried, "Now you-all got to fight a duel!"

"Precisely, miss," said the Philosopher, still stiffly at attention. "Why else do you think I struck him?"

The goose grease dripped slowly off his ornate vest, but you never would have guessed for so much as an instant that he thought he was anything but faultlessly turned out.

"But it should have been a glove," protested the Proper Young Man.

"I didn't have a glove, sir," said the Philosopher, speaking a truth that was self-evident.

"It's frightfully improper," persisted the Proper Young Man.

The Mustached Villain flipped back his coattails and reaching into his back pockets, brought out two pistols.

"I always carry them," he said with a frightful leer, "for occasions such as this."

We have to break it up, thought Lodge. We have to stop it. We can't let it go on!

He made the Rustic Slicker say, "Now lookit here, now. I don't want to fool around with firearms. Someone might get hurt."

"You have to fight," said the leering Villain, holding both pistols in one hand and twirling his mustaches with the other.

"He has the choice of weapons," observed the Proper Young Man. "As the challenged party . . ."

The Beautiful Bitch stopped clapping her hands.

"You keep out of this," she screamed. "You sissy—you just don't want to see them fight."

The Villain bowed. "The Slicker has the choice," he said.

The Extra-Terrestrial Ally piped up. "This is ridiculous," it said. "All you humans are ridiculous."

The Alien Monster stuck his head out from behind the tree.

"Leave 'em alone," he bellowed in his frightful brogue. "If they want to fight, let 'em go ahead and fight."

Then he curled himself into a wheel by the simple procedure of putting his tail into his mouth and started to roll. He rolled around the duck pond at a fearful pace, chanting all the while: "Leave 'em fight. Leave 'em fight. Leave 'em fight." Then he popped behind his tree again.

The Defenseless Orphan complained, "I thought this was a picnic."

And so did all the rest of us, thought Lodge.

Although you could have bet, even before it started, that it wouldn't stay a picnic.

"Your choice, please," said the Villain to the Slicker, far too politely. "Pistols, knives, swords, battle axes—"

Ridiculous, thought Lodge.

Make it ridiculous.

He made the Slicker say, "Pitchforks at three paces."

The Sweet Young Thing tripped lightly on the stage. She was humming a drinking song, and you could see that she'd picked up quite a glow.

But she stopped at what she saw before her: the Philosopher dripping goose grease, the Villain clutching a pistol in each hand, the Beautiful Bitch jangling a diamond necklace, and she asked, "What is going on here?"

The Out-At-Elbows Philosopher relaxed his pose and rubbed his hands together with smirking satisfaction.

"Now," he said, oozing good fellowship and cheer, "isn't this a cozy situation. All nine of us are here—"

In the audience, Alice Page leaped to her feet, put her hands up to her face, pressed her palms tight against her temples, closed her eyes quite shut and screamed and screamed and screamed.

V

There had been, not eight characters, but nine.

Henry Griffith's character had walked on with the rest of them.

"You're crazy, Bayard," Forester said. "When a man is dead, he's dead. Whether he still exists or not, I don't profess to know, but if he does exist it is not on the level of his previous existence; it is on another plane, in another state of being, in another dimension, call it what you will, religionist or spiritualist, the answer is the same."

Lodge nodded his agreement. "I was grasping at straws. Trying to dredge up every possibility. I know that Henry's dead. I know the dead stay dead. And yet, you'll have to admit, it is a natural thought. Why did Alice scream? Not because the nine characters were there. But because of why there might be nine of them. The ghost in us dies hard."

"It's not only Alice," Forester told him. "It's all the others, too. If we don't get this business under control, there'll be a flare-up. The emotional index was already stretched pretty thin when this happened—doubt over the purpose of the research, the inevitable wear and tear of nine people living together for months on end, a sort of cabin fever. It all built up. I've watched it building up and I've held my breath."

"Some joker out there subbed for Henry," Lodge said. "How does that sound to you? Someone handled his own character and Henry's too."

"No one could handle more than one character," said Forester.

"Someone put a whale into that duck pond."

"Sure, but it didn't last long. The whale jumped a time or two and then was gone. Whoever put it there couldn't keep it there."

"We all co-operate on the setting and the props. Why couldn't someone pull quietly out of that co-operation and concentrate all his mind on two characters?"

Forester looked doubtful. "I suppose it could be done. But the second character probably would be out of whack. Did you notice any of them that seemed a little strange?"

"I don't know about strange," said Lodge, "but the Alien Monster hid—"

"Henry's character wasn't the Alien Monster."

"How can you be sure?"

"Henry wasn't the kind of mind to cook up an alien monster."

"All right, then. Which one is Henry's character?"

Forester slapped the arm of his chair impatiently. "I've told you, Bayard, that I don't know who any of them are. I've tried to match them up and it can't be done."

"It would help if we knew. Especially . . ."

"Especially Henry's character," said Forester. He left the chair and paced up and down the office.

"Your theory of some joker putting on Henry's character is all wrong," he said. "How would he know which one?"

Lodge raised his hand and smote the desk. "The Sweet Young Thing!" he shouted.

"What's that?"

"The Sweet Young Thing. She was the last to walk on. Don't you remember? The Mustached Villain asked where she was and the Rustic Slicker said he saw her in a saloon and—"

"Good Lord!" breathed Forester. "And the Out-At-Elbows Philosopher was at great pains to announce that all of them were there. Needling us! Jeering at us!"

"You think the Philosopher is the one, then? He's the joker. The one who produced the Sweet Young Thing—the ninth member of the cast. The ninth one to appear would have to be Henry's character, don't you see. You said yourself it couldn't be done because you wouldn't know which one it was. But you could know—you'd know when eight were on the stage that the missing one was Henry's character."

"Either there was a joker," Forester said, "or the cast itself is somehow sentient—has come halfway alive."

Lodge scowled. "I can't buy that one, Kent. They're images of our minds. We call them up, we put them through their paces, we dismiss them. They depend utterly on us. They couldn't have a separate identity. They're creatures of our mind and that is all."

"It wasn't exactly along that line that I was thinking," said Forester. "I was thinking of the machine itself. It takes the impressions from our minds and shapes them. It translates what we think into the images on the screen. It transforms our thoughts into seeming actualities. . . ."

"A memory . . ."

"I think the machine may have a memory," Forester declared. "God knows it has enough sensitive equipment packed into it to have almost anything. The machine is an extension of our imagery."

"I don't know," protested Lodge. "I simply do not know. This going around in circles. This incessant speculation."

But he did know, he told himself. He did know that the machine could act independently, for it had made the Slicker throw the goose. But that was different from handling a character from scratch, different from putting on a character that should not appear. It had simply been a matter of an induced, automatic action—and it didn't mean a thing.

Or did it?

"The machine could walk on Henry's character," Forester persisted. "It could have the Philosopher mock us."

"But why?" asked Lodge and even as he asked it, he knew why the machine might do just that, and the thought of it made icy worms go crawling up his back.

"To show us," Forester said, "that it was sentient, too."

"But it wouldn't do that," Lodge argued. "If it were sentient it would keep quiet about it. That would be its sole defense. We could smash it. We probably would smash it if we thought it had come alive. We could dismantle it; we could put an end to it."

He sat in the silence that fell between them and felt the dread that had settled on this place—a strange dread compounded of an intellectual and a moral doubt, of a man who had fallen dead, of one character too many, of the guarded loneliness that hemmed in their lives.

"I can't think" he said. "Let's sleep on it."

"Okay," said Forester.

"A drink?"

Forester shook his head.

He's glad to drop it, too, thought Lodge. He's glad to get away.

Like a hurt animal, he thought. All of us, like hurt animals, crawling off to be alone, sick of one another, poisoned by the same faces eternally sitting across the table or meeting in the halls, of the same mouths saying the same inane phrases over and over again until, when you meet the owner of a particular mouth, you know before he says it what he is going to say.

"Good night, Bayard."

"Night, Kent. Sleep tight."

"See you."

"Sure," said Lodge.

The door shut softly.

Good night. Sleep tight. Don't let the bedbugs bite.

VI

He woke, screaming in the night.

He sat bolt upright in the middle of the bed and searched with numbed mind for the actuality, slowly, clumsily separating the actuality from the dream becoming aware again of the room he slept in, of the furniture, of his own place and who he was and what he did and why he happened to be there.

It was all right, he told himself. It had been just a dream. The kind of dream that was common here. The kind of dream that everyone was having.

The dream of walking down a street or road, or walking up a staircase, of walking almost anywhere and of meeting something—a spiderlike thing, or a wormlike thing, or a squatting monstrosity with horns and drooling mouth or perhaps something such as could be fabricated only in a dream and have it stop and say hello and chat—for it was human, too, just the same as you.

He sat and shivered at the memory of the one he'd met, of how it had put a hairy, taloned claw around his shoulder, of how it had drooled upon him with great affection and had asked him if he had the time to catch a drink because it had a thing or two it wanted to talk with him about. Its odor had been overpowering and its shape obscene, and he tried to shrink from it, and tried to run from it, but could neither shrink nor run, for it was a man like him, clothed in different flesh.

He swung his legs off the bed and found his slippers with searching toes and scuffed his feet into them. He found his robe and stood up and put it on and went out to the office.

There he mixed himself a drink.

Sleep tight, he thought. God, how can a man sleep tight? Now it's got me as well as all the others.

The guilt of it—the guilt of what mankind meant to do.

Although, despite the guilt, there was a lot of logic in it.

There were planets upon which no human could have lived for longer than a second, because of atmospheric pressure, because of overpowering gravity, because of lack of atmosphere or poison atmosphere, or because of any one of any combination of a hundred other reasons.

And yet those planets had economic and strategic value, every one of them. Some of them had both great economic and great strategic value. And if Man were to hold the galactic empire which he was carving out against the possible appearance of some as yet unknown alien foe, he must man all economic and strategic points, must make full use of all the resources of his new empire.

For that somewhere in the galaxy there were other intelligences as yet unmet by men there could be little doubt. The sheer mathematics of pure chance said there had to be. Given an infinite space, the possibility of such an intelligence also neared infinity. Friend or foe: you couldn't know. But you couldn't take a chance. So you planned and built against the day of meeting.

And in such planning, to bypass planets of economic and strategic value was sheer insanity.

Human colonies must be planted on those planets—must be planted there and grow against the day of meeting so that their numbers and their resources and their positioning in space might be thrown into the struggle if the struggle came to be.

And if Man, in his natural form, could not exist there—why, then you changed his form. You manufactured bodies that could live there, that could fit into the planets' many weird conditions, that could live on those planets and grow and build and carry out Man's plans.

Man could build those bodies. He had the technique to compound the flesh and bone and nerve, he had the skill to duplicate the mechanisms that produced the hormones, he had ferreted out the secrets of the enzymes and the amino acids and had at his fingertips all the other know-how to construct a body—any body, not just a human body. Biological engineering had become an exact science and biological blueprints could be drawn up to meet any conceivable set of planetary conditions. Man was all set to go on his project for colonization by humans in strange nonhuman forms.

Ready except for one thing: he could make everything but life.

Now the search for life went on, a top-priority, highly classified research program carried out here and on other asteroids, with the teams of biochemists, metabolists, endocrinologists and others isolated on the tumbling slabs of rock, guarded by military patrols operating out in space, hemmed in by a million regulations and uncounted security checks.

They sought for life, working down in that puzzling gray area where nonlife was separated from life by a shadow zone and a strange unpredictability that was enough to drive one mad, working with the viruses and crystals which at one moment might be dead and the next moment half alive and no man as yet who could tell why this was or how it came about.

That there was a definite key to life, hidden somewhere against Man's searching, was a belief that never wavered in the higher echelons, but on the guarded asteroids there grew up a strange and perhaps unscientific belief that life was not a matter of fact to be pinned down by formula or equation, but rather a matter of spirit, with some shading to the supernatural—that it was not something that Man was ever meant to know, that to seek it was presumptuous and perhaps sacrilegious, that it was a tangled trap into which Man had lured himself by his madcap hunt for knowledge.

And I, thought Bayard Lodge, I am one of those who drive them on in this blind and crazy search for a thing that we were never meant to find, that for our peace of mind and for our security of soul we never should have sought. I reason with them when they whisper out their fears, I kid them out of it when they protest the inhumanity of the course we plan, I keep them working and I kill each of them just a little every day, kill the humanity of them inch by casual inch—and I wake up screaming because a *human* thing I met put its arm around me and asked me to have a drink with it.

He finished off his drink and poured another one and this time did not bother with the mix.

"Come on," he said to the monster of the dream. "Come on, friend. I'll have that drink with you."

He stared around the room, waiting for the monster.

"What the hell," he said, "we're all human, aren't we?"

He poured another one and held it in a fist that suddenly was shaky.

"Us humans," he said, still talking to the monster, "have got to stick together."

VII

All of them met in the lounge after breakfast, and Lodge, looking from face to face, saw the terror that lay behind the masks they kept in front of them, could sense the unvoiced shrieking that lay inside of them, held imprisoned by the iron control of breeding and of discipline.

Kent Forester carefully lit a cigarette and when he spoke his voice was conversationally casual, and Lodge, watching him as he talked, knew the price he paid to keep his voice casual.

"This is something," Forester said, "that we can't allow to keep on eating on us. We have to talk it out."

"You mean rationalize it?" said Sifford.

Forester shook his head. "Talk it out, I said. This is once we can't kid ourselves.

"There were nine characters last night," said Craven.

"And a whale," said Forester.

"You mean one of . . ."

"I don't know. If one of us did, let's speak up and say so. There's not a one among us who can't appreciate a joke."

"A grisly joke," said Craven.

"But a joke," said Forester.

"I would like to think it was a joke," Maitland declared. "I'd feel a lot easier if I knew it was a joke."

"That's the point," said Forester. "That's what I'm getting at."

He paused a moment. "Anyone?" he asked.

No one said a word.

They waited.

"No one, Kent," said Lodge.

"Perhaps the joker doesn't want to reveal himself," said Forester. "I think all of us could understand that. Maybe we could hand out slips of paper."

"Hand them out," Sifford grumbled.

Forester took sheets of folded paper from his pocket, carefully tore the strips. He handed out the strips.

"If anyone played a joke," Lodge pleaded, "for God's sake let us know."

The slips came back. Some of them said "no," others said "no joke," one said "I didn't do it."

Forester wadded up the strips.

"Well, that lets the idea out," he said. "I must admit I didn't have much hope."

Craven lumbered to his feet. "There's one thing that all of us have been thinking," he said, "and it might as well be spoken. It's not a pleasant subject."

He paused and looked around him at the others, as if defying them to stop him.

"No one liked Henry too well," he said. "Don't deny it. He was a hard man to like. A hard man any way you look at him. I was closer to him than any of you. I've agreed to say a few words for him at the service this afternoon.

I am glad to do it, for he was a good man despite his hardness. He had a tenacity of will, a stubbornness such as you seldom find even in a hard man. And he had moral scruples that none of us could guess. He would talk to me a little—really talk—and that's something that he never did with the rest of you.

"Henry was close to something. He was scared. He died."

"There was nothing wrong with him."

Craven looked at Dr. Lawrence.

"Was there, Susan?" he asked. "Was there anything wrong with him?"

"Not a thing," said Dr. Susan Lawrence. "He should not have died."

Craven turned to Lodge. "He talked with you recently."

"A day or two ago," said Lodge. "He seemed quite normal then."

"What did he talk about?"

"Oh, the usual things. Minor matters."

"Minor matters?" Mocking.

"All right, then. If you want it that way. He talked about not wanting to go on. He said our work was unholy. That's the word he used—unholy."

Lodge looked around the room. "That's one the rest of you have never thought to use. Unholy."

"He was more insistent than usual?"

"Well, no," said Lodge. "It was the first time he had ever talked to me about it. The only person engaged in the research here, I believe, who had not talked with me about it at one time or another."

"And you talked him into going back."

"We discussed it."

"You killed the man."

"Perhaps," said Lodge. "Perhaps I'm killing all of you. Perhaps you're killing yourselves and I myself. How am I to know?"

He said to Dr. Lawrence, "Sue, could a man die of a psychosomatic illness brought about by fear?"

"Clinically, no," said Susan Lawrence. "Practically, I'm afraid, the answer might be yes."

"He was trapped," said Craven.

"Mankind's trapped," snapped Lodge. "If you must point your finger, point it at all of us. Point it at the whole community of Man."

"I don't think," Forester interrupted, "that this is pertinent."

"It is," insisted Craven, "and I will tell you why. I'd be the last to admit the existence of a ghost—"

Alice Page came swiftly to her feet. "Stop it!" she cried. "Stop it! Stop it! Stop it!"

"Miss Page, please," said Craven.

"But you're saying . . ."

"I'm saying that if there ever were a situation where a departed spirit had a motive—and I might even say a right—to come back and haunt his place of death, this is it."

"Sit down, Craven," Lodge commanded, sharply.

Craven hesitated angrily, then sat down, grumbling to himself. Lodge said, "If there's any point in continuing the discussion along these lines, I insist that it be done objectively."

Maitland said, "There's no point to it I can see. As scientists who are most intimately concerned with life we must recognize that death is an utter ending."

"That," objected Sifford, "is open to serious question and you know it."

Forester broke in, his voice cool. "Let's defer the matter for a moment. We can come back to it. There is another thing."

He hurried on. "Another thing that we should know. Which of the characters was Henry's character?"

No one said a word.

"I don't mean," said Forester, "to try to find which belonged to whom. But by a process of elimination . . ."

"All right," said Sifford. "Hand out the slips again."

Forester brought out the paper in his pocket, tore more strips.

Craven protested. "Not just slips," he said. "I won't fall for a trick like that."

Forester looked up from the slips.

"Trick?"

"Of course," said Craven, harshly. "Don't deny it. You've been trying to find out."

"I don't deny it," Forester told him. "I'd have been derelict in my duty if I hadn't tried."

Lodge said, "I wonder why we keep this secret thing so closely to ourselves. It might be all right under normal circumstances, but these aren't normal circumstances. I think it might be best if we made a clean breast of it. I, for one, am willing. I'll lead off if you only say the word."

He waited for the word.

There was no word.

They all stared back at him and there was nothing in their faces—no anger, no fear, nothing at all that a man could read.

Lodge shrugged the defeat from his shoulders.

He said to Craven, "All right, then. What were you saying?"

"I was saying that if we wrote down the names of our characters it would be no better than standing up and shouting them aloud. Forester knows our handwriting. He could spot every slip."

Forester protested. "I hadn't thought of it. I ask you to believe I hadn't. But what Craven says is true."

"All right, then?" asked Lodge.

"Ballots," Craven said. "Fix up ballots with the characters' names upon them."

"Aren't you afraid we might be able to identify your X's?"

Craven looked levelly at Lodge. "Since you mention it, I might be."

Forester said, wearily, "We have a batch of dies down in the labs. Used for stamping specimens. I think there's an X among them."

"That would satisfy you?" Lodge asked Craven.

Craven nodded that it would.

Lodge heaved himself out of the chair.

"I'll get the stamp," he said. "You can fix the ballots while I'm after it."

Children, he thought. Just so many children. Suspicious and selfish and frightened, like cornered animals. Cornered between the converging walls of fear and guilt, trapped in the corner of their own insecurity.

He walked down the stairs to the laboratories, his heels ringing on the metal treads, with the sound of his walking echoing from the hidden corners of the fear and guilt.

If Henry hadn't died right now, he thought, it might have been all right. We might have muddled through.

But he knew that probably was wrong. For if it had not been Henry's death, it would have been something else. They were ready for it—more than ready for it. It would not have taken much at any time in the last few weeks to have lit the fuse.

He found the die and ink pad and tramped back upstairs again. The ballots lay upon the table and someone had found a shoe box and cut a slit out of its lid to make a ballot box.

"We'll all sit over on this side of the room," said Forester, "and we'll go up, one by one, and vote."

And if anyone saw the ridiculous side of speaking of what they were about to do as voting, he pointedly ignored it.

Lodge put the die and ink pad down on the table top and walked across the room to take his seat.

"Who wants to start it off?" asked Forester.

No one said a word.

Even afraid of this, thought Lodge.

Then Maitland said he would.

They sat in utter silence as each walked forward to mark a ballot, to fold it and to drop it in the box. Each of them waited for the one to return before another walked out to the table.

Finally it was done, and Forester went to the table, took up the box and shook it, turning it this way and that to change the order of the ballots, so that no one might guess by their position to whom they might belong.

"I'll need two monitors," he said.

His eyes looked them over. "Craven," he said. "Sue."

They stood up and went forward.

Forester opened the box. He took out a ballot, unfolded it and read it, passed it on to Dr. Lawrence, and she passed it on to Craven.

"The Defenseless Orphan."

"The Rustic Slicker."

"The Alien Monster."

"The Beautiful Bitch."

"The Sweet Young Thing."

Wrong on that one, Lodge told himself. But who else could it be? She had been the last one on. She had been the ninth.

Forester went on, unfolding the ballots and reading them.

"The Extra-Terrestrial Ally."

"The Proper Young Man."

Only two left now. Only two. The Out-At-Elbows Philosopher and the Mustached Villian.

I'll make a guess, Lodge said to himself. I'll make a bet. I'll bet on which one was Henry.

He was the Mustached Villain.

Forester unfolded the last ballot and read aloud the name.

"The Mustached Villain."

So I lose the bet, thought Lodge.

He heard the rippling hiss of indrawn breath from those around him, the swift, stark terror of what the balloting had meant.

For Henry's character had been the most self-assertive and dominant in last night's Play: the Philosopher.

VIII

The script in Henry's notebook was close and crabbed, with a curtness to it, much like the man himself. His symbols and his equations were a triumph of clarity, but the written words had a curious backward, petulant slant and the phrases that he used were laconic to the point of rudeness—although whom he was being rude to, unless it were himself, was left a matter of conjecture.

Maitland closed the book with a snap and shoved it away from him, out into the center of the table.

"So that was it," he said.

They sat in quietness, their faces pale and drawn, as if in bitter fact they might have seen the ghost of Craven's hinting.

"That's the end of it," snapped Sifford. "I won't—"

"You won't what?" asked Lodge.

Sifford did not answer. He just sat there with his hands before him on the table, opening and closing them, making great tight fists of them, then straightening out his fingers, stretching them as if he meant by sheer power of will to bend them back farther than they were meant to go.

"Henry was crazy," said Susan Lawrence curtly. "A man would have to be to dream up that sort of evidence."

"As a medical person," Maitland said, "we could expect that reaction from you."

"I work with life," said Susan Lawrence. "I respect it and it is my job to preserve it as long as it can be kept within the body. I have a great compassion for the things possessing it."

"Meaning we haven't?"

"Meaning you have to live with it and come to know it for its power and greatness, for the fine thing that it is, before you can appreciate or understand its wondrous qualities."

"But, Susan—"

"And I know," she said, rushing on to head him off. "I know that is more than decay and breakdown, more than the senility of matter. It is something greater than disease. To argue that life is the final step to which matter is reduced, the final degradation of the nobility of soil and ore and water is to argue that a static, unintelligent, purposeless existence is the norm of the universe."

"We're getting all tangled up semantically," suggested Forester. "As living things the terms we use have no comparative values with the terms that might be used for universal purpose, even if we knew those universal terms."

"Which we don't," said Helen Gray. "What you say would be true especially if what Henry had thought he had found was right."

"We'll check Henry's notes," Lodge told them grimly. "We'll follow him step by step. I think he's wrong, but on the chance he isn't, we can't pass up an angle."

Sifford bristled. "You mean even if he were right you would go ahead? That you would use even so humanly degrading a piece of evidence to achieve our purpose?"

"Of course I would," said Lodge. "If life is a disease and a senility, all right, then, it is disease and senility. As Kent and Helen pointed out, the terms are not comparative when used in a universal sense. What is poison for the universe is—well, is life for us. If Henry was right, his discovery is no more than the uncovering of a fact that has existed since time untold."

"You don't know what you're saying," Sifford said.

"But I do," Lodge told him bluntly. "You have grown neurotic. You and some of the others. Maybe I, myself. Maybe all of us. We are ruled by fear —you by the fear of your job, I by the fear that the job will not be done. We've been penned up, we've been beating out our brains against the stone walls of our conscience and a moral value suddenly furbished up and polished until it shines like the shield of Galahad. Back on the Earth you wouldn't give this thing a second thought. You'd gulp a little, maybe, then you'd swallow it, if it were proved true, and you'd go ahead to track down that principle of decay and of disease we happen to call life. The principle itself would be only one more factor for your consideration, one more tool to work with, another bit of knowledge. But here you claw at the wall and scream."

"Bayard!" shouted Forester. "Bayard, you can't—"

"I can," Lodge told him, "and I am. I'm sick of all their whimpering and baying. I'm tired of spoonfed fanatics who drove themselves to their own fanaticism by their own synthetic fears. It takes men and women with knife-sharp minds to lick this thing we're after. It takes guts and intelligence."

Craven was white-lipped with fury. "We've worked," he shouted. "Even when everything within us, even when all our decency and intelligence and our religious instincts told us not to work, we worked. And don't say you kept us at it, you with your mealy words and your kidding and your back slapping. Don't say you laughed us into it."

Forester pounded the table with a fist. "Let's quit this arguing," he cried. "Let's get down to cases."

Craven settled back in his chair, face still white with anger. Sifford kept on making fists.

"Henry wrote a conclusion," said Forester. "Well, hardly a conclusion. Let's call it a suspicion. Now what do you want to do about it? Ignore it, run from it, test it for its proof?"

"I say, test it," Craven said. "It was Henry's work. Henry's gone and can't speak for his own beliefs. We owe at least that much to him."

"If it can be tested," Maitland qualified. "To me it sounds more like philosophy than science."

"Philosophy runs hand in hand with science," said Alice Page. "We can't simply brush it off because it sounds involved."

"I didn't say involved," Maitland objected. "What I meant was—oh, hell, let's go ahead and check it."

"Check it," Sifford said.

He swung around on Lodge. "And if it checks out, if it comes anywhere near to checking, if we can't utterly disprove it, I'm quitting. I'm serving notice now."

"That's your privilege, Sifford, any time you wish."

"It might be hard to prove anything one way or the other," said Helen Gray. "It might not be any easier to disprove than prove."

Lodge saw Sue Lawrence looking at him and there was grim laughter and something of grudging admiration and a touch of confused cynicism in her face, as if she might be saying to him, *Well, you've done it again. I didn't think you would—not this time, I didn't. But you did. Although you won't always do it. There'll come a time . . .*

"Want to bet?" he whispered at her.

She said, "Cyanide."

And although he laughed back at her, he knew that she was right—righter than she knew. For the time had already come and this was the end of Life Team No. 3.

They would go on, of course, stung by the challenge Henry Griffith had written in his notebook, still doggedly true to their training and their charge, but the heart was out of them, the fear and the prejudice too deeply ingrained within their souls. the confused tangle of their thinking too much a part of them.

If Henry Griffith had sought to sabotage the project, Lodge told himself, he had done it perfectly. In death he had done it far better than he could have, alive.

He seemed to hear in the room the dry, acerbic chuckling of the man and he wondered at the imagined chuckle, for Henry had had no humor in him.

Although Henry had been the Out-At-Elbows Philosopher and it was hard to think of Henry as that sort of character—an old humbug who hid behind a polished manner and a golden tongue. For there was nothing of the humbug in Henry, either, and his manner was not polished nor did he have the golden gift of words. He slouched and he rarely talked, and when he did he growled.

A joker, Lodge thought—had he been, after all, a joker?

Could he have used the Philosopher to lampoon the rest of them, a character who derided them and they not knowing it?

He shook his head, arguing with himself.

If the Philosopher had kidded them, it had been gentle kidding, so gentle that none of them had known it was going on, so subtle that it had slid off them without notice.

But that wasn't the terrifying aspect of it—that Henry might have been quietly making fun of them. The terrifying thing was that the Philosopher had been second on the stage. He had followed the Rustic Slicker and during the whole time had been much in evidence—munching on the turkey leg and waving it to emphasize the running fire of pompous talk that had never slacked. The Philosopher had been, in fact, the most prominent player in the entire Play.

And that meant that no one could have put him on the stage, for no one, in the first place, could have known so soon which of the nine was Henry's character, and no one, not having handled him before, could have put the Philosopher so realistically through his paces. And none of those who had sent on their characters early in the Play could have handled two characters convincingly for any length of time—especially when the Philosopher had talked all the blessed time.

And that would cancel out at least four of those sitting in the room.

Which could mean:

That there was a ghost.

Or that the machine itself retained a memory.

Or that the eight of them had suffered mass hallucination.

He considered that last alternative and it wilted in the middle. So did the other two. None of the three made sense. Not any of it made sense—none of it at all.

Take a team of trained men and women, trained objectively, trained to look for facts, conditioned to skepticism and impatience of anything outside the pale of fact: What did it take to wreck a team like that? Not simply the cabin fever of a lonely asteroid. Not simply the nagging of awakened conscience against well established ethics. Not the atavistic, Transylvanian fear of ghosts.

There was some other factor. Another factor that had not been thought of yet—like the new approach that Maitland had talked about at dinner, saying they would have to take a new direction to uncover the secret that they sought. We're going at it wrong, Maitland had said. We'll have to find a new approach.

And Maitland had meant, without saying so, that in their research the old methods of ferreting out the facts were no longer valid, that the scientific mind had operated for so long in the one worn groove that it knew no other, that they must seek some fresh concept to arrive at the fact of life.

Had Henry, Lodge wondered, supplied that fresh approach? And in the supplying of it and in dying, wrecked the team as well?

Or was there another factor, as Maitland had said there must be a new approach—a factor that did not fit in with conventional thinking or standard psychology?

The Play, he wondered. Was the Play a factor? Had the Play, designed to keep the team intact and sane, somehow turned into a two-edged sword?

They were rising from the table now, ready to leave, ready to go to their rooms and to dress for dinner. And after dinner, there would be the Play again.

Habit, Lodge thought. Even with the whole thing gone to pot, they still conformed to habit.

They would dress for dinner; they would stage the Play. They would go back tomorrow morning to their workrooms and they'd work again, but the work would be a futile work, for the dedicated purpose of their calling had been burned out of them by fear, by the conflict of their souls, by death, by ghosts.

Someone touched his elbow and he saw that Forester stood beside him.

"Well, Kent?"

"How do you feel?"

"Okay," said Lodge. Then he said, "You know, of course, it's over."

"We'll try again," said Forester.

Lodge shook his head. "Not me. You, maybe. You're a younger man than I. I'm burned out too."

IX

The Play started in where it had left off the night before, with the Sweet Young Thing coming on the stage and all the others there, with the Out-At-Elbows Philosopher rubbing his hands together smugly and saying, "Now this is a cozy situation. All of us are here."

Sweet Young Thing (*tripping lightly*): Why, Philosopher, I know that I am late, but what a thing to say. Of course we all are here. I was unavoidably detained.

Rustic Slicker (*speaking aside, with a rural leer*): By a Tom Collins and a slot machine.

Alien Monster (*sticking out its head from behind the tree*): Tsk hrstlgn vglater, tsk . . .

And there was something wrong, Lodge told himself.

There was a certain mechanical wrongness, something out of place, a horrifying alienness that sent a shiver through you even when you couldn't spot the alienness.

There was something wrong with the Philosopher, and the wrongness was not that he should not be there, but something else entirely. There was a wrongness about the Sweet Young Thing and the Proper Young Man and the Beautiful Bitch and all the others.

There was a great deal wrong with the Rustic Slicker, and he, Bayard Lodge, knew the Rustic Slicker as he knew no other man—knew the blood and guts and brains of him, knew his thoughts and dreams and his hidden yearnings, his clodhopperish conceit, his smart-aleck snicker, the burning inferiority complex that drove him to social exhibitionism.

He knew him as every member of the audience must know his own character, as something more than an imagined person, as someone more than another person, something more than friend. For the bond was strong—the bond of the created and creator.

And tonight the Rustic Slicker had drawn a little way apart, had cut the apron strings, had stood on his own with the first dawning of independence.

The Philosopher was saying: "It's quite natural that I should have commented on all of us being here. For one of us is dead. . . . "

There was no gasp from the audeince, no hiss of indrawn breath, no stir, but you could feel the tension snap tight like a whining violin string.

"We have been consciences," said the Mustached Villain. "Projected conscience playing out our parts. . . . "

The Rustic Slicker said: "The consciences of mankind."

Lodge half rose out of his chair.

I didn't make him say that! I didn't want him to say that. I thought it, that was all. So help me God, I just thought it, that was all!

And now he knew what was wrong. At last, he knew the strangeness of the characters this night.

They weren't on the screen at all! They were on the stage, the little width of stage which ran before the screen!

They were no longer projected imaginations—they were flesh and blood. They were mental puppets come to sudden life.

He sat there, cold at the thought of it—cold and rigid in the quickening knowledge that by the power of mind alone—by the power of mind and electronic mysteries, Man had created life.

A new approach, Maitland had said.

Oh, Lord! A new approach!

They had failed at their work and triumphed in their play, and there'd be no longer any need of life teams, grubbing down into that gray area where life and death were interchangeable. To make a human monster you'd sit before a screen and you'd dream him up, bone by bone, hair by hair, brains, innards, special abilities and all. There'd be monsters by the billions to plant on those other planets. And the monsters would be human, for they'd be dreamed by brother humans working from a blueprint.

In just a little while the characters would step down off the stage and would mingle with them. And their creators? What would their creators do? Go screaming, raving mad?

What would he say to the Rustic Slicker?

What *could* he say to the Rustic Slicker?

And, more to the point, what would the Rustic Slicker have to say to him?

He sat, unable to move, unable to say a word or cry out a warning, waiting for the moment when they would step down.

John Updike

Incest

"I WAS IN A MOVIE HOUSE, FAIRLY PLUSH, IN A SORT OF MEZZANINE, OR balcony. It was a wide screen. On it there were tall people—it seemed to be at a dance or at least *function*—talking and bending toward each other gracefully, in that misty technicolor Japanese pictures have. I *knew* that this was the movie version of *Remembrance of Things Past*. I had the impression sitting there that I had been looking forward to it for a long time, and I felt slightly guilty at not being home, you know. There was a girl sitting down one row, catty-corner from me. She had a small head with a thin, rather touching neck, like Moira Lengel, but it wasn't her, or anyone we know. At any rate there was this feeling of great affection toward her, and it seemed, in the light of the movie—the movie was taking place entirely in a bright yellow ballroom, so the faces of the audience were clear—it seemed somehow that the entire chance to make my life good was wrapped up in this girl, who was strange to me. Then she was in the seat beside me, and I was giving her a back rub."

"*Uh*-oh," his wife said, pausing in her stooping. She was grazing the carpet, picking up the toys, cards, matches, and spoons scattered by their daughter Jane, a year and seven months old. Big Jane, as she had dreaded being called when they named the child, held quite still to catch what next he had to tell. Lee had begun the recitation ironically, to register his irritation with her for asking him, her own day had been so dull and wearing, to talk, to tell her of *his* day. Nothing interested him less than his own day, done. It made his jaws ache, as with a smothered yawn, to consider framing one sentence about it. So, part desperation, part discipline, he had begun the account of the dream he had been careful to keep from her at breakfast. He protected his wife here, at the place where he recalled feeling his hands leave the lean girl's comforted shoulder blades and travel thoughtfully around the cool, strait, faintly ridged sides of the rib case to the always surprising boon in front—sensations momentarily more vivid in the nerves of his fingers than the immediate texture of the bamboo chair he occupied.

"Through the blouse."

"Good," she said. "Good for you both."

Jane appeared so saucy saying this he was emboldened to add a true detail: "I think I did undo her bra strap. By pinching through the cloth." To judge by his wife's expression—tense for him, as if he were bragging before company

361

—the addition was a mistake. He hastened on. "Then we were standing in back of the seats, behind one of those walls that comes up to your chest, and I was being introduced to her father. I had the impression he was a doctor. He was rather pleasant, really: gray hair, and a firm grip. He seemed cordial, and I had a competent feeling, as if I couldn't help making a good impression. But behind this encounter—with the girl standing off to one side—there was the sadness of the movie itself continuing on the screen; the music soared; Proust's face was shown—a very young face—with the eyelids closed, and this shimmered and spun and turned into a slow pink vortex that then solidified into a huge motionless rose, filling the whole screen. And I thought, *Now I know how the book ends.*"

"How exciting! It's like 'The Dream of the Rood.' " Jane resumed cleaning up after her daughter. Lee was abruptly oppressed by a belief that he had made her life harder to bear.

He said, "The girl must have been you because you're the only person I know who likes to have their back rubbed."

"You find my neck touching?"

"Well for God's sake, I can't be held accountable for the people I meet in dreams. I don't invite them." He was safe, of course, as long as they stayed away from the real issue, which was why he had told her the dream at all. "That girl means nothing to me now. In the dream obviously I was still in high school and hadn't met you. I remember sitting there and wondering, because it was such a long movie, if my mother would give me hell when I got back."

"I say, it's a very exciting dream. How far *are* you in Proust?"

"Sodom and Gomorrah." It occurred to him, what a queer mediocre thing it was, to scorn the English title yet not dare pronunciation of the French, and apropos of this self-revelation he said, "I'll never get out; I'm just the sort of person who begins Proust and can't finish. Lowest of the low. The humiliated and oppressed. Won't even tell his wife what his day was like." He changed his tone. "Which is better—to finish *Remembrance of Things Past,* or to never begin it?"

Unexpectedly, so profound was her fatigue, she did not recognize the question as a piece of sport rhetoric, and, after a moment's thought, seriously answered, "To finish it."

Then she turned, and her lovely pale face—in photographs like a white water-smoothed stone, so little did the indentations and markings of it have harshness—lengthened, and the space between her eyebrows creased vertically; into the kitchen she shouted, *"Jane!* What are you *doing?"*

While they had been talking, the child had been keeping herself quiet with the sugar bowl. It was a new trick of hers, to push a chair and climb up on it; in this way a new world, a fresh stratum of things, was made available to her curiosity. The sugar bowl, plump Swedish pewter, lived casually on the counter of a waist-high cabinet, near the wall. Little Jane had taken and inverted it, and with an eerie, repetitious, patient dabbling motion had reduced the one shining Alp to a system of low ranges. She paid no attention to her mother's shout, but when her parents drew closer and sighed together, she quickly turned her face toward them as if for admiration, her chin and lips frosted. Her upper lip, when she smiled, curved like the handlebar of a bicycle. The sight of her incredibly many, perfect, blue, inturned teeth struck joy into Lee's heart.

With an audience now, little Jane accelerated her work. Her right hand, unattended by her eyes, which remained with her parents, scrabbled in a panicky way among the white drifts and then, palm down, swept a quantity onto the floor, where it hit with a sound like one stroke of a drummer's brush. On the spatter-pattern linoleum the grains of sugar were scarcely visible. The child looked down, wondering where they had gone.

"Damn you," his wife said to Lee, "you never do a damn thing to help. Now, why can't you play with her a minute? You're her father. *I'm* not going to clean it up." She walked out of the kitchen.

"I *do* play with her," he said, helplessly amiable (he understood his wife so well, divined so exactly what confused pain the scattered sugar caused her heart, as neatness-loving as her mother's), although he recognized that in her distraught state his keeping cheerful figured as mockery of her, one more cross to carry toward the day's end.

Lee asked his daughter, "Want to run around?"

Jane hunched her shoulders and threw back her head, her sugar-gritty teeth gleefully clenched. "Pay roun," she said, wagging her hand on her wrist.

He made the circular motion she had intended, and said, "In a minute. Now we must help poor Mommy." With two sheets of typing paper, using one as a brush and the other as a pan, he cleaned up what she had spilled on the counter, reaching around her, since she kept her position standing on the chair. Her breath floated randomly, like a butterfly, on his forearms as he swept. They seemed two conspirators. He folded the pan into a chute and returned the sugar to the bowl. Then there was the sugar on the floor—when you moved your feet, atoms of it crackled. He stooped, the two pieces of paper in his hands, knowing they wouldn't quite do.

Jane whimpered and recklessly jogged her body up and down on her legs, making the chair tip and slap the cabinet. "*Jane,*" he said.

"Pay roun," the girl whined feebly, her strength sapped by frustration.

"*What?*" his wife answered from the living room in a voice as cross as his. She had fought giving the baby her name, but he had insisted; there was no other woman's name he liked, he had said.

"Nothing, I was shouting at the kid. She was going to throw herself off the chair. She wants to play Round."

"Well, why don't you? She's had an awfully dismal day. I don't think we make her happy enough."

"O.K., dammit. I will." He crumpled the sheets of paper and stuffed them into the wastepaper can, letting the collected sugar fly where it would.

Round was a simple game. Jane ran from the sofa in one room to the bed in the other, through the high white double doorway, with pilasters, that had persuaded them to take the small apartment. He chased her. When his hands nicked her bottom or touched her swollen waist, she laughed wildly her double laugh, which originated deep in her lungs and ricocheted, shrill, off her palate. Lee's problem was to avoid overtaking her, in the great length of his strides, and stepping on her. When she wobbled or slowed, he clapped twice or thrice, to give her the sense of his hands right behind her ears, like two nipping birds. If she toppled, he swiftly picked her up, tickling her briefly if she seemed stunned or indignant. When she reached the bed—two low couches, box springs on short legs, set side by side and made up as one—he leapfrogged over her and fell full-length on the mattresses. This, for him, was the strenuous part of the game. Jane, finding herself between her father's ankles after the rush of his body above her head, laughed her loudest, pivoted, and ran the other way, flailing her arms, which she held so stiffly the elbows were indentations. At the sofa end of the track there could be no leapfrogging. Lee merely stopped and stood with his back toward her until the little girl calculated she dare make a break for it. Her irises swivelled in their blue whites; it was the first strategy of her life. The instant she decided to move, her bottled excitement burst forth; as she clumped precipitately toward the high white arch laughter threatened to upend her world. The game lasted until the child's bath. Big Jane, for the first time that day free of her daughter, was not hurrying toward this moment.

After four times back and forth Lee was exhausted and damp. He flopped on the bed the fifth time and instead of rising rolled onto his back. This was ruining the crease in his pants. His daughter, having started off, felt his absence behind her and halted. Her mother was coming from the kitchen, carrying washed diapers and a dust brush. Like her own mother, big Jane held a cigarette in the left corner of her mouth. Her left eye fluttered against the smoke. Lee's mother-in-law was shorter than his wife, paler, more sarcastic —very different, he had thought. But this habit was hers right down to the tilt of the cigarette and the droop of the neglected ash. Looking, Lee saw that as Jane squinted, the white skin at the outside corner of her eye crinkled finely, as dry as her mother's, and that his wife's lids were touched with the lashless, grainy, humiliated quality of the lids of the middle-aged woman he had met not a dozen times, mostly in Indianapolis, where she kept a huge brick house spotlessly clean and sipped sherry from breakfast to bed. All unknowing he had married her.

Jane, as she passed him, glanced down with an untypical, sardonic, cigarette-stitched expression. By shifting his head on the pillow he could watch her in the bathroom. She turned her back to hang the diapers on a brown cord strung between mirror and window. This was more his Jane: the wide rounded shoulders, the back like two halves of a peach, the big thighs, the narrow ankles. In the mirror her face, straining up as she attached the clothespins, showed age and pallor. It was as if there could exist a coin one side of which wears thin while the other keeps all the gloss and contour of the minting.

"Da-*tee*." A coral flush had overspread his daughter's face; in another moment she would whimper and throw herself on the floor.

With an ostentatious groan—he didn't know which of his women he was rebuking—Lee rose from the bed and chased his daughter again. Then they played in the living room with the bolsters, two prism-shaped pieces of foam rubber that served as a back to the sofa, an uncomfortable modernist slab that could, when a relative visited, be used for sleeping. Stood on end, the stiff bolsters were about the baby's height, and little Jane hugged them like brothers, and preferred them to dolls. Though to her human-sized, they were light enough to lift. Especially she loved to unzip the skin of mongrel linen fabric and prod with her finger the grayish, buoyant flesh beneath.

Catching them at this, big Jane said, "It kills me, it just is more depressing than anything she does, the way she's always trying to undress those bolsters. Don't en*courage* her at it."

"I don't. It's not my idea. It was *you* who took the covers to the Launderette so she saw them naked. It made a big impression. It's a state of primal innocence she wants to get them back to."

Wavering between quarrel and honest discussion—that there was a way of "talking things out" was an idea she had inherited from her father, a rigorously liberal civic leader and committeeman—she chose discussion. "It's not just those bolsters, you know. About three times a day she takes all the books out of their jackets. And spills matches in a little heap. You have no idea how much cleaning up I have to do to keep this place from looking like a pigpen. Yesterday I was in the bathroom washing my hair and when I came out she had gotten our camera open. I guess the whole roll's exposed. I put it back. Today she wanted to get the works out of the music box and threw a tantrum. And I don't know how often she brings those nasty frustrating little Chinese eggs you got her to me and says, 'Opo. Opo.' "

Reminded of the word, little Jane said, of a bolster, "Opo, opo." The zipper was stuck.

"Japanese," Lee said. "Those eggs were made in Genuine Occupied Japan. They're antiques." The child's being balked by the zipper preyed on his nerves. He hated fiddling with things like zippers caught on tiny strips of cloth. It was like squinting into a specific detail of Hell. Further, as he leaned back on the bolsterless sofa to rest his neck against the wall, he was irritated to feel the glass-capped legs skid on the uneven floor. "It's a very healthy instinct," he went on. "She's an empiricist. She's throwing open doors long locked by superstition."

Jane said, "I looked up 'unwrapping instinct' in Spock and the only thing in the index was 'underweight.' " Her tone was listless and humorous, and for the moment this concession put the family, to Lee's mind, as right as three Japanese eggs, each inside the other.

His wife gave his daughter her bath as day turned to evening. He had to go into the bathroom himself and while there studied the scene. The child's silky body, where immersed, was of a graver tint that that of her skin smarting in air. Two new cakes of unwrapped soap drifted around her. When her mother put a washrag to her face, blinding and scratching her, her fingers turned pale green with the pressure of her grip on the edge of the tub. She didn't cry, though. "She seems to like her bath better now," he said.

"She loves it. From five on, until you come, she talks about it. Daddy. Bath. Omelet."

"Omma net," his daughter said, biting her lower lip in a smile for him.

It had become, in one of those delicate mutations of routine whereby Jane shifted duties to him, his job to feed the little girl. The child's soft mouth had been burned and she was wary; the sample bites Lee took to show her that the food was safe robbed of sharpness his appetite for his own dinner. Fore-knowledge of the emotion caused in his wife by the sight of half-clean plates and half-full cups led him to complete little Jane's portion of tomato juice, omelet-with-toast, and, for dessert, applesauce. Handling the tiny cup and tiny knife and fork and spoon set his stomach slightly on edge. Though not fussy about food, he was disturbed by eating implements of improper weight or length. Jane, hidden in the kitchen, was unable to see, or if she had seen, to appreciate—for all their three years of marriage, she had a stunted aware-ness of his niceties—the discomfort he was giving himself. This annoyed him.

So he was unfortunately brusque with little Jane's bottle. Ideally the bottle was the happiest part of the meal. Steaming and dewy, it soared, white angel, out of the trembling pan, via Mommy's hands, with a kiss, into hers. She grabbed it, and Lee, his hand behind her head, steered her toward the bed-room and her crib.

"Nice maugham," she said, conscientiously echoing the infinity of times they had told her that the bottle was nice and warm.

Having lifted her into the crib and seen her root the bottle in her mouth, he dropped the fuzzy pink blanket over her and left quickly, gently closing the doors and sealing her into the darkness that was to merge with sleep. It was no doubt this quickness that undid the process. Though the child was drugged with heated milk, she still noticed a light.

He suspected this at the time. When, their own meal barely begun, the crib springs creaked unmistakably, he said, "Son of a bitch." Stan Lomax, on their faint radio, was giving an account of Williams' latest verbal outrage; Lee was desperate to hear every word. Like many Americans he was spiritually de-pendent on Ted Williams. He asked his wife, "God damn it, doesn't that kid do anything in the day? Didn't you take her to the park? Why isn't she worn out?"

The one answer to this could be his own getting up, after a silence, and going in to wait out the baby's insomnia. The hollow goodness of the act, like a coin given to a beggar with embarrassment, infuriated his tongue: "I work like a fool all day and come home and run the kid up and down until my legs ache and I have a headache and then I can't even eat my pork chop in peace."

In the aquarium of the dark room his child's face floated spectrally, and her eyes seemed discrete pools of the distant, shy power that had put them all there, and had made these walls, and the single tree outside, showing the first stages of leaf under the yellow night sky of New York. "Do you want to go on the big bed?"

"Big—*bed!*"

"O.K."

"Ogay."

Adjusting to the lack of light, he perceived that the bottle, nested in a crumpled sheet, was drained. Little Jane had been standing in her crib, one foot on the edge, as in ballet school. For two weeks she had been gathering nerve for the time she would climb the crib's wall and drop free outside. He lifted her out, breathing "Ooh, *heavy*," and took her to the wide low bed made of two beds. She clung to the fuzzy blanket—with milk, her main soporific.

Beside her on the bed, he began their story. "Once upon a time, in the big, big woods—" She flipped ecstatically at the known cadence. "Now you relax. There was a tiny little creature name of Barry Mouse."

"Mouff!" she cried, and sat straight up, as if she had heard one. She looked down at him for confirmation.

"Barry Mouse," he said. "And one day when Barry Mouse was walking through the woods, he came to a great big tree, and in the top of the great big tree what do you think there was?"

At last she yielded to the insistent pressure of his hand and fell back, her heavy blond head sinking into the pillow. He repeated, "What do you think there was?"

"Owl."

"That's right. Up at the top of the tree there was an owl, and the owl said, 'I'm going to eat you, Barry Mouse.' And Barry Mouse said, 'No, no.' So Owl said, 'O.K., then why don't you *hop* on my *back* and we'll *fly* to the *moon!*' And so Barry Mouse hopped on Owl's back and awaay they went—"

Jane turned on her side, so her great face was an inch from his. She giggled and drummed her feet against his abdomen, solidly. Neither Lee nor his wife, who shared the one bedtime story, had ever worked out what happened on the moon. Once the owl and the mouse were aloft, their imaginations collapsed. Knowing his voice daren't stop now, when her state was possibly transitional and he felt as if he were bringing to his lips an absolutely brimful glass of liquid, he continued with some nonsense about cinnamon trees and Chinese maidens, no longer bothering to keep within her vocabulary. She began touching his face with her open mouth, a sure sigh she was sleepy. "Hey," he murmured when one boneless moist kiss landed directly on his lips.

"Jane is so sleepy," he said, "because Daddy is sleepy, and Mommy is sleepy, and Bear is ssleepy, and Doll is sssleepy. . . . "

She lay quiet, her face in shadow, her fine straight yellow hair fanned across the pillow. Neither he nor his wife was blond; they had brown hair, rat color. There was little blondness in either family: just Jane's Aunt Ruth, and Lee's sister Margaret, eight years older than he and married before he had left grade school. She had been the fetching one of the children and he the bright one. So he imagined, though his parents loved them all impeccably.

Presuming his daughter asleep, he lifted himself on one elbow. She kicked his belly, rolled onto her back, and said in a voice loud with drowsiness, "Baaiy Mouff."

Stroking her strange hair, he began again, "Once upon a time, in the deep, deep woods, there lived a little creature," and this time succeeded.

As he lowered her into her crib, her eyes opened. He said, "O.K.?"

She pronounced beautifully, "O.K."

"Gee, she's practically epileptic with energy," he said, blinded by the brilliant light of the room where his wife had remained.

"She's a good child," Jane affirmed, speaking out of her thoughts while left alone rather than in answer to his remark. "Your dessert is on the table." She had kept hers intact on the sofa beside her, so they could eat their raspberry whip together. She also had beside her an orange-juice glass half full of sherry.

When the clock said 7:50, he said, "Why don't you run off to the movie? You never have any fun."

"All right," she said. "Go ahead. Go."

"No, I don't mean that. I mean you should go." Still, he smiled.

"You can go as a reward for putting her to sleep."

"Venus, I don't *want* to go," he said, without great emphasis, since at that moment he was rustling through the paper. He had difficulty finding the theatre section, and decided. "No, if you're too tired, no one will. I can't leave you. You need me too much."

"If you want to, go; don't torment me about it," she said, drawing on her sherry and staring into the *New Republic.* When she had the chance, she worked at being liberal.

"Do you think," he asked, "when Jane is sixteen, she'll go around in the back seat of Chevrolets and leave her poor old Daddy?"

"I hope so," Jane said.

"Will she have your bosom?"

"Not immediately."

He earnestly tried to visualize his daughter matured, and saw little but a charm bracelet on a slim, fair wrist. The forearms of teen-age girls tapered amazingly, toward little cages of bird bones. Charm bracelets were *démodé* already, he supposed.

Lee, committed to a long leisured evening at home, of the type that seemed precious on the nights when they had to go out and be entertained, was made nervous by its wide opportunities. He nibbled at the reading matter closest to hand—an article, "Is the Individual a Thing of the Past?," and last Sunday's comic section. At Alley Oop he checked himself and went into the kitchen. Thinking of the oatmeal cookies habitual in his parents' home, he opened the cupboard and found four kinds of sugar and seven of cereal, five infants' and two adults'. Jane was always buying some esoteric grind of sugar for a pastrymaking project, then discovering she couldn't use it. He smiled at this foible and carried his smile like an egg on a spoon into the living room, where his wife saw it but of course not the point of it, that it was in love of her. He leaned his forehead against the bookcase, by the anthology shelf, and considered all the poetry he had once read evaporating in him, a vast dying sea.

As he stood there, his father floated from behind and possessed him, occupying specifically the curved area of the jawbone. He understood perfectly why that tall stoical man was a Mason, Booster, deacon, and Scout troop leader.

Jane, concentrating all the pleasures her day had withheld into the hour remaining before she became too dopey to think, put Bach on the record-player. As she did so, her back and arms made angles signifying to him a whole era of affection and, more, awe.

When she returned to the sofa, he asked, "What makes you so pretty?" Then, having to answer it, he said, "Childbearing."

Preoccupied with some dim speckled thinker in her magazine, she fondled the remark briefly and set it aside, mistakenly judging it to be a piece of an obscure, ill-tempered substance. He poured a little sherry for himself and struck a pose by the mantel, trying to find with his legs and shoulders angles equivalent in effect to those she had made putting on the record. As she sat there, studious, he circumscribed her, every detail, with the tidal thought *Mine, mine.* She wasn't watching. She thought she knew what to expect from him, tonight at least.

He resolved, *Later,* and, in a mood of resolution, read straight through the Jones Very section of Matthiessen's anthology. The poet's stubborn sensibility aroused a readerly stubbornness; when Lee had finished, it was too late, the hour had slipped by. By the clock it was 10:30; for his wife, it was after one. Her lids were pink. This was the sort of day when you sow and not reap.

Two hissing, clattering elves working a minor fairy-tale transposition, together they lifted the crib containing the sleeping girl and carried it into the living room, and shut the doors. Instead of undressing, Jane picked up odds and ends of his—spare shoes and the socks he had worn yesterday and the tie he had worn today. Next she went into the bathroom and emerged wearing a cotton nightie. In bed beside him she read a page of *Swan's Way* and fell asleep under the harsh light. He turned it off and thought furiously, the family's second insomniac. The heat of Jane's body made the bed stuffy. He hated these low beds; he lay miles below the ceiling, deep in the pit. The radiator, hidden in the window sill by his head, breathed lavishly. High above, through a net of crosses, a few stars strove where the yellow gave out. The child cried once, but, thank God, in her sleep.

He recalled what he always forgot in the interval of day, his insomnia game. Last night he had finished D in a burst of glory: Yvonne Dione, Zuleika Dobson. He let the new letter be G. Senator Albert Gore. Benny Goodman, Constance Garnett, *David* Garnett, Edvard Grieg. Goethe was Wolfgang and Gorki was Maxim. Farley Granger, Graham Greene (or Greta Garbo, *or* George Gobel), Henry Green. I was always difficult. You kept thinking of Ilka Chase. He wrestled and turned and cursed his wife, her heedless rump way on his side. To choke the temptation to thump her awake, he padded after a glass of water, scowling into the mirror. As he returned his head to the cooled pillow, it came to him, Christian name and surname both at once: Ira

Gershwin. Ira Gershwin: he savored it before proceeding. John Galsworthy, Kathryn Grayson . . . Lou Gehrig, poor devil . . .

He and Jane walked along a dirt road, in high, open-field country, like the farm owned by Mark, his mother's brother. He was glad that Jane was seeing the place, because while he was growing up it had given him a sense of wealth to have an uncle attached to a hundred such well-kept acres. His relationship with Jane seemed to be at that stage when it was important for each side of the betrothal to produce external signs of respectability. "But I am even richer," he abruptly announced. She appeared not to notice. They walked companionably but in silence, and seemed responsible for the person with them, a female their height. Lee gathered the impression, despite a veil against his eyes, that this extra girl was blond and sturdy and docile. His sense of her sullenness may have been nothing but his anxiety to win her approval, reflected; though her features were hard to make out, the emotion he bore her was precise: the coppery, gratified, somewhat adrift feeling he would get when physically near girls he admired in high school. The wind had darkened and grown purposeful.

Jane went back, though the countryside remained the same, and he was dousing, with a lawn hose attached to the side of the house, the body of this third person. Her head rested on the ground; he held her ankles and slowly, easily turned the light, stiff mass, to wet every area. It was important that water wash over every bit of skin. He was careful; the task, like rinsing an automobile, was more absorbing than pleasant or unpleasant.

The Sword

Doris Betts

THE DAYS FELL OUT OF THE SICK MAN'S LIFE SLUGGISHLY, LIKE DEAD coals slipping finally onto the hearth from an old fire. Every evening when he blew the lamp and raised the shade, Bert would stand in the dark thinking, This is the last one. Tomorrow he will be gone.

But the next morning, when Bert started awake in the leather chair and strained his ears for silence, he could still hear the tired in-and-out of breathing and his arms and legs would loosen in the chair as he listened to it.

Bert was almost never out of the sick man's room, until the smell of it seemed right to him and he could look at the flowers on the wall and not know if they were blue or green.

His mother would enter and leave the room all day long, standing with one hand curled around the bed rail and looking down at the sick man, her face set into awkward squares like blocks heaped up by some clumsy child.

"Is he any better, Bert?"

"No, I think he is about the same. Maybe a little weaker."

Then she would whisper it under her breath as if it hurt her mouth to make the words. "A little weaker . . . "

At first Bert had put out his hand to her, but she had not seemed to notice, and after a while he stood at the window when his mother came in and stared at the leaves that tossed and shifted on the grass when the wind went by. She wanted to be left alone, he supposed. She had been left to herself for a long time now.

Always she would say hopefully, "Lester? How are you today, Lester?" But there was the suck and push of the old man's breathing and nothing else, and she would go away, watching her feet.

He had been sick for three weeks when Bert first came home, and he was still able to talk a little and smile and look around him.

He had been smiling when Bert came into the room that first day and put his coat on the leather chair and walked over to the bed.

"Hello, Father," Bert said.

The old man said slowly, "It's Bert, isn't it? Have you come home awhile, Bert?"

And he said, "Yes, Father. I've come home a little while."

But there were two more weeks gone now since that day and the old man still lay in bed—no longer smiling—and breathing in and out while Bert watched him.

This morning the doctor had come early, so that Bert was out of his chair before the sun was well into the room.

"Morning, Bert."

"Hello, Dr. Herman. You're early today."

"This is going to be a busy one. Did he rest last night?"

"Yes sir, he sleeps almost all the time now."

Only once during the examination had the sick man opened his eyes and then he had looked at the doctor without interest and closed them again.

"How is he, Dr. Herman?"

The doctor made a shrugging motion. "Holding his own. We're just waiting, I'm afraid."

Later, putting his things away, he had added, "I'm glad you've come home, Bert. Your father was always talking about you. He was very proud."

Was he? thought Bert.

Bert stood by the window and watched the doctor go down the walk, his black bag banging against his knee every other step. We're just waiting, the doctor had said. Once he stopped in the walk to tie his shoe and the wind rose in the oak tree—almost bare now—and came to flap the doctor's coat, impatiently.

After the doctor was out of sight, his mother came and stood by the bed and put her head against the post, as if she were tired of holding it up.

"Does the doctor think he is any better, Bert?" she said.

Bert said, "No, he seems about the same."

She sat down in the leather chair stiffly, leaning her head back, and he saw the hairs springing up from her braid like grass after feet go by.

She said to herself, "At first I thought he would get well. Even after the first week or so I thought he would get well."

"We both thought so," said Bert.

She said, "I wish he knew things. He'd be so glad you were home again. These last years all he could talk about before Christmas was that you would be home awhile. He looked forward to it so."

He looked forward to it, Bert thought. Always forward. What was I expected to do? The sick man moved and coughed and Bert went closer to the bed to see if he was all right. Nothing else was said, and after awhile his mother got up from the chair and went out to the kitchen.

No one else came in the rest of the morning, although Jubah put her head at the door once and smiled at him and Bert sat alone in the room and watched his father's face. He wondered how in five years features he had once known well could fold in upon themselves until the face was strange to him, with its pinched nose and sharp chin, and the cheeks that looked as if they had been pressed deep inside the mouth.

Sometimes Bert would try to remember how his father had looked a long time ago—when he had driven him to school on winter mornings, or across a hundred dinner tables, or on those few special times when he had gone hunting with his father and three other men. But all Bert could remember of those times was the bigness of the other hunters, and the early morning smell of woods and rain, and once his father stopping to put a hand against a poplar tree and smile.

His father had been a very poor hunter; he almost never made a successful shot. But he had been proud when Bert learned to shoot well. And when Bert began bringing home almost all the game, he could remember his father coming into the kitchen at dusk and calling, "Ruth? Come see what your son did!" And the rabbits would be spread on the table for his mother to exclaim about, while his father stood quietly at the sink, washing his hands.

After Bert became such a good shot his father complimented and praised him but gradually they went hunting less and less until one Christmas he had given his gun to Bert. "I was never much with guns," he said then. And after that, the two of them never went hunting again, and the gun was finally stacked away in some closet.

The only time Bert could remember his father's face clearly was that time he had come home from the army and they had set up after the others were in bed—his father oddly expectant, with waiting eyebrows and a half-formed smile, and his own feelings of awkwardness and discomfort, until the two of them had fallen into separate silences and finally gone to bed. He remembered how his father had looked then.

At noon Mother brought the tray and they whispered at the sick man until he lifted his eyelids and looked at them, waiting, expecting nothing and yet seeming to expect anything.

Mother said, "It's lunchtime, Lester. Hot soup." And the sick man made a noise in his throat that might have meant yes or no, and might have meant nothing at all. She fed him slowly and all the time he never looked at the soup or the spoon or her hand holding it; he lay there watching her mouth with that funny look on his face.

Bert watched them for awhile, but he could not keep his hands still; they kept plunging into his pockets or picking at each other until he went to the window and made them into fists and leaned them against the glass. Sometimes the wind would catch a leaf and drive it against the glass where it paused and then tumbled off. Bert thought, My father is going to die, but he did not believe it. He believed the wind and the leaves and the window-glass; but he did not believe that about his father.

When the sick man had eaten, Mother came over to the window and touched Bert's arm; it startled him for a minute and he snapped his head over one shoulder and stared at her; then the muscles that had grown tight around his eyes and forehead let themselves go and he smiled.

She said, "He will sleep some more, Bert. Why don't you come sit out front with me?"

"All right," said Bert.

She whispered, "We'll leave the door open."

He took the tray from her and carried it out into the kitchen where he put it down on the table. His mother called, "Can you bring me a glass of water?" and he filled a glass at the sink and carried it into the front room to her.

She had put her feet up into a big chair and rested an arm against her eyes, and fine hairs were standing up out of her braid all over her head. Bert put the glass into her other hand, and she rubbed at her forehead with the arm and thanked him. He sat down opposite her.

She said, "I wish you'd let me stay with him, Bert. You've hardly been out of that room since you came home."

Bert shook his head. He had to stay with his father now. He had to do that much.

For a time neither of them spoke and he looked thoughtfully around the room. Here he had sat with his father when he came home from the army —his father had been in the big chair smiling, and Bert had sat just where he was now, moving his feet back and forth against the rug and looking now and then at his father thinking, What does he want of me?

His mother said, "At first I thought he would get well, Bert. I thought he would get well at first." For a minute Bert wanted to say, Did you like him? Did you really like my father? Do you know something I don't? But he didn't say anything; he just watched the movement in her face. He thought she was going to shed her first tears then, but she took her feet off the chair and moved around and shifted until the desire for tears went away. She looked suddenly like a brave little girl: a fat girl with chubby features and hair that would not stay in place. Bert wondered what she would do after the sick man died and if it would mean any real change in her life. Sometimes he thought he knew his mother very well and yet this thing he did not know. Does it mean a lot to her? Is there something in me that does not understand him? She'll just have me then, he thought, and he didn't feel quite so helpless for a minute. She's got to prepare herself.

Aloud he said, "Father is very weak now and his age is against him."

She said, "I know now he's not ever going to be well again. I know it and I don't know it all at the same time and that's a queer feeling, Bert, both at the same time."

When she said that, Bert felt his whole body tighten. His mother was right; that's the way it was for him too, maybe for everybody. Nobody believed it. The one thing that was glaring and obvious and unmistakable in the universe and nobody really believed it. Bert wondered if his father believed it now, waiting every day in bed to see if it were true.

He said, "Dr. Herman will be back tomorrow." He said it rapidly as if he had just thought of it, but it was because he couldn't think of anything else to tell her. "We're to call him if we need him for anything."

His mother said, "Yes," and drank the water very fast so that it must have hurt her throat to swallow so hard. Bert took the glass back into the kitchen.

He stacked the dishes off the tray into the sink and began to pour water on them from the kettle and then to wash them with a soapy rag. He thought, it seems to me now that if it were new again, I would be different than I was; but he didn't know exactly what he meant by that. Jubah came in from the back porch; she stopped in the doorway and stood there straight as a knife handle and watched him.

"What you doing, Mister Bert?" she said.

He said, "Dishes."

She came on into the kitchen and wiped her hands on a paper towel and threw it away.

"I'll do them," she said. "How's Mr. Lester?"

Bert watched her brown hands go down into the water and slush it up into soapsuds.

He said, "No different, Jubah. He just lies there but there isn't any change."

Jubah shook her head back and forth and made a tut-tut sound with her tongue. "Sometimes it comes up slow," she said.

When he went back into the front room, his mother looked as if she had been crying, but it was hard to tell. She had not cried before. That night he had come in from the station, she had stood in the hall holding one hand with another, looking something like a queen, he thought. She's said, "I'm sorry to call you from your business, Bert. But it seemed best . . ."

He'd dropped his bag at the door and come to put his arm around her. "How is he?"

Just for a minute, she'd put her head down on his shoulder and rested it there and then she'd caught his arm in tight fingers and made a little smile. "He'll be glad you're here," she'd said.

Now, coming into the front room, he thought perhaps she had been crying, but he could not be sure. He sat down in the chair again and looked at her, trying to decide about it.

His mother said rapidly, "Do you know what Jubah said this morning? I was just walking through the kitchen and Jubah said—Death comes up slow like an old cat but after she waits a long time she jumps and it's all gone then —I was just walking by her and she looked up from the stove and said that, Bert, and I thought I would fall down right there to hear her say it."

Bert said, "Jubah talks too much," but he turned it over in his mind and looked at it in front and behind and on both sides. Death comes up slow like an old cat but after she waits a long time she jumps and it's all gone then.

He tried to remember what it had been like in the army, but he couldn't remember what he had thought about death then. He and Charlie used to talk about it sometimes, but always in terms of somebody else—the fellow in the next bunk, or the ship that left yesterday, or the list in the paper.

Charlie always said, "I don't believe nothing can hurt you till your time comes." He used to say it over and over, confidently, and Bert had listened just as confidently, because both of them knew their time hadn't come.

And it didn't seem to, because they got through all right and Charlie went home to his filling station in Maine and he'd never heard from him.

There'd been another boy, confident as they were, who said that ever since he was a kid he'd known he was going to die during a storm. Every time they had any kind of storm, he'd walk the floor smoking on a cigar, and jumping at the sound of thunder. They'd laughed at him.

"It's whenever your time comes," Charlie always told him.

But as it turned out Bert and Charlie had come home all right, and the other boy (funny that he couldn't remember his name) had died in Africa, they said, and there wasn't even a cloud in the sky.

But that didn't prove anything about what Charlie had said. It didn't prove anything except what his mother had said, that nobody really believed in it. Bert felt tired.

He frowned. "Sometimes," he began, "sometimes, Mother, I wish I could . . ." but he stopped there and didn't know what he wished. It had something to do with the old hunting trips and with his father and with Jubah, but he didn't know what it was. He put his head into his hands and smashed the palms into his eyes. He thought, I have known people and been known by people. That proves something, doesn't it?

His mother was looking at him. She said, "Your father loved you so, Bert." He kept his palms tight against his eyes where the pressure made him see sparks and gray wheels spinning and something like a Roman candle. He wondered, Was that it? Was that all it was all these years? And that made him tired too.

Bert said, "I'll see if he's awake now."

He tiptoed into the room and looked down at the sick man, who was awake —lying there with that look on his face. Bert looked down at him, at his faded eyes on each side of the pinched nose and the mouth, bent in now as if the corners had been tugged from the inside. Slow, he thought, slow like a big cat, and for a minute he hated Jubah for telling his mother about the cat.

The old man closed his eyes and Bert felt suddenly that two doors had been shut against him and he no longer had anything to do with his father. He came back into the front room and sat down, then he got up and took a magazine and sat again. He thought, I'm trying, damn it. I've always been trying.

Big letters crawling crookedly on the magazine said CHILDBIRTH, IT CAN BE PAINLESS. OUR GROWING TRAFFIC DEATHS. RUSSIA AND THE ATOM. He leafed through it, not reading anything.

Sometimes since his father had been sick, Bert had tried to remember some vivid detail, some special time, some conversation that had happened when he was a boy that was important. That's where a psychologist began, with the little boy, and he could say, "It is here that it began to go wrong, when you were three, or seven, or nine." But Bert could never find anything.

He remembered the time he came home from the army only because it was so much like everything else that it seemed important in itself.

His father and mother had met him at the train-station; she had hugged him and Father had shaken his hand and stood there smiling, looking at him curiously and—yes, he was sure of it, warmly—until he stammered, "Well, let's go home now." So they had piled into the Ford and gone home, making a lot of noise on the road about souvenirs and about old friends, and about what-he-was-going-to-do-now.

And that night, when Mother and Aunt Mary had gone to bed, and Jubah had called good night from the back-door and thanked him again for the silk shawl, Bert and his father had sat in this same front room; his father in the big chair, looking expectant, with his eyebrows up and an underdeveloped smile fooling with his mouth. Bert felt then the same way he did when he and his father came in from hunting and put the rabbits down on the kitchen table.

But his father hadn't seemed uncomfortable at all; he just sat across from him smiling, and Bert moved his feet back and forth against the rug thinking, What is it you want of me?

Finally he said, "You know, Father, I brought souvenirs to the others, but I didn't know what to bring you. I didn't know what you would like."

And his father had gone on smiling, looking at him out of a quiet face, his faded eyes making a question and yet not a curious question.

And Bert had said nervously, "So I just thought I'd give you the money, Sir, and let you get something you liked and wanted for yourself," holding out the envelope in a hand that was carved from wood or clay, but was not his hand.

His father had said slowly, "That was nice of you, Bert. Thank you very much," and had taken the envelope and turned it over and over in his hands, not opening it, just turning it over in his fingers.

After that the two of them had sat for a little longer until they fell into separate silences and went to bed.

Sometimes now, when Bert sat in the leather chair and watched his father breathe in and out, he would remember that night and try to think what else he should have done. The pistol? But his father had never been much with guns. Silk shawls or bits of jade? And what would his father have done with a Japanese sword or a rising-sun flag?

When his mother spoke now it frightened him because he had forgotten she was in the room.

She said, "What are you reading, Bert?" and he jumped and his eyes caught at the words in the magazine like fingers.

He said, "Childbirth. Painless Childbirth," and she almost smiled.

She said thoughtfully, "I remember the day you were born," but she didn't say any more. Bert tried to picture his father on that day. Had he been proud? Had he said perhaps, softly and to himself, "My son?"

Jubah called them to supper and Bert ate it automatically, watching Jubah's sharp hipbones shift when she moved about the kitchen. Jubah was very thin. She was almost as old as his father and she had been with them a long time. That was a funny thing, Jubah's loyalty to Mr. Lester. They were often laughing as if old and yellowed secrets were between them. I should have known Jubah better, Bert thought now, watching her go about the kitchen. Perhaps she would have told me.

Jubah said, "I'll stay over tonight, Mister Bert," and he didn't argue with her.

His mother said, "Your bed's fixed, Jubah," and she thanked her.

Later, when Bert blew out the lamp and raised the shade in the sick man's room he thought how tired he was, and he went to sleep quickly in the chair.

When he woke again, it was almost day and he heard the old man choking and wheezing on the bed and he knew this was the last day. He called his mother and they lit the lamp and stood by the bed while Jubah telephoned the doctor.

His mother didn't say anything or bend down to touch the sick man; she just stood there listening to him cough and the tears ran out her eyes and down her cheeks and fell off.

Now that it had come, Bert found his hands were trembling and the lamplight jiggled and splashed against the flowered wall every time his father made a noise with his throat, but even when he squeezed his eyes together they were dry.

Suddenly his father said, "Ruth," and she sat down on the side of the bed and took both his hands in hers and his eyelids flew up and he looked at her, until Bert felt he could not bear that look.

Bert put the lamp on the table and bent over the old man, feeling the hiccoughing begin in his throat and the tightness clamp across his chest. He put a hand against the old man's shoulder and said suddenly, "I should have given you the sword," and his voice was too loud.

The sick man's eyes flashed to him once, flicked his face and went away and he gargled a sound in his throat. His mother frowned at Bert and shook her head sharply.

"Hush," she said sternly. "Hush, he does not know anything," and the old man raised his head off the pillow stiffly and put it down again and was dead.

Bert backed out the door when Jubah came in; his mother had put her head down on the bed and begun to cry with a great sucking sound, and Bert went heavily into the front room and fell into the big chair, saying aloud over and over, "He is dead. He is already dead. He is dead."

He put his forehead down against his arm, but he could not even cry.

The Girl at the Window

THIS WAS THE OLD HOUSE WE HAD BOUGHT: A VAST AND CUMBERSOME island afloat upon the land, towers and cupolas and gables rendering the sky complex with their anfractuous horizon of darkness that galloped against the rose-pink of twilights. Deep and heavy walls of liver rock held this circus of wood afloat, but one could see where the impossible weight had sunk even these rocks waist-deep into the clay. Weeds and grass and wild roses thickened everywhere about the house, the smoke-colored sheds and the roofed well.

A double wagon track was worn like a paradigm of memory into the depths of the yard. Otherwise, all was overgrown and blurred with desuetude and the brainless vigor of an inhuman and unwanted growth.

But it wasn't the house itself that was the secret; rather, this house was only the vessel of—not simply the secret, but the inner vessel of life; and it was life that was the secret, only this particular and induplicable form of life.

On the third floor of the house, there were rooms complicated with the detritus of a century—old shawls draped over the backs of cold and dusty love seats, clothes forms made in the shapes of young women long turned to air and loam, scrapbooks containing the portraits of staring, somber faces without names . . . high-topped shoes, bent stiffly at the ankles, books and magazines, rolled-up blinds, clothes hangers, broken oil lamps, chairs with burst cane bottoms and splintered arms, chests heaped with diaphanous black garments and flowered hats, as strange as extinct birds . . . all of these things, covered with the oat-smelling dust of soil and time.

For three days, we cleaned and rearranged these objects, and there was such a multitude that after a while they all began to look alike—the books and the letters, the chairs and the photographs.

But not quite. There was one photograph—at least a century old—that caught my attention. Not at first, for I was sorting out different papers, and it merely lay among them; but later the thought of it came back to me so strongly that I returned to the room and looked for it. (The room was like the others—slanted beneath the gable and dim with a light that seemed peculiarly adapted to the thought of a long distant past.)

I found it again, and this time—holding it in my hands—I was troubled by the elusive strangeness before me. The photograph dated surely from the 1850's or 1860's, and it was simply the photograph of a large building. Apparently an apartment building. There were no human presences that I could detect in the scene, and yet the immanence of something human was as certain and palpable as an odor. Indeed, there was no tangible life in the picture at all, except for a sorry-looking horse standing in harness before a quaint little carriage. The head of the horse was blurred, obviously from a sudden movement in a day when photographic exposures required seconds rather than fractions of a second.

What was there about the picture that magnetized my attention? I stared at it in the darkness of that room until my eyes blurred and the everyday sounds of the world subsided into something half-unreal and half-silent. Then I closed my eyes and concentrated upon the scene that remained fixed in my mind.

The more I thought, the stranger it all seemed. And yet, I was close to experiencing some sort of recognition in it. In some way the photograph seemed to be meant for me alone, in a sense that was ineffably mysterious. This photograph had been waiting for me, and for no one else.

Although I was not able to define this unsettling power, I did in fact accomplish something with all that thought: whatever the mystery was, it had to do with the windows.

In spite of this fascination, I had to put the photograph aside for several weeks while we settled in the house, and made it fit our family the way new shoes or a new suit is made to fit the body.

But eventually I sought out the photograph again, and sat before it and stared into that strange scene of a building that had existed in an unknown city at least a century before, and was now undoubtedly disbursed into soil, mud, brick dust and air.

I decided to take it to a room in the basement, which I had set aside as my dark room, where I intended to develop all my own photographs. I proposed to make a negative and enlarge it. I was aware of the problems, of course, and scarcely hoped to learn much from the photograph, for the techniques of that distant time were impossibly crude, and upon enlargement, the details of that scene would undoubtedly be lost in the hypertrophied grain—elements of vision that had an atomic absoluteness, and would wax thick and gross, like anonymous golf balls of gray and white inhabiting the expanded view.

But this was not so. For I was astonished to discover upon my first enlargement that the grain did not expand with the view, and that the images of people appeared in the windows of that building.

I did not really study that first enlargement at all. Someone watching me might have thought I was simply impatient, or in a hurry. All I did was throw the photograph aside, after that first discovery, switch out the light, and leave my dark room to go upstairs and join my family.

The children were sitting around the television, eating peanut butter and banana sadwiches. My wife was preparing supper. Everything was normal, and as it should be. I went into the kitchen and fixed drinks for my wife and me. The children were laughing in the other room, and the tv was turned up too loud, as usual.

I have sometimes pretended that the people you meet in recurring dreams have an independent, suspended reality during the intervals between their appearances in your dreams. Not suspended entirely, perhaps, but only as actors. That is, I have fancied that between their appearances in dreams, they might live an existence as divorced from their roles in your dreams as it is divorced from the reality of everyday life. That they actually might meet for rehearsals somewhere, in some totally unknowable realm, and discuss the terms of what they will do on the stage of your next dream, memorize lines, and strive to control and predict certain effects upon the audience. In this situation, it is the dreamer who (like an audience) is the only unpredictable element, the only unrehearsed participant in what happens, the only uncertainty, as of jury or God.

It was this way with the people in that photograph. While I turned back to the daily affairs that called for my immediate attention, those people whose faces had just begun to emerge sat back in their darkened rooms and waited for me. They were waiting for that quiet and secret moment when I would come back to them, and enlarge their images until they became cogently human in the text of my attention. Perhaps they talked with one another, and lived lives beyond the scope of my imagining, imprisoned as they were in the crepuscular rooms of an ancient building . . . which in turn existed only in the flattened image of the photograph of a dead, past time.

Still, everything that could be said to be *there* once had access to the light, and this suggested to me that it was somehow accessible to the understanding. It might *not* be beyond recall. It was possible that the people in those rooms continued to exist with their own lucidity, no matter how intangible this lucidity might seem.

It was a week or ten days before I found time to go back. It was evening, and when the children turned on the tv, I descended the steps and went into the dark room. I enlarged the upper right section of the photograph, showing one window completely, and two half windows to each side. When the image began to come forth, like something emerging from the deep water of time, rather than from the tray before me, I saw that there was the face of a young girl to be seen in the room beyond the window. It was perfectly clear; and the eyes of the face were fixed intently, unmistakably, upon mine. That is to say, upon the lens of the camera.

Whoever had been taking that photograph over a hundred years ago, he had been watched by this young girl. Probably without knowing it.

In the two half windows that showed at the side of each window, there was nothing at all. Merely the darkness of unlighted rooms.

I studied the face of the girl. It was a beautiful face, but somber. She must have been only nine or ten years old; but already, I could imagine, there was something old in her features.

I could see dark combs in her light hair. Her chin was slightly raised, and one hand was cupped softly on her throat, almost in a theatrical gesture of surprise or fear. Whatever it was, the emotion on her face was clearly one of some force. There was something of unease upon it, but there was fascination, too.

It occurred to me that she might not have seen a camera before this instant, and she was staring out through the window at a man leaning over, seeming to peer absorbedly into nothing but a shrouded black box.

Nevertheless, she probably knew what the camera was, even if she had never seen one. Possibly she saw something else that disturbed or frightened her.

Then I considered the strange impossibility that she might have seen into the lens, into the camera itself, and even into that very future to which the camera would bring her image. In other words, that she might be looking at me, just as I was looking at her.

A whimsical idea, which I put out of my mind immediately. Then I studied her face closely for several minutes before going back upstairs, having had enough of such communion for a while.

But of course I returned, and enlarged that single window with the girl in it. There was surely some revelation in that face, if it could be brought closer. The closer it came, I was thinking, the more life-like it would be. And I even fancied that I might eventually see the face grow to life-size, and feel something like a breath on my hands as I worked with it.

Ridiculous, of course. But all of this was part of the hypnotic effect the photograph had upon me. And my wild fancies were not discouraged when I found that, upon this latest enlargement, the girl's face actually began to show something almost like color. As did her hair, which might have been a pale gold with slight rednesses in it.

The eyes, of course, were even more life-like. And behind the girl I could now identify an asymmetrical shadow. This was the back of a man who appeared to be stooped and leaning forward with his face in his hands, weeping. It was impossible to see clearly, but he appeared to be elderly.

Whatever condition he was in, or whoever he was, the girl continued to stare in fascination out upon the world, and into the camera lens, and even (as I have suggested) at myself, as if I were a voyeur god gazing upon her from so much distance and so much time.

Beyond the man, there was something else, a long horizontal shadow that the man seemed to be facing. But at this stage of the enlargement, I could not tell what it was. Still, I studied it very closely for a long time, and then I looked once more at the man. I was almost certain that his hair was silver and long, curling over the collar of his dark coat.

And when I finished studying these two things, I looked back once more at the face of the girl as it continued to gaze at me. I am sure I imagined it, but the face seemed older. The girl might have been as old as twelve or thirteen. It was very difficult to tell.

And there was a slight mole on her right cheek. No larger than the tip of a lead pencil, but there it was, clear before my gaze. I was sure it was not a defect in the photograph, but an actual mole on the girl's cheek.

With the next enlargement, I discovered that the long shape beyond the old man was a casket. No figure was visible in it, but the ornate satin upon the lid glowed faintly in the dim light, and the shape of the lid was unmistakable.

Therefore, the photograph had caught this old man in a moment of grief, weeping into his hands before a loved one who had just died. And it had caught the girl, too.

However, the girl had happened to turn around and look outside, where she had seen something that surprised or puzzled or·terrified her, so that she had clutched vaguely at her throat while the shutter opened and closed, fastening their image permanently by the witnessing of their light upon a chemically treated plate.

But what was it the girl saw? What precisely was the landscape of her fear or grief? That window she was staring through was not so different from the lens of a camera, I told myself. Nor so different from the images I busied myself with, enlarging them without either attenuating or fragmenting them, in contradiction of all law. It was as if one could increase the power of a microscope without destroying the surface appearance of that which he regarded, but only rendering it clearer and more unmistakably itself with each enlargement.

Only in this, the mystery grew with each enlargement, precisely as the human discoveries increased, defying all expectations.

And yet the girl's face was no different; merely more human, in its strange way, and perhaps still a little older than even that second discovery had suggested.

There was something else, however: her lips were slightly parted. The realization was beyond question. Her lips were open just a fraction of an inch, and I realized that the camera had caught her in the act of speaking a word.

But how could this be? The camera of that day had disastrously slow shutter speeds, as I have said. The horse harnessed to the cart outside the building gave evidence that this was so, for his head was blurred. So why didn't I conclude that the girl's lips were simply parted . . . from an adenoidal condition, perhaps, or because of something else? But no. This was not so, and I could see it was not so. Although I could not have proved it to anyone else, I was certain that the girl had been caught in the act of saying something.

Possibly something to the old man behind her. Her grandfather, perhaps; speaking a word of consolation to him as he stooped before the casket weeping for the loss of a loved one.

But this would not do either. The girl was looking out the window. Her eyes were focused. She was looking at the anonymous cameraman, at the camera itself . . . at the lens, at me.

And she was speaking a word. Not only her lips, but her eyes gave testimony to the truth of this hypothesis.

It was the next and the last enlargement that conveyed to me the final revelation. And this was the revelation I had been waiting for, although it might in itself seem arcane and impossibly ambiguous. For the answer is really, in one sense, a non-answer. But even a non-answer is an answer of sorts . . . or it can be, as when it signifies that no categorical answer is possible because the terms of the question are wrong, or the implications of the question are somehow unthinkable.

This happened on the very next night, and I was excited when I descended the steps to my dark room and prepared my enlarger.

When the image grew before my eyes, it was almost like the entrance of someone I had known all my life. The girl's face, looking still older than I would have thought possible the first time, appeared between my hands, and her lips were now so clearly parted that no one could have doubted that she was in the act of speaking a word . . . as no one could have doubted the deep, unequivocal focus of her eyes upon the person who gazed upon her.

As I studied her image, it came to me—suddenly and irrefutably. I mean, the word she was speaking (whispering, I think, so that the old man behind her could not possibly have heard).

The word was, "No."

That was all. "No." Nothing else at all.

For who else might have seen this possibility, or might have understood the burden of her prescient fear? What strange Cassandra was this girl? And what dreams might she have had before and after this one instant, when she stared outwards into time as well as into space?

These are questions that undoubtedly deserve non-answers. Whatever they might have led to, however, I decided that evening to destroy all my enlargements, along with the original photograph.

Good and evil had nothing to do with it. Although it seemed to me to be an act of cleansing, as well as liberation. I mean the act of destroying everything that had to do with the photograph.

Sometimes I wake up in the night and wonder about the girl, and fear for her, and feel pity for her.

Did she, I wonder, worship the future, or the judgment of the future, as a kind of God? Was she, in short, as poisoned by this error as we are? (I speak of the error of believing that the future is wiser, or more nearly infallible, than we are; an error that is an inevitable corollary to the myth of progress.)

Was I like a God to her, to the extent that she guessed at, or imagined, my presence? Consider this: if she were mad, she might have dreamed that some unknown man was staring at her through a glass, and that this man lived a hundred years beyond that instant. The man might have been her great grandson, or the great grandson of people she had never known. All would be the same to her.

What I am asking is this: if one might have a glimpse of the future, might it not occur in such a manner as this? Wouldn't the camera still seem to her in that day a marvelous, a magical invention? And if something of her could pass through the lens of the camera in one direction, might she not conceive that something, or some vestige of someone, pass in the other direction?

But it isn't really the girl who is at the heart of this mystery (although God knows she embodies enough!). For I am thinking of all those other windows. And I am thinking of the poor horse and the strange little carriage it was harnessed to. I wonder if they belonged to the photographer.

And the photographer himself. What was he like? Who was he? And the camera. I would have liked to have a photograph of this man. I would have liked to see him as that girl saw him.

As it is, I only conceive of him as huddled behind the old camera, his head covered with the stiff dark cloth that kept out all the adventitious light of day. He is gazing into the lens before him, and the building he sees is inverted and upside down. All the windows are upside down. The horse and the carriage are upside down. The horse moves his head, but the girl speaks the word "No," and already the picture has been taken.

Date Due

MAR 09 2005			